Praise for

LETHAL WHITE

"Even if the world is the seedy underbelly of contemporary London and not magical Hogwarts, cracking the cover of a Galbraith novel is like stepping through a portal. You're immersed, all at once."
— *Bustle*

"One of contemporary crime fiction's most delightful partnerships."
— *Seattle Times*

"If you love the intricate, character-driven mysteries written by Tana French and Kate Atkinson, then chances are good that you'll enjoy the ones by Robert Galbraith...Galbraith knows how to tell a story every bit as deftly as does J.K. Rowling. Cormoran Strike, who lost a leg in Afghanistan, may limp painfully through much of the book, but the tale being told never misses a step."
— *Dallas Morning News*

"Rowling's emotionally intelligent portrayal of her protagonists never overwhelms the whodunit story line."
— *Publishers Weekly* (starred review)

"Rowling deftly circumnavigates all of the tropes and constructs that have long since relegated the male-author-dominated thriller genre to a place of ridicule and sheer inanity."
— *Tablet* magazine

LETHAL WHITE

ROBERT GALBRAITH

MULHOLLAND BOOKS

LITTLE, BROWN AND COMPANY

NEW YORK BOSTON LONDON

Copyright © 2018 by J.K. Rowling

Hachette Book Group supports the right to free expression and the value of copyright. The purpose of copyright is to encourage writers and artists to produce the creative works that enrich our culture.

The scanning, uploading, and distribution of this book without permission is a theft of the author's intellectual property. If you would like permission to use material from the book (other than for review purposes), please contact permissions@hbgusa.com. Thank you for your support of the author's rights.

Mulholland Books / Little, Brown and Company
Hachette Book Group
1290 Avenue of the Americas, New York, NY 10104
mulhollandbooks.com

Originally published in hardcover in North America by Mulholland Books, September 2018
Published simultaneously in Great Britain by Sphere, September 2018
First Mulholland Books trade paperback edition, June 2019

Mulholland Books is an imprint of Little, Brown and Company, a division of Hachette Book Group, Inc. The Mulholland Books name and logo are trademarks of Hachette Book Group, Inc.

The publisher is not responsible for websites (or their content) that are not owned by the publisher.

The Hachette Speakers Bureau provides a wide range of authors for speaking events. To find out more, go to hachettespeakersbureau.com or call (866) 376-6591.

Permission credits appear on page 650.

ISBN 978-0-316-42273-4 (hc) / 978-0-316-45339-4 (lp) / 978-0-316-49159-4 (int'l tpb) / 978-0-316-422772 (trade pb)
LCCN 2018952121

10 9 8 7 6 5 4 3 2 1

LSC-C

Printed in the United States of America

To Di and Roger,

and in memory

of the lovely white Spike

PROLOGUE

Happiness, dear Rebecca, means first and foremost the calm, joyous sense of innocence.

Henrik Ibsen, *Rosmersholm*

If only the swans would swim side by side on the dark green lake, this picture might turn out to be the crowning achievement of the wedding photographer's career.

He was loath to change the couple's position, because the soft light beneath the canopy of trees was turning the bride, with her loose red-gold curls, into a pre-Raphaelite angel and emphasizing the chiseled cheekbones of her husband. He couldn't remember when he had last been commissioned to photograph so handsome a couple. There was no need for tactful tricks with the new Mr. and Mrs. Matthew Cunliffe, no need to angle the lady so that rolls of back fat were hidden (she was, if anything, fractionally too slender, but that would photograph well), no need to suggest the groom "try one with your mouth closed," because Mr. Cunliffe's teeth were straight and white. The only thing that needed concealing, and it could be retouched out of the final pictures, was the ugly scar running down the bride's forearm: purple and livid, with the puncture marks of stitches still visible.

She had been wearing a rubber and stockinette brace when the photographer arrived at her parents' house that morning. It had given him quite a start when she had removed it for the photographs. He had even wondered whether she had made a botched attempt to kill herself before the wedding, because he had seen it all. You did, after twenty years in the game.

"I was assaulted," Mrs. Cunliffe—or Robin Ellacott, as she had been two hours ago—had said. The photographer was a squeamish man. He had fought off the mental image of steel slicing into that soft, pale flesh. Thankfully, the ugly mark was now hidden in the shadow cast by Mrs. Cunliffe's bouquet of creamy roses.

The swans, the damned swans. If both would clear out of the background it wouldn't matter, but one of them was repeatedly diving, its fluffy pyramid of a backside jutting out of the middle of the lake like a feathered iceberg, its contortions ruffling the surface of the water so that its digital removal would be far more complicated than young Mr. Cunliffe, who had already suggested this remedy, realized. The swan's mate, meanwhile, continued to lurk over by the bank: graceful, serene and determinedly out of shot.

"Have you got it?" asked the bride, her impatience palpable.

"You look gorgeous, flower," said the groom's father, Geoffrey, from behind the photographer. He sounded tipsy already. The couple's parents, best man and bridesmaids were all watching from the shade of nearby trees. The smallest bridesmaid, a toddler, had had to be restrained from throwing pebbles into the lake, and was now whining to her mother, who talked to her in a constant, irritating whisper.

"Have you got it?" Robin asked again, ignoring her father-in-law.

"Almost," lied the photographer. "Turn in to him a little bit more, please, Robin. That's it. Nice big smiles. Big smiles, now!"

There was a tension about the couple that could not be wholly attributed to the difficulty of getting the shot. The photographer didn't care. He wasn't a marriage counselor. He had known couples to start screaming at each other while he read his light meter. One bride had stormed out of her own reception. He still kept, for the amusement of friends, the blurred shot from 1998 that showed a groom head-butting his best man.

Good-looking as they were, he didn't fancy the Cunliffes' chances. That long scar down the bride's arm had put him off her from the start. He found the whole thing ominous and distasteful.

"Let's leave it," said the groom suddenly, releasing Robin. "We've got enough, haven't we?"

"Wait, wait, the other one's coming now!" said the photographer crossly.

The moment Matthew had released Robin, the swan by the far shore had begun to paddle its way across the dark green water towards its mate.

"You'd think the buggers were doing it on purpose, eh, Linda?" said Geoffrey with a fat chuckle to the bride's mother. "Bloody things."

"It doesn't matter," said Robin, pulling her long skirt up clear of her shoes, the heels of which were a little too low. "I'm sure we've got something."

She strode out of the copse of trees into the blazing sunlight and off across the lawn towards the seventeenth-century castle, where most of the wedding guests were already milling, drinking champagne as they admired the view of the hotel grounds.

"I think her arm's hurting her," the bride's mother told the groom's father.

Bollocks it is, thought the photographer with a certain cold pleasure. *They rowed in the car.*

The couple had looked happy enough beneath the shower of confetti in which they had departed the church, but on arrival at the country house hotel they had worn the rigid expressions of those barely repressing their rage.

"She'll be all right. Just needs a drink," said Geoffrey comfortably. "Go keep her company, Matt."

Matthew had already set off after his bride, gaining on her easily as she navigated the lawn in her stilettos. The rest of the party followed, the bridesmaids' mint-green chiffon dresses rippling in the hot breeze.

"Robin, we need to talk."

"Go on, then."

"Wait a minute, can't you?"

"If I wait, we'll have the family on us."

Matthew glanced behind him. She was right.

"Robin—"

"Don't touch my arm!"

Her wound was throbbing in the heat. Robin wanted to find the holdall containing the sturdy rubber protective brace, but it would be somewhere out of reach in the bridal suite, wherever that was.

The crowd of guests standing in the shadow of the hotel was coming into clearer view. The women were easy to tell apart, because of their hats. Matthew's Aunt Sue wore an electric blue wagon wheel, Robin's sister-in-law, Jenny, a startling confection of yellow feathers. The male guests blurred into conformity in their dark suits. It was impossible to see from this distance whether Cormoran Strike was among them.

"Just stop, will you?" said Matthew, because they had fast outstripped the family, who were matching their pace to his toddler niece.

Robin paused.

"I was shocked to see him, that's all," said Matthew carefully.

"I suppose you think I was expecting him to burst in halfway through the service and knock over the flowers?" asked Robin.

Matthew could have borne this response if not for the smile she was trying to suppress. He had not forgotten the joy in her face when her ex-boss had crashed into their wedding ceremony. He wondered whether he would ever be able to forgive the fact that she had said "I do" with her eyes fastened upon the big, ugly, shambolic figure of Cormoran Strike, rather than her new husband. The entire congregation must have seen how she had beamed at him.

Their families were gaining on them again. Matthew took Robin's upper arm gently, his fingers inches above the knife wound, and walked her on. She came willingly, but he suspected that this was because she hoped she was moving closer to Strike.

"I said in the car, if you want to go back to work for him—"

"—I'm an 'effing idiot,'" said Robin.

The men grouped on the terrace were becoming distinguishable now, but Robin could not see Strike anywhere. He was a big man. She ought to have been able to make him out even among her brothers and uncles, who were all over six foot. Her spirits, which had soared when Strike had appeared, tumbled earthwards like rain-soaked fledglings. He must have left after the service rather than boarding a minibus to the hotel. His brief appearance had signified a gesture of goodwill, but nothing more. He had not come to rehire her, merely to congratulate her on a new life.

"Look," said Matthew, more warmly. She knew that he, too, had scanned the crowd, found it Strike-less and drawn the same conclusion. "All I was trying to say in the car was: it's up to you what you do, Robin. If he wanted—if he wants you back—I was just worried, for Christ's sake. Working for him wasn't exactly safe, was it?"

"No," said Robin, with her knife wound throbbing. "It wasn't safe."

She turned back towards her parents and the rest of the family group, waiting for them to catch up. The sweet, ticklish smell of hot grass filled her nostrils as the sun beat down on her uncovered shoulders.

"Do you want to go to Auntie Robin?" said Matthew's sister.

Toddler Grace obligingly seized Robin's injured arm and swung on it, eliciting a yelp of pain.

"Oh, I'm so sorry, Robin—Gracie, let go—"

"Champagne!" shouted Geoffrey. He put his arm around Robin's shoulders and steered her on towards the expectant crowd.

The gents' bathroom was, as Strike would have expected of this upmarket country hotel, odor-free and spotless. He wished he could have brought a pint into the cool, quiet toilet cubicle, but that might have reinforced the impression that he was some disreputable alcoholic who had been bailed from jail to attend the wedding. Reception staff had met his assurances that he was part of the Cunliffe-Ellacott wedding party with barely veiled skepticism as it was.

Even in an uninjured state Strike tended to intimidate, given that he was large, dark, naturally surly-looking and sported a boxer's profile. Today he might have just climbed out of the ring. His nose was broken, purple and swollen to twice its usual size, both eyes were bruised and puffy, and one ear was inflamed and sticky with fresh black stitches. At least the knife wound across the palm of his hand was concealed by bandages, although his best suit was crumpled and stained from a wine spill on the last occasion he had worn it. The best you could say for his appearance was that he had managed to grab matching shoes before heading for Yorkshire.

He yawned, closed his aching eyes and rested his head momentarily against the cold partition wall. He was so tired he might easily fall asleep here, sitting on the toilet. He needed to find Robin, though, and ask her—beg her, if necessary—to forgive him for sacking her and come back to work. He had thought he read delight in her face when their eyes met in church. She had certainly beamed at him as she walked past on Matthew's arm on the way out, so he had hurried back through the graveyard to ask his friend Shanker, who was now asleep in the car park in the Mercedes he had borrowed for the journey, to follow the minibuses to the reception.

Strike had no desire to stay for a meal and speeches: he had not RSVPed the invitation he had received before sacking Robin. All he wanted was a few minutes to talk to her, but so far this had proved impossible. He had forgotten what weddings were like. As he sought Robin on the crowded terrace he had found himself the uncomfortable focus of a hundred pairs of curious eyes. Turning down champagne, which he disliked, he had retreated into the bar in search of a pint. A dark-haired young man who had a look of Robin about the mouth and forehead had followed, a gaggle of other young people trailing in his wake, all of them wearing similar expressions of barely suppressed excitement.

"You're Strike, aye?" said the young man.

The detective agreed to it.

"Martin Ellacott," said the other. "Robin's brother."

"How d'you do?" said Strike, raising his bandaged hand to show that he could not shake without pain. "Where is she, d'you know?"

"Having photos done," said Martin. He pointed at the iPhone clutched in his other hand. "You're on the news. You caught the Shacklewell Ripper."

"Oh," said Strike. "Yeah."

In spite of the fresh knife wounds on his palm and ear, he felt as though the violent events of twelve hours previously had happened long ago. The contrast between the sordid hideout where he had cornered the killer and this four-star hotel was so jarring that they seemed separate realities.

A woman whose turquoise fascinator was trembling in her

white-blonde hair now arrived in the bar. She, too, was holding a phone, her eyes moving rapidly upwards and downwards, checking the living Strike against what he was sure was a picture of him on her screen.

"Sorry, need a pee," Strike had told Martin, edging away before anybody else could approach him. After talking his way past the suspicious reception staff, he had taken refuge in the bathroom.

Yawning again, he checked his watch. Robin must, surely, have finished having pictures taken by now. With a grimace of pain, because the painkillers they had given him at the hospital had long since worn off, Strike got up, unbolted the door and headed back out among the gawping strangers.

A string quartet had been set up at the end of the empty dining room. They started to play while the wedding group organized themselves into a receiving line that Robin assumed she must have agreed to at some point during the wedding preparations. She had abnegated so much responsibility for the day's arrangements that she kept receiving little surprises like this. She had forgotten, for instance, that they had agreed to have photographs taken at the hotel rather than the church. If only they had not sped away in the Daimler immediately after the service, she might have had a chance to speak to Strike and to ask him—beg him, if necessary—to take her back. But he had left without talking to her, leaving her wondering whether she had the courage, or the humility, to call him after this and plead for her job.

The room seemed dark after the brilliance of the sunlit gardens. It was wood-paneled, with brocade curtains and gilt-framed oil paintings. Scent from the flower arrangements lay heavy in the air, and glass- and silverware gleamed on snow-white tablecloths. The string quartet, which had sounded loud in the echoing wooden box of a room, was soon drowned out by the sound of guests clambering up the stairs outside, crowding onto the landing, talking and laughing, already full of champagne and beer.

"Here we go, then!" roared Geoffrey, who seemed to be enjoying the day more than anybody else. "Bring 'em on!"

If Matthew's mother had been alive, Robin doubted that Geoffrey would have felt able to give his ebullience full expression. The late Mrs. Cunliffe had been full of cool side-stares and nudges, constantly checking any signs of unbridled emotion. Mrs. Cunliffe's sister, Sue, was one of the first down the receiving line, bringing a fine frost with her, for she had wanted to sit at the top table and been denied that privilege.

"How are you, Robin?" she asked, pecking the air near Robin's ear. Miserable, disappointed and guilty that she was not feeling happy, Robin suddenly sensed how much this woman, her new aunt-in-law, disliked her. "Lovely dress," said Aunt Sue, but her eyes were already on handsome Matthew.

"I wish your mother—" she began, then, with a gasp, she buried her face in the handkerchief that she held ready in her hand.

More friends and relatives shuffled inside, beaming, kissing, shaking hands. Geoffrey kept holding up the line, bestowing bear hugs on everybody who did not actively resist.

"He came, then," said Robin's favorite cousin, Katie. She would have been a bridesmaid had she not been hugely pregnant. Today was her due date. Robin marveled that she could still walk. Her belly was watermelon-hard as she leaned in for a kiss.

"Who came?" asked Robin, as Katie sidestepped to hug Matthew.

"Your boss. Strike. Martin was just haranguing him down in the—"

"You're over there, I think, Katie," said Matthew, pointing her towards a table in the middle of the room. "You'll want to get off your feet, must be difficult in the heat, I guess?"

Robin barely registered the passage of several more guests down the line. She responded to their good wishes at random, her eyes constantly drawn to the doorway through which they were all filing. Had Katie meant that Strike was here at the hotel, after all? Had he followed her from the church? Was he about to appear? Where had he been hiding? She had searched everywhere—on the terrace, in the hallway, in the bar. Hope surged only to fail again. Perhaps Martin, famous for his lack of tact, had driven him away? Then she reminded herself that Strike was not such a feeble creature as that and hope bubbled up once more, and while her inner self performed these peregrinations of expectation and dread, it was impossible to simulate the more conventional wedding day emotions whose absence, she knew, Matthew felt and resented.

"Martin!" Robin said joyfully, as her younger brother appeared, already three pints to the bad, accompanied by his mates.

"S'pose you already knew?" said Martin, taking it for granted that she must. He was holding his mobile in his hand. He had slept at a friend's house the previous evening, so that his bedroom could be given to relatives from Down South.

"Knew what?"

"That he caught the Ripper last night."

Martin held up the screen to show her the news story. She gasped at the sight of the Ripper's identity. The knife wound that man had inflicted was throbbing on her forearm.

"Is he still here?" asked Robin, throwing pretense to the wind. "Strike? Did he say he was staying, Mart?"

"For Christ's sake," muttered Matthew.

"Sorry," said Martin, registering Matthew's irritation. "Holding up the queue."

He slouched off. Robin turned to look at Matthew and saw, as though in thermal image, the guilt glowing through him.

"You knew," she said, shaking hands absently with a great aunt who had leaned in, expecting to be kissed.

"Knew what?" he snapped.

"That Strike had caught—"

But her attention was now demanded by Matthew's old university friend and workmate, Tom, and his fiancée, Sarah. She barely heard a word that Tom said, because she was constantly watching the door, where she hoped to see Strike.

"You knew," Robin repeated, once Tom and Sarah had walked away. There was another hiatus. Geoffrey had met a cousin from Canada. "Didn't you?"

"I heard the tail end of it on the news this morning," muttered Matthew. His expression hardened as he looked over Robin's head towards the doorway. "Well, here he is. You've got your wish."

Robin turned. Strike had just ducked into the room, one eye gray and purple above his heavy stubble, one ear swollen and stitched. He raised a bandaged hand when their eyes met and attempted a rueful smile, which ended in a wince.

"Robin," said Matthew. "Listen, I need—"

"In a minute," she said, with a joyfulness that had been conspicuously absent all day.

"Before you talk to him, I need to tell—"

"Matt, please, can't it wait?"

Nobody in the family wanted to detain Strike, whose injury meant that he could not shake hands. He held the bandaged one in front of him and shuffled sideways down the line. Geoffrey glared at him and even Robin's mother, who had liked him on their only previous encounter, was unable to muster a smile as he greeted her by name. Every guest in the dining room seemed to be watching.

"You didn't have to be so dramatic," Robin said, smiling up into his swollen face when at last he was standing in front of her. He grinned back, painful though it was: the two-hundred-mile journey he had undertaken so recklessly had been worth it, after all, to see her smile at him like that. "Bursting into church. You could have just called."

"Yeah, sorry about knocking over the flowers," said Strike, including the sullen Matthew in his apology. "I did call, but—"

"I haven't had my phone on this morning," said Robin, aware that she was holding up the queue, but past caring. "Go round us," she said gaily to Matthew's boss, a tall redheaded woman.

"No, I called—two days ago, was it?" said Strike.

"What?" said Robin, while Matthew had a stilted conversation with Jemima.

"A couple of times," said Strike. "I left a message."

"I didn't get any calls," said Robin, "or a message."

The chattering, chinking, tinkling sounds of a hundred guests and the gentle melody of the string quartet seemed suddenly muffled, as though a thick bubble of shock had pressed in upon her.

"When did—what did you—two days ago?"

Since arriving at her parents' house she had been occupied nonstop with tedious wedding chores, yet she had still managed to check her phone frequently and surreptitiously, hoping that Strike had called or texted. Alone in bed at one that morning she had checked her entire call history in the vain hope that she would find a missed communication, but had found the history deleted. Having barely slept in the last couple of weeks, she had concluded that she had made an exhausted blunder, pressed the wrong button, erased it accidentally...

"I don't want to stay," Strike mumbled. "I just wanted to say I'm sorry, and ask you to come—"

"You've got to stay," she said, reaching out and seizing his arm as though he might escape.

Her heart was thudding so fast that she felt breathless. She knew that she had lost color as the buzzing room seemed to wobble around her.

"Please stay," she said, still holding tight to his arm, ignoring Matthew as he bristled beside her. "I need—I want to talk to you. Mum?" she called.

Linda stepped out of the receiving line. She seemed to have been waiting for the summons, and she didn't look happy.

"Please could you add Cormoran to a table?" said Robin. "Maybe put him with Stephen and Jenny?"

Unsmiling, Linda led Strike away. There were a few last guests waiting to offer their congratulations. Robin could no longer muster smiles and small talk.

"Why didn't I get Cormoran's calls?" she asked Matthew, as an elderly man shuffled away towards the tables, neither welcomed nor greeted.

"I've been trying to tell you—"

"Why didn't I get the calls, Matthew?"

"Robin, can we talk about this later?"

The truth burst upon her so suddenly that she gasped.

"*You* deleted my call history," she said, her mind leaping rapidly from deduction to deduction. "You asked for my passcode number when I came back from the bathroom at the service station." The last two guests took one look at the bride and groom's expressions and hurried past without demanding their greeting. "You took my phone away. You said it was about the honeymoon. Did you listen to his message?"

"Yes," said Matthew. "I deleted it."

The silence that seemed to have pressed in on her had become a high-pitched whine. She felt light-headed. Here she stood in the big white lace dress she didn't like, the dress she had had altered because the wedding had been delayed once, pinned to the spot by ceremonial obligations. On the periphery of her vision, a hundred blurred faces swayed. The guests were hungry and expectant.

Her eyes found Strike, who was standing with his back to her, waiting beside Linda while an extra place was laid at her elder brother Stephen's table. Robin imagined striding over to him and saying: "Let's get out of here." What would he say if she did?

Her parents had spent thousands on the day. The packed room was waiting for the bride and groom to take their seats at the top table. Paler than her wedding dress, Robin followed her new husband to their seats as the room burst into applause.

The finicky waiter seemed determined to prolong Strike's discomfort. He had no choice but to stand in full view of every table while he waited for his extra place to be laid. Linda, who was almost a foot shorter than the detective, remained at Strike's elbow while the youth made imperceptible adjustments to the dessert fork and turned the plate so that the design aligned with its neighbors'. The little Strike could see of Linda's face below the silvery hat looked angry.

"Thanks very much," he said at long last, as the waiter stepped out of the way, but as he took hold of the back of his chair, Linda laid a light hand on his sleeve. Her gentle touch might as well have been a shackle, accompanied as it was by an aura of outraged motherhood and offended hospitality. She greatly resembled her daughter. Linda's fading hair was red-gold, too, the clear gray-blue of her eyes enhanced by her silvery hat.

"Why are you here?" she asked through clenched teeth, while waiters bustled around them, delivering starters. At least the arrival of food had distracted the other guests. Conversation broke out as people's attention turned to their long-awaited meal.

"To ask Robin to come back to work with me."

"You sacked her. It broke her heart."

There was much he could have said to that, but he chose not to say it out of respect for what Linda must have suffered when she had seen that eight-inch knife wound.

"Three times she's been attacked, working for you," said Linda, her color rising. "Three times."

Strike could, with truth, have told Linda that he accepted liability only for the first of those attacks. The second had happened after Robin disregarded his explicit instructions and the third as a consequence of her not only disobeying him, but endangering a murder investigation and his entire business.

"She hasn't been sleeping. I've heard her at night..."

Linda's eyes were over-bright. She let go of him, but whispered, "You haven't got a daughter. You can't understand what we've been through."

Before Strike could muster his exhausted faculties, she had marched away to the top table. He caught Robin's eye over her untouched starter. She pulled an anguished expression, as though afraid that he might walk out. He raised his eyebrows slightly and dropped, at last, into his seat.

A large shape to his left shifted ominously. Strike turned to see more eyes like Robin's, set over a pugnacious jaw and surmounted by bristling brows.

"You must be Stephen," said Strike.

Robin's elder brother grunted, still glaring. They were both large men; packed together, Stephen's elbow grazed Strike's as he reached for his pint. The rest of the table was staring at Strike. He raised his right hand in a kind of halfhearted salute, remembered that it was bandaged only when he saw it, and felt that he was drawing even more attention to himself.

"Hi, I'm Jenny, Stephen's wife," said the broad-shouldered brunette on Stephen's other side. "You look as though you could use this."

She passed an untouched pint across Stephen's plate. Strike was so grateful he could have kissed her. In deference to Stephen's scowl, he confined himself to a heartfelt "thanks" and downed half of it in one go. Out of the corner of his eye he saw Jenny mutter something in Stephen's ear. The latter watched Strike set the pint glass down again, cleared his throat and said gruffly:

"Congratulations in order, I s'pose."

"Why?" said Strike blankly.

Stephen's expression became a degree less fierce.

"You caught that killer."

"Oh yeah," said Strike, picking up his fork in his left hand and stabbing the salmon starter. Only after he had swallowed it in its entirety and noticed Jenny laughing did he realize he ought to have treated it with more respect. "Sorry," he muttered. "Very hungry."

Stephen was now contemplating him with a glimmer of approval.

"No point in it, is there?" he said, looking down at his own mousse. "Mostly air."

"Cormoran," said Jenny, "would you mind just waving at Jonathan? Robin's other brother—over there."

Strike looked in the direction indicated. A slender youth with the same coloring as Robin waved enthusiastically from the next table. Strike gave a brief, sheepish salute.

"Want her back, then, do you?" Stephen fired at him.

"Yeah," said Strike. "I do."

He half-expected an angry response, but instead Stephen heaved a long sigh.

"S'pose I've got to be glad. Never seen her happier than when she was working for you. I took the piss out of her when we were kids for saying she wanted to be a policewoman," he added. "Wish I hadn't," he said, accepting a fresh pint from the waiter and managing to down an impressive amount before continuing. "We were dicks to her, looking back, and then she... well, she stands up for herself a bit better these days."

Stephen's gaze wandered to the top table and Strike, who had his back to it, felt justified in stealing a look at Robin, too. She was silent, neither eating nor looking at Matthew.

"Not now, mate," he heard Stephen say and turned to see his neighbor holding out a long thick arm to form a barrier between Strike and one of Martin's friends, who was on his feet and already bending low to ask Strike a question. The friend retreated, abashed.

"Cheers," said Strike, finishing Jenny's pint.

"Get used to it," said Stephen, demolishing his own mousse in a mouthful. "You caught the Shacklewell Ripper. You're going to be famous, mate."

People talked of things passing in a blur after a shock, but it was not like that for Robin. The room around her remained only too visible, every detail distinct: the brilliant squares of light that fell through the curtained windows, the enamel brightness of the azure sky beyond the glass, the damask tablecloths obscured by elbows and disarranged glasses, the gradually flushing cheeks of the scoffing and quaffing guests, Aunt Sue's patrician profile unsoftened by her neighbors' chat, Jenny's silly yellow hat quivering as she joked with Strike. She saw Strike. Her eyes returned so often to his back that she could have sketched with perfect accuracy the creases in his suit jacket, the dense dark curls of the back of his head, the difference in the thickness of his ears due to the knife injury to the left.

No, the shock of what she had discovered in the receiving line had not rendered her surroundings blurred. It had instead affected her perception of both sound and time. At one point, she knew that Matthew had urged her to eat, but it did not register with her until after her full plate had been removed by a solicitous waiter, because everything said to her had to permeate the thick walls that had closed in on her in the aftermath of Matthew's admission of perfidy. Within the invisible cell that separated her entirely from everyone else in the room, adrenaline thundered through her, urging her again and again to stand up and walk out.

If Strike had not arrived today, she might never have known that he wanted her back, and that she might be spared the shame, the anger, the humiliation, the hurt with which she had been racked since that awful night when he had sacked her. Matthew had sought to deny her the thing that might save her, the thing for which she had cried in the small hours of the night when everybody else was asleep: the restoration of her self-respect, of the job that had meant everything to her, of the friendship she had not known was one of the prizes of her life until it was torn away from her. Matthew had lied and kept lying. He had smiled and laughed as she dragged herself through the days before the wedding trying to pretend that she was happy that she had lost a life she had loved. Had she fooled him? Did he believe that she was truly glad her life with Strike was over? If he did, she had married a man who did not know her at all, and if he didn't...

The puddings were cleared away and Robin had to fake a smile for the concerned waiter who this time asked whether he could bring her something else, as this was the third course that she had left uneaten.

"I don't suppose you've got a loaded gun?" Robin asked him.

Fooled by her serious manner, he smiled, then looked confused.

"It doesn't matter," she said. "Never mind."

"For Christ's sake, Robin," Matthew said, and she knew, with a throb of fury and pleasure, that he was panicking, scared of what she would do, scared of what was going to happen next.

Coffee was arriving in sleek silver pots. Robin watched the waiters pouring, saw the little trays of petits fours placed upon the tables. She saw Sarah Shadlock in a tight turquoise sleeveless dress, hurrying across the room to the bathroom ahead of the speeches, watched heavily pregnant Katie following her in her flat shoes, swollen and tired, her enormous belly to the fore, and, again, Robin's eyes returned to Strike's back. He was scoffing petits fours and talking to Stephen. She was glad she had put him beside Stephen. She had always thought they would get on.

Then came the call for quiet, followed by rustling, fidgeting and a mass scraping of chairs as all those who had their backs to the top table dragged themselves around to watch the speakers. Robin's eyes met Strike's. She could not read his expression. He didn't look away from her until her father stood up, straightened his glasses and began to speak.

Strike was longing to lie down or, failing that, to get back into the car with Shanker, where he could at least recline the seat. He had had barely two hours' slumber in the past forty-eight, and a mixture of heavy-duty painkillers and what was now four pints was rendering him so sleepy that he kept dozing off against the hand supporting his head, jerking back awake as his temple slid off his knuckles.

He had never asked Robin what either of her parents did for a living. If Michael Ellacott alluded to his profession at any point during his speech, Strike missed it. He was a mild-looking man, almost professorial, with his horn-rimmed glasses. The children had all got his height, but only Martin had inherited his dark hair and hazel eyes.

The speech had been written, or perhaps rewritten, when Robin was jobless. Michael dwelled with patent love and appreciation on Robin's personal qualities, on her intelligence, her resilience, her generosity and her kindness. He had to stop and clear his throat when he started to speak of his pride in his only daughter, but there was a blank where her achievements ought to have been, an empty space for what she had actually done, or lived through. Of course, some of the things that Robin had survived were unfit to be spoken in this giant humidor of a room, or heard by these feathered and button-holed guests, but the fact of her survival was, for Strike, the highest proof of those qualities and to him it seemed, sleep-befuddled though he was, that an acknowledgment ought to have been made.

Nobody else seemed to think so. He even detected a faint relief in the crowd as Michael drew to a conclusion without alluding to knives or scars, gorilla masks or balaclavas.

The time had come for the bridegroom to speak. Matthew got to his feet amid enthusiastic applause, but Robin's hands remained in her lap as she stared at the window opposite, where the sun now hung low in the cloudless sky, casting long dark shadows over the lawn.

Somewhere in the room, a bee was buzzing. Far less concerned about offending Matthew than he had been about Michael, Strike adjusted his position in his chair, folding his arms and closing his eyes. For a minute or so, he listened as Matthew told how he and Robin had known each other since childhood, but only in their sixth form had he noticed how very good-looking the little girl who had once beaten him in the egg-and-spoon race had become...

"Cormoran!"

He jerked awake suddenly and, judging by the wet patch on his chest, knew that he had been drooling. Blearily he looked around at Stephen, who had elbowed him.

"You were snoring," Stephen muttered.

Before he could reply the room broke into applause again. Matthew was sitting down, unsmiling.

Surely it had to be nearly over...but no, Matthew's best man was getting to his feet. Now that he was awake again, Strike had become aware just how full his bladder was. He hoped to Christ this bloke would speak fast.

"Matt and I first met on the rugby pitch," he said and a table towards the rear of the room broke into drunken cheers.

"Upstairs," said Robin. "Now."

They were the first words she had spoken to her husband since they had sat down at the top table. The applause for the best man's speech had barely died away. Strike was standing, but she could tell that he was only heading for the bathroom because she saw him stop a waiter and ask directions. In any case, she knew, now, that he wanted her back, and was convinced that he would stay long enough to hear her agreement. The look they had exchanged during the starters had told her as much.

"They'll be bringing in the band in half an hour," said Matthew. "We're s'posed to—"

But Robin walked off towards the door, taking with her the invisible isolation cell that had kept her cold and tearless through her father's speech, through Matthew's nervous utterings, through the tedium of the familiar old anecdotes from the rugby club regurgitated by the best man. She had the vague impression that her mother tried to waylay her as she plowed through the guests, but paid no attention. She had sat obediently through the meal and the speeches. The universe owed her an interlude of privacy and freedom.

Up the staircase she marched, her skirt held out of the way of her cheap shoes, and off along a plush carpeted corridor, unsure where she was going, with Matthew's footsteps hurrying behind her.

"Excuse me," she said to a waistcoated teenager who was wheeling a linen basket out of a cupboard, "where's the bridal suite?"

He looked from her to Matthew and smirked, actually smirked.

"Don't be a jerk," said Robin coldly.

"Robin!" said Matthew, as the teenager blushed.

"That way," said the youth hoarsely, pointing.

Robin marched on. Matthew, she knew, had the key. He had stayed at the hotel with his best man the previous evening, though not in the bridal suite.

When Matthew opened the door, she strode inside, registering the rose petals on the bed, the champagne standing in its cooler, the large envelope inscribed to Mr. and Mrs. Cunliffe. With relief, she saw the holdall that she had intended to take as hand luggage to their mystery honeymoon. Unzipping it, she thrust her uninjured arm inside and found the brace that she had removed for the photographs. When she had pulled it back over her aching forearm, with its barely healed wound, she wrenched the new wedding ring off her finger and slammed it down on the bedside table beside the champagne bucket.

"What are you doing?" said Matthew, sounding both scared and aggressive. "What—you want to call it off? You don't want to be married?"

Robin stared at him. She had expected to feel release once they were alone and she could speak freely, but the enormity of what he had done mocked her attempts to express it. She read his fear of her silence in his darting eyes, his squared shoulders. Whether he was aware of it or not, he had placed himself precisely between her and the door.

"All right," he said loudly, "I know I should've—"

"You knew what that job meant to me. You knew."

"I didn't want you to go back, all right?" Matthew shouted. "You got attacked and stabbed, Robin!"

"That was my own fault!"

"He fucking sacked you!"

"Because I did something he'd told me not to do—"

"*I knew you'd fucking defend him!*" Matthew bellowed, all control gone. "I knew if you spoke to him you'd go scurrying back like some fucking lapdog!"

"You don't get to make those decisions for me!" she yelled. "Nobody's got the right to intercept my fucking calls and delete my messages, Matthew!"

Restraint and pretense were gone. They heard each other only by

accident, in brief pauses for breath, each of them howling their resentment and pain across the room like flaming spears that burned into
dust before touching their target. Robin gesticulated wildly, then
screeched with pain as her arm protested sharply, and Matthew
pointed with self-righteous rage at the scar she would carry forever
because of her reckless stupidity in working with Strike. Nothing
was achieved, nothing was excused, nothing was apologized for: the
arguments that had defaced their last twelve months had all led to
this conflagration, the border skirmishes that presage war. Beyond
the window, afternoon dissolved rapidly into evening. Robin's
head throbbed, her stomach churned, her sense of being stifled threatened to overcome her.

"You hated me working those hours—you didn't give a damn
that I was happy in my job for the first time in my life, so you *lied!*
You knew what it meant to me, and you *lied!* How could you delete
my call history, how could you delete my voicemail—?"

She sat down suddenly in a deep, fringed chair, her head in her
hands, dizzy with the force of her anger and shock on an empty
stomach.

Somewhere, distantly in the carpeted hush of the hotel corridors,
a door closed, a woman giggled.

"Robin," said Matthew hoarsely.

She heard him approaching her, but she put out a hand, holding him away.

"Don't touch me."

"Robin, I shouldn't have done it, I know that. I didn't want you
hurt again."

She barely heard him. Her anger was not only for Matthew, but
also for Strike. He should have called back. He should have tried and
kept trying. *If he had, I might not be here now.*

The thought scared her.

If I'd known Strike wanted me back, would I have married Matthew?

She heard the rustle of Matthew's jacket and guessed that he was
checking his watch. Perhaps the guests waiting downstairs would
think that they had disappeared to consummate the marriage. She
could imagine Geoffrey making ribald jokes in their absence. The

band must have been in place for an hour. Again she remembered how much this was all costing her parents. Again, she remembered that they had lost deposits on the wedding that had been postponed.

"All right," she said, in a colorless voice. "Let's go back down and dance."

She stood up, automatically smoothing her skirt. Matthew looked suspicious.

"You're sure?"

"We've got to get through today," she said. "People have come a long way. Mum and Dad have paid a lot of money."

Hoisting her skirt up again, she set off for the suite door.

"Robin!"

She turned back, expecting him to say "I love you," expecting him to smile, to beg, to urge a truer reconciliation.

"You'd better wear this," he said, holding out the wedding ring she had removed, his expression as cold as hers.

Strike had not been able to think of a better course of action, given that he intended to stay until he had spoken to Robin again, than continuing to drink. He had removed himself from Stephen and Jenny's willing protection, feeling that they ought to be free to enjoy the company of friends and family, and fallen back on the methods by which he usually repelled strangers' curiosity: his own intimidating size and habitually surly expression. For a while he lurked at the end of the bar, nursing a pint on his own, and then repaired to the terrace, where he had stood apart from the other smokers and contemplated the dappled evening, breathing in the sweet meadow smell beneath a coral sky. Even Martin and his friends, now full of drink themselves and smoking in a circle like teenagers, failed to muster sufficient nerve to badger him.

After a while, the guests were skillfully rounded up and ushered *en masse* back into the wood-paneled room, which had been transformed in their absence into a dance floor. Half the tables had been removed, the others shifted to the sides. A band stood ready behind amplifiers, but the bride and groom remained absent. A man whom Strike understood to be Matthew's father, sweaty, rotund and red-faced, had already made several jokes about what they might be getting up to when Strike found himself addressed by a woman in a tight turquoise dress whose feathery hair adornment tickled his nose as she closed in for a handshake.

"It's Cormoran Strike, isn't it?" she said. "What an honor! Sarah Shadlock."

Strike knew all about Sarah Shadlock. She had slept with Matthew at university, while he was in a long-distance relationship with Robin. Once again, Strike indicated his bandage to show why he could not shake her hand.

"Oh, you poor thing!"

A drunk, balding man who was probably younger than he looked loomed up behind Sarah.

"Tom Turvey," he said, fixing Strike with unfocused eyes. "Bloody good job. Well done, mate. *Bloody good job*."

"We've wanted to meet you for ages," said Sarah. "We're old friends of Matt and Robin's."

"Shacklewell Rip—Ripper," said Tom, on a slight hiccup. "Bloody good job."

"*Look* at you, you poor thing," said Sarah again, touching Strike on the bicep as she smiled up into his bruised face. "*He* didn't do that to you, did he?"

"Ev'ryone wants to know," said Tom, grinning blearily. "Can hardly contain their bloody selves. You should've made a speech instead of Henry."

"Ha ha," said Sarah. "Last thing you'd want to do, I expect. You must have come here straight from catching—well, I don't know—*did* you?"

"Sorry," said Strike, unsmiling, "police have asked me not to talk about it."

"Ladies and gentlemen," said the harried MC, who had been caught unawares by Matthew and Robin's unobtrusive entrance into the room, "please welcome Mr. and Mrs. Cunliffe!"

As the newlyweds moved unsmilingly into the middle of the dance floor, everybody but Strike began to applaud. The lead singer of the band took the microphone from the MC.

"This is a song from their past that means a lot to Matthew and Robin," the singer announced, as Matthew slid his hand around Robin's waist and grasped her other hand.

The wedding photographer moved out of the shadows and began clicking away again, frowning a little at the reappearance of the ugly rubber brace on the bride's arm.

The first acoustic bars of "Wherever You Will Go" by The Calling struck up. Robin and Matthew began to revolve on the spot, their faces averted from each other.

So lately, been wondering,
Who will be there to take my place
When I'm gone, you'll need love
To light the shadows on your face . . .

Strange choice for an "our song," Strike thought . . . but as he watched he saw Matthew move closer to Robin, saw his hand tighten on her narrow waist as he bent his handsome face to whisper something in her ear.

A jolt somewhere around the solar plexus pierced the fug of exhaustion, relief and alcohol that had cushioned Strike all day long from the reality of what this wedding meant. Now, as Strike watched the newlyweds turn on the dance floor, Robin in her long white dress, with a circlet of roses in her hair, Matthew in his dark suit, his face close to his bride's cheek, Strike was forced to recognize how long, and how deeply, he had hoped that Robin would not marry. He had wanted her free, free to be what they had been together. Free, so that if circumstances changed . . . so the possibility was there . . . free, so that one day, they might find out what else they could be to each other.

Fuck this.

If she wanted to talk, she would have to call him. Setting down his empty glass on a windowsill, he turned and made his way through the other guests, who shuffled aside to let him pass, so dark was his expression.

*

As she turned, staring into space, Robin saw Strike leaving. The door opened. He was gone.

"Let go of me."

"What?"

She pulled free, hoisted up her dress once more for freedom of movement, then half-walked, half-ran off the dance floor, almost careering into her father and Aunt Sue, who were waltzing sedately nearby. Matthew was left standing alone in the middle of the room as Robin fought her way through the startled onlookers towards the door that had just swung shut.

"Cormoran!"

He was already halfway down the stairs, but on hearing his name he turned back. He liked her hair in its long loose waves beneath the crown of Yorkshire roses.

"Congratulations."

She walked down another couple of steps, fighting the lump in her throat.

"You really want me back?"

He forced a smile.

"I've just driven for bloody hours with Shanker in what I strongly suspect is a stolen car. Of course I want you back."

She laughed, though tears sprang to her eyes.

"Shanker's here? You should have brought him in!"

"Shanker? In here? He'd have been through everyone's pockets then nicked the reception till."

She laughed some more, but tears spilled out of her brimming eyes and bounced down her cheek.

"Where are you going to sleep?"

"In the car, while Shanker drives me home. He's going to charge me a fortune for this. Doesn't matter," he added gruffly, as she opened her mouth. "Worth it if you're coming back. More than worth it."

"I want a contract this time," said Robin, the severity of her tone belied by the expression of her eyes. "A proper one."

"You've got it."

"OK, then. Well, I'll see you..."

When would she see him? She was supposed to be on honeymoon for two weeks.

"Let me know," said Strike.

He turned and began to descend the stairs again.

"Cormoran!"

"What?"

She walked towards him until she stood on the step above. Their eyes were on a level now.

"I want to hear all about how you caught him and everything."

He smiled.

"It'll keep. Couldn't have done it without you, though."

Neither of them could tell who had made the first move, or whether they acted in unison. They were holding each other tightly before they knew what had happened, Robin's chin on Strike's shoulder, his face in her hair. He smelled of sweat, beer and surgical spirits, she, of roses and the faint perfume that he had missed when she was no longer in the office. The feel of her was both new and familiar, as though he had held her a long time ago, as though he had missed it without knowing it for years. Through the closed door upstairs the band played on:

> *I'll go wherever you will go*
> *If I could make you mine . . .*

As suddenly as they had reached for each other, they broke apart. Tears were rolling down Robin's face. For one moment of madness, Strike yearned to say, "Come with me," but there are words that can never be unsaid or forgotten, and those, he knew, were some of them.

"Let me know," he repeated. He tried to smile, but it hurt his face. With a wave of his bandaged hand, he continued down the stairs without looking back.

She watched him go, wiping the hot tears frantically from her face. If he had said "come with me," she knew she would have gone: but then what? Gulping, wiping her nose on the back of her hand, Robin turned, hoisted up her skirts again, and climbed slowly back towards her husband.

ONE YEAR LATER

1

I hear that he means to enlarge . . . that he is looking for a competent assistant.

Henrik Ibsen, *Rosmersholm*

Such is the universal desire for fame that those who achieve it accidentally or unwillingly will wait in vain for pity.

For many weeks after the capture of the Shacklewell Ripper, Strike had feared that his greatest detective triumph might have dealt his career a fatal blow. The smatterings of publicity his agency had hitherto attracted seemed now like the two submersions of the drowning man before his final descent to the depths. The business for which he had sacrificed so much, and worked so hard, relied largely on his ability to pass unrecognized in the streets of London, but with the capture of a serial killer he had become lodged in the public imagination, a sensational oddity, a jokey aside on quiz shows, an object of curiosity all the more fascinating because he refused to satisfy it.

Having wrung every last drop of interest out of Strike's ingenuity in catching the Ripper, the papers had exhumed Strike's family history. They called it "colorful," though to him it was a lumpen internal mass that he had carried with him all his life and preferred not to probe: the rock star father, the dead groupie mother, the army career that ended with the loss of half his right leg. Grinning journalists bearing checkbooks had descended on the only sibling with whom he had shared a childhood, his half-sister, Lucy. Army acquaintances had given off-the-cuff remarks that, shorn of what

Strike knew was rough humor, assumed the appearance of envy and disparagement. The father whom Strike had only met twice, and whose surname he did not use, released a statement through a publicist, implying a non-existent, amicable relationship that was proceeding far from prying eyes. The aftershocks of the Ripper's capture had reverberated through Strike's life for a year, and he was not sure they were spent yet.

Of course, there was an upside to becoming the best-known private detective in London. New clients had swarmed to Strike in the aftermath of the trial, so that it had become physically impossible for him and Robin to cover all the jobs themselves. Given that it was advisable for Strike to keep a low profile for a while, he had remained largely office-bound for several months while subcontracted employees—mostly ex-police and military, many from the world of private security—took on the bulk of the work, Strike covering nights and paperwork. After a year of working on as many jobs as the enlarged agency could handle, Strike had managed to give Robin an overdue pay rise, settle the last of his outstanding debts and buy a thirteen-year-old BMW 3 series.

Lucy and his friends assumed that the presence of the car and additional employees meant that Strike had at last achieved a state of prosperous security. In fact, once he had paid the exorbitant costs of garaging the car in central London and met payroll, Strike was left with almost nothing to spend on himself and continued to live in two rooms over the office, cooking on a single-ringed hob.

The administrative demands freelance contractors made and the patchy quality of the men and women available to the agency were a constant headache. Strike had found only one man whom he had kept on semi-permanently: Andy Hutchins, a thin, saturnine ex-policeman ten years older than his new boss, who had come highly recommended by Strike's friend in the Met, Detective Inspector Eric Wardle. Hutchins had taken early retirement when he had been struck by a sudden bout of near-paralysis of his left leg, followed by a diagnosis of multiple sclerosis. When he had applied for contract work, Hutchins had warned Strike that he might not always be fit; it was, he explained, an unpredictable disease, but he had not relapsed in three years. He followed a special low-fat diet that to Strike sounded positively punitive: no red meat, no cheese, no chocolate, nothing deep-fried. Methodical and patient, Andy could be trusted to get the job done without constant supervision, which was more than could be said for any of Strike's other hires apart from Robin. It seemed incredible to him, still, that she had walked into his life as a temporary secretary to become his partner and outstanding colleague.

Whether they were still friends, though, was another question.

Two days after Robin and Matthew's wedding, when the press had driven him out of his flat, while it was still impossible to turn on the TV without hearing his own name, Strike had sought refuge, in spite of invitations from friends and his sister, in a Travelodge near Monument station. There he had attained the solitude and privacy he craved; there he had been free to sleep for hours undisturbed; and there he had downed nine cans of lager and become increasingly desirous of speaking to Robin with each empty can that he threw, with diminishing accuracy, across the room into the bin.

They had had no contact since their hug on the stairs, to which Strike's thoughts had turned repeatedly in the ensuing days. He was sure that Robin would be going through a hellish time, holed up in Masham while deciding whether to pursue a divorce or an annulment, arranging the sale of their flat while dealing with both press and family fallout. What exactly he was going to say when he reached her, Strike did not know. He only knew that he wanted to hear her voice. It was at this point, drunkenly searching his kit bag, that he discovered that in his sleep-deprived haste to leave his flat, he had not packed a recharging lead for his mobile, which was out of battery. Undeterred, he had dialed directory inquiries and succeeded, after many requests to repeat himself more clearly, in getting connected to Robin's parents' house.

Her father had answered.

"Hi, c'n'I speak t'Robinplease?"

"To Robin? I'm afraid she's on her honeymoon."

For a muzzy moment or two, Strike had not quite comprehended what he had been told.

"Hello?" Michael Ellacott had said, and then, angrily, "I suppose this is another journalist. My daughter's abroad and I would like you to stop calling my house."

Strike had hung up, then continued to drink until he passed out.

His anger and disappointment had lingered for days and were in no way abated by his awareness that many would say that he had no claims upon his employee's private life. Robin wasn't the woman he had thought her if she could have got meekly on a plane with the man he mentally referred to as "that twat." Nevertheless, something close to depression weighed upon him while he sat in his Travelodge with his brand-new recharging lead and more lager, waiting for his name to disappear from the news.

Consciously seeking to distract himself from thoughts of Robin, he had ended his self-imposed isolation by accepting an invitation that he would usually have avoided: dinner with Detective Inspector Eric Wardle, Wardle's wife April and their friend Coco. Strike knew perfectly well that he was being set up. Coco had previously tried to find out through Wardle whether Strike was single.

She was a small, lithe, very pretty girl with tomato-red hair, a tattoo artist by trade and a part-time burlesque dancer. He ought to have read the danger signs. She was giggly and slightly hysterical even before they started drinking. Strike had taken her to bed in the Travelodge in the same way he had drunk nine cans of Tennent's.

Coco had taken some shaking loose in the weeks that followed. Strike did not feel good about it, but one advantage of being on the run from the press was that one-night stands found it far harder to track you down.

One year on, Strike had no idea why Robin had chosen to remain with Matthew. He supposed her feelings for her husband ran so deep that she was blind to what he really was. He was in a new relationship himself, now. It had lasted ten months, the longest since he had split up with Charlotte, who had been the only woman whom he had ever contemplated marrying.

The emotional distance between the detective partners had become a simple fact of daily existence. Strike could not fault Robin's work. She did everything she was told promptly, meticulously and with initiative and ingenuity. Nevertheless, he had noticed a pinched look that had never been there before. He thought her slightly jumpier than usual and, once or twice while parceling out work between his partner and subcontractors, he had caught an uncharacteristic blank, unfocused expression that troubled him. He knew some of the signs of post-traumatic stress disorder and she had now survived two near-fatal attacks. In the immediate aftermath of losing half his leg in Afghanistan, he, too, had experienced dissociation, finding himself suddenly and abruptly removed from his present surroundings to those few seconds of acute foreboding and terror that had preceded the disintegration of the Viking in which he had been sitting, and of his body and military career. He had been left with a deep dislike of being driven by anybody else and, to this day, with dreams of blood and agony that sometimes woke him, bathed in sweat.

However, when he had attempted to discuss Robin's mental health in the calm, responsible tones of her employer, she had cut him off with a finality and a resentment that he suspected could be traced to the sacking. Thereafter, he had noticed her volunteering for trickier, after-dark assignments and it had been something of a headache to arrange work so that he did not appear to be trying, as in fact he was, to keep her on the safest, most mundane jobs.

They were polite, pleasant and formal with each other, talking about their private lives in the broadest brushstrokes, and then only when necessary. Robin and Matthew had just moved house and Strike had insisted that she take a full week off to do it. Robin had been resistant, but Strike had overruled her. She had taken very little leave all year, he reminded her, in a tone that brooked no argument.

On Monday, the latest of Strike's unsatisfactory subcontractors, a cocky ex–Red Cap Strike had not known while in the service, had driven his moped into the rear of a taxi he was supposed to be tailing. Strike had enjoyed sacking him. It had given him somebody on whom to vent his anger, because his landlord had also chosen this week to inform Strike that, along with nearly every other owner of office space in Denmark Street, he had sold out to a developer.

The threat of losing both office and home now loomed over the detective.

To set the seal on a particularly shitty few days, the temp he had hired to cover basic paperwork and answer the phone in Robin's absence was as irritating a woman as Strike had ever met. Denise talked nonstop in a whiny, nasal voice that carried even through the closed door of his inner office. Strike had latterly resorted to listening to music on headphones, with the result that she had had to bang on the door repeatedly and shout before he heard her.

"What?"

"I've just found this," said Denise, brandishing a scribbled note in front of him. "It says 'clinic'...there's a word beginning with 'V' in front...the appointment's for half an hour's time—should I have reminded you?"

Strike saw Robin's handwriting. The first word was indeed illegible.

"No," he said. "Just throw it away."

Mildly hopeful that Robin was quietly seeking professional help for any mental problems she might be suffering, Strike replaced his earphones and returned to the report he was reading, but found it hard to concentrate. He therefore decided to leave early for the interview he had scheduled with a possible new subcontractor. Mainly to get away from Denise, he was meeting the man in his favorite pub.

Strike had had to avoid the Tottenham for months in the aftermath of his capture of the Shacklewell Ripper, because journalists had lain in wait for him here, word having got out that he was a regular. Even today, he glanced around suspiciously before deciding that it was safe to advance on the bar, order his usual pint of Doom Bar and retire to a corner table.

Partly because he had made an effort to give up the chips that were a staple of his diet, partly because of his workload, Strike was thinner now than he had been a year ago. The weight loss had relieved pressure on his amputated leg, so that both the effort and the relief of sitting were less noticeable. Strike took a swig of his pint, stretching his knee from force of habit and enjoying the relative ease of movement, then opened the cardboard file he had brought with him.

The notes within had been made by the idiot who had crashed his moped into the back of the taxi, and they were barely adequate. Strike couldn't afford to lose this client, but he and Hutchins were struggling to cover workload as it was. He urgently needed a new hire, and yet he wasn't entirely sure that the interview he was about to conduct was wise. He had not consulted Robin before making the bold decision to hunt down a man he had not seen for five years, and even as the door of the Tottenham opened to admit Sam Barclay, who was punctual to the minute, Strike was wondering whether he was about to make an almighty mistake.

He would have known the Glaswegian almost anywhere as an ex-squaddie, with his T-shirt under his thin V-neck jumper, his close-cropped hair, his tight jeans and over-white trainers. As Strike stood up and held out his hand, Barclay, who appeared to have recognized him with similar ease, grinned and said:

"Already drinking, aye?"

"Want one?" asked Strike.

While waiting for Barclay's pint, he watched the ex-Rifleman in the mirror behind the bar. Barclay was only a little over thirty, but his hair was prematurely graying. He was otherwise exactly as Strike remembered. Heavy browed, with large round blue eyes and a strong jaw, he had the slightly beaky appearance of an affable owl. Strike had liked Barclay even while working to court-martial him.

"Still smoking?" Strike asked, once he'd handed over the beer and sat down.

"Vapin' now," said Barclay. "We've had a baby."

"Congratulations," said Strike. "On a health kick, then?"

"Aye, somethin' like that."

"Dealing?"

"I wasnae dealin'," said Barclay hotly, "as you fuckin' well know. Recreational use only, pal."

"Where are you buying it now, then?"

"Online," said Barclay, sipping his pint. "Easy. First time I did it, I thought, this cannae fuckin' work, can it? But then I thought, 'Och, well, it's an adventure.' They send it to you disguised in fag packets and that. Choose off a whole menu. Internet's a great thing."

He laughed and said, "So whut's this all about? Wasnae expectin' to hear from *you* anytime soon."

Strike hesitated.

"I was thinking of offering you a job."

There was a beat as Barclay stared at him, then he threw back his head and roared with laughter.

"Fuck," he said. "Why didn't ye say that straight off, like?"

"Why d'you think?"

"I'm no vapin' every night," said Barclay earnestly. "I'm no, seriously. The wife doesnae like it."

Strike kept his hand closed on the file, thinking.

He had been working a drugs case in Germany when he had run across Barclay. Drugs were bought and sold within the British army as in every other part of society, but the Special Investigation Branch had been called in to investigate what appeared to be a rather more professional operation than most. Barclay had been fingered as a key player and the discovery of a kilo brick of prime Moroccan hash among his effects had certainly justified an interview.

Barclay insisted that he had been stitched up and Strike, who was sitting in on his interrogation, was inclined to agree, not least because the Rifleman seemed far too intelligent not to have found a better hiding place for his hashish than the bottom of an army kit bag. On the other hand, there was ample evidence that Barclay had been using regularly, and there was more than one witness to the fact that his behavior was becoming erratic. Strike felt that Barclay had been lined up as a convenient scapegoat, and decided to undertake a little side excavation on his own.

This threw up interesting information relating to building materials and engineering supplies that were being reordered at a thoroughly implausible rate. While it was not the first time that Strike had uncovered this kind of corruption, it so happened that the two officers in charge of these mysteriously vanishing and highly resalable commodities were the very men so keen to secure Barclay's court martial.

Barclay was startled, during a one-to-one interview with Strike, to find the SIB sergeant suddenly interested, not in hashish, but in anomalies relating to building contracts. At first wary, and sure he would not be believed given the situation in which he found himself, Barclay finally admitted to Strike that he had not only noticed what others had failed to see, or chosen not to inquire into, but begun to tabulate and document exactly how much these officers were stealing. Unfortunately for Barclay, the officers in question had got wind of the fact that he was a little too interested in their activities, and it was shortly after this that a kilo of hashish had turned up in Barclay's effects.

When Barclay showed Strike the record he had been keeping (the notebook had been hidden a good deal more skillfully than the hashish), Strike had been impressed by the method and initiative it displayed, given that Barclay had never been trained in investigative technique. Asked why he had undertaken the investigation for which nobody was paying, and which had landed him in so much trouble, Barclay had shrugged his broad shoulders and said "no right, is it? That's the army they're robbin'. Taxpayers' money they're fuckin' pocketin'."

Strike had put in many more hours on the case than his colleagues felt was merited, but finally, with Strike's additional investigations into the matter to add weight, the dossier on his superiors' activities that Barclay had compiled led to their conviction. The SIB took credit for it, of course, but Strike had made sure that accusations against Barclay were quietly laid to rest.

"When ye say 'work,'" Barclay wondered aloud now, as the pub hummed and tinkled around them, "ye mean detective stuff?"

Strike could see that the idea appealed.

"Yeah," said Strike. "What have you been doing since I last saw you?"

The answer was depressing, though not unexpected. Barclay had found it hard to get or keep a regular job in the first couple of years out of the army and had been doing a bit of painting and decorating for his brother-in-law's company.

"The wife's bringin' in most o' the money," he said. "She's got a good job."

"OK," said Strike, "I reckon I can give you a couple of days a week for starters. You'll bill me as a freelancer. If it doesn't work out, either of us can walk away at any time. Sound fair?"

"Aye," said Barclay, "aye, fair enough. What are you paying, like?"

They discussed money for five minutes. Strike explained how his other employees set themselves up as private contractors and how receipts and other professional expenses should be brought into the office for reimbursement. Finally he opened the file and slid it around to show Barclay the contents.

"I need this guy followed," he said, pointing out a photograph of a chubby youth with thick curly hair. "Pictures of whoever he's with and what he's up to."

"Aye, all right," said Barclay, getting out his mobile and taking pictures of the target's photograph and address.

"He's being watched today by my other guy," said Strike, "but I need you outside his flat from six o'clock tomorrow morning."

He was pleased to note that Barclay did not query the early start.

"Whut happened to that lassie, though?" Barclay inquired as he put his phone back into his pocket. "The one who was in the papers with ye?"

"Robin?" said Strike. "She's on holiday. Back next week."

They parted with a handshake, Strike enjoying a moment's fleeting optimism before remembering that he would now have to return to the office, which meant proximity to Denise, with her parrot-like chatter, her habit of talking with her mouth full and her inability to remember that he detested pale, milky tea.

He had to pick his way through the ever-present roadworks at the top of Tottenham Court Road to get back to his office. Waiting until he was past the noisiest stretch, he called Robin to tell her that he had hired Barclay, but his call went straight to voicemail. Remembering that she was supposed to be at the mysterious clinic right now, he cut the call without leaving a message.

Walking on, a sudden thought occurred to him. He had assumed that the clinic related to Robin's mental health, but what if—?

The phone in his hand rang: the office number.

"Hello?"

"Mr. Strike?" said Denise's terrified squawk in his ear. "Mr. Strike, could you come back quickly, please? Please—there's a gentle-man—he wants to see you very urgently—"

Behind her, Strike heard a loud bang and a man shouting.

"Please come back as soon as you can!" screamed Denise.

"On my way!" Strike shouted and he broke into an ungainly run.

2

. . . he doesn't look the sort of man one ought to allow in here.
Henrik Ibsen, *Rosmersholm*

Panting, his right knee aching, Strike used the handrail to pull himself up the last few steps of the metal staircase leading to his office. Two raised voices were reverberating through the glass door, one male, the other shrill, frightened and female. When Strike burst into the room, Denise, who was backed against the wall, gasped, "Oh, thank God!"

Strike judged the man in the middle of the room to be in his mid-twenties. Dark hair fell in straggly wisps around a thin and dirty face that was dominated by burning, sunken eyes. His T-shirt, jeans and hoodie were all torn and filthy, the sole of one of his trainers peeling away from the leather. An unwashed animal stench hit the detective's nostrils.

That the stranger was mentally ill could be in no doubt. Every ten seconds or so, in what seemed to be an uncontrollable tic, he touched first the end of his nose, which had grown red with repeated tapping, then, with a faint hollow thud, the middle of his thin sternum, then let his hand drop to his side. Almost immediately, his hand would fly to the tip of his nose again. It was as though he had forgotten how to cross himself, or had simplified the action for speed's sake. Nose, chest, hand at his side; nose, chest, hand at his side; the mechanical movement was distressing to watch, and the more so as he seemed barely conscious that he was doing it. He was one of those ill and desperate people you saw in the capital who were always somebody else's problem, like the traveler on the Tube everybody tried to avoid making eye contact with and the ranting woman on the street corner whom people crossed the street to avoid, fragments of shattered humanity who were too common to trouble the imagination for long.

"You him?" said the burning-eyed man, as his hand touched nose and chest again. "You Strike? You the detective?"

With the hand that was not constantly flying from nose to chest, he suddenly tugged at his flies. Denise whimpered, as if scared he might suddenly expose himself, and, indeed, it seemed entirely possible.

"I'm Strike, yeah," said the detective, moving around to place himself between the stranger and the temp. "You OK, Denise?"

"Yes," she whispered, still backed against the wall.

"I seen a kid killed," said the stranger. "Strangled."

"OK," said Strike, matter-of-factly. "Why don't we go in here?"

He gestured to him that he should proceed into the inner office.

"I need a piss!" said the man, tugging at his zip.

"This way, then."

Strike showed him the door to the toilet just outside the office. When the door had banged shut behind him, Strike returned quietly to Denise.

"What happened?"

"He wanted to see you, I said you weren't here and he got angry and started punching things!"

"Call the police," said Strike quietly. "Tell them we've got a very ill man here. Possibly psychotic. Wait until I've got him into my office, though."

The bathroom door banged open. The stranger's flies were gaping. He did not seem to be wearing underpants. Denise whimpered again as he frantically touched nose and chest, nose and chest, unaware of the large patch of dark pubic hair he was exposing.

"This way," said Strike pleasantly. The man shuffled through the inner door, the stench of him doubly potent after a brief respite.

On being invited to sit down, the stranger perched himself on the edge of the client's chair.

"What's your name?" Strike asked, sitting down on the other side of the desk.

"Billy," said the man, his hand flying from nose to chest three times in quick succession. The third time his hand fell, he grabbed it with his other hand and held it tightly.

"And you saw a child strangled, Billy?" said Strike, as in the next room Denise gabbled:

"Police, quickly!"

"What did she say?" asked Billy, his sunken eyes huge in his face as he glanced nervously towards the outer office, one hand clasping the other in his effort to suppress his tic.

"That's nothing," said Strike easily. "I've got a few different cases on. Tell me about this child."

Strike reached for a pad and paper, all his movements slow and cautious, as though Billy were a wild bird that might take fright.

"He strangled it, up by the horse."

Denise was now gabbling loudly into the phone beyond the flimsy partition wall.

"When was this?" asked Strike, still writing.

"Ages...I was a kid. Little girl it was, but after they said it was a little boy. Jimmy was there, he says I never saw it, but I did. I saw him do it. Strangled. I saw it."

"And this was up by the horse, was it?"

"Right up by the horse. That's not where they buried her, though. Him. That was down in the dell, by our dad's. I seen them doing it, I can show you the place. She wouldn't let me dig, but she'd let you."

"And Jimmy did it, did he?"

"Jimmy never strangled nobody!" said Billy angrily. "He saw it with me. He says it didn't happen but he's lying, he was there. He's frightened, see."

"I see," lied Strike, continuing to take notes. "Well, I'll need your address if I'm going to investigate."

He half-expected resistance, but Billy reached eagerly for the proffered pad and pen. A further gust of body odor reached Strike. Billy began to write, but suddenly seemed to think better of it.

"You won't come to Jimmy's place, though? He'll fucking tan me. You can't come to Jimmy's."

"No, no," said Strike soothingly. "I just need your address for my records."

Through the door came Denise's grating voice.

"I need someone here quicker than that, he's very disturbed!"

"What's she saying?" asked Billy.

To Strike's chagrin, Billy suddenly ripped the top sheet from the pad, crumpled it, then began to touch nose and chest again with his fist enclosing the paper.

"Don't worry about Denise," said Strike, "she's dealing with another client. Can I get you a drink, Billy?"

"Drink of what?"

"Tea? Or coffee?"

"Why?" asked Billy. The offer seemed to have made him even more suspicious. "Why do you want me to drink something?"

"Only if you fancy it. Doesn't matter if you don't."

"I don't need medicine!"

"I haven't got any medicine to give you," said Strike.

"I'm not mental! He strangled the kid and they buried it, down in the dell by our dad's house. Wrapped in a blanket it was. Pink blanket. It wasn't my fault. I was only a kid. I didn't want to be there. I was just a little kid."

"How many years ago, do you know?"

"Ages...years...can't get it out of my head," said Billy, his eyes burning in his thin face as the fist enclosing the piece of paper fluttered up and down, touching nose, touching chest. "They buried her in a pink blanket, down in the dell by my dad's house. But afterwards they said it was a boy."

"Where's your dad's house, Billy?"

"She won't let me back now. *You* could dig, though. *You* could go. Strangled her, they did," said Billy, fixing Strike with his haunted eyes. "But Jimmy said it was a boy. Strangled, up by the—"

There was a knock on the door. Before Strike could tell her not to enter, Denise had poked her head inside, much braver now that Strike was here, full of her own importance.

"They're coming," she said, with a look of exaggerated meaning that would have spooked a man far less jumpy than Billy. "On their way now."

"Who's coming?" demanded Billy, jumping up. "Who's on their way?"

Denise whipped her head out of the room and closed the door. There was a soft thud against the wood, and Strike knew that she was leaning against it, trying to hold Billy in.

"She's just talking about a delivery I'm expecting," Strike said soothingly, getting to his feet. "Go on about the—"

"What have you done?" yelped Billy, backing away towards the door while he repeatedly touched nose and chest. "Who's coming?"

"Nobody's coming," said Strike, but Billy was already trying to push the door open. Meeting resistance, he flung himself hard against it. There was a shriek from outside as Denise was thrown aside. Before Strike could get out from around the desk, Billy had sprinted through the outer door. They heard him jumping down the metal stairs three at a time and Strike, infuriated, knowing that he had no hope of catching a younger and, on the evidence, fitter man, turned and ran back into his office. Throwing up the sash window, he leaned outside just in time to see Billy whipping around the corner of the street out of sight.

"*Bollocks!*"

A man heading inside the guitar shop opposite stared around in some perplexity for the source of the noise.

Strike withdrew his head and turned to glare at Denise, who was dusting herself down in the doorway to his office. Incredibly, she looked pleased with herself.

"I tried to hold him in," she said proudly.

"Yeah," said Strike, exercising considerable self-restraint. "I saw."

"The police are on their way."

"Fantastic."

"Would you like a cup of tea?"

"No," he said through gritted teeth.

"Then I think I'll go and freshen up the bathroom," she said, adding in a whisper, "I don't think he used the flush."

3

As she walked along the unfamiliar Deptford street, Robin was raised to temporary light-heartedness, then wondered when she had last felt this way and knew that it had been over a year. Energized and uplifted by the afternoon sunshine, the colorful shopfronts and general bustle and noise, she was currently celebrating the fact that she never need see the inside of the Villiers Trust Clinic again.

Her therapist had been unhappy that she was terminating treatment.

"We recommend a full course," she had said.

"I know," Robin replied, "but, well, I'm sorry, I think this has done me as much good as it's going to."

The therapist's smile had been chilly.

"The CBT's been great," Robin had said. "It's really helped with the anxiety, I'm going to keep that up..."

She had taken a deep breath, eyes fixed on the woman's low-heeled Mary Janes, then forced herself to look her in the eye.

"...but I'm not finding this part helpful."

Another silence had ensued. After five sessions, Robin was used to them. In normal conversation, it would be considered rude or passive aggressive to leave these long pauses and simply watch the other person, waiting for them to speak, but in psychodynamic therapy, she had learned, it was standard.

Robin's doctor had given her a referral for free treatment on the NHS, but the waiting list had been so long that she had decided, with Matthew's tight-lipped support, to pay for treatment. Matthew, she knew, was barely refraining from saying that the ideal solution would be to give up the job that had landed her with PTSD and which in his view paid far too poorly considering the dangers to which she had been exposed.

"You see," Robin had continued with the speech she had prepared, "my life is pretty much wall to wall with people who think they know what's best for me."

"Well, yes," said the therapist, in a manner that Robin felt would have been considered condescending beyond the clinic walls, "we've discussed—"

"—and..."

Robin was by nature conciliatory and polite. On the other hand, she had been urged repeatedly by the therapist to speak the unvarnished truth in this dingy little room with the spider plant in its dull green pot and the man-sized tissues on the low pine table.

"...and to be honest," she said, "you feel like just another one of them."

Another pause.

"Well," said the therapist, with a little laugh, "I'm here to help you reach your own conclusions about—"

"Yes, but you do it by—by *pushing* me all the time," said Robin. "It's combative. You challenge everything I say."

Robin closed her eyes, as a great wave of weariness swept her. Her muscles ached. She had spent all week putting together flat-pack furniture, heaving around boxes of books and hanging pictures.

"I come out of here," said Robin, opening her eyes again, "feeling wrung out. I go home to my husband, and he does it, too. He leaves big sulky silences and challenges me on the smallest things. Then I phone my mother, and it's more of the same. The only person who isn't *at me* all the time to sort myself out is—"

She pulled up short, then said:

"—is my work partner."

"Mr. Strike," said the therapist sweetly.

It had been a matter of contention between Robin and the therapist that she had refused to discuss her relationship with Strike, other than to confirm that he was unaware of how much the Shacklewell Ripper case had affected her. Their personal relationship, she had stated firmly, was irrelevant to her present issues. The therapist had raised him in every session since, but Robin had consistently refused to engage on the subject.

"Yes," said Robin. "Him."

"By your own admission you haven't told him the full extent of your anxiety."

"So," said Robin, ignoring the last comment, "I really only came today to tell you I'm leaving. As I say, I've found the CBT really useful and I'm going to keep using the exercises."

The therapist had seemed outraged that Robin wasn't even prepared to stay for the full hour, but Robin had paid for the entire session and therefore felt free to walk out, giving her what felt like a bonus hour in the day. She felt justified in not hurrying home to do more unpacking, but to buy herself a Cornetto and enjoy it as she wandered through the sun-drenched streets of her new area.

Chasing her own cheerfulness like a butterfly, because she was afraid it might escape, she turned up a quieter street, forcing herself to concentrate, to take in the unfamiliar scene. She was, after all, delighted to have left behind the old flat in West Ealing, with its many bad memories. It had become clear during his trial that the Shacklewell Ripper had been tailing and watching Robin for far longer than she had ever suspected. The police had even told her that they thought he had hung around Hastings Road, lurking behind parked cars, yards from her front door.

Desperate though she had been to move, it had taken her and Matthew eleven months to find a new place. The main problem was that Matthew had been determined to "take a step up the property ladder," now that he had a better-paid new job and a legacy from his late mother. Robin's parents, too, had expressed a willingness to help them, given the awful associations of the old flat, but London was excruciatingly expensive. Three times had Matthew set his heart on flats that were, realistically, well out of their price range. Three times had they failed to buy what Robin could have told him would sell for thousands more than they could offer.

"It's ridiculous!" he kept saying, "it isn't worth that!"

"It's worth whatever people are prepared to pay," Robin had said, frustrated that an accountant didn't understand the operation of market forces. She had been ready to move anywhere, even a single room, to escape the shadow of the killer who continued to haunt her dreams.

On the point of doubling back towards the main road, her eye was caught by the opening in a brick wall, which was flanked by gateposts topped with the strangest finials she had ever seen.

A pair of gigantic, crumbling stone skulls sat on top of carved bones on gateposts, beyond which a tall square tower rose. The finials would have looked at home, Robin thought, moving closer to examine the empty black eye sockets, garnishing the front of a pirate's mansion in some fantasy film. Peering through the opening, Robin saw a church and mossy tombs lying amid an empty rose garden in full bloom.

She finished her ice cream while wandering around St. Nicholas's, a strange amalgam of an old red-brick school grafted onto the rough stone tower. Finally she sat down on a wooden bench that had grown almost uncomfortably hot in the sun, stretched her aching back, drank in the delicious scent of warm roses and was suddenly transported, entirely against her will, back to the hotel suite in Yorkshire, almost a year ago, where a blood-red bouquet of roses had witnessed the aftermath of her abandonment of Matthew on the dance floor at her wedding reception.

Matthew, his father, his Aunt Sue, Robin's parents and brother Stephen had all converged on the bridal suite where Robin had retreated to escape Matthew's fury. She had been changing out of her wedding dress when they had burst in, one after another, all demanding to know what was going on.

A cacophony had ensued. Stephen, first to grasp what Matthew had done in deleting Strike's calls, started to shout at him. Geoffrey was drunkenly demanding to know why Strike had been allowed to stay for dinner given he hadn't RSVPed. Matthew was bellowing at all of them to butt out, that this was between him and Robin, while Aunt Sue said over and over, "I've never seen a bride walk out of her first dance. *Never!* I've *never* seen a bride walk out of her first dance."

Then Linda had finally grasped what Matthew had done, and began telling him off, too. Geoffrey had leapt to his son's defense, demanding to know why Linda wanted her daughter to go back to a man who allowed her to get stabbed. Martin had arrived, extremely drunk, and had taken a swing at Matthew for reasons that nobody had ever explained satisfactorily, and Robin had retreated to the bathroom where, incredibly, given that she had barely eaten all day, she had thrown up.

Five minutes later, she had been forced to let Matthew in because his nose was bleeding and there, with their families still shouting at each other in the next door bedroom, Matthew had asked her, a wodge of toilet roll pressed to his nostrils, to come with him to the Maldives, not as a honeymoon, not anymore, but to sort things out in private, "away," as he put it thickly, gesturing towards the source of the yelling, "from *this*. And there'll be press," he added, accusingly. "They'll be after you, for the Ripper business."

He was cold-eyed over the bloody toilet paper, furious with her for humiliating him on the dance floor, livid with Martin for hitting him. There was nothing romantic in his invitation to board the plane. He was proposing a summit, a chance for calm discussion. If, after serious consideration, they came to the conclusion that the marriage was a mistake, they would come home at the end of the fortnight, make a joint announcement, and go their separate ways.

And at that moment, the wretched Robin, arm throbbing, shaken to the core by the feelings that had risen inside when she had felt Strike's arms around her, knowing that the press might even now be trying to track her down, had seen Matthew, if not as an ally, at least as an escape. The idea of getting on a plane, of flying out of reach of the tsunami of curiosity, gossip, anger, solicitude and unsought advice that she knew would engulf her as long as she remained in Yorkshire, was deeply appealing.

So they had left, barely speaking during the flight. What Matthew had been thinking through those long hours, she had never inquired.

She knew only that she had thought about Strike. Over and again, she had returned to the memory of their embrace as she watched the clouds slide past the window.

Am I in love with him? she had asked herself repeatedly, but without reaching any firm conclusion.

Her deliberations on the subject had lasted days, an inner torment she could not reveal to Matthew as they walked on white beaches, discussing the tensions and resentments that lay between the two of them. Matthew slept on the living-room sofa at night, Robin in the net-draped double bed upstairs. Sometimes they argued, at other times they retreated into hurt and furious silences. Matthew was keeping tabs on Robin's phone, wanting to know where it was, constantly picking it up and checking it, and she knew that he was looking for messages or calls from her boss.

What made things worse was that there were none. Apparently Strike wasn't interested in talking to her. The hug on the stairs, to which her thoughts kept scampering back like a dog to a blissfully pungent lamppost, seemed to have meant far less to him than it had to her.

Night after night, Robin walked by herself on the beach, listening to the sea's deep breathing, her injured arm sweating beneath its rubber protective brace, her phone left at the villa so that Matthew had no excuse to tail her and find out whether she was talking secretly to Strike.

But on the seventh night, with Matthew back at the villa, she had decided to call Strike. Almost without acknowledging it to herself, she had formulated a plan. There was a landline at the bar and she knew the office number off by heart. It would be diverted to Strike's mobile automatically. What she was going to say when she reached him, she didn't know, but she was sure that if she heard him speak, the truth about her feelings would be revealed to her. As the phone rang in distant London, Robin's mouth had become dry.

The phone was answered, but nobody spoke for a few seconds. Robin listened to the sounds of movement, then heard a giggle, and then at last somebody spoke.

"Hello? This is Cormy-Warmy—"

As the woman broke into loud, raucous laughter, Robin heard Strike somewhere in the background, half-amused, half-annoyed and certainly drunk:

"Gimme that! Seriously, give it—"

Robin had slammed the receiver back onto its rest. Sweat had broken out on her face and chest: she felt ashamed, foolish, humiliated. He was with another woman. The laughter had been unmistakably intimate. The unknown girl had been teasing him, answering his mobile, calling him (how revolting) "Cormy."

She would deny phoning him, she resolved, if ever Strike asked her about the dropped call. She would lie through her teeth, pretend not to know what he was talking about...

The sound of the woman on the phone had affected her like a hard slap. If Strike could have taken somebody to bed so soon after their hug—and she would have staked her life on the fact that the girl, whoever she was, had either just slept with Strike, or was about to—then he wasn't sitting in London torturing himself about his true feelings for Robin Ellacott.

The salt on her lips made her thirsty as she trudged through the night, wearing a deep groove in the soft white sand as the waves broke endlessly beside her. Wasn't it possible, she asked herself, when she was cried out at last, that she was confusing gratitude and friendship with something deeper? That she had mistaken her love of detection for love of the man who had given her the job? She admired Strike, of course, and was immensely fond of him. They had passed through many intense experiences together, so that it was natural to feel close to him, but was that love?

Alone in the balmy, mosquito-buzzing night, while the waves sighed on the shore and she cradled her aching arm, Robin reminded herself bleakly that she had had very little experience with men for a woman approaching her twenty-eighth birthday. Matthew was all she had ever known, her only sexual partner, a place of safety to her for ten long years now. If she *had* developed a crush on Strike—she employed the old-fashioned word her mother might have used—mightn't it also be the natural side effect of the lack of variety and experimentation most women of her age had enjoyed? For so long faithful to Matthew, hadn't she been bound to look up one day and remember that there were other lives, other choices? Hadn't she been long overdue to notice that Matthew was not the only man in the world? Strike, she told herself, was simply the one with whom she had been spending the most time, so naturally it had been he onto whom she projected her wondering, her curiosity, her dissatisfaction with Matthew.

Having, as she told herself, talked sense into that part of her that kept yearning for Strike, she reached a hard decision on the eighth evening of her honeymoon. She wanted to go home early and announce their separation to their families. She must tell Matthew that it had nothing to do with anybody else, but after agonizing and serious reflection, she did not believe they were well suited enough to continue in the marriage.

She could still remember her feeling of mingled panic and dread as she had pushed open the cabin door, braced for a fight that had never materialized. Matthew had been sitting slumped on the sofa and when he saw her, he mumbled, "Mum?"

His face, arms and legs had been shining with sweat. As she moved towards him, she saw an ugly black tracing of veins up the inside of his left arm, as though somebody had filled them with ink.

"Matt?"

Hearing her, he had realized that she was not his dead mother.

"Don't...feel well, Rob..."

She had dashed for the phone, called the hotel, asked for a doctor. By the time he arrived, Matthew was drifting in and out of delirium. They had found the scratch on the back of his hand and, worried, concluded that he might have cellulitis, which Robin could tell, from the faces of the worried doctor and nurse, was serious. Matthew kept seeing figures moving in the shadowy corners of the cabin, people who weren't there.

"Who's that?" he kept asking Robin. "Who's that over there?"

"There's nobody else here, Matt."

Now she was holding his hand while the nurse and doctor discussed hospitalization.

"Don't leave me, Rob."

"I'm not going to leave you."

She had meant that she was going nowhere just now, not that she would stay forever, but Matthew had begun to cry.

"Oh, thank God. I thought you were going to walk...I love you, Rob. I know I fucked up, but I love you..."

The doctor gave Matthew oral antibiotics and went to make telephone calls. Delirious, Matthew clung to his wife, thanking her. Sometimes he drifted into a state where, again, he thought he saw shadows moving in the empty corners of the room, and twice more he muttered about his dead mother. Alone in the velvety blackness of the tropical night, Robin listened to winged insects colliding with the screens at the windows, alternately comforting and watching over the man she had loved since she was seventeen.

It hadn't been cellulitis. The infection had responded, over the next twenty-four hours, to antibiotics. As he recovered from the sudden, violent illness, Matthew watched her constantly, weak and vulnerable as she had never seen him, afraid, she knew, that her promise to stay had been temporary.

"We can't throw it all away, can we?" he had asked her hoarsely from the bed where the doctor had insisted he stay. "All these years?"

She had let him talk about the good times, the shared times, and she had reminded herself about the giggling girl who had called Strike "Cormy." She envisioned going home and asking for an annulment, because the marriage had still not been consummated. She remembered the money her parents had spent on the wedding day she had hated.

Bees buzzed in the churchyard roses around her as Robin wondered, for the thousandth time, where she would be right now if Matthew hadn't scratched himself on coral. Most of her now-terminated therapy sessions had been full of her need to talk about the doubts that had plagued her ever since she had agreed to remain married.

In the months that had followed, and especially when she and Matthew were getting on reasonably well, it seemed to her that it had been right to give the marriage a fair trial, but she never forgot to think of it in terms of a trial, and this in itself sometimes led her, sleepless at night, to castigate herself for the pusillanimous failure to pull herself free once Matthew had recovered.

She had never explained to Strike what had happened, why she had agreed to try and keep the marriage afloat. Perhaps that was why their friendship had grown so cold and distant. When she had returned from her honeymoon, it was to find Strike changed towards her—and perhaps, she acknowledged, she had changed towards him, too, because of what she had heard on the line when she had called, in desperation, from the Maldives bar.

"Sticking with it, then, are you?" he had said roughly, after a glance at her ring finger.

His tone had nettled her, as had the fact that he had never asked why she was trying, never asked about her home life from that point onwards, never so much as hinted that he remembered the hug on the stairs.

Whether because Strike had arranged matters that way or not, they had not worked a case together since that of the Shacklewell Ripper. Imitating her senior partner, Robin had retreated into a cool professionalism.

But sometimes she was afraid that he no longer valued her as he once had, now that she had proven herself so conventional and cowardly. There had been an awkward conversation a few months ago in which he had suggested that she take time off, asked whether she felt she was fully recovered after the knife attack. Taking this as a slight upon her bravery, afraid that she would again find herself sidelined, losing the only part of her life that she currently found fulfilling, she had insisted that she was perfectly well and redoubled her professional efforts.

The muted mobile in her bag vibrated. Robin slipped her hand inside and looked to see who was calling. Strike. She also noticed that he had called earlier, while she was saying a joyful goodbye to the Villiers Trust Clinic.

"Hi," she said. "I missed you earlier, sorry."

"Not a problem. Move gone all right?"

"Fine," she said.

"Just wanted to let you know, I've hired us a new subcontractor. Name of Sam Barclay."

"Great," said Robin, watching a fly shimmering on a fat, blush-pink rose. "What's his background?"

"Army," said Strike.

"Military police?"

"Er—not exactly."

As he told her the story of Sam Barclay, Robin found herself grinning.

"So you've hired a dope-smoking painter and decorator?"

"Vaping, dope *vaping*," Strike corrected her, and Robin could tell that he was grinning, too. "He's on a health kick. New baby."

"Well, he sounds...interesting."

She waited, but Strike did not speak.

"I'll see you Saturday night, then," she said.

Robin had felt obliged to invite Strike to her and Matthew's house-warming party, because she had given their most regular and reliable subcontractor, Andy Hutchins, an invitation, and felt it would be odd to leave out Strike. She had been surprised when he had accepted.

"Yeah, see you then."

"Is Lorelei coming?" Robin asked, striving for casualness, but not sure she had succeeded.

Back in central London, Strike thought he detected a sardonic note in the question, as though challenging him to admit that his girl-friend had a ludicrous moniker. He would once have pulled her up on it, asked what her problem was with the name "Lorelei," enjoyed sparring with her, but this was dangerous territory.

"Yeah, she's coming. The invitation was to both—"

"Yes, of course it was," said Robin hastily. "All right, I'll see you—"

"Hang on," said Strike.

He was alone in the office, because he had sent Denise home early. The temp had not wanted to leave: she was paid by the hour, after all, and only after Strike had assured her that he would pay for a full day had she gathered up all her possessions, talking nonstop all the while.

"Funny thing happened this afternoon," said Strike.

Robin listened intently, without interrupting, to Strike's vivid account of the brief visit of Billy. By the end of it, she had forgotten to worry about Strike's coolness. Indeed, he now sounded like the Strike of a year ago.

"He was definitely mentally ill," said Strike, his eyes on the clear sky beyond the window. "Possibly psychotic."

"Yeah, but—"

"I know," said Strike. He picked up the pad from which Billy had ripped his half-written address and turned it absently in his free hand. "Is he mentally ill, *so* he thinks he saw a kid strangled? Or is he mentally ill *and* he saw a kid strangled?"

Neither spoke for a while, during which time both turned over Billy's story in their minds, knowing that the other was doing the same. This brief, companionable spell of reflection ended abruptly when a cocker spaniel, which Robin had not noticed as it came snuffling through the roses, laid its cold nose without warning on her bare knee and she shrieked.

"What the fuck?"

"Nothing—a dog—"

"Where are you?"

"In a graveyard."

"What? Why?"

"Just exploring the area. I'd better go," she said, getting to her feet. "There's another flat-pack waiting for me at home."

"Right you are," said Strike, with a return to his usual briskness. "See you Saturday."

"I'm so sorry," said the cocker spaniel's elderly owner, as Robin slid her mobile back into her bag. "Are you frightened of dogs?"

"Not at all," said Robin, smiling and patting the dog's soft golden head. "He surprised me, that's all."

As she headed back past the giant skulls towards her new home, Robin thought about Billy, whom Strike had described with such vividness that Robin felt as though she had met him, too.

So deeply absorbed in her thoughts was she, that for the first time all week, Robin forgot to glance up at the White Swan pub as she passed it. High above the street, on the corner of the building, was a single carved swan, which reminded Robin, every time she passed it, of her calamitous wedding day.

4

But what do you propose to do in the town, then?

Henrik Ibsen, *Rosmersholm*

Six and a half miles away, Strike set his mobile down on his desk and lit a cigarette. Robin's interest in his story had been soothing after the interview he had endured half an hour after Billy had fled. The two policemen who had answered Denise's call had seemed to relish their opportunity to make the famous Cormoran Strike admit his fallibility, taking their time as they ascertained that he had succeeded in finding out neither full name nor address of the probably psychotic Billy.

The late afternoon sun hit the notebook on his desk at an angle, revealing faint indentations. Strike dropped his cigarette into an ashtray he had stolen long ago from a German bar, picked up the notepad and tilted it this way and that, trying to make out the letters formed by the impressions, then reached for a pencil and lightly shaded over them. Untidy capital letters were soon revealed, clearly spelling the words "Charlemont Road." Billy had pressed less hard on the house or flat number than the street name. One of the faint indents looked like either a 5 or an incomplete 8, but the spacing suggested more than one figure, or possibly a letter.

Strike's incurable predilection for getting to the root of puzzling incidents tended to inconvenience him quite as much as other people. Hungry and tired though he was, and despite the fact that he had sent his temp away so he could shut up the office, he tore the paper carrying the revealed street name off the pad and headed into the outer room, where he switched the computer back on.

There were several Charlemont Roads in the UK, but on the assumption that Billy was unlikely to have the means to travel very far, he suspected that the one in East Ham had to be the right one. Online records showed two Williams living there, but both were over sixty. Remembering that Billy had been scared that Strike might turn up at "Jimmy's place," he had searched for Jimmy and then James, which turned up the details of James Farraday, 49.

Strike made a note of Farraday's address beneath Billy's indented scribbles, though not at all confident that Farraday was the man he sought. For one thing, his house number contained no fives or eights and, for another, Billy's extreme unkemptness suggested that whomever he lived with must take a fairly relaxed attitude to his personal hygiene. Farraday lived with a wife and what appeared to be two daughters.

Strike turned off the computer, but continued to stare abstractedly at the dark screen, thinking about Billy's story. It was the detail of the pink blanket that kept nagging at him. It seemed such a specific, unglamorous detail for a psychotic delusion.

Remembering that he needed to be up early in the morning for a paying job, he pulled himself to his feet. Before leaving the office, he inserted the piece of paper bearing both the impressions of Billy's handwriting and Farraday's address into his wallet.

London, which had recently been at the epicenter of the Queen's Diamond Jubilee celebrations, was preparing to host the Olympics. Union Jacks and the London 2012 logo were everywhere—on signs, banners, bunting, keyrings, mugs and umbrellas—while jumbles of Olympic merchandise cluttered virtually every shop window. In Strike's opinion, the logo resembled shards of fluorescent glass randomly thrown together and he was equally unenamored of the official mascots, which looked to him like a pair of cycloptic molars.

There was a tinge of excitement and nervousness about the capital, born, no doubt, of the perennially British dread that the nation might make a fool of itself. Complaints about non-availability of Olympics tickets were a dominant theme in conversation, unsuccessful applicants decrying the lottery that was supposed to have given everybody a fair and equal chance of watching events live. Strike, who had hoped to see some boxing, had not managed to get tickets, but laughed out loud at his old school friend Nick's offer to take his place at the dressage, which Nick's wife Ilsa was overjoyed to have bagged.

Harley Street, where Strike was due to spend Friday running surveillance on a cosmetic surgeon, remained untouched by Olympic fever. The grand Victorian façades presented their usual implacable faces to the world, unsullied by garish logos or flags.

Strike, who was wearing his best Italian suit for the job, took up a position near the doorway of a building opposite and pretended to be talking on his mobile, actually keeping watch over the entrance of the expensive consulting rooms of two partners, one of whom was Strike's client.

"Dodgy Doc," as Strike had nicknamed his quarry, was taking his time living up to his name. Possibly he had been scared out of his unethical behavior by his partner, who had confronted him after realizing that Dodgy had recently performed two breast augmentations that had not been run through the business's books. Suspecting the worst, the senior partner had come to Strike for help.

"His justification was feeble, full of holes. He is," said the white-haired surgeon, stiff-lipped but full of foreboding, "and always has been a...ah...womanizer. I checked his internet history before confronting him and found a website where young women solicit cash contributions for their cosmetic enhancements, in return for explicit pictures. I fear...I hardly know what...but it might be that he has made an arrangement with these women that is not...monetary. Two of the younger women had been asked to call a number I did not recognize, but which suggested surgery might be arranged free in return for an 'exclusive arrangement.'"

Strike had not so far witnessed Dodgy meeting any women outside his regular hours. He spent Mondays and Fridays in his Harley Street consulting rooms and the mid-week at the private hospital where he operated. Whenever Strike had tailed him outside his places of work, he had merely taken short walks to purchase chocolate, to which he seemed addicted. Every night, he drove his Bentley home to his wife and children in Gerrards Cross, tailed by Strike in his old blue BMW.

Tonight, both surgeons would be attending a Royal College of Surgeons dinner with their wives, so Strike had left his BMW in its expensive garage. The hours rolled by in tedium, Strike mostly concerned with shifting the weight off his prosthesis at regular intervals as he leaned up against railings, parking meters and doorways. A steady trickle of clients pressed the bell at Dodgy's door and were admitted, one by one. All were female and most were sleek and well-groomed. At five o'clock, Strike's mobile vibrated in his breast pocket and he saw a text from his client.

Safe to clock off, about to leave with him for the Dorchester.

Perversely, Strike hung around, watching as the partners left the building some fifteen minutes later. His client was tall and white-haired; Dodgy, a sleek, dapper olive-skinned man with shiny black hair, who wore three-piece suits. Strike watched them get into a taxi and leave, then yawned, stretched and contemplated heading home, possibly with a takeaway.

Almost against his will, he pulled out his wallet and extracted the piece of crumpled paper on which he had managed to reveal Billy's street name.

All day, at the back of his mind, he had thought he might go and seek out Billy in Charlemont Road if Dodgy Doc left work early, but he was tired and his leg sore. If Lorelei knew that he had the evening off, she would expect Strike to call. On the other hand, they were going to Robin's house-warming together tomorrow night and if he spent tonight at Lorelei's, it would be hard to extricate himself tomorrow, after the party. He never spent two nights in a row at Lorelei's flat, even when the opportunity had occurred. He liked to set limits on her rights to his time.

As though hoping to be dissuaded by the weather, he glanced up at the clear June sky and sighed. The evening was clear and perfect, the agency so busy that he did not know when he would next have a few hours to spare. If he wanted to visit Charlemont Road, it would have to be tonight.

5

I can quite understand your having a horror of public meetings and . . . of the rabble that frequents them.

Henrik Ibsen, *Rosmersholm*

His journey coinciding with rush hour, it took Strike over an hour to travel from Harley Street to East Ham. By the time he had located Charlemont Road his stump was aching and the sight of the long residential street made him regret that he was not the kind of man who could simply write off Billy as a mental case.

The terraced houses had a motley appearance: some were bare brick, others painted or pebble-dashed. Union Jacks hung at windows: further evidence of Olympics fever or relics of the Royal Jubilee. The small plots in front of the houses had been made into pocket gardens or dumps for debris, according to preference. Halfway along the road lay a dirty old mattress, abandoned to whoever wanted to deal with it.

His first glimpse of James Farraday's residence did not encourage Strike to hope that he had reached journey's end, because it was one of the best-maintained houses in the street. A tiny porch with colored glass had been added around the front door, ruched net curtains hung at each window and the brass letterbox gleamed in the sunshine. Strike pressed the plastic doorbell and waited.

After a short wait, a harried woman opened the door, releasing a silver tabby, which appeared to have been waiting, coiled behind the door, for the first chance to escape. The woman's cross expression sat awkwardly above an apron printed with a "Love Is..." cartoon. A strong odor of cooking meat wafted out of the house.

"Hi," said Strike, salivating at the smell. "Don't know whether you can help me. I'm trying to find Billy."

"You've got the wrong address. There's no Billy here."

She made to close the door.

"He said he was staying with Jimmy," said Strike, as the gap narrowed.

"There's no Jimmy here, either."

"Sorry, I thought somebody called James—"

"Nobody calls him Jimmy. You've got the wrong house."

She closed the door.

Strike and the silver tabby eyed each other; in the cat's case, superciliously, before it sat down on the mat and began to groom itself with an air of dismissing Strike from its thoughts.

Strike returned to the pavement, where he lit a cigarette and looked up and down the street. By his estimate there were two hundred houses on Charlemont Road. How long would it take to knock on every household's door? More time than he had this evening, was the unfortunate answer, and more time than he was likely to have anytime soon. He walked on, frustrated and increasingly sore, glancing in through windows and scrutinizing passersby for a resemblance to the man he had met the previous day. Twice, he asked people entering or leaving their houses whether they knew "Jimmy and Billy," whose address he claimed to have lost. Both said no.

Strike trudged on, trying not to limp.

At last he reached a section of houses that had been bought up and converted into flats. Pairs of front doors stood crammed side by side and the front plots had been concreted over.

Strike slowed down. A torn sheet of A4 had been pinned to one of the shabbiest doors, from which the white paint was peeling. A faint but familiar prickle of interest that he would never have dignified with the name "hunch" led Strike to the door.

The scribbled message read:

7.30 Meeting moved from pub to Well Community Centre in Vicarage Lane—end of street turn left Jimmy Knight

Strike lifted the sheet of paper with a finger, saw a house number ending in 5, let the note fall again and moved to peer through the dusty downstairs window.

An old bed sheet had been pinned up to block out sunlight, but a corner had fallen down. Tall enough to squint through the uncovered portion of glass, Strike saw a slice of empty room containing an open sofa bed with a stained duvet on it, a pile of clothes in the corner and a portable TV standing on a cardboard box. The carpet was obscured by a multitude of empty beer cans and overflowing ashtrays. This seemed promising. He returned to the peeling front door, raised a large fist and knocked.

Nobody answered, nor did he hear any sign of movement within.

Strike checked the note on the door again, then set off. Turning left into Vicarage Lane, he saw the community center right in front of him, "The Well" spelled out boldly in shining Perspex letters.

An elderly man wearing a Mao cap and a wispy, graying beard was standing just outside the glass doors with a pile of leaflets in his hand. As Strike approached, the man, whose T-shirt bore the washed-out face of Che Guevara, eyed him askance. Though tieless, Strike's Italian suit struck an inappropriately formal note. When it became clear that the community center was Strike's destination, the leaflet-holder shuffled sideways to bar the entrance.

"I know I'm late," said Strike, with well-feigned annoyance, "but I've only just found out the bloody venue's been changed."

His assurance and his size both seemed to disconcert the man in the Mau cap, who nevertheless appeared to feel that instant capitulation to a man in a suit would be unworthy of him.

"Who are you representing?"

Strike had already taken a swift inventory of the capitalized words visible on the leaflets clutched against the other man's chest: DISSENT — DISOBEDIENCE — DISRUPTION and, rather incongruously, ALLOTMENTS. There was also a crude cartoon of five obese businessmen blowing cigar smoke to form the Olympic rings.

"My dad," Strike said. "He's worried they're going to concrete over his allotment."

"Ah," said the bearded man. He moved aside. Strike tugged a leaflet out of his hand and entered the community center.

There was nobody in sight except for a gray-haired woman of West Indian origin, who was peering through an inner door that she had opened an inch. Strike could just hear a female voice in the room beyond. Her words were hard to distinguish, but her cadences suggested a tirade. Becoming aware that somebody was standing immediately behind her, the woman turned. The sight of Strike's suit seemed to affect her in opposite fashion to the bearded man at the door.

"Are you from the Olympics?" she whispered.

"No," said Strike. "Just interested."

She eased the door open to admit him.

Around forty people were sitting on plastic chairs. Strike took the nearest vacant seat and scanned the backs of the heads in front of him for the matted, shoulder-length hair of Billy.

A table for speakers had been set up at the front. A young woman was currently pacing up and down in front of it as she addressed the audience. Her hair was dyed the same bright red shade as Coco's, Strike's hard-to-shake one-night stand, and she was speaking in a series of unfinished sentences, occasionally losing herself in secondary clauses and forgetting to drop her "h"s. Strike had the impression that she had been talking for a long time.

". . . think of the squatters and artists who're all being—'cause this is a proper community, right, and then in they come wiv like clipboards and it's, like, get out if you know what's good for you, thin end of the, innit, oppressive laws, it's the Trojan 'orse—it's a coordinated campaign of, like . . ."

Half the audience looked like students. Among the older members, Strike saw men and women who he marked down as committed protestors, some wearing T-shirts with leftist slogans like his friend on the door. Here and there he saw unlikely figures who he guessed were ordinary members of the community who had not taken kindly to the Olympics' arrival in East London: arty types who had perhaps been squatting, and an elderly couple, who were currently whispering to each other and who Strike thought might be genuinely worried about their allotment. Watching them resume the attitudes of meek endurance appropriate to those sitting in church, Strike guessed that they had agreed that they could not easily leave without drawing too much attention to themselves. A much-pierced boy covered in anarchist tattoos audibly picked his teeth.

Behind the girl who was speaking sat three others: an older woman and two men, who were talking quietly to each other. One of them was at least sixty, barrel-chested and lantern-jawed, with the pugnacious air of a man who had served his time on picket lines and in successful showdowns with recalcitrant management. Something about the dark, deep-set eyes of the other made Strike scan the leaflet in his hand, seeking confirmation of an immediate suspicion.

COMMUNITY OLYMPIC RESISTANCE (CORE)

15 June 2012

7.30 p.m. White Horse Pub East Ham E6 6EJ

Speakers:

Lilian Sweeting	Wilderness Preservation, E. London
Walter Frett	Workers' Alliance/CORE activist
Flick Purdue	Anti-poverty campaigner/CORE activist
Jimmy Knight	Real Socialist Party/CORE organizer

Heavy stubble and a general air of scruffiness notwithstanding, the man with the sunken eyes was nowhere near as filthy as Billy and his hair had certainly been cut within the last couple of months. He appeared to be in his mid-thirties, and while squarer of face and more muscular, he had the same dark hair and pale skin as Strike's visitor. On the available evidence, Strike would have put a sizable bet on Jimmy Knight being Billy's older brother.

Jimmy finished his muttered conversation with his Workers' Alliance colleague, then leaned back in his seat, thick arms folded, wearing an expression of abstraction that showed he was not listening to the young woman any more than her increasingly fidgety audience.

Strike now became aware that he was under observation from a nondescript man sitting in the row in front of him. When Strike met the man's pale blue gaze, he redirected his attention hastily towards Flick, who was still talking. Taking note of the blue-eyed man's clean jeans, plain T-shirt and the short, neat hair, Strike thought that he would have done better to have forgone the morning's close shave, but perhaps, for a ramshackle operation like CORE, the Met had not considered it worthwhile to send their best. The presence of a plain-clothes officer was to be expected, of course. Any group currently planning to disrupt or resist the arrangements for the Olympics was likely to be under surveillance.

A short distance from the plainclothes policeman sat a professional-looking young Asian man in shirtsleeves. Tall and thin, he was watching the speaker fixedly, chewing the fingernails of his left hand. As Strike watched, the man gave a little start and took his finger away from his mouth. He had made it bleed.

"All right," said a man loudly. The audience, recognizing a voice of authority, sat a little straighter. "Thanks very much, Flick."

Jimmy Knight got to his feet, leading the unenthusiastic applause for Flick, who walked back around the table and sat down in the empty chair between the two men.

In his well-worn jeans and unironed T-shirt, Jimmy Knight reminded Strike of the men his dead mother had taken as lovers. He might have been the bass player in a grime band or a good-looking roadie, with his muscled arms and tattoos. Strike noticed that the back of the nondescript blue-eyed man had tensed. He had been waiting for Jimmy.

"Evening, everyone, and thanks very much for coming."

His personality filled the room like the first bar of a hit song. Strike knew him from those few words as the kind of man who, in the army, was either outstandingly useful or an insubordinate bastard. Jimmy's accent, like Flick's, revealed an uncertain provenance. Strike thought that Cockney might have been grafted, in his case more successfully, onto a faint, rural burr.

"So, the Olympic threshing machine's moved into East London!"

His burning eyes swept the newly attentive crowd.

"Flattening houses, knocking cyclists to their deaths, churning up land that belongs to all of us. Or it did.

"You've heard from Lilian what they're doing to animal and insect habitats. I'm here to talk about the encroachment on human communities. They're concreting over our common land, and for what? Are they putting up the social housing or the hospitals we need? Of course not! No, we're getting stadiums costing billions, showcases for the capitalist system, ladies and gentlemen. We're being asked to celebrate elitism while, beyond the barriers, ordinary people's freedoms are encroached, eroded, removed.

"They tell us we should be celebrating the Olympics, all the glossy press releases the right-wing media gobbles up and regurgitates. Fetishize the flag, whip up the middle classes into a frenzy of jingoism! Come worship our glorious medalists—a shiny gold for everyone who passes over a big enough bribe with a pot of someone else's piss!"

There was a murmur of agreement. A few people clapped.

"We're supposed to get excited about the public schoolboys and girls who got to practice sports while the rest of us were having our playing fields sold off for cash! Sycophancy should be our national Olympic sport! We deify people who've had millions invested in them because they can ride a bike, when they've sold themselves as fig leaves for all the planet-raping, tax-dodging bastards who are queuing up to get their names on the barriers—barriers shutting working people off their own land!"

The applause, in which Strike, the old couple beside him and the Asian man did not join, was as much for the performance as the words. Jimmy's slightly thuggish but handsome face was alive with righteous anger.

"See this?" he said, sweeping from the table behind him a piece of paper with the jagged "2012" that Strike disliked so much. "Welcome to the Olympics, my friends, a fascist's wet dream. See the logo? D'you see it? It's a broken swastika!"

The crowd laughed and applauded some more, masking the loud rumble of Strike's stomach. He wondered whether there might be a takeaway nearby. He had even started to calculate whether he might have time to leave, buy food and return, when the gray-haired West Indian woman whom he had seen earlier opened the door to the hall and propped it open. Her expression clearly indicated that CORE had now outstayed its welcome.

Jimmy, however, was still in full flow.

"This so-called celebration of the Olympic spirit, of fair play and amateurism is normalizing repression and authoritarianism! Wake up: London's being militarized! The British state, which has honed the tactics of colonization and invasion for centuries, has seized on the Olympics as the perfect excuse to deploy police, army, helicopters and guns against ordinary citizens! One thousand extra CCTV cameras—extra laws hurried through—and you think they'll be repealed when this carnival of capitalism moves on?"

"Join us!" shouted Jimmy, as the community center worker edged along the wall towards the front of the hall, nervous but determined. "CORE is part of a broader global justice movement that meets repression with resistance! We're making common cause with all leftist, anti-oppressive movements across the capital! We're going to be staging lawful demonstrations and using every tool of peaceful protest still permitted to us in what is rapidly becoming an occupied city!"

More applause followed, though the elderly couple beside Strike seemed thoroughly miserable.

"All right, all right, I know," added Jimmy to the community center worker, who had now reached the front of the audience and was gesturing timidly. "They want us out," Jimmy told the crowd, smirking and shaking his head. "Of course they do. Of course."

A few people hissed at the community center worker.

"Anyone who wants to hear more," said Jimmy, "we'll be in the pub down the road. Address on your leaflets!"

Most of the crowd applauded. The plainclothes policeman got to his feet. The elderly couple was already scuttling towards the door.

6

I . . . have the reputation of being a wicked fanatic, I am told.
                                    Henrik Ibsen, *Rosmersholm*

Chairs clattered, bags were hoisted onto shoulders. The bulk of the audience began to head for the doors at the back, but some appeared reluctant to leave. Strike took a few steps towards Jimmy, hoping to talk to him, but was outpaced by the young Asian man, who was striding jerkily towards the activist with an air of nervous determination. Jimmy exchanged a few more words with the man from the Workers' Alliance, then noticed the newcomer, bade Walter goodbye and moved forward with every appearance of goodwill to speak to what he clearly assumed was a convert.

As soon as the Asian man began to speak, however, Jimmy's expression clouded. As they talked in low voices in the middle of the rapidly emptying room, Flick and a cluster of young people loitered nearby, waiting for Jimmy. They seemed to consider themselves above manual labor. The community center worker cleared away chairs alone.

"Let me do that," Strike offered, taking three from her and ignoring the sharp twinge in his knee as he hoisted them onto a tall stack.

"Thanks very much," she panted. "I don't think we'll be letting this lot—"

She allowed Walter and a few others to pass before continuing. None of them thanked her.

"—use the center again," she finished resentfully. "I didn't realize what they were all about. Their leaflet's on about civil disobedience and I don't know what else."

"Pro-Olympics, are you?" Strike asked, placing a chair onto a pile.

"My granddaughter's in a running club," she said. "We got tickets. She can't wait."

Jimmy was still locked in conversation with the young Asian man. A minor argument seemed to have developed. Jimmy seemed tense, his eyes shifting constantly around the room, either seeking an escape or checking that nobody else was within earshot. The hall was emptying. The two men began to move towards the exit. Strike strained his ears to hear what they were saying to each other, but the clumping footsteps of Jimmy's acolytes on the wooden floor obliterated all but a few words.

"...for years, mate, all right?" Jimmy was saying angrily. "So do whatever the fuck you want, you're the one who volunteered yourself..."

They passed out of earshot. Strike helped the community center volunteer stack the last of the chairs and, as she turned off the light, asked for directions to the White Horse.

Five minutes later, and in spite of his recent resolution to eat more healthily, Strike bought a bag of chips at a takeaway and proceeded along White Horse Road, at the end of which he had been told he would find the eponymous pub.

As he ate, Strike pondered the best way to open conversation with Jimmy Knight. As the reaction of the elderly Che Guevara fan on the door had shown, Strike's current attire did not tend to foster trust with anti-capitalist protestors. Jimmy had the air of an experienced hard-left activist and was probably anticipating official interest in his activities in the highly charged atmosphere preceding the opening of the Games. Indeed, Strike could see the nondescript, blue-eyed man walking behind Jimmy, hands in his jean pockets. Strike's first job would be to reassure Jimmy that he was not there to investigate CORE.

The White Horse turned out to be an ugly prefabricated building, which stood on a busy junction facing a large park. A white war memorial with neatly ranged poppy wreaths at its base rose like an eternal reproach to the outside drinking area opposite, where old cigarette butts lay thickly on cracked concrete riven with weeds. Drinkers were milling around the front of the pub, all smoking. Strike spotted Jimmy, Flick and several others standing in a group in front of a window that was decorated with an enormous West Ham banner. The tall young Asian man was nowhere to be seen, but the plainclothes policeman loitered alone on the periphery of their group.

Strike went inside to fetch a pint. The décor inside the pub consisted mostly of Cross of St. George flags and more West Ham paraphernalia. Having bought a pint of John Smith's, Strike returned to the forecourt, lit a fresh cigarette and advanced on the group around Jimmy. He was at Flick's shoulder before they realized that the large stranger in a suit wanted something from them. All talk ceased as suspicion flared on every face.

"Hi," said Strike, "my name's Cormoran Strike. Any chance of a quick word, Jimmy? It's about Billy."

"Billy?" repeated Jimmy sharply. "Why?"

"I met him yesterday. I'm a private detect—"

"Chizzle's sent him!" gasped Flick, turning, frightened, to Jimmy.

"'K'up!" he growled.

While the rest of the group surveyed Strike with a mixture of curiosity and hostility, Jimmy beckoned to Strike to follow him to the edge of the crowd. To Strike's surprise, Flick tagged along. Men with buzz cuts and West Ham tops nodded at the activist as he passed. Jimmy came to a halt beside two old white bollards topped by horse heads, checked that nobody else was within earshot, then addressed Strike.

"What did you say your name was again?"

"Cormoran, Cormoran Strike. Is Billy your brother?"

"Younger brother, yeah," said Jimmy. "Did you say he came to see you?"

"Yep. Yesterday afternoon."

"You're a private—?"

"Detective. Yes."

Strike saw dawning recognition in Flick's eyes. She had a plump, pale face that would have been innocent without the savage eyeliner and the uncombed tomato-red hair. She turned quickly to Jimmy again.

"Jimmy, he's—"

"Shacklewell Ripper?" asked Jimmy, eyeing Strike over his lighter as he lit another cigarette. "Lula Landry?"

"That's me," said Strike.

Out of the corner of Strike's eye, he noticed Flick's eyes traveling down his body to his lower legs. Her mouth twisted in seeming contempt.

"Billy came to see you?" repeated Jimmy. "Why?"

"He told me he'd witnessed a kid being strangled," said Strike.

Jimmy blew out smoke in angry gusts.

"Yeah. He's fucked in the head. Schizoid affective disorder."

"He seemed ill," agreed Strike.

"Is that all he told you? That he saw a kid being strangled?"

"Seemed enough to be getting on with," said Strike.

Jimmy's lips curved in a humorless smile.

"You didn't believe him, did you?"

"No," said Strike truthfully, "but I don't think he should be roaming the streets in that condition. He needs help."

"I don't think he's any worse than usual, do you?" Jimmy asked Flick, with a somewhat artificial air of dispassionate inquiry.

"No," she said, turning to address Strike with barely concealed animosity. "He has ups and downs. He's all right if he takes his meds."

Her accent had become markedly more middle-class away from the rest of their friends. Strike noticed that she had painted eyeliner over a clump of sleep in the corner of one eye. Strike, who had spent large portions of his childhood living in squalor, found a disregard for hygiene hard to like, except in those people so unhappy or ill that cleanliness became an irrelevance.

"Ex-army, aren't you?" she asked, but Jimmy spoke over her.

"How did Billy know how to find you?"

"Directory inquiries?" suggested Strike. "I don't live in a bat cave."

"Billy doesn't know how to use directory inquiries."

"He managed to find my office OK."

"There's no dead kid," Jimmy said abruptly. "It's all in his head. He goes on about it when he's having an episode. Didn't you see his tic?"

Jimmy imitated, with brutal accuracy, the compulsive nose to chest movement of a twitching hand. Flick laughed.

"Yeah, I saw that," said Strike, unsmiling. "You don't know where he is, then?"

"Haven't seen him since yesterday morning. What do you want him for?"

"Like I say, he didn't seem in any fit state to be wandering around on his own."

"Very public spirited of you," said Jimmy. "Rich and famous detective worrying about our Bill."

Strike said nothing.

"Army," Flick repeated, "weren't you?"

"I was," said Strike, looking down at her. "How's that relevant?"

"Just saying." She had flushed a little in her righteous anger. "Haven't always been this worried about people getting hurt, have you?"

Strike, who was familiar with people who shared Flick's views, said nothing. She would probably believe him if he told her he had joined the forces in the hope of bayoneting children.

Jimmy, who also seemed disinclined to hear more of Flick's opinions on the military, said:

"Billy'll be fine. He crashes at ours sometimes, then goes off. Does it all the time."

"Where does he stay when he's not with you?"

"Friends," said Jimmy, shrugging. "I don't know all their names." Then, contradicting himself, "I'll ring around tonight, make sure he's OK."

"Right you are," said Strike, downing his pint and handing the empty to a tattooed bar worker, who was marching through the forecourt, grabbing glasses from all who had finished with them. Strike took a last drag on his cigarette, dropped it to join the thousands of its brethren on the cracked forecourt, ground it out beneath his prosthetic foot, then pulled out his wallet.

"Do me a favor," he said to Jimmy, taking out a card and handing it over, "and contact me when Billy turns up, will you? I'd like to know he's safe."

Flick gave a derisive snort, but Jimmy seemed caught off guard.

"Yeah, all right. Yeah, I will."

"D'you know which bus would get me back to Denmark Street quickest?" Strike asked them. He could not face another long walk to the Tube. Buses were rolling past the pub with inviting frequency. Jimmy, who seemed to know the area well, directed Strike to the appropriate stop.

"Thanks very much." As he put his wallet back inside his jacket, Strike said casually, "Billy told me you were there when the child was strangled, Jimmy."

Flick's rapid turn of the head towards Jimmy was the giveaway. The latter was better prepared. His nostrils flared, but otherwise he did a creditable job of pretending not to be alarmed.

"Yeah, he's got the whole sick scene worked out in his poor fucked head," he said. "Some days he thinks our dead mum might've been there, too. Pope next, I expect."

"Sad," said Strike. "Hope you manage to track him down."

He raised a hand in farewell and left them standing on the forecourt. Hungry in spite of the chips, his stump now throbbing, he was limping by the time he reached the bus stop.

After a fifteen-minute wait, the bus arrived. Two drunk youths a few seats in front of Strike got into a long, repetitive argument about the merits of West Ham's new signing, Jussi Jääskeläinen, whose name neither of them could pronounce. Strike stared unseeingly out of the grimy window, leg sore, desperate for his bed, but unable to relax.

Irksome though it was to admit it, the trip to Charlemont Road had not rid him of the tiny niggling doubt about Billy's story. The memory of Flick's sudden, frightened peek at Jimmy, and above all her blurted exclamation "Chizzle's sent him!" had turned that niggling doubt into a significant and possibly permanent impediment to the detective's peace of mind.

7

Do you think you will remain here? Permanently, I mean?
Henrik Ibsen, *Rosmersholm*

Robin would have been happy to spend the weekend relaxing after her long week unpacking and putting together furniture, but Matthew was looking forward to the house-warming party, to which he had invited a large number of colleagues. His pride was piqued by the interesting, romantic history of the street, which had been built for shipwrights and sea captains back when Deptford had been a shipbuilding center. Matthew might not yet have arrived in the postcode of his dreams, but a short cobbled street full of pretty old houses was, as he had wanted, a "step up," even if he and Robin were only renting the neat brick box with its sash windows and the moldings of cherubs over the front door.

Matthew had objected when Robin first suggested renting again, but she had overridden him, saying that she could not stand another year in Hastings Road while further purchases of overpriced houses fell through. Between the legacy and Matthew's new job, they were just able to make rent on the smart little three-bedroomed house, leaving the money they had received from the sale of their Hastings Road flat untouched in the bank.

Their landlord, a publisher who was off to New York to work at head office, had been delighted with his new tenants. A gay man in his forties, he admired Matthew's clean-cut looks and made a point of handing over the keys personally on their moving day.

"I agree with Jane Austen on the ideal tenant," he told Matthew, standing in the cobbled street. " 'A married man, and without children; the very state to be wished for.' A house is never well cared for without a lady! Or do you two share the hoovering?"

"Of course," Matthew had said, smiling. Robin, who was carrying a box of plants over the threshold behind the two men, had bitten back a caustic retort.

She had a suspicion that Matthew was not disclosing to friends and workmates that they were tenants rather than owners. She deplored her own increasing tendency to watch Matthew for shabby or duplicitous behavior, even in small matters, and imposed private penances on herself for thinking the worst of him all the time. It was in this spirit of self-castigation that she had agreed to the party, bought alcohol and plastic tumblers, made food and set everything up in the kitchen. Matthew had rearranged the furniture and, over several evenings, organized a playlist now blaring out of his iPod in its dock. The first few bars of "Cutt Off" by Kasabian started as Robin hurried upstairs to change.

Robin's hair was in foam rollers, because she had decided to wear it as she had on their wedding day. Running out of time before guests were due, she pulled out the rollers one-handed as she yanked open the wardrobe door. She had a new dress, a form-fitting pale gray affair, but she was afraid that it drained her of color. She hesitated, then took out the emerald-green Roberto Cavalli that she had never worn in public. It was the most expensive item of clothing she owned, and the most beautiful: the "leaving" present that Strike had bought her after she had gone to him as a temp and helped him catch their first killer. The expression on Matthew's face when she had excitedly shown him the gift had prevented her ever wearing it.

For some reason her mind drifted to Strike's girlfriend, Lorelei, as she held the dress up against herself. Lorelei, who always wore jewel-bright colors, affected the style of a 1940s pin-up. As tall as Robin, she had glossy brunette hair that she wore over one eye like Veronica Lake. Robin knew that Lorelei was thirty-three, and that she co-owned and ran a vintage and theatrical clothing store on Chalk Farm Road. Strike had let slip this information one day and Robin, making a mental note of the name, had gone home and looked it up online. The shop appeared to be glamorous and successful.

"It's a quarter to," said Matthew, hurrying into the bedroom, stripping off his T-shirt as he came. "I might shower quickly."

He caught sight of her, holding the green dress against herself.

"I thought you were wearing the gray one?"

Their eyes met in the mirror. Bare-chested, tanned and handsome, Matthew's features were so symmetrical that his reflection was almost identical to his real appearance.

"I think it makes me look pale," said Robin.

"I prefer the gray one," he said. "I like you pale."

She forced a smile.

"All right," she said. "I'll wear the gray."

Once changed, she ran fingers through her curls to loosen them, pulled on a pair of strappy silver sandals and hurried back downstairs. She had barely reached the hall when the doorbell rang.

If she had been asked to guess who would arrive first, she would have said Sarah Shadlock and Tom Turvey, who had recently got engaged. It would be like Sarah to try and catch Robin on the hop, to make sure she had an opportunity to nose around the house before anybody else, and to stake out a spot where she could look over all the arrivals. Sure enough, when Robin opened up, there stood Sarah in shocking pink, a big bunch of flowers in her arms, Tom carrying beer and wine.

"Oh, it's *gorgeous*, Robin," crooned Sarah, the moment she got over the doorstep, staring around the hall. She hugged Robin absentmindedly, her eyes on the stairs as Matthew descended, doing up his shirt. "*Lovely.* These are for you."

Robin found herself encumbered by an armful of stargazer lilies.

"Thanks," she said. "I'll just go and put them in water."

They didn't have a vase big enough for the flowers, but Robin could hardly leave them in the sink. She could hear Sarah's laugh from the kitchen, even over Coldplay and Rihanna, who were now belting out "Princess of China" from Matthew's iPod. Robin dragged a bucket out of the cupboard and began to fill it, splattering herself with water in the process.

The idea had once been mooted, she remembered, that Matthew would refrain from taking Sarah out for lunches during their office lunch hours. There had even been talk of stopping socializing with her, after Robin had found out that Matthew had been cheating with Sarah in their early twenties. However, Tom had helped Matthew get the higher-paid position he now enjoyed at Tom's firm, and now that Sarah was the proud owner of a large solitaire diamond, Matthew did not seem to think that there should be the slightest awkwardness attached to social events including the future Mr. and Mrs. Turvey.

Robin could hear the three of them moving around upstairs. Matthew was giving a tour of the bedrooms. She heaved the lily-filled bucket out of the sink and shoved it into a corner beside the kettle, wondering whether it was mean-spirited to suspect that Sarah had brought flowers just to get Robin out of the way for a bit. Sarah had never lost the flirtatious manner towards Matthew she had had since their shared years at university.

Robin poured herself a glass of wine and emerged from the kitchen as Matthew led Tom and Sarah into the sitting room.

"...and Lord Nelson and Lady Hamilton are supposed to have stayed in number 19, but it was called Union Street then," he said. "Right, who wants a drink? It's all set up in the kitchen."

"Gorgeous place, Robin," said Sarah. "Houses like this don't come up that often. You must've got really lucky."

"We're only renting," said Robin.

"Really?" said Sarah beadily, and Robin knew that Sarah was drawing her own conclusions, not about the housing market, but about Robin and Matthew's marriage.

"Nice earrings," said Robin, keen to change the subject.

"Aren't they?" said Sarah, pulling back her hair to give Robin a better view. "Tom's birthday present."

The doorbell rang again. Robin went to answer it, hoping that it would be one of the few people she had invited. She had no hope of Strike, of course. He was bound to be late, as he had been to every other personal event to which she had invited him.

"Oh, thank God," said Robin, surprised at her own relief when she saw Vanessa Ekwensi.

Vanessa was a police officer: tall, black, with almond-shaped eyes, a model's figure and a self-possession Robin envied. She had come to the party alone. Her boyfriend, who worked in Forensic Services at the Met, had a prior commitment. Robin was disappointed: she had looked forward to meeting him.

"You all right?" Vanessa asked as she entered. She was carrying a bottle of red wine and wearing a deep purple slip dress. Robin thought again of the emerald-green Cavalli upstairs and wished she had worn it.

"I'm fine," she said. "Come through to the back, you can smoke there."

She led Vanessa through the sitting room, past Sarah and Matthew, who were now mocking Tom's baldness to his face.

The rear wall of the small courtyard garden was covered in ivy. Well-maintained shrubs stood in terra-cotta tubs. Robin, who did not smoke, had put ashtrays and a few fold-up chairs out there, and dotted tea candles around. Matthew had asked her with an edge in his voice why she was taking so much trouble over the smokers. She had known perfectly well why he was saying it and pretended not to.

"I thought Jemima smoked?" she asked, with a feigned air of confusion. Jemima was Matthew's boss.

"Oh," he said, caught off balance. "Yeah—yeah, but only socially."

"Well, I'm pretty sure this is a social occasion, Matt," said Robin sweetly.

She fetched Vanessa a drink and came back to find her lighting up, her lovely eyes fixed on Sarah Shadlock, who was still mocking Tom's hairline, with Matthew her hearty accomplice.

"That's her, is it?" Vanessa asked.

"That's her," said Robin.

She appreciated the small show of moral support. Robin and Vanessa had been friends for months before Robin had confided the history of her relationship with Matthew. Before that they had talked police work, politics and clothes on evenings that took them to the cinema, or to cheap restaurants. Robin found Vanessa better company than any other woman she knew. Matthew, who had met her twice, told Robin he found her "cold," but said he could not explain why.

Vanessa had had a succession of partners; she had been engaged once, but broken it off when he had cheated. Robin sometimes wondered whether Vanessa found her laughably inexperienced: the woman who'd married her boyfriend from school.

A few moments later, a dozen people, colleagues of Matthew's with their partners, who had obviously been to the pub first, streamed into the sitting room. Robin watched Matthew greeting them and showing them where the drinks were. He had adopted the loud, bantering tone that she had heard him using on work nights out. It irritated her.

The party quickly became crowded. Robin effected introductions, showed people where to find drink, set out more plastic cups and handed a couple of plates of food around because the kitchen was becoming packed. Only when Andy Hutchins and his wife arrived did she feel she could relax for a moment and spend some more time with her own guests.

"I made you some special food," Robin told Andy, after she had shown him and Louise out into the courtyard. "This is Vanessa. She's Met. Vanessa, Andy and Louise—stay there, Andy, I'll get it, it's dairy-free."

Tom was standing against the fridge when she got to the kitchen.

"Sorry, Tom, need to get in—"

He blinked at her, then moved aside. He was already drunk, she thought, and it was barely nine o'clock. Robin could hear Sarah's braying laugh from the middle of the crowd outside.

"Lemmelp," said Tom, holding the fridge door that threatened to close on Robin as she bent down to the lower shelf to get the tray of dairy-free, non-fried food she had saved for Andy. "God, you've got a nice arse, Robin."

She straightened up without comment. In spite of the drunken grin, she could feel the unhappiness flowing from behind it, like a cool draft. Matthew had told her how self-conscious Tom was about his hairline, that he was even considering a transplant.

"That's a nice shirt," said Robin.

"Wha' this? You like it? She bought it for me. Matt's got one like it, hasn't he?"

"Er—I'm not sure," said Robin.

"You're not sure," repeated Tom, with a short, nasty laugh. "So much f' surveillance training. You wanna pay more attention at home, Rob."

Robin contemplated him for a moment in equal amounts of pity and anger, then, deciding that he was too drunk to argue with, she left, carrying Andy's food.

The first thing she saw as people cleared out of the way to let her back into the courtyard was that Strike had arrived. He had his back to her and was talking to Andy. Lorelei was beside him, wearing a scarlet silk dress, the gleaming fall of dark hair down her back like an advertisement for expensive shampoo. Somehow, Sarah had inveigled her way into the group in Robin's brief absence. When Vanessa caught Robin's eye, the corner of her mouth twitched.

"Hi," said Robin, setting the platter of food down on the wrought iron table beside Andy.

"Robin, hi!" said Lorelei. "It's such a pretty street!"

"Yes, isn't it?" said Robin, as Lorelei kissed the air behind Robin's ear.

Strike bent down, too. His stubble grazed Robin's face, but his lips did not touch skin. He was already opening one of the six-pack of Doom Bar he had brought with him.

Robin had mentally rehearsed things to say to Strike once he was in her new house: calm, casual things that made it sound as though she had no regrets, as though there were some wonderful counterweight that he couldn't appreciate that tipped the scales in Matthew's favor. She also wanted to question him about the strange matter of Billy and the strangled child. However, Sarah was currently holding forth on the subject of the auction house, Christie's, where she worked, and the whole group was listening to her.

"Yeah, we've got 'The Lock' coming up at auction on the third," she said. "Constable," she added kindly, for the benefit of anyone who did not know art as well as she did. "We're expecting it to make over twenty."

"Thousand?" asked Andy.

"Million," said Sarah, with a patronizing little snort of laughter.

Matthew laughed behind Robin and she moved automatically to let him join the circle. His expression was rapt, Robin noticed, as so often when large sums of money were under discussion. Perhaps, she thought, this is what he and Sarah talk about when they have lunch: money.

" 'Gimcrack' went for over twenty-two last year. Stubbs. Third most valuable Old Master ever sold."

Out of the corner of her eye, Robin saw Lorelei's scarlet-tipped hand slide into Strike's, which had been marked across the palm with the very same knife that had forever scarred Robin's arm.

"Anyway, boring, boring, boring!" said Sarah insincerely. "Enough work chat! Anyone got Olympics tickets? Tom—my fiancé—he's furious. We got *ping pong*." She pulled a droll face. "How have you lot got on?"

Robin saw Strike and Lorelei exchange a fleeting look, and knew that they were mutually consoling each other for having to endure the tedium of the Olympics ticket conversation. Suddenly wishing that they hadn't come, Robin backed out of the group.

An hour later, Strike was in the sitting room, discussing the England football team's chances in the European Championships with one of Matthew's friends from work while Lorelei danced. Robin, with whom he had not exchanged a word since they had met outside, crossed the room with a plate of food, paused to talk to a redheaded woman, then continued to offer the plate around. The way she had done her hair reminded Strike of her wedding day.

The suspicions provoked by her visit to that unknown clinic uppermost in his mind, he appraised her figure in the clinging gray dress. She certainly didn't appear to be pregnant, and the fact that she was drinking wine seemed a further counter-indication, but they might only just have begun the process of IVF.

Directly opposite Strike, visible through the dancing bodies, stood DI Vanessa Ekwensi, whom Strike had been surprised to find at the party. She was leaning up against the wall, talking to a tall blond man who seemed, by his over-attentive attitude, to have temporarily forgotten that he was wearing a wedding ring. Vanessa glanced across the room at Strike and by a wry look signaled that she would not mind him breaking up the tête-à-tête. The football conversation was not so fascinating that he would be disappointed to leave it, and at the next convenient pause he circumnavigated the dancers to talk to Vanessa.

"Evening."

"Hi," she said, accepting his peck on the cheek with the elegance that characterized all her gestures. "Cormoran, this is Owen—sorry, I didn't catch your surname?"

It didn't take long for Owen to lose hope of whatever he had wanted from Vanessa, whether the mere pleasure of flirting with a good-looking woman, or her phone number.

"Didn't realize you and Robin were this friendly," said Strike, as Owen walked away.

"Yeah, we've been hanging out," said Vanessa. "I wrote her a note after I heard you sacked her."

"Oh," said Strike, swigging Doom Bar. "Right."

"She rang to thank me and we ended up going for a drink."

Robin had never mentioned this to Strike, but then, as Strike knew perfectly well, he had been at pains to discourage anything but work talk since she had come back from her honeymoon.

"Nice house," he commented, trying not to compare the tastefully decorated room with his combined kitchen and sitting room in the attic over the office. Matthew must be earning very good money to have afforded this, he thought. Robin's pay rise certainly couldn't have done it.

"Yeah, it is," said Vanessa. "They're renting."

Strike watched Lorelei dance for a few moments while he pondered this interesting piece of information. An arch something in Vanessa's tone told him that she, too, read this as a choice not entirely related to the housing market.

"Blame sea-borne bacteria," said Vanessa.

"Sorry?" said Strike, thoroughly confused.

She threw him a sharp look, then shook her head, laughing.

"Nothing. Forget it."

"Yeah, we didn't do too badly," Strike heard Matthew telling the redheaded woman in a lull in the music. "Got tickets for the boxing."

Of course you fucking did, thought Strike irritably, feeling in his pocket for more cigarettes.

"Enjoy yourself?" asked Lorelei in the taxi, at one in the morning.

"Not particularly," said Strike, who was watching the headlights of oncoming cars.

He had had the impression that Robin had been avoiding him. After the relative warmth of their conversation on Thursday, he had expected—what? A conversation, a laugh? He had been curious to know how the marriage was progressing, but was not much the wiser. She and Matthew seemed amicable enough together, but the fact that they were renting was intriguing. Did it suggest, even subconsciously, a lack of investment in a joint future? An easier arrangement to untangle? And then there was Robin's friendship with Vanessa Ekwensi, which Strike saw as another stake in the life she led independently of Matthew.

Blame sea-borne bacteria.

What the hell did that mean? Was it connected to the mysterious clinic? Was Robin ill?

After a few minutes' silence it suddenly occurred to Strike that he ought to ask Lorelei how her evening had been.

"I've had better," sighed Lorelei. "I'm afraid your Robin's got a lot of boring friends."

"Yeah," said Strike. "I think that's mainly her husband. He's an accountant. And a bit of a tit," he added, enjoying saying it.

The taxi bowled on through the night, Strike remembering how Robin's figure had looked in the gray dress.

"Sorry?" he said suddenly, because he had the impression that Lorelei had spoken to him.

"I said, 'What are you thinking about?'"

"Nothing," lied Strike, and because it was preferable to talking, he slid an arm around her, pulled her close and kissed her.

8

...my word! Mortensgaard has risen in the world. There are lots of people who run after him now.

Henrik Ibsen, *Rosmersholm*

Robin texted Strike on Sunday evening to ask what he wanted her to do on Monday, because she had handed over all her jobs before taking a week's leave. His terse response had been "come to office," which she duly entered at a quarter to nine the following day, glad, no matter how matters stood between her and her partner, to be back in the shabby old rooms.

The door to Strike's inner office was standing open when she arrived. He was sitting behind his desk, listening to someone on his mobile. Sunlight fell in treacle-gold pools across the worn carpet. The soft mumble of traffic was soon obliterated by the rattle of the old kettle and, five minutes after her arrival, Robin set a mug of steaming dark brown Typhoo in front of Strike, who gave her a thumbs up and a silent "thanks." She returned to her desk, where a light was flashing on the phone to indicate a recorded message. She dialed their answering service and listened while a cool female voice informed her that the call had been made ten minutes before Robin had arrived and, presumably, while Strike was either upstairs, or busy with the other call.

A cracked whisper hissed in Robin's ear.

"I'm sorry I ran out on you, Mr. Strike, I'm sorry. I can't come back, though. He's keeping me here, I can't get out, he's wired the doors..."

The end of the sentence was lost in sobs. Worried, Robin tried to attract Strike's attention, but he had turned in his swivel chair to look out of the window, still listening to his mobile. Random words reached Robin through the pitiable sounds of distress on the phone.

"...can't get out...I'm all alone..."

"Yeah, OK," Strike was saying in his office. "Wednesday, then, OK? Great. Have a good one."

"...*please help me, Mr. Strike!*" wailed the voice in Robin's ear.

She smacked the button to switch to speakerphone and at once the tortured voice filled the office.

"The doors will explode if I try and escape, Mr. Strike, please help me, please come and get me, I shouldn't have come, I told him I know about the little kid and it's bigger, much bigger, I thought I could trust him—"

Strike spun in his desk chair, got up and came striding through to the outer office. There was a clunk as though the receiver had been dropped. The sobbing continued at a distance, as though the distraught speaker was stumbling away from the phone.

"That's him again," said Strike. "Billy, Billy Knight."

The sobbing and gasping grew louder again and Billy said in a frantic whisper, his lips evidently pressed against the mouthpiece:

"There's someone at the door. Help me. Help me, Mr. Strike."

The call was cut.

"Get the number," said Strike. Robin reached for the receiver to dial 1471, but before she could do so, the phone rang again. She snatched it up, her eyes on Strike's.

"Cormoran Strike's office."

"Ah...yes, good morning," said a deep, patrician voice.

Robin grimaced at Strike and shook her head.

"Shit," he muttered, and moved back into his office to get his tea.

"I'd like to speak to Mr. Strike, please."

"I'm afraid he's on another call right now," lied Robin.

Their standard practice for a year had been to phone the client back. It weeded out journalists and cranks.

"I'll hold," said the caller, who sounded captious, unused to not getting his way.

"He'll be a while, I'm afraid. Could I take a number and get him to call you back?"

"Well, it needs to be within the next ten minutes, because I'm about to go into a meeting. Tell him I want to discuss a job I'd like him to do for me."

"I'm afraid I can't guarantee that Mr. Strike will be able to undertake the job in person," said Robin, which was also the standard response to deflect press. "Our agency's quite booked up at the moment."

She pulled pen and paper towards her.

"What kind of job are you—?"

"It has to be Mr. Strike," said the voice firmly. "Make that clear to him. It has to be Mr. Strike himself. My name's Chizzle."

"How are you spelling that?" asked Robin, wondering whether she had heard correctly.

"C-H-I-S-W-E-L-L. Jasper Chiswell. Ask him to call me on the following number."

Robin copied down the digits Chiswell gave her and bade him good morning. As she set down the receiver, Strike sat down on the fake leather sofa they kept in the outer room for clients. It had a disobliging habit of making unexpected farting noises when you shifted position.

"A man called Jasper Chizzle, spelled 'Chiswell,' wants you to take on a job for him. He says it's got to be you, nobody else." Robin screwed up her forehead in perplexity. "I know the name, don't I?"

"Yeah," said Strike. "He's Minister for Culture."

"Oh my God," said Robin, realization dawning. "*Of course!* The big man with the weird hair!"

"That's him."

A clutch of vague memories and associations assailed Robin. She seemed to remember an old affair, resignation in disgrace, rehabilitation and, somewhat more recently, a fresh scandal, another nasty news story . . .

"Didn't his son get sent to jail for manslaughter not that long ago?" she said. "That was Chiswell, wasn't it? His son was stoned and driving and he killed a young mother?"

Strike recalled his attention, it seemed, from a distance. He was wearing a peculiar expression.

"Yeah, that rings a bell," said Strike.

"What's the matter?"

"A few things, actually," said Strike, running a hand over his stubbly chin. "For starters: I tracked down Billy's brother on Friday."

"How?"

"Long story," said Strike, "but turns out Jimmy's part of a group that's protesting against the Olympics. 'CORE,' they call themselves. Anyway, he was with a girl, and the first thing she said when I told them I was a private detective was: 'Chiswell's sent him.'"

Strike pondered this point while drinking his perfectly brewed tea.

"But Chiswell wouldn't need me to keep an eye on CORE," he went on, thinking aloud. "There was already a plainclothes guy there."

Though keen to hear what other things troubled Strike about Chiswell's call, Robin did not prompt him, but sat in silence, allowing him to mull the new development. It was precisely this kind of tact that Strike had missed when she was out of the office.

"And get this," he went on at last, as though there had been no interruption. "The son who went to jail for manslaughter isn't—or wasn't—Chiswell's only boy. His eldest was called Freddie and he died in Iraq. Yeah. Major Freddie Chiswell, Queen's Royal Hussars. Killed in an attack on a convoy in Basra. I investigated his death in action while I was still SIB."

"So you *know* Chiswell?"

"No, never met him. You don't meet families, usually... I knew Chiswell's daughter years ago, as well. Only slightly, but I met her a few times. She was an old school friend of Charlotte's."

Robin experienced a tiny frisson at the mention of Charlotte. She had a great curiosity, which she successfully concealed, about Charlotte, the woman Strike had been involved with on and off for sixteen years, whom he had been supposed to marry before the relationship ended messily and, apparently, permanently.

"Pity we couldn't get Billy's number," said Strike, running a large, hairy-backed hand over his jaw again.

"I'll make sure I get it if he calls again," Robin assured him. "Are you going to ring Chiswell back? He said he was about to go into a meeting."

"I'm keen to find out what he wants, but the question is whether we've got room for another client," said Strike. "Let's think..."

He put his hands behind his head, frowning up at the ceiling, on which many fine cracks were exposed by the sunlight. *Screw that now* ... the office would soon be a developer's problem, after all...

"I've got Andy and Barclay watching the Webster kid. Barclay's doing well, by the way. I've had three solid days' surveillance out of him, pictures, the lot.

"Then there's old Dodgy Doc. He still hasn't done anything newsworthy."

"Shame," said Robin, then she caught herself. "No, I don't mean that, I mean good." She rubbed her eyes. "This job," she sighed. "It messes with your ethics. Who's watching Dodgy today?"

"I was going to ask you to do it," said Strike, "but the client called yesterday afternoon. He'd forgotten to tell me Dodgy's at a symposium in Paris."

Eyes still on the ceiling, brow furrowed in thought, Strike said:

"We've got two days at that tech conference starting tomorrow. Which do you want to do, Harley Street or a conference center out in Epping Forest? We can swap over if you want. D'you want to spend tomorrow watching Dodgy, or with hundreds of stinking geeks in superhero T-shirts?"

"Not all tech people smell," Robin reprimanded him. "Your mate Spanner doesn't."

"You don't want to judge Spanner by the amount of deodorant he puts on to come here," said Strike.

Spanner, who had overhauled their computer and telephone system when the business had received its dramatic boost in business, was the younger brother of Strike's old friend Nick. He fancied Robin, as she and Strike were equally aware.

Strike mulled over options, rubbing his chin again.

"I'll call Chiswell back and find out what he's after," he said at last. "You never know, it might be a bigger job than that lawyer whose wife's sleeping around. He's next on the waiting list, right?"

"Him, or that American woman who's married to the Ferrari dealer. They're both waiting."

Strike sighed. Infidelity formed the bulk of their workload.

"I hope Chiswell's wife isn't cheating. I fancy a change."

The sofa made its usual flatulent noises as Strike quit it. As he strode back to the inner office, Robin called after him:

"Are you happy for me to finish up this paperwork, then?"

"If you don't mind," said Strike, closing the door behind him.

Robin turned back to her computer feeling quite cheerful. A busker had just started singing "No Woman, No Cry" in Denmark Street and for a while there, while they talked about Billy Knight and the Chiswells, she had felt as though they were the Strike and Robin of a year ago, before he had sacked her, before she had married Matthew.

Meanwhile, in the inner office, Strike's call to Jasper Chiswell had been answered almost instantly.

"Chiswell," he barked.

"Cormoran Strike here," said the detective. "You spoke to my partner a short while ago."

"Ah, yes," said the Minister for Culture, who sounded as though he were in the back of a car. "I've got a job for you. Nothing I want to discuss over the phone. I'm busy today and this evening, unfortunately, but tomorrow would suit."

"*Ob-observing the hypocrites . . .*" sang the busker down in the street.

"Sorry, no chance tomorrow," said Strike, watching motes of dust fall through the bright sunlight. "No chance until Friday, actually. Can you give me an idea what kind of job we're talking about, Minister?"

Chiswell's response was both tense and angry.

"I can't discuss it over the phone. I'll make it worth your while to meet me, if that's what you want."

"It isn't a question of money, it's time. I'm solidly booked until Friday."

"Oh, for Christ's sake—"

Chiswell suddenly removed his phone from his mouth and Strike heard him talking furiously to somebody else.

"—*left* here, you moron! *Lef*—for fuck's sake! No, I'll walk. I'll bloody walk, open the door!"

In the background, Strike heard a nervous man say:

"I'm sorry, Minister, it was No Entry—"

"Never mind that! Open this—*open this bloody door!*"

Strike waited, eyebrows raised. He heard a car door slam, rapid footsteps and then Jasper Chiswell spoke again, his mouth close to the receiver.

"The job's urgent!" he hissed.

"If it can't wait until Friday, you'll have to find someone else, I'm afraid."

"*My feet is my only carriage,*" sang the busker.

Chiswell said nothing for a few seconds; then, finally:

"It's got to be you. I'll explain when we meet, but—all right, if it *has* to be Friday, meet me at Pratt's Club. Park Place. Come at twelve, I'll give you lunch."

"All right," Strike agreed, now thoroughly intrigued. "See you at Pratt's."

He hung up and returned to the office where Robin was opening and sorting mail. When he told her the upshot of the conversation, she Googled Pratt's for him.

"I didn't think places like this still existed," she said in disbelief, after a minute's reading off the monitor.

"Places like what?"

"It's a gentleman's club . . . very Tory . . . no women allowed, except as guests of club members at lunchtime . . . and 'to avoid confusion,'" Robin read from the Wikipedia page, "'all male staff members are called George.'"

"What if they hire a woman?"

"Apparently they did in the eighties," said Robin, her expression midway between amusement and disapproval. "They called her Georgina."

9

It is best for you not to know. Best for us both.

Henrik Ibsen, *Rosmersholm*

At half past eleven the following Friday, a suited and freshly shaven Strike emerged from Green Park Tube station and proceeded along Piccadilly. Double-deckers rolled past the windows of luxury shops, which were capitalizing on Olympics fever to push an eclectic mix of goods: gold-wrapped chocolate medals, Union Jack brogues, antique sporting posters and, over and again, the jagged logo that Jimmy Knight had compared to a broken swastika.

Strike had allowed a generous margin of time to reach Pratt's, because his leg was again aching after two days in which he had rarely been able to take the weight off his prosthesis. He had hoped that the tech conference in Epping Forest, where he had spent the previous day, might have offered intervals of rest, but he had been disappointed. His target, the recently fired partner of a start-up, was suspected of trying to sell key features of their new app to competitors. For hours, Strike had tailed the young man from booth to booth, documenting all his movements and his interactions, hoping at some point that he would tire and sit. However, between the coffee bar where customers stood at high tables, to the sandwich bar where everyone stood and ate sushi with their fingers out of plastic boxes, the target had spent eight hours walking or standing. Coming after long hours of lurking in Harley Street the day before, it was hardly surprising that the removal of his prosthesis the previous evening had been an uncomfortable affair, the gel pad that separated stump from artificial shin difficult to prize off. As Strike passed the cool off-white arches of the Ritz, he hoped Pratt's contained at least one comfortable chair of generous proportions.

He turned right into St. James's Street, which led him in a gentle slope straight down to the sixteenth-century St. James's Palace. This was not an area of London that Strike usually visited on his own account, given that he had neither the means nor the inclination to buy from gentlemen's outfitters, long-established gun shops or centuries-old wine dealers. As he drew nearer to Park Place, though, he was visited by a personal memory. He had walked this street more than ten years previously, with Charlotte.

They had walked up the slope, not down it, heading for a lunch date with her father, who was now dead. Strike had been on leave from the army and they had recently resumed what was, to everyone who knew them, an incomprehensible and obviously doomed affair. On neither side of their relationship had there ever been a single supporter. His friends and family had viewed Charlotte with everything from mistrust to loathing, while hers had always considered Strike, the illegitimate son of an infamous rock star, as one more manifestation of Charlotte's need to shock and rebel. Strike's military career had been nothing to her family, or rather, it had been just another sign of his plebeian unfitness to aspire to the well-bred beauty's hand, because gentlemen of Charlotte's class did not enter the Military Police, but Cavalry or Guards regiments.

She had clutched his hand very tightly as they entered an Italian restaurant somewhere nearby. Its precise location escaped Strike now. All he remembered was the expression of rage and disapproval on Sir Anthony Campbell's face as they had approached the table. Strike had known before a word was spoken that Charlotte had not told her father that she and Strike had resumed their affair, or that she would be bringing him with her. It had been a thoroughly Charlottian omission, prompting the usual Charlottian scene. Strike had long since come to believe that she engineered situations out of an apparently insatiable need for conflict. Prone to outbursts of lacerating honesty amid her general mythomania, she had told Strike towards the end of their relationship that at least, while fighting, she knew she was alive.

As Strike drew level with Park Place, a line of cream-painted townhouses leading off St. James's Street, he noted that the sudden memory of Charlotte clinging to his hand no longer hurt, and felt like an alcoholic who, for the first time, catches a whiff of beer without breaking into a sweat or having to grapple with his desperate craving. *Perhaps this is it*, he thought, as he approached the black door of Pratt's, with its wrought iron balustrade above. Perhaps, two years after she had told him the unforgivable lie and he had left for good, he was healed, clear of what he sometimes, even though not superstitious, saw as a kind of Bermuda triangle, a danger zone in which he feared being pulled back under, dragged to the depths of anguish and pain by the mysterious allure Charlotte had held for him.

With a faint sense of celebration, Strike knocked on the door of Pratt's.

A petite, motherly woman opened up. Her prominent bust and alert, bright-eyed mien put him in mind of a robin or a wren. When she spoke, he caught a trace of the West Country.

"You'll be Mr. Strike. The minister's not here yet. Come along in."

He followed her across the threshold into a hall through which could be glimpsed an enormous billiard table. Rich crimsons, greens and dark wood predominated. The stewardess, who he assumed was Georgina, led him down a set of steep stairs, which Strike took carefully, maintaining a firm grip on the banister.

The stairs led to a cozy basement. The ceiling had sunk so low that it appeared partially supported by a large dresser on which sundry porcelain platters were displayed, the topmost ones half embedded into the plaster.

"We aren't very big," she said, stating the obvious. "Six hundred members, but we can only serve fourteen a meal at a time. Would you like a drink, Mr. Strike?"

He declined, but accepted an invitation to sit down in one of the leather chairs grouped around an aged cribbage board.

The small space was divided by an archway into sitting and dining areas. Two places had been set at the long table in the other half of the room, beneath small, shuttered windows. The only other person in the basement apart from himself and Georgina was a white-coated chef working in a minuscule kitchen a mere yard from where Strike sat. The chef bade Strike welcome in a French accent, then continued carving cold roast beef.

Here was the very antithesis of the smart restaurants where Strike tailed errant husbands and wives, where the lighting was chosen to complement glass and granite, and sharp-tongued restaurant critics sat like stylish vultures on uncomfortable modern chairs. Pratt's was dimly lit. Brass picture lights dotted walls papered in dark red, which was largely obscured by stuffed fish in glass cases, hunting prints and political cartoons. In a blue and white tiled niche along one side of the room sat an ancient iron stove. The china plates, the threadbare carpet, the table bearing its homely load of ketchup and mustard all contributed to an ambience of cozy informality, as though a bunch of aristocratic boys had dragged all the things they liked about the grown-up world—its games, its drink and its trophies—down into the basement where Nanny would dole out smiles, comfort and praise.

Twelve o'clock arrived, but Chiswell did not. "Georgina," however, was friendly and informative about the club. She and her husband, the chef, lived on the premises. Strike could not help but reflect that this must be some of the most expensive real estate in London. To maintain the little club, which, Georgina told him, had been established in 1857, was costing somebody a lot of money.

"The Duke of Devonshire owns it, yes," said Georgina brightly. "Have you seen our betting book?"

Strike turned the pages of the heavy, leather-bound tome, where long ago wagers had been recorded. In a gigantic scrawl dating back to the seventies, he read: "Mrs. Thatcher to form the next government. Bet: one lobster dinner, the lobster to be larger than a man's erect cock."

He was grinning over this when a bell rang overhead.

"That'll be the minister," said Georgina, bustling away upstairs.

Strike replaced the betting book on its shelf and returned to his seat. From overhead came heavy footsteps and then, descending the stairs, the same irascible, impatient voice he had heard on Monday.

"—no, Kinvara, I can't. I've just told you why, I've got a lunch meeting...no, you can't...Five o'clock, then, yes...yes...*yes!*...Goodbye!"

A pair of large, black-shod feet descended the stairs until Jasper Chiswell emerged into the basement, peering around with a truculent air. Strike rose from his armchair.

"Ah," said Chiswell, scrutinizing Strike from beneath his heavy eyebrows. "You're here."

Jasper Chiswell wore his sixty-eight years reasonably well. A big, broad man, though round-shouldered, he still had a full head of gray hair which, implausible though it seemed, was his own. This hair made Chiswell an easy target for cartoonists, because it was coarse, straight and rather long, standing out from his head in a manner that suggested a wig or, so the unkind suggested, a chimney brush. To the hair was added a large red face, small eyes and a protuberant lower lip, which gave him the air of an overgrown baby perpetually on the verge of a tantrum.

"M'wife," he told Strike, brandishing the mobile still in his hand. "Come up to town without warning. Sulking. Thinks I can drop everything."

Chiswell stretched out a large, sweaty hand, which Strike shook, then eased off the heavy overcoat he was wearing despite the heat of the day. As he did so, Strike noticed the pin on his frayed regimental tie. The uninitiated might think it a rocking horse, but Strike recognized it at once as the White Horse of Hanover.

"Queen's Own Hussars," said Strike, nodding at it as both men sat down.

"Yerse," said Chiswell. "Georgina, I'll have some of that sherry you gave me when I was in with Alastair. You?" he barked at Strike.

"No thanks."

Though nowhere near as dirty as Billy Knight, Chiswell did not smell very fresh.

"Yerse, Queen's Own Hussars. Aden and Singapore. Happy days."

He didn't seem happy at the moment. His ruddy skin had an odd, plaque-like appearance close up. Dandruff lay thick in the roots of his coarse hair and large patches of sweat spread around the underarms of his blue shirt. The minister bore the unmistakable appearance, not unusual in Strike's clients, of a man under intense strain, and when his sherry arrived, he swallowed most of it in a single gulp.

"Shall we move through?" he suggested, and without waiting for an answer he barked, "We'll eat straight away, Georgina."

Once they were seated at the table, which had a stiff, snowy-white tablecloth like those at Robin's wedding, Georgina brought them thick slices of cold roast beef and boiled potatoes. It was English nursery food, plain and unfussy, and none the worse for it. Only when the stewardess had left them in peace, in the dim dining room full of oil paintings and more dead fish, did Chiswell speak again.

"You were at Jimmy Knight's meeting," he said, without preamble. "A plainclothes officer there recognized you."

Strike nodded. Chiswell shoved a boiled potato in his mouth, masticated angrily, and swallowed before saying:

"I don't know who's paying you to get dirt on Jimmy Knight, or what you may already have on him, but whoever it is and whatever you've got, I'm prepared to pay double for the information."

"I haven't got anything on Jimmy Knight, I'm afraid," said Strike. "Nobody was paying me to be at the meeting."

Chiswell looked stunned.

"But then, why were you there?" he demanded. "You're not telling me *you* intend to protest against the Olympics?"

So plosive was the "p" of "protest" that a small piece of potato flew out of his mouth across the table.

"No," said Strike. "I was trying to find somebody I thought might be at the meeting. They weren't."

Chiswell attacked his beef again as though it had personally wronged him. For a while, the only sounds were those of their knives and forks scraping the china. Chiswell speared the last of his boiled potatoes, put it whole into his mouth, let his knife and fork fall with a clatter onto his plate and said:

"I'd been thinking of hiring a detective before I heard you were watching Knight."

Strike said nothing. Chiswell eyed him suspiciously.

"You have the reputation of being very good."

"Kind of you to say so," said Strike.

Chiswell continued to glare at Strike with a kind of furious desperation, as though wondering whether he dared hope that the detective would not prove yet another disappointment in a life beset with them.

"I'm being blackmailed, Mr. Strike," he said abruptly. "Blackmailed by a pair of men who have come together in a temporary, though probably unstable, alliance. One of them is Jimmy Knight."

"I see," said Strike.

He, too, put his knife and fork together. Georgina appeared to know by some psychic process that Strike and Chiswell had eaten their fill of the main course. She arrived to clear away, reappearing with a treacle tart. Only once she had retired to the kitchen, and both men had helped themselves to large slices of pudding, did Chiswell resume his story.

"There's no need for sordid details," he said, with an air of finality. "All you need to know is that Jimmy Knight is aware that I did something that I would not wish to see shared with the gentlemen of the fourth estate."

Strike said nothing, but Chiswell seemed to think his silence had an accusatory flavor, because he added sharply:

"No crime was committed. Some might not like it, but it wasn't illegal at the—but that's by the by," said Chiswell, and took a large gulp of water. "Knight came to me a couple of months ago and asked for forty thousand pounds in hush money. I refused to pay. He threatened me with exposure, but as he didn't appear to have any proof of his claim, I dared hope he would be unable to follow through on the threat.

"No press story resulted, so I concluded that I was right in thinking he had no proof. He returned a few weeks later and asked for half the former sum. Again, I refused.

"It was then, thinking to increase the pressure on me, I assume, that he approached Geraint Winn."

"I'm sorry, I don't know who—?"

"Della Winn's husband."

"Della Winn, the Minister for Sport?" said Strike, startled.

"Yes, of course Della-Winn-the-Minister-for-Sport," snapped Chiswell.

The Right Honorable Della Winn, as Strike knew well, was a Welshwoman in her early sixties who had been blind since birth. No matter their party affiliation, people tended to admire the Liberal Democrat, who had been a human rights lawyer before standing for Parliament. Usually photographed with her guide dog, a pale yellow Labrador, she had been much in evidence in the press of late, her current bailiwick being the Paralympics. She had visited Selly Oak while Strike had been in the hospital, readjusting to the loss of his leg in Afghanistan. He had been left with a favorable impression of her intelligence and her empathy. Of her husband, Strike knew nothing.

"I don't know whether Della knows what Geraint's up to," said Chiswell, spearing a piece of treacle tart and continuing to speak while he chewed it. "Probably, but keeping her nose clean. Plausible deniability. Can't have the sainted Della involved in black-mail, can we?"

"Her husband's asked you for money?" asked Strike, incredulous.

"Oh no, no. Geraint wants to force me from office."

"Any particular reason why?" said Strike.

"There's an enmity between us dating back many years, rooted in a wholly baseless—but that's irrelevant," said Chiswell, with an angry shake of the head. "Geraint approached me, 'hoping it isn't true,' and 'offering me a chance to explain.' He's a nasty, twisted little man who's spent his life holding his wife's handbag and answering her telephone calls. Naturally he's relishing the idea of wielding some actual power."

Chiswell took a swig of sherry.

"So, as you can see, I'm in something of a cleft stick, Mr. Strike. Even if I were minded to pay off Jimmy Knight, I still have to con-tend with a man who wants my disgrace, and who may well be able to lay hands on proof."

"How could Winn get proof?"

Chiswell took another large mouthful of treacle tart and glanced over his shoulder to check that Georgina remained safely in the kitchen.

"I've heard," he muttered, and a fine mist of pastry flew from the slack lips, "that there may be photographs."

"Photographs?" repeated Strike.

"Winn can't *have* them, of course. If he had, it would all be over. But he might be able to find a way of getting hold of them. Yerse."

He shoved the last piece of tart into his mouth, then said:

"Of course, there's a chance the photographs don't incriminate me. There are no distinguishing marks, so far as I'm aware."

Strike's imagination frankly boggled. He yearned to ask, "Distinguishing marks on what, Minister?" but refrained.

"It all happened six years ago," continued Chiswell. "I've been over and over the damn thing in my head. There were others involved who might have talked, but I doubt it, I doubt it very much. Too much to lose. No, it's all going to come down to what Knight and Winn can dig up. I strongly suspect that if he gets hold of the photographs, Winn will go straight to the press. I don't think that would be Knight's first choice. He simply wants money.

"So here I am, Mr. Strike, *a fronte praecipitium, a tergo lupi*. I've lived with this hanging over me for weeks now. It hasn't been enjoyable."

He peered at Strike through his tiny eyes, and the detective was irresistibly put in mind of a mole, blinking up at a hovering spade that waited to crush it.

"When I heard you were at that meeting I assumed you were investigating Knight and had some dirt on him. I've come to the conclusion that the only way out of this diabolical situation is to find something that I can use against each of them, before they get their hands on those photographs. Fight fire with fire."

"Blackmail with blackmail?" said Strike.

"I don't want anything from them except to leave me the hell alone," snapped Chiswell. "Bargaining chips, that's all I want. I acted within the law," he said firmly, "and in accordance with my conscience."

Chiswell was not a particularly likable man, but Strike could well imagine that the ongoing suspense of waiting for public exposure would be torture, especially to a man who had already endured his fair share of scandals. Strike's scant research on his prospective client the previous evening had unearthed gleeful accounts of the affair that had ended his first marriage, of the fact that his second wife had spent a week in a clinic for "nervous exhaustion" and of the grisly drug-induced car crash in which his younger son had killed a young mother.

"This is a very big job, Mr. Chiswell," said Strike. "It'll take two or three people to thoroughly investigate Knight and Winn, especially if there's time pressure."

"I don't care what it costs," said Chiswell. "I don't care if you have to put your whole agency on it.

"I refuse to believe there isn't anything dodgy about Winn, sneaking little toad that he is. There's something funny about them as a couple. She, the blind angel of light," Chiswell's lip curled, "and he, her potbellied henchman, always scheming and backstabbing and grubbing up every freebie he can get. There must be something there. Must be.

"As for Knight, Commie rabble rouser, there's bound to be something the police haven't yet caught up with. He was always a tearaway, a thoroughly nasty piece of work."

"You knew Jimmy Knight before he started trying to blackmail you?" asked Strike.

"Oh, yes," said Chiswell. "The Knights are from my constituency. The father was an odd-job man who did a certain amount of work for our family. I never knew the mother. I believe she died before the three of them moved into Steda Cottage."

"I see," said Strike.

He was recalling Billy's anguished words, *"I seen a child strangled and nobody believes me,"* the nervous movement from nose to chest as he made his slipshod half-cross, and the prosaic, precise detail of the pink blanket in which the dead child had been buried.

"There's something I think I should tell you before we discuss terms, Mr. Chiswell," said Strike. "I was at the CORE meeting because I was trying to find Knight's younger brother. His name's Billy."

The crease between Chiswell's myopic eyes deepened a fraction.

"Yerse, I remember that there were two of them, but Jimmy was the elder by a considerable amount—a decade or more, I would guess. I haven't seen—Billy, is it?—in many years."

"Well, he's seriously mentally ill," said Strike. "He came to me last Monday with a peculiar story, then bolted."

Chiswell waited, and Strike was sure he detected tension.

"Billy claims," said Strike, "that he witnessed the strangling of a small child when he was very young."

Chiswell did not recoil, horrified; he did not bluster or storm. He did not demand whether he was being accused, or ask what on earth that had to do with him. He responded with none of the flamboyant defenses of the guilty man, and yet Strike could have sworn that to Chiswell, this was not a new story.

"And who does he claim strangled the child?" he asked, fingering the stem of his wine glass.

"He didn't tell me—or wouldn't."

"You think this is what Knight is blackmailing me over? Infanticide?" asked Chiswell roughly.

"I thought you ought to know why I went looking for Jimmy," said Strike.

"I have no deaths on my conscience," said Jasper Chiswell forcefully. He swallowed the last of his water. "One cannot," he added, replacing the empty glass on the table, "be held accountable for unintended consequences."

10

I have believed that we two together would be equal to it.
                                        Henrik Ibsen, *Rosmersholm*

The detective and the minister emerged from 14 Park Place an hour later and walked the few yards that took them back to St. James's Street. Chiswell had become less curmudgeonly and gnomic over coffee, relieved, Strike suspected, to have put in train some action that might lift from him what had clearly become an almost intolerable burden of dread and suspense. They had agreed terms and Strike was pleased with the deal, because this promised to be a better-paid and more challenging job than the agency had been given in a while.

"Well, thank you, Mr. Strike," said Chiswell, staring off down St. James's as they both paused on the corner. "I must leave you here. I have an appointment with my son."

Yet he did not move.

"You investigated Freddie's death," he said abruptly, glancing at Strike out of the corner of his eyes.

Strike had not expected Chiswell to raise the subject, and especially not here, as an afterthought, after the intensity of their basement discussion.

"Yes," he replied. "I'm sorry."

Chiswell's eyes remained fixed on a distant art gallery.

"I remembered your name on the report," said Chiswell. "It's an unusual one."

He swallowed, still squinting at the gallery. He seemed strangely unwilling to depart for his appointment.

"Wonderful boy, Freddie," he said. "Wonderful. Went into my old regiment—well, as good as. Queen's Own Hussars amalgamated with the Queen's Royal Irish back in 'ninety-three, as you'll know. So it was the Queen's Royal Hussars he joined.

"Full of promise. Full of life. But of course, you never knew him."

"No," said Strike.

Some polite comment seemed necessary.

"He was your eldest, wasn't he?"

"Of four," said Chiswell, nodding. "Two girls," and by his inflection he waved them away, mere females, chaff to wheat, "and this other boy," he added darkly. "He went to jail. Perhaps you saw the newspapers?"

"No," lied Strike, because he knew what it felt like to have your personal details strewn across the newspapers. It was kindest, if at all credible, to pretend you hadn't read it all, politest to let people tell their own story.

"Been trouble all his life, Raff," said Chiswell. "I got him a job in there."

He pointed a thick finger at the distant gallery window.

"Dropped out of his History of Art degree," said Chiswell. "Friend of mine owns the place, agreed to take him on. M'wife thinks he's a lost cause. He killed a young mother in a car. He was high."

Strike said nothing.

"Well, goodbye," said Chiswell, appearing to come out of a melancholy trance. He offered his sweaty hand once more, which Strike shook, then strode away, bundled up in the thick coat that was so inappropriate on this fine June day.

Strike proceeded up St. James's Street in the opposite direction, pulling out his mobile as he went. Robin picked up on the third ring.

"Need to meet you," said Strike without preamble. "We've got a new job, a big one."

"Damn!" she said. "I'm in Harley Street. I didn't want to bother you, knowing you were with Chiswell, but Andy's wife broke her wrist falling off a stepladder. I said I'd cover Dodgy while Andy takes her to hospital."

"Shit. Where's Barclay?"

"Still on Webster."

"Is Dodgy in his consulting room?"

"Yes."

"We'll risk it," said Strike. "He usually goes straight home on Fridays. This is urgent. I need to tell you about it face to face. Can you meet me in the Red Lion in Duke of York Street?"

Having refused all alcohol during his meal with Chiswell, Strike fancied a pint rather than returning to the office. If he had stuck out in his suit at the White Horse in East Ham, he was perfectly dressed for Mayfair, and two minutes later he entered the Red Lion in Duke of York Street, a snug Victorian pub whose brass fittings and etched glass reminded him of the Tottenham. Taking a pint of London Pride off to a corner table, he looked up Della Winn and her husband on his phone and began reading an article about the forthcoming Paralympics, in which Della was extensively quoted.

"Hi," said Robin, twenty-five minutes later, dropping her bag onto the seat opposite him.

"Want a drink?" he asked.

"I'll get it," said Robin. "Well?" she said, rejoining him a couple of minutes later, holding an orange juice. Strike smiled at her barely contained impatience. "What was it all about? What did Chiswell want?"

The pub, which comprised only a horseshoe space around a single bar, was already tightly packed with smartly dressed men and women, who had started their weekend early or, like Strike and Robin, were finishing work over a drink. Lowering his voice, Strike told her what had passed between him and Chiswell.

"Oh," said Robin blankly, when at last Strike had finished filling her in. "So we're . . . we're going to try and get dirt on Della Winn?"

"On her husband," Strike corrected her, "and Chiswell prefers the phrase 'bargaining chips.'"

Robin said nothing, but sipped her orange juice.

"Blackmail's illegal, Robin," said Strike, correctly reading her uneasy expression. "Knight's trying to screw forty grand out of Chiswell and Winn wants to force him out of his job."

"So he's going to blackmail them back and we're going to help him do it?"

"We get dirt on people every day," said Strike roughly. "It's a bit late to start getting a conscience about it."

He took a long pull on his pint, annoyed not only by her attitude, but by the fact that he had let his resentment show. She lived with her husband in a desirable sash-windowed house in Albury Street, while he remained in two drafty rooms, from which he might soon be ejected by the redevelopment of the street. The agency had never before been offered a job that gave three people full employment, possibly for months. Strike was not about to apologize for being keen to take it. He was tired, after years of graft, of being plunged back into the red whenever the agency hit a lean patch. He had ambitions for his business that couldn't be achieved without building up a far healthier bank balance. Nevertheless, he felt compelled to defend his position.

"We're like lawyers, Robin. We're on the client's side."

"You turned down that investment banker the other day, who wanted to find out where his wife—"

"—because it was bloody obvious he'd do her harm if he found her."

"Well," said Robin, a challenging look in her eye, "what if the thing they've found out about Chiswell—"

But before she could finish her sentence, a tall man in deep conversation with a colleague walked straight into Robin's chair, flinging her forward into the table and knocking over her orange juice.

"Oi!" barked Strike, as Robin tried to wipe the juice off her sopping dress. "Fancy apologizing?"

"Oh dear," said the man in a drawl, eyeing the juice-soaked Robin as several people turned to stare. "Did I do that?"

"Yes, you bloody did," said Strike, heaving himself up and moving around the table. "And that's not an apology!"

"Cormoran!" said Robin warningly.

"Well, I'm sorry," said the man, as though making an enormous concession, but taking in Strike's size, his regret seemed to become more sincere. "Seriously, I do apol—"

"Bugger off," snarled Strike. "Swap seats," he said to Robin. "Then if some other clumsy tosser walks by they'll get me, not you."

Half-embarrassed, half-touched, she picked up her handbag, which was also soaked, and did as he had requested. Strike returned to the table clutching a fistful of paper napkins, which he handed to her.

"Thanks."

It was difficult to maintain a combative stance given that he was voluntarily sitting in a chair covered in orange juice to spare her. Still dabbing off the juice, Robin leaned in and said quietly:

"You know what I'm worried about. The thing Billy said."

The thin cotton dress was sticking to her everywhere: Strike kept his gaze resolutely on her eyes.

"I asked Chiswell about that."

"Did you?"

"Of course I did. What else was I going to think, when he said he was being blackmailed by Billy's brother?"

"And what did he say?"

"He said he had no deaths on his hands, but 'one cannot be held accountable for unintended consequences.' "

"What on earth does *that* mean?"

"I asked. He gave me the hypothetical example of a man dropping a mint, on which a small child later choked to death."

"*What?*"

"Your guess is as good as mine. Billy hasn't called back, I suppose?"

Robin shook her head.

"Look, the overwhelming probability is Billy's delusional," said Strike. "When I told Chiswell what Billy had said, I didn't get any sense of guilt or fear..."

As he said it, he remembered the shadow that had passed over Chiswell's face, and the impression he had received that the story was not, to Chiswell, entirely new.

"So what are they blackmailing Chiswell about?" asked Robin.

"Search me," said Strike. "He said it happened six years ago, which doesn't fit with Billy's story, because he wouldn't have been a little kid six years ago. Chiswell said some people would think what he did was immoral, but it wasn't illegal. He seemed to be suggesting that it wasn't against the law when he did it, but is now."

Strike suppressed a yawn. Beer and the heat of the afternoon were making him drowsy. He was due at Lorelei's later.

"So you trust him?" Robin asked.

"Do I trust Chiswell?" Strike wondered aloud, his eyes on the extravagantly engraved mirror behind Robin. "If I had to bet on it, I'd say he was being truthful with me today because he's desperate. Do I think he's generally trustworthy? Probably no more than anyone else."

"You didn't *like* him, did you?" asked Robin, incredulously. "I've been reading about him."

"And?"

"Pro-hanging, anti-immigration, voted against increasing maternity leave—"

She didn't notice Strike's involuntary glance down her figure as she continued:

"—banged on about family values, then left his wife for a journalist—"

"All right, I wouldn't choose him for a drinking buddy, but there's something slightly pitiable about him. He's lost one son, the other one's just killed a woman—"

"Well, yes, there you are," said Robin. "He advocates locking up petty criminals and throwing away the key, then his son runs over someone's mother and he pulls out all the stops to get him a short sen—"

She broke off suddenly as a loud female voice said: "Robin! How lovely!"

Sarah Shadlock had entered the pub with two men.

"Oh God," muttered Robin, before she could help herself, then, more loudly, "Sarah, hi!"

She would have given much to avoid this encounter. Sarah would be delighted to tell Matthew that she had found Robin and Strike having a tête-à-tête in a Mayfair pub, when she herself had told Matthew by phone only an hour ago that she was alone in Harley Street.

Sarah insisted on wiggling around the table to embrace Robin,

something the latter was sure she would not have done had she not
been with men.

"Darling, what's happened to you? You're all sticky!"

She was just a little posher here, in Mayfair, than anywhere else
Robin had met her, and several degrees warmer to Robin.

"Nothing," muttered Robin. "Spilled orange juice, that's all."

"Cormoran!" said Sarah blithely, swooping in for a kiss on his
cheek. Strike, Robin was pleased to note, sat impassive and did not
respond. "Bit of R and R?" said Sarah, embracing them both in her
knowing smile.

"Work," said Strike bluntly.

Receiving no encouragement to stay, Sarah moved along the bar,
taking her colleagues with her.

"I forgot Christie's is round the corner," muttered Robin.

Strike checked his watch. He didn't want to have to wear his suit
to Lorelei's, and indeed, it was now stained with orange juice from
having taken Robin's seat.

"We need to talk about how we're going to do this job, because it
starts tomorrow."

"OK," said Robin with some trepidation, because it had been a
long time since she had worked a weekend. Matthew had got used
to her coming home.

"It's all right," said Strike, apparently reading her mind, "I won't
need you till Monday.

"The job's going to take three people at a minimum. I reckon
we've already got enough on Webster to keep the client happy, so
we'll put Andy full time on Dodgy Doc, let the two waiting-list
clients know we're not going to be able to do them this month and
Barclay can come in with us on the Chiswell case.

"On Monday, you're going into the House of Commons."

"I'm what?" said Robin, startled.

"You're going to go in as Chiswell's goddaughter, who's interested
in a career in Parliament, and get started on Geraint, who runs Della's
constituency office at the other end of the corridor to Chiswell's.
Chat him up . . ."

He took a swig of beer, frowning at her over the top of the glass.

"What?" said Robin, unsure what was coming.

"How d'you feel," said Strike, so quietly that she had to lean in to hear him, "about breaking the law?"

"Well, I tend to be opposed to it," said Robin, unsure whether to be amused or worried. "That's sort of why I wanted to do investigative work."

"And if the law's a bit of a gray area, and we can't get the information any other way? Bearing in mind that Winn's definitely breaking the law, trying to blackmail a Minister of the Crown out of his job?"

"Are you talking about bugging Winn's office?"

"Right in one," said Strike. Correctly reading her dubious expression, he went on. "Listen, by Chiswell's account, Winn's a slapdash loudmouth, which is why he's stuck in the constituency office and kept well away from his wife's work at the Department for Sport. Apparently he leaves his office door open most of the time, shouts about constituents' confidential affairs and leaves private papers lying around in the communal kitchen. There's a good chance you'll be able to inveigle indiscretions out of him without needing the bug, but I don't think we can count on it."

Robin swilled the last of her orange juice in her glass, deliberating, then said:

"All right, I'll do it."

"Sure?" said Strike. "OK, well you won't be able to take devices in, because you'll have to go through a metal detector. I've said I'm going to get a handful to Chiswell tomorrow. He'll pass them to you once you're inside.

"You'll need a cover name. Text it to me when you've thought of one so I can let Chiswell know. You could use 'Venetia Hall' again, actually. Chiswell's the kind of bloke who'd have a goddaughter called Venetia."

"Venetia" was Robin's middle name, but Robin was too full of apprehension and excitement to care that Strike, from his smirk, continued to find it amusing.

"You're going to have to work a disguise as well," said Strike. "Nothing major, but Chiswell remembered what you look like from the Ripper coverage, so we've got to assume Winn might, too."

"It'll be too hot for a wig," she said. "I might try colored contact lenses. I could go and buy some now. Maybe some plain-lensed glasses on top." A smile she could not suppress surfaced again. "The House of Commons!" she repeated excitedly.

Robin's excited grin faded as Sarah Shadlock's white-blonde head intruded on the periphery of her vision, on the other side of the bar. Sarah had just repositioned herself to keep Robin and Strike in her sights.

"Let's go," Robin said to Strike.

As they walked back towards the Tube, Strike explained that Barclay would be tailing Jimmy Knight.

"I can't do it," said Strike regretfully. "I've blown my cover with him and his CORE mates."

"So what will you be up to?"

"Plug gaps, follow up leads, cover nights if we need them," said Strike.

"Poor Lorelei," said Robin.

It had slipped out before she could stop herself. Increasingly heavy traffic was rolling past, and when Strike did not answer, Robin hoped that he hadn't heard her.

"Did Chiswell mention his son who died in Iraq?" she asked, rather like a person hastily coughing to hide a laugh that has already escaped them.

"Yeah," said Strike. "Freddie was clearly his favorite child, which doesn't say much for his judgment."

"What d'you mean?"

"Freddie Chiswell was a prize shit. I investigated a lot of Killed in Actions, and I never had so many people ask me whether the dead officer had been shot in the back by his own men."

Robin looked shocked.

"*De mortuis nil nisi bonum?*" asked Strike.

Robin had learned quite a lot of Latin, working with Strike.

"Well," she said quietly, for the first time finding some pity in her heart for Jasper Chiswell, "you can't expect his father to speak ill of him."

They parted at the top of the street, Robin to shop for colored contact lenses, Strike heading for the Tube.

He felt unusually cheerful after the conversation with Robin: as they contemplated this challenging job, the familiar contours of their friendship had suddenly resurfaced. He had liked her excitement at the prospect of entering the House of Commons; liked being the one who had offered the chance. He had even enjoyed the way she stress-tested his assumptions about Chiswell's story.

On the point of entering the station, Strike turned suddenly aside, infuriating the irate businessman who had been walking six inches in his wake. Tutting furiously, the man barely avoided a collision and strode off huffily into the Underground while the indifferent Strike leaned up against the sun-soaked wall, enjoying the sensation of heat permeating his suit jacket as he phoned Detective Inspector Eric Wardle.

Strike had told Robin the truth. He didn't believe that Chiswell had ever strangled a child, yet there had been something undeniably odd about his reaction to Billy's story. Thanks to the minister's revelation that the Knight family had lived in proximity to his family home, Strike now knew that Billy had been a "little kid" in Oxfordshire. The first logical step in assuaging his continued unease about that pink blanket was to find out whether any children in the area had disappeared a couple of decades ago, and never been found.

11

. . . let us stifle all memories in our sense of freedom, in joy, in passion.

Henrik Ibsen, *Rosmersholm*

Lorelei Bevan lived in an eclectically furnished flat over her thriving vintage clothes store in Camden. Strike arrived that night at half past seven, a bottle of Pinot Noir in one hand and his mobile clamped to his ear with the other. Lorelei opened the door, smiled good-naturedly at the familiar sight of him on the phone, kissed him on the mouth, relieved him of his wine and returned to the kitchen, from which a welcome smell of Pad Thai was issuing.

"...or try and get into CORE itself," Strike told Barclay, closing the door behind him and proceeding to Lorelei's sitting room, which was dominated by a large print of Warhol's Elizabeth Taylors. "I'll send you everything I've got on Jimmy. He's involved with a couple of different groups. No idea whether he's working. His local's the White Horse in East Ham. Think he's a Hammers fan."

"Could be worse," said Barclay, who was speaking quietly, as he had just got the teething baby to sleep. "Could be Chelsea."

"You'll have to admit to being ex-army," said Strike, sinking into an armchair and hoisting his leg up onto a conveniently positioned square pouf. "You look like a squaddie."

"Nae problem," said Barclay. "I'll be the poor wee laddie who didnae know whut he was gettin' himself intae. Hard lefties love that shit. Let 'em patronize me."

Grinning, Strike took out his cigarettes. For all his initial doubts, he was starting to think that Barclay might have been a good hire.

"All right, hang fire till you hear from me again. Should be sometime Sunday."

As Strike rang off, Lorelei appeared with a glass of red for him.

"Want some help in the kitchen?" Strike asked, though without moving.

"No, stay there. I won't be long," she replied, smiling. He liked her fifties-style apron.

As she returned to the kitchen, he lit up. Although Lorelei did not smoke, she had no objection to Strike's Benson & Hedges as long as he used the kitsch ashtray, decorated with cavorting poodles, that she had provided for the purpose.

Smoking, he admitted to himself that he envied Barclay infiltrating Knight and his band of hard-left colleagues. It was the kind of job Strike had relished in the Military Police. He remembered the four soldiers in Germany who had become enamored of a local far-right group. Strike had managed to persuade them that he shared their belief in a white ethno-nationalist super-state, infiltrated a meeting and secured four arrests and prosecutions that had given him particular satisfaction.

Turning on the TV, he watched Channel 4 News for a while, drinking his wine, smoking in pleasurable anticipation of Pad Thai and other sensual delights, and for once enjoying what so many of his fellow workers took for granted, but which he had rarely experienced: the relief and release of a Friday night.

Strike and Lorelei had met at Eric Wardle's birthday party. It had been an awkward evening in some ways, because Strike had seen Coco there for the first time since telling her by phone that he had no interest in another date. Coco had got very drunk; at one in the morning, while he was sitting on a sofa deep in conversation with Lorelei, she had marched across the room, thrown a glass of wine over both of them and stormed off into the night. Strike had not been aware that Coco and Lorelei were old friends until the morning after he woke up in Lorelei's bed. He considered that this was really more Lorelei's problem than his. She seemed to think the exchange, for Coco wanted nothing more to do with her, more than fair.

"How d'you do it?" Wardle had asked, the next time they met, genuinely puzzled. "Blimey, I'd like to know your—"

Strike raised his heavy eyebrows and Wardle appeared to gag on what had come perilously close to a compliment.

"There's no secret," said Strike. "Some women just like fat one-legged pube-headed men with broken noses."

"Well, it's a sad indictment of our mental health services that they're loose on the streets," Wardle had said, and Strike had laughed.

Lorelei was her real name, taken not from the mythical siren of the Rhine, but from Marilyn Monroe's character in *Gentlemen Prefer Blondes*, her mother's favorite film. Men's eyes swiveled when she passed them in the street, but she evoked neither the profound longing nor the searing pain that Charlotte had caused Strike. Whether this was because Charlotte had stunted his capacity to feel so intensely, or because Lorelei lacked some essential magic, he did not know. Neither Strike nor Lorelei had said "I love you." In Strike's case this was because, desirable and amusing though he found her, he could not have said it honestly. It was convenient to him to assume that Lorelei felt the same way.

She had recently ended a five-year-long live-in relationship when, after several lingering looks across Wardle's dark sitting room, he had strolled across to talk to her. He had wanted to believe her when she had told him how glorious it was to have her flat to herself and her freedom restored, yet lately he had felt tiny spots of displeasure when he had told her he had to work weekends, like the first heavy drops of rain that presage a storm. She denied it when challenged: *no, no, of course not, if you've got to work . . .*

But Strike had set out his uncompromising terms at the outset of the relationship: his work was unpredictable and his finances poor. Hers was the only bed he intended to visit, but if she sought predictability or permanence, he was not the man for her. She had appeared content with the deal, and if, over the course of ten months, she had grown less so, Strike was ready to call things off with no hard feelings. Perhaps she sensed this, because she had forced no argument. This pleased him, and not merely because he could do without the aggravation. He liked Lorelei, enjoyed sleeping with her and found it desirable—for a reason he did not bother to dwell on, being perfectly aware what it was—to be in a relationship just now.

The Pad Thai was excellent, their conversation light and amusing. Strike told Lorelei nothing about his new case, except that he hoped it would be both lucrative and interesting. After doing the dishes together, they repaired to the bedroom, with its candy-pink walls and its curtains printed with cartoonish cowgirls and ponies.

Lorelei liked to dress up. To bed that night, she wore stockings and a black corset. She had the talent, by no means usual, of staging an erotic scene without tipping into parody. Perhaps, with his one leg and his broken nose, Strike ought to have felt ludicrous in this boudoir, which was all frivolity and prettiness, but she played Aphrodite to his Hephaestus so adeptly that thoughts of Robin and Matthew were sometimes driven entirely from his mind.

There was, after all, little pleasure to compare with that given by a woman who really wanted you, he thought next day at lunchtime, as they sat side by side at a pavement café, reading separate papers, Strike smoking, Lorelei's perfectly painted nails trailing absently along the back of his hand. So why had he already told her that he needed to work this afternoon? It was true that he needed to drop off the listening devices at Chiswell's Belgravia flat, but he could easily have spent another night with her, returned to the bedroom, the stockings and the basque. The prospect was certainly tempting.

Yet something implacable inside him refused to give in. Two nights in a row would break the pattern; from there, it would be a short slide into true intimacy. In the depths of himself Strike could not imagine a future in which he lived with a woman, married or fathered children. He had planned some of those things with Charlotte, in the days when he had been readjusting to life minus half his leg. An IED on a dusty road in Afghanistan had blasted Strike out of his chosen life into an entirely new body and a new reality. Sometimes he saw his proposal to Charlotte as the most extreme manifestation of his temporary disorientation in the aftermath of his amputation. He had needed to relearn how to walk, and, almost as hard, to live a life outside the military. From a distance of two years, he saw himself trying to hold tight to some part of his past as everything else slipped away. The allegiance he had given the army, he had transferred to a future with Charlotte.

"Good move," his old friend Dave Polworth had said without missing a beat, when Strike told him of the engagement. "Shame to waste all that combat training. Slightly increased risk of getting killed, though, mate."

Had he ever really thought the wedding would happen? Had he truly imagined Charlotte settling for the life he could give her? After everything they had been through, had he believed that they could achieve redemption together, each of them damaged in their own untidy, personal and peculiar ways? It seemed to Strike sitting in the sunshine with Lorelei that for a few months he had both believed it wholeheartedly and known that it was impossible, never planning more than a few weeks ahead, holding Charlotte at night as though she were the last human on earth, as though only Armageddon could separate them.

"Want another coffee?" murmured Lorelei.

"I'd better make a move," said Strike.

"When will I see you?" she asked, as Strike paid the waiter.

"Told you, I've got this big new job on," he said. "Timings are going to be a bit unpredictable for a while. I'll call you tomorrow. We'll go out as soon as I can get a clear evening."

"All right," she said, smiling, and added softly, "Kiss me."

He did so. She pressed her full lips against his, irresistibly recalling certain highlights of the early morning. They broke apart. Strike grinned, bade her goodbye and left her sitting in the sun with her newspaper.

The Minister for Culture did not invite Strike inside when he opened the door of his house in Ebury Street. Chiswell seemed keen, in fact, for the detective to leave as quickly as possible. After taking the box of listening devices, he muttered, "Good, right, I'll make sure she gets them," and was on the point of closing the door when he suddenly called after Strike, "What's her name?"

"Venetia Hall," said Strike.

Chiswell shut the door, and Strike turned his tired footsteps back along the street of quiet golden townhouses, towards the Tube and Denmark Street.

His office seemed stark and gloomy after Lorelei's flat. Strike threw open the windows to let in the noise of Denmark Street down below, where music lovers continued to visit the instrument stores and old record shops that Strike feared were doomed by the forthcoming redevelopment. The sound of engines and horns, of conversation and footsteps, of guitar riffs played by would-be purchasers and the distant bongos of another busker were pleasant to Strike as he settled to work, knowing that he had hours ahead in the computer chair if he were to wrest the bare bones of his targets' lives from the internet.

If you knew where to search and had time and expertise, the outline of many existences could be unearthed in cyberspace: ghostly exoskeletons, sometimes partial, sometimes unnervingly complete, of the lives led by their flesh and blood counterparts. Strike had learned many tricks and secrets, become adept ferreting in even the darkest corners of the internet, but often the most innocent social media sites held untold wealth, a minor amount of cross-referencing all that was necessary to compile detailed private histories that their careless owners had never meant to share with the world.

Strike first consulted Google Maps to examine the place where Jimmy and Billy had grown up. Steda Cottage was evidently too small and insignificant to be named, but Chiswell House was clearly marked, a short way outside the village of Woolstone. Strike spent five minutes fruitlessly scanning the patches of woodland around Chiswell House, noticing a couple of tiny squares that might be estate cottages—*they buried it down in the dell by my dad's house*—before resuming his investigation of the older, saner brother.

CORE had a website where Strike found, sandwiched between lengthy polemics about celebration capitalism and neo-liberalism, a useful schedule of protests at which Jimmy was planning to demonstrate or speak, which the detective printed out and added to his file. He then followed a link to the Real Socialist Party website, which was an even busier and more cluttered affair than that of CORE. Here he found another lengthy article by Jimmy, arguing for the dissolution of the "apartheid state" of Israel and the defeat of the "Zionist lobby" which had a stranglehold on the Western capitalist establishment. Strike noted that Jasper Chiswell was among the "Western Political Elite" listed at the bottom of this article as a "publicly declared Zionist."

Jimmy's girlfriend, Flick, appeared in a couple of photographs on the Real Socialist website, sporting black hair as she marched against Trident and blonde shaded to pink as she cheered Jimmy, who was speaking on an open-air stage at a Real Socialist Party rally. Following a link to Flick's Twitter handle, he perused her timeline, which was a strange mixture of the cloying and the vituperative. "I hope you get fucking arse cancer, you Tory cunt" sat directly above a video clip of a kitten sneezing so hard that it fell out of its basket.

As far as Strike could tell, neither Jimmy nor Flick owned or ever had owned property, something that he had in common with both of them. He could find no indication online of how they were supporting themselves, unless writing for far-left websites paid better than he had imagined. Jimmy was renting the miserable flat in Charlemont Road from a man called Kasturi Kumar, and while Flick made casual mention on social media of living in Hackney, he could not find an address for her anywhere online.

Digging deeper into online records, Strike discovered a James Knight of the correct age who seemed to have cohabited for five years with a woman called Dawn Clancy, and upon delving into Dawn's highly informative, emoji-strewn Facebook page, Strike discovered that they had been married. Dawn was a hairdresser who had run a successful business in London before returning to her native Manchester. Thirteen years older than Jimmy, she seemed to have neither children nor any present-day contact with her ex-husband. However, a comment she had made to a jilted girlfriend's "all men are trash" post, caught Strike's eye: "Yeah, he's a shit, but at least he hasn't sued you! I win (again)!"

Intrigued, Strike turned his attention to court records and, after a little digging, found several useful nuggets of information. Jimmy had been charged with affray twice, once on an anti-capitalism march, once at an anti-Trident protest, but this, Strike had expected.

What was far more interesting was to find Jimmy on a list of vexatious litigants on the website of HM Courts and Tribunals Service. Due to a longstanding habit of beginning frivolous legal actions, Knight was now "forbidden from starting civil cases in courts without permission."

Jimmy had certainly had a good run for his, or the state's, money. Over the past decade he had brought civil actions against sundry individuals and organizations. The law had taken his side only once, when, in 2007, he had won compensation from Zanet Industries, who were found not to have followed due process when dismissing him.

Jimmy had represented himself in court against Zanet and, presumably elated by his win, had gone on to represent himself in suing several others, among them a garage owner, two neighbors, a journalist he alleged had defamed him, two officers in the Metropolitan Police he claimed had assaulted him, two more employers and, finally, his ex-wife, who he said had harassed him and caused him loss of earnings.

In Strike's experience, those who disdained the use of representation in court were either unbalanced or so arrogant that it came to the same thing. Jimmy's litigious history suggested that he was greedy and unprincipled, sharp without being wise. It was always useful to have a handle on a man's vulnerabilities when trying to ferret out his secrets. Strike added the names of all the people Jimmy had tried to sue, plus the current address of his ex-wife, to the file beside him.

At close to midnight Strike retired to his flat for some much-needed sleep, rose early on Sunday, and transferred his attention to Geraint Winn, remaining hunched at the computer until the light began to fade again, by which time a new cardboard file labeled CHISWELL sat beside him, fat with miscellaneous but crosschecked information on Chiswell's two blackmailers.

Stretching and yawning, he became suddenly aware of the noises reaching him through the open windows. The music shops had closed at last, the bongos had ceased, but traffic continued to swish and rumble along Charing Cross Road. Strike heaved himself up, supporting himself on the desk because his remaining ankle was numb after hours in the computer chair, and stooped to look through the inner office window at a tangerine sky spread beyond the rooftops.

It was Sunday evening and in less than two hours England would be playing Italy at the quarter-finals of the European Football Championships in Kiev. One of the few personal indulgences Strike had allowed himself was a subscription to Sky so that he could watch football. The small portable TV that was all his flat upstairs could comfortably accommodate might not be the ideal medium on which to watch such an important game, but he could not justify a night in a pub given that he had an early start on Monday, covering Dodgy Doc again, a prospect that gave him little pleasure.

He checked his watch. He had time to get a Chinese takeaway before the match, but he still needed to call both Barclay and Robin with instructions for the next few days. As he was on the point of picking up the phone, a musical alert told him that he had received an email.

The subject line read: "Missing Kids in Oxfordshire." Strike laid his mobile and keys back on the desk and clicked it open.

Strike —
This is best I can do on a quick search. Obviously without exact time frame it's difficult. 2 missing child cases in Oxfordshire/ Wiltshire from the early/mid 90s unresolved as far as I can tell. Suki Lewis, 12, went missing from care October 1992. Also Immamu Ibrahim, 5-year-old, disappeared 1996. Father disappeared at the same time, is believed to be in Algeria. Without further information, not much to be done.
Best, E

12

The atmosphere we breathe is heavy with storms.

Henrik Ibsen, *Rosmersholm*

The sunset cast a ruddy glow across the duvet behind Robin as she sat at the dressing table in her and Matthew's spacious new bedroom. Next-door's barbecue was now smoking the air that had earlier been fragrant with honeysuckle. She had just left Matthew downstairs, lying on the sofa watching the warm-up to the England–Italy game, a cold bottle of Peroni in his hand.

Opening the dressing table drawer, she took out a pair of colored contact lenses she had concealed there. After trial and error the previous day, she had decided the hazel ones appeared most natural with her strawberry-blonde hair. Gingerly, she extracted first one, then the other, placing them over her watering blue-gray irises. It was essential that she get used to wearing them. Ideally she would have had them in all weekend, but Matthew's reaction when he had seen her in them had dissuaded her.

"Your eyes!" he had said, after staring at her, perplexed, for a few seconds. "Bloody hell, that looks horrible, take them out!"

As Saturday had already been ruined by one of their tense disagreements about her job, she had chosen not to wear the lenses all weekend, because they would serve as a constant reminder to Matthew about what she was up to the following week. He seemed to think that working undercover in the House of Commons was tantamount to treason, and her refusal to tell him who either her client or her targets were had further aggravated him.

Robin kept telling herself that Matthew was worried about her safety and that he could hardly be blamed for it. It had become a mental exercise she performed like a penance: *you can't blame him for being concerned, you nearly got killed last year, he wants you to be safe.* However, the fact that she had gone for a drink with Strike on Friday seemed to be worrying Matthew far more than any potential killer.

"Don't you think you're being bloody hypocritical?" he said.

Whenever he was angry, the skin around his nose and upper lip became taut. Robin had noticed it years ago, but lately it gave her a sensation close to revulsion. She had never mentioned this to her therapist. It had felt too nasty, too visceral.

"How am I hypocritical?"

"Going for cozy little drinks with him—"

"Matt, I work with—"

"—then complaining when I have lunch with Sarah."

"Have lunch with her!" said Robin, her pulse quickening in anger. "Do it! As a matter of fact, I met her in the Red Lion, out with some men from work. Do you want to call Tom and tell him his fiancée's drinking with colleagues? Or am I the only one who's not allowed to do it?"

The skin around his nose and mouth looked like a muzzle as it tightened, Robin thought: a pale muzzle on a snarling dog.

"Would you have told me you'd gone for a drink with him if Sarah hadn't seen you?"

"Yes," said Robin, her temper snapping, "and I'd've known you'd be a dick about it, too."

The tense aftermath of this argument, by no means their most serious of the last month, had lingered all through Sunday. Only in the last couple of hours, with the prospect of the England game to cheer him, had Matthew become amiable again. Robin had even volunteered to fetch him a Peroni from the kitchen and kissed him on the forehead before leaving him, with a sense of liberation, for her colored contact lenses and her preparations for the following day.

Her eyes felt gradually less uncomfortable with repeated blinking. Robin moved across to the bed, where her laptop lay. Pulling it towards her, she saw that an email from Strike had just arrived.

Robin,
Bit of research on the Winns attached. I'll call you shortly for quick brief before tomorrow.
CS

Robin was annoyed. Strike was supposed to be "plugging gaps" and working nights. Did he think she had done no research of her own over the weekend? Nevertheless, she clicked on the first of several attachments, a document summarizing the fruits of Strike's online labor.

Geraint Winn

Geraint Ifon Winn, d.o.b. 15th July 1950. Born Cardiff. Father a miner. Grammar school educated, met Della at University of Cardiff. Was "property consultant" prior to acting as her election agent and running her Parliamentary office post-election. No details of former career available online. No company ever registered in his name. Lives with Della, Southwark Park Road, Bermondsey.

Strike had managed to dig up a couple of poor-quality pictures of Geraint with his well-known wife, both of which Robin had already found and saved to her laptop. She knew how hard Strike had had to work to find an image of Geraint, because it had taken her a long time the previous night, while Matthew slept, to find them. Press photographers did not seem to feel he added much to pictures. A thin, balding man who wore heavy-framed glasses, he had a lipless mouth, a weak chin and a pronounced overbite, which taken together put Robin in mind of an overweight gecko.

Strike had also attached information on the Minister for Sport.

Della Winn

D.o.b. 8th August 1947. Née Jones. Born and raised Vale of Glamorgan, Wales. Both parents teachers. Blind from birth due to bilateral microphthalmia. Attended St. Enodoch Royal School for the Blind from age 5–18. Won multiple swimming awards as teenager. (See attached articles for further details, also of The Playing Field charity.)

Even though Robin had read as much as she could about Della over the weekend, she plowed diligently through both articles. They told her little that she did not already know. Della had worked for a prominent human rights charity before successfully standing for election in the Welsh constituency in which she had been born. She was a long-time advocate for the benefit of sports in deprived areas, a champion of disabled athletes and a supporter for projects that used sport to rehabilitate injured veterans. The founding of her charity, the Level Playing Field, to support young athletes and sportspeople facing challenges, whether of poverty or physical impairment, had received a fair amount of press coverage. Many high-profile sports-people had given their time to fundraisers.

The articles that Strike had attached both mentioned something that Robin already knew from her own research: the Winns, like the Chiswells, had lost a child. Della and Geraint's daughter and only offspring had killed herself at the age of sixteen, a year before Della had stood for Parliament. The tragedy was mentioned in every profile Robin had read on Della Winn, even those lauding her substantial achievements. Her maiden speech in Parliament had supported a proposed bullying hotline, but she had never otherwise discussed her child's suicide.

Robin's mobile rang. After checking that the bedroom door was closed, Robin answered.

"That was quick," said Strike thickly, through a mouthful of Singapore noodles. "Sorry—took me by surprise—just got a takeaway."

"I've read your email," said Robin. She heard a metallic snap and was sure he was opening a can of beer. "Very useful, thanks."

"Got your disguise sorted?" Strike asked.

"Yes," said Robin, turning to examine herself at the mirror. It was strange how much a change of eye color transformed your face. She was planning to wear a pair of clear-lensed glasses over her hazel eyes.

"And you know enough about Chiswell to pretend to be his goddaughter?"

"Of course," said Robin.

"Go on then," said Strike, "impress me."

"Born 1944," Robin said at once, without reading her notes. "Studied Classics at Merton College, Oxford, then joined Queen's Own Hussars, saw active service in Aden and Singapore.

"First wife, Lady Patricia Fleetwood, three children: Sophia, Isabella and Freddie. Sophia's married and lives in Northumberland, Isabella runs Chiswell's Parliamentary office—"

"Does she?" said Strike, sounding vaguely surprised, and Robin was pleased to know that she had discovered something he did not.

"Is she the daughter you knew?" she asked, remembering what Strike had said in the office.

"Wouldn't go as far as 'knew.' I met her a couple of times with Charlotte. Everyone called her 'Izzy Chizzy.' One of those upper-class nicknames."

"Lady Patricia divorced Chiswell after he got a political journalist pregnant—"

"—which resulted in the disappointing son at the art gallery."

"Exactly—"

Robin moved the mouse around to bring up a saved picture, this time of a dark and rather beautiful young man in a charcoal suit, heading up courtroom steps accompanied by a stylish, black-haired woman in sunglasses whom he closely resembled, though she looked hardly old enough to be his mother.

"—but Chiswell and the journalist split up not long after Raphael was born," said Robin.

"The family calls him 'Raff,'" said Strike, "and the second wife doesn't like him, thinks Chiswell should have disowned him after the car crash."

Robin made a further note.

"Great, thanks. Chiswell's current wife, Kinvara, was unwell last year," Robin continued, bringing up a picture of Kinvara, a curvaceous redhead in a slinky black dress and heavy diamond necklace. She was some thirty years younger than Chiswell and pouting at the camera. Had she not known, Robin would have guessed them father and daughter rather than a married couple.

"With nervous exhaustion," said Strike, beating her to it. "Yeah. Drink or drugs, d'you reckon?"

Robin heard a clang and surmised that Strike had just dropped an empty Tennent's can in the office bin. He was alone, then. Lorelei never stayed in the tiny flat upstairs.

"Who knows?" said Robin, her eyes still on Kinvara Chiswell.

"One last thing," said Strike. "Just in. A couple of kids went missing in Oxfordshire around the right time to tally with Billy's story."

There was a brief pause.

"You still there?" asked Strike.

"Yes...I thought you don't believe Chiswell strangled a child?"

"I don't," said Strike. "The timescale doesn't fit, and if Jimmy knew a Tory minister had strangled a kid, he wouldn't have waited twenty years to try and monetise it. But I'd still like to know whether Billy's imagining that he saw someone throttled. I'm going to do a bit of digging on the names Wardle's given me and if either seem credible I might ask you to sound Izzy out. She might remember something about a kid disappearing in the vicinity of Chiswell House."

Robin said nothing.

"Like I said in the pub, Billy's very ill. It's probably nothing," said Strike, with a trace of defensiveness. As he and Robin were both well aware, he had previously jettisoned paid cases and rich clients to pursue mysteries that others might have let lie. "I just—"

"—can't rest easy until you've looked into it," said Robin. "All right. I understand."

Unseen by her, Strike grinned and rubbed his tired eyes.

"Well, best of luck tomorrow," he said. "I'll be on my mobile if you need me."

"What are you going to be up to?"

"Paperwork. Jimmy Knight's ex doesn't work Mondays. I'm off to Manchester to find her on Tuesday."

Robin experienced a sudden wave of nostalgia for the previous year, when she and Strike had undertaken a road trip together to interrogate women left behind in the wake of dangerous men. She wondered whether he had thought about it while he planned this journey.

"Watching England–Italy?" she asked.

"Yeah," said Strike. "There's nothing else, is there?"

"No," said Robin hurriedly. She had not meant to sound as though she wanted to detain him. "Speak soon, then."

She cut the call on his farewell and tossed the mobile aside onto the bed.

13

I am not going to let myself be beaten to the ground by the dread of what may happen.

Henrik Ibsen, *Rosmersholm*

The following morning, Robin woke, gasping, her fingers at her own throat, trying to loosen a non-existent hold. She was already at the bedroom door when Matthew woke, confused.

"It's nothing, I'm fine," she muttered, before he could articulate a question, groping to find the handle that would let her out of the bedroom.

The surprise was that it hadn't happened more often since she had heard the story of the strangled child. Robin knew exactly how it felt to have fingers close tightly around your neck, to feel your brain flood with darkness, to know that you were seconds from being blotted out of existence. She had been driven into therapy by sharp-edged fragments of recollection that were unlike normal memories and which had the power to drag her suddenly out of her body and plunge her back into a past where she could smell the strangler's nicotine-stained fingers, and feel the stabber's soft, sweatshirted belly against her back.

She locked the bathroom door and sat down on the floor in the loose T-shirt she had worn to bed, focusing on her breathing, on the feel of the cool tiles beneath her bare legs, observing, as she had been taught, the rapid beating of her heart, the adrenaline jolting through her veins, not fighting her panic, but watching it. After a while, she consciously noticed the faint smell of the lavender body wash she had used last night, and heard the distant passing of an airplane.

You're safe. Just a dream. Just a dream.

Through two closed doors, she heard Matthew's alarm go off. A few minutes later, he knocked on the door.

"You all right?"

"Fine," Robin called back, over the running tap.

She opened the door.

"Everything OK?" he asked, watching her closely.

"Just needed a pee," said Robin brightly, heading back to the bedroom for her colored contact lenses.

Before starting work with Strike, Robin had signed on with an agency called Temporary Solutions. The offices to which they had sent her were jumbled in her memory now, so that only anomalies, eccentrics and oddities remained. She remembered the alcoholic boss whose dictated letters she had reworded out of kindness, the desk drawer she had opened to find a complete set of dentures and a pair of stained underpants, the hopeful young man who had nicknamed her "Bobbie" and tried, ineptly, to flirt over their back-to-back monitors, the woman who had plastered the interior of her cubicle workspace with pictures of the actor Ian McShane and the girl who had broken up with her boyfriend on the telephone in the middle of the open-plan office, indifferent to the prurient hush falling over the rest of the room. Robin doubted whether any of the people with whom she had come into glancing contact remembered her any better than she remembered them, even the timid romancer who had called her "Bobbie."

However, from the moment that she arrived at the Palace of Westminster, she knew that what happened here would live in her memory forever. She felt a ripple of pleasure simply to leave the tourists behind and pass through the gate where the policeman stood guard. As she approached the palace, with its intricate gold moldings starkly shadowed in the early morning sun, the famous clock tower silhouetted against the sky, her nerves and her excitement mounted.

Strike had told her which side door to use. It led into a long, dimly lit stone hall, but first she must pass through a metal detector and

X-ray machine of the kind used at airports. As she took off her shoulder bag to be scanned, Robin noticed a tall, slightly disheveled natural blonde in her thirties waiting a short distance away, holding a small package wrapped in brown paper. The woman watched as Robin stood for an automated picture that would appear on a paper day pass, to be worn on a lanyard around her neck, and when the security man waved Robin on, stepped forwards.

"Venetia?"

"Yes," said Robin.

"Izzy," said the other, smiling and holding out a hand. She was wearing a loose blouse with a splashy pattern of oversize flowers on it, and wide-legged trousers. "This is from Papa." She pressed the package she was holding into Robin's hands. "I'm *rilly* sorry, we've got to dash—so glad you got here on time—"

She set off at a brisk walk, and Robin hastened to follow.

"—I'm in the middle of printing off a bunch of papers to take over to Papa at DCMS—I'm *snowed under* just now. Papa being Minister for Culture, with the Olympics coming, it's just crazy—"

She led Robin at a near jog through the hall, which had stained-glass windows at the far end, and off along labyrinthine corridors, talking all the while in a confident, upper-class accent, leaving Robin impressed by her lungpower.

"Yah, I'm leaving at the summer recess—setting up a decorating company with my friend Jacks—I've been here for five years—Papa's not happy—he needs somebody *rilly* good and the only applicant he liked turned us down."

She talked over her shoulder at Robin, who was hurrying to keep up.

"I don't s'pose you know any *fabulous* PAs?"

"I'm afraid not," said Robin, who had retained no friends from her temping career.

"Nearly there," said Izzy, who had led Robin through a bewildering number of narrow corridors, all carpeted in the same forest green as the leather seats Robin had seen in the Commons on TV. At last they reached a side-passage off which led several heavy wooden doors, arched in the gothic style.

"That," said Izzy in a stage whisper, pointing as they passed the first door on the right, "is Winn's. This," she said, marching to the last door on the left, "is ours."

She stood aside to let Robin pass into the room first.

The office was cramped and cluttered. The arched stone windows were hung with net curtains, beyond which lay the terrace bar, where shadowy figures moved against the dazzling brightness of the Thames. There were two desks, a multitude of bookshelves and a sagging green armchair. Green drapes hung at the overflowing book-shelves that covered one wall, only partially concealing the untidy stacks of files stacked there. On top of a filing cabinet stood a TV monitor, showing the currently empty interior of the Commons, its green benches deserted. A kettle sat beside mismatched mugs on a low shelf and had stained the wallpaper above it. The desktop printer whirred wheezily in a corner. Some of the papers it was disgorging had slid onto the threadbare carpet.

"Oh, shit," said Izzy, dashing over and scooping them up, while Robin closed the door behind her. As she tapped the fallen papers back into a neat stack on her desk, Izzy said:

"I'm *thrilled* Papa's brought you in. He's been under *so much* strain, which he really doesn't need with everything we've got on now, but you and Strike will sort it out, won't you? Winn's a horrible little man," said Izzy, reaching for a leather folder. "*Inadequate*, you know. How long have you worked with Strike?"

"A couple of years," said Robin, as she undid the package Izzy had given her.

"I've met him, did he tell you? Yah—I was at school with his ex, Charlie Campbell. Gorgeous but trouble, Charlie. D'you know her?"

"No," said Robin. A long-ago near-collision outside Strike's office had been her only contact with Charlotte.

"I always quite fancied Strike," said Izzy.

Robin glanced around, surprised, but Izzy was matter-of-factly inserting papers into the folder.

"Yah, people couldn't see it, but *I* could. He was so butch and so ...well...unapologetic."

"Unapologetic?" Robin repeated.

"Yah. He never took any crap from anyone. Didn't give a toss that people thought he wasn't, you know—"

"Good enough for her?"

As soon as the words escaped her, Robin felt embarrassed. She had felt suddenly strangely protective of Strike. It was absurd, of course: if anybody could look after themselves, it was he.

"S'pose so," said Izzy, still waiting for her papers to print. "It's been ghastly for Papa, these past couple of months. And it isn't as though what he did was wrong!" she said fiercely. "One minute it's legal, the next it isn't. That's not Papa's fault."

"What wasn't legal?" asked Robin innocently.

"Sorry," Izzy replied, pleasantly but firmly. "Papa says, the fewer people know, the better."

She peeked through the net curtains at the sky. "I won't need a jacket, will I? No...sorry to dash, but Papa needs these and he's off to meet Olympic sponsors at ten. Good luck."

And in a rush of flowered fabric and tousled hair, she was gone, leaving Robin curious but strangely reassured. If Izzy could take this robust view of her father's misdemeanor, it surely could not be anything dreadful—always assuming, of course, that Chiswell had told his daughter the truth.

Robin ripped the last piece of wrapping from the small parcel Izzy had given her. It contained, as she had known it would, the half-dozen listening devices that Strike had given to Jasper Chiswell over the weekend. As a Minister of the Crown, Chiswell was not required to pass through the security scanner every morning, as Robin was. She examined the bugs carefully. They had the appearance of normal plastic power points, and were designed to be fitted over genuine plug sockets, allowing the latter to function as normal. They would begin to record only when somebody spoke in their vicinity. She could hear her own heartbeat in the silence left by Izzy's departure. The difficulty of her task was only just beginning to sink in.

She took off her coat, hung it up, then removed from her shoulder bag a large box of Tampax, which she had brought for the purpose of concealing the listening devices she wasn't using. After hiding all but one of the bugs inside it, she placed the box in the bottom drawer of her desk. Next, she searched the cluttered shelves until she found an empty box file, in which she hid the remaining device beneath a handful of letters with typos that she took out of a pile labeled "for shredding." Thus armed, Robin took a deep breath and left the room.

Winn's door had opened since she had arrived. As Robin walked past, she saw a tall young Asian man wearing thick-lensed glasses and carrying a kettle.

"Hi!" said Robin at once, imitating Izzy's bold, cheery approach. "I'm Venetia Hall, we're neighbors! Who are you?"

"Aamir," muttered the other, in a working-class London accent. "Mallik."

"Do you work for Della Winn?" asked Robin.

"Yeah."

"Oh, she's *so* inspirational," gushed Robin. "One of my heroines, actually."

Aamir did not reply, but radiated a desire to be left alone. Robin felt like a terrier trying to harass a racehorse.

"Have you worked here long?"

"Six months."

"Are you going to the café?"

"No," said Aamir, as though she had propositioned him, and he turned sharply away towards the bathroom.

Robin walked on, holding her box file, wondering whether she had imagined animosity rather than shyness in the young man's demeanor. It would have been helpful to make a friend in Winn's office. Having to pretend to be an Izzy-esque goddaughter of Jasper Chiswell was hampering her. She couldn't help but feel that Robin Ellacott from Yorkshire might have befriended Aamir more easily.

Having set off with fake purpose, she decided to explore for a while before returning to Izzy's office.

Chiswell's and Winn's offices were in the Palace of Westminster itself, which, with its vaulted ceilings, libraries, tearooms and air of comfortable grandeur, might have been an old university college.

A half-covered passageway, watched over by large stone statues of a unicorn and lion, led to an escalator to Portcullis House. This was a modern crystal palace, with a folded glass roof, triangular panes held in place by thick black struts. Beneath was a wide, open-plan area including a café, where MPs and civil servants mingled. Flanked by full-grown trees, large water features consisting of long blocks of covered-in shallow pools became dazzling strips of quicksilver in the June sunshine.

There was a shiver of ambition in the thrumming air, and the sense of being part of a vital world. Beneath the ceiling of artfully fragmented glass, Robin passed political journalists perched on leather benches, all of whom were checking or talking on their mobiles, typing onto laptops or intercepting politicians for comment. Robin wondered whether she might have enjoyed working here if she had never been sent to Strike.

Her explorations ended in the third, dingiest and least interesting of the buildings that housed MPs' offices, which resembled nothing so much as a three-star hotel, with worn carpets and cream walls and row upon row of identical doors. Robin doubled back, still clutching her file, and passed Winn's door again fifty minutes after she had last seen it. Quickly checking that the corridor was deserted, she pressed her ear against the thick oak and thought she heard movement within.

"How's it going?" asked Izzy, when Robin re-entered her office a couple of minutes later.

"I haven't seen Winn yet."

"He might be over at DCMS. He goes to see Della on any excuse," said Izzy. "Fancy a coffee?"

But before she could leave her desk, her telephone rang.

While Izzy fielded a call from an irate constituent who had been unable to secure tickets for the Olympic diving—"yes, I like Tom Daley, too," she said, rolling her eyes at Robin, "but it's a *lottery*, madam"—Robin spooned out instant coffee and poured UHT milk, wondering how many times she had done this in offices she hated, and feeling suddenly extraordinarily grateful that she had escaped that life forever.

"Hung up," said Izzy indifferently, setting down the receiver. "What were we talking about? Oh, Geraint, yah. He's furious Della didn't make him a SPAD."

"What's a SPAD?" Robin asked, setting Izzy's coffee down and taking a seat at the other desk.

"Special Adviser. They're like temporary civil servants. Lots more prestige, but you don't hand the posts out to family, it's not done. Anyway, Geraint's hopeless, she wouldn't want him even if it were possible."

"I just met the man who works with Winn," said Robin. "Aamir. He wasn't too friendly."

"Oh, he's odd," said Izzy, dismissively. "Barely civil to me. It's probably because Geraint and Della hate Papa. I've never really got to the bottom of why, but they seem to hate all of us—oh, that reminds me: Papa texted a minute ago. My brother Raff's going to be coming in later this week, to help out in here. Maybe," Izzy added, though she did not sound particularly hopeful, "if Raff's any good, he might be able to take over from me. But Raff doesn't know anything about the blackmail or who you really are, so don't say anything, will you? Papa's got about fourteen godchildren. Raff'll never know the difference."

Izzy sipped her coffee again, then, suddenly subdued, she said:

"I suppose you know about Raff. It was all over the papers. That poor woman...it was awful. She had a four-year-old daughter..."

"I did see something," said Robin, noncommittally.

"I was the only one in the family who visited him in jail," said Izzy. "Everyone was so disgusted by what he'd done. Kinvara—Papa's wife—said he should have got life, but she's got no idea," she continued, "how *ghastly* it was in there...people don't realize what prison's like...I mean, I *know* he did a terrible thing, but..."

Her words trailed away. Robin wondered, perhaps ungenerously, whether Izzy was suggesting that jail was no place for a young man as refined as her half-brother. Doubtless it *had* been a horrible experience, Robin thought, but after all, he had taken drugs, climbed into a car and mown down a young mother.

"I thought he was working in an art gallery?" Robin asked.

"He's gone and messed up at Drummond's," sighed Izzy. "Papa's really taking him in to keep an eye on him."

Public money paid for these salaries, Robin thought, remembering again the unusually short prison sentence the son of the minister had served for that drug-induced fatal accident.

"How did he mess up at the gallery?"

To her great surprise, Izzy's doleful expression vanished in a sudden spurt of laughter.

"Oh, God, I'm sorry, I shouldn't laugh. He shagged the other sales assistant in the loo," she said, quaking with giggles. "I know it isn't funny really—but he'd just got out of jail, and Raff's lovely looking and he's always pulled anyone he wants. They shoved him into a suit and put him in close proximity with some pretty little blonde art graduate, what did they think was going to happen? But as you can imagine, the gallery owner wasn't too chuffed. He heard them going at it and put Raff on a final warning. Then Raff and the girl went and did it again, so Papa had a total fit and says he's coming here instead."

Robin didn't feel particularly amused, but Izzy appeared not to notice, lost in her own thoughts.

"You never know, it could be the making of them, Papa and Raff," she said hopefully, then checked her watch.

"Better return some calls," she sighed, setting down her coffee mug, but as she reached for her phone she froze, fingers on the receiver as a sing-song male voice rang out in the corridor beyond the closed door.

"That's him! Winn!"

"Well, here I go," said Robin, snatching up her box file again.

"Good luck!" whispered Izzy.

Emerging into the corridor, Robin saw Winn standing in the doorway of his office, apparently talking to Aamir, who was inside. Winn was holding a folder with orange lettering on it saying "The Level Playing Field." At the sound of Robin's footsteps, he turned to face her.

"Well, hello there," he said with a Cardiff lilt, stepping back into the corridor.

His gaze dribbled down Robin's neck, fell onto her breasts, then up again to her mouth and her eyes. Robin knew him from that single look. She had met plenty of them in offices, the type who watched you in a way that made you feel clumsy and self-conscious, who would place a hand in the small of the back as they sidled behind you or ushered you through doors, who peered over your shoulder on the excuse of reading your monitor and made chancy little comments on your clothes that progressed to comments on your figure during after-work drinks. They cried "joke!" if you got angry, and became aggressive in the face of complaints.

"Where d'you fit in, then?" asked Geraint, making the question sound salacious.

"I'm interning for Uncle Jasper," said Robin, smiling brightly.

"*Uncle* Jasper?"

"Jasper Chiswell, yes," said Robin, pronouncing the name, as the Chiswells did themselves, "Chizzle." "He's my godfather. Venetia Hall," said Robin, holding out her hand.

Everything about Winn seemed faintly amphibian, down to his damp palm. He was less like a gecko in the flesh, she thought, and more like a frog, with a pronounced potbelly and spindly arms and legs, his thinning hair rather greasy.

"And how did it come about that you're Jasper's goddaughter?"

"Oh, Uncle Jasper and Daddy are old friends," said Robin, who had a full backstory prepared.

"Army?"

"Land management," said Robin, sticking to her prearranged story.

"Ah," said Geraint; then, "Lovely hair. Is it natural?"

"Yes," said Robin.

His eyes slid down her body again. It cost Robin an effort to keep smiling at him. At last, gushing and giggling until her check muscles ached, agreeing that she would indeed give him a shout should she need any assistance, Robin walked on down the corridor. She could feel him watching her until she turned out of sight.

Just as Strike had felt after discovering Jimmy Knight's litigious habits, Robin was sure that she had just gained a valuable insight into Winn's weakness. In her experience, men like Geraint were astoundingly prone to believe that their scattergun sexual advances were appreciated and even reciprocated. She had spent no inconsiderable part of her temping career trying to rebuff and avoid such men, all of whom saw lubricious invitations in the merest pleasantry, and for whom youth and inexperience were an irresistible temptation.

How far, she asked herself, was she prepared to go in her quest to find out things to Winn's discredit? Walking with sham purpose through endless corridors to support her pretense of having papers to deliver, Robin pictured herself leaning over his desk while the inconvenient Aamir was elsewhere, breasts at eye-level, asking for help and advice, giggling at smutty jokes.

Then, with a sudden, dreadful lurch of imagination she saw, clearly, Winn's lunge, saw the sweaty face swooping for her, its lipless mouth agape, felt hands gripping her arms, pinning them to her sides, felt the potbelly press itself into her, squashing her backwards into a filing cabinet...

The endless green of carpet and chairs, the dark wood arches and the square panels seemed to blur and contract as Winn's imagined pass became an attack. She pushed through the door ahead as though she could physically force herself past her panic...

Breathe. Breathe. Breathe.

"Bit overwhelming the first time you see it, eh?"

The man sounded kindly and not very young.

"Yes," said Robin, barely knowing what she said. *Breathe.*

"Temporary, eh?" And then, "You all right, dear?"

"Asthma," said Robin.

She had used the excuse before. It gave her an excuse to stop, to breathe deeply, to re-anchor herself to reality.

"Got an inhaler?" asked the elderly steward in concern.

He wore a frock coat, white tie and tails and an ornate badge of office. In his unexpected grandeur, Robin thought wildly of the white rabbit, popping up in the middle of madness.

"I left it in my office. I'll be fine. Just need a second..."

She had blundered into a blaze of gold and color that was increasing her feeling of oppression. The Members' Lobby, that familiar, ornate, Victorian-gothic chamber she had seen on television, stood right outside the Commons, and on the periphery of her vision loomed four gigantic bronze statues of previous prime ministers—Thatcher, Atlee, Lloyd George and Churchill—while busts of all the others lined the walls. They appeared to Robin like severed heads and the gilding, with its intricate tracery and richly colored embellishments, danced around her, jeering at her inability to cope with its ornate beauty.

She heard the scraping of a chair's legs. The steward had brought her a seat and was asking a colleague to fetch a glass of water.

"Thank you...thank you..." said Robin numbly, feeling inadequate, ashamed and embarrassed. Strike must never know about this. He would send her home, tell her she wasn't fit to do the job. Nor must she tell Matthew, who treated these episodes as shameful, inevitable consequences of her stupidity in continuing surveillance work.

The steward talked to her kindly while she recovered and within a few minutes she was able to respond appropriately to his well-intentioned patter. While her breathing returned to normal, he told her the tale of how Edward Heath's bust had begun to turn green on the arrival of the full-sized Thatcher statue beside him, and how it had had to be treated to turn it back to its dark brown bronze.

Robin laughed politely, got to her feet and handed him the empty glass with renewed thanks.

What treatment would it take, she wondered as she set off again, to return her to what she had once been?

14

. . . how happy I should feel if I could succeed in bringing a little
light into all this murky ugliness.

Henrik Ibsen, *Rosmersholm*

Strike rose early on Tuesday morning. After showering, putting on his prosthesis and dressing, he filled a thermos with dark brown tea, took the sandwiches he had made the previous evening out of the fridge, stowed them in a carrier bag along with two packets of Club biscuits, chewing gum and a few bags of salt and vinegar crisps, then headed out into the sunrise and off to the garage where he kept his BMW. He had an appointment for a haircut at half past twelve, with Jimmy Knight's ex-wife, in Manchester.

Once settled in the car, his bag of provisions within easy reach, Strike pulled on the trainers he kept in the car, which gave his fake foot better purchase on the brake. He then took out his mobile and began to compose a text to Robin.

Starting with the names that Wardle had given him, Strike had spent much of Monday researching, as best as he could, the two children the policemen had told him had vanished from the Oxfordshire area twenty years previously. Wardle had misspelled the boy's first name, which had cost Strike time, but Strike had finally dug out archived press reports about Imamu Ibrahim, in which Imamu's mother had asserted that her estranged husband had kidnapped the boy and taken him to Algeria. Strike had finally dredged up two lines about Imamu and his mother on the website of an organization that worked to resolve international custody issues. From this, Strike had to conclude that Imamu had been found alive and well with his father.

The fate of Suki Lewis, the twelve-year-old runaway from a care home, was more mysterious. Strike had finally discovered an image of her, buried in an old news story. Suki had vanished from her residential care home in Swindon in 1992 and Strike could find no other mention of her since. Her blurry picture showed a rather toothy, undersized child, fine-featured, with short dark hair.

Little girl it was, but after they said it was a little boy.

So a vulnerable, androgynous child might have disappeared off the face of the earth around the same time, and in the approximate area, that Billy Knight claimed to have witnessed the strangling of a boy-girl.

In the car, he composed a text to Robin.

If you can make it sound natural, ask Izzy if she remembers anything about a 12-year-old called Suki Lewis. She ran away 20 years ago from a care home near their family house.

The dirt on his windscreen shimmered and blurred in the rising sun as he left London. Driving was no longer the pleasure it had once been. Strike could not afford a specially adapted vehicle, and even though it was an automatic, the operation of the BMW's pedals remained challenging with his prosthesis. In challenging conditions, he sometimes reverted to operating brake and accelerator with his left foot.

When he finally joined the M6, Strike hoped to settle in at sixty miles an hour, but some arsehole in a Vauxhall Corsa decided to tailgate him.

"Fucking overtake," growled Strike. He was not minded to alter his own speed, having settled in comfortably without needing to use his false foot more than was necessary, and for a while he glowered into his rearview mirror until the Vauxhall driver got the hint and took himself off.

Relaxing to the degree that was ever possible behind the wheel these days, Strike wound down the window to admit the fine, fresh summer's day and allowed his thoughts to return to Billy and the missing Suki Lewis.

She wouldn't let me dig, he had said in the office, compulsively tapping his nose and his chest, *but she'd let you.*

Who, Strike wondered, was "she"? Perhaps the new owner of Steda Cottage? They might well object to Billy asking to dig up flowerbeds in search of bodies.

After feeling around with his left hand inside his provisions bag, extracting and ripping open a bag of crisps with his teeth, Strike reminded himself for the umpteenth time that Billy's whole story might be a chimera. Suki Lewis could be anywhere. Not every lost child was dead. Perhaps Suki, too, had been stolen away by an errant parent. Twenty years previously, in the infancy of the internet, imperfect communication between regional police forces could be exploited by those wishing to reinvent themselves or others. And even if Suki was no longer alive, there was nothing to suggest that she had been strangled, let alone that Billy Knight had witnessed it. Most people would surely conclude that this was a case of much smoke, but no fire.

Chewing crisps by the handful, Strike reflected that whenever it came to a question of what "most people" would think, he usually envisaged his half-sister Lucy, the only one of his seven half-siblings with whom he had shared his chaotic and peripatetic childhood. To him, Lucy represented the acme of all that was conventional and unimaginative, even though they had both grown up on intimate terms with the macabre, the dangerous and the frightening.

Before Lucy had gone to live permanently with their aunt and uncle in Cornwall, at the age of fourteen, their mother had hauled her and Strike from squat to commune to rented flat to friend's floor, rarely remaining in the same place more than six months, exposing her children to a parade of eccentric, damaged and addicted human beings along the way. Right hand on the wheel, left hand now groping around for biscuits, Strike recalled some of the nightmarish spectacles that he and Lucy had witnessed as children: the psychotic youth fighting an invisible devil in a basement flat in Shoreditch, the teenager literally being whipped at a quasi-mystical commune in Norfolk (still, for Strike's money, the worst place that Leda had ever taken them) and Shayla, one of the most fragile of Leda's friends and a part-time prostitute, sobbing about the brain damage inflicted on her toddler son by a violent boyfriend.

That unpredictable and sometimes terrifying childhood had left Lucy with a craving for stability and conformity. Married to a quantity surveyor whom Strike disliked, with three sons he barely knew, she would probably dismiss Billy's story of the strangled boy-girl as the product of a broken mind, sweeping it swiftly away into the corner with all the other things she could not bear to think about. Lucy needed to pretend that violence and strangeness had vanished into a past as dead as their mother; that with Leda gone, life was unshakably secure.

Strike understood. Profoundly different though they were, often though she exasperated him, he loved Lucy. Nevertheless, he could not help comparing her with Robin as he bowled towards Manchester. Robin had grown up in what seemed to Strike the very epitome of middle-class stability, but she was courageous in a way that Lucy was not. Both women had been touched by violence and sadism. Lucy had reacted by burying herself where she hoped it would never reach her again; Robin, by facing it almost daily, investigating and resolving other crimes and traumas, driven to do so by the same impulse to actively disentangle complications and disinter truths that Strike recognized in himself.

As the sun climbed higher, still dappling the grubby windscreen, he experienced a powerful regret that she wasn't here with him now. She was the best person he had ever met to run a theory past. She'd unscrew the thermos for him and pour him tea. *We'd have a laugh.*

They had slipped back into their old bantering ways a couple of times lately, since Billy had entered the office with a story troubling enough to break down the reserve that had, over a year, hardened into a permanent impediment to their friendship . . . *or whatever it was*, thought Strike, and for a moment or two he felt her again in his arms on the stairs, breathed in the scent of white roses and of the perfume that hung around the office when Robin was at her desk...

With a kind of mental grimace, he reached for another cigarette, lit up and forced his mind towards Manchester, and the line of questioning he intended to take with Dawn Clancy, who, for five years, had been Mrs. Jimmy Knight.

15

Yes, she is a queer one, she is. She has always been very much on the high horse . . .

Henrik Ibsen, *Rosmersholm*

While Strike was speeding northwards, Robin was summoned without explanation to a personal meeting with the Minister for Culture himself.

Walking in the sunshine towards the Department for Culture, Media and Sport, which stood in a large white Edwardian building a few minutes away from the Palace of Westminster, Robin found herself almost wishing that she were one of the tourists cluttering the pavement, because Chiswell had sounded bad tempered on the phone.

Robin would have given a great deal to have something useful to tell the minister about his blackmailer, but as she had only been on the job a day and a half, all she could say with any certainty was that her first impressions of Geraint Winn had now been confirmed: he was lazy, lecherous, self-important and indiscreet. The door of his office stood open more often than not, and his sing-song voice rang down the corridor as he talked with injudicious levity about his constituents' petty concerns, name-dropped celebrities and senior politicians and generally sought to give the impression of a man for whom running a mere constituency office was an unimportant sideshow.

He hailed Robin jovially from his desk whenever she passed his open door, showing a pronounced eagerness for further contact.

However, whether by chance or design, Aamir Mallik kept thwarting Robin's attempts to turn these greetings into conversations, either interrupting with questions for Winn or, as he had done just an hour previously, simply closing the door in Robin's face.

The exterior of the great block that housed the DCMS, with its stone swags, its columns and its neoclassical façade, was not reassuring. The interior had been modernized and hung with contemporary art, including an abstract glass sculpture that hung from the cupola over the central staircase, up which Robin was led by an efficient-seeming young woman. Believing her to be the minister's goddaughter, her companion was at pains to show her points of interest.

"The Churchill Room," she said, pointing left as they turned right. "That's the balcony he gave his speech from, on VE Day. The minister's just along here..."

She led Robin down a wide, curving corridor that doubled as an open-plan workspace. Smart young people sat at an array of desks in front of lengthy windows to the right, which looked out onto a quadrangle, which, in size and scale, bore the appearance of a colosseum, with its high white windowed walls. It was all very different from the cramped office where Izzy made their instant coffee from a kettle. Indeed, a large, expensive machine complete with pods sat on one desk for that purpose.

The offices to the left were separated from this curving space by glass walls and doors. Robin spotted the Minister for Culture from a distance, sitting at his desk beneath a contemporary painting of the Queen, talking on the telephone. He indicated by a brusque gesture that her escort should show Robin inside the office and continued talking on the telephone as Robin waited, somewhat awkwardly, for him to finish his call. A woman's voice was issuing from the earpiece, high-pitched and to Robin, even eight feet away, hysterical.

"I've got to go, Kinvara!" barked Chiswell into the mouthpiece. "Yes...we'll talk about this later. *I've got to go.*"

Setting down the receiver harder than was necessary, he pointed Robin to a chair opposite him. His coarse, straight gray hair stood out around his head in a wiry halo, his fat lower lip giving him an air of angry petulance.

"The newspapers are sniffing around," he growled. "That was m'wife. The *Sun* rang her this morning, asking whether the rumors are true. She said 'what rumors?' but the fella didn't specify. Fishing, obviously. Trying to surprise something out of her."

He frowned at Robin, whose appearance he seemed to find wanting.

"How old are you?"

"Twenty-seven," she said.

"You look younger."

It didn't sound like a compliment.

"Managed to plant the surveillance device yet?"

"I'm afraid not," said Robin.

"Where's Strike?"

"In Manchester, interviewing Jimmy Knight's ex-wife," said Robin.

Chiswell made the angry, subterranean noise usually rendered as "harrumph," then got to his feet. Robin jumped up, too.

"Well, you'd better get back and get on with it," said Chiswell. "The National Health Service," he added, with no change of tone, as he headed towards the door. "People are going to think we're bloody mad."

"Sorry?" said Robin, entirely thrown.

Chiswell pulled open the glass door and indicated that Robin should pass through it ahead of him, out into the open-plan area where all the smart young people sat working beside their sleek coffee machine.

"Olympics opening ceremony," he explained, following her. "Lefty bloody crap. We won two bloody world wars, but we're not supposed to celebrate that."

"Nonsense, Jasper," said a deep, melodious Welsh voice close at hand. "We celebrate military victories all the time. This is a different kind of celebration."

Della Winn, the Minister for Sport, was standing just outside Chiswell's door, holding the leash of her near-white Labrador. A woman of stately appearance, with gray hair swept back off a broad forehead, she wore sunglasses so dark that Robin could make out nothing behind them. Her blindness, Robin knew from her research, had been due to a rare condition in which neither eyeball had grown *in utero*. She sometimes wore prosthetic eyes, especially when she was to be photographed. Della was sporting a quantity of heavy, tactile jewelry in gold, with a large necklace of intaglios, and dressed from head to foot in sky blue. Robin had read in one of Strike's printed profiles of the politician that Geraint laid out Della's clothes for her every morning and that it was simplest for him, not having a great feel for fashion, to select things in the same color. Robin had found this rather touching when she read it.

Chiswell did not appear to relish the sudden appearance of his colleague and indeed, given that her husband was blackmailing him, Robin supposed that this was hardly surprising. Della, on the other hand, gave no sign of embarrassment.

"I thought we might share the car over to Greenwich," she said to Chiswell, while the pale Labrador snuffled gently at the hem of Robin's skirt. "Give us a chance to go over the plans for the twelfth. What are you doing, Gwynn?" she added, feeling the Labrador's head tugging.

"She's sniffing me," said Robin nervously, patting the Labrador.

"This is my goddaughter, ah..."

"Venetia," said Robin, as Chiswell was evidently struggling to remember her name.

"How do you do?" said Della, holding out her hand. "Visiting Jasper?"

"No, I'm interning in the constituency office," said Robin, shaking the warm, be-ringed hand, as Chiswell walked away to examine the document held by a hovering young man in a suit.

"Venetia," repeated Della, her face still turned towards Robin. A faint frown appeared on the handsome face, half-masked behind the impenetrable black glasses. "What's your surname?"

"Hall," said Robin.

She felt a ridiculous flutter of panic, as though Della were about to unmask her. Still poring over the document he had been shown, Chiswell moved away, leaving Robin, or so it felt, entirely at Della's mercy.

"You're the fencer," said Della.

"Sorry?" said Robin, totally confused again, her mind on posts and rails. Some of the young people around the space-age coffee machine had turned around to listen, expressions of polite interest on their faces.

"Yes," said Della. "Yes, I remember you. You were on the English team with Freddie."

Her friendly expression had hardened. Chiswell was now leaning over a desk while he struck through phrases on the document.

"No, I never fenced," said Robin, thoroughly out of her depth. She had realized at the mention of the word "team" that swords were under discussion, rather than fields and livestock.

"You certainly did," said Della flatly. "I remember you. Jasper's goddaughter, on the team with Freddie."

It was a slightly unnerving display of arrogance, of complete self-belief. Robin felt inadequate to the job of continuing to protest, because there were now several listeners. Instead, she merely said, "Well, nice to have met you," and walked away.

"*Again*, you mean," said Della sharply, but Robin made no reply.

16

. . . a man with as dirty a record as his! . . . This is the sort of
man that poses as a leader of the people! And successfully, too!
                        Henrik Ibsen, *Rosmersholm*

After four and a half hours in the driving seat, Strike's exit from the
BMW in Manchester was far from graceful. He stood for a while in
Burton Road, a broad, pleasant street with its mixture of shops and
houses, leaning on the car, stretching his back and leg, grateful that
he had managed to find a parking space only a short way from
"Stylz." The bright pink shopfront stood out between a café and a
Tesco Express, pictures of moody models with unnaturally tinted
hair in the window.

With its black and white tiled floor and pink walls that reminded
Strike of Lorelei's bedroom, the interior of the small shop was determinedly trendy, but it did not appear to cater to a particularly youthful or adventurous clientele. There were currently only two clients,
one of whom was a large woman of at least sixty, who was reading
Good Housekeeping in front of a mirror, her hair a mass of foil. Strike
made a bet with himself as he entered that Dawn would prove to be
the slim peroxide blonde with her back to him, chatting animatedly
to an elderly lady whose blue hair she was perming.

"I've got an appointment with Dawn," Strike told the young
receptionist, who looked slightly startled to see anything so large and
male in this fug of perfumed ammonia. The peroxided blonde turned
at the sound of her name. She had the leathery, age-spotted skin of
a committed sunbed user.

"With you in a moment, cock," she said, smiling. He settled to wait on a bench in the window.

Five minutes later, she was leading him to an upholstered pink chair at the back of the shop.

"What are you after, then?" she asked him, inviting him with a gesture to sit down.

"I'm not here for a haircut," said Strike, still standing. "I'll happily pay for one, I don't want to waste your time, but," he pulled a card and his driver's license from his pocket, "my name's Cormoran Strike. I'm a private detective and I was hoping to talk to you about your ex-husband, Jimmy Knight."

She looked stunned, as well she might, but then fascinated.

"Strike?" she repeated, gaping. "You aren't him that caught that Ripper guy?"

"That's me."

"Jesus, what's Jimmy done?"

"Nothing much," said Strike easily. "I'm just after background."

She didn't believe him, of course. Her face, he suspected, was full of filler, her forehead suspiciously smooth and shiny above the carefully penciled eyebrows. Only her stringy neck betrayed her age.

"That's over. It was over ages ago. I never talk about Jimmy. Least said, soonest mended, don't they say?"

But he could feel the curiosity and excitement radiating from her like heat. Radio 2 jangled in the background. She glanced towards the two women sitting at the mirrors.

"Sian!" she said loudly, and the receptionist jumped and turned. "Take out her foils and keep an eye on the perm for me, love." She hesitated, still holding Strike's card. "I'm not sure I should," she said, wanting to be talked into it.

"It's only background," he said. "No strings."

Five minutes later she was handing him a milky coffee in a tiny staffroom at the rear of the shop, talking merrily, a little haggard in the fluorescent overhead light, but still good-looking enough to explain why Jimmy had first shown interest in a woman thirteen years his senior.

"...yeah, a demonstration against nuclear weapons. I went with this friend of mine, Wendy, she was big into all that. Vegetarian," she added, nudging the door into the shop closed with her foot and taking out a pack of Silk Cut. "You know the type."

"Got my own," said Strike, when she offered the pack. He lit her cigarette for her, then one of his Benson & Hedges. They blew out simultaneous streams of smoke. She crossed her legs towards him and rattled on.

"...yeah, so Jimmy gave a speech. Weapons and how much we could save, give to the NHS and everything, what was the point...he talks well, you know," said Dawn.

"He does," agreed Strike, "I've heard him."

"Yeah, and I fell for it, hook, line and sinker. Thought he was some kind of Robin Hood."

Strike heard the joke coming before she made it. He knew it was not the first time.

"*Robbing* Hood, more like," she said.

She was already divorced when she had met Jimmy. Her first husband had left her for another girl at the London salon they had owned together. Dawn had done well out of the divorce, managing to retain the business. Jimmy had seemed a romantic figure after her wide-boy first husband and, on the rebound, she had fallen for him hard.

"But there were always girls," she said. "Lefties, you know. Some of them were really young. He was like a pop star to them or something. I only found out how many of them there were later, after he'd set up cards on all my accounts."

Dawn told Strike at length how Jimmy had persuaded her to bankroll a lawsuit against his ex-employer, Zanet Industries, who had failed to follow due process in firing him.

"Very keen on his rights, Jimmy. He's not stupid, though, you know. Ten grand payout he got from Zanet. I never saw a penny of it. He pissed it all away, trying to sue other people. He tried to take me to court, after we split up. Loss of earnings, don't make me laugh. I'd kept him for five years and he claimed he'd been working with me, building up the business for no pay and left with occupational asthma from the chemicals—so much shit he talked—they chucked it out of court, thank God. And then he tried to get me on a harassment charge. Said I'd keyed his car."

She ground out her cigarette and reached for another one.

"I had, too," she said, with a sudden, wicked smile. "You know he's been put on a list, now? Can't sue anyone without permission."

"I did know, yeah," said Strike. "Was he ever involved in any criminal activity while you were together, Dawn?"

She lit up again, watching Strike over her fingers, still hoping to hear what Jimmy was supposed to have done to have Strike after him. Finally she said:

"I'm not sure he was too careful about checking all the girls he was playing around with were sixteen. I heard, after, one of them...but we'd split up by then. It wasn't my problem anymore," said Dawn, as Strike made a note.

"And I wouldn't trust him if it was anything to do with Jews. He doesn't like them. Israel's the root of all evil, according to Jimmy. Zionism: I got sick of the bloody sound of the word. You'd think they'd suffered enough," said Dawn vaguely. "Yeah, his manager at Zanet was Jewish and they hated each other."

"What was his name?"

"What was it?" Dawn drew heavily on her cigarette, frowning. "Paul something...Lobstein, that's it. Paul Lobstein. He's probably still at Zanet."

"D'you still have any contact with Jimmy, or any of his family?"

"Christ, no. Good riddance. The only one of his family I ever met was little Billy, his brother."

She softened a little as she said the name.

"He wasn't right. He stayed with us for a bit at one point. He was a sweetheart, really, but not right. Jimmy said it was their father. Violent alkie. Raised them on his own and knocked the shit out of them, from what the boys said, used the belt and everything. Jimmy got away to London, and poor little Billy was left alone with him. No surprise he was how he was."

"What d'you mean?"

"He 'ad a—a tic, do they call it?"

She mimicked with perfect accuracy the nose to chest tapping Strike had witnessed in his office.

"He was put on drugs, I know that. Then he left us, went to share a flat with some other lads for a bit. I never saw him again after Jimmy and I split. He was a sweet boy, yeah, but he annoyed Jimmy."

"In what way?" Strike asked.

"Jimmy didn't like him talking about their childhood. I dunno, I think Jimmy felt guilty he'd left Billy in the house alone. There was something funny about that whole business..."

Strike could tell she hadn't thought about these things for a while.

"Funny?" he prompted.

"A couple of times, when he'd had a few, Jimmy went on about how his dad would burn for how he made his living."

"I thought he was an odd-job man?"

"Was he? They told me he was a joiner. He worked for that politician's family, what's his name? The one with the hair."

She mimed stiff bristles coming out of her head.

"Jasper Chiswell?" Strike suggested, pronouncing the name the way it was spelled.

"Him, yeah. Old Mr. Knight had a rent-free cottage in the family grounds. The boys grew up there."

"And he said his father would go to hell for what he did for a living?" repeated Strike.

"Yeah. It's probably just because he was working for Tories. It was all about politics with Jimmy. I don't get it," said Dawn restlessly. "You've got to live. Imagine me asking my clients how they vote before I'll—

"Bloody hell," she gasped suddenly, grinding out her cigarette and jumping to her feet, "Sian had better've taken out Mrs. Horridge's rollers or she'll be bald."

17

I see he is altogether incorrigible.

Henrik Ibsen, *Rosmersholm*

Watching for an opportunity to plant the bug in Winn's office, Robin spent most of the afternoon hanging around the quiet corridor on which both his and Izzy's offices lay, but her efforts were fruitless. Even though Winn had left for a lunchtime meeting, Aamir remained inside. Robin paced up and down, box file in her arms, waiting for the moment when Aamir might go to the bathroom and returning to Izzy's office whenever any passerby tried to engage her in conversation.

Finally, at ten past four, her luck changed. Geraint Winn swaggered around the corner, rather tipsy after what seemed to have been a prolonged lunch, and in sharp contrast to his wife, he seemed delighted to meet her as she set off towards him.

"There she is!" he said, over-loudly. "I wanted a word with you! Come in here, come in!"

He pushed open the door of his office. Puzzled, but only too eager to see the interior of the room she was hoping to bug, Robin followed him.

Aamir was working in shirtsleeves at his desk, which formed a tiny oasis of order in the general clutter. Stacks of folders lay around Winn's desk. Robin noticed the orange logo of the Level Playing Field on a pile of letters in front of him. There was a power point directly under Geraint's desk that would be an ideal position for the listening device.

"Have you two met?" Geraint asked jovially. "Venetia, Aamir."

He sat down and invited Robin to take the armchair on which a sliding pile of card folders lay.

"Did Redgrave call back?" Winn asked Aamir, struggling out of his suit jacket.

"Who?" said the latter.

"Sir Steve Redgrave!" said Winn, with the suspicion of an eye roll in Robin's direction. She felt embarrassed for him, especially as Aamir's muttered "no" was cold.

"Level Playing Field," Winn told Robin.

He had managed to get his jacket off. With an attempted flourish, he threw it onto the back of his chair. It slid limply onto the floor, but Geraint appeared not to notice, and instead tapped the orange logo on the topmost letter in front of him. "Our cha—" he belched. "Pardon me—our charity. Disadvantaged and disabled athletes, you know. Lots of high profile supporters. Sir Steve keen to—" he belched again, "—pardon—help. Well, now. I wanted to apologize. For my poor wife."

He seemed to be enjoying himself hugely. Out of the corner of her eye, Robin saw Aamir fling Geraint a sharp look, like the flash of a claw, swiftly retracted.

"I don't understand," said Robin.

"Gets names wrong. Does it all the time. If I didn't keep an eye on her, we'd have all sorts going on, wrong letters going out to the wrong people...she thought you were someone else. I had her on the phone over lunch, insisting you were somebody our daughter ran across years ago. Verity Pulham. 'Nother of your godfather's god-children. Told her straight away it wasn't you, said I'd pass on her apologies. Silly girl, she is. Very stubborn when she thinks she's right, but," he rolled his eyes again and tapped his forehead, the long-suffering husband of an infuriating wife, "I managed to penetrate in the end."

"Well," said Robin carefully, "I'm glad she knows she was mistaken, because she didn't seem to like Verity very much."

"Truth to tell, Verity *was* a little bitch," said Winn, still beaming. Robin could tell he enjoyed using the word. "Nasty to our daughter, you see."

"Oh dear," said Robin, with a thud of dread beneath her ribs as she remembered that Rhiannon Winn had killed herself. "I'm sorry. How awful."

"You know," said Winn, sitting down and tipping back his chair against the wall, hands behind his head, "you seem far too sweet a girl to be associated with the Chiswell family." He was definitely a little drunk. Robin could smell faint wine dregs on his breath and Aamir threw him another of those sharp, scathing looks. "What were you doing before this, Venetia?"

"PR," said Robin, "but I'd like to do something more worthwhile. Politics, or maybe a charity. I was reading about the Level Playing Field," she said truthfully. "It seems wonderful. You do a lot with veterans, too, don't you? I saw an interview with Terry Byrne yesterday. The Paralympian cyclist?"

Her attention had been caught by the fact that Byrne had the same below the knee amputation as Strike.

"You'll have a personal interest in veterans, of course," said Winn.

Robin's stomach swooped and fell again.

"Sorry?"

"Freddie Chiswell?" Winn prompted.

"Oh, yes, of course," said Robin. "Although I didn't know Freddie very well. He was a bit older than me. Obviously, it was dreadful when he—when he was killed."

"Oh, yes, awful," said Winn, though he sounded indifferent. "Della was very much against the Iraq war. Very much against it. Your Uncle Jasper was all for it, mind you."

For a moment, the air seemed to thrum with Winn's unexpressed implication that Chiswell had been well served for his enthusiasm.

"Well, I don't know about that," said Robin carefully. "Uncle Jasper thought military action justified on the evidence we had at the time. Anyway," she said bravely, "nobody can accuse him of acting out of self-interest, can they, when his son had to go and fight?"

"Ah, if you're going to take that line, who can argue?" said Winn.

He raised his hands in mock surrender, his chair slipped a little on the wall and for a few seconds he struggled to maintain balance, seizing the desk and pulling himself and the chair upright again. With a substantial effort, Robin managed not to laugh.

"Geraint," said Aamir, "we need those letters signed if we're going to get them off by five."

"'S'only half four," said Winn, checking his watch. "Yes, Rhiannon was on the British junior fencing team."

"How marvelous," said Robin.

"Sporty, like her mother. Fencing for the Welsh juniors at fourteen. I used to drive her all over the place for tournaments. Hours on the road together! She made the British juniors at sixteen."

"But the English lot were very stand-offish to her," said Winn, with a glimmer of Celtic resentment. "She wasn't at one of your big public schools, you see. It was all about connections with them. Verity Pulham, she didn't have the ability, not really. As a matter of fact, it was only when Verity broke her ankle that Rhiannon, who was a far better fencer, got on the British team at all."

"I see," said Robin, trying to balance sympathy with a feigned allegiance to the Chiswells. Surely this could not be the grievance that Winn had against the family? Yet Geraint's fanatic tone spoke of longstanding resentment. "Well, these things should come down to ability, of course."

"That's right," said Winn. "They should. Look at this, now..."

He fumbled for his wallet and pulled from it an old photograph. Robin held out her hand, but Geraint, keeping a firm hold on the picture, got up clumsily, stumbled over a stack of books lying beside his chair, walked around the desk, came so close that Robin could feel his breath on her neck, and showed her the image of his daughter.

Dressed in fencing garb, Rhiannon Winn stood beaming and holding up the gold medal around her neck. She was pale and small-featured, and Robin could see very little of either parent in her face, although perhaps there was a hint of Della in the broad, intelligent brow. But with Geraint's loud breathing in her ear, trying to stop herself leaning away from him, Robin had a sudden vision of Geraint Winn striding, with his wide, lipless grin, through a large hall of sweaty teenage girls. Was it shameful to wonder whether it had been parental devotion that had spurred him to chauffeur his daughter all over the country?

"What have you done to yourself, eh?" Geraint asked, his hot breath in her ear. Leaning in, he touched the purple knife scar on her bare forearm.

Unable to prevent herself, Robin snatched her arm away. The nerves around the scar had not yet fully healed: she hated anyone touching it.

"I fell through a glass door when I was nine," she said, but the confidential, confiding atmosphere had been dispersed like cigarette smoke.

Aamir hovered on the edge of her vision, rigid and silent at his desk. Geraint's smile had become forced. She had worked too long in offices not to know that a subtle transfer of power had just taken place within the room. Now she stood armed with his little drunken inappropriateness and Geraint was resentful and a little worried. She wished that she had not pulled away from him.

"I wonder, Mr. Winn," she said breathily, "whether you'd mind giving me some advice about the charitable world? I just can't make up my mind, politics—charity—and I don't know anyone else who's done both."

"Oh," said Geraint, blinking behind his thick glasses. "Oh, well...yes, I daresay I could..."

"Geraint," said Aamir again, "we really do need to get those letters—"

"Yes, all right, all right," said Geraint loudly. "We'll talk later," he said to Robin, with a wink.

"Wonderful," she said, with a smile.

As Robin walked out she threw Aamir a small smile, which he didn't return.

18

After nearly nine hours at the wheel, Strike's neck, back and legs were stiff and sore and his bag of provisions long since empty. The first star was glimmering out of the pale, inky wash above when his mobile rang. It was the usual time for his sister, Lucy, to call "for a chat"; he ignored three out of four of her calls, because, much as he loved her, he could muster no interest in her sons' schooling, the PTA's squabbles or the intricacies of her husband's career as a quantity surveyor. Seeing that it was Barclay on the line, however, he turned into a rough and ready lay-by, really the turnoff to a field, cut the engine and answered.

"'M in," said Barclay laconically. "Wi' Jimmy."

"Already?" said Strike, seriously impressed. "How?"

"Pub," said Barclay. "Interrupted him. He was talkin' a load o' pish about Scottish independence. The grea' thing about English lefties," he continued, "is they love hearin' how shit England is. Havenae hadtae buy a pint all afternoon."

"Bloody hell, Barclay," said Strike, lighting himself another cigarette on top of the twenty he had already had that day, "that was good work."

"That was just fer starters," said Barclay. "You shoulda heard them when I told them how I've seen the error of the army's imperialist ways. Fuck me, they're gullible. I'm off tae a CORE meetin' the morrow."

"How's Knight supporting himself? Any idea?"

"He told me he's a journalist on a couple o' lefty websites and he sells CORE T-shirts and a bit o' dope. Mind, his shit's worthless. We went back tae his place, after the pub. Ye'd be better off smokin' fuckin' Oxo cubes. I've said I'll get him better. We can run that through office expenses, aye?"

"I'll put it under 'sundries,'" said Strike. "All right, keep me posted."

Barclay rang off. Deciding to take the opportunity to stretch his legs, Strike got out of the car, still smoking, leaned on the five-bar gate facing a wide, dark field, and rang Robin.

"It's Vanessa," Robin lied, when she saw Strike's number come up on her phone.

She and Matthew had just eaten a takeaway curry off their knees while watching the news. He had arrived home late and tired; she didn't need another argument.

Picking up the mobile, she headed out through the French doors onto the patio that had served as the smoking area for the party. After making sure that the doors were completely closed, she answered.

"Hi. Everything OK?"

"Fine. All right to talk for a moment?"

"Yes," said Robin, leaning against the garden wall, and watching a moth banging fruitlessly against the bright glass, trying to enter the house. "How did it go with Dawn Clancy?"

"Nothing usable," said Strike. "I thought I might have a lead, some Jewish ex-boss Jimmy had a vendetta against, but I rang the company and the poor bloke died of a stroke last September. Then I got a call from Chiswell just after I left her. He says the *Sun*'s sniffing around."

"Yes," said Robin. "They called his wife."

"We could've done without that," said Strike, with what Robin felt was considerable understatement. "I wonder who's tipped off the papers?"

"I'd bet on Winn," said Robin, remembering the way that Geraint had talked that afternoon, the name-dropping, the self-importance. "He's just the type to hint to a journalist that there's a story on Chiswell, even if he hasn't got proof of it yet. Seriously," she said again, with no real hope of an answer, "what d'you think Chiswell did?"

"Be nice to know, but it doesn't really matter," said Strike, who sounded tired. "We aren't being paid to get the goods on *him*. Speaking of which—"

"I haven't been able to plant the bug yet," said Robin, anticipating the question. "I hung around as late as possible, but Aamir locked the door after they both left."

Strike sighed.

"Well, don't get overeager and balls it up," he said, "but we're up against it if the *Sun*'s involved. Anything you can do. Get in early or something."

"I will, I'll try," said Robin. "I did get something odd about the Winns today, though," and she told him about the confusion Della had made between herself and one of Chiswell's real goddaughters, and the story of Rhiannon on the fencing team. Strike seemed only distantly interested.

"Doubt that explains the Winns wanting Chiswell out of office. Anyway—"

"—means before motive," she said, quoting Strike's own, oft-repeated words.

"Exactly. Listen, can you meet me after work tomorrow, and we'll have a proper debrief?"

"All right," said Robin.

"Barclay's doing good work, though," said Strike, as though the thought of it cheered him up. "He's already well in with Jimmy."

"Oh," said Robin. "Good."

After telling her that he would text the name of a convenient pub, Strike rang off, leaving Robin alone and pensive in the quiet dark of the yard, while stars grew pin-bright overhead.

Barclay's doing good work, though.

As opposed to Robin, who had found out nothing but an irrelevancy about Rhiannon Winn.

The moth was still fluttering desperately against the sliding doors, frantic to get at the light.

Idiot, Robin thought. *It's better out here.*

The ease with which the lie about Vanessa being on the phone had slid out of her mouth ought, she reflected, to have made her feel guilty, but she was merely glad that she had got away with it. As she watched the moth continuing to bang its wings hopelessly against the brilliant glass, Robin remembered what her therapist had said to her during one of the sessions when Robin had dwelled at length on her need to discern where the real Matthew ended and her illusions about him began.

"People change in ten years," the therapist had responded. "Why does it have to be a question of you being mistaken in Matthew? Perhaps it's simply that you've both changed?"

The following Monday would mark their first wedding anniversary. At Matthew's suggestion, they were going to spend next weekend at a fancy hotel near Oxford. In a funny kind of way, Robin was looking forward to it, because she and Matthew seemed to get along better these days with a change of scene. Being surrounded by strangers nudged them out of their tendency to bicker. She had told him the story of Ted Heath's bust turning green, along with several other (to her) interesting facts about the House of Commons. He had maintained a bored expression through all of them, determined to signal his disapproval of the whole venture.

Reaching a decision, she opened the French window and the moth fluttered merrily inside.

"What did Vanessa want?" asked Matthew, his eyes on the news as Robin sat down again. Sarah Shadlock's stargazer lilies were sitting on a table beside her, still in bloom ten days after they had arrived in the house, and Robin could smell their heady scent even over the curry.

"I picked up her sunglasses by mistake last time we went out," said Robin, feigning exasperation. "She wants them back, they're Chanel. I said I'll meet her before work."

"Chanel, eh?" said Matthew, with a smile that Robin found patronizing. She knew that he thought he had discovered a weakness in Vanessa, but perhaps he liked her better to think that she valued designer labels and wanted to make sure she got them back.

"I'll have to leave at six," said Robin.

"Six?" he said, annoyed. "Christ, I'm knackered, I don't want to wake up at—"

"I was going to suggest I sleep in the spare room," Robin said.

"Oh," said Matthew, mollified. "Yeah, OK. Thanks."

19

Robin left the house at a quarter to six the next morning. The sky was a faint blush pink and the morning already warm, justifying her lack of jacket. Her eyes flickered towards the single carved swan as she passed their local pub, but she forced her thoughts back onto the day ahead and not the man she had left behind.

On arrival in Izzy's corridor an hour later, Robin saw that Geraint's office door was already open. A swift peek inside showed her an empty room, but Aamir's jacket hanging on the back of his chair.

Running to Izzy's office, Robin unlocked it, dashed to her desk, pulled one of the listening devices from the box of Tampax, scooped up a pile of out-of-date agendas as an alibi, then ran back out into the corridor.

As she approached Geraint's office, she slid off the gold bangle that she had worn for this purpose, and threw it lightly so that it rolled into Geraint's office.

"Oh damn," she said out loud.

Nobody responded from inside the office. Robin knocked on the open door, said "hello?" and put her head inside. The room was still empty.

Robin dashed across the room to the double power point just above the skirting board beside Geraint's desk. Kneeling, she took the listening device out of her bag, unplugged the fan on his desk, pressed the device into place over the dual socket, reinserted the fan's plug, checked that it worked, then, panting as though she had just sprinted a hundred yards, looked around for her bangle.

"What are you doing?"

Aamir was standing in the doorway in his shirtsleeves, a fresh tea in his hand.

"I did knock," Robin said, sure that she was bright pink. "I dropped my bangle and it rolled—oh, there it is."

It was lying just beneath Aamir's computer chair. Robin scrambled to pick it up.

"It's my mother's," she lied. "I wouldn't be popular if that went missing."

She slid the bangle back over her wrist, picked up the papers she had left on Geraint's desk, smiled as casually as she could manage, then walked out of the office past Aamir, whose eyes, she saw out of the corner of her own, were narrowed in suspicion.

Jubilant, Robin re-entered Izzy's office. At least she would have some good news for Strike when they met in the pub that evening. Barclay was no longer the only one doing good work. So absorbed was she in her thoughts that Robin didn't realize that there was somebody else in the room until a man said, right behind her: "Who are you?"

The present dissolved. Both of her attackers had lunged at her from behind. With a scream, Robin spun around, ready to fight for her life: the papers flew into the air and her handbag slipped off her shoulder, fell to the floor and burst open, scattering its contents everywhere.

"Sorry!" said the man. "Christ, I'm sorry!"

But Robin was finding it hard to draw breath. There was a thundering in her ears and sweat had broken out all over her body. She bent down to scoop everything back up, trembling so much that she kept dropping things.

Not now. Not now.

He was talking to her, but she couldn't understand a word. The world was fragmenting again, full of terror and danger, and he was a blur as he handed her eyeliner and a bottle of drops to moisten her contact lenses.

"Oh," Robin gasped at random. "Great. Excuse me. Bathroom."

She stumbled to the door. Two people were coming towards her down the corridor, their voices fuzzy and indistinct as they greeted her. Hardly knowing what she responded, she half-ran past them towards the Ladies.

A woman from the Secretary for Health's office greeted her from the sink where she was applying lipstick. Robin blundered blindly past, locking the cubicle door with fumbling fingers.

It was no use trying to suppress the panic: that only made it fight back, trying to bend her to its will. She must ride it out, as though the fear was a bolting horse, easing it onto a more manageable course. So she stood motionless, palms pressed against the partition walls, speaking to herself inside her head as though she were an animal handler, and her body, in its irrational terror, a frantic prey creature.

You're safe, you're safe, you're safe . . .

Slowly, the panic began to ebb, though her heart was still leaping erratically. At last, Robin removed her numb hands from the walls of the cubicle and opened her eyes, blinking in the harsh lights. The bathroom was quiet.

Robin peered out of the cubicle. The woman had left. There was nobody there except her own pale reflection in the mirror. After splashing cold water on her face and patting it dry with paper towels, she readjusted her clear-lensed glasses and left the bathroom.

An argument seemed to be in progress in the office she had just left. Taking a deep breath, she re-entered the room.

Jasper Chiswell turned to glare at her, his wiry mass of gray hair sticking out around his pink face. Izzy was standing behind her desk. The stranger was still there. In her shaken state, Robin would have preferred not to be the focus of three pairs of curious eyes.

"What just happened?" Chiswell demanded of Robin.

"Nothing," said Robin, feeling cold sweat erupting again under her dress.

"You ran out of the room. Did he—" Chiswell pointed at the dark man, "—do something to you? Make a pass?"

"Wha—? No! I didn't realize he was in here, that's all—he spoke and I jumped. And," she could feel herself blushing harder than ever, "then I needed the loo."

Chiswell rounded on the dark man.

"So why are you here so early, eh?"

Now, at last, Robin realized that this was Raphael. She had known from the pictures she had found online that this half-Italian was an exotic in a family that was otherwise uniformly blond and very English in appearance, but had been wholly unprepared for how handsome he was in the flesh. His charcoal-gray suit, white shirt and a conventional dark blue spotted tie were worn with an air that none of the other men along the corridor could muster. So dark-skinned as to appear swarthy, he had high cheekbones, almost black eyes, dark hair worn long and floppy, and a wide mouth that, unlike his father's, had a full upper lip that added vulnerability to his face.

"I thought you liked punctuality, Dad," he said, raising his arms and letting them fall in a slightly hopeless gesture.

His father turned to Izzy. "Give him something to do."

Chiswell marched out. Mortified, Robin headed for her desk. Nobody spoke until Chiswell's footsteps had died away, then Izzy spoke.

"He's under all kinds of stress just now, Raff, babes. It isn't you. He's honestly going berserk about the smallest things."

"I'm so sorry," Robin forced herself to say to Raphael. "I completely overreacted."

"No problem," he replied, in the kind of accent that is routinely described as "public school." "For the record, I'm not, in fact, a sex offender."

Robin laughed nervously.

"You're the goddaughter I didn't know about? Nobody tells me anything. Venetia, yeah? I'm Raff."

"Um—yes—hi."

They shook hands and Robin retook her seat, busying herself with some pointless paper shuffling. She could feel her color fluctuating.

"It's just crazy at the moment," Izzy said, and Robin knew that she was trying, for not entirely unselfish reasons, to persuade Raphael that their father wasn't as bad to work with as he might appear. "We're understaffed, we've got the Olympics coming up, TTS is constantly going off on Papa—"

"*What's* going off on him?" asked Raphael, dropping down into the sagging armchair, loosening his tie and crossing his long legs.

"TTS," Izzy repeated. "Lean over and put on the kettle while you're there, Raff, I'm dying for a coffee. TTS. It stands for Tinky the Second. It's what Fizz and I call Kinvara."

The many nicknames of the Chiswell family had been explained to Robin during her office interludes with Izzy. Izzy's older sister Sophia was "Fizzy," while Sophia's three children rejoiced in the pet names of "Pringle," "Flopsy" and "Pong."

"Why 'Tinky the Second'?" asked Raff, unscrewing a jar of instant coffee with long fingers. Robin was still very aware of all his movements, though keeping her eyes on her supposed work. "What was Tinky the First?"

"Oh, come on, Raff, you must have heard about Tinky," said Izzy. "That ghastly Australian nurse Grampy married last time round, when he was getting senile. He blew most of the money on her. He was the second silly old codger she'd married. Grampy bought her a dud racehorse and loads of horrible jewelry. Papa nearly had to go to court to get her out of the house when Grampy died. She dropped dead of breast cancer before it got really expensive, thank God."

Startled by this sudden callousness, Robin looked up.

"How d'you take it, Venetia?" Raphael asked as he spooned coffee into mugs.

"White, no sugar, please," said Robin. She thought it best if she maintained a low profile for a while, after her recent incursion into Winn's office.

"TTS married Papa for his dosh," Izzy plowed on, "*and* she's horse-mad like Tinky. You know she's got nine now? Nine!"

"Nine what?" said Raphael.

"Horses, Raff!" said Izzy impatiently. "Bloody uncontrollable, bad-mannered, hot-blooded horses that she mollycoddles and keeps as child substitutes and spends all the money on! *God*, I wish Papa would leave her," said Izzy. "Pass the biscuit tin, babes."

He did so. Robin, who could feel him looking at her, maintained the pretense of absorption in her work.

The telephone rang.

"Jasper Chiswell's office," said Izzy, trying to prize off the lid of the biscuit tin one-handed, the receiver under her chin. "Oh," she said, suddenly cool. "Hello, Kinvara. You've just missed Papa..."

Grinning at his half-sister's expression, Raphael took the biscuits from her, opened them and offered the tin to Robin, who shook her head. A torrent of indistinguishable words was pouring from Izzy's earpiece.

"No...no, he's gone...he only came over to say hello to Raff..."

The voice at the end of the phone seemed to become more strident.

"Back at DCMS, he's got a meeting at ten," said Izzy. "I can't—well, because he's very busy, you know, the Olymp—yes...goodbye."

Izzy slammed the receiver down and struggled out of her jacket.

"She should take another *rest cure*. The last one doesn't seem to have done her much good."

"Izzy doesn't believe in mental illness," Raphael told Robin.

He was contemplating her, still slightly curious and, she guessed, trying to draw her out.

"Of course I believe in mental illness, Raff!" said Izzy, apparently stung. "Of course I do! I was sorry for her when it happened—I *was*, Raff—Kinvara had a stillbirth two years ago," Izzy explained, "and *of course* that's sad, *of course* it is, and it was quite understandable that she was a bit, you know, afterwards, but—no, I'm sorry," she said crossly, addressing Raphael, "but she uses it. She *does*, Raff. She thinks it entitles her to everything she wants and—well, she'd have been a dreadful mother, anyway," said Izzy defiantly. "She can't stand not being the center of attention. When she's not getting enough she starts her little girl act—*don't leave me alone, Jasper, I get scared when you're not here at night.* Telling stupid lies...funny phone calls to the house, men hiding in the flowerbeds, fiddling with the horses."

"*What?*" said Raphael, half-laughing, but Izzy cut him short.

"Oh, Christ, look, Papa's left his briefing papers."

She hurried out from behind her desk, snatched a leather folder off the top of the radiator and called over her shoulder, "Raff, you can listen to the phone messages and transcribe them for me while I'm gone, OK?"

The heavy wooden door thudded shut behind her, leaving Robin and Raphael alone. If she had been hyperaware of Raphael before Izzy had gone, now he seemed to Robin to fill the entire room, his olive dark eyes on her.

He took Ecstasy and ran his car into a mother of a four-year-old. He barely served a third of his sentence and now his father's put him on the taxpayer's payroll.

"How do I do this, then?" asked Raphael, moving behind Izzy's desk.

"Just press play, I expect," Robin muttered, sipping her coffee and pretending to make notes on a pad.

Canned messages began to issue from the answering machine, drowning out the faint hum of conversation from the terrace beyond the net-curtained window.

A man named Rupert asked Izzy to call him back about "the AGM."

A constituent called Mrs. Ricketts spoke for two solid minutes about traffic along the Banbury road.

An irate woman said crossly that she ought to have expected an answering machine and that MPs ought to be answering to the public personally, then spoke until cut off by the machine about her neighbors' failure to lop overhanging branches from a tree, in spite of repeated requests from the council.

Then a man's growl, almost theatrically menacing, filled the quiet office:

"They say they piss themselves as they die, Chiswell, is that true? Forty grand, or I'll find out how much the papers will pay."

20

Strike had selected the Two Chairmen for his Wednesday evening catch-up with Robin because of its proximity to the Palace of Westminster. The pub was tucked away on a junction of centuries-old back streets—Old Queen Street, Cockpit Steps—amid a motley collection of quaint, sedate buildings that stood at oblique angles to each other. Only as he limped across the road and saw the hanging metal sign over the front door did Strike realize that the "two chairmen" for whom the pub was named were not, as he had assumed, joint managers of a board, but lowly servants carrying the heavy load of a sedan chair. Tired and sore as Strike was, the image seemed appropriate, although the occupant of the sedan chair in the pub sign was a refined lady in white, not a large, curmudgeonly minister with wiry hair and a short temper.

The bar was crowded with after-work drinkers and Strike had a sudden apprehension that he might not get a seat inside, an unwelcome prospect, because leg, back and neck were tight and sore after yesterday's long drive and the hours he had spent in Harley Street today, watching Dodgy Doc.

Strike had just bought a pint of London Pride when the table by the window became free. With a turn of speed born of necessity, he nabbed the high bench with its back to the street before the nearest group of suited men and women could annex it. There was no question of anybody challenging his right to sole occupancy of a table made for four. Strike was large enough, and surly enough in appearance to make even this group of civil servants doubt their ability to negotiate a compromise.

The wooden-floored bar was what Strike mentally categorized as "upmarket utilitarian." A faded mural on the back wall depicted bewigged eighteenth-century men gossiping together, but otherwise all was pared-back wood and monochrome prints. He peered out of the window to see whether Robin was within sight, but as there was no sign of her he drank his beer, read the day's news on his phone and tried to ignore the menu lying on the table in front of him, which was taunting him with a picture of battered fish.

Robin, who had been due to arrive at six, was still absent at half past. Unable to resist the picture on the menu any longer, Strike ordered himself cod and chips and a second pint, and read a long article in *The Times* about the upcoming Olympics opening cere-mony, which was really a long list of the ways in which the journalist feared it might misrepresent and humiliate the nation.

By a quarter to seven, Strike was starting to worry about Robin. He had just decided to call her when she came hurrying in through the door, flushed, wearing glasses that Strike knew she did not need and with an expression that he recognized as the barely contained excitement of one who has something worthwhile to impart.

"Hazel eyes," he noted, as she sat down opposite him. "Good one. Changes your whole look. What've you got?"

"How do you know I've—? Well, loads, actually," she said, decid-ing it was not worthwhile toying with him. "I nearly called you earlier but there have been people around all day, and I had a close shave this morning placing the listening device."

"You did it? Bloody well done!"

"Thanks. I really want a drink, hang on."

She came back with a glass of red wine and launched immediately into an account of the message that Raphael had found on the answering machine that morning.

"I had no chance of getting the caller's number, because there were four messages after it. The phone system's antiquated."

Frowning, Strike asked: "How did the caller pronounce 'Chiswell,' can you remember?"

"They said it right. *Chizzle.*"

"Fits with Jimmy," said Strike. "What happened after the call?"

"Raff told Izzy about it when she got back to the office," said Robin, and Strike thought he detected a touch of self-consciousness as she said the name "Raff." "He didn't understand what he was passing on, obviously. Izzy called her dad straight away and he went berserk. We could hear him shouting on the end of the line, though not much of what he was actually saying."

Strike stroked his chin, thinking.

"What did the anonymous caller sound like?"

"London accent," Robin said. "Threatening."

"'They piss themselves as they die,'" repeated Strike in an undertone.

There was something that Robin wanted to say, but a brutal personal memory made it hard for her to articulate.

"Strangling victims—"

"Yeah," said Strike, cutting her off. "I know."

Both of them drank.

"Well, assuming the call was Jimmy," Robin went on, "he's phoned the department twice today."

She opened her handbag and showed Strike the listening device hidden inside it.

"You retrieved it?" he asked, staggered.

"And replaced it with another one," said Robin, unable to suppress a triumphant smile. "That's why I'm late. I took a chance. Aamir, who works with Winn, left and Geraint came into our office while I was packing up, to chat me up."

"He did, did he?" asked Strike, amused.

"I'm glad you find it funny," said Robin coolly. "He isn't a nice man."

"Sorry," said Strike. "In what way is he not a nice man?"

"Just take it from me," said Robin. "I've met plenty of them in offices. He's a pervert, but with creepy add-ons. He was just telling me," she said, and her indignation showed in the rising tide of pink in her face, "that I remind him of his dead daughter. Then he touched my hair."

"Touched your hair?" repeated Strike, unamused.

"Picked a bit of it off my shoulder and ran it through his fingers," said Robin. "Then I think he saw what I thought of him and tried to pass it off as fatherly. Anyway, I said I needed the loo but asked him to stay put so we could keep chatting about charities. I nipped down the corridor and swapped the devices."

"That was bloody good going, Robin."

"I listened to it on the way here," said Robin, pulling headphones out of her pocket, "and—"

Robin handed Strike the headphones.

"—I've cued up the interesting bit."

Strike obediently inserted the earbuds and Robin switched on the tape in her handbag.

"...at three thirty, Aamir."

The Welsh male voice was interrupted by the sound of a mobile phone ringing. Feet scuffled near the power point, the ring ceased and Geraint said:

"Oh, hello Jimmy...half a mo'—Aamir, close that door."

More scuffling, footsteps.

"Jimmy, yes...?"

There followed a long stretch in which Geraint seemed to be attempting to stem the flow of a mounting tirade.

"Whoa—now, wai...Jimmy, lis...Jimmy, listen—*listen!* I know you've lost out, Jimmy, I understand how bitter you—*Jimmy, please!* We understand your feelings—that's unfair, Jimmy, neither Della nor I grew up wealth—my father was a coalminer, Jimmy! Now listen, please! *We're close to getting the pictures!*"

There followed a spell in which Strike thought he heard, very faintly, the rise and fall of Jimmy Knight's fluent speech at the end of the telephone.

"I take your point," said Geraint finally, "but I urge you to do nothing rash, Jimmy. He isn't going to give you—Jimmy, listen! He isn't going to give you your money, he's made that perfectly clear. It's the newspapers now or nothing, so...proof, Jimmy! Proof!"

Another, shorter period of unintelligible gabbling followed.

"I've just told you, haven't I? Yes...no, but the Foreign Office...well, hardly...no, Aamir has a contact...yes...yes...all right then...I will, Jimmy. Good—yes, all right. Yes. Goodbye."

The clunk of a mobile being set down was followed by Geraint's voice.

"Stupid prick," he said.

There were more footsteps. Strike glanced at Robin, who by a rolling gesture of the hand indicated that he should keep listening. After perhaps thirty seconds, Aamir spoke, diffident and strained.

"Geraint, Christopher didn't promise anything about the pictures."

Even on the tinny little tape, with the nearby shufflings of paper at Geraint's desk, the silence sounded charged.

"Geraint, did you h—?"

"Yes, I heard!" snapped Winn. "Good God, boy, a first from the LSE and you can't think of a way to persuade that bastard to give you pictures? I'm not asking you to take them out of the department, just to get copies. That shouldn't be beyond the wit of man."

"I don't want more trouble," muttered Aamir.

"Well, I should have thought," said Geraint, "after everything Della in particular has done for you..."

"And I'm grateful," said Aamir swiftly. "You know I am...all right, I'll—I'll try."

For the next minute there were no sounds but scuffing footsteps and papers, followed by a mechanical click. The device automatically switched off after a minute of no talking, activated again when somebody spoke. The next voice was that of a different man asking whether Della would be attending "the sub-committee" this afternoon.

Strike removed the earbuds.

"Did you catch it all?" Robin asked.

"I think so," said Strike.

She leaned back, watching Strike expectantly.

"The Foreign Office?" he repeated quietly. "What the hell can he have done that means the *Foreign Office* has got pictures?"

"I thought we weren't supposed to be interested in what he did?" said Robin, eyebrows raised.

"I never said I wasn't interested. Just that I'm not being paid to find out."

Strike's fish and chips arrived. He thanked the barmaid and proceeded to add a generous amount of ketchup to his plate.

"Izzy was completely matter of fact about whatever it is," said Robin, thinking back. "She couldn't possibly have spoken about it the way she did if he'd—you know—murdered anybody."

She deliberately avoided the word "strangled." Three panic attacks in three days were quite sufficient.

"Got to say," said Strike, now chewing chips, "that anonymous call makes you—unless," he said, struck by a thought, "Jimmy's had the bright idea of trying to drag Chiswell into the Billy business on top of whatever else he's genuinely done. A child-killing doesn't have to be true to make trouble for a government minister who's already got the press on his tail. You know the internet. Plenty of people out there think being a Tory as tantamount to being a child killer. This might be Jimmy's idea of adding pressure."

Strike stabbed a few chips moodily with his fork.

"I'd be glad to know where Billy is, if we had somebody free to look for him. Barclay hasn't seen any sign of him and says Jimmy hasn't mentioned having a brother."

"Billy said he was being held captive," Robin said tentatively.

"Don't think we can set much store on anything Billy's saying right now, to be honest. I knew a guy in the Shiners who had a psychotic episode on exercises. Thought he had cockroaches living under his skin."

"In the—?"

"Shiners. Fusiliers. Want a chip?"

"I'd better not," sighed Robin, though she was hungry. Matthew, whom she had warned by text that she would be late, had told her he would wait for her to get home, so they could eat dinner together. "Listen, I haven't told you everything."

"Suki Lewis?" asked Strike, hopefully.

"I haven't been able to work her into the conversation yet. No, it's that Chiswell's wife claims men have been lurking in the flowerbeds and fiddling with her horses."

"Men?" Strike repeated. "In the plural?"

"That's what Izzy said—but she also says Kinvara's hysterical and attention-seeking."

"Getting to be a bit of a theme, that, isn't it? People who're supposed to be too crazy to know what they've seen."

"D'you think that could have been Jimmy, as well? In the garden?"

Strike thought it over as he chewed.

"I can't see what he's got to gain from lurking in the garden or fiddling with horses, unless he's at the point where he just wants to frighten Chiswell. I'll check with Barclay and see whether Jimmy's got a car or mentioned going to Oxfordshire. Did Kinvara call the police?"

"Raff asked that, when Izzy got back," said Robin, and once again, Strike thought he detected a trace of self-consciousness as she spoke the man's name. "Kinvara claims the dogs barked, she saw the shadow of a man in the garden, but he ran away. She says there were footprints in the horses' field next morning and that one of them had been cut with a knife."

"Did she call a vet?"

"I don't know. It's harder to ask questions with Raff in the office. I don't want to look too nosy, because he doesn't know who I am."

Strike pushed his plate away from him and felt for his cigarettes.

"Photos," he mused, returning to the central point. "Photos at the Foreign Office. What the hell can they show that would incriminate Chiswell? He's never worked at the Foreign Office, has he?"

"No," said Robin. "The highest post he's ever held is Minister for Trade. He had to resign from there because of the affair with Raff's mother."

The wooden clock over the fireplace was telling her it was time to leave. She didn't move.

"You're liking Raff, then?" Strike said suddenly, catching her off guard.

"What?"

Robin was scared that she had blushed.

"What do you mean, I'm 'liking' him?"

"Just an impression I got," said Strike. "You disapproved of him before you met him."

"D'you want me to be antagonistic towards him, when I'm supposed to be his father's goddaughter?" demanded Robin.

"No, of course not," said Strike, though Robin had the sense that he was laughing at her, and resented it.

"I'd better get going," she said, sweeping the headphones off the table and back into her bag. "I told Matt I'd be home for dinner."

She got up, bade Strike goodbye and left the pub.

Strike watched her go, dimly sorry that he had commented on her manner when mentioning Raphael Chiswell. After a few minutes' solitary beer consumption, he paid for his food and ambled out onto the pavement, where he lit a cigarette and called the Minister for Culture, who answered on the second ring.

"Wait there," said Chiswell. Strike could hear a murmuring crowd behind him. "Crowded room."

The clunk of a door closing and the noise of the crowd was muted.

"'M at a dinner," said Chiswell. "Anything for me?"

"It isn't good news, I'm afraid," said Strike, walking away from the pub, up Queen Anne Street, between white painted buildings that gleamed in the dusk. "My partner succeeded in planting the listening device in Mr. Winn's office this morning. We've got a recording of him talking to Jimmy Knight. Winn's assistant—Aamir, is it?—is trying to get copies of those photographs you told me about. At the Foreign Office."

The ensuing silence lasted so long that Strike wondered whether they had been cut off.

"Minist—?"

"I'm here!" snarled Chiswell. "That boy Mallik, is it? Dirty little bastard. *Dirty little bastard.* He's already lost one job—let him try, that's all. Let him try! Does he think I won't—I know things about Aamir Mallik," he said. "Oh yes."

Strike waited, in some surprise, for elucidation of these remarks, but none were forthcoming. Chiswell merely breathed heavily into the telephone. Soft, muffled thuds told Strike that Chiswell was pacing up and down on carpet.

"Is that all you had to say to me?" demanded the MP at last.

"There was one other thing," said Strike. "My partner says your wife's seen a man or men trespassing on your property at night."

"Oh," said Chiswell, "yerse." He did not sound particularly concerned. "My wife keeps horses and she takes their security very seriously."

"You don't think this has any connection with—?"

"Not in the slightest, not in the slightest. Kinvara's sometimes—well, to be candid," said Chiswell, "she can be bloody hysterical. Keeps a bunch of horses, always fretting they're going to be stolen. I don't want you wasting time chasing shadows through the undergrowth in Oxfordshire. My problems are in London. Is that everything?"

Strike said that it was and, after a curt farewell, Chiswell hung up, leaving Strike to limp towards St. James's Park station.

Settled in a corner seat of the Tube ten minutes later, Strike folded his arms, stretched out his legs and stared unseeingly at the window opposite.

The nature of this investigation was highly unusual. He had never before had a blackmail case where the client was so unforthcoming about his offense—but then, Strike reasoned with himself, he had never had a government minister as a client before. Equally, it was not every day that a possibly psychotic young man burst into Strike's office and insisted that he had witnessed a child murder, though Strike had certainly received his fair share of unusual and unbalanced communications since hitting the newspapers: what he had once called, over Robin's occasional protests, "the nutter drawer," now filled half a filing cabinet.

It was the precise relationship between the strangled child and Chiswell's case of blackmail that was preoccupying Strike, even though, on the face of it, the connection was obvious: it lay in the fact of Jimmy and Billy's brotherhood. Now somebody (and Strike thought it overwhelmingly likely to be Jimmy, judging from Robin's account of the call) seemed to have decided to tie Billy's story to Chiswell, even though the blackmailable offense that had brought Chiswell to Strike could not possibly have been infanticide, or

Geraint Winn would have gone to the police. Like a tongue probing a pair of ulcers, Strike's thoughts kept returning fruitlessly to the Knight brothers: Jimmy, charismatic, articulate, thuggishly good-looking, a chancer and a hothead, and Billy, haunted, filthy, unquestionably ill, bedeviled by a memory no less dreadful for the fact that it might be false.

They piss themselves as they die.

Who did? Again, Strike seemed to hear Billy Knight.

They buried her in a pink blanket, down in the dell by my dad's house. But afterwards they said it was a boy . . .

He had just been specifically instructed by his client to restrict his investigations to London, not Oxfordshire.

As he checked the name of the station at which they had just arrived, Strike remembered Robin's self-consciousness when talking about Raphael Chiswell. Yawning, he took out his mobile again and succeeded in Googling the youngest of his client's offspring, of whom there were many pictures going up the courtroom steps to his trial for manslaughter.

As he scrolled through multiple pictures of Raphael, Strike felt a rising antipathy towards the handsome young man in his dark suit. Setting aside the fact that Chiswell's son resembled an Italian model more than anything British, the images caused a latent resentment, rooted in class and personal injuries, to glow a little redder inside Strike's chest. Raphael was of the same type as Jago Ross, the man whom Charlotte had married after splitting with Strike: upper class, expensively clothed and educated, their peccadillos treated more leniently for being able to afford the best lawyers, for resembling the sons of the judges deciding their fates.

The train set off again and Strike, losing his connection, stuffed his phone back into his pocket, folded his arms and resumed his blank stare at the dark window, trying to deny an uncomfortable idea headspace, but it nosed up against him like a dog demanding food, impossible to ignore.

He now realized that he had never imagined Robin being interested in any man other than Matthew, except, of course, for that moment when he himself had held her on the stairs at her wedding, when, briefly...

Angry with himself, he kicked the unhelpful thought aside, and forced his wandering mind back onto the curious case of a government minister, slashed horses and a body buried in a pink blanket, down in a dell.

21

. . . certain games are going on behind your back in this house.

Henrik Ibsen, *Rosmersholm*

"Why are you so busy and I've got bugger all to do?" Raphael asked Robin, late on Friday morning.

She had just returned from tailing Geraint to Portcullis House. Observing him from a distance, she had seen how the polite smiles of the many young women he greeted turned to expressions of dislike as he passed. Geraint had disappeared into a meeting room on the first floor, so Robin had returned to Izzy's office. Approaching Geraint's room she had hoped she might be able to slip inside and retrieve the second listening device, but through the open door she saw Aamir working at his computer.

"Raff, I'll give you something to do in a moment, babes," muttered a fraught Izzy, who was hammering at her keyboard. "I've got to finish this, it's for the local party chairwoman. Papa's coming to sign it in five minutes."

She threw a harried glance at her brother, who was sprawled in the armchair, his long legs spread out in front of him, shirtsleeves rolled up, tie loosened, playing with the paper visitor's pass that hung around his neck.

"Why don't you go and get yourself a coffee on the terrace?" Izzy suggested. Robin knew she wanted him out the way when Chiswell turned up.

"Want to come for a coffee, Venetia?" asked Raphael.

"Can't," said Robin. "Busy."

The fan on Izzy's desk swept Robin's way and she enjoyed a few seconds of cool breeze. The net-curtained window gave but a misty impression of the glorious June day. Truncated parliamentarians appeared as glowing wraiths on the terrace beyond the glass. It was stuffy inside the cluttered office. Robin was wearing a cotton dress, her hair in a ponytail, but still she occasionally blotted her upper lip with the back of her hand as she pretended to be working.

Having Raphael in the office was, as she had told Strike, a disadvantage. There had been no need to come up with excuses for lurking in the corridor when she had been alone with Izzy. What was more, Raphael watched her a lot, in an entirely different way to Geraint's lewd up-and-down looks. She didn't approve of Raphael, but every now and then she found herself coming perilously close to feeling sorry for him. He seemed nervy around his father, and then—well, *anybody* would think him handsome. That was the main reason she avoided looking at him: it was best not to, if you wanted to preserve any objectivity.

He kept trying to foster a closer relationship with her, which she was attempting to discourage. Only the previous day he had interrupted her as she hovered outside Geraint and Aamir's door, listening with all her might to a conversation that Aamir was having on the phone about an "inquiry." From the scant details that Robin had so far heard, she was convinced that the Level Playing Field was under discussion.

"But this isn't a *statutory* inquiry?" Aamir was asking, sounding worried. "It isn't official? I thought this was just a routine...but Mr. Winn understood that his letter to the fundraising regulator had answered all their concerns."

Robin could not pass up the opportunity to listen, but knew her situation to be perilous. What she had not expected was to be surprised by Raphael rather than Winn.

"What are you doing, skulking there?" he had asked, laughing.

Robin walked hastily away, but she heard Aamir's door slam behind her and suspected that he, at least, would make sure that it was closed in future.

"Are you always this jumpy, or is it just me?" Raphael had asked, hurrying after her. "Come for a coffee, come on, I'm so bloody bored."

Robin had declined brusquely, but even as she pretended to be busy again, she had to admit that part of her—a tiny part—was flattered by his attentions.

There was a knock on the door and, to Robin's surprise, Aamir Mallik entered the room, holding a list of names. Nervous but determined, he addressed Izzy.

"Yeah, uh, hi. Geraint would like to add the Level Playing Field trustees to the Paralympian reception on the twelfth of July," he said.

"I've got nothing to do with that reception," snapped Izzy. "DCMS are organizing it, not me. *Why,*" she erupted, wiping her sweaty fringe off her forehead, "does everyone come to *me?*"

"Geraint needs them to come," said Aamir. The list of names quivered in his hand.

Robin wondered whether she dared creep into Aamir's empty office right now and swap the listening devices. She got to her feet quietly, trying not to draw attention to herself.

"Why doesn't he ask Della?" asked Izzy.

"Della's busy. It's only eight people," said Aamir. "He really needs—"

"'*Hear the word of Lachesis, the daughter of Necessity!*'"

The Minister for Culture's booming tones preceded him into the room. Chiswell stood in the doorway, wearing a crumpled suit and blocking Robin's exit. She sat down quietly again. Aamir, or so it seemed to Robin, braced himself.

"Know who Lachesis was, Mr. Mallik?" asked Chiswell.

"Can't say I do," said Aamir.

"No? Didn't study the Greeks in your Harringay Comprehensive? You seem to have time on your hands, Raff. Teach Mr. Mallik about Lachesis."

"I don't know, either," said Raphael, peering up at his father through his thick, dark lashes.

"Playing stupid, eh? Lachesis," said Chiswell, "was one of the Fates. She measured out each man's allotted lifespan. Knew when everyone's number would be up. Not a fan of Plato, Mr. Mallik? Catullus more up your street, I expect. He produced some fine poetry about men of your habits. *Pedicabo ego vos et irrumabo, Aureli pathice et cinaede Furi,* eh? Poem 16, look it up, you'll enjoy it."

Raphael and Izzy were both staring at their father. Aamir stood for a few seconds as though he had forgotten what he had come for, then stalked out of the room.

"A little Classics education for everyone," said Chiswell, turning to watch him go with what appeared to be malicious satisfaction. "We are never too old to learn, eh, Raff?"

Robin's mobile vibrated on her desk. Strike had texted. They had agreed not to contact each other during working hours unless it was urgent. She slid the phone into her bag.

"Where's my signing pile?" Chiswell asked Izzy. "Have you finished that letter for Brenda Bloody Bailey?"

"Printing it now," said Izzy.

While Chiswell scribbled his signature on a stack of letters, breathing like a bulldog in the otherwise quiet room, Robin muttered something about needing to get going, and hurried out into the corridor.

Wanting to read Strike's text without fear of interruption, she followed a wooden sign to the crypt, hastened down the narrow stone staircase indicated and found, at the bottom, a deserted chapel.

The crypt was decorated like a medieval jewel casket, every inch of gold wall embellished with motifs and symbols, heraldic and religious. There were jewel-bright saints' pictures above the altar and the sky-blue organ pipes were wrapped in gold ribbon and scarlet *fleurs-de-lys*. Robin hurried into a red velvet pew and opened Strike's text.

Need a favor. Barclay's done a 10-day stretch on Jimmy Knight, but he's just found out his wife's got to work over the weekend & he can't get anyone else to look after the baby. Andy leaves for a week in Alicante with the family tonight. I can't tail Jimmy, he knows me. CORE are joining an anti-missile march tomorrow. Starts at 2, in Bow. Can you do it?

Robin contemplated the message for several seconds, then let out a groan that echoed around the crypt.

It was the first time in over a year that Strike had asked her to work extra hours at such short notice, but this was her anniversary weekend. The pricey hotel was booked, the bags packed and ready in the car. She was supposed to be meeting Matthew after work in a couple of hours. They were to drive straight to Le Manoir aux Quat'Saisons. Matthew would be furious if she said she couldn't go.

In the gilded hush of the crypt, the words Strike had said to her when he had agreed to give her detective training came back to her.

I need someone who can work long hours, weekends... you've got a lot of aptitude for the job, but you're getting married to someone who hates you doing it...

And she had told him that it didn't matter what Matthew thought, that it was up to her what she did.

Where did her allegiance lie now? She had said that she would stay in the marriage, promised to give it a chance. Strike had had many hours of unpaid overtime out of her. He could not claim that she was workshy.

Slowly, deleting words, replacing them, overthinking every syllable, she typed out a response.

I'm really sorry, but it's my anniversary weekend. We've got a hotel booked, leaving this evening.

She wanted to write more, but what was there to say? "My marriage isn't going well, so it's important I celebrate it"? "I'd much rather disguise myself as a protestor and stalk Jimmy Knight"? She pressed "send."

Sitting waiting for his response, feeling as though she were about to get the results of medical tests, Robin's eyes followed the course of twisting vines that covered the ceiling. Strange faces peered down at her out of the molding, like the wild Green Man of myth. Heraldic and pagan imagery mingled with angels and crosses. It was more than a place of God, this chapel. It harked back to an age of superstition, magic and feudal power.

The minutes slid by and still Strike hadn't answered. Robin got up and walked around the chapel. At the very back she found a cupboard. Opening it, she saw a plaque to suffragette Emily Davison. Apparently, she had slept there overnight so that she could give her place of residence as the House of Commons on the census of 1911, seven years before women were given the vote. Emily Davison, she could not help but feel, would not have approved of Robin's choice to place a failing marriage above freedom to work.

Robin's mobile buzzed again. She looked down, afraid of what she was going to read. Strike had answered with two letters:

OK

A lead weight seemed to slide from her chest to her stomach. Strike, as she was well aware, was still living in the glorified bedsit over the office and working through weekends. The only unmarried person at the agency, the boundary between his professional and private lives was, if not precisely non-existent, then flexible and porous, whereas hers, Barclay's and Hutchins's were not. And the worst of it was that Robin could think of no way of telling Strike that she was sorry, that she understood, that she wished things were different, without reminding both of them of that hug on the stairs at her wedding, now so long unmentioned that she wondered whether he even remembered it.

Feeling utterly miserable, she retraced her steps out of the crypt, still holding the papers she had been pretending to deliver.

Raphael was alone in the office when she returned, sitting at Izzy's PC and typing at a third of her speed.

"Izzy's gone with Dad to do something so tedious it just bounced off my brain," he said. "They'll be back in a bit."

Robin forced a smile, returned to her desk, her mind on Strike.

"Bit weird, that poem, wasn't it?" Raphael asked.

"What? Oh—oh, that Latin thing? Yes," said Robin. "It was, a bit."

"It was like he'd memorized it to use on Mallik. Nobody's got that at their fingertips."

Reflecting that Strike seemed to know strange bits of Latin off by heart, too, Robin said, "No, you wouldn't think so."

"Has he got it in for that Mallik, or something?"

"I really don't know," lied Robin.

Running out of ways to occupy her time at the desk, she shuffled papers again.

"How long are you staying, Venetia?"

"I'm not sure. Until Parliament goes into recess, probably."

"You seriously want to work here? Permanently?"

"Yes," she said. "I think it's interesting."

"What were you doing before this?"

"PR," said Robin. "It was quite fun, but I fancied a change."

"Hoping to bag an MP?" he said, with a faint smile.

"I can't say I've seen anyone round here I'd like to marry," said Robin.

"Hurtful," said Raphael, with a mock sigh.

Afraid that she had blushed, Robin tried to cover up by bending down to open a drawer and taking a few objects out at random.

"So, is Venetia Hall seeing anyone?" he persisted, as she straightened up.

"Yes," she said. "His name's Tim. We've been together a year now."

"Yeah? What does Tim do?"

"He works at Christie's," said Robin.

She had got the idea from the men she had seen with Sarah Shadlock in the Red Lion: immaculate, suited public-school types of the kind she imagined Chiswell's goddaughter would know.

"What about you?" she asked. "Izzy said something—"

"At the gallery?" said Raphael, cutting her off. "That was nothing. She was too young for me. Her parents have sent her to Florence now, anyway."

He had swung his chair around to face her, his expression grave and searching, contemplating her as though he wanted to know something that common conversation would not yield. Robin broke their mutual gaze. Holding a look that intense was not compatible with being the contented girlfriend of the imaginary Tim.

"D'you believe in redemption?"

The question caught Robin totally by surprise. It had a kind of gravity and beauty, like the gleaming jewel of the chapel at the foot of a winding stair.

"I . . . yes, I do," she said.

He had picked up a pencil from Izzy's desk. His long fingers turned it over and over as he watched her intently. He seemed to be sizing her up.

"You know what I did? In the car?"

"Yes," she answered.

The silence that unspooled between them seemed to Robin to be peopled with flashing lights and shadowy figures. She could imagine Raphael bloody at the steering wheel, and the broken figure of the young mother on the road, and the police cars and the incident tape and the gawpers in passing cars. He was watching her intently, hoping, she thought, for some kind of benison, as though her forgiveness mattered. And sometimes, she knew, the kindness of a stranger, or even a casual acquaintance, could be transformative, something to cling to while those closest to you dragged you under in their efforts to help. She thought of the elderly steward in the Members' Lobby, uncomprehending but immensely consoling, his hoarse, kindly words a thread to hold on to, which would lead her back to sanity.

The door opened again. Both Robin and Raphael jumped as a curvy redhead entered the room, a visitor's pass hanging around her neck on a lanyard. Robin recognized her at once from online photographs as Jasper Chiswell's wife, Kinvara.

"Hello," said Robin, because Kinvara was merely staring blankly at Raphael, who had swung hastily back to his computer and began typing again.

"You must be Venetia," said Kinvara, switching her clear golden gaze onto Robin. She had a high-pitched, girlish voice. Her eyes were catlike in a slightly puffy face. "Aren't you pretty? Nobody told me you were so pretty."

Robin had no idea how to respond to this. Kinvara dropped down into the sagging chair where Raff usually sat, took off the designer sunglasses holding her long red hair off her face and shook it loose. Her bare arms and legs were heavily freckled. The top buttons of her sleeveless green shirt-dress were straining across her heavy bust.

"*Whose* daughter are you?" asked Kinvara with a trace of petulance. "Jasper didn't tell me. He doesn't tell me anything he doesn't *have* to tell me, actually. I'm used to it. He just said you're a goddaughter."

Nobody had warned Robin that Kinvara did not know who she really was. Perhaps Izzy and Chiswell had not expected them to come face to face.

"I'm Jonathan Hall's daughter," said Robin nervously. She had come up with a rudimentary background for Venetia-the-goddaughter, but had never expected to have to elaborate for the benefit of Chiswell's own wife, who presumably knew all Chiswell's friends and acquaintances.

"Who's he?" asked Kinvara. "I should probably know, Jasper'll be cross I haven't paid attention—"

"He's in land management up in—"

"Oh, was it the Northumberland property?" interrupted Kinvara, whose interest had not seemed particularly profound. "That was before my time."

Thank God, thought Robin.

Kinvara crossed her legs and folded her arms across her large chest. Her foot bounced up and down. She shot Raphael a hard, almost spiteful look.

"Aren't you going to say hello, Raphael?"

"Hello," he said.

"Jasper told me to meet him here, but if you'd rather I waited in the corridor I can," Kinvara said in her high, tight voice.

"Of course not," muttered Raphael, frowning determinedly at his monitor.

"Well, I wouldn't want to interrupt anything," said Kinvara, turning from Raphael to Robin. The story of the blonde in the art gallery bathroom swam back into Robin's mind. For a second time she pretended to be searching for something in a drawer and it was with relief that she heard the sounds of Chiswell and Izzy coming along the corridor.

"...and by ten o'clock, no later, or I won't have time to read the whole bloody thing. And tell Haines *he'll* have to talk to the BBC, I haven't got time for a bunch of idiots talking about inclu—Kinvara."

Chiswell stopped dead in the office door and said, without any trace of affection, "I told you to meet me at DCMS, not here."

"And it's lovely to see you, too, Jasper, after three days apart," said Kinvara, getting to her feet and smoothing her crumpled dress.

"Hi, Kinvara," said Izzy.

"I forgot you said DCMS," Kinvara told Chiswell, ignoring her stepdaughter. "I've been trying to call you all morning—"

"I told you," growled Chiswell, "I'd be in meetings till one, and if it's about those bloody stud fees again—"

"No, it isn't about the stud fees, Jasper, *actually*, and I'd have preferred to tell you in private, but if you want me to say it in front of your children, I will!"

"Oh, for heaven's sake," Chiswell blustered. "Come away, then, come on, we'll find a private room—"

"There was a man last night," said Kinvara, "who—*don't look at me like that, Isabella!*"

Izzy's expression was indeed conveying naked skepticism. She raised her eyebrows and walked into the room, acting as though Kinvara had become invisible to her.

"I said you can tell me in a private room!" snarled Chiswell, but Kinvara refused to be deflected.

"I saw a man in the woods by the house last night, Jasper!" she said, in a loud, high-pitched voice that Robin knew would be echoing all the way along the narrow corridor. "I'm *not* imagining things—there was a man with a spade in the woods, I saw him, and he ran when the dogs chased him! You keep telling me not to make a fuss, but I'm alone in that house at night and if *you're* not going to do anything about this, Jasper, *I'm* going to call the police!"

22

. . . don't you feel called upon to undertake it, for the sake of the good cause?

Henrik Ibsen, *Rosmersholm*

Strike was in a thoroughly bad temper.

Why the fuck, he asked himself, as he limped towards Mile End Park the following morning, was *he*, the senior partner and founder of the firm, having to stake out a protest march on a hot Saturday morning, when he had three employees and a knackered leg? Because, he answered himself, *he* didn't have a baby who needed watching, or a wife who'd booked plane tickets or broken her wrist, or a fucking anniversary weekend planned. *He* wasn't married, so it was his downtime that had to be sacrificed, *his* weekend that became just two more working days.

Everything that Robin feared Strike to be thinking about her, he was, in fact, thinking: of her house on cobbled Albury Street versus his drafty two rooms in a converted attic, of the rights and status conferred by the little gold ring on her finger, set against Lorelei's disappointment when he had explained that lunch and possibly dinner would now be impossible, of Robin's promises of equal responsibility when he had taken her on as a partner, contrasted with the reality of her rushing home to her husband.

Yes, Robin had worked many hours of unpaid overtime in her two years at the agency. Yes, he knew that she had gone way beyond the call of duty for him. Yes, he was, in theory, fucking grateful to her. The fact remained that today, while he was limping along the street towards hours of probably fruitless surveillance, she and her arsehole of a husband were speeding off to a country hotel weekend, a thought that made his sore leg and back no easier to bear.

Unshaven, clad in an old pair of jeans, a frayed, washed-out hoodie and ancient trainers, with a carrier bag swinging from his hand, Strike entered the park. He could see the massing protestors in the distance. The risk of Jimmy recognizing him had almost decided Strike to let the march go unwatched, but the most recent text from Robin (which he had, out of sheer bad temper, left unanswered) had changed his mind.

Kinvara Chiswell came into the office. She claims she saw a man with a spade in the woods near their house last night. From what she said, Chiswell's been telling her not to call the police about these intruders, but she says she's going to do it unless he does something about them. Kinvara didn't know Chiswell's called us in, btw, she thought I really was Venetia Hall. Also, there's a chance the charity commission's investigating the Level Playing Field. I'm trying to get more details.

This communication had served only to aggravate Strike. Nothing short of a concrete piece of evidence against Geraint Winn would have satisfied him right now, with the *Sun* on Chiswell's case and their client so tetchy and stressed.

According to Barclay, Jimmy Knight owned a ten-year-old Suzuki Alto, but it had failed its MOT and was currently off the road. Barclay could not absolutely guarantee that Jimmy wasn't sneaking out under cover of darkness to trespass in Chiswell's gardens and woods seventy miles away, but Strike thought it unlikely.

On the other hand, he thought it just possible that Jimmy might have sent a proxy to intimidate Chiswell's wife. He probably still had friends or acquaintances in the area where he grew up. An even more disturbing idea was that Billy had escaped from the prison, real or imaginary, in which he had told Strike he was being held, and decided to dig for proof that the child lay in a pink blanket by his father's old cottage or, gripped by who knew what paranoid fantasy, to slash one of Kinvara's horses.

Worried by these inexplicable features of the case, by the interest the *Sun* was taking in the minister, and aware that the agency was no closer to securing a "bargaining chip" against either of Chiswell's blackmailers than on the day that Strike had accepted the minister as a client, he felt he had little choice but to leave no stone unturned. In spite of his tiredness, his aching muscles and his strong suspicion that the protest march would yield nothing useful, he had dragged himself out of bed on Saturday morning, strapped his prosthesis back onto a stump that was already slightly puffy and, unable to think of much he'd like to do less than walk for two hours, set off for Mile End Park.

Once close enough to the crowd of protestors to make out individuals, Strike pulled from the carrier bag swinging from his hand a plastic Guy Fawkes mask, white with curling eyebrows and mustache and now mainly associated with the hacking organization Anonymous, and put it on. Balling up the carrier bag, he shoved it into a handy bin, then hobbled on towards the cluster of placards and banners: "No missiles on homes!" "No snipers on streets!" "Don't play games with our lives!" and several "He's got to go!" posters featuring the prime minister's face. Strike's fake foot always found grass one of the most difficult surfaces to navigate. He was sweating by the time he finally spotted the orange CORE banners, with their logo of broken Olympic rings.

There were about a dozen of them. Lurking behind a group of chattering youths, Strike readjusted the slipping plastic mask, which had not been constructed for a man whose nose had been broken, and spotted Jimmy Knight, who was talking to two young women, both of whom had just thrown back their heads, laughing delightedly at something Knight had said. Clamping the mask to his face to make sure the slits aligned with his eyes, Strike scanned the rest of the CORE members and concluded that the absence of tomato-red hair was not because Flick had dyed it another color, but because she wasn't there.

Stewards now started herding the crowd into something resembling a line. Strike moved into the mass of protestors, a silent, lumbering figure, acting a little obtusely so that the youthful organizers, intimidated by his size, treated him like a rock around which the current must be channeled as he took up a position right behind CORE. A skinny boy who was also wearing an Anonymous mask gave Strike a double thumbs up as he was shunted towards the rear of the line. Strike returned it.

Now smoking a roll-up, Jimmy continued to joke with the two young girls beside him, who were vying for his attention. The darker of the two, who was particularly attractive, was holding a double-sided banner carrying a highly detailed painting of David Cameron as Hitler overlooking the 1936 Olympic Stadium. It was quite an impressive piece of art, and Strike had time to admire it as the procession finally set off at a steady pace, flanked by police and stewards in high visibility jackets, moving gradually out of the park and onto the long, straight Roman Road.

The smooth tarmac was slightly easier on Strike's prosthesis, but his stump was still throbbing. After a few minutes a chant was got up: "Missiles OUT! Missiles OUT!"

A couple of press photographers were walking backwards in the road ahead, taking pictures of the front of the march.

"Hey, Libby," said Jimmy, to the girl with the hand-painted Hitler banner. "Wanna get on my shoulders?"

Strike noted her friend's poorly concealed envy as Jimmy crouched down so that Libby could straddle his neck and be lifted up above the crowd, her banner raised high enough for the photographers in front to see.

"Show 'em your tits, we'll be front page!" Jimmy called up to her.

"*Jimmy!*" she squealed, in mock outrage. Her friend's smile was forced. The cameras clicked, and Strike, grimacing with pain behind the plastic mask, tried not to limp too obviously.

"Guy with the biggest camera was focused on you the whole time," said Jimmy, when he finally lowered the girl back to the ground.

"Fuck, if I'm in the papers my mum'll go apeshit," said the girl excitedly, and she fell into step on Jimmy's other side, taking any opportunity to nudge or slap him as he teased her about being scared of what her parents would say. She was, Strike judged, at least fifteen years younger than he was.

"Enjoying yourself, Jimmy?"

The mask restricted Strike's peripheral vision, so that it was only when the uncombed, tomato-red hair appeared immediately in front of him that Strike realized Flick had joined the march. Her sudden appearance had taken Jimmy by surprise, too.

"There you are!" he said, with a feeble show of pleasure.

Flick glared at the girl called Libby, who sped up, intimidated. Jimmy tried to put his arm around Flick, but she shrugged it off.

"Oi," he said, feigning innocent indignation. "What's up?"

"Three fucking guesses," snarled Flick.

Strike could tell that Jimmy was debating which tack to take with her. His thuggishly handsome face showed irritation but also, Strike thought, a certain wariness. For a second time, he tried to put his arm around her. This time, she slapped it away.

"Oi," he said again, this time aggressively. "The fuck was that for?"

"I'm off doing your dirty work and you're fucking around with *her*? What kind of fucking idiot do you think I am, Jimmy?"

"Missiles OUT!" bellowed a steward with a megaphone, and the crowd took up the chant once more. The cries made by the Mohicaned woman beside Strike were as shrill and raucous as a peacock's. The one bonus of the renewed shouting was that it left Strike at liberty to grunt with pain every time he set his prosthetic foot on the road, which was a kind of release and made the plastic mask reverberate in a ticklish fashion against his sweating face. Squinting through the eyeholes he watched Jimmy and Flick argue, but he couldn't hear a word over the din of the crowd. Only when the chant subsided at last could he make out a little of what they were saying to each other.

"I'm fucking sick of this," Jimmy was saying. "*I'm* not the one who picks up students in bars when—"

"You'd ditched me!" said Flick, in a kind of whispered scream. "You'd fucking ditched me! You told me you didn't want anything exclusive—"

"Heat of the moment, wasn't it?" said Jimmy roughly. "I was stressed. Billy was doing my fucking head in. I didn't expect you to go straight to a bar and pick up some fucking—"

"You told me you were sick of—"

"Fuck's sake, I lost my temper and said a bunch of shit I didn't mean. If I went and shagged another woman every time you give me grief—"

"Yeah, well I sometimes think the only reason you even keep me around is Chis—"

"Keep your fucking voice down!"

"—and today, you think it was fun at that creep's house—"

"I said I was grateful, fuck's sake, we discussed this, didn't we? I had to get those leaflets printed or I'd've come with you—"

"And I do that cleaning," she said, with a sudden sob, "and it's disgusting and then today you send me—it was horrible, Jimmy, he should be in hospital, he's in a right state—"

Jimmy glanced around. Coming briefly within Jimmy's eye-line, Strike attempted to walk naturally, though every time he asked his stump to bear his full weight, he felt as though he was pressing it down on a thousand fire ants.

"We'll get him to hospital after," said Jimmy. "We will, but he'll screw it all up if we let him loose now, you know what he's like...once Winn's got those photos...hey," said Jimmy gently, putting his arm around her for a third time. "Listen. I'm so fucking grateful to you."

"Yeah," choked Flick, wiping her nose on the back of her hand, "because of the money. Because you wouldn't even know what Chiswell had done if—"

Jimmy pulled her roughly towards him and kissed her. For a second she resisted, then opened her mouth. The kiss went on and on as they walked. Strike could see their tongues working in each other's mouths. They staggered slightly as they walked, locked together, while other CORE members grinned, and the girl whom Jimmy had lifted into the air looked crestfallen.

"Jimmy," murmured Flick at last, when the kiss had ended, but his arm was still around her. She was doe-eyed with lust now, and soft-spoken. "I think you should come and talk to him, seriously. He keeps talking about that bloody detective."

"What?" said Jimmy, though Strike could tell he'd heard.

"Strike. That bastard soldier with the one leg. Billy's fixated on him. Thinks he's going to rescue him."

The end point of the march came into sight at last: Bow Quarter in Fairfield Road, where the square brick tower of an old match factory, proposed site of some of the planned missiles, punctured the skyline.

" 'Rescue him'?" repeated Jimmy scornfully. "Fuck's sake. It's not like he's being fucking tortured."

The marchers were breaking ranks now, dissolving back into a formless crowd that milled around a dark green pond in front of the proposed missile site. Strike would have given much to sit down on a bench or lean up against a tree, as many of the protestors were doing, so as to take the weight off his stump. Both the end, where skin that was never meant to bear his weight was irritated and inflamed, and the tendons in his knee were begging for ice and rest. Instead, he limped on after Jimmy and Flick as they walked around the edge of the crowd, away from their CORE colleagues.

"He wanted to see you and I told him you were busy," he heard Flick say, "and he cried. It was horrible, Jimmy."

Pretending to be watching the young black man with a microphone, who was ascending a stage at the front of the crowd, Strike edged closer to Jimmy and Flick.

"I'll look after Billy when I get the money," Jimmy was telling Flick. He seemed guilty and conflicted now. "Obviously I'll look after him . . . and you. I won't forget what you've done."

She liked hearing that. Out of the corner of his eye, Strike saw her grubby face flush with excitement. Jimmy took a pack of tobacco and some Rizlas from his jeans pocket and began to roll himself another cigarette.

"Still talking about that fucking detective, is he?"

"Yeah."

Jimmy lit up and smoked in silence for a while, his eyes roving abstractedly over the crowd.

"Tell you what," he said suddenly, "I'll go see him now. Calm him down a bit. We just need him to stay put a bit longer. Coming?"

He held out his hand and Flick took it, smiling. They walked away.

Strike let them get a short head start, then stripped off the mask and the old gray hoodie, replaced the former with the sunglasses he had pocketed for this eventuality and set off after them, dumping the mask and hoodie on top of their banners.

The pace Jimmy now set was completely different to the leisurely march. Every few strides, Flick had to jog to keep up, and Strike was soon gritting his teeth as the nerve endings at the inflamed skin at the end of his stump rubbed against the prosthesis, his overworked thigh muscles groaning in protest.

He was perspiring hard, his gait becoming more and more unnatural. Passersby were starting to stare. He could feel their curiosity and pity as he dragged his prosthetic leg along. He knew he should have been doing his bloody physio exercises, that he ought to have kept to the no chips rule, that in an ideal world he'd have taken the day off today, and rested up, the prosthesis off, an ice pack on his stump. On he limped, refusing to listen to the body pleading with him to stop, the distance between himself, Jimmy and Flick growing ever wider, the compensating movement of his upper body and arms becoming grotesque. He could only pray that neither Jimmy nor Flick would turn and look behind them, because there was no way Strike could remain incognito if they saw him hobbling along like this. They were already disappearing into the neat little brick box that was Bow station, while Strike was panting and swearing on the opposite side of the road.

As he stepped off the curb, an excruciating pain shot through the back of his right thigh, as though a knife had sliced through the muscle. The leg buckled and he fell, his outstretched hand skidding along asphalt, hitting hip, shoulder and head on the open road. Somewhere in the vicinity a woman yelped in shock. Onlookers would think he was drunk. It had happened before when he had fallen. Humiliated, furious, groaning in agony, Strike crawled back onto the pavement, dragging his right leg out of the way of oncoming traffic. A young woman approached nervously to see whether he needed help, he barked at her, then felt guilty.

"Sorry," he croaked, but she was gone, hurrying away with two friends.

He dragged himself to the railings bordering the pavement and sat there, back against metal, sweating and bleeding. He doubted whether he would be able to stand again without assistance. Running his hands over the back of his stump, he felt an egg-shaped swelling and, with a groan, guessed that he had torn a hamstring. The pain was so sharp that it was making him feel sick.

He tugged his mobile out of his pocket. The screen was cracked where he had fallen on it.

"Fuck. It. All," he muttered, closing his eyes and leaning his head back against the cold metal.

He sat motionless for several minutes, dismissed as a tramp or a drunk by the people navigating around him, while he silently assessed his limited options. At last, with a sense of being utterly cornered, he opened his eyes, wiped his face with his forearm, and punched in Lorelei's number.

23

. . . ailing and languishing in the gloom of such a marriage . . .
Henrik Ibsen, *Rosmersholm*

In retrospect, Robin knew that her anniversary weekend had been doomed before it had even begun, down in the House of Commons crypt where she had turned down Strike's request to tail Jimmy.

Trying to throw off her sense of guilt, she had confided Strike's request to Matthew when he picked her up after work. Already tense due to the demands of navigating the Friday night traffic in the Land Rover, which he disliked, Matthew went on the offensive, demanding to know why she felt bad after all the slave labor Strike had had out of her over the past two years and proceeding to badmouth Strike so viciously that Robin had felt compelled to defend him. They were still arguing about her job an hour later, when Matthew suddenly noticed that there was neither wedding nor engagement ring on Robin's gesticulating left hand. She never wore these when playing the unmarried Venetia Hall, and had entirely forgotten that she would not be able to retrieve them from Albury Street before leaving for the hotel.

"It's our bloody anniversary and you can't even remember to put your rings back on?" Matthew had shouted.

They drew up outside the soft golden brick hotel an hour and a half later. A beaming man in uniform opened the door for Robin. Her "thank you" was almost inaudible due to the hard, angry lump in her throat.

They barely spoke over their Michelin-starred dinner. Robin, who might as well have been eating polystyrene and dust, looked around at the surrounding tables. She and Matthew were by far the youngest couple there, and she wondered whether any of these husbands and wives had been through this kind of trough in their marriages, and survived it.

They slept back to back that night.

Robin woke on Saturday in the awareness that every moment in the hotel, every step through the beautifully cultivated grounds, with the lavender walk, the Japanese garden, the orchard and organic vegetable beds, was costing them a small fortune. Perhaps Matthew was thinking the same, because he became conciliatory over breakfast. Nevertheless, their conversation felt perilous, straying regularly into dangerous territory from which they retreated precipitately. A tension headache began pounding behind Robin's temple, but she did not want to ask hotel staff for painkillers, because any sign of dissatisfaction might lead to another argument. Robin wondered what it would be like to have a wedding day and honeymoon about which it was safe to reminisce. They eventually settled on talking about Matthew's job as they strolled the grounds.

There was to be a charity cricket match between his firm and another the following Saturday. Matthew, who was as good at cricket as he had been at rugby, was greatly looking forward to the game. Robin listened to his boasts about his own prowess and jokes about Tom's inadequate bowling, laughed at the appropriate moments and made sounds of agreement, and all the time a chilled and miserable part of her was wondering what was happening right now in Bow, whether Strike had gone on the march, whether he was getting anything useful on Jimmy and wondering how she, Robin, had ended up with the pompous, self-involved man beside her, who reminded her of a handsome boy she had once loved.

For the first time ever, Robin had sex with Matthew that night purely because she could not face the row that would ensue if she refused. It was their anniversary, so they had to have sex, like a notary's stamp on the weekend, and about as pleasurable. Tears stung her eyes as Matthew climaxed, and that cold, unhappy self buried deep in her compliant body wondered why he could not feel her unhappiness even though she was trying so hard to dissemble, and how he could possibly imagine that the marriage was a success.

She put her arm over her wet eyes in the darkness after he had rolled off her and said all the things you were supposed to say. For the first time, when she said "I love you, too," she knew, beyond doubt, that she was lying.

Very carefully, once Matthew was asleep, Robin reached out in the darkness for the phone that lay on her bedside table, and checked her texts. There was nothing from Strike. She Googled pictures of the march in Bow and thought she recognized, in the middle of the crowd, a tall man with familiar curly hair, who was wearing a Guy Fawkes mask. Robin turned her mobile face down on the bedside table to shut out its light, and closed her eyes.

24

...her ungovernable, wild fits of passion—which she expected me to reciprocate...

Henrik Ibsen, *Rosmersholm*

Strike returned to his two attic rooms in Denmark Street six days later, early on Friday morning. Leaning on crutches, his prosthesis in a holdall over his shoulder and his right trouser leg pinned up, his expression tended to repel the sidelong glances of sympathy that passersby gave him as he swung along the short street to number twenty-four.

He hadn't seen a doctor. Lorelei had called her local practice once she and the lavishly tipped cabbie had succeeded in supporting Strike upstairs to her flat, but the GP had asked Strike to come into his surgery for an examination.

"What d'you want me to do, hop there? It's my hamstring, I can feel it," he had snapped down the phone. "I know the drill: rest, ice, all that bollocks. I've done it before."

He had been forced to break his no-consecutive-overnights-at-a-woman's rule, spending four full days and five nights at Lorelei's. He now regretted it, but what choice had he had? He had been caught, as Chiswell would have put it, *a fronte praecipitium, a tergo lupi.* He and Lorelei had been supposed to have dinner on Saturday night. Having chosen to tell her the truth rather than make an excuse not to meet, he had been forced to let her help. Now he wished that he had phoned his old friends Nick and Ilsa, or even Shanker, but it was too late. The damage was done.

The knowledge that he was being unfair and ungrateful was hardly calculated to improve Strike's mood as he dragged himself and his holdall up the stairs. In spite of the fact that parts of the sojourn at Lorelei's flat had been thoroughly enjoyable, all had been ruined by what had happened the previous evening, and it was entirely his own fault. He had let it happen, the thing that he had tried to guard against ever since leaving Charlotte, let it happen because he'd dropped his guard, and accepted mugs of tea, home-cooked meals and gentle affection, until finally, last night in the darkness, she had whispered onto his bare chest, "I love you."

Grimacing again with the effort of balancing on his crutches as he unlocked his front door, Strike almost fell into his flat. Slamming the door behind him, he dropped the holdall, crossed to the small chair at the Formica table in his kitchen-cum-living room, fell into it and cast his crutches aside. It was a relief to be home and alone, however difficult it was to manage with his leg in this state. He ought to have returned sooner, of course, but being in no condition to tail anyone and in considerable discomfort, it had been easier to remain in a comfortable armchair, his stump resting on a large square pouf, texting Robin and Barclay instructions while Lorelei fetched him food and drink.

Strike lit a cigarette and thought back over all the women there had been since he'd left Charlotte. First, Ciara Porter, a gorgeous one-night stand, with no regrets on either side. A few weeks after he had hit the press for solving the Landry case, Ciara had called him. He had become elevated in the model's mind from casual shag to possible boyfriend material by his newsworthiness, but he had turned down further meetings with her. Girlfriends who wanted to be photographed with him were no good to him in his line of work.

Next had come Nina, who had worked for a publisher, and whom he had used to get information on a case. He had liked her, but insufficiently, as he looked back on it, to treat her with common consideration. He had hurt Nina's feelings. He wasn't proud of it, but it hardly kept him up at nights.

Elin had been different, beautiful and, best of all, convenient, which was why he'd hung around. She had been in the process of divorcing a wealthy man and her need for discretion and compartmentalization had been at least as great as his own. They had managed a few months together before he'd spilled wine all over her, and walked out of the restaurant where they were having dinner. He had called her afterwards to apologize and she had dumped him before he finished the sentence. Given that he had left her humiliated in Le Gavroche with a hefty dry-cleaning bill, he felt that it would have been in poor taste to respond with "that's what I was going to say next."

After Elin there had been Coco, on whom he preferred not to dwell, and now there was Lorelei. He liked her better than any of the others, which was why he was sorry that it had been she who said "I love you."

Strike had made a vow to himself two years previously, and he made very few vows, because he trusted himself to keep them. Having never said "I love you" to any woman but Charlotte, he would not say it to another unless he knew, beyond reasonable doubt, that he wanted to stay with that woman and make a life with her. It would make a mockery of what he'd been through with Charlotte if he said it under circumstances any less serious. Only love could have justified the havoc they had lived together, or the many times he had resumed the relationship, even while he knew in his soul that it couldn't work. Love, to Strike, was pain and grief sought, accepted, endured. It was not in Lorelei's bedroom, with the cowgirls on the curtains.

And so he had said nothing after her whispered declaration, and then, when she'd asked whether he'd heard her, he'd said, "Yeah, I did."

Strike reached for his cigarettes. *Yeah, I did.* Well, that had been honest, as far as it went. There was nothing wrong with his hearing. After that, there'd been a fairly lengthy silence, then Lorelei had got out of bed and gone to the bathroom and stayed there for thirty minutes. Strike assumed that she'd gone there to cry, though she'd been kind enough to do it quietly, so that he couldn't hear her. He had lain in bed, wondering what he could say to her that was both kind and truthful, but he knew that nothing short of "I love you, too" would be acceptable, and the fact was that he didn't love her, and he wasn't going to lie.

When she came back to bed, he had reached out for her in the bed. She'd let him stroke her shoulder for a while, then told him she was tired and needed some sleep.

What was I supposed to fucking do? he demanded of an imaginary female inquisitor who strongly resembled his sister, Lucy.

You could try not accepting tea and blow jobs, came the snide response, to which Strike, with his stump throbbing, answered, *fuck you.*

His mobile rang. He had sellotaped up the shattered screen, and through this distorted carapace he saw an unknown number.

"Strike."

"Hi, Strike, Culpepper here."

Dominic Culpepper, who had worked for the *News of the World* until its closure, had previously put work Strike's way. Relations between them, never personally warm, had become slightly antagonistic when Strike had refused Culpepper the inside story on his two most recent murder cases. Now working for the *Sun*, Culpepper had been one of those journalists who had most enthusiastically raked over Strike's personal life in the aftermath of the Shacklewell Ripper arrest.

"Wondered if you were free to do a job for us," said Culpepper.

You've got a fucking nerve.

"What kind of thing're you after?"

"Digging up dirt on a government minister."

"Which one?"

"You'll know if you take the job."

"I'm pretty stretched just now. What kind of dirt are we talking?"

"That's what we need you to find out."

"How do you know there's dirt there?"

"A well-placed source," said Culpepper.

"Why do you need me if there's a well-placed source?"

"He's not ready to talk. He just hinted that there are beans to be spilled. Lots of them."

"Sorry, can't do it, Culpepper," said Strike. "I'm booked solid."

"Sure? We're paying good money, Strike."

"I'm not doing too badly these days," said the detective, lighting a second cigarette from the tip of his first.

"No, I'll bet you aren't, you jammy bastard," said Culpepper. "All right, it'll have to be Patterson. D'you know him?"

"The ex-Met guy? Run across him a couple of times," said Strike.

The call finished with mutually insincere good wishes, leaving Strike with an increased feeling of foreboding. He Googled Culpepper's name and found his byline on a story about the Level Playing Field from two weeks previously.

Of course, it was possible that more than one government minister was currently in danger of being exposed by the *Sun* for an offense against public taste or morals, but the fact that Culpepper had recently been in close proximity with the Winns strongly suggested Robin had been right in suspecting Geraint of tipping off the *Sun*, and that it was Chiswell whom Patterson would shortly be investigating.

Strike wondered whether Culpepper knew that he, Strike, was already working for Chiswell, whether his call had been designed to startle information out of the detective, but it seemed unlikely. The newspaperman would have been very stupid to tell Strike whom he was about to hire, if he was aware that Strike was already in the minister's pay.

Strike knew of Mitch Patterson by reputation: they had twice been hired by different halves of divorcing couples in the last year. Previously a senior officer in the Metropolitan Police who had "taken early retirement," Patterson was prematurely silver-haired and had the face of an angry pug. Though personally unpleasant, or so Eric Wardle had told Strike, Patterson was a man who "got results."

"Course, he won't be able to kick the shit out of people in his new career," Wardle had commented, "so that's one useful tool in his arsenal gone."

Strike didn't much relish the thought that Patterson would shortly be on the case. Picking up his mobile again, he noted that neither Robin nor Barclay had called in an update within the last twelve hours. Only the previous day, he had had to reassure Chiswell, who had called to express his doubts about Robin, given her lack of results thus far.

Frustrated by his employees and his own incapacity, Strike texted Robin and Barclay the same message:

Sun just tried to hire me to investigate Chiswell. Call with update asap. Need usable info NOW.

Pulling his crutches back towards him, he got up to examine the contents of his fridge and kitchen cupboards, discovering that he would be eating nothing but tinned soup for the next four meals unless he made a trip to the supermarket. After pouring spoiled milk down the sink, he made himself a mug of black tea and returned to the Formica table, where he lit a third cigarette and contemplated, without pleasure, the prospect of doing his hamstring stretches.

His phone rang again. Seeing that it was Lucy, he let it go to voicemail. The last thing he needed right now was updates on the school board's last meeting.

A few minutes after that, when Strike was in the bathroom, she called back. He had hopped back into the kitchen with his trousers at half-mast, in the hope that it was either Robin or Barclay. When he saw his sister's number for a second time, he merely swore loudly and returned to the bathroom.

The third call told him that she was not about to give up. Slamming down the can of soup he had been opening, Strike swept up the mobile.

"Lucy, I'm busy, what is it?" he said testily.

"It's Barclay."

"Ah, about time. Any news?"

"A bit on Jimmy's bird, if that helps. Flick."

"It all helps," said Strike. "Why didn't you let me know earlier?"

"Only found out ten minutes ago," said Barclay, unfazed. "I've just heard her tellin' Jimmy in the kitchen. She's been bumpin' money from her work."

"What work?"

"Didnae tell me. Trouble is, Jimmy's no that keen on her, from whut I've seen. I'm no sure he'd care if she got nicked."

A distracting beeping sounded in Strike's ear. Another caller was trying to get him. Glancing at the phone, he saw that it was Lucy again.

"Tell ye somethin' else I got out o' him, though," said Barclay. "Last night, when he was stoned. He said he knew a government minister who had blood on his hands."

Beep. Beep. Beep.

"Strike? Ye there?"

"Yeah, I'm here."

Strike had never told Barclay about Billy's story.

"What exactly did he say, Barclay?"

"He was ramblin' on about the government, the Tories, whut a bunch o' bastards they are. Then, out o' nowhere, he says 'and fuckin' killers.' I says, what d'ye mean? An' he says, 'I know one who's got blood on his fuckin' hands. Kids.'"

Beep. Beep. Beep.

"Mind you, they're a bunch o' bampots, CORE. He might be talkin' about benefit cuts. That's as good as murder to this lot. Not that I think too much of Chiswell's politics meself, Strike."

"Seen any sign of Billy? Jimmy's brother?"

"Nothin'. Naebody's mentioned him, neither."

Beep. Beep. Beep.

"And no sign of Jimmy nipping off to Oxfordshire?"

"Not on my watch."

Beep. Beep. Beep.

"All right," said Strike. "Keep digging. Let me know if you get anything."

He rang off, jabbed at his phone's screen and brought up Lucy's call, instead.

"Lucy, hi," he said impatiently. "Bit busy now, can I—?"

But as she began to talk, his expression became blank. Before she had finished gasping out the reason for her call, he had grabbed his door keys and was scrabbling for his crutches.

25

We shall try if we cannot make you powerless to do any harm.
Henrik Ibsen, *Rosmersholm*

Strike's text requesting an update reached Robin at ten to nine, as she arrived in the corridor where Izzy and Winn's offices lay. So keen was she to see what he had to say that she stopped dead in the middle of the deserted passage to read it.

"Oh shit," she murmured, reading that the *Sun* was becoming ever more interested in Chiswell. Leaning up against the wall of the corridor with its curved stone jambs, every oak door shut, she braced herself to call Strike back.

They had not spoken since she had refused to tail Jimmy. When she had phoned him on Monday to apologize directly, Lorelei had answered.

"Oh, hi, Robin, it's me!"

One of the awful things about Lorelei was that she was likable. For reasons Robin preferred not to explore, she would have much preferred Lorelei to be unpleasant.

"He's in the shower, sorry! He's been here all weekend, he did his knee in following somebody. He won't tell me the details, but I suppose you know! He had to call me from the street, it was dreadful, he couldn't stand up. I got a cabbie to take me there and paid him to help me get Corm upstairs. He can't wear the prosthesis, he's on crutches..."

"Just tell him I was checking in," said Robin, her stomach like ice. "Nothing important."

Robin had replayed the conversation several times in her head since. There had been an unmistakably proprietorial note in Lorelei's voice as she talked about Strike. It had been Lorelei whom he had called when he was in trouble (*well, of course it was. What was he going to do, call you in Oxfordshire?*), Lorelei in whose flat he had spent the rest of the weekend (*they're dating, where else was he going to go?*), Lorelei who was looking after him, consoling him and, perhaps, uniting with him in abuse of Robin, without whom this injury might not have happened.

And now she had to call Strike and tell him that, five days on, she had no useful information. Winn's office, which had been so conveniently accessible when she had started work two weeks ago, was now carefully locked up whenever Geraint and Aamir had to leave it. Robin was sure that this was Aamir's doing, that he had become suspicious of her after the incidents of the dropped bangle, and of Raphael calling loud attention to her eavesdropping on Aamir's phone call.

"Post."

Robin whirled around to see the cart trundling towards her, pushed by a genial gray-haired man.

"I'll take anything for Chiswell and Winn. We're having a meeting," Robin heard herself say. The postman handed over a stack of letters, along with a box with a clear cellophane window, through which Robin saw a life-size and very realistic plastic fetus. The legend across the top read: *It Is Legal To Murder Me.*

"Oh God, that's horrible," said Robin.

The postman chortled.

"That's nothing compared to some of what they get," he said comfortably. "Remember the white powder that was on the news? Anthrax, they claimed. Proper hoo-hah, that was. Oh, and I delivered a turd in a box once. Couldn't smell it through all the wrapping. The baby's for Winn, not Chiswell. She's the pro-choice one. Enjoying it here, are you?" he said, showing a disposition for chat.

"Loving it," Robin said, whose attention had been caught by one of the envelopes she had so rashly taken. "Excuse me."

Turning her back on Izzy's office, she hurried past the postman, and five minutes later emerged onto the Terrace Café, which sat on the bank of the Thames. It was separated from the river by a low stone wall, which was punctuated with black iron lamps. To the left and right stood Westminster and Lambeth bridges respectively, the former painted the green of the seats in the House of Commons, the latter, scarlet like those in the House of Lords. On the opposite bank rose the white façade of County Hall, while between palace and hall rolled the broad Thames, its oily surface lucent gray over muddy depths.

Sitting down out of earshot of the few early morning coffee drinkers, Robin turned her attention to one of the letters addressed to Geraint Winn that she had so recklessly taken from the postman. The sender's name and address had been carefully inscribed on the reverse of the envelope in a shaky cursive: Sir Kevin Rodgers, 16 The Elms, Fleetwood, Kent, and she happened to know, due to her extensive background reading on the Winns' charity, that the elderly Sir Kevin, who had won a silver at the hurdles in the 1956 Olympics, was one of the Level Playing Field's trustees.

What things, Robin asked herself, did people feel the need to put in writing these days, when phone calls and emails were so much easier and faster?

Using her mobile, she found a number for Sir Kevin and Lady Rodgers at the correct address. They were old enough, she thought, to still use a landline. Taking a fortifying gulp of coffee, she texted Strike back:

Following a lead, will call asap.

She then turned off caller ID on her mobile, took out a pen and the notebook in which she had written Sir Kevin's number and punched in the digits.

An elderly woman answered within three rings. Robin affected what she was afraid was a poor Welsh accent.

"Could I speak to Sir Kevin, please?"

"Is that Della?"

"Is Sir Kevin there?" asked Robin again, a little louder. She had been hoping to avoid actually claiming to be a government minister.

"Kevin!" called the woman. "Kevin! It's Della!"

There was a noise of shuffling that made Robin think of tartan bedroom slippers.

"Hello?"

"Kevin, Geraint's just got your letter," said Robin, wincing as her accent wobbled somewhere between Cardiff and Lahore.

"Sorry, Della, what?" said the man feebly.

He seemed to be deaf, which was both help and hindrance. Robin spoke more loudly, enunciating as clearly as she could. Sir Kevin grasped what she was saying on her third attempt.

"I told Geraint I'd have to resign unless he took urgent steps," he said miserably. "You're an old friend, Della, and it was—it is—a worthy cause, but I have to think of my own position. I did warn him."

"But why, Kevin?" said Robin, picking up her pen.

"Hasn't he shown you my letter?"

"No," said Robin truthfully, pen poised.

"Oh dear," said Sir Kevin weakly. "Well, for one thing...twenty-five thousand pounds unaccounted for is a serious matter."

"What else?" asked Robin, making rapid notes.

"What's that?"

"You said 'for one thing.' What else are you worried about?"

Robin could hear the woman who'd answered the phone talking in the background. Her voice sounded irate.

"Della, I'd rather not go into it all on the phone," said Sir Kevin, sounding embarrassed.

"Well, this is disappointing," said Robin, with what she hoped was a touch of Della's mellifluous grandeur. "I hoped you'd at least tell me why, Kevin."

"Well, there's the Mo Farah business—"

"Mo Farah?" repeated Robin, in unaffected surprise.

"What was that?"

"*Mo—Farah?*"

"You didn't know?" said Sir Kevin. "Oh dear. Oh dear..."

Robin heard footsteps and then the woman came back on the line, first muffled, then clear.

"Let me speak to her—Kevin, let go—look, Della, Kevin's very upset about all this. He suspected you didn't know what's been going on and, well, here we are, he was right. Nobody ever wants to worry you, Della," she said, sounding as though she thought this a mistaken protectiveness, "but the fact of the matter is—no, she's got to know, Kevin—Geraint's been promising people things he can't deliver. Disabled children and their families have been told they're getting visits from David Beckham and Mo Farah and I don't know who else. It's all going to come out, Della, now the Charity Commission's involved, and I'm not having Kevin's name dragged through the mud. He's a conscientious man and he's done his best. He's been urging Geraint to sort out the accounts for months now, and then there's what Elspeth...no, Kevin, I'm *not*, I'm just telling her...well, it could get very nasty, Della. It might yet come to the police as well as the press, and I'm sorry, but I'm thinking of Kevin's health."

"What's Elspeth's story?" said Robin, still writing fast.

Sir Kevin said something plaintive in the background.

"I'm not going into that on the phone," said Lady Rodgers repressively. "You'll have to ask Elspeth."

There was more shuffling and Sir Kevin took the receiver again. He sounded almost tearful.

"Della, you know how much I admire you. I wish it could have been otherwise."

"Yes," said Robin, "well, I'll have to call Elspeth, then."

"What was that?"

"I'll—call—Elspeth."

"Oh dear," said Sir Kevin. "But you know, there might be nothing in it."

Robin wondered whether she dared ask for Elspeth's number, but decided not. Della would surely have it.

"I wish you'd tell me what Elspeth's story is," she said, her pen poised over her notebook.

"I don't like to," said Sir Kevin wheezily. "The damage these kinds of rumors do to a man's reputation—"

Lady Rodgers came back on the line.

"That's all we've got to say. This whole business has been very hard on Kevin, very stressful. I'm sorry, but that's our final word on the matter, Della. Goodbye."

Robin set her mobile down on the table beside her and checked that nobody was looking her way. She picked up her mobile again and scrolled down the list of The Level Playing Field's trustees. One of them was called Dr. Elspeth Curtis-Lacey, but her personal number was not listed on the charity's website and appeared, from a search of directory inquiries, to be unlisted.

Robin phoned Strike. The call went straight to voicemail. She waited a couple of minutes and tried again, with the same result. After her third failed attempt to reach him, she texted:

Got some stuff on GW. Call me.

The dank shadow that had lain on the terrace when she had first arrived was moving incrementally backwards. The warm sun slid over Robin's table as she eked out her coffee, waiting for Strike to call back. At last her phone vibrated to show that she had a text: heart leaping, she picked it up, but it was only Matthew.

Fancy a drink with Tom and Sarah tonight after work?

Robin contemplated the message with a mixture of lassitude and dread. Tomorrow was the charity cricket match about which Matthew was so excited. After-work drinks with Tom and Sarah would doubtless mean plenty of banter on the subject. She could already picture the four of them at the bar: Sarah, with her perennially flirtatious attitude towards Matthew, Tom fending off Matthew's jokes about his lousy bowling with increasingly clumsy, angry ripostes, and Robin, as was increasingly the case these days, pretending to be amused and interested, because that was the cost of not being harangued by Matthew for seeming bored, or feeling superior to her company or (as happened during their worst rows) wishing that she were drinking with Strike instead. At least, she consoled herself, it couldn't be a late or drunken night, because Matthew, who took all sporting fixtures seriously, would want a decent sleep before the match. So she texted back:

OK, where?

and continued to wait for Strike to ring her.

After forty minutes, Robin began to wonder whether Strike was somewhere he couldn't call, which left open the question of whether she ought to inform Chiswell of what she had just found out. Would Strike consider that a liberty, or would he be more annoyed if she failed to give Chiswell his bargaining chip, given the time pressure?

After debating the matter inwardly for a while longer, she called Izzy, the upper half of whose office window she could see from where she sat.

"Izzy, it's me. Venetia. I'm calling because I can't say this in front of Raphael. I think I've got some information on Winn for your father—"

"Oh, fabulous!" said Izzy loudly, and Robin heard Raphael in the background saying, "Is that Venetia? Where is she?" and the clicking of computer keys.

"Checking the diary, Venetia...He'll be at DCMS until eleven, but then he's in meetings all afternoon. Do you want me to call him? He could probably see you straight away if you hurry."

So Robin replaced her mobile, notebook and pen in her bag, gulped down the last of her coffee and hurried off to the Department for Culture, Media and Sport.

Chiswell was pacing up and down his office, speaking on the phone, when Robin arrived outside the glass partition. He beckoned her inside, pointed to a low leather sofa at a short distance from his desk, and continued to talk to somebody who appeared to have displeased him.

"It was a gift," he was saying distinctly into the receiver, "from my eldest son. Twenty-four-karat gold, inscribed *Nec Aspera Terrent.* Bloody hell's bells!" he roared suddenly, and Robin saw the heads of the bright young people just outside the office turning towards Chiswell. "It's Latin! Pass me to somebody who can speak *English! Jasper Chiswell.* I'm the *Minister for Culture.* I've given you the date...no, you can't...I haven't got all bloody day—"

Robin gathered, from the side of the conversation that she could hear, that Chiswell had lost a money clip of sentimental value, which he thought he might have left at a hotel where he and Kinvara had spent the night of her birthday. As far as she could hear, the hotel staff had not only failed to find the clip, they were showing insufficient deference to Chiswell for having deigned to stay at one of their hotels.

"I want somebody to call me back. Bloody useless," muttered Chiswell, hanging up and peering at Robin as though he had forgotten who she was. Still breathing heavily, he dropped down on the sofa opposite her. "I've got ten minutes, so this had better be worthwhile."

"I've got some information on Mr. Winn," said Robin, taking out her notebook. Without waiting for his response, she gave him a succinct summary of the information she had gleaned from Sir Kevin.

"...and," she concluded, barely a minute and a half later, "there may be further impropriety on Mr. Winn's part, but that information is allegedly held by Dr. Elspeth Curtis-Lacey, whose number is unlisted. It shouldn't take us long to find a way of contacting her, but I thought," Robin said apprehensively, because Chiswell's tiny eyes were screwed up in what might have been displeasure, "I should bring you this immediately."

For a few seconds he simply stared at her, his expression petulant as ever, but then he slapped his thigh in what was clearly pleasure.

"Well, well, well," he said. "He told me you were his best. Yerse. Said so."

Pulling a crumpled handkerchief out of his pocket he wiped his face, which had become sweaty during his phone call with the unfortunate hotel.

"Well, well, well," he said again, "this is turning out to be a rather good day. One by one, they trip themselves up ... so Winn's a thief and a liar and maybe more?"

"Well," said Robin cautiously, "he can't account for the twenty-five thousand pounds, and he's certainly promised things he can't deliver..."

"Dr. Elspeth Curtis-Lacey," said Chiswell, following his own train of thought. "Name's familiar..."

"She used to be a Liberal Democrat councilor from Northumberland," said Robin, who had just read this on the Level Playing Field's website.

"Child abuse," said Chiswell suddenly. "That's how I know her. Child abuse. She was on some committee. She's a bloody crank about it, sees it everywhere. Course, it's full of cranks, the Lib Dems. It's where they congregate. Stuffed to the gunnels with oddballs."

He stood up, leaving a smattering of dandruff behind him on the black leather, and paced up and down, frowning.

"All this charity stuff's bound to come out sooner or later," he said, echoing Sir Kevin's wife. "But, my Christ, they wouldn't want it to break right now, not with Della up to her neck in the Paralympics. Winn's going to panic when he finds out I know. Yerse. I think this might well neutralize him...in the short term, anyway. If he's been fiddling with children, though—"

"There's no proof of that," said Robin.

"—that would stymie him for good," said Chiswell, pacing again. "Well, well, well. This explains why Winn wanted to bring his trustees to our Paralympian reception next Thursday, doesn't it? He's clearly trying to keep them sweet, stop anyone else deserting the sinking ship. Prince Harry's going to be there. These charity people love a royal. Only reason half of them are in it."

He scratched his thick mop of gray hair, revealing large patches of underarm sweat.

"Here's what we'll do," he said. "We'll add his trustees to the guest list and you can come too. Then you can corner this Curtis-Lacey, find out what she's got. All right? Night of the twelfth?"

"Yes," said Robin, making a note, "Fine."

"In the meantime, I'll let Winn know I know he's had his fingers in the till."

Robin was almost at the door when Chiswell said abruptly:

"You don't want a PA's job, I suppose?"

"Sorry?"

"Take over from Izzy? What does that detective pay you? I could probably match it. I need somebody with brains and a bit of backbone."

"I'm...happy where I am," said Robin.

Chiswell grunted.

"Hmm. Well, perhaps it's better this way. I might well have a bit more work for you, once we've got rid of Winn and Knight. Off you go, then."

He turned his back to her, his hand already on the phone.

Out in the sunshine, Robin took out her mobile again. Strike still hadn't called, but Matthew had texted the name of a pub in Mayfair, conveniently close to Sarah's work. Nevertheless, Robin was now able to contemplate the evening with slightly more cheerfulness than she had felt prior to her meeting with Chiswell. She even started humming Bob Marley as she walked back towards the Houses of Parliament.

He told me you were his best. Yerse. Said so.

26

I am not so entirely alone, even now. There are two of us to bear the solitude together here.

Henrik Ibsen, Rosmersholm

It was four in the morning, the hopeless hour when shivering insomniacs inhabit a world of hollow shadow, and existence seems frail and strange. Strike, who had fallen into a doze, woke abruptly in the hospital chair. For a second, all he felt was his aching body and the hunger that tore at his stomach. Then he saw his nine-year-old nephew, Jack, who lay motionless in the bed beside him, jelly pads over his eyes, a tube running down his throat, lines coming out of neck and wrist. A bag of urine hung from the side of the bed, while three separate drips fed their contents into a body that appeared tiny and vulnerable amid the softly humming machines, in the hushed, cavernous space of the intensive care ward.

He could hear the padding of a nurse's soft shoes somewhere beyond the curtain surrounding Jack's bed. They hadn't wanted Strike to spend the night in the chair, but he had dug in and his celebrity, minor though it was, combined with his disability, had worked in his favor. His crutches stood propped against the bedside cabinet. The ward was overwarm, as hospitals always were. Strike had spent many weeks in a series of iron beds after his leg had been blown off. The smell transported him back to a time of pain and brutal readjustment, when he had been forced to recalibrate his life against a backdrop of endless obstacles, indignities and privations.

The curtain rustled and a nurse entered the cubicle, stolid and practical in her overalls. Seeing that he was awake, she gave Strike a brief, professional smile, then took the clipboard off the end of Jack's bed and went to take readings from the screens monitoring his blood pressure and oxygen levels. When she had finished, she whispered, "Fancy a cup of tea?"

"Is he doing all right?" Strike asked, not bothering to disguise the plea in his voice. "How's everything looking?"

"He's stable. No need to worry. This is what we expect at this stage. Tea?"

"Yeah, that'd be great. Thanks very much."

He realized that his bladder was full once the curtain had closed behind the nurse. Wishing he'd thought to ask her to pass his crutches, Strike hoisted himself up, holding the arm of the chair to steady himself, hopped to the wall and grabbed them, then swung out from behind the curtain and off towards the brightly lit rectangle at the far end of the dark ward.

Having relieved himself at a urinal beneath a blue light that was supposed to thwart junkies' ability to locate veins, he headed into the waiting room close to the ward where, late yesterday afternoon, he had sat waiting for Jack to come out of emergency surgery. The father of one of Jack's school friends, with whom Jack was meant to be staying the night when his appendix burst, had kept him company. The man had been determined not to leave Strike alone until they had "seen the little chap out of the woods," and had talked nervously all the time Jack had been in surgery, saying things like "they bounce at that age," "he's a tough little bugger," "lucky we only live five minutes from school" and, over and over again, "Greg and Lucy'll be going frantic." Strike had said nothing, barely listening, holding himself ready for the worst news, texting Lucy every thirty minutes with an update.

Not yet out of surgery.

No news yet.

At last the surgeon had come to tell them that Jack, who had had to be resuscitated on arrival at hospital, had made it through surgery, that he had had "a nasty case of sepsis" and that he would shortly be arriving in intensive care.

"I'll bring his mates in to see him," said Lucy and Greg's pal excitedly. "Cheer him up—Pokémon cards—"

"He won't be ready for that," said the surgeon repressively. "He'll be under heavy sedation and on a ventilator for at least the next twenty-four hours. Are you the next of kin?"

"No, that's me," croaked Strike, speaking at last, his mouth dry. "I'm his uncle. His parents are in Rome for their wedding anniversary. They're trying to get a flight back right now."

"Ah, I see. Well, he's not quite out of the woods yet, but the surgery was successful. We've cleaned out his abdomen and put a drain in. They'll be bringing him down shortly."

"Told you," said Lucy and Greg's friend, beaming at Strike with tears in his eyes, "told you they bounce!"

"Yeah," said Strike, "I'd better let Lucy know."

But in a calamity of errors, Jack's panic-stricken parents had arrived at the airport, only to realize that Lucy had somehow lost her passport between hotel room and departure gate. In fruitless desperation they retraced their steps, trying to explain their dilemma to everyone from hotel staff, police and the British embassy, with the upshot that they had missed the last flight of the night.

At ten past four in the morning, the waiting room was mercifully deserted. Strike turned on the mobile he had kept switched off while on the ward and saw a dozen missed calls from Robin and one from Lorelei. Ignoring them, he texted Lucy who, he knew, would be awake in the Rome hotel to which, shortly past midnight, her passport had been delivered by the taxi driver who had found it. Lucy had implored Strike to send a picture of Jack when he got out of surgery. Strike had pretended that the picture wouldn't load. After the stress of the day, Lucy didn't need to see her son ventilated, his eyes covered in pads, his body swamped by the baggy hospital gown.

All looking good, he typed. **Still sedated but nurse confident.**

He pressed send and waited. As he had expected, she responded within two minutes.

You must be exhausted. Have they given you a bed at the hospital?

No, I'm sitting next to him, Strike responded. **I'll stay here until you get back. Try and get some sleep and don't worry x.**

Strike switched off his mobile, dragged himself back onto his one foot, reorganized his crutches and returned to the ward.

The tea was waiting for him, as pale and milky as anything Denise had made, but after emptying two sachets of sugar into it, he drank it in a couple of gulps, eyes moving between Jack and the machines both supporting and monitoring him. He had never before examined the boy so closely. Indeed, he had never had much to do with him, in spite of the pictures he drew for Strike, which Lucy passed on.

"He hero-worships you," Lucy had told Strike several times. "He wants to be a soldier."

But Strike avoided family get-togethers, partly because he disliked Jack's father, Greg, and partly because Lucy's desire to cajole her brother into some more conventional mode of existence was enervating even without the presence of her sons, the eldest of whom Strike found especially like his father. Strike had no desire to have children and while he was prepared to concede that some of them were likable—was prepared to admit, in fact, that he had conceived a certain detached fondness for Jack, on the back of Lucy's tales of his ambition to join the Red Caps—he had steadfastly resisted birthday parties and Christmas get-togethers at which he might have forged a closer connection.

But now, as dawn crept through the thin curtains blocking Jack's bed from the rest of the ward, Strike saw for the first time the boy's resemblance to his grandmother, Strike's own mother, Leda. He had the same very dark hair, pale skin and finely drawn mouth. He would, in fact, have made a beautiful girl, but Leda's son knew what puberty was about to do to the boy's jaw and neck...if he lived.

Course he's going to bloody live. The nurse said—

He's in intensive fucking care. They don't put you in here for hiccups.

He's tough. Wants to join the military. He'll be OK.

He'd fucking better be. I never even sent him a text to say thank you for his pictures.

It took Strike a while to drop back into an uneasy doze.

He was woken by early morning sunshine penetrating his eyelids. Squinting against the light, he heard footsteps squeaking on the floor. Next came a loud rattle as the curtain was pulled back, opening Jack's bed to the ward again and revealing more motionless figures, lying in beds all around them. A new nurse stood beaming at him, younger, with a long dark ponytail.

"Hi!" she said brightly, taking Jack's clipboard. "It's not often we get anyone famous in here! I know all about you, I read everything about how you caught that serial—"

"This is my nephew, Jack," he said coldly. The idea of discussing the Shacklewell Ripper now was repugnant to him. The nurse's smile faltered.

"Would you mind waiting outside the curtain? We need to take bloods, change his drips and his catheter."

Strike dragged himself back onto his crutches and made his way laboriously out of the ward again, trying not to focus on any of the other inert figures wired to their own buzzing machines.

The canteen was already half-full when he got there. Unshaven and heavy-eyed, he had slid his tray all the way to the till and paid before he realized he could not carry it and manage his crutches. A young girl clearing tables spotted his predicament and came to help.

"Cheers," said Strike gruffly, when she had placed the tray on a table beside a window.

"No probs," said the girl. "Leave it there after, I'll get it."

The small kindness made Strike feel disproportionately emotional. Ignoring the fry-up he had just bought, he took out his phone and texted Lucy again.

All fine, nurse changing his drip, will be back with him shortly. X

As he had half-expected, his phone rang as soon as he had cut into his fried egg.

"We've got a flight," Lucy told him without preamble, "but it's not until eleven."

"No problem," he told her. "I'm not going anywhere."

"Is he awake yet?"

"No, still sedated."

"He'll be so chuffed to see you, if he wakes up before—before—"

She burst into tears. Strike could hear her still trying to talk through her sobs.

"...just want to get home...want to see him..."

For the first time in Strike's life, he was glad to hear Greg, who now took the phone from his wife.

"We're bloody grateful, Corm. This is our first weekend away together in five years, can you believe it?"

"Sod's law."

"Yeah. He said his belly was sore, but I thought he was at it. Thought he didn't want us to go away. I feel a right bastard now, I can tell you."

"Don't worry," said Strike, and again, "I'm going nowhere."

After a few more exchanges and a tearful farewell from Lucy, Strike was left to his full English. He ate methodically and without pleasure amid the clatter and jangle of the canteen, surrounded by other miserable and anxious people tucking into fatty, sugar-laden food.

As he was finishing the last of his bacon, a text from Robin arrived.

I've been trying to call with an update on Winn. Let me know when it's convenient to talk.

The Chiswell case seemed a remote thing to Strike just now, but as he read her text he suddenly had a simultaneous craving for nicotine and to hear Robin's voice. Abandoning his tray with thanks to the kind girl who had helped him to his table, he set off again on his crutches.

A cluster of smokers stood around the entrance to the hospital, hunch-shouldered like hyenas in the clean morning air. Strike lit up, inhaled deeply, and called Robin back.

"Hi," he said, when she answered. "Sorry I haven't been in touch, I've been at a hospital—"

"What's happened? Are you OK?"

"Yeah, I'm fine. It's my nephew, Jack. His appendix burst yesterday and he—he's got—"

To Strike's mortification, his voice cracked. As he fought to conquer himself, he wondered how long it had been since he had cried. Perhaps not since the tears of pain and rage he had shed in the hospital in Germany to which he had been airlifted away from the patch of bloody ground where the IED had ripped off his leg.

"Fuck," he muttered at last, the only syllable he seemed able to manage.

"Cormoran, what's happened?"

"He's—they've got him in intensive care," said Strike, his face crumpled up in the effort to hold himself together, to speak normally. "His mum—Lucy and Greg are stuck in Rome, so they asked me—"

"Who's with you? Is Lorelei there?"

"Christ, no."

Lorelei saying "I love you" seemed weeks in the past, though it was only two nights ago.

"What are the doctors saying?"

"They think he'll be OK, but, you know, he's—he's in intensive care. Shit," croaked Strike, wiping his eyes, "sorry. It's been a rough night."

"Which hospital is it?"

He told her. Rather abruptly, she said goodbye and rang off. Strike was left to finish his cigarette, intermittently wiping his face and nose on the sleeve of his shirt.

The quiet ward was bright with sun when he returned. He propped his crutches against the wall, sat down again at Jack's bedside with the day-old newspaper he had just pilfered from the waiting room and read an article about how Arsenal might soon be losing Robin van Persie to Manchester United.

An hour later, the surgeon and the anesthetist in charge of the ward arrived at the foot of Jack's bed to inspect him, while Strike listened uneasily to their muttered conversation.

"...haven't managed to get his oxygen levels below fifty percent...persistent pyrexia...urine outputs have tailed off in the last four hours..."

"...another chest X-ray, check there's nothing going on in the lungs..."

Frustrated, Strike waited for somebody to throw him digestible information. At last the surgeon turned to speak to him.

"We'll be keeping him sedated just now. He's not ready to come off the oxygen and we need to get his fluid balance right."

"What does that mean? Is he worse?"

"No, it often goes like this. He had a very nasty infection. We had to wash out the peritoneum pretty thoroughly. I'd just like to X-ray the chest as a precaution, make sure we haven't punctured anything resuscitating him. I'll pop in to see him again later."

They walked away to a heavily bandaged teenager covered in even more tubes and lines than Jack, leaving Strike anxious and destabilized in their wake. Through the hours of the night Strike had come to see the machines as essentially friendly, assisting his nephew to recovery. Now they seemed implacable judges holding up numbers indicating that Jack was failing.

"Fuck," Strike muttered again, shifting the chair nearer to the bed. "Jack...your mum and dad..." He could feel a traitorous prickle behind the eyelids. Two nurses were walking past. "...shit..."

With an almighty effort he controlled himself and cleared his throat.

"...sorry, Jack, your mum wouldn't like me swearing in your ear...it's Uncle Cormoran here, by the way, if you didn't...anyway, Mum and Dad are on their way back, OK? And I'll be with you until they—"

He stopped mid-sentence. Robin was framed in the distant doorway of the ward. He watched her asking directions from a ward sister, and then she came walking towards him, wearing jeans and a T-shirt, her eyes their usual blue-gray and her hair loose, and holding two polystyrene cups.

Seeing Strike's unguarded expression of happiness and gratitude, Robin felt amply repaid for the bruising argument with Matthew, the two changes of bus and the taxi it had taken to get here. Then the slight prone figure beside Strike came into view.

"Oh no," she said softly, coming to a halt at the foot of the bed.

"Robin, you didn't have to—"

"I know I didn't," said Robin. She pulled a chair up beside Strike's. "But I wouldn't want to have to deal with this alone. Be careful, it's hot," she added, passing him a tea.

He took the cup from her, set it down on the bedside cabinet, then reached out and gripped her hand painfully tightly. He had released her before she could squeeze back. Then both sat staring at Jack for a few seconds, until Robin, her fingers throbbing, asked:

"What's the latest?"

"He still needs the oxygen and he's not peeing enough," said Strike. "I don't know what that means. I'd rather have a score out of ten or—I don't fucking know. Oh, and they want to X-ray his chest in case they punctured his lungs putting that tube in."

"When was the operation?"

"Yesterday afternoon. He collapsed doing cross-country at school. Some friend of Greg and Lucy's who lives right by the school came with him in the ambulance and I met them here."

Neither spoke for a while, their eyes on Jack.

Then Strike said, "I've been a bloody terrible uncle. I don't know any of their birthdays. I couldn't have told you how old he was. The dad of his mate's who brought him in knew more than me. Jack wants to be a soldier, Luce says he talks about me and he draws me pictures and I never even bloody thank him."

"Well," said Robin, pretending not to see that Strike was dabbing roughly at his eyes with his sleeve, "you're here for him right now when he needs you and you've got plenty of time to make it up to him."

"Yeah," said Strike, blinking rapidly. "You know what I'll do if he—? I'll take him to the Imperial War Museum. Day trip."

"Good idea," said Robin kindly.

"Have you ever been?"

"No," said Robin.

"Good museum."

Two nurses, one male, one the woman whom Strike had earlier snubbed, now approached.

"We need to X-ray him," said the girl, addressing Robin rather than Strike. "Would you mind waiting outside the ward?"

"How long will you be?" asked Strike.

"Half an hour. Forty minutes-ish."

So Robin fetched Strike's crutches and they went to the canteen.

"This is really good of you, Robin," Strike said over two more pallid teas and some ginger biscuits, "but if you've got things to do—"

"I'll stay until Greg and Lucy come," said Robin. "It'll be awful for them, being so far away. Matt's twenty-seven and his dad was still worried sick when Matt was so ill in the Maldives."

"Was he?"

"Yeah, you know, when he—oh, of course. I never told you, did I?"

"Told me what?"

"He got a nasty infection on our honeymoon. Scratched himself on some coral. They were talking about airlifting him off to hospital at one point, but it was OK. Wasn't as bad as they first thought."

As she said it, she remembered pushing open the wooden door still hot from the daylong sun, her throat constricted with fear as she prepared to tell Matthew she wanted an annulment, little knowing what she was about to face.

"You know, Matt's mum died not that long ago, so Geoffrey was really scared about Matt... but it was all OK," Robin repeated, taking a sip of her tepid tea, her eyes on the woman behind the counter, who was ladling baked beans onto a skinny teenager's plate.

Strike watched her. He had sensed omissions in her story. *Blame sea-borne bacteria.*

"Must've been scary," he said.

"Well, it wasn't fun," said Robin, examining her short, clean fingernails, then checking her watch. "If you want a cigarette we should go now, he'll be back soon."

One of the smokers they joined outside was wearing pajamas. He had brought his drip with him, and held it tightly like a shepherd's crook to keep himself steady. Strike lit up and exhaled towards a clear blue sky.

"I haven't asked about your anniversary weekend."

"I'm sorry I couldn't work," said Robin quickly. "It had been booked and—"

"That's not why I was asking."

She hesitated.

"It wasn't great, to be honest."

"Ah, well. Sometimes when there's pressure to have a good time—"

"Yes, exactly," said Robin.

After another short pause she asked:

"Lorelei's working today, I suppose?"

"Probably," said Strike. "What is this, Saturday? Yeah, I suppose so."

They stood in silence while Strike's cigarette shrank, millimeter by millimeter, watching visitors and arriving ambulances. There was no awkwardness between them, but the air seemed charged, somehow, with things wondered and unspoken. Finally Strike pressed out the stub of his cigarette in a large open ashtray that most smokers had ignored and checked his phone.

"They boarded twenty minutes ago," he said, reading Lucy's last text. "They should be here by three."

"What happened to your mobile?" asked Robin, looking at the heavily sellotaped screen.

"Fell on it," said Strike. "I'll get a new one when Chiswell pays us."

They passed the X-ray machine being rolled out of the ward as they walked back inside.

"Chest looks fine!" said the radiographer pushing it.

They sat by Jack's side talking quietly for another hour, until Robin went to buy more tea and chocolate bars from nearby vending machines, which they consumed in the waiting room while Robin filled Strike in about everything she had discovered about Winn's charity.

"You've outdone yourself," said Strike, halfway down his second Mars bar. "That was excellent work, Robin."

"You don't mind that I told Chiswell?"

"No, you had to. We're up against it time-wise with Mitch Patterson sniffing round. Has this Curtis-Lacey woman accepted the invitation to the reception?"

"I'll find out on Monday. What about Barclay? How's he getting on with Jimmy Knight?"

"Still nothing we can use," Strike sighed, running a hand over the stubble that was rapidly becoming a beard, "but I'm hopeful. He's good, Barclay. He's like you. Got an instinct for this stuff."

A family shuffled into the waiting room, the father sniffing and the mother sobbing. The son, who looked barely older than six, stared at Strike's missing leg as though it was merely one more horrible detail in the nightmarish world he had suddenly entered. Strike and Robin glanced at each other and left, Robin carrying Strike's tea as he swung along on his crutches.

Once settled beside Jack again, Strike asked, "How did Chiswell react when you told him everything you'd got on Winn?"

"He was delighted. As a matter of fact, he offered me a job."

"I'm always surprised that doesn't happen more often," said Strike, unperturbed.

Just then, the anesthetist and surgeon converged at the foot of Jack's bed again.

"Well, things are looking up," said the anesthetist. "His X-ray's clear and his temperature's coming down. That's the thing with children," he said, smiling at Robin. "They travel fast in both directions. We're going to see how he manages with a little less oxygen, but I think we're getting on top of things."

"Oh, thank God," said Robin.

"He's going to live?" said Strike.

"Oh yes, I think so," said the surgeon, with a touch of patronage. "We know what we're doing in here, you know."

"Gotta let Lucy know," muttered Strike, trying and failing to get up, feeling weaker at good news than he'd felt at bad. Robin fetched his crutches and helped him into a standing position. As she watched him swinging towards the waiting room, she sat back down, exhaled loudly and put her face briefly into her hands.

"Always worst for the mothers," said the anesthetist kindly.

She didn't bother to correct him.

Strike was away for twenty minutes. When he returned, he said:

"They've just landed. I've warned her how he looks, so they're prepared. They should be here in about an hour."

"Great," said Robin.

"You can head off, Robin. I didn't mean to balls up your Saturday."

"Oh," said Robin, feeling oddly deflated. "OK."

She stood up, took her jacket off the back of the chair and collected her bag.

"If you're sure?"

"Yeah, yeah, I'll probably try and get a kip in now we know he's going to be all right. I'll walk you out."

"There's no need—"

"I want to. I can have another smoke."

But when they reached the exit, Strike walked on with her, away from the huddled smokers, past the ambulances and the car park that seemed to stretch for miles, roofs glimmering like the backs of marine creatures, surfacing through a dusty haze.

"How did you get here?" he asked, once they were away from the crowds, beside a patch of lawn surrounded by stocks whose scent mingled with the smell of hot tarmac.

"Bus, then cab."

"Let me give you the cab fare—"

"Don't be ridiculous. Seriously, no."

"Well…thanks, Robin. It made all the difference."

She smiled up at him.

"'S'what friends are for."

Awkwardly, leaning on his crutches, he bent towards her. The hug was brief and she broke away first, afraid that he was going to overbalance. The kiss that he had meant to plant on her cheek landed on her mouth as she turned her face towards him.

"Sorry," he muttered.

"Don't be silly," she said again, blushing.

"Well, I'd better get back."

"Yes, of course."

He turned away.

"Let me know how he is," she called after him, and he raised one hand in acknowledgment.

Robin walked away without looking back. She could still feel the shape of his mouth on hers, her skin tingling where his stubble had scratched her, but she did not rub the sensation away.

Strike had forgotten that he had meant to have another cigarette. Whether because he was now confident that he would be able to take his nephew to the Imperial War Museum, or for some other reason, his exhaustion was now stippled with a crazy light-heartedness, as though he had just taken a shot of spirits. The dirt and heat of a London afternoon, with the smell of stocks in the air, seemed suddenly full of beauty.

It was a glorious thing, to be given hope, when all had seemed lost.

27

They cling to their dead a long time at Rosmersholm.

Henrik Ibsen, *Rosmersholm*

By the time Robin found her way back across London to the unfamiliar cricket ground, it was five in the afternoon and Matthew's
charity match was over. She found him back in his street clothes in
the bar, fuming and barely speaking to her. Matthew's side had lost.
The other team was crowing.

Facing an evening of being ignored by her husband, and having
no friends among his colleagues, Robin decided against going on to
the restaurant with the two teams and their partners, and made her
way home alone.

The following morning, she found Matthew fully dressed on the
sofa, snoring drunkenly. They argued when he woke up, a row that
lasted hours and resolved nothing. Matthew wanted to know why it
was Robin's job to hurry off and hold Strike's hand, given that he
had a girlfriend. Robin maintained that you were a lousy person if
you left a friend alone to cope with a possibly dying child.

The row escalated, attaining levels of spite that had never yet been
reached in a year of marital bickering. Robin lost her temper, and
asked whether she was not owed time off for good behavior, after a
decade spent watching Matthew strut around various sports fields.
He was genuinely stung.

"Well, if you don't enjoy it, you should have said!"

"Never occurred to you I might not, did it? Because I'm supposed to see all your victories as mine, aren't I, Matt? Whereas *my* achievements—"

"Sorry, remind me what they are again?" Matthew said, a low blow he had never thrown at her before. "Or are we counting *hi*s achievements as yours?"

Three days passed, and they had not forgiven each other. Robin had slept in the spare room every night since their row, rising early each morning so she could leave the house before Matthew was out of the shower. She felt a constant ache behind the eyes, an unhappiness which was easier to ignore while at work, but which settled back over her like a patch of low pressure once she turned her footsteps homewards each night. Matthew's silent anger pressed against the walls of their house, which, while twice the size of any space they had shared before, seemed darker and more cramped.

He was her husband. She had promised to try. Tired, angry, guilty and miserable, Robin felt as though she were waiting for something definitive to happen, something that would release them both with honor, without more filthy rows, with reasonableness. Over and again, her thoughts returned to the wedding day, when she had discovered that Matthew had deleted Strike's messages. With her whole heart, she regretted not leaving then, before he could scratch himself on coral, before she could be trapped, as she now saw it, by cowardice disguised as compassion.

As Robin approached the House of Commons on Wednesday morning, not yet focused on the day ahead, but pondering her marital problems, a large man in an overcoat peeled away from the railings where he had been mingling with the first tourists of the day and walked towards her. He was tall and broad-shouldered, with thick silver hair and a squashed, deeply pitted and lined face. Robin did not realize that she was his object until he halted right in front of her, large feet placed firmly at right angles, blocking her onward progress.

"Venetia? Can I have a quick word, love?"

She took a panicked half-step backwards, looking up into the hard, flat face, peppered with wide pores. He had to be press. Did he recognize her? The hazel contact lenses were a little more discernible at close quarters, even through her plain-lensed glasses.

"Just started working for Jasper Chiswell, haven't you, love? I was wondering how that came about. How much is he paying you? Known him long?"

"No comment," said Robin, trying to sidestep him. He moved with her. Fighting the rising feeling of panic, Robin said firmly, "Get out of my way. I need to get to work."

A couple of tall Scandinavian youths with rucksacks were watching the encounter with clear concern.

"I'm only giving you a chance to tell your side of the story, darling," said her accoster, quietly. "Think about it. Might be your only chance."

He moved aside. Robin knocked into her would-be rescuers as she pushed past them. *Shit, shit, shit . . . who was he?*

Once safely past the security scanner, she moved aside in the echoing stone hall where workers were striding past her and called Strike. He didn't pick up.

"Call me, please, urgently," she muttered to his voicemail.

Rather than heading for Izzy's office, or the wide echoing space of Portcullis House, she took refuge in one of the smaller tearooms, which without its counter and till would have resembled a dons' common room, paneled in dark wood and carpeted in the ubiquitous forest green. A heavy oak screen divided the room, MPs sitting at the far end, away from the lesser employees. She bought a cup of coffee, took a table beside the window, hung her coat on the back of her chair and waited for Strike to call her. The quiet, sedate space did little to calm Robin's nerves.

It was nearly three-quarters of an hour before Strike phoned.

"Sorry, missed you, I was on the Tube," he said, panting. "Then Chiswell called. He's only just rung off. We've got trouble."

"Oh God, what now?" said Robin, setting her coffee down as her stomach contracted in panic.

"The *Sun* think you're the story."

And at once, Robin knew whom she had just met outside the Houses of Parliament: Mitch Patterson, the private detective the newspaper had hired.

"They've been digging for anything new in Chiswell's life, and there you are, good-looking new woman in his office, of course they're going to check you out. Chiswell's first marriage split up because he had an affair at work. Thing is, it isn't going to take them long to find out you aren't really his goddaughter. *Ouch*—fuck—"

"What's the matter?"

"First day back on two legs and Dodgy Doc's finally decided to go and meet a girl on the sly. Chelsea Physic Garden, Tube to Sloane Square and a bugger of a walk. Anyway," he panted, "what's *your* bad news?"

"It's more of the same," said Robin. "Mitch Patterson just accosted me outside Parliament."

"Shit. D'you think he recognized you?"

"He didn't seem to, but I don't know. I should clear out, shouldn't I?" said Robin, contemplating the cream ceiling, which was stuccoed in a pattern of overlapping circles. "We could put someone else in here. Andy, or Barclay?"

"Not yet," said Strike. "If you walk out the moment you meet Mitch Patterson, it'll look like you're the story for sure. Anyway, Chiswell wants you to go to this reception tomorrow night, to try and get the rest of the dirt on Winn from that other trustee—what was her name, Elspeth? *Bollocks*—sorry—having trouble here, it's a bloody woodchip path. Dodgy's taking the girl for a walk into the undergrowth. She looks about seventeen."

"Don't you need your phone, to take photographs?"

"I'm wearing those glasses with the inbuilt camera...oh, here we go," he added quietly. "Dodgy's copping a feel in some bushes."

Robin waited. She could hear a very faint clicking.

"And here come some genuine horticulturalists," Strike muttered. "That's driven them back out into the open...

"Listen," he continued, "meet me at the office tomorrow after work, before you go to that reception. We'll take stock of everything we've got so far and make a decision on what to do next. Try your best to get the second listening device back, but don't replace it, just in case we need to take you out of there."

"All right," said Robin, full of foreboding, "but it's going to be difficult. I'm sure Aamir is suspic—Cormoran, I'm going to have to go."

Izzy and Raphael had just walked into the tearoom. Raphael had his arm around his half-sister, who, Robin saw at once, was distressed to the point of tears. He saw Robin, who hastily hung up on Strike, made a grimace indicating that Izzy was in a bad way, then muttered something to his sister, who nodded and headed towards Robin's table, leaving Raphael to buy drinks.

"Izzy!" said Robin, pulling out a chair for her. "Are you all right?"

As Izzy sat down, tears leaked out of her eyes. Robin passed her a paper napkin.

"Thanks, Venetia," she said huskily. "I'm so sorry. Making a fuss. Silly."

She took a deep shuddering breath and sat upright, with the posture of a girl who had been told for years to sit up straight and pull herself together.

"Just silly," she repeated, tears welling again.

"Dad's just been a total bastard to her," said Raphael, arriving with a tray.

"Don't say that, Raff," hiccuped Izzy, another tear trickling down her nose. "I know he didn't mean it. He was upset when I arrived and then I made it worse. Did you know he's lost Freddie's gold money clip?"

"No," said Raphael, without much interest.

"He thinks he left it at some hotel on Kinvara's birthday. They'd just called him back when I arrived. They haven't got it. You know what Papa's like about Freddie, even now."

An odd look passed over Raphael's face, as though he had been struck by an unpleasant thought.

"And then," said Izzy, shakily, "I'd misdated a letter and he flew off the handle..."

Izzy twisted the damp napkin between her hands.

"Five years," she burst out. "Five years I've worked for him, and I can count on one hand how many times he's thanked me for anything. When I told him I was thinking of leaving he said 'not till after the Olympics,'" her voice quavered, "'because I don't want to have to break in someone new before then.'"

Raphael swore under his breath.

"Oh, but he's not that bad, really," said Izzy quickly, in an almost comical *volte-face*. Robin knew that she had just remembered her hope that Raphael would take over her job. "I'm just upset, making it sound worse than it—"

Her mobile rang. She read the caller's name and let out a moan.

"Not TTS, not now, I can't. Raff, you speak to her."

She held out the mobile to him, but Raphael recoiled as though asked to hold a tarantula.

"Please, Raff—*please*..."

With extreme reluctance, Raphael took the phone.

"Hi, Kinvara. Raff here, Izzy's out of the office. No... Venetia's not here...no...I'm at the office, obviously, I just picked up Izzy's phone...He's just gone to the Olympic Park. No...no, I'm not...I don't know where Venetia is, all I know is, she's not here...yes... yes...OK...bye, then—" He raised his eyebrows. "Hung up."

He pushed the phone back across the table to Izzy, who asked:

"Why's she so interested in where Venetia is?"

"Three guesses," said Raphael, amused. Catching his drift, Robin looked out of the window, feeling the color rising in her face. She wondered whether Mitch Patterson had called Kinvara, and planted this idea in her head.

"Oh, come orf it," said Izzy. "She thinks Papa's...? Venetia's young enough to be his daughter!"

"In case you haven't noticed, so's his wife," said Raphael, "and you know what she's like. The further down the tubes their marriage goes, the more jealous she gets. Dad's not picking up his phone to her, so she's drawing paranoid conclusions."

"Papa doesn't pick up because she drives him crazy," said Izzy, her resentment towards her father suddenly submerged by dislike for her stepmother. "For the last two years she's refused to budge from home or leave her bloody horses. Suddenly the Olympics are nearly here and London's full of celebrities and all she wants to do is come up to town, dressed up to the nines and play the minister's wife."

She took another deep breath, blotted her face again, then stood up.

"I'd better get back, we're so busy. Thanks, Raff," she said, cuffing him lightly on the shoulder.

She walked away. Raphael watched her go, then turned back to Robin.

"Izzy was the only one who bothered to visit me when I was inside, you know."

"Yes," said Robin. "She said."

"And when I used to have to go to bloody Chiswell House as a kid, she was the only one who'd talk to me. I was the little bastard who'd broken up their family, so they all hated my guts, but Izzy used to let me help her groom her pony."

He swilled the coffee in his cup, looking sullen.

"I suppose you were in love with swashbuckling Freddie, were you, like all the other girls? He hated me. Used to call me 'Raphaela' and pretend Dad had told the family I was another girl."

"How horrible," said Robin, and Raphael's scowl turned into a reluctant smile.

"You're so sweet."

He seemed to be debating with himself whether or not to say something. Suddenly he asked:

"Ever meet Jack o'Kent when you were visiting?"

"Who?"

"Old boy who used to work for Dad. Lived in the grounds of Chiswell House. Scared the hell out of me when I was a kid. He had a kind of sunken face and mad eyes and he used to loom out of nowhere when I was in the gardens. He never said a word except to swear at me if I got in his way."

"I . . . vaguely remember someone like that," lied Robin.

"Jack o'Kent was Dad's nickname for him. Who *was* Jack o'Kent? Didn't he have something to do with the devil? Anyway, I used to have literal nightmares about the old boy. One time he caught me trying to get into a barn and gave me hell. He put his face up close to mine and said words to the effect of, I wouldn't like what I saw in there, or it was dangerous for little boys, or . . . I can't remember exactly. I was only a kid."

"That sounds scary," Robin agreed, her interest awakened now. "What was he doing in there, did you ever find out?"

"Probably just storing farm machinery," said Raphael, "but he made it sound like he was conducting Satanic rituals.

"He was a good carpenter, mind you. He made Freddie's coffin. An English oak had come down...Dad wanted Freddie buried in wood from the estate..."

Again, he seemed to be wondering whether he ought to say what was on his mind. He scrutinized her through his dark lashes and finally said:

"Does Dad seem...well, normal to you at the moment?"

"What d'you mean?"

"You don't think he's acting a bit strangely? Why's he bawling Izzy out for nothing?"

"Pressure of work?" suggested Robin.

"Yeah...maybe," said Raphael. Then, frowning, he said, "He phoned me the other night, which is strange in itself, because he can't normally stand the sight of me. Just to talk, he said, and that's never happened before. Mind you, he'd had a few too many, I could tell as soon as he spoke.

"Anyway, he started rambling on about Jack o'Kent. I couldn't make out what he was going on about. He mentioned Freddie dying, and Kinvara's baby dying and then," Raphael leaned in closer. Robin felt his knees touch hers under the table, "remember that phone call we got, my first day here? That bloody creepy message about people pissing themselves as they die?"

"Yes," said Robin.

"He said, 'It's all punishment. That was Jack o'Kent calling. He's coming for me.'"

Robin stared at him.

"But whoever it was on the phone," said Raphael, "it can't have been Jack o'Kent. He died years ago."

Robin said nothing. She had suddenly remembered Matthew's delirium, the depth of that subtropical night, when he had thought she was his dead mother. Raphael's knees seemed to press harder into hers. She moved her chair back slightly.

"I was awake half the night wondering whether he's cracking up. We can't afford to have Dad go bonkers as well, can we? We've already got Kinvara hallucinating horse slashers and gravediggers—"

"Gravediggers?" repeated Robin sharply.

"Did I say gravediggers?" said Raphael restlessly. "Well, you know what I mean. Men with spades in the woods."

"You think she's imagining them?" asked Robin.

"No idea. Izzy and the rest of them think she is, but then they've treated her like a hysteric ever since she lost that kid. She had to go through labor even though they knew it had died, did you know that? She wasn't right afterwards, but when you're a Chiswell you're supposed to suck that sort of thing up. Put on a hat and go open a fête or something."

He seemed to read Robin's thoughts in her face, because he said:

"Did you expect me to hate her, just because the others do? She's a pain in the arse, and she thinks I'm a total waste of space, but I don't spend my life mentally subtracting everything she spends on her horses from my niece and nephews' inheritance. She's not a gold-digger, whatever Izzy and *Fizzy* think," he said, laying arch emphasis on his other sister's nickname. "They thought my mother was a gold-digger, too. It's the only motivation they understand. I'm not supposed to know they've got cozy Chiswell family nicknames for me and my mother, as well…" His dark skin flushed. "Unlikely as it might seem, Kinvara genuinely fell for Dad, I could tell. She could have done a damn sight better if it was money she was after. He's skint."

Robin, whose definition of "skint" did not comprise owning a large house in Oxfordshire, nine horses, a mews flat in London or the heavy diamond necklace she had seen around Kinvara's neck in photographs, maintained an impassive expression.

"Have you been to Chiswell House lately?"

"Not lately," said Robin.

"It's falling apart. Everything's moth-eaten and miserable."

"The one time I really remember being at Chiswell House, the grown-ups were talking about a little girl who'd disappeared."

"Really?" said Raphael, surprised.

246 • ROBERT GALBRAITH

"Yes, I can't remember her name. I was young myself. Susan? Suki? Something like that."

"Doesn't ring any bells," said Raphael. His knees brushed hers again. "Tell me, does everyone confide their dark family secrets to you after five minutes of knowing you, or is it just me?"

"Tim always says I look sympathetic," said Robin. "Perhaps I should forget politics and go into counseling."

"Yeah, maybe you should," he said, looking into her eyes. "That isn't a very strong prescription. Why bother with glasses? Why not just wear contacts?"

"Oh, I . . . find these more comfortable," said Robin, pushing the glasses back up her nose and gathering her things. "You know, I really ought to get going."

Raphael leaned back in his chair with a rueful smile.

"Message received . . . he's a lucky man, your Tim. Tell him so, from me."

Robin gave a half-laugh and stood up, catching herself on the corner of the table as she did so. Self-conscious and slightly flustered, she walked out of the tearoom.

Making her way back to Izzy's office, she mulled over the Minister for Culture's behavior. Explosions of bad temper and paranoid ramblings were not, she thought, surprising in a man currently at the mercy of two blackmailers, but Chiswell's suggestion that a dead man had telephoned him was undeniably odd. He had not struck her on either of their two encounters as the kind of man who would believe in either ghosts or divine retribution, but then, Robin reflected, drink brought out strange things in people . . . and suddenly, she remembered Matthew's snarling face as he had shouted across the sitting room on Sunday.

She was almost level with Winn's office door when she registered the fact that it was standing ajar again. Robin peered into the room beyond. It seemed to be empty. She knocked twice. Nobody answered.

It took her less than five seconds to reach the power socket beneath Geraint's desk. Unplugging the fan, she prized the recording device loose and had just opened her handbag when Aamir's voice said:

"What the hell do you think you're doing?"

Robin gasped, attempted to stand up, hit her head hard on the desk and yelped in pain. Aamir had just unfolded himself from an armchair angled away from the door, was taking headphones from his ears. He seemed to have been taking a few minutes for himself, while listening to an iPod.

"I knocked!" Robin said, her eyes watering as she rubbed the top of her head. The recording device was still in her hand and she hid it behind her back. "I didn't think anyone was in here!"

"What," he repeated, advancing on her, "are you *doing?*"

Before she could answer, the door was pushed fully open. Geraint walked in.

There was no lipless grin this morning, no air of bustling self-importance, no ribald comment at finding Robin on the floor of his office. Winn seemed somehow smaller than usual, with purplish shadows beneath the lens-shrunken eyes. In perplexity he turned from Robin to Aamir, and as Aamir began to tell him that Robin had just walked in uninvited, the latter managed to stuff the recording device into her handbag.

"I'm so sorry," she said, getting to her feet, sweating profusely. Panic lapped at the edges of her thought, but then an idea bobbed up like a life raft. "I really am. I was going to leave a note. I was only going to borrow it."

As the two men frowned at her, she gestured to the unplugged fan.

"Ours is broken. Our room's like an oven. I didn't think you'd mind," she said, appealing to Geraint. "I was just going to borrow it for thirty minutes." She smiled piteously. "Honestly, I felt faint earlier."

She plucked the front of her shirt away from her skin, which was indeed clammy. His gaze fell to her chest and the usual lecherous grin resurfaced.

"Though I shouldn't say so, overheating rather suits you," said Winn, with the ghost of a smirk, and Robin forced a giggle.

"Well, well, we can spare it for thirty minutes, can't we?" he said, turning to Aamir. The latter said nothing, but stood ramrod straight, staring at Robin with undisguised suspicion. Geraint lifted the fan carefully off the desk and passed it to Robin. As she turned to go, he patted her lightly on the lower back.

"Enjoy."

"Oh, I will," she said, her flesh crawling. "Thank you so much, Mr. Winn."

28

Do I take it to heart, to find myself so hampered and thwarted in my life's work?

Henrik Ibsen, *Rosmersholm*

The long hike to and around Chelsea Physic Garden the previous day had not benefited Strike's hamstring injury. As his stomach was playing up from a constant diet of Ibuprofen, he had eschewed painkillers for the past twenty-four hours, with the result that he was in what his doctors liked to describe as "some discomfort" as he sat with his one and a half legs up on the office sofa on Thursday afternoon, his prosthesis leaning against the wall nearby while he reviewed the Chiswell file.

Silhouetted like a headless watchman against the window of his inner office was Strike's best suit, plus a shirt and tie, which hung from the curtain rail, shoes and clean socks sitting below the limp trouser legs. He was going out to dinner with Lorelei tonight and had organized himself so that he need not climb the stairs to his attic flat again before bed.

Lorelei had been typically understanding about his lack of communication during Jack's hospitalization, saying with only the slightest edge to her voice that it must have been a horrible thing to go through on his own. Strike had too much sense to tell her that Robin had been there, too. Lorelei had then requested, sweetly and without rancor, dinner, "to talk a few things through."

They had been dating for just over ten months and she had just nursed him through five days of incapacity. Strike felt that it was neither fair, nor decent, to ask her to say what she had to say over the phone. Like the hanging suit, the prospect of having to find an answer to the inevitable question "where do you see this relationship going?" loomed ominously on the periphery of Strike's consciousness.

Dominating his thoughts, however, was what he saw as the perilous state of the Chiswell case, for which he had so far seen not a penny in payment, but which was costing him a significant outlay in salaries and expenses. Robin might have succeeded in neutralizing the immediate threat of Geraint Winn, but after a promising start Barclay had nothing whatsoever to use against Chiswell's first blackmailer, and Strike foresaw disastrous consequences should the *Sun* newspaper find its way to Jimmy Knight. Balked of the mysterious photographs at the Foreign Office that Winn had promised him, and notwithstanding Chiswell's assertion that Jimmy would not want the story in the press, Strike thought an angry and frustrated Jimmy was overwhelmingly likely to try and profit from a chance that seemed to be slipping through his fingers. His history of litigation told its own story: Jimmy was a man prone to cutting off his own nose to spite his face.

To compound Strike's bad mood, after several straight days and nights hanging out with Jimmy and his mates, Barclay had told Strike that unless he went home soon, his wife would be initiating divorce proceedings. Strike, who owed Barclay expenses, had told him to come into the office for a check, after which he could take a couple of days off. To his extreme annoyance, the normally reliable Hutchins had then caviled at having to take over the tailing of Jimmy Knight at short notice, rather than hanging around Harley Street, where Dodgy Doc was once again consulting patients.

"What's the problem?" Strike had asked roughly, his stump throbbing. Much as he liked Hutchins, he had not forgotten that the ex-policeman had recently taken time off for a family holiday and to drive his wife to hospital when she broke her wrist. "I'm asking you to switch targets, that's all. I can't follow Knight, he knows me."

"Yeah, all right, I'll do it."

"Decent of you," Strike had said, angrily. "Thanks."

The sound of Robin and Barclay climbing the metal stairs to the office at half past five made a welcome distraction from Strike's increasingly dark mood.

"Hi," said Robin, walking into the office with a holdall over her shoulder. Answering Strike's questioning look, she explained, "Outfit for the Paralympic reception. I'll change in the loo, I won't have time to go home."

Barclay followed Robin into the room and closed the door.

"We met downstairs," he told Strike cheerfully. "Firs' time."

"Sam was just telling me how much dope he's had to smoke to keep in with Jimmy," said Robin, laughing.

"I've no been inhalin'," said Barclay, deadpan. "That'd be remiss, on a job."

The fact that the pair of them seemed to have hit it off was perversely annoying to Strike, who was now making heavy weather of hoisting himself off the fake leather cushions, which made their usual farting noises.

"It's the sofa," he snapped at Barclay, who had looked around, grinning. "I'll get your money."

"Stay there, I'll do it," Robin said, setting down her holdall and reaching for the checkbook in the lower drawer of the desk, which she handed to Strike, with a pen. "Want some tea, Cormoran? Sam?"

"Aye, go on, then," said Barclay.

"You're both bloody cheerful," said Strike sourly, writing Barclay his check, "considering we're about to lose the job that's keeping us all in employment. Unless either of you have got information I don't know about, of course."

"Only excitin' thing tae happen in Knightville this week was Flick havin' a big bust up wi' one o' her flatmates," said Barclay. "Lassie called Laura. She reckoned Jimmy had stolen a credit card out o' her handbag."

"Had he?" asked Strike sharply.

"I'd say it was more likely to be Flick herself. Told ye she was boastin' about helpin' herself to cash from her work, didn't I?"

"Yeah, you did."

"It all kicked off in the pub. The girl, Laura, was scunnered. She and Flick got intae a row about who was more middle class."

In spite of the pain he was in, and his grumpy mood, Strike grinned.

"Aye, it got nasty. Ponies and foreign holidays dragged in. Then this Laura said she reckoned Jimmy nicked her new credit card off her, months back. Jimmy got aggressive, said that was slander—"

"Shame he's banned, or he could've sued her," said Strike, ripping out the check.

"—and Laura ran off intae the night, bawlin'. She's left the flat."

"Got a surname for her?"

"I'll try and find out."

"What's Flick's background, Barclay?" asked Strike as Barclay put his check into his wallet.

"Well, she told me she dropped out o' uni," said Barclay. "Failed her first-year exams and gave up."

"Some of the best people drop out," said Robin, carrying two mugs of tea over. She and Strike had both left their degree courses without a qualification.

"Cheers," said Barclay, accepting a mug from Robin. "Her parents are divorced," he went on, "and she's no speaking tae either of them. They don't like Jimmy. Cannae blame them. If my daughter ever hooks up wi' a bawbag like Knight, I'll know what tae do about it. When she's not around, he tells the lads what he gets up to wi' young girls. They all think they're shaggin' a great revolutionary, doin' it for the cause. Flick doesnae know the half o' what he's up tae."

"Any of them underage? His wife suggested he's got form there. That'd be a bargaining chip."

"All over sixteen so far's I know."

"Pity," said Strike. He caught Robin's eye, as she returned to them holding her own tea. "You know what I mean." He turned to Barclay again. "From what I heard on that march, she's not so monogamous herself."

"Aye, one o' her pals made a gag about an Indian waiter."

"A waiter? I heard a student."

"No reason it couldn'ta been both," said Barclay. "I'd say she's a—"

But catching Robin's eye, Barclay decided against saying the word, and instead drank his tea.

"Anything new your end?" Strike asked Robin.

"Yes. I got the second listening device back."

"You're kidding," said Strike, sitting up straighter.

"I've only just finished transcribing it all, there was hours of stuff on there. Most of it's useless, but..."

She set down her tea, unzipped the holdall and took out the recording device.

"...there's one strange bit. Listen to this."

Barclay sat down on the arm of the sofa. Robin straightened up in her desk chair and flicked the switch on the device.

Geraint's lilting accent filled the office.

"...keep them sweet, make sure I introduce Elspeth to Prince Harry," said Geraint. "Right, that's me off, I'll see you tomorrow."

"G'night," said Aamir.

Robin shook her head at Strike and Barclay and mouthed, "Wait."

They heard the door close. After the usual thirty-second silence, there was a click, where the tape had stopped then restarted. A deep, Welsh female voice spoke.

"Are you there, sweetheart?"

Strike raised his eyebrows. Barclay stopped chewing.

"Yes," said Aamir, in his flat London accent.

"Come and give me a kiss," said Della.

Barclay made a small choking noise into his tea. The sound of lips smacking emanated from the bug. Feet shuffled. A chair was moved. There was a faint, rhythmic thudding.

"What's that?" muttered Strike.

"The guide dog's tail wagging," said Robin.

"Let me hold your hand," said Della. "Geraint won't be back, don't worry, I've sent him out to Chiswick. There. Thank you. Now, I needed a little private word with you. The thing is, darling, your neighbors have complained. They say they've been hearing funny noises through the walls."

"Like what?" He sounded apprehensive.

"Well, they thought they *might* be animal," said Della. "A dog whining or whimpering. You haven't—?"

"Of course I haven't," said Aamir. "It must've been the telly. Why would I get a dog? I'm at work all day."

"I thought it would be like you to bring home some poor little stray," she said. "Your soft heart..."

"Well, I haven't," said Aamir. He sounded tense. "You don't have to take my word for it. You can go and check if you want, you've got a key."

"Darling, don't be like that," said Della. "I wouldn't dream of letting myself in without your permission. I don't snoop."

"You're within your rights," he said, and Strike thought he sounded bitter. "It's your house."

"You're upset. I knew you would be. I had to mention it, because if Geraint picks up the phone to them next time—it was the purest good luck the neighbor caught me—"

"I'll make sure and keep the volume down from now on," said Aamir. "OK? I'll be careful."

"You understand, my love, that as far as I'm concerned, you're free to do whatever—"

"Look, I've been thinking," Aamir interrupted. "I really think I should be paying you some rent. What if—"

"We've been over this. Don't be silly, I don't want your money."

"But—"

"Apart from everything else," she said, "you couldn't afford it. A three-bedroomed house, on your own?"

"But—"

"We've been through this. You seemed happy when you first moved in...I thought you liked it—"

"Obviously, I like it. It was very generous of you," he said stiffly.

"Generous...it's not a question of generosity, for heaven's sake...Now, listen: how would you like to come and have a curry? I've got a late vote and I was going to nip over to the Kennington Tandoori. My treat."

"Sorry, I can't," said Aamir. He sounded stressed. "I've got to get home."

"Oh," said Della, with a great deal less warmth. "Oh...that's disappointing. What a pity."

"I'm sorry," he said again. "I said I'd meet a friend. University friend."

"Ah. I see. Well, next time, I'll make sure to call ahead. Find a slot in your diary."

"Della, I—"

"Don't be silly, I'm only teasing. You can walk out with me, at least?"

"Yes. Yes, of course."

There was more scuffling, then the sound of the door opening. Robin turned off the tape.

"They're *shaggin'*?" said Barclay loudly.

"Not necessarily," said Robin. "The kiss might've been on the cheek."

"'Let me hold your hand'?" repeated Barclay. "Since when's that normal office procedure?"

"How old's this Aamir bloke?" asked Strike.

"I'd guess mid-twenties," said Robin.

"And she's, what...?"

"Mid-sixties," said Robin.

"And she's provided him with a house. He's not related to her, is he?"

"There's no family connection as far as I'm aware," said Robin. "But Jasper Chiswell knows something personal about him. He quoted a Latin poem at Aamir when they met in our office."

"You didn't tell me that."

"Sorry," said Robin, remembering that this had happened shortly before she had refused to tail Jimmy on the march. "I forgot. Yes, Chiswell quoted something Latin, then mentioned 'a man of your habits.'"

"What was the poem?"

"I don't know, I never did Latin."

She checked her watch.

"I'd better get changed, I'm supposed to be at DCMS in forty minutes."

"Aye, that's me off as well, Strike," said Barclay.

"Two days, Barclay," Strike said, as the other headed to the door, "then you're back on Knight."

"Nae bother," said Barclay, "I'll be wantin' a break from the wean by then."

"I like him," said Robin, as Barclay's footsteps died away down the metal stairs.

"Yeah," grunted Strike, as he reached for his prosthesis. "He's all right."

He and Lorelei were meeting early, at his request. It was time to begin the onerous process of making himself presentable. Robin retired to the cramped toilet on the landing to change, and Strike, having put his prosthesis back on, withdrew to the inner office.

He had got as far as pulling on his suit trousers when his mobile rang. Half-hoping that it was Lorelei to say that she could not make dinner, he picked up the cracked phone and saw, with an inexplicable sense of foreboding, that it was Hutchins.

"Strike?"

"What's wrong?"

"Strike...I've fucked up."

Hutchins sounded weak.

"What's happened?"

"Knight's with some mates. I followed them into a pub. They're planning something. He's got a placard with Chiswell's face on it—"

"And?" said Strike loudly.

"Strike, I'm sorry...my balance has gone...I've lost them."

"You stupid fucker!" roared Strike, losing his temper completely. "Why didn't you tell me you were ill?"

"I've had a lot of time off lately...knew you were stretched..."

Strike switched Hutchins to speakerphone, laid his mobile onto his desk, took his shirt off the hanger and began to dress as fast as possible.

"Mate, I'm so sorry...I'm having trouble walking..."

"I know the fucking feeling!"

Fuming, Strike stabbed off the call.

"Cormoran?" Robin called through the door. "Everything OK?"

"No, it's fucking not!"

He opened the office door.

In one part of his brain, he registered that Robin was wearing the green dress he had bought her two years ago, as a thank you for helping him catch their first killer. She looked stunning.

"Knight's got a placard with Chiswell's face on it. He's planning something with a bunch of mates. I *knew* it, I fucking *knew* this would happen now Winn's bailed on him . . . I'll bet you anything he's heading for your reception. Shit," said Strike, realizing he didn't have shoes on and doubling back. "And Hutchins has lost them," he shouted over his shoulder. "The stupid tit didn't tell me he's ill."

"Maybe you can get Barclay back?" suggested Robin.

"He'll be on the Tube by now. I'm going to have to fucking do it, aren't I?" said Strike. He dropped back into the sofa and slid his feet into his shoes. "There are going to be press all round that place tonight if Harry's going to be there. All it needs is for a journo to twig what Jimmy's stupid fucking sign means, and Chiswell's out of a job and so're we." He heaved himself back to his feet. "Where is this thing, tonight?"

"Lancaster House," said Robin. "Stable Yard."

"Right," said Strike, heading for the door. "Stand by. You might have to bail me out. There's a good chance I'm going to have to punch him."

29

It became impossible for me to remain an idle spectator any longer.

Henrik Ibsen, *Rosmersholm*

The taxi that Strike had picked up in Charing Cross Road turned into St. James's Street twenty minutes later, while he was still talking to the Minister for Culture on his mobile.

"A placard? What's on it?"

"Your face," said Strike. "That's all I know."

"And he's heading for the reception? Well, this is bloody it, isn't it?" shouted Chiswell, so loudly that Strike winced and removed the phone from his ear. "If the press see this, it's all over! You were supposed to stop something like this bloody happening!"

"And I'm going to try," said Strike, "but in your shoes I'd want to be forewarned. I'd advise—"

"I don't pay you for advice!"

"I'll do whatever I can," promised Strike, but Chiswell had already hung up.

"I'm not going to be able to go any further, mate," said the taxi driver, addressing Strike in the rearview mirror from which dangled a swinging mobile, outlined in tufts of multi-colored cotton and embossed with a golden Ganesh. The end of St. James's Street had been blocked off. A swelling crowd of royal watchers and Olympics fans, many clutching small Union Jacks, was congregating behind portable barriers, waiting for the arrival of Paralympians and Prince Harry.

"OK, I'll get out here," said Strike, fumbling for his wallet.

He was once again facing the crenellated frontage of St. James's Palace, its gilded, diamond-shaped clock gleaming in the early evening sun. Strike limped down the slope again towards the crowd, passing the side street where Pratt's stood, while smartly dressed passersby, workers and customers of galleries and wine merchants moved aside courteously as his uneven gait became progressively more pronounced.

"*Fuck, fuck, fuck,*" he muttered, pain shooting up into his groin every time he put his weight onto the prosthesis as he drew closer to the assembled sports fans and royal watchers. He could see no placards or banners of a political nature, but as he joined the back of the crowd and looked down Cleveland Row, he spotted a press pen and ranks of photographers, which stood waiting for the prince and famous athletes. It was only when a car slid past, containing a glossy-haired brunette Strike vaguely recognized from the television, that he remembered he had not called Lorelei to tell her he would be late to dinner. He hastily dialed her number.

"Hi, Corm."

She sounded apprehensive. He guessed that she thought he was going to cancel.

"Hi," he said, his eyes still darting around for some sign of Jimmy. "I'm really sorry, but something's come up. I might be late."

"Oh, that's fine," she said, and he could tell that she was relieved that he was still intending to come. "Shall I try and change the booking?"

"Yeah—maybe make it eight instead of seven?"

Turning for the third time to scan Pall Mall behind him, Strike spotted Flick's tomato-red hair. Eight CORE members were heading for the crowd, including a stringy, blond-dreadlocked youth and a short, thickset man who resembled a bouncer. Flick was the only woman. All bar Jimmy were holding placards with the broken Olympic rings on them, and slogans such as "Fair Play Is Fair Pay" and "Homes Not Bombs." Jimmy was holding his own placard upside down, the picture on it turned inwards, parallel with his leg.

"Lorelei, I've got to go. Speak later."

Uniformed police were walking around the perimeter fencing

keeping the crowds back, walkie-talkies in hand, eyes roving constantly over the cheerful spectators. They, too, had spotted CORE, who were trying to reach a spot opposite the press pen.

Gritting his teeth, Strike began to forge a path through the pressing crowd, eyes on Jimmy.

30

There is no denying it would have been more fortunate if we had succeeded in checking the stream at an earlier point.

Henrik Ibsen, *Rosmersholm*

Slightly self-conscious in her clinging green dress and heels, Robin attracted a considerable number of appreciative glances from male passersby as she climbed out of her taxi at the entrance to the Department for Culture, Media and Sport. As she reached the doorway, she saw approaching from fifty yards away Izzy, who was wearing bright orange, and Kinvara, in what appeared to be the slinky black dress and heavy diamond necklace that she had worn in the photograph that Robin had seen of her online.

Acutely anxious about what was happening with Jimmy and Strike, Robin nevertheless registered that Kinvara appeared to be upset. Izzy rolled her eyes at Robin as they approached. Kinvara gave Robin a pointed up-and-down look that suggested she found the green dress inappropriate, if not indecent.

"We were supposed," said a booming male voice in Robin's near vicinity, "to be meeting *here*."

Jasper Chiswell had just emerged from the building, carrying three engraved invitations, one of which he held out to Robin.

"Yes, I know that now, Jasper, thank you," said Kinvara, puffing slightly as she approached. "Very sorry for getting it wrong again. Nobody bothered to check I knew what the arrangements were."

Passersby stared at Chiswell, finding him vaguely familiar with his chimney-brush hair. Robin saw a suited man nudge his companion and point. A sleek black Mercedes drew up at the curb. The chauffeur got out; Kinvara walked around the back of the car to sit behind him. Izzy wriggled over into the middle of the back seat, leaving Robin to take the back seat directly behind Chiswell.

The car pulled away from the curb, the atmosphere inside unpleasant. Robin turned her head to watch the after-work drinkers and evening shoppers, wondering whether Strike had found Knight yet, scared of what might happen when he did, and wishing she could spirit the car directly to Lancaster House.

"You haven't invited Raphael, then?" Kinvara shot at the back of her husband's head.

"No," said Chiswell. "He angled for an invitation, but that will be because he's smitten with Venetia."

Robin felt her face flood with color.

"Venetia seems to have quite the fan base," said Kinvara tersely.

"Going to have a little chat with Raphael tomorrow," said Chiswell. "I'm seeing him rather differently these days, I don't mind telling you."

Out of the corner of her eye, Robin saw Kinvara's hands twist around the chain on her ugly evening bag, which sported a horse's head picked out in crystals. A tense silence settled over the car's interior as it purred on through the warm city.

31

. . . the result was, that he got a thrashing . . .
                    Henrik Ibsen, *Rosmersholm*

Adrenaline made it easier for Strike to block out the mounting pain in his leg. He was closing on Jimmy and his companions, who were being thwarted in their desire to show themselves clearly to the press, because the excitable crowd had pressed forwards as the first official cars began to glide past, hoping to spot some celebrities. Late to the party, CORE now found themselves faced by an impenetrable mass.

Mercedes and Bentleys swished past, affording the crowd glimpses of the famous and the not-so-famous. A comedian got a loud cheer as he waved. A few flashes went off.

Clearly deciding that he could not hope for a more prominent spot, Jimmy began to drag his homemade banner out of the tangle of legs around him, preparatory to hoisting it aloft.

A woman ahead of Strike gave a shriek of indignation as he pushed her out of the way. In three strides, Strike had closed his large left hand around Jimmy's right wrist, preventing him from raising the placard above waist height, forcing it back towards the ground. Strike had time to see the recognition in his eyes before Jimmy's fist came hurtling at his throat. A second woman saw the punch coming and screamed.

Strike dodged it and brought his left foot down hard on the placard, splintering the pole, but his amputated leg was not equal to bearing all his weight, especially as Jimmy's second punch connected.

As Strike crumpled, he hit Jimmy in the balls. Knight gave a soft scream of pain, doubled up, hit the falling Strike and both of them toppled over, knocking bystanders sideways, all of whom shouted their indignation. As Strike hit the pavement, one of Jimmy's companions aimed a kick at his head. Strike caught his foot and twisted it. Through the mounting furore, he heard a third woman shriek:

"They're attacking that man!"

Strike was too intent on seizing hold of Jimmy's mangled cardboard banner to care whether he was being cast as victim or aggressor. Tugging on the banner, which like himself was being trampled underfoot, he succeeded in ripping it. One of the pieces attached to the spike heel of a panicking woman trying to get out of the way of the fight, and was carried away.

Fingers closed around his neck from behind. He aimed an elbow at Jimmy's face and his hold loosened, but then somebody kicked Strike in the stomach and another blow hit him on the back of the head. Red spots popped in front of his eyes.

More shouting, a whistle, and the crowd was suddenly thinning around them. Strike could taste blood, but, from what he could see, the splintered and torn remnants of Jimmy's placard had been scattered by the mêlée. Jimmy's hands were again scrabbling at Strike's neck, but then Jimmy was pulled away, swearing fluently at the top of his voice. The winded Strike was seized and dragged to his feet as well. He put up no resistance. He doubted he could have stood of his own accord.

32

. . . and now we can go in to supper. Will you come in, Mr. Kroll?

Henrik Ibsen, *Rosmersholm*

Chiswell's Mercedes turned the corner of St. James's Street onto Pall Mall and set off along Cleveland Row.

"What's going on?" growled Chiswell, as the car slowed, then stopped.

The shouting ahead was not of the excited, enthusiastic kind that royalty or celebrities might expect. Several uniformed officers were converging on the crowd on the left-hand side of the street which was jostling and pushing as it tried to move away from what appeared to be a confrontation between police and protestors. Two disheveled men in jeans and T-shirts emerged from the fray, both held in armlocks by uniformed officers: Jimmy Knight, and a youth with limp blond dreadlocks.

Then Robin bit back a cry of dismay as a hobbling, bloody Strike appeared, also being led along by police. Behind them, an altercation in the crowd had not subsided, but was growing. A barrier swayed.

"Pull up, PULL UP!" bellowed Chiswell at the driver, who had just begun to accelerate again. Chiswell wound down his window. "Door open—Venetia, open your door!—that man!" Chiswell roared at a nearby policeman, who turned, startled, to see the Minister for Culture shouting at him and pointing at Strike. "He's my guest—that man—bloody well let him go!"

Confronted by an official car, a government minister, the steely, patrician voice, the brandishing of a thick embossed invitation, the policeman did as he was told. Most people's attention was focused on the increasingly violent brawl between police and CORE, and the consequent trampling and pushing of the crowd trying to get away from it. A couple of cameramen had broken away from the press pen up ahead, and were running towards the fracas.

"Izzy, move up—get in, GET IN!" Chiswell snarled at Strike through the window.

Robin squeezed backwards, half-sitting in Izzy's lap to accommodate Strike as he clambered into the back seat. The door slammed. The car rolled on.

"Who are you?" squealed the frightened Kinvara, who was now pinned against the opposite door by Izzy. "What's going on?"

"He's a private detective," growled Chiswell. His decision to bring Strike into the car seemed born of panic. Twisting around in his seat to glare at Strike, he said, "How does it help me if you get bloody arrested?"

"They weren't arresting me," said Strike, dabbing his nose with the back of his hand. "They wanted to take a statement. Knight attacked me when I went for his placard. Cheers," he added, as, with difficulty given how tightly compressed they all were, Robin passed him a box of tissues that had been lying on the ledge behind the rear seat. He pressed one to his nose. "I got rid of the placard," Strike added, through the blood-stained tissue, but nobody congratulated him.

"Jasper," said Kinvara, "what's going—?"

"Shut up," snapped Chiswell, without looking at her. "I can't let you out in front of all these people," he told Strike angrily, as though the latter had suggested it. "There are more photographers...You'll have to come in with us. I'll fix it."

The car was now proceeding towards a barrier where police and security were checking ID and invitations.

"Nobody say anything," Chiswell instructed. "*Shut up*," he added pre-emptively to Kinvara, who had opened her mouth.

A Bentley up ahead was admitted and the Mercedes rolled forwards.

In pain, because she was bearing a good proportion of Strike's weight across her left hip and leg, Robin heard screeching from behind the car. Turning, she saw a young woman running after the car, a female police officer chasing her. The girl had wild tomato-red hair, a T-shirt with a logo of broken Olympic rings on it, and she screamed after Chiswell's car:

"He put the fucking horse on them, Chiswell! He put the horse on them, you cheating, thieving bastard, you *murderer*—"

"I have a guest here who didn't get his invitation," Chiswell was shouting through his wound-down window to the armed policeman at the barrier. "Cormoran Strike, the amputee. He's been in the papers. There was a balls-up at my department, his invitation didn't go. The prince," he said, with breathtaking chutzpah, "asked to meet him specifically!"

Strike and Robin were watching what was happening behind the car. Two policemen had seized the struggling Flick and were escorting her away. A few more cameras flashed. Caving under the weight of ministerial pressure, the armed policeman requested ID of Strike. Strike, who always carried a couple of forms of identification, though not necessarily in his own name, passed over his genuine driving license. A queue of stationary cars grew longer behind them. The prince was due in fifteen minutes' time. Finally, the policeman waved them through.

"Shouldn't have done that," said Strike in an undertone to Robin. "Shouldn't have let me in. Bloody lax."

The Mercedes swung around the inner courtyard and arrived, finally, at the foot of a shallow flight of red-carpeted steps, in front of an enormous, honey-colored building that resembled a stately home. Wheelchair ramps had been set either side of the carpet, and a celebrated wheelchair basketball player was already maneuvering his way up one.

Strike pushed open the door, clambered out of the car, then turned and reached back inside to assist Robin. She accepted the offer of help. Her left leg was almost completely numb from where he'd sat on her.

"Nice to see you again, Corm," said Izzy, beaming, as she got out behind Robin.

"Hi, Izzy," said Strike.

Now burdened with Strike whether he wanted him or not,

Chiswell hurried up the steps to explain to one of the liveried men standing outside the front door that Strike must be admitted without his invitation. They heard a recurrence of the word "amputee." All around them, more cars were releasing their smartly dressed passengers.

"What's all this about?" Kinvara said, who had marched around the rear of the Mercedes to address Strike. "What's going on? What does my husband need a private detective for?"

"*Will you be quiet, you stupid, stupid bitch?*"

Stressed and disturbed though Chiswell undoubtedly was, his naked hostility shocked Robin. *He hates her,* she thought. *He genuinely hates her.*

"You two," said the minister, pointing at his wife and daughter, "get inside.

"Give me one good reason I should keep paying you," he added, turning on Strike as still more people spilled past them. "You realize," said Chiswell, and in his necessarily quiet fury, spit flew from his mouth onto Strike's tie, "I've just been called a bloody murderer in front of twenty people, including press?"

"They'll think she's a crank," said Strike.

If the suggestion brought Chiswell any comfort, it didn't show.

"I want to see you tomorrow morning at ten o'clock," he told Strike. "Not at my office. Come to the flat in Ebury Street." He turned away, then, as an afterthought, turned back. "You too," he barked at Robin.

Side by side, they watched him lumbering up the steps.

"We're about to get sacked, aren't we?" whispered Robin.

"I'd say it's odds on," said Strike, who, now that he was on his feet, was in considerable pain.

"Cormoran, what was on the placard?" said Robin.

Strike allowed a woman in peach chiffon to pass, then said quietly:

"Picture of Chiswell hanging from a gallows and, beneath him, a bunch of dead children. One odd thing, though."

"What?"

"All the kids were black."

Still dabbing at his nose, Strike reached inside his pocket for a cigarette, then remembered where he was and let his hand fall back to his side.

"Listen, if that Elspeth woman's in here, you might as well try and find out what else she knows about Winn. It'll help justify our final invoice."

"OK," said Robin. "The back of your head's bleeding, by the way."

Strike dabbed at it ineffectually with the tissues he had pocketed and began to limp up the steps beside Robin.

"We shouldn't be seen together any more tonight," he told her, as they passed over the threshold into a blaze of ochre, scarlet and gold. "There was a café in Ebury Street, not far from Chiswell's house. I'll meet you there at nine o'clock tomorrow, and we can face the firing squad together. Go on, you go ahead."

But as she moved away from him, towards the grand staircase, he called after her:

"Nice dress, by the way."

33

I believe you could bewitch anyone — if you set yourself to do it.
Henrik Ibsen, *Rosmersholm*

The grand hallway of the mansion constituted a vast empty block of space. A red-and-gold-carpeted central staircase led to an upper balcony that split left and right. The walls, which appeared to be of marble, were ochre, dull green and rose. Sundry Paralympians were being shown to a lift on the left of the entrance, but the limping Strike made his way laboriously to the stairs and heaved himself upwards by liberal use of the banister. The sky visible through a huge and ornate skylight, supported by columns, was fading through technicolor variations that intensified the colors of the massive Venetian paintings of classical subjects hanging on every wall.

Doing his best to walk naturally, because he was afraid he might be mistaken for some veteran Paralympian and perhaps asked to expound on past triumphs, Strike followed the crowd up the right staircase, around the balcony and into a small anteroom overlooking the courtyard where the official cars were parked. From here, the guests were ushered left into a long and spacious picture gallery, where the carpet was apple green and decorated with a rosette pattern. Tall windows stood at either end of the room and almost every inch of white wall was covered in paintings.

"Drink, sir?" said a waiter just inside the doorway.

"Is it champagne?" asked Strike.

"English sparkling wine, sir," said the waiter.

Strike helped himself, though without enthusiasm, and continued through the crowd, passing Chiswell and Kinvara, who were listening (or, Strike thought, pretending to listen) to a wheelchair-bound athlete. Kinvara shot Strike a swift, suspicious side glance as he passed, aiming for the far wall where he hoped to find either a chair, or something on which he could conveniently lean. Unfortunately, the gallery walls were so densely packed with pictures that leaning was impossible, nor were there any seats, so Strike came to rest beside an enormous painting by Count d'Orsay of Queen Victoria riding a dapple-gray horse. While he sipped his sparkling wine, he tried discreetly to staunch the blood still leaking from his nose, and wipe the worst of the dirt off his suit trousers.

Waiters were circulating, carrying trays of canapés. Strike managed to grab a couple of miniature crab cakes as they passed, then fell to examining his surroundings, noting another spectacular skylight, this one supported by a number of gilded palm trees.

The room had a peculiar energy. The prince's arrival was imminent and the guests' gaiety came and went in nervous spurts, with increasingly frequent glances at the doors. From his vantage point beside Queen Victoria, Strike spotted a stately figure in a primrose-yellow dress standing almost directly opposite him, close beside an ornate black and gold fireplace. One hand was keeping a gentle hold on the harness of a pale yellow Labrador, who sat panting gently at her feet in the overcrowded room. Strike had not immediately recognized Della, because she was not wearing sunglasses, but prosthetic eyes. Her slightly sunken, opaque, china-blue gaze gave her an odd innocence. Geraint stood a short distance from his wife, gabbling at a thin, mousy woman whose eyes darted around, searching for a rescuer.

A sudden hush fell near the doors through which Strike had entered. Strike saw the top of a ginger head and a flurry of suits. Self-consciousness spread through the packed room like a petrifying breeze. Strike watched the top of the ginger head move away, towards the far right side of the room. Still sipping his English wine and wondering which of the women in the room was the trustee with dirt on Geraint Winn, his attention was suddenly caught by a tall woman nearby with her back to him.

Her long dark hair was twisted up into a messy bun and, unlike every other woman present, her outfit gave no suggestion of party best. The straight black knee-length dress was plain to the point of severity, and though barelegged she wore a pair of spike-heeled, open-toed ankle boots. For a sliver of a second Strike thought he must be mistaken, but then she moved and he knew for sure that it was her. Before he could move away from her vicinity, she turned around and looked straight into his eyes.

Color flooded her face, which as he knew was normally cameo pale. She was heavily pregnant. Her condition had not touched her anywhere but the swollen belly. She was as fine-boned as ever in face and limbs. Less adorned than any other woman in the room, she was easily the most beautiful. For a few seconds they contemplated each other, then she took a few tentative steps forwards, the color ebbing from her cheeks as fast as it had come.

"Corm?"

"Hello, Charlotte."

If she thought of kissing him, his stony face deterred her.

"What on earth are you doing here?"

"Invited," lied Strike. "Celebrity amputee. You?"

She seemed dazed.

"Jago's niece is a Paralympian. She's..."

Charlotte looked around, apparently trying to spot the niece, and took a sip of water. Her hand was shaking. A few drops spilled from the glass. He saw them break like glass beads on her swollen belly.

"...well, she's here somewhere," she said, with a nervous laugh. "She's got cerebral palsy and she's remarkable, actually, an incredible rider. Her father's in Hong Kong, so her mum invited me, instead."

His silence was unnerving her. She rattled on:

"Jago's family like to make me go out and do things, only my sister-in-law's cross because I got the dates mixed up. I thought tonight was dinner at the Shard and this thing was Friday, tomorrow, I mean, so I'm not dressed properly for royalty, but I was late and I didn't have time to change."

She gestured hopelessly at her plain black dress and her spike-heeled boots.

"Jago not here?"

Her gold-flecked green eyes flickered slightly.

"No, he's in the States."

Her focus moved to his upper lip.

"Have you been in a fight?"

"No," he said, dabbing at his nose with the back of his hand again. He straightened up, lowering his weight carefully back onto his prosthesis, ready to walk away. "Well, nice to—"

"Corm, don't go," she said, reaching out. Her fingers did not quite make contact with his sleeve; she let her hand fall back by her side. "Don't, not yet, I—you've done such incredible things. I read about them all in the papers."

The last time they had seen each other he had been bleeding, too, because of the flying ashtray that had caught him in the face as he left her. He remembered the text, "It was yours," sent on the eve of her wedding to Ross, referring to another baby she had claimed to be bearing, which had vanished before he ever saw proof of its existence. He remembered, too, the picture she had sent to his office of herself, minutes after saying "I do" to Jago Ross, beautiful and stricken, like a sacrificial victim.

"Congratulations," he said, keeping his eyes on her face.

"I'm huge because it's twins."

She did not, as he had seen other pregnant women do, touch her belly as she talked about the babies, but looked down as though slightly surprised to see her changed shape. She had never wanted children when they had been together. It was one of the things they had had in common. The baby that she had claimed was his had been an unwelcome surprise to both of them.

In Strike's imagination, Jago Ross's progeny were curled under the black dress like a pair of white whelps, not entirely human, emissaries of their father, who resembled a dissolute arctic fox. He was glad they were there, if such a joyless emotion could be called gladness. All impediments, all deterrents, were welcome, because it now became apparent to him that the gravitational pull Charlotte had so long exerted over him, even after hundreds of fights and scenes and a thousand lies, was not yet spent. As ever, he had the sense that behind the green-and-gold-flecked eyes, she knew exactly what he was thinking.

"They aren't due for ages. I had a scan, it's a boy and a girl. Jago's pleased about the boy. Are you here with anyone?"

"No."

As he said it, he caught a flash of green over Charlotte's shoulder. Robin, who was now talking brightly to the mousy woman in purple brocade who had finally escaped Geraint.

"Pretty," said Charlotte, who had looked to see what had caught his attention. She had always had a preternatural ability to detect the slightest flicker of interest towards other women. "No, wait," she said slowly, "isn't that the girl who works with you? She was in all the papers—what's her name, Rob—?"

"No," said Strike, "that's not her."

He wasn't remotely surprised that Charlotte knew Robin's name, or that she had recognized her, even with the hazel contact lenses. He had known Charlotte would keep tabs on him.

"You've always liked girls with that coloring, haven't you?" said Charlotte with a kind of synthetic gaiety. "That little American you started dating after you pretended we'd broken up in Germany had the same kind of—"

There was a kind of hushed scream in their vicinity.

"Ohmigod, *Charlie!*"

Izzy Chiswell was bearing down upon them, beaming, her pink face clashing with her orange dress. She was, Strike suspected, not on her first glass of wine.

"Hello, Izz," said Charlotte, forcing a smile. Strike could almost feel the effort it cost her to tug herself free of that tangle of ancient grudges and wounds in which their relationship had gradually strangled to death.

Again, he prepared to walk away, but the crowd parted and Prince Harry was suddenly revealed in all his hyper-real familiarity, some ten feet away from where Strike and the two women stood, so that moving away from the area would be done under the scrutiny of half the room. Trapped, Strike startled a passing waiter by reaching out a long arm and snatching another glass of wine from his tray. For a few seconds, both Charlotte and Izzy watched the prince. Then, when it became apparent that he was not about to approach them any time soon, they turned back to each other.

"Showing already!" Izzy said, admiring Charlotte's belly. "Have you had a scan? D'you know what it is?"

"Twins," said Charlotte, without enthusiasm. She indicated Strike, "You remember—?"

"Corm, yah, of course, we brought him here!" said Izzy, beaming and clearly unconscious of any indiscretion.

Charlotte turned from her old schoolfriend to her ex, and Strike could feel her sniffing the air for the reason that Strike and Izzy would have traveled together. She shifted very slightly, apparently allowing Izzy into the conversation, but boxing Strike in so that he couldn't walk away without asking one of them to get out of his way. "Oh, wait, of course. You investigated Freddie's death in action, didn't you?" she said. "I remember you telling me about it. Poor Freddie."

Izzy acknowledged this tribute to her brother with a slight tip of her glass, then peeked back over her shoulder at Prince Harry.

"He gets sexier every passing day, doesn't he?" she whispered.

"Ginger pubes, though, darling," said Charlotte, deadpan.

Against his will, Strike grinned. Izzy snorted with laughter.

"Speaking of which," said Charlotte (she never acknowledged that she had been funny), "isn't that Kinvara Hanratty over there?"

"My ghastly stepmother? Yes," said Izzy. "D'you know her?"

"My sister sold her a horse."

During the sixteen years of Strike's on-off relationship with Charlotte, he had been privy to countless conversations like this. People of Charlotte's class all seemed to know each other. Even if they had never met, they knew siblings or cousins or friends or classmates, or else their parents knew somebody else's parents: all were connected, forming a kind of web that constituted a hostile habitat for outsiders. Rarely did these web-dwellers leave to seek companionship or love among the rest of society. Charlotte had been unique in her circle in choosing somebody as unclassifiable as Strike, whose invisible appeal and low status had, he knew, been subjects of perennial, horrified debate among most of her friends and family.

"Well, I hope it wasn't a horse Amelia liked," Izzy said, "because Kinvara will ruin it. Awful hands and a horrible seat, but she thinks she's Charlotte Dujardin. D'you ride, Cormoran?" Izzy asked.

"No," said Strike.

"He doesn't trust horses," said Charlotte, smiling at him.

But he did not respond. He had no desire to touch upon old jokes or shared memories.

"Kinvara's livid, look at her," said Izzy, with some satisfaction. "Papa's just dropped a heavy hint he's going to try and talk my brother Raff into taking over from me, which is *fabulous*, and what I hoped would happen. Papa used to let Kinvara boss him around about Raff, but he's putting his foot down these days."

"I think I've met Raphael," said Charlotte. "Wasn't he working at Henry Drummond's art gallery a couple of months ago?"

Strike checked at his watch and then back around the room. The prince was moving away from their part of the room and Robin was nowhere to be seen. With any luck, she had followed the trustee who had dirt on Winn into the bathroom and was eliciting confidences over the sink.

"Oh Lord," said Izzy. "Look out. Geraint Bloody—hello, Geraint!"

Geraint's object, it soon became clear, was Charlotte.

"Hello, hello," he said, peering at her through heavily smudged glasses, his lipless smile a leer. "You've just been pointed out to me by your niece. What an extraordinary young woman she is, quite extraordinary. Our charity's involved in supporting the equestrian team. Geraint Winn," he said, holding out a hand, "The Level Playing Field."

"Oh," said Charlotte. "Hello."

Strike had watched her repel lecherous men for years. Having acknowledged his presence, she stared coldly at Geraint, as though quite puzzled to know why he was still in her vicinity.

Strike's mobile vibrated in his pocket. Reaching for it, he saw an unknown number. This was his excuse to leave.

"Need to get going, sorry. 'Scuse me, Izzy."

"Oh, that's a shame," Izzy said, pouting. "I wanted to ask you all about the Shacklewell Ripper!"

Strike saw Geraint's eyes widen. Inwardly cursing her, he said, "Night. Bye," he added to Charlotte.

Limping away as fast as he could manage, he accepted the call, but by the time he had raised it to his ear, the caller had gone.

"Corm."

Somebody lightly touched his arm. He turned. Charlotte had followed him.

"I'm leaving, too."

"What about your niece?"

"She's met Harry, she'll be thrilled. She doesn't actually like me that much. None of them do. What happened to your mobile?"

"I fell on it."

He walked on, but, long-legged as she was, she caught up with him.

"I don't think I'm going your way, Charlotte."

"Well, unless you're tunneling out, we have to walk two hundred yards together."

He limped on without answering. To his left, he caught another flash of green. As they reached the grand staircase in the hall, Charlotte reached out and lightly grasped his arm, wobbly in the heels that were so unsuitable for a pregnant woman. He resisted the urge to shake her loose.

His mobile rang again. The same unknown number had appeared on the screen. Charlotte drew up beside him, watching his face as he answered it.

The moment the mobile touched his ear he heard a desperate, haunting scream.

"They're going to kill me, Mr. Strike, help me, help me, please help me . . ."

34

But who could really foresee what was coming? I am sure I could not.

Henrik Ibsen, *Rosmersholm*

The hazy, clear-skied promise of another summer's day hadn't yet translated itself into actual warmth when Robin arrived next morning at the café closest to Chiswell's house. She could have chosen one of the circular tables outside on the pavement, but instead she huddled down in a corner of the café where she was to meet Strike, hands clasped around her latte for comfort, her reflection in the espresso machine pale and heavy-eyed.

Somehow, she had known that Strike would not be here when she arrived. Her mood was simultaneously depressed and nervy. She would rather not have been alone with her thoughts, but here she was, with only the hiss of the coffeemaker for company, chilly in spite of the jacket she had grabbed on the way out of the house and full of anxiety about the imminent confrontation with Chiswell, who might quibble his bill, after the catastrophe of Strike's fight with Jimmy Knight.

But that wasn't all that was worrying Robin. She had woken that morning from a confused dream in which the dark, spike-booted figure of Charlotte Ross figured. Robin had recognized Charlotte immediately when she spotted her at the reception. She had tried not to watch the once-engaged couple as they'd talked, angry with herself for being so sharply interested in what was passing between them, yet, even as she had moved from group to group, shamelessly insinuating herself into conversations in the hope of finding the elusive Elspeth Curtis-Lacey, her eyes had sought out Strike and Charlotte, and when they left the reception together she had experienced a nasty sensation in her stomach, akin to the drop of an elevator.

She had arrived home unable to think of anything else, which had made her feel guilty when Matthew emerged from the kitchen, eating a sandwich. She had the impression that he had not been home long. He subjected the green dress to an up-and-down look very like the one Kinvara had given her. She made to walk past him upstairs, but he had moved to block her.

"Robin, come on. Please. Let's talk."

So they had gone into the sitting room and talked. Tired of conflict, she had apologized for hurting Matthew's feelings by missing the cricket match, and for forgetting her wedding ring on their anniversary weekend. Matthew in turn had expressed regret for the things he had said during Sunday's row, and especially for the remark about her lack of achievements.

Robin felt as though they were moving chess pieces on a board that was vibrating in the preliminary tremors of an earthquake. *It's too late. You know, surely, that none of this matters anymore?*

But when the talk was finished, Matthew said, "So we're OK?"

"Yes," she replied. "We're fine."

He had stood up, held out a hand and helped her up from her chair. She had forced a smile and then he had kissed her, hard, on the mouth, and begun to tug at the green dress. She heard the fabric around the zip tear and when she began to protest, he clamped his mouth on hers again.

She knew that she could stop him, she knew that he was waiting for her to stop him, that she was being tested in an ugly, underhand way, that he would deny what he was really doing, that he would claim to be the victim. She hated him for doing it this way, and part of her wanted to be the kind of woman who could have disengaged from her own revulsion and from her own reluctant flesh, but she had fought too long and too hard to regain possession of her own body to barter it in this way.

"No," she said, pushing him away. "I don't want to."

He released her at once, as she had known he would, with an expression compounded of anger and triumph. Suddenly, she knew that she had not fooled him when they had had sex on their anniversary weekend, and paradoxically that made her feel tender towards him.

"I'm sorry," she said. "I'm tired."

"Yeah," said Matthew. "So am I."

And he had walked out of the room, leaving Robin with a chill down her back where the green dress had torn.

Where the hell was Strike? It was five past nine and she wanted company. She also wanted to know what had happened after he left the reception with Charlotte. Anything would be preferable to sitting here, thinking about Matthew.

As though the thought had summoned him, her phone rang.

"Sorry," he said, before she could speak. "Suspicious package at bloody Green Park. I've been stuck on the Tube for twenty minutes and I've only just got reception. I'll be there as quick as I can, but you might have to start without me."

"Oh, God," said Robin, closing her tired eyes.

"Sorry," Strike repeated, "I'm on my way. Got something to tell you, actually. Funny thing happened last night—oh, hang on, we're moving. See you shortly."

He hung up, leaving Robin with the prospect of having to deal alone with the first effusions of Jasper Chiswell's anger, and still grappling formless feelings of dread and misery that swirled around a dark, graceful woman who was sixteen years' worth of knowledge and memories ahead of her when it came to Cormoran Strike, which, Robin told herself, *shouldn't matter, for God's sake, haven't you got enough problems without worrying about Strike's love life, it's nothing whatsoever to do with you* . . .

She felt a sudden guilty prickle around her lips, where Strike's missed kiss had landed outside the hospital. As though she could wash it away, she downed the dregs of her coffee, got up and left the café for the broad, straight street, which comprised two symmetrical lines of identical nineteenth-century houses.

She walked briskly, not because she was in any hurry to bear the brunt of Chiswell's anger and disappointment, but because activity helped dispel her uncomfortable thoughts.

Arriving outside Chiswell's house precisely on time, she lingered for a few hopeful seconds beside the glossy black front door, just in case Strike were to appear at the last moment. He didn't. Robin therefore steadied herself, walked up the three clean white steps from the pavement and knocked on the front door, which was on the latch and opened a few inches. A man's muffled voice shouted something that might have been "come in."

Robin passed into a small, dingy hall dominated by vertiginous stairs. The olive-green wallpaper was drab and peeling in places. Leaving the front door as she had found it, she called out:

"Minister?"

He didn't answer. Robin knocked gently on the door to the right, and opened it.

Time froze. The scene seemed to fold in upon her, crashing through her retinas into a mind unprepared for it, and shock kept her standing in the doorway, her hand still on the handle and her mouth slightly open, trying to comprehend what she was seeing.

A man was sitting in a Queen Anne chair, his legs splayed, his arms dangling, and he seemed to have a shiny gray turnip for a head, in which a carved mouth gaped, but no eyes.

Then Robin's struggling comprehension grasped the fact that it was not a turnip, but a human head shrink-wrapped in a clear plastic bag, into which a tube ran from a large canister. The man looked as though he had suffocated. His left foot lay sideways on the rug, revealing a small hole in the sole, his thick fingers dangled, almost touching the carpet, and there was a stain at his groin where his bladder had emptied.

And next she understood that it was Chiswell himself who sat in the chair, and that his thick mass of gray hair was pressed flat against his face in the vacuum created by the bag, and that the gaping mouth had sucked the plastic into itself, which was why it gaped so darkly.

35

...the White Horse! In broad daylight!

Henrik Ibsen, *Rosmersholm*

Somewhere in the distance, outside the house, a man shouted. He sounded like a workman, and in some part of her brain Robin knew that that was who she had heard when she was expecting to hear "come in." Nobody had invited her into the house. The door had simply been left ajar.

Now, when it might have been expected, she didn't panic. There was no threat here, however horrifying the sight of that awful dummy, with the turnip head and the tube, this poor lifeless figure could not hurt her. Knowing that she must check that life was extinct, Robin approached Chiswell and gently touched his shoulder. It was easier, not being able to see his eyes, because of the coarse hair that obscured them like a horse's forelock. The flesh felt hard beneath his striped shirt and cooler than she had expected.

But then she imagined the gaping mouth speaking, and took several quick steps backwards, until her foot landed with a crunch on something hard on the carpet and she slipped. She had cracked a pale blue plastic tube of pills lying on the carpet. She recognized them as the sort of homeopathic tablets sold in her local chemist.

Taking out her mobile, she called 999 and asked for the police. After explaining that she had found a body and giving the address, she was told that someone would be with her shortly.

Trying not to focus on Chiswell, she took in the frayed curtains, which were of an indeterminate dun color, trimmed with sad little bobbles, the antiquated TV in its faux wood cladding, the patch of darker wallpaper over the mantelpiece where a painting had once hung, and the silver-framed photographs. But the shrink-wrapped head, the rubber piping and the cold glint of the canister seemed to turn all of this everyday normality into pasteboard. The nightmare alone was real.

So Robin turned her mobile onto its camera function and began to take photographs. Putting a lens between herself and the scene mitigated the horror. Slowly and methodically, she documented the scene.

A glass sat on the coffee table in front of the body, with a few millimeters of what looked like orange juice in it. Scattered books and papers lay beside it. There was a piece of thick cream writing paper headed with a red Tudor rose, like a drop of blood, and the printed address of the house in which Robin stood. Somebody had written in a rounded, girlish hand.

> *Tonight was the final straw. How stupid do you think I am, putting that girl in your office right under my nose? I hope you realize how ridiculous you look, how much people are laughing at you, chasing a girl who's younger than your daughters.*
>
> *I've had enough. Make a fool of yourself, I don't care anymore, it's over.*
>
> *I've gone back to Woolstone. Once I've made arrangements for the horses, I'll clear out for good. Your bloody horrible children will be happy, but will you, Jasper? I doubt it, but it's too late.*
>
> *K*

As Robin bent to take a picture of the note, she heard the front door snap shut, and with a gasp, she spun around. Strike was standing on the threshold, large, unshaven, still in the suit he had worn to the reception. He was staring at the figure in the chair.

"The police are on their way," said Robin. "I just called them."

Strike moved carefully into the room.

"Holy shit."

He spotted the cracked tube of pills on the floor, stepped over them, and scrutinized the tubing and the plastic-covered face.

"Raff said he was behaving strangely," said Robin, "but I don't think he ever dreamed..."

Strike said nothing. He was still examining the body.

"Was that there yesterday evening?"

"What?"

"That," said Strike, pointing.

There was a semi-circular mark on the back of Chiswell's hand, dark red against the coarse, pallid skin.

"I can't remember," said Robin.

The full shock of what had happened was starting to hit her and she was finding it hard to arrange her thoughts, which floated, unmoored and disconnected, through her head: Chiswell barking through the car window to persuade the police to let Strike into last night's reception, Chiswell calling Kinvara a stupid bitch, Chiswell demanding that they meet him here this morning. It was unreasonable to expect her to remember the backs of his hands.

"Hmm," said Strike. He noticed the mobile in Robin's hand. "Have you taken pictures of everything?"

She nodded.

"All of this?" he asked, waving a hand over the table. "That?" he added, pointing at the cracked pills on the carpet.

"Yes. That was my fault. I trod on them."

"How did you get in?"

"The door was open. I thought he'd left it on the latch for us," said Robin. "A workman shouted in the street and I thought it was Chiswell saying 'come in.' I was expecting—"

"Stay here," said Strike.

He left the room. She heard him climbing the stairs and then his heavy footsteps on the ceiling above, but she knew that there was nobody there. She could feel the house's essential lifelessness, its flimsy cardboard unreality, and, sure enough, Strike returned less than five minutes later, shaking his head.

"Nobody."

He walked past her through a door that led off the sitting room and, hearing his footsteps hit tile, Robin knew that it was the kitchen.

"Completely empty," Strike said, re-emerging.

"What happened last night?" Robin asked. "You said something funny happened."

She wanted to discuss a subject other than the awful form that dominated the room in its grotesque lifelessness.

"Billy called me. He said people were trying to kill him—chasing him. He claimed to be in a phone box in Trafalgar Square. I went to try and find him, but he wasn't there."

"Oh," said Robin.

So he hadn't been with Charlotte. Even in this extremity, Robin registered the fact, and was glad.

"The hell?" said Strike quietly, looking past her into a corner of the room.

A buckled sword was leaning against the wall in a dark corner. It looked as though it had been forced or stood on and deliberately bent. Strike walked carefully around the body to examine it, but then they heard the police car pulling up outside the house and he straightened up.

"We'll tell them everything, obviously," said Strike.

"Yes," said Robin.

"Except the surveillance devices. Shit—they'll find them in your office—"

"They won't," said Robin. "I took them home yesterday, in case we decided I needed to clear out because of the *Sun*."

Before Strike could express admiration for this clear-eyed foresight, somebody rapped hard on the front door.

"Well, it's been nice while it's lasted, hasn't it?" Strike said, with a grim smile, as he moved towards the hall. "Being out of the papers?"

PART TWO

36

What has happened can be hushed up—or at any rate can be explained away...

Henrik Ibsen, *Rosmersholm*

The Chiswell case maintained its singular character even when their client was no more.

As the usual cumbersome procedures and formalities enveloped the corpse, Strike and Robin were escorted from Ebury Street to Scotland Yard, where they were separately interviewed. Strike knew that a tornado of speculation must be whirling through the newsrooms of London at the death of a government minister, and sure enough, by the time they emerged from Scotland Yard six hours later, the colorful details of Chiswell's private life were being broadcast across TV and radio, while opening the internet browsers on their phones revealed brief news items from news sites, as a tangle of baroque theories spread across blogs and social media, in which a multitude of cartoonish Chiswells died at the hand of myriad nebulous foes. As he rode in a taxi back to Denmark Street, Strike read how Chiswell the corrupt capitalist had been murdered by the Russian mafia after failing to pay back interest on some seedy, illegal transaction, while Chiswell the defender of solid English values had surely been dispatched by vengeful Islamists after his attempts to resist the rise of sharia law.

Strike returned to his attic flat only to collect his belongings, and decamped to the house of his old friends Nick and Ilsa, respectively a gastroenterologist and a lawyer. Robin, who at Strike's insistence had taken a taxi directly home to Albury Street, was given a peremptory hug by Matthew, whose tissue-thin pretense of sympathy was worse, Robin felt, than outright fury.

When he heard that Robin had been summoned back to Scotland Yard for further interrogation the next day, Matthew's self-control crumbled.

"Anyone could have seen this coming!"

"Funny, it seemed to take most people by surprise," Robin said. She had just ignored her mother's fourth call of the morning.

"I don't mean Chiswell killing himself—"

"—it's pronounced 'Chizzle'—"

"—I mean you getting yourself into trouble for sneaking around the Houses of Parliament!"

"Don't worry, Matt. I'll make sure the police know you were against it. Wouldn't want your promotion prospects compromised."

But she wasn't sure that her second interviewer was a policeman. The softly spoken man in a dark gray suit didn't reveal whom he worked for. Robin found this gentleman far more intimidating than yesterday's police, even though they had, at times, been forceful to the point of aggression. Robin told her new interviewer everything she had seen and heard in the Commons, omitting only the strange conversation between Della Winn and Aamir Mallik, which had been captured on the second listening device. As the interaction had taken place behind a closed door after normal working hours, she could only have heard it by using surveillance equipment. Robin assuaged her conscience by telling herself that this conversation could not possibly have anything to do with Chiswell's death, but squirming feelings of guilt and terror pursued her as she left the building for the second time. So consumed was she by what she hoped was paranoia by this brush with the security services, that she called Strike from a payphone near the Tube, instead of using her mobile.

"I've just had another interview. I'm pretty sure it was MI5."

"Bound to happen," said Strike, and she took solace from his matter-of-fact tone. "They've got to check you out, make sure you are who you claim to be. Isn't there anywhere you can go, other than home? I can't believe the press aren't onto us yet, but it must be imminent."

"I could go back to Masham, I suppose," Robin said, "but they're bound to try there if they want to find me. That's where they came after the Ripper stuff."

Unlike Strike, she had no friends of her own into whose anonymous homes she felt she could vanish. All her friends were Matthew's, too, and she had no doubt that, like her husband, they would be scared of harboring anybody who was of interest to the security services. At a loss as to what to do, she went back to Albury Street.

Yet the press didn't come for her, even though the newspapers were hardly holding back on the subject of Chiswell. The *Mail* had already run a double-page spread on the various tribulations and scandals that had plagued Jasper Chiswell's life. *"Once mentioned as a possible prime minister," "sexy Italian Ornella Serafin, with whom he had the affair that broke up his first marriage," "voluptuous Kinvara Hanratty, who was thirty years his junior," "Lieutenant Freddie Chiswell, eldest son, died in the Iraq war his father had staunchly supported," "youngest child Raphael, whose drug-filled joy ride ended in the death of a young mother."*

Broadsheets contained tributes from friends and colleagues: *"a fine mind, a supremely able minister, one of Thatcher's bright young men," "but for a somewhat tumultuous private life, there were no heights he might not have reached," "the public persona was irascible, even abrasive, but the Jasper Chiswell I knew at Harrow was a witty and intelligent boy..."*

Five days of lurid press coverage passed, yet still, the press's mysterious restraint on the subject of Strike and Robin's involvement held, and still, nobody had printed a word about blackmail.

On the Friday morning following the discovery of Chiswell's body, Strike was sitting quietly at Nick and Ilsa's kitchen table, sunlight pouring through the window behind him.

His host and hostess were at work. Nick and Ilsa, who had been trying for some years to have a baby, had recently adopted a pair of kittens whom Nick had insisted on calling Ossie and Ricky, after the two Spurs players he had revered in his teens. The cats, who had only recently consented to sit on the knees of their adoptive parents, had not appreciated the arrival of the large and unfamiliar Strike. Finding themselves alone with him, they had sought refuge on top of a kitchen wall cabinet. He was currently conscious of the scrutiny of four pale green eyes, which followed his every movement from on high.

Not that he was currently moving a great deal. Indeed, for much of the past half an hour he had been almost motionless, as he pored over the photographs that Robin had taken in Ebury Street, which he had printed out in Nick's study for convenience. Finally, causing Ricky to jump up in a flurry of upended fur, Strike isolated nine of the photographs and put the rest in a pile. While Strike scrutinized his selected images, Ricky settled back down, the tip of a black tail swaying as he awaited the detective's next move.

The first photograph that Strike had selected showed a close-up of the small, semi-circular puncture mark on Chiswell's left hand.

The second and third pictures showed different angles of the glass that had sat on the coffee table in front of Chiswell. A powdery residue was visible on the sides, above an inch of orange juice.

The fourth, fifth and sixth photographs Strike laid together side by side. Each showed a slightly different angle of the body, with slices of the surrounding room caught within its frame. Once again, Strike studied the ghostly outline of the buckled sword in the corner, the dark patch over the mantelpiece where a picture had previously hung and, beneath this, barely noticeable against the dark wallpaper, a pair of brass hooks spaced nearly a yard apart.

The seventh and eighth photographs, when placed side by side, showed the entirety of the coffee table. Kinvara's farewell letter sat on top of a number of papers and books, of which only a sliver of one letter was visible, signed by "Brenda Bailey." Of the books, Strike could see nothing but a partial title on an old cloth edition— "CATUL"—and the lower part of a Penguin paperback. Also in shot was the upturned corner of the threadbare rug beneath the table.

The ninth and final picture, which Strike had enlarged from yet another shot of the body, showed Chiswell's gaping trouser pocket, in which something shiny and golden had been caught in the flash of Robin's camera. While he was still contemplating this gleaming object, Strike's mobile rang. It was his hostess, Ilsa.

"Hi," he said, standing up and grabbing the packet of Benson &

Hedges and lighter that lay on the side behind him. With an eruption of claws on wood, Ossie and Ricky streaked along the top of the kitchen cabinets, in case Strike was about to start throwing things at them. Checking to see that they were too far away to make a break for the garden, Strike let himself outside and swiftly closed the back door. "Any news?"

"Yes. Looks like you were right."

Strike sat down on a wrought iron garden chair and lit up.

"Go on."

"I've just had coffee with my contact. He can't speak freely, given the nature of what we're talking about, but I put your theory to him and he said 'That sounds *very* plausible.' Then I said, 'Fellow politician?' and he said that sounded very likely, too, and I said I supposed that in that situation, the press would appeal, and he said, yes, he thought so, too."

Strike exhaled.

"I owe you, Ilsa, thanks. The good news is, I'll be able to get out of your hair."

"Corm, we don't mind you staying, you know that."

"The cats don't like me."

"Nick says they can tell you're a Gooner."

"The comedy circuit lost a shining light when your husband decided on medicine. Dinner's on me tonight and I'll clear out afterwards."

Strike then rang Robin. She picked up on the second ring.

"Everything OK?"

"I've found out why the press aren't all over us. Della's taken out a super-injunction. The papers aren't allowed to report that Chiswell hired us, in case it breaks the blackmail story. Ilsa's just met her High Court contact and he confirmed it."

There was a pause, while Robin digested this information.

"So Della convinced a judge that Chiswell made up the blackmail?"

"Exactly, that he was using us to dig dirt on enemies. I'm not surprised the judge swallowed it. The whole world thinks Della's whiter than white."

"But Izzy knew why I was there," protested Robin. "The family will have confirmed that he was being blackmailed."

Strike tapped ash absentmindedly into Ilsa's pot of rosemary.

"Will they? Or will they want it all hushed up, now he's dead?"

He took her silence as reluctant agreement.

"The press will appeal the injunction, won't they?"

"They're already trying, according to Ilsa. If I were a tabloid editor, I'd be having us watched, so I think we'd better be careful. I'm going back to the office tonight, but I think you should stay home."

"For how long?" said Robin.

He heard the strain in her voice and wondered whether it was entirely due to the stress of the case.

"We'll play it by ear. Robin, they know you were the one inside the Houses of Parliament. You became the story while he was alive and you're sure as hell the story now they know who you really are, and he's dead."

She said nothing.

"How're you getting on with the accounts?" he asked.

She had insisted on being given this job, little though either of them enjoyed it.

"They'd look a lot healthier if Chiswell had paid his bill."

"I'll try and tap the family," said Strike, rubbing his eyes, "but it feels tasteless asking for money before the funeral."

"I've been looking through the photos again," said Robin. In daily contact since finding the body, every one of their conversations wound its way back to the pictures of Chiswell's corpse and the room in which they had found him.

"Me too. Notice anything new?"

"Yes, two little brass hooks on the wall. I think the sword was usually—"

"—displayed beneath the missing painting?"

"Exactly. D'you think it was Chiswell's, from the army?"

"Very possibly. Or some ancestor's."

"I wonder why it was taken down? And how it got bent?"

"You think Chiswell grabbed it off the wall to try and defend himself against his murderer?"

"That's the first time," said Robin quietly, "you've said it. 'Murderer.'"

A wasp swooped low over Strike but, repelled by his cigarette smoke, buzzed away again.

"I was joking."

"Were you?"

Strike stretched out his legs in front of him, contemplating his feet. Stuck in the house, which was warm, he had not bothered with shoes and socks. His bare foot, which rarely saw sunlight, was pale and hairy. The prosthetic foot, a single piece of carbon fiber with no individual toes, had a dull gleam in the sunshine.

"There are odd features," Strike said, as he waggled his remaining toes, "but it's been a week and no arrest. The police will have noticed everything we did."

"Hasn't Wardle heard anything? Vanessa's dad's ill. She's on compassionate leave, or I'd've asked her."

"Wardle's deep in anti-terrorist stuff for the Olympics. Considerately spared the time to call my voicemail and piss himself laughing at my client dying on me, though."

"Cormoran, did you notice the name on those homeopathic pills I trod on?"

"No," said Strike. This wasn't one of the photographs he had isolated. "What was it?"

"Lachesis. I saw it when I enlarged the picture."

"Why's that significant?"

"When Chiswell came into our office and quoted that Latin poem at Aamir, and said something about a man of your habits, he mentioned Lachesis. He said she was—"

"One of the Fates."

"—exactly. The one who 'knew when everyone's number was up.'"

Strike smoked in silence for a few seconds.

"Sounds like a threat."

"I know."

"You definitely can't remember which poem it was? Author, perhaps?"

"I've been trying, but no—wait—" said Robin suddenly. "He gave it a number."

"Catullus," said Strike, sitting up straighter on the iron garden chair. "How d'you know?"

"Because Catullus's poems are numbered, not titled, there was an old copy on Chiswell's coffee table. Catullus described plenty of interesting habits: incest, sodomy, child rape...he might've missed out bestiality. There's a famous one about a sparrow, but nobody buggers it."

"Funny coincidence, isn't it?" said Robin, ignoring the witticism.

"Maybe Chiswell was prescribed the pills and that put him in mind of the Fate?"

"Did he seem to you like the kind of man who'd trust homeopathy?"

"No," admitted Strike, "but if you're suggesting the killer dropped a tube of lachesis as an artistic flourish—"

He heard a distant trill of bells.

"There's someone at the door," said Robin, "I'd better—"

"Check who it is, before you answer," said Strike. He had had a sudden presentiment.

Her footsteps were muffled by what he knew was carpet.

"Oh, God."

"Who is it?"

"Mitch Patterson."

"Has he seen you?"

"No, I'm upstairs."

"Then don't answer."

"I won't."

But her breathing had become noisy and ragged.

"You all right?"

"Fine," she said, her voice constricted.

"What's he—?"

"I'm going to go. I'll call you later."

The line went dead.

Strike lowered the mobile. Feeling a sudden heat in the fingers of the hand not holding his phone, he realized his cigarette had burned to the filter. Stubbing it out on the hot paving stone, he flicked it over the wall into the garden of a neighbor whom Nick and Ilsa disliked, and immediately lit another, thinking about Robin.

He was concerned about her. It was to be expected, of course, that she was experiencing anxiety and stress after finding a body and being interviewed by the security services, but he had noticed lapses in concentration over the phone, where she asked him the same thing two or three times. There was also what he considered her unhealthy eagerness to get back to the office, or out on the street.

Convinced that she ought to be taking some time out, Strike hadn't told Robin about a line of investigation he was currently pursuing, because he was sure she would insist on being allowed to help.

The fact was that, for Strike, the Chiswell case had begun, not with the dead man's story of blackmail, but with Billy Knight's tale of a strangled child wrapped in a pink blanket in the ground. Ever since Billy's last plea for help, Strike had been phoning the telephone number from which it had been made. Finally, on the previous morning, he had got an answer from a curious passerby, who had confirmed the phone box's position on the edge of Trafalgar Square.

Strike. That bastard soldier with the one leg. Billy's fixated on him. Thinks he's going to rescue him.

Surely there was a chance, however tiny, that Billy might gravitate back to the place where he had last sought help? Strike had spent a few hours wandering Trafalgar Square on the previous afternoon, knowing how remote was the possibility that Billy would show up, yet feeling compelled to do something, however pointless.

Strike's other decision, which was even harder to justify, because it cost money the agency could currently ill afford, was to keep Barclay embedded with Jimmy and Flick.

"It's your money," the Glaswegian said, when the detective gave him this instruction, "but what'm I looking for?"

"Billy," said Strike, "and in the absence of Billy, anything strange."

Of course, the next lot of accounts would show Robin exactly what Barclay was up to.

Strike had a sudden feeling that he was being watched. Ossie, the bolder of Nick and Ilsa's kittens, was sitting at the kitchen window, beside the kitchen taps, staring through the window with eyes of pale jade. His gaze felt judgmental.

37

*I shall never conquer this completely. There will always be a
doubt confronting me—a question.*

Henrik Ibsen, *Rosmersholm*

Wary of breaching the conditions of the super-injunction, photographers stayed away from Chiswell's funeral in Woolstone. News organizations restricted themselves to brief, factual announcements that the service had taken place. Strike, who had considered sending flowers, had decided against it on the basis that the gesture might be taken as a tasteless reminder that his bill remained unpaid. Meanwhile the inquest into Chiswell's death was opened and adjourned, pending further investigations.

And then, quite suddenly, nobody was very interested in Jasper Chiswell. It was as though the corpse that had been borne aloft for a week upon a swell of newsprint, gossip and rumor, now sank beneath stories of sportsmen and women, of Olympic preparations and predictions, the country in the grip of an almost universal preoccupation, for whether they approved or disapproved of the event, it was impossible to ignore or avoid.

Robin was still phoning Strike daily, pressuring him to let her come back to work, but Strike continued to refuse. Not only had Mitch Patterson twice more appeared in her street, but an unfamiliar young busker had spent the whole week playing on the pavement opposite Strike's office, missing chord changes every time he saw the detective and regularly breaking off halfway through songs to answer his mobile. The press, it seemed, had not forgotten that the Olympics would eventually end, and that there was still a juicy story to be run on the reason Jasper Chiswell had hired private detectives.

None of Strike's police contacts knew anything about the progress of their colleagues' investigation into the case. Usually able to fall asleep under even the most unpropitious conditions, Strike found himself unusually restless and wakeful by night, listening to the increased noise from the London now heaving with Olympics visitors. The last time he had endured such a long stretch of sleeplessness had been his first week of consciousness after his leg had been borne off by the IED in Afghanistan. Then he had been kept awake by a tormenting itch impossible to scratch, because he felt it on his missing foot.

Strike hadn't seen Lorelei since the night of the Paralympic reception. After leaving Charlotte in the street, he had set off for Trafalgar Square to try and locate Billy, with the result that he had been even later to dinner with Lorelei than he had expected. Tired, sore, frustrated at his failure to find Billy and jarred by the unexpected meeting with his ex, he had arrived at the curry house in the expectation, and perhaps the hope, that Lorelei would have already left.

However, she had not only been waiting patiently at the table, she had immediately wrong-footed him with what he mentally characterized as a strategic retreat. Far from forcing a discussion about the future of their relationship, she had apologized for what she claimed to have been a foolish and precipitate declaration of love in bed, which she knew had embarrassed him and which she sincerely regretted.

Strike, who had drunk most of a pint on sitting down, bolstering himself, as he had imagined, for the unpleasant task of explaining that he did not want their relationship to become either more serious or permanent, was stymied. Her claim that she had said "I love you" as a kind of *cri de joie* rendered his prepared speech useless, and given that she had looked very lovely in the lamp-lit restaurant, it had been easier and pleasanter to accept her explanation at face value rather than force a rupture that, clearly, neither of them wanted. They had texted and spoken a few times during the subsequent week apart, though nowhere near as often as he had talked to Robin. Lorelei had been perfectly understanding about his need to keep a low profile for a while once he explained that his late client had been the government minister who had suffocated in a plastic bag.

Lorelei had even been unfazed when he refused her invitation to watch the opening ceremony of the Olympics with her, because he'd already agreed to spend the evening at Lucy and Greg's. Strike's sister was as yet unwilling to let Jack out of her sight, and had therefore declined Strike's offer to take him to the Imperial War Museum over the weekend, offering dinner instead. When he explained to Lorelei how matters stood, Strike could tell that she was hoping that he would ask her to come with him to meet some of his family for the first time. He said, truthfully, that his motive for going alone was to spend time with the nephew whom he felt he had neglected, and Lorelei accepted this explanation good-naturedly, merely asking whether he was free the following night.

As the taxi bore him from Bromley South station towards Lucy and Greg's, Strike found himself mulling the situation with Lorelei, because Lucy usually demanded a bulletin on his love life. This was one of the reasons he avoided these kinds of get-togethers. It troubled Lucy that her brother was still, at the age of nearly thirty-eight, unmarried. She had gone so far, on one embarrassing occasion, as to invite to dinner a woman whom she imagined he might fancy, which had taught him only that his sister grossly misjudged his taste and needs.

As the taxi bore him deeper and deeper into middle-class suburbia, Strike found himself face to face with the uncomfortable truth, which was that Lorelei's willingness to accept the casualness of their current arrangement did not stem from a shared sense of disengagement, but from a desperation to keep him on almost any terms.

Staring out of the window at the roomy houses with double garages and neat lawns, his thoughts drifted to Robin, who called him daily when her husband was out, and then to Charlotte, holding lightly to his arm as she walked down the Lancaster House staircase in her spike-heeled boots. It had been convenient and pleasurable to have Lorelei in his life these past ten and a half months, affectionately undemanding, erotically gifted and pretending not to be in love with him. He could let the relationship continue, tell himself that he was, in that meaningless phrase, "seeing how things went," or he could face the fact that he had merely postponed what must be done, and the longer he let things drift, the more mess and pain would result.

These reflections were hardly calculated to cheer him up, and as the taxi drew up outside his sister's house, with the magnolia tree in the front garden, and the net curtain twitching excitedly, he felt an irrational resentment towards his sister, as though all of it was her fault.

Jack opened the front door before Strike could even knock. Given his state the last time Strike had seen him, Jack looked remarkably well, and the detective was torn between pleasure at his recovery, and annoyance that he hadn't been allowed to take his nephew out, rather than making the long and inconvenient journey to Bromley.

However, Jack's delight in Strike's arrival, his eager questions about everything Strike remembered about their time together in hospital, because he himself had been glamorously unconscious, were touching, as was the fact that Jack insisted upon sitting next to his uncle at dinner, and monopolized his attention throughout. It was clear that Jack felt that they had become more closely bonded for each having passed through the tribulation of emergency surgery. He demanded so many details of Strike's amputation that Greg put down his knife and fork and pushed away his plate with a nauseated expression. Strike had previously formed the impression that Jack, the middle son, was Greg's least favorite. He took a slightly malicious pleasure in satisfying Jack's curiosity, especially as he knew that Greg, who would usually have shut the conversation down, was exercising unusual restraint given Jack's convalescent state. Unconscious of all undercurrents, Lucy beamed throughout, her eyes barely leaving Strike and Jack. She asked Strike nothing about his private life. All she seemed to ask was that he would be kind and patient with her son.

Uncle and nephew left the dinner table on excellent terms, Jack choosing a seat next to Strike on the sofa to watch the Olympics opening ceremony and chattering nonstop while they waited for the live broadcast to start, expressing the hope, among other things, that there would be guns, cannons and soldiers.

This innocent remark reminded Strike of Jasper Chiswell and his annoyance, reported by Robin, that Britain's military prowess was not to be celebrated on this largest of national stages. This made Strike wonder whether Jimmy Knight was sitting in front of a TV somewhere, readying himself to sneer at what he had castigated as a carnival of capitalism.

Greg handed Strike a bottle of Heineken.

"Here we go!" said Lucy excitedly.

The live broadcast began with a countdown. A few seconds in, a numbered balloon failed to burst. *Let it not be shit*, thought Strike, suddenly forgetting everything else in an upsurge of patriotic paranoia.

But the opening ceremony had been so very much the reverse of shit that Strike stayed to watch the whole thing, voluntarily missing his last train, accepting the offer of the sofa bed and breakfasting on Saturday morning with the family.

"Agency doing well, is it?" Greg asked him over the fry-up Lucy had cooked.

"Not bad," said Strike.

He generally avoided discussing his business with Greg, who seemed to have been wrong-footed by Strike's success. His brother-in-law had always given the impression of being irritated by Strike's distinguished military career. As he fielded Greg's questions about the structure of the business, the rights and responsibilities of his freelance hires, Robin's special status as salaried partner and the potential for expansion, Strike detected, not for the first time, Greg's barely disguised hope that there might be something Strike had forgotten or overlooked, too much the soldier to easily navigate the civilian business world.

"What's the ultimate aim, though?" he asked, while Jack sat patiently at Strike's side, clearly hoping to talk more about the military. "I suppose you'll be looking to build up the business so that you don't need to be out on the street? Direct them all from the office?"

"No," said Strike. "If I'd wanted a desk job I'd've stayed in the army. The aim is to build up enough reliable employees that we can sustain a steady workload, and make some decent money. Short term, I want to build up enough money in the bank to see us through the lean times."

"Seems under-ambitious," said Greg. "With the free advertising you got after the Ripper case—"

"We're not talking about that case now," said Lucy sharply, from beside the frying pan, and with a glance at his son Greg fell silent, permitting Jack to re-enter the conversation with a question about assault courses.

Lucy, who had loved every moment of her brother's visit, glowed with pleasure as she hugged him goodbye after breakfast.

"Let me know when I can take Jack out," said Strike, while his nephew beamed up at him.

"I will, and thanks so much, Stick. I'll never forget what you—"

"I didn't do anything," Strike said, thumping her gently on the back. "He did it himself. He's tough, aren't you, Jack? Thanks for a nice evening, Luce."

Strike considered that he had got out just in time. Finishing his cigarette outside the station, with ten minutes to kill before the next train to central London, he reflected that Greg had reverted over breakfast to that combination of chirpiness and heartiness with which he usually treated his brother-in-law, while Lucy's inquiries after Robin as he put on his coat had shown signs of becoming a wide-ranging inquiry into his relationships with women in general. His thoughts had just returned dispiritedly towards Lorelei when his mobile rang.

"Hello?"

"Is this Cormoran?" said an upper-class female voice he did not immediately recognize.

"Yes. Who's this?"

"Izzy Chiswell," she said, sounding as though she had a head cold.

"Izzy!" repeated Strike, surprised. "Er…how are you?"

"Oh, bearing up. We, ah, got your invoice."

"Right," said Strike, wondering whether she was about to dispute the total, which was large.

"I'd be very happy to give you payment immediately, if you could...I wonder whether you could possibly come and see me? Today, if that's convenient? How are you fixed?"

Strike checked his watch. For the first time in weeks he had nothing to do except make his way to Lorelei's later for dinner, and the prospect of collecting a large check was certainly welcome.

"Yeah, that should be fine," he said. "Where are you, Izzy?"

She gave him her address in Chelsea.

"I'll be about an hour."

"Perfect," she said, sounding relieved. "I'll see you then."

38

Oh, this killing doubt!

Henrik Ibsen, *Rosmersholm*

It was almost midday when Strike arrived at Izzy's mews house in Upper Cheyne Row in Chelsea, a quietly expensive stretch of houses which, unlike those of Ebury Street, were tastefully mismatched. Izzy's was small and painted white, with a carriage lamp beside the front door, and when Strike rang the doorbell she answered within a few seconds.

In her loose black trousers and a black sweater too warm for such a sunny day, Izzy reminded Strike of the first time he had met her father, who had been sporting an overcoat in June. A sapphire cross hung around her neck. Strike thought that she had gone as far into official mourning as modern-day dress and sensibilities would permit.

"Come in, come in," she said nervously, not making eye contact, and standing back, waved him into an airy open-plan sitting and kitchen area, with white walls, brightly patterned sofas and an Art Nouveau fireplace with sinuous, molded female figures supporting the mantelpiece. The long rear windows looked out onto a small, private courtyard, where expensive wrought iron furniture sat among carefully tended topiary.

"Sit down," said Izzy, waving him towards one of the colorful sofas. "Tea? Coffee?"

"Tea would be great, thanks."

Strike sat down, unobtrusively extracted a number of uncomfortable, beaded cushions from beneath him, and took stock of the room. In spite of the cheery modern fabrics, a more traditional English taste predominated. Two hunting prints stood over a table laden with silver-framed photographs, including a large black-and-white study of Izzy's parents on their wedding day, Jasper Chiswell dressed in the uniform of the Queen's Own Hussars, Lady Patricia toothy and blonde in a cloud of tulle. Over the mantelpiece hung a large watercolor of three blond toddlers, which Strike assumed represented Izzy and her two older siblings, dead Freddie and the unknown Fizzy.

Izzy clattered around, dropping teaspoons and opening and closing cupboards without finding what she was looking for. At last, turning down Strike's offer of help, she carried a tray bearing a teapot, bone china mugs and biscuits the short distance between kitchenette and coffee table, and set it down.

"Did you watch the opening ceremony?" she asked politely, busy with teapot and strainer.

"I did, yeah," said Strike. "Great, wasn't it?"

"Well, I liked the first part," said Izzy, "all the industrial revolution bit, but I thought it went, well, a bit PC after that. I'm not sure foreigners will really get why we were talking about the National Health Service, and I must say, I could have done without all the rap music. Help yourself to milk and sugar."

"Thanks."

There was a brief silence, broken only by the tinkling of silver and china; that plush kind of silence achievable in London only by people with plenty of money. Even in winter, Strike's attic flat was never completely quiet: music, footsteps and voices filled the Soho street below, and when pedestrians forsook the area, traffic rumbled through the night, while the slightest breath of wind rattled his insecure windows.

"Oh, your check," gasped Izzy, jumping up again to fetch an envelope on the kitchen side. "Here."

"Thanks very much," said Strike, taking it from her.

Izzy sat down again, took a biscuit, changed her mind about eating it and put it on her plate instead. Strike sipped tea that he suspected was of the finest quality, but which, to him, tasted unpleasantly of dried flowers.

"Um," said Izzy at last, "it's quite hard to know where to begin."

She examined her fingers, which were unmanicured.

"I'm scared you'll think I'm bonkers," she muttered, glancing up at him through her fair lashes.

"I doubt that," said Strike, putting down his tea and adopting what he hoped was an encouraging expression.

"Have you heard what they found in Papa's orange juice?"

"No," said Strike.

"Amitriptyline tablets, ground up into powder. I don't know whether you—they're anti-depressants. The police say it's quite an efficient, painless suicide method. Sort of belt and—belt and braces, the pills and the—the bag."

She took a sloppy gulp of tea.

"They were quite kind, really, the police. Well, they have training, don't they? They told us, if the helium's concentrated enough, one breath and you're . . . you're asleep."

She pursed her lips together.

"The thing is," she said loudly, in a sudden rush of words, "I absolutely *know* that Papa would never have killed himself, because it was something he detested, he always said it was the coward's way out, awful for the family and everybody left behind.

"And it was strange: there was no packaging for the amitriptyline anywhere in the house. No empty boxes, no blister packs, nothing. Of course, a box would have Kinvara's name on it. Kinvara's the one who's prescribed amitriptyline. She's been taking them for over a year."

Izzy glanced at Strike to see what effect her words had had. When he said nothing, she plunged on.

"Papa and Kinvara rowed the night before, at the reception, right before I came over to talk to you and Charlie. Papa had just told us he'd asked Raff to come over to the Ebury Street house next morning. Kinvara was furious. She asked why and Papa wouldn't tell her, he just smiled, and that infuriated her."

"Why would—?"

"Because she hates all of us," said Izzy, correctly anticipating Strike's question. Her hands were clutched together, the knuckles white. "She's always hated anything and anyone that competed with her for Papa's attention or his affection, and she *particularly* hates Raff, because he looks just like his mother, and Kinvara's always been insecure about Ornella, because she's still very glamorous, but Kinvara doesn't like that Raff's a boy, either. She's always been frightened he'd replace Freddie, and maybe get put back in the will. Kinvara married Papa for his money. She never loved him."

"When you say 'put back'—"

"Papa wrote Raff out of his will when Raff ran—when he did the thing—in the car. Kinvara was behind that, of course, she was egging Papa on to have nothing more to do with Raff at all—anyway, Papa told us at Lancaster House he'd invited Raff around next day and Kinvara went quiet, and a couple of minutes later she suddenly announced that she was leaving and walked out. She claims she went back to Ebury Street, wrote Papa a farewell note—but you were there. Maybe you saw it?"

"Yes," said Strike. "I did."

"Yes, so, she claims she wrote that note, packed her bag, then caught the train back to Woolstone.

"The way the police were questioning us, they seemed to think Kinvara leaving him would have made Papa kill himself, but that's just too ridiculous for words! Their marriage has been in trouble for ages. I think he'd been able to see through her for months and months before then. She's been telling crazy fibs and doing all kinds of melodramatic things to try and keep Papa's interest. I promise you, if Papa had believed she was about to leave him, he'd have been relieved, not suicidal, but of course, he wouldn't have taken that note seriously, he'd have known perfectly well it was more play-acting. Kinvara's got nine horses and no income. She'll have to be dragged out of Chiswell House, just like Tinky the First—my Grandpa's third wife," Izzy explained. "The Chiswell men seem to have a thing for women with big boobs and horses."

Flushed beneath her freckles, Izzy drew breath, and said:

"I think Kinvara killed Papa. I can't get it out of my head, can't focus, can't think about anything else. She was convinced there was something going on between Papa and Venetia—she was suspicious from the first moment she saw Venetia, and then the *Sun* snooping around convinced her she was right to be worried—and she probably thought Papa reinstating Raff proved that he was getting ready for a new era, and I think she ground up her anti-depressants and put them in his orange juice when he wasn't looking—he always had a glass of juice first thing, that was his routine—then, when he became sleepy and couldn't fight her off, she put the bag over his head and *then*, after she'd killed him, she wrote that note to try and make it look as though she was the one who was going to divorce *him* and I think she sneaked out of the house after she'd done it, went home to Woolstone and pretended she'd been there when Papa died."

Running out of breath, Izzy felt for the cross around her neck and played with it nervously, watching for Strike's reaction, her expression both nervous and defiant.

Strike, who had dealt with several military suicides, knew that survivors were nearly always left with a particularly noxious form of grief, a poisoned wound that festered even beyond that of those whose relatives had been dispatched by enemy bullets. He might have his own doubts about the way in which Chiswell had met his end, but he was not about to share them with the disoriented, grief-stricken woman beside him. What struck him chiefly about Izzy's diatribe was the hatred she appeared to feel for her stepmother. It was no trivial charge that she laid against Kinvara, and Strike wondered what it was that convinced Izzy that the rather childish, sulky woman with whom he had shared five minutes in a car could be capable of planning what amounted to a methodical execution.

"The police," he said at last, "will have looked into Kinvara's movements, Izzy. In a case like this, the spouse is usually the first one to be investigated."

"But they're accepting her story," said Izzy feverishly. "I can tell they are."

Then it's true, thought Strike. He had too high an opinion of the Met to imagine that they would be slapdash in confirming the movements of the wife who had had easy access to the murder scene, and who had been prescribed the drugs that had been found in the body.

"Who else knew Papa always drank orange juice in the mornings? Who else had access to amitriptyline and the helium—?"

"Does she admit to buying the helium?" Strike asked.

"No," said Izzy, "but she wouldn't, would she? She just sits there doing her hysterical little girl act." Izzy affected a higher-pitched voice. "'I don't know how it got into the house! Why are you all pestering me, leave me alone, I've been widowed!'

"I told the police, she attacked Papa with a hammer, over a year ago."

Strike froze in the act of raising his unappetizing tea to his lips.

"What?"

"She attacked Papa with a hammer," said Izzy, her pale blue eyes boring into Strike, willing him to understand. "They had a massive row, because—well, it doesn't matter why, but they were out in the stables—this was at home, at Chiswell House, obviously—and Kinvara grabbed the hammer off the top of a toolbox and smashed Papa over the head with it. She was bloody lucky she didn't kill him *then*. It left him with olfactory dysfunction. He couldn't smell and taste as well afterwards, and he got cross at the smallest things, but he insisted on hushing it all up. He bundled her off into some residential center and told everyone she was ill, 'nervous exhaustion.'

"But the stable girl witnessed the whole thing and told us what had really happened. She had to call the local GP because Papa was bleeding so badly. It would have been all over the papers if Papa hadn't got Kinvara admitted to a psychiatric ward and warned the papers off."

Izzy picked up her tea, but her hand was now shaking so badly that she was forced to put it back down again.

"She isn't what men think she is," said Izzy vehemently. "They all buy the little girl nonsense, even Raff. 'She *did* lose a baby, Izzy...' But if he heard a *quarter* of what Kinvara says about him behind his back, he'd soon change his tune."

"And what about the open front door?" Izzy said, jumping subject. "You know all about that, it's how you and Venetia got in, isn't it? That door's never closed properly unless you slam it. Papa knew that. He'd have made sure he closed it properly if he'd been in the house alone, wouldn't he? But if Kinvara was sneaking out early in the morning without wanting to be heard, she'd have had to pull it to and leave it, wouldn't she?

"She isn't very bright, you know. She'd have tidied away all the amitriptyline packaging, thinking it would incriminate her if she left it. I know the police think the absence of packaging is odd, but I can tell they're all leaning towards suicide and that's why I wanted to speak to you, Cormoran," Izzy finished, edging a little forward in her armchair. "I want to hire you. I want you to investigate Papa's death."

Strike had known the request was coming almost from the moment the tea had arrived. The prospect of being paid to investigate what was, in any case, preoccupying Strike to the point of obsession, was naturally inviting. However, clients who sought nothing but confirmation of their own theories were always troublesome. He could not accept the case on Izzy's terms, but compassion for her grief led him to seek a gentler mode of refusal.

"The police won't want me under their feet, Izzy."

"They don't have to know it's Papa's death you're investigating," said Izzy eagerly. "We could pretend we want you to investigate all those stupid trespasses into the garden that Kinvara claims have been going on. It would serve her bloody well right if we took her seriously now."

"Do the rest of the family know you're meeting me?"

"Oh, yes," said Izzy eagerly. "Fizzy's all for it."

"Is she? Does she suspect Kinvara, too?"

"Well, no," said Izzy, sounding faintly frustrated, "but she agrees a hundred percent that Papa couldn't have killed himself."

"Who does she think did it, if not Kinvara?"

"Well," said Izzy, who seemed uneasy at this line of questioning, "actually, Fizz has got this crazy idea that Jimmy Knight was involved somehow, but obviously, that's ridiculous. Jimmy was in custody when Papa died, wasn't he? You and I saw him being led away by the police the evening before, but Fizz doesn't want to hear that, she's *fixated* on Jimmy! I've said to her, 'how did Jimmy Knight know where the amitriptyline and the helium were?' but she won't listen, she keeps going on about how Knight was after revenge—"

312 • ROBERT GALBRAITH

"Revenge for what?"

"What?" said Izzy restlessly, though Strike knew she had heard him. "Oh—that doesn't matter now. That's all over."

Snatching up the teapot, Izzy marched away into the kitchen area, where she added more hot water from the kettle.

"Fizz is irrational about Jimmy," she said, returning with her teapot refilled and setting it down with a bang on the table. "She's never been able to stand him since we were teenagers."

She poured herself a second cup of tea, her color heightened. When Strike said nothing, she repeated nervously:

"The blackmail business can't have anything to do with Papa dying. That's all over."

"You didn't tell the police about it, did you?" asked Strike quietly.

There was a pause. Izzy turned steadily pinker. She sipped her tea, then said:

"No."

Then she said, in a rush, "I'm sorry, I can imagine how you and Venetia feel about that, but we're more concerned about Papa's legacy now. We can't face it all getting into the press, Cormoran. The only way the blackmail can have any bearing on his death is if it drove him to suicide, and I just don't believe he'd have killed himself over that, or anything else."

"Della must have found it easy to get her super-injunction," said Strike, "if Chiswell's own family were backing her up, saying nobody was blackmailing him."

"We care more about how Papa's remembered. The blackmail... that's all over and done with."

"But Fizzy still thinks Jimmy might've had something to do with your father's death."

"That's not—that would be a separate matter, from what he was blackmailing about," said Izzy incoherently. "Jimmy had a grudge... it's hard to explain... Fizz is just silly about Jimmy."

"How does the rest of the family feel about bringing me in again?"

"Well... Raff isn't awfully keen, but it's nothing to do with him. I'd be paying you."

"Why isn't he keen?"

"Because," said Izzy, "well, because the police questioned Raff more than any of the rest of us, because—look, Raff doesn't matter," she repeated. "I'll be the client, I'm the one who wants you. Just break Kinvara's alibis, I know you can do it."

"I'm afraid," said Strike, "I can't take the job on those terms, Izzy."

"Why not?"

"The client doesn't get to tell me what I can and can't investigate. Unless you want the whole truth, I'm not your man."

"You *are*, I know you're the best, that's why Papa hired you, and that's why I want you."

"Then you'll need to answer questions when I ask them, instead of telling me what does and doesn't matter."

She glared at him over the rim of her teacup, then, to his surprise, gave a brittle laugh.

"I don't know why I'm surprised. I knew you were like this. Remember when you argued with Jamie Maugham in Nam Long Le Shaker? Oh, you must remember. You wouldn't back down—the whole table was at you at one point—what was the argument about, d'you—?"

"The death penalty," said Strike, caught off guard. "Yeah. I remember."

For the space of a blink, he seemed to see, not Izzy's clean, bright sitting room, with its relics of a wealthy English past, but the louche, dimly lit interior of a Vietnamese restaurant in Chelsea where, twelve years previously, he and one of Charlotte's friends had got into an argument over dinner. Jamie Maugham's face was smoothly porcine in his memory. He had wanted to show up the oik whom Charlotte had insisted on bringing to dinner instead of Jamie's old friend, Jago Ross.

"...and Jamie got rilly, rilly angry with you," Izzy said. "He's quite a successful QC now, you know."

"Must've learned to keep his temper in an argument, then," said Strike, and Izzy gave another little giggle. "Izzy," he said, returning to the main issue, "if you mean what you say—"

"—I do—"

"—then you'll answer my questions," said Strike, drawing a notebook out of his pocket.

Irresolute, she watched him take out a pen.

"I'm discreet," said Strike. "In the past couple of years, I've been told the secrets of a hundred families and not shared one of them. Nothing irrelevant to your father's death will ever be mentioned again outside my agency. But if you don't trust me—"

"I do," said Izzy desperately, and to his slight surprise, she leaned forward and touched him on the knee. "I do, Cormoran, honestly, but it's...it's hard...talking about Papa..."

"I understand that," he said, readying his pen. "So let's start with why the police questioned Raphael so much more than the rest of you."

He could tell that she didn't want to answer, but after a moment's hesitation she said:

"Well, I think it was partly because Papa phoned Raff early on the morning he died. It was the last call he made."

"What did he say?"

"Nothing that mattered. It can't have had anything to do with Papa dying. But," she rushed on, as though wanting to extinguish any impression her last words might have made, "I think the *main* reason Raff isn't keen on me hiring you is that he rather fell for your Venetia while she was in the office and now, well, obviously, he feels a bit of an idiot that he poured his heart out to her."

"Fell for her, did he?" said Strike.

"Yes, so it's hardly surprising he feels everyone's made a fool of him."

"The fact remains—"

"I know what you're going to say, but—"

"—if you want me to investigate, it'll be me who decides what matters, Izzy. Not you. So I want to know," he ticked off all the times she had said that information "didn't matter" on his fingers as he named them, "what your father called Raphael about the morning he died, what your father and Kinvara were rowing about when she hit him around the head with a hammer—and what your father was being blackmailed about."

The sapphire cross winked darkly as Izzy's chest rose and fell. When at last she spoke, it was jerkily.

"It's not up to me to tell you about what Papa and Raff said to each other, the last t-time they spoke. That's for Raff to say."

"Because it's private?"

"Yes," she said, very pink in the face. He wondered whether she was telling the truth.

"You said your father had asked Raphael over to the house in Ebury Street the day he died. Was he rearranging the time? Canceling?"

"Canceling. Look, you'll have to ask Raff," she reiterated.

"All right," said Strike, making a note. "What caused your stepmother to hit your father around the head with a hammer?"

Izzy's eyes filled with tears. Then, with a sob, she pulled a handkerchief out of her sleeve and pressed it to her face:

"I d–didn't want to tell you that b–because I d–didn't want you to think badly of Papa now he's... now he's... you see, he d–did something that..."

Her broad shoulders shook as she emitted unromantic snorts. Strike, who found this frank and noisy anguish more touching than he would have found delicate eye dabbing, sat in impotent sympathy while she tried to gasp out her apologies.

"I'm—I'm s—"

"Don't be silly," he said gruffly. "Of course you're upset."

But she seemed deeply ashamed of this loss of control, and her hiccuping return to calm was punctuated with further flustered "sorrys." At last, she wiped her face dry as roughly as though cleaning a window, said one final "I'm so sorry," straightened her spine and said with a forcefulness Strike rather admired, given the circumstances:

"If you take the case... once we've signed on the dotted line... I'll tell you what Papa did that made Kinvara hit him."

"I assume," said Strike, "the same goes for the reason that Winn and Knight were blackmailing your father?"

"Look," she said, tears welling again, "don't you see, it's Papa's memory, his legacy, now. I don't want those things to be the thing people remember about him—please help us, Corm. *Please*. I know it wasn't suicide, I *know* it wasn't..."

He let his silence do the work for him. At last, her expression piteous, she said with a catch in her voice:

"All right. I'll tell you all about the blackmail, but only if Fizz and Torks agree."

"Who's Torks?" inquired Strike.

"Torquil. Fizzy's husband. We swore we wouldn't ever tell anyone, but I'll t-talk to them and if they agree, I'll t-tell you everything."

"Doesn't Raphael get consulted?"

"He never knew anything about the blackmail business. He was in jail when Jimmy first came to see Papa and anyway, he didn't grow up with us, so he couldn't—Raff never knew."

"And what about Kinvara?" asked Strike. "Did she know?"

"Oh, yes," said Izzy, and a look of malice hardened her usually friendly features, "but she *definitely* won't want us to tell you. Oh, not to protect Papa," she said, correctly reading Strike's expression, "to protect herself. Kinvara benefited, you see. She didn't mind what Papa was up to, so long as she reaped the rewards."

39

...naturally I talk as little about it as possible; it is better to be silent about such things.

Henrik Ibsen, *Rosmersholm*

Robin was having a bad Saturday, following an even worse night.

She had woken with a yelp at 4 a.m., with the sensation of being still tangled in the nightmare in which she had been carrying a whole bag full of listening devices through darkened streets, knowing that men in masks were following her. The old knife wound on her arm had been gaping open and it was the trail of her spurting blood that her pursuers were following, and she knew she would never make it to the place where Strike was waiting for the bag of bugs...

"What?" Matthew had said groggily, half asleep.

"Nothing," Robin had replied, before lying sleepless until seven, when she felt entitled to get up.

A scruffy young blond man had been lurking in Albury Street for the past two days. He barely bothered to conceal the fact that he was keeping their house under observation. Robin had discussed him with Strike, who was sure that he was a journalist rather than a private detective, probably a junior one, dispatched to keep tabs on her because Mitch Patterson's hourly rate had become an unjustifiable expense.

She and Matthew had moved to Albury Street to escape the place where the Shacklewell Ripper had lurked. It was supposed to be a place of safety, yet it, too, had become contaminated by contact with unnatural death. Mid-morning, Robin had taken refuge in the bathroom before Matthew could realize she was hyperventilating again. Sitting on the bathroom floor, she had recourse to the technique she had learned in therapy, cognitive restructuring, which sought to identify the automatic thoughts of pursuit, pain and danger that sprang into her mind given certain triggers. *He's just some idiot who works for the* Sun. *He wants a story, that's all. You're safe. He can't get at you. You're completely safe.*

When Robin emerged from the bathroom and went downstairs, she found her husband slamming kitchen doors and drawers as he threw together a sandwich. He did not offer to make one for her.

"What are we supposed to tell Tom and Sarah, with that bastard staring through the windows?"

"Why would we tell Tom and Sarah anything?" asked Robin blankly.

"We're going to theirs for dinner tonight!"

"Oh, no," groaned Robin. "I mean, yes. Sorry. I forgot."

"Well, what if the bloody journalist follows us?"

"We ignore him," said Robin. "What else can we do?"

She heard her mobile ringing upstairs and, glad of the excuse to get out of Matthew's vicinity, went to answer it.

"Hi," said Strike. "Good news. Izzy's hired us to look into Chiswell's death. Well," he corrected himself, "what she actually wants is for us to prove Kinvara did it, but I managed to broaden the remit."

"That's fantastic!" whispered Robin, carefully closing the bedroom door and sitting down on the bed.

"I thought you'd be pleased," said Strike. "Now, what we need for starters is a line on the police investigation, especially forensics. I've just tried Wardle, but he's been warned not to talk to us. They seem to have guessed I'd still be sniffing around. Then I tried Anstis, but nothing doing, he's full time on the Olympics and doesn't know anyone on the case. So I was going to ask, is Vanessa back off compassionate leave?"

"Yes!" said Robin, suddenly excited. It was the first time she had had the useful contact, rather than Strike. "But even better than Vanessa—she's dating a guy in forensics, Oliver, I've never met him, but—"

"If Oliver would agree to talk to us," said Strike, "that would be fantastic. Tell you what, I'll call Shanker, see whether he'll sell me something we can offer in exchange. Call you back."

He hung up. Though hungry, Robin did not go back downstairs, but stretched out on the smart mahogany bed, which had been a wedding gift from Matthew's father. It was so cumbersome and heavy that it had taken the full complement of removal men, sweating and swearing under their breath, to haul it up the stairs in pieces and reassemble it in the bedroom. Robin's dressing table, on the other hand, was old and cheap. Light as an orange crate without its drawers in, it had required only one man to pick it up and place it between the bedroom windows.

Ten minutes later, her mobile rang again.

"That was quick."

"Yeah, we're in luck. Shanker's having a rest day. Our interests happen to coincide. There's somebody he wouldn't mind the police picking off. Tell Vanessa we're offering information on Ian Nash."

"Ian Nash?" repeated Robin, sitting up to grab pen and paper and make a note of the name. "Who exactly—?"

"Gangster. Vanessa will know who he is," said Strike.

"How much did it cost?" asked Robin. The personal bond between Strike and Shanker, profound in its way, never interfered with Shanker's rules of business.

"Half the first week's fee," said Strike, "but it'll be money well spent if Oliver comes across with the goods. How're you?"

"What?" said Robin, disconcerted. "I'm fine. Why d'you ask?"

"Don't suppose it's ever occurred to you that I've got a duty of care, as your employer?"

"We're partners."

"You're a salaried partner. You could sue for poor working conditions."

"Don't you think," said Robin, examining the forearm where the eight-inch purple scar still stood out, livid, against her pale skin, "I'd've already done that, if I was going to? But if you're offering to sort out the loo on the landing—"

"I'm just saying," persisted Strike, "it'd be natural if you'd had a bit of reaction. Finding a body isn't many people's idea of fun."

"I'm absolutely fine," lied Robin.

I have to be fine, she thought, after they had bidden each other goodbye. *I'm not losing everything, all over again.*

40

Your starting-point is so very widely removed from his, you see.
                    Henrik Ibsen, *Rosmersholm*

At six o'clock on Wednesday morning, Robin, who had again slept in the spare room, got up and dressed herself in jeans, T-shirt, sweat-shirt and trainers. Her backpack contained a dark wig that she had bought online and which had been delivered the previous morning, under the very nose of the skulking journalist. She crept quietly downstairs, so as not to wake Matthew, with whom she had not discussed her plan. She knew perfectly well that he would disapprove.

There was a precarious peace between them, even though dinner on Saturday night with Tom and Sarah had been an awful affair: in fact, precisely because dinner had been so dreadful. It had started inauspiciously because the journalist had indeed followed them up the street. They had succeeded in shaking him off, largely due to Robin's counter-surveillance training, which had led them to dodge unseen out of a crowded Tube compartment just before the doors closed, leaving Matthew aggravated by what he considered undigni-fied, childish tricks. But even Matthew could not lay the blame for the rest of the evening at Robin's door.

What had begun as light-hearted analysis over dinner of their failure to win the charity cricket match had turned suddenly nasty and aggressive. Tom had suddenly lashed out drunkenly at Matthew, telling him he was not half as good as he thought he was, that his arrogance had grated on the rest of the team, that, indeed, he was not popular in the office, that he put people's backs up, rubbed them the wrong way. Rocked by the sudden attack, Matthew had tried to ask what he had done wrong at work, but Tom, so drunk that Robin thought he must have started on the wine long before their arrival, had taken Matthew's hurt incredulity as provocation.

"Don't play the fucking innocent with me!" he had shouted. "I'm not going to stand for it any more! Belittling me and fucking needling me—"

"Was I?" Matthew asked Robin, shaken, as they walked back towards the Tube in the darkness.

"No," said Robin, honestly. "You didn't say anything nasty to him at all."

She added "tonight" only in her head. It was a relief to be taking a hurt and bewildered Matthew home, rather than the man she usually lived with, and her sympathy and support had won her a couple of days' ceasefire at home. Robin was not about to jeopardize their truce by telling Matthew what she was planning this morning to throw the still-lurking journalist off her trail. She couldn't afford to be followed to a meeting with a forensic pathologist, especially as Oliver, according to Vanessa, had needed a great deal of persuasion to meet Strike and Robin in the first place.

Letting herself quietly out of the French windows into the courtyard behind the house, Robin used one of the garden chairs to clamber onto the top of the wall that divided their garden from that of the house directly behind them, of which the curtains were, mercifully, closed. With a muffled, earthy thud, she slid off the wall onto the neighbors' lawn.

The next part of her escape was a little trickier. She had first to drag a heavy ornamental bench in their neighbor's garden several feet, until it stood plumb with the fence, then, balancing on the back of it, she climbed over the top of the creosoted panel, which swayed precariously as she dropped down into a flowerbed on the other side, where she staggered and fell. Scrambling up again, she hurried across the new lawn to the opposite fence, in which there was a door to the car park on the other side.

To Robin's relief, the bolt opened easily. As she pulled the garden gate closed behind her, she thought ruefully of the footprints she had just left across the dewy lawns. If the neighbors woke early, it would be only too easy to discover whence had come the intruder who had invaded their gardens, shifted their garden furniture and squashed their begonias. Chiswell's killer, if killer there was, had been far more adept at covering their tracks.

Crouching down behind a parked Skoda in the deserted car park that served the garage-less street, Robin used the wing mirror to adjust the dark wig she had taken out of her backpack, then walked off briskly along the street that ran parallel with Albury Street, until she turned right into Deptford High Street.

Other than a couple of vans making early morning deliveries and the proprietor of a newsagent raising the metal security roller door from his shop front, there was hardly anybody around. Glancing over her shoulder, Robin felt a sudden rush, not of panic, but of elation: nobody was following her. Even so, she didn't remove her wig until she was safely on the Tube, giving the young man who had been eyeing her covertly over his Kindle something of a surprise.

Strike had chosen the Corner Café on Lambeth Road for its proximity to the forensics laboratory where Oliver Bargate worked. When Robin arrived, she found Strike standing outside, smoking. His gaze fell to the muddy knees of her jeans.

"Rough landing in a flowerbed," she explained, as she came within earshot. "That journalist is still hanging around."

"Matthew give you a leg up?"

"No, I used garden furniture."

Strike ground out his cigarette on the wall beside him and followed her into the café, which smelled pleasantly of frying food. In Strike's opinion, Robin looked paler and thinner than usual, but her manner was cheerful as she ordered coffee and two bacon rolls.

"One," Strike corrected her. "One," he repeated regretfully to the man behind the counter. "Trying to lose weight," he told Robin, as they took a recently vacated table. "Better for my leg."

"Ah," said Robin. "Right."

As he swept the crumbs from the table with his sleeve, Strike reflected, not for the first time, that Robin was the only woman he had ever met who had shown no interest in improving him. He knew that he could have changed his mind now and ordered five bacon rolls, and she would simply have grinned and handed them over. This thought made him feel particularly affectionate towards her as she joined him at the table in her muddy jeans.

"Everything OK?" he asked, salivating as he watched her put ketchup on her roll.

"Yes," lied Robin, "all good. How *is* your leg?"

"Better than it was. What does this bloke we're meeting look like?"

"Tall, black, glasses," said Robin thickly, through a mouthful of bread and bacon. Her early morning activity had made her hungrier than she had been in days.

"Vanessa back on Olympics duty?"

"Yeah," said Robin. "She's badgered Oliver into meeting us. I don't think he was that keen, but she's after promotion."

"Dirt on Ian Nash will definitely help," said Strike. "From what Shanker told me, the Met's been trying—"

"I think this is him," whispered Robin.

Strike turned to see a lanky, worried-looking black man in rimless glasses standing in the doorway. He was holding a briefcase. Strike raised a hand in greeting and Robin slid her sandwich and coffee over to the next seat, to allow Oliver to sit opposite Strike.

Robin was not sure what she had expected: he was handsome, with his high-rise hairstyle and pristine white shirt, but seemed suspicious and disapproving, neither of which trait she associated with Vanessa. Nevertheless, he shook the hand Strike proffered and, turning to Robin, said:

"You're Robin? We've always missed each other."

"Yes," said Robin, shaking hands, too. Oliver's spotless appearance was making her feel self-conscious about her disheveled hair and muddy jeans. "Nice to meet you, at last. It's counter service, shall I get you a tea or coffee?"

"Er—coffee, yeah, that'd be good," said Oliver. "Thanks."

As Robin went to the counter, Oliver turned back to Strike.

"Vanessa says you've got some information for her."

"Might have," said Strike. "It all depends on what you've got for us, Oliver."

"I'd like to know exactly what you're offering before we take this any further."

Strike drew an envelope out of his jacket pocket and held it up.

"A car registration number and a hand-drawn map."

Apparently this meant something to Oliver.

"Can I ask where you got this?"

"You can ask," said Strike cheerfully, "but that information's not included in the deal. Eric Wardle will tell you my contact's got a record of hundred percent reliability, though."

A group of workmen entered the café, talking loudly.

"This'll all be off the record," said Strike quietly. "No one'll ever know you talked to us."

Oliver sighed, then bent down, opened his briefcase and extracted a large notebook. As Robin returned with a mug of coffee for Oliver and sat back down at the table, Strike readied himself to make notes.

"I've spoken to one of the guys on the team who did forensics," Oliver said, glancing at the workmen who were now bantering loudly at the next table, "and Vanessa's had a word with someone who knows where the wider investigation's going." He addressed Robin. "They don't know Vanessa is friendly with you. If it gets out that we helped—"

"They won't hear it from us," Robin assured him.

Frowning slightly, Oliver opened his notebook and consulted the details he had jotted there in a small but legible hand.

"Well, forensics are fairly clear-cut. I don't know how much technical detail you want—"

"Minimal," said Strike. "Give us the highlights."

"Chiswell had ingested around 500mg of amitriptyline, dissolved in orange juice, on an empty stomach."

"That's a sizable dose, isn't it?" asked Strike.

"It could have been fatal on its own, even without the helium, but it wouldn't have been as quick. On the other hand, he had heart disease, which would have made him more susceptible. Amitriptyline causes dysrhythmia and cardiac arrest in overdose."

"Popular suicide method?"

"Yeah," said Oliver, "but it's not always as painless as people hope. Most of it was still in his stomach. Very small traces in the duodenum. Suffocation is what actually killed him, on analysis of the lung and brain tissue. Presumably the amitriptyline was a back-up."

"Prints on the glass and the orange juice carton?"

Oliver turned a page in his notebook.

"The glass only had Chiswell's prints on it. They found the carton in the bin, empty, also with Chiswell's prints on, and others. Nothing suspicious. Just as you'd expect if it had been handled during purchase. Juice inside tested negative for drugs. The drugs went directly into the glass."

"The helium canister?"

"That had Chiswell's prints on it, and some others. Nothing suspicious. Same as the juice carton, like it had been handled during purchase."

"Does amitriptyline have a taste?" asked Robin.

"Yeah, it's bitter," said Oliver.

"Olfactory dysfunction," Strike reminded Robin. "After the head injury. He might not have tasted it."

"Would it have made him groggy?" Robin asked Oliver.

"Probably, especially if he wasn't used to taking it, but people can have unexpected reactions. He might've become agitated."

"Any sign of how or where the pills were crushed up?" asked Strike.

"In the kitchen. There were traces of powder found on the pestle and mortar there."

"Prints?"

"His."

"D'you know whether they tested the homeopathic pills?" asked Robin.

"The what?" said Oliver.

"There was a tube of homeopathic pills on the floor. I trod on them," Robin explained. "Lachesis."

"I don't know anything about them," said Oliver, and Robin felt a little foolish for mentioning them.

"There was a mark on the back of his left hand."

"Yes," said Oliver, turning back to his notes. "Abrasions to face and a small mark on the hand."

"On the face, too?" said Robin, freezing with her sandwich in her hand.

"Yes," said Oliver.

"Any explanation?" asked Strike.

"You're wondering whether the bag was forced over his head," said Oliver; it was a statement, not a question. "So did MI5. They know he didn't make the marks himself. Nothing under his own nails. On the other hand, there was no bruising to the body to show force, nothing disarranged in the room, no signs of a struggle—"

"Other than the bent sword," said Strike.

"I keep forgetting you were there," said Oliver. "You know all this."

"Marks on the sword?"

"It had been cleaned recently, but Chiswell's prints were on the handle."

"What time of death are we looking at?"

"Between 6 and 7 a.m.," said Oliver.

"But he was fully dressed," mused Robin.

"From what I've heard about him, he was quite literally the kind of bloke who wouldn't have been caught dead in pajamas," said Oliver drily.

"Met's inclining to suicide, then?" asked Strike.

"Off the record, I think an open verdict is quite likely. There are a few discrepancies that need explaining. You know about the open front door, of course. It's warped. It won't close unless you shut it with force, but it sometimes jumps back open again if you slam it too hard. So it could have been accidental, the fact that it was open. Chiswell might not have realized he'd left it ajar, but equally, a killer might not have known the trick to closing it."

"You don't happen to know how many keys to the door there were?" asked Strike.

"No," said Oliver. "As I'm sure you'll appreciate, Van and I had to sound only casually interested, asking all these questions."

"He's a dead government minister," said Strike. "Surely you didn't have to sound too casual?"

"I know one thing," said Oliver. "He had plenty of reasons to kill himself."

"Such as?" inquired Strike, pen poised over his notebook.

"His wife was leaving him—"

"Allegedly," said Strike, writing.

"—they'd lost a baby, his eldest son died in Iraq, the family say he was acting strangely, drinking heavily and so on, and he had serious money problems."

"Yeah?" said Strike. "Like what?"

"He was almost wiped out in the 2008 crash," said Oliver. "And then there was...well, that business you two were investigating."

"D'you know where the blackmailers were, at the time of—?"

Oliver made a swift, convulsive movement that nearly knocked over his coffee. Leaning towards Strike he hissed:

"There's a super-injunction out, in case you haven't—"

"Yeah, we've heard," said Strike.

"Well, I happen to like my job."

"OK," said Strike, unperturbed, but lowering his voice. "I'll rephrase my question. Have they looked into the movements of Geraint Winn and Jimmy—?"

"Yes," said Oliver curtly, "and both have alibis."

"What are they?"

"The former was in Bermondsey with—"

"Not Della?" blurted Robin, before she could stop herself. The idea of his blind wife being Geraint's alibi had struck her, somehow, as indecent. She had formed the impression, whether naively or not, that Della stood apart from Geraint's criminal activity.

"No," said Oliver tersely, "and do we have to use names?"

"Who, then?" asked Strike.

"Some employee. He claims he was with the employee and the bloke confirmed it."

"Were there other witnesses?"

"I don't know," said Oliver, with a trace of frustration. "I assume so. They're happy with the alibi."

"What about Ji—the other man?"

"He was in East Ham with his girlfriend."

"Was he?" said Strike, making a note of it. "I saw him being marched off to a police van, the night before Chiswell died."

"He was let off with a caution. But," Oliver said quietly, "blackmailers don't generally kill their victims, do they?"

"Not if they're getting money out of them," said Strike, still writing. "But Knight wasn't."

Oliver looked at his watch.

"Couple more things," said Strike equably, his elbow still planted on the envelope containing Ian Nash's details. "Does Vanessa know anything about a phone call to his son that Chiswell made on the morning of his death?"

"Yeah, she said something about that," said Oliver, flicking backwards and forwards through his notebook to find the information. "Yeah, he made two calls just after 6 a.m. First to his wife, then to his son."

Strike and Robin looked at each other again.

"We knew about the call to Raphael. He called his wife as well?"

"Yeah, he called her first."

Oliver seemed to read their reaction correctly, because he said:

"The wife's totally in the clear. She was the first person they investigated, once they were satisfied it wasn't politically motivated, obviously.

"A neighbor saw her go into the house on Ebury Street the evening before and come out shortly afterwards with a bag, two hours before her husband came back. A taxi driver picked her up halfway down the street and took her to Paddington. She was caught on camera on the train back to wherever she lives—is it Oxfordshire?—and apparently there was someone at the house when she got home, who can vouch for the fact that she arrived there before midnight and never left again until the police came round to tell her Chiswell was dead. Multiple witnesses to her whole journey."

"Who was at the house with her?"

"That, I don't know." Oliver's eyes moved to the envelope still lying beneath Strike's elbow. "And that really is everything I've got."

Strike had asked everything he had wanted to know, and had gained a couple of bits of information he had not expected, including the abrasions to Chiswell's face, his poor finances and the phone call to Kinvara in the early morning.

"You've been a big help," he told Oliver, sliding the envelope across the table. "Much appreciated."

Oliver appeared relieved that the encounter was over. He stood up and, with one more hasty handshake and a nod to Robin, departed the café. Once Oliver had stridden out of sight, Robin sat back in her chair and sighed.

"What's that glum expression for?" asked Strike, draining his mug of tea.

"This is going to be the shortest job on record. Izzy wants us to prove it was Kinvara."

"She wants the truth about her father's death," said Strike, but he grinned at Robin's skeptical expression, "and, yeah, she's hoping it was Kinvara. Well, we'll have to see whether we can break all those alibis, won't we? I'm going to Woolstone on Saturday. Izzy's invited me over to Chiswell House, so I can meet her sister. Are you in? I'd rather not drive, the state my leg's in at the moment."

"Yes, of course," said Robin immediately.

The idea of getting out of London with Strike, even for a day, was so appealing that she did not bother to consider whether she and Matthew had plans, but surely, in the glow of their unexpected rapprochement, he would raise no difficulties. After all, she had not worked for a week and a half. "We can take the Land Rover. It'll be better on country roads than your BMW."

"You might need diversionary tactics if that hack's still watching you," said Strike.

"I think I could probably throw them off more easily in a car than on foot."

"Yeah, you probably could," said Strike.

Robin was in possession of an advanced driving qualification. Though he had never told her so, Robin was the only person by whom he would willingly be driven.

"What time are we supposed to be at Chiswell House?"

"Eleven," said Strike, "but plan to be away for the whole day. I fancy taking a look at the Knights' old place while we're there." He hesitated. "I can't remember whether I told you... I kept Barclay undercover with Jimmy and Flick."

He was braced for annoyance that he had not discussed it with her, resentment that Barclay had been working when she wasn't, or, perhaps most justifiably, a demand to know what he was playing at, given the state of the agency's finances, but she simply said, with more amusement than rancor:

"You know you didn't tell me. Why did you keep him there?"

"Because I've got a gut feeling there's a lot more to the Knight brothers than meets the eye."

"You always tell me to mistrust gut feelings."

"Never claimed not to be a hypocrite, though. And brace yourself," Strike added, as they got up from the table, "Raphael's not happy with you."

"Why not?"

"Izzy says he fell for you. Quite upset you turned out to be an undercover detective."

"Oh," said Robin. A faint pink blush spread over her face. "Well, I'm sure he'll bounce back fast enough. He's that type."

41

*I was thinking of what brought us together from the first, what
links us so closely to one another...*

Henrik Ibsen, *Rosmersholm*

Strike had spent many hours of his life trying to guess what he had
done to cause the sullen silence of a woman in his vicinity. The best
that could be said for the prolonged sulk in which Lorelei spent most
of Friday evening was that he knew exactly how he had offended her,
and was even prepared to concede that her displeasure was, to some
extent, justified.

Within five minutes of his arrival at her flat in Camden, Izzy had
called his mobile, partly to tell him about a letter that she had received
from Geraint Winn, but mainly, he knew, to talk. She was not the
first of his clients to assume that they had purchased, along with
detective services, a mixture of father-confessor and therapist. Izzy
gave every sign that she was settling in to spend her entire Friday
evening talking to Strike, and the flirtatiousness that had been apparent in the knee touching of their last encounter was even more
pronounced by phone.

A tendency to size Strike up as a potential lover was not uncom-
mon in the sometimes fragile and lonely women he dealt with in his
professional life. He had never slept with a client, in spite of occasional temptation. The agency meant too much to him, but even had
Izzy held attraction for him, he would have been careful to keep his
manner on the antiseptic side of professional, because she would be
forever tainted in his mind by association with Charlotte.

In spite of his genuine desire to cut the call short—Lorelei had cooked, and was looking particularly lovely in a silky sapphire blue dress that resembled nightwear—Izzy had displayed the persistent adhesiveness of a teasel. It took Strike nearly three-quarters of an hour to disentangle himself from his client, who laughed long and loudly at even his mildest jokes, so that Lorelei could hardly fail to know that it was a woman who was at the end of the line. Hardly had he got rid of Izzy and begun to explain to Lorelei that she was a grief-stricken client, than Barclay had called with an update on Jimmy Knight. The mere fact that he had taken the second call, considerably briefer though it was, had, in Lorelei's eyes, compounded his original offense.

This was the first time he and Lorelei had met since she had retracted her declaration of love. Her wounded and affronted demeanor over dinner confirmed him in the unwilling belief that, far from wanting their no-strings arrangement to continue, she had clung to the hope that if she stopped pressuring him, he would be free to reach the realization that he was, in fact, deeply in love with her. Talking on the phone for the best part of an hour, while dinner slowly shriveled in the oven, had dashed her hopes of a perfect evening, and the reset of their relationship.

Had Lorelei only accepted his sincere apology, he might have felt like sex. However, by half-past two in the morning, at which time she finally burst into tears of mingled self-recrimination and self-justification, he was too tired and bad-tempered to accept physical overtures which would, he feared, assume an importance in her mind that he did not want to give them.

This has to end, he thought, as he rose, hollow-eyed and dark-jawed, at six o'clock, moving as quietly as possible in the hope that she would not wake before he made his way out of her flat. Forgoing breakfast, because Lorelei had replaced the kitchen door with an amusingly retro bead curtain that rattled loudly, Strike made it all the way to the top of the stairs to the street before Lorelei emerged from the dark bedroom, sleep tousled, sad and desirable in a short kimono.

"Weren't you even going to say goodbye?"

Don't cry. Please don't fucking cry.

"You looked very peaceful. I've got to go, Robin's picking me up at—"

"Ah," said Lorelei. "No, you wouldn't want to keep Robin hanging around."

"I'll call you," said Strike.

He thought he caught a sob as he reached the front door, but by making a noisy business of opening it, he could credibly claim not to have heard.

Having left in plenty of time, Strike made a detour to a handy McDonald's for an Egg McMuffin and a large coffee, which he consumed at an unwiped table, surrounded by other early Saturday risers. A young man with a boil on the back of his neck was reading the *Independent* right ahead of Strike, who read the words *Sports Minister in Marriage Split* over the youth's shoulder before he turned a page.

Drawing out his phone, Strike Googled "Winn marriage." The news stories popped up immediately: *Minister for Sport Splits from Husband: Separation "Amicable." Della Winn Calls Time on Marriage. Blind Paralympics Minister to Divorce.*

The stories from major newspapers were all factual and on the short side, a few padded out with details of Della's impressive career within politics and outside. The press's lawyers would, of course, be particularly careful around the Winns just now, with their superinjunction still in place. Strike finished his McMuffin in two bites, jammed an unlit cigarette in his mouth and limped out of the restaurant. Out on the pavement he lit up, then brought up the website of a well-known and scurrilous political blogger on his phone.

The brief paragraph had been written only a few hours previously.

Which creepy Westminster couple known to share a predilection for youthful employees are rumored to be splitting at last? He is about to lose access to the nubile political wannabes on whom he has preyed so long, but she has already found a handsome young "helper" to ease the pain of separation.

Less than forty minutes later, Strike emerged from Barons Court Tube station to lean up against the pillar-box in front of the entrance. Cutting a solitary figure beneath the Art Nouveau lettering and open segmented pediment of the grand station behind him, he took out his phone again and continued to read about the Winns' separation. They had been married over thirty years. The only couple he knew who had been together that long were the aunt and uncle back in Cornwall, who had served as surrogate parents to Strike and his sister during those regular intervals when his mother had been unwilling or unable to care for them.

A familiar roar and rattle made Strike look up. The ancient Land Rover that Robin had taken off her parents' hands was trundling towards him. The sight of Robin's bright gold head behind the wheel caught the tired and faintly depressed Strike off-guard. He experienced a wave of unexpected happiness.

"Morning," said Robin, thinking that Strike looked terrible as he opened the door and shoved in a holdall. "Oh, sod off," she added, as a driver behind her slammed on his horn, aggravated by the time Strike was taking to get inside.

"Sorry…leg's giving me trouble. Dressed in a hurry."

"No problem—*and you!*" Robin shouted at the driver now overtaking them, who was gesticulating and mouthing obscenities at her.

Finally dropping down into the passenger seat, Strike slammed the door and Robin pulled away from the curb.

"Any trouble getting away?" he asked.

"What d'you—?"

"The journalist."

"Oh," she said. "No—he's gone. Given up."

Strike wondered just how difficult Matthew had been about Robin giving up a Saturday for work.

"Heard about the Winns?" he asked her.

"No, what's happened?"

"They've split up."

"*No!*"

"Yep. In all the papers. Listen to this…"

He read aloud the blind item on the political website.

"God," said Robin quietly.

"I had a couple of interesting calls last night," Strike said, as they sped towards the M4.

"Who from?"

"One from Izzy, the other from Barclay. Izzy got a letter from Geraint yesterday," said Strike.

"Really?" said Robin.

"Yeah. It was sent to Chiswell House a few days back, not her London flat, so she only opened it when she went back to Woolstone. I got her to scan and email it to me. Want to hear?"

"Go on," said Robin.

"'My very dear Isabella—'"

"Ugh," said Robin, with a small shudder.

"'As I hope you will understand,'" read Strike, "'Della and I did not feel it appropriate to contact you in the immediate, shocking aftermath of your father's death. We do so now in a spirit of friendliness and compassion.'"

"If you need to point that out..."

"'Della and I may have had political and personal differences with Jasper, but I hope we never forgot that he was a family man, and we are aware that your personal loss will be severe. You ran his office with courtesy and efficiency and our little corridor will be the poorer for your absence.'"

"He always cut Izzy dead!" said Robin.

"Exactly what Izzy said on the phone last night," replied Strike. "Stand by, you're about to get a mention.

"'I cannot believe that you had anything to do with the almost certainly illegal activities of the young woman calling herself "Venetia." We feel it only fair to inform you that we are currently investigating the possibility that she may have accessed confidential data on the multiple occasions she entered this office without consent.'"

"I never looked at anything except the plug socket," said Robin, "and I didn't access the office on 'multiple occasions.' Three. That's 'a few,' at most."

"'As you know, the tragedy of suicide has touched our own family. We know that this will be an extremely difficult and painful time for you. Our families certainly seem fated to bump into each other in their darkest hours.

"'Sending our very best wishes, our thoughts are with all of you, etc, etc.'"

Strike closed the letter on his phone.

"That's not a letter of condolence," said Robin.

"Nope, it's a threat. If the Chiswells blab about anything you found out about Geraint or the charity, he'll go after them, hard, using you."

She turned onto the motorway.

"When did you say that letter was sent?"

"Five, six days ago," said Strike, checking.

"It doesn't sound as though he knew his marriage was over then, does it? All that 'our corridor will be poorer for your absence' guff. He's lost his job if he's split with Della, surely?"

"You'd think so," agreed Strike. "How handsome would you say Aamir Mallik is?"

"What?" said Robin, startled. "Oh...the 'young helper'? Well, he's OK looking, but not model material."

"It must be him. How many other young men's hands is she holding and calling darling?"

"I can't imagine him as her lover," said Robin.

"'A man of your habits,'" quoted Strike. "Pity you can't remember what number that poem was."

"Is there one about sleeping with an older woman?"

"The best-known ones are on that very subject," said Strike. "Catullus was in love with an older woman."

"Aamir isn't in love," said Robin. "You heard the tape."

"He didn't sound smitten, I grant you. I wouldn't mind knowing what causes the animal noises he makes at night, though. The ones the neighbors complain about."

His leg was throbbing. Reaching down to feel the join between prosthesis and stump, he knew that part of the problem was having put on the former hurriedly, in the dark.

"D'you mind if I readjust—?"

"Carry on," said Robin.

Strike rolled up his trouser leg and proceeded to remove the prosthesis. Ever since he had been forced to take two weeks off wearing it, the skin at the end of his stump had shown a tendency to object to renewed friction. Retrieving E45 cream from his holdall, he applied it liberally to the reddened skin.

"Should've done this earlier," he said apologetically.

Deducing from the presence of Strike's holdall that he had come from Lorelei's, Robin found herself wondering whether he had been too pleasurably occupied to worry about his leg. She and Matthew had not had sex since their anniversary weekend.

"I'll leave it off for a bit," said Strike, heaving both prosthesis and holdall into the back of the Land Rover, which he now saw was empty but for a tartan flask and two plastic cups. This was a disappointment. There had always been a carrier bag full of food on the previous occasions they had ventured out of London by car.

"No biscuits?"

"I thought you were trying to lose weight?"

"Nothing eaten on a car journey counts, any competent dietician will tell you that."

Robin grinned.

"'Calories Are Bollocks: the Cormoran Strike Diet.'"

"'Hunger Strike: Car Journeys I Have Starved On.'"

"Well, you should've had breakfast," said Robin, and to her own annoyance, she wondered for the second time whether he had been otherwise engaged.

"I did have breakfast. Now I want a biscuit."

"We can stop somewhere if you're hungry," said Robin. "We should have plenty of time."

As Robin accelerated smoothly to overtake a couple of dawdling cars, Strike was aware of an ease and restfulness that could not be entirely ascribed to the relief of removing his prosthesis, nor even of having escaped Lorelei's flat, with its kitschy décor and its heartsore occupant. The very fact that he had removed his leg while Robin drove, and was not sitting with all muscles clenched, was highly unusual. Not only had he had to work hard to overcome anxiety at being driven by other people in the aftermath of the explosion that had blown off his leg, he had a secret but deep-rooted aversion to women drivers, a prejudice he ascribed largely to early, nerve-wracking experiences with all his female relatives. Yet it was not merely a prosaic appreciation of her competence that had caused that sudden lifting of the heart when he had seen her driving towards him this morning. Now, watching the road, he experienced a spasm of memory, sharp with both pleasure and pain; his nostrils seemed to be full again with the smell of white roses, as he held her on the stairs at her wedding and he felt her mouth beneath his in the hot fug of a hospital car park.

"Could you pass me my sunglasses?" asked Robin. "In my bag there."

He handed them over.

"Want a tea?"

"I'll wait," said Robin, "you carry on."

He reached into the back for the thermos and poured himself a plastic cup full. The tea was exactly as he liked it.

"I asked Izzy about Chiswell's will last night," Strike told Robin.

"Did he leave a lot?" asked Robin, remembering the shabby interior of the house in Ebury Street.

"Much less than you might've thought," said Strike, taking out the notebook in which he had jotted everything Izzy had told him. "Oliver was right. The Chiswells are on their uppers—in a relative sense, obviously," he added.

"Apparently Chiswell's father spent most of the capital on women and horses. Chiswell had a very messy divorce from Lady Patricia. Her family was wealthy and could afford better lawyers. Izzy and her sister are all right for cash through their mother's family. There's a trust fund, which explains Izzy's smart flat in Chelsea.

"Raphael's mother walked away with hefty child support, which seems to have nearly cleaned Chiswell out. After that, he plunged the little he had left into some risky equities advised by his stockbroker son-in-law. 'Torks' feels pretty bad about that, apparently. Izzy would rather we didn't mention it today. The 2008 crash virtually wiped Chiswell out.

"He tried to do some planning against death duties. Shortly after he lost most of his cash, some valuable family heirlooms and Chiswell House itself were made over to the eldest grandson—"

"Pringle," said Robin.

"What?"

"Pringle. That's what they call the eldest grandson. Fizzy's got three children," Robin explained, "Izzy was always banging on about them: Pringle, Flopsy and Pong."

"Jesus Christ," muttered Strike. "It's like interviewing the Teletubbies."

Robin laughed.

"—and otherwise, Chiswell seems to have been hoping he could put himself right by selling off land around Chiswell House and objects of less sentimental value. The house in Ebury Street's been remortgaged."

"So Kinvara and all her horses are living in her step-grandson's house?" said Robin, changing up a gear to overtake a lorry.

"Yeah, Chiswell left a letter of wishes with his will, asking that Kinvara has the right to remain in the house lifelong, or until she remarries. How old's this Pringle?"

"About ten, I think."

"Well, it'll be interesting to see whether the family honor Chiswell's request given that one of them thinks Kinvara killed him. Mind you, it's a moot point whether she'll have enough money to keep the place running, from what Izzy told me last night. Izzy and her sister were each left fifty grand, and the grandchildren get ten grand apiece, and there's hardly enough cash to honor those bequests. That leaves Kinvara with what's left from the house in Ebury Street once it's sold off and all other personal effects, minus the valuable stuff that was already put into the grandson's name. Basically, he's leaving her with the junk that wasn't worth selling and any personal gifts he gave her during the marriage."

"And Raphael gets nothing?"

"I wouldn't feel too sorry for him. According to Izzy, his glamorous mother's made a career out of asset-stripping wealthy men. He's in line to inherit a flat in Chelsea from her."

"So all in all, it's hard to make a case for Chiswell being killed for his money," said Strike. "What *is* the other sister's bloody name? I'm not calling her Fizzy."

"Sophia," said Robin, amused.

"Right, well, we can rule her out. I've checked, she was taking a

Riding for the Disabled lesson in Northumberland on the morning he died. Raphael had nothing to gain from his father's death, and Izzy thinks he knew it, although we'll need to check that. Izzy herself got what she called 'a bit squiffy' at Lancaster House and felt a bit fragile the following day. Her neighbor can vouch for the fact that she was having tea in the shared courtyard behind their flats at the time of death. She told me that quite naturally last night."

"Which leaves Kinvara," said Robin.

"Right. Now, if Chiswell didn't trust her with the information that he'd called in a private detective, he might not have been honest about the state of the family finances, either. It's possible she thought she was going to get a lot more than she has, but—"

"—she's got the best alibi in the family," said Robin.

"Exactly," said Strike.

They had now left behind the clearly man-made border shrubs and bushes that had lined the motorway as it passed Windsor and Maidenhead. There were real old trees left and right now, trees that had predated the road, and which would have seen their fellows felled to make way for it.

"Barclay's call was interesting," Strike went on, turning a couple of pages in his notebook. "Knight's been in a nasty mood ever since Chiswell died, though he hasn't told Barclay why. On Wednesday night he was goading Flick, apparently, said he agreed with her ex-flatmate that Flick had bourgeois instincts—d'you mind if I smoke? I'll wind down the window."

The breeze was bracing, though it made his tired eyes water. Holding his burning cigarette out of the car between drags, he went on:

"So Flick got really angry, said she'd been doing 'that shitty job for you' and then said it wasn't her fault they hadn't got forty grand, at which Jimmy went, to quote Barclay, 'apeshit.' Flick stormed out and on Thursday morning, Jimmy texted Barclay and told him he was going back to where he grew up, to visit his brother."

"Billy's in Woolstone?" said Robin, startled. She realized that she had come to think of the younger Knight brother as an almost mythical person.

"Jimmy might've been using him as a cover story. Who knows where he's really got to...Anyway, Jimmy and Flick reappeared last night in the pub, all smiles. Barclay says they'd obviously made up over the phone and in the two days he was away, she's managed to find herself a nice non-bourgeois job."

"That was good going," said Robin.

"How d'you feel about shop work?"

"I did a bit in my teens," said Robin. "Why?"

"Flick's got herself a few hours part time in a jewelry shop in Camden. She told Barclay it's run by some mad Wiccan woman. It's minimum wage and the boss sounds barking mad, so they're having trouble finding anyone else."

"Don't you think they might recognize me?"

"The Knight lot have never seen you in person," said Strike. "If you did something drastic with your hair, broke out the colored contact lenses again...I've got a feeling," he said, drawing deeply on his cigarette, "that Flick's hiding a lot. How did she know what Chiswell's blackmailable offense was? She was the one who told Jimmy, don't forget, which is strange."

"Wait," said Robin. "What?"

"Yeah, she said, when I was following them on the march," said Strike. "Didn't I tell you?"

"No," said Robin.

As she said it, Strike remembered that he had spent the week after the march at Lorelei's with his leg up, when he had still been so angry at Robin for refusing to work that he had barely spoken to her. Then they had met at the hospital, and he had been far too distracted and worried to pass on information in his usual methodical fashion.

"Sorry," he said. "It was that week after..."

"Yes," she said, cutting him off. She, too, preferred not to think about the weekend of the march. "So what exactly did she say?"

"That he wouldn't know what Chiswell had done, but for her."

"That's weird," said Robin, "seeing as he's the one who grew up right beside them."

"But the thing they were blackmailing him about only happened six years ago, after Jimmy had left home," Strike reminded her. "If you ask me, Jimmy's been keeping Flick around because she knows too much. He might be scared of ending it, in case she starts talking.

"If you can't get anything useful out of her, you can pretend selling earrings isn't for you and leave, but the state their relationship's in, I think Flick might be in the mood to confide in a friendly stranger. Don't forget," he said, throwing the end of his cigarette out of the window and winding it back up, "she's also Jimmy's alibi for the time of death."

Excited about the prospect of going back undercover, Robin said: "I hadn't forgotten."

She wondered how Matthew would react if she shaved the sides of her head, or dyed her hair blue. He had not put up much of a show of resentment at her spending Saturday with Strike. Her long days of effective house arrest, and her sympathy about the argument with Tom, seemed to have bought her credit.

Shortly after half past ten, they turned off the motorway onto a country road that wound down into the valley where the tiny village of Woolstone lay nestled. Robin parked beside a hedgerow full of Traveler's Joy, so that Strike could reattach his prosthesis. Replacing her sunglasses in her handbag, Robin noticed two texts from Matthew. They had arrived two hours earlier, but the alert of her mobile must have been drowned out by the racket of the Land Rover.

The first read:

All day. What about Tom?

The second, which had been sent ten minutes later, said:

Ignore last, was meant for work.

Robin was rereading these when Strike said:
"Shit."

He had already reattached his prosthesis, and was staring through his window at something she could not see.

"What?"

"Look at that."

Strike pointed back up the hill down which they had just driven. Robin ducked her head so that she could see what had caught his attention.

A gigantic prehistoric white chalk figure had been cut into the hillside. To Robin, it resembled a stylised leopard, but the realization of what it was supposed to be had already hit her when Strike said:

"'Up by the horse. He strangled the kid, up by the horse.'"

42

In a family there is always something or other going awry . . .
Henrik Ibsen, *Rosmersholm*

A flaking wooden sign marked the turning to Chiswell House. The drive, which was overgrown and full of potholes, was bordered on the left by a dense patch of woodland and on the right, by a long field that had been separated into paddocks by electric fences, and contained a number of horses. As the Land Rover lurched and rumbled towards the out-of-sight house, two of the largest horses, spooked by the noisy and unfamiliar car, took off. A chain reaction then occurred, as most of their companions began to canter around, too, the original pair kicking out at each other as they went.

"Wow," said Robin, watching the horses as the Land Rover swayed over the uneven ground. "She's got stallions in together."

"That's bad, is it?" asked Strike, as a hairy creature the color of jet lashed out with teeth and back legs at an equally large animal he would have categorized as brown, though doubtless the coat color had some rarefied equine name.

"It's not usually done," said Robin, wincing as the black stallion's rear legs made contact with its companion's flank.

They turned a corner and saw a plain-faced neo-classical house of dirty yellow stone. The graveled forecourt, like the drive, had several potholes and was strewn with weeds, the windows were grubby and a large tub of horse feed sat incongruously beside the front door. Three cars were already sitting there: a red Audi Q3, a racing green

Range Rover and an old and muddy Grand Vitara. To the right of the house lay a stable block and to the left, a wide croquet lawn that had long since been given over to the daisies. More dense woodland lay beyond.

As Robin braked, an overweight black Labrador and a rough-coated terrier came shooting out of the front door, both barking. The Labrador seemed keen to make friends but the Norfolk terrier, which had a face like a malevolent monkey, barked and growled until a fair-haired man, dressed in stripy shirt and mustard-colored corduroy trousers, appeared at the doorway and bellowed:

"SHUT UP, RATTENBURY!"

Cowed, the dog subsided into low growls, all directed at Strike.

"Torquil D'Amery," drawled the fair-haired man, approaching Strike with his hand outstretched. There were deep pockets beneath his pale blue eyes and his shiny pink face looked as though it never needed a razor. "Ignore the dog, he's a bloody menace."

"Cormoran Strike. This is—"

Robin had just held out her hand when Kinvara erupted out of the house, wearing old jodhpurs and a washed-out T-shirt, her loose red hair falling everywhere.

"For God's *sake*...don't you know *anything* about horses?" she shrieked at Strike and Robin. "Why did you come up the drive so fast?"

"You should wear a hard hat if you're going in there, Kinvara!" Torquil called at her retreating figure, but she stormed away giving no sign that she had heard him. "Not your fault," he assured Strike and Robin, rolling his eyes. "Got to take the drive at speed or you'll get stuck in one of the bloody holes, ha ha. Come on in—ah, here's Izzy."

Izzy emerged from the house, wearing a navy shirtdress, the sapphire cross still around her neck. To Robin's slight surprise, she embraced Strike as though he was an old friend come to offer condolences.

"Hi, Izzy," he said, taking half a step backwards to extricate himself from the embrace. "You know Robin, obviously."

"Oh, yah, got to get used to calling you 'Robin' now," said Izzy, smiling and kissing Robin on both cheeks. "Sorry if I slip up and call you Venetia—I'm bound to, that's how I still think of you.

"Did you hear about the Winns?" she asked, in almost the same breath.

They nodded.

"Horrible, *horrible* little man," said Izzy. "I'm delighted Della's given him the push.

"Anyway, come along in...where's Kinvara?" she asked her brother-in-law as she led them into the house, which seemed gloomy after the brightness outside.

"Bloody horses are upset again," said Torquil, over the renewed barking of the Norfolk terrier. "No, fuck off, Rattenbury, you're staying outside."

He banged the front door closed on the terrier, which began to whine and scratch at it instead. The Labrador padded quietly in Izzy's wake as she led them through a dingy hallway with wide stone stairs, into a drawing room on the right.

Long windows faced out over the croquet lawn and the woods. As they entered, three white-blond children raced through the overgrown grass outside with raucous cries, then passed out of sight. There was nothing of modernity about them. In their dress and their hairstyles they might have walked straight out of the 1940s.

"They're Torquil and Fizzy's," said Izzy fondly.

"Guilty as charged," said Torquil, proudly. "M'wife's upstairs, I'll go and get her."

As Robin turned away from the window she caught a whiff of a strong, heady scent that gave her an unaccountable feeling of tension until she spotted the vase of stargazer lilies standing on a table behind a sofa. They matched the faded curtains, once scarlet and now a washed-out pale rose, and the frayed fabric on the walls, where two patches of darker crimson showed that pictures had been removed. Everything was threadbare and worn. Over the mantelpiece hung one of the few remaining paintings, which showed a stabled horse with a splashy brown and white coat, its nose touching a starkly white foal curled in the straw.

Beneath this painting, and standing so quietly that they had not immediately noticed him, was Raphael. With his back to the empty grate, hands in the pockets of his jeans, he appeared more Italian than ever in this very English room, with its faded tapestry cushions, its gardening books piled in a heap on a small table and its chipped Chinoiserie lamps.

"Hi, Raff," said Robin.

"Hello, Robin," he said, unsmiling.

"This is Cormoran Strike, Raff," said Izzy. Raphael didn't move, so Strike walked over to him to shake hands, which Raphael did reluctantly, returning his hand to his jeans immediately afterwards.

"Yah, so, Fizz and I were just talking about Winn," said Izzy, who seemed greatly preoccupied with the news of the Winns' split. "We just hope to God he's going to keep his mouth shut, because now Papa's gorn, he can say whatever he likes about him and get away with it, can't he?"

"You've got the goods on Winn, if he tries," Strike reminded her.

She cast him a look of glowing gratitude.

"You're right, of course, and we wouldn't have that if it weren't for you...and Venetia—Robin, I mean," she added, as an afterthought.

"Torks, I'm downstairs!" bellowed a woman from just outside the room, and a woman who was unmistakably Izzy's sister backed into the room carrying a laden tray. She was older, heavily freckled and weather-beaten, her blonde hair streaked with silver, and she wore a striped shirt very like her husband's, though she had twinned hers with pearls. "TORKS!" she bellowed at the ceiling, making Robin jump. "I'M DOWN HERE!"

She set the tray with a clatter on the needlepoint ottoman that stood in front of Raff and the fireplace.

"Hi, I'm Fizzy. Where's Kinvara gorn?"

"Faffing around with the horses," said Izzy, edging around the sofa and sitting down. "Excuse not to be here, I expect. Grab a pew, you two."

Strike and Robin took two sagging armchairs that stood side by side, at right angles to the sofa. The springs beneath them seemed to have worn out decades ago. Robin felt Raphael's eyes on her.

"Izz tells me you know Charlie Campbell," Fizzy said to Strike, pouring everybody tea.

"That's right," said Strike.

"Lucky man," said Torquil, who had just re-entered the room. Strike gave no sign he had heard this.

"Did you ever meet Jonty Peters?" Fizzy continued. "Friend of the Campbells? He had something to do with the police...no, Badger, these aren't for you...Torks, what did Jonty Peters do?"

"Magistrate," said Torquil promptly.

"Yah, of course," said Fizzy, "magistrate. Did you ever meet Jonty, Cormoran?"

"No," said Strike, "afraid not."

"He was married to what's-her-name, lovely gel, Annabel. Did masses for Save the Children, got her CBE last year, so well-deserved. Oh, but if you knew the Campbells, you must have met Rory Moncrieff?"

"Don't think so," said Strike patiently, wondering what Fizzy would have said if he'd told her that the Campbells had kept him as far from their friends and family as was possible. Perhaps she was equal even to that: *oh, but then, you must have run across Basil Plumley? They loathed him, yah, violent alcoholic, but his wife did climb Kilimanjaro for Dogs Trust...*

Torquil pushed the fat Labrador away from the biscuits and it ambled away into a corner, where it flopped down for a doze. Fizzy sat down between her husband and Izzy on the sofa.

"I don't know whether Kinvara's intending to come back," said Izzy. "We might as well get started."

Strike asked whether the family had heard any more about the progress of the police investigation. There was a tiny pause, during which the distant shrieks of children echoed across the overgrown lawn.

"We don't know much more than I've already told you," said Izzy, "though I think we all get the sense—don't we?" she appealed to the other family members, "that the police think it's suicide. On the other hand, they clearly feel they have to investigate thoroughly—"

"That's because of who he was, Izz," Torquil interrupted. "Minister of the Crown, obviously they're going to look into it more deeply than they would for the bloke in the street. You should know, Cormoran," he said portentously, adjusting his substantial weight on the sofa, "sorry, gels, but I'm going to say it—personally, I think it *was* suicide.

"I understand, of course I do, that that's a hard thought to bear, and don't think I'm not happy you've been brought in!" he assured Strike. "If it puts the gels' minds at rest, that's all to the good. But the, ah, male contingent of the family—eh, Raff?—think there's nothing more to it than, well, m'father-in-law felt he couldn't go on. Happens. Not in his right mind, clearly. Eh, Raff?" repeated Torquil.

Raphael did not seem to relish the implicit order. Ignoring his brother-in-law, he addressed Strike directly.

"My father was acting strangely in the last couple of weeks. I didn't understand why, at the time. Nobody had told me he was being blackm—"

"We're not going into that," said Torquil quickly. "We agreed. Family decision."

Izzy said anxiously:

"Cormoran, I know you wanted to know what Papa was being blackmailed about—"

"Jasper broke no law," said Torquil firmly, "and that's the end of it. I'm sure you're discreet," he said to Strike, "but these things get out, they always do. We don't want the papers crawling all over us again. We're agreed, aren't we?" he demanded of his wife.

"I suppose so," said Fizzy, who seemed conflicted. "No, of course we don't want it all over the papers, but Jimmy Knight had good reason to wish Papa harm, Torks, and I think it's important Cormoran knows that, at least. You know he was *here*, in Woolstone, this week?"

"No," said Torquil, "I didn't."

"Yah, Mrs. Ankill saw him," said Fizzy. "He asked her whether she'd seen his brother."

"Poor little Billy," said Izzy vaguely. "He wasn't right. Well, you wouldn't be, would you, if you were brought up by Jack o'Kent? Papa was out with the dogs one night years ago," she told Strike and Robin, "and he saw Jack *kicking* Billy, literally *kicking* him, all around their garden. The boy was naked. When he saw Papa, Jack o'Kent stopped, of course."

The idea that this incident should have been reported to either police or social work seemed not to have occurred to Izzy, or indeed her father. It was as though Jack o'Kent and his son were wild creatures in the wood, behaving, regrettably, as such animals naturally behaved.

"I think the less said about Jack o'Kent," said Torquil, "the better. And you say Jimmy had reason to wish your father harm, Fizz, but what he really wanted was money, and killing your father certainly wasn't going—"

"He was angry with Papa, though," said Fizzy determinedly. "Maybe, when he realized Papa wasn't going to pay up, he saw red. He was a holy terror when he was a teenager," she told Strike. "Got into far-left politics early. He used to be down in the local pub with the Butcher brothers, telling everybody that Tories should be hung, drawn and quartered, trying to sell people the *Socialist Worker*..."

Fizzy glanced sideways at her younger sister, who rather determinedly, Strike thought, ignored her.

"He was trouble, always trouble," Fizzy said. "The girls liked him, but—"

The drawing room door opened and, to the rest of the family's evident surprise, Kinvara strode in, flushed and agitated. After a little difficulty extricating himself from his sagging armchair, Strike succeeded in standing up and held out a hand.

"Cormoran Strike. How do you do?"

Kinvara looked as though she would have liked to ignore his friendly overture, but shook the offered hand with bad grace. Torquil pulled up another chair beside the ottoman, and Fizzy poured an extra cup of tea.

"Horses all right, Kinvara?" Torquil asked heartily.

"Well, Mystic's taken another chunk out of Romano," she said with a nasty glance at Robin, "so I've had to call the vet again. He gets upset every time somebody comes up the drive too fast, otherwise he's absolutely fine."

"I don't know why you've put the stallions in together, Kinvara," said Fizzy.

"It's a myth that they don't get along," Kinvara snapped back. "Bachelor herds are perfectly common in the wild. There was a study in Switzerland that proved they can coexist peacefully once they've established the hierarchy among themselves."

She spoke in dogmatic, almost fanatic, tones.

"We were just telling Cormoran about Jimmy Knight," Fizzy told Kinvara.

"I thought you didn't want to go into—?"

"Not the blackmail," said Torquil hastily, "but what a horror he was when he was younger."

"Oh," said Kinvara, "I see."

"Your stepdaughter's worried that he may have had something to do with your husband's death," said Strike, watching her for a reaction.

"I know," said Kinvara, with apparent indifference, her eyes following Raphael, who had just walked away from the grate to fetch a pack of Marlboro Lights that lay beside a table lamp. "I never knew Jimmy Knight. The first time I ever laid eyes on him was when he turned up at the house a year ago to speak to Jasper. There's an ashtray beneath that magazine, Raphael."

Her stepson lit his cigarette and returned, carrying the ashtray, which he placed on a table beside Robin, before resuming his position in front of the empty fireplace.

"That was the start of it," Kinvara continued. "The blackmail. Jasper wasn't actually there that night, so Jimmy talked to me. Jasper was furious when he came home and I told him."

Strike waited. He suspected that he wasn't the only one in the room who thought Kinvara might break the family vow of *omerta* and blurt out what Jimmy had come to say. She refrained, however, so Strike drew out his notebook.

"Would you mind if I run through a few routine questions? I doubt there'll be anything you haven't already been asked by the police. Just a couple of points I'd like clarified, if you don't mind.

"How many keys are there, to the house in Ebury Street?"

"Three, as far as *I'm* aware," said Kinvara. The emphasis suggested that the rest of the family might have been hiding keys from her.

"And who had them?" asked Strike.

"Well, Jasper had his own," she said, "and I had one and there was a spare that Jasper had given to the cleaning woman."

"What's her name?"

"I've no idea. Jasper let her go a couple of weeks before he—he died."

"Why did he sack her?" asked Strike.

"Well, if you must know, we got rid of her because we were tightening our belts."

"Had she come from an agency?"

"Oh no. Jasper was old-fashioned. He put up a card up in a local shop and she applied. I think she was Romanian or Polish or something."

"Have you got her details?"

"No. Jasper hired and fired her. I never even met her."

"What happened to her key?"

"It *was* in the kitchen drawer at Ebury Street, but after he died we found out that Jasper had removed it and locked it up in his desk at work," said Kinvara. "It was handed back by the ministry, with all his other personal effects."

"That seems odd," Strike said. "Anyone know why he'd have done that?"

The rest of the family looked blank, but Kinvara said:

"He was always security conscious and he'd been paranoid lately — except when it came to the horses, of course. All the keys to Ebury Street are a special kind. Restricted. Impossible to copy."

"Tricky to copy," said Strike, making a note, "but not impossible, if you know the right people. Where were the other two keys at the time of death?"

"Jasper's was in his jacket pocket and mine was here, in my handbag," said Kinvara.

"The canister of helium," said Strike, moving on. "Does anybody know when it was purchased?"

Total silence greeted these words.

"Was there ever a party," Strike asked, "perhaps for one of the children —?"

"Never," said Fizzy. "Ebury Street was the place Papa used for work. He never hosted a party there that I can remember."

"You, Mrs. Chiswell," Strike asked Kinvara. "Can you remember any occasion —?"

"No," she said, cutting across him. "I've already told the police this. Jasper must have bought it himself, there's no other explanation."

"Has a receipt been found? A credit card bill?"

"He probably paid cash," said Torquil helpfully.

"Another thing I'd like to clear up," Strike said, working down the list he had made himself, "is this business of the phone calls the minister made on the morning of his death. Apparently he called you, Mrs. Chiswell, and then you, Raphael."

Raphael nodded. Kinvara said:

"He wanted to know whether I meant it when I said I was leaving and I said yes, I did. It wasn't a long conversation. I didn't know—I didn't know who your assistant really was. She appeared out of nowhere and Jasper was odd in his manner when I asked about her and I—I was very upset. I thought there was something going on."

"Were you surprised that your husband waited until the morning to call you about the note you'd left?" asked Strike.

"He told me he hadn't spotted it when he came in."

"Where had you left it?"

"On his bedside table. He was probably drunk when he got back. He's been—he *was*—drinking heavily. Ever since the blackmail business started."

The Norfolk terrier that had been shut out of the house suddenly popped up at one of the long windows and began barking at them again.

"Bloody dog," said Torquil.

"He misses Jasper," said Kinvara. "He was Jasper's d-dog—"

She stood up abruptly and walked away to snatch some tissues from a box sitting on top of the gardening books. Everybody looked uncomfortable. The terrier barked on and on. The sleeping Labrador woke and let out a single deep bark in return, before one of the tow-headed children reappeared on the lawn, shouting for the Norfolk terrier to come and play ball. It bounded off again.

"Good boy, Pringle!" shouted Torquil.

In the absence of barking, Kinvara's small gulps and the sounds of the Labrador flopping down to sleep again filled the room. Izzy, Fizzy and Torquil exchanged awkward glances, while Raphael stared rather stonily ahead. Little though she liked Kinvara, Robin found the family's inaction unfeeling.

"Where did that picture come from?" asked Torquil, with an artificial air of interest, squinting at the equine painting over Raphael's head. "New, isn't it?"

"That was one of Tinky's," said Fizzy, squinting up at it. "She brought a bunch of horsey junk over from Ireland with her."

"See that foal?" said Torquil, staring critically at the picture. "You know what it looks like? Lethal white syndrome. Heard of it?" he asked his wife and sister-in-law. "*You'll* know all about that, Kinvara," he said, clearly under the impression that he was graciously offering a way back into polite conversation. "Pure white foal, seems healthy when it's born, but defective bowel. Can't pass feces. M'father bred horses," he explained to Strike. "They can't survive, lethal whites. The tragedy is that they're born alive, so the mare feeds them, gets attached and then—"

"Torks," said Fizzy tensely, but it was too late. Kinvara blundered out of the room. The door slammed.

"What?" said Torquil, surprised. "What have I—?"

"*Baby*," whispered Fizzy.

"Oh, Lord," he said, "I clean forgot."

He got to his feet, hitched up his mustard corduroys, embarrassed and defensive.

"Oh, come on," he said, to the room at large. "I couldn't expect her to take it that way. Horses in a bloody painting!"

"You know what she's like," said Fizzy, "about *anything* connected with birth. Sorry," she said to Strike and Robin. "She had a baby that didn't survive, you see. Very sensitive on the subject."

Torquil approached the painting and squinted over Raphael's head at words etched on a small plaque set into the frame.

"'Mare Mourning,'" he read. "There you are, you see," he said, with an air of triumph. "Foal *is* dead."

"Kinvara likes it," said Raphael unexpectedly, "because the mare reminds her of Lady."

"Who?" said Torquil.

"The mare that got laminitis."

"What's laminitis?" asked Strike.

"A disease of the hoof," Robin told him.

"Oh, do you ride?" asked Fizzy keenly.

"I used to."

"Laminitis is serious," Fizzy told Strike. "It can cripple them. They need a lot of care, and sometimes nothing can be done, so it's kindest—"

"My stepmother had been nursing this mare for weeks," Raphael told Strike, "getting up in the middle of the night and so on. My father waited—"

"Raff, this really hasn't got anything to do with anything," said Izzy.

"—waited," continued Raphael doggedly, "until Kinvara went out one day, called in the vet without telling her and had the horse put down."

"Lady was suffering," said Izzy. "Papa told me what a state she was in. It was pure selfishness, keeping her alive."

"Yeah, well," said Raphael, his eyes on the lawn beyond the windows, "if I'd gone out and come back to the corpse of an animal I loved, I might've reached for the nearest blunt instrument as well."

"Raff," said Izzy, "please!"

"You're the one who wanted this, Izzy," he said, with grim satisfaction. "D'you really think Mr. Strike and his glamorous assistant aren't going to find Tegan and talk to her? They'll soon know what a shit Dad could—"

"Raff!" said Fizzy sharply.

"Steady on, old chap," said Torquil, something that Robin had never thought to hear outside a book. "This whole thing's been bloody upsetting, but there's no need for that."

Ignoring all of them, Raphael turned back to Strike.

"I suppose your next question was going to be, what did my father say to *me*, when he called me that morning?"

"That's right," said Strike.

"He ordered me down here," said Raphael.

"Here?" repeated Strike. "Woolstone?"

"*Here*," said Raphael. "This house. He told me he thought Kinvara was going to do something stupid. He sounded wooly. A bit odd. Like he had a heavy hangover."

"What did you understand by 'something stupid'?" asked Strike, his pen poised over his pad.

"Well, she's got form at threatening to top herself," said Raff, "so that, I suppose. Or he might've been afraid she was going to torch what little he had left." He gestured around the shabby room. "As you can see, that wasn't much."

"Did he tell you she was leaving him?"

"I got the impression that things were bad between them, but I can't remember his exact words. He wasn't very coherent."

"Did you do as he asked?" asked Strike.

"Yep," said Raphael. "Got in my car like an obedient son, drove all the way here and found Kinvara alive and well in the kitchen, raging about Venetia—Robin, I mean," he corrected himself. "As you may have gathered, Kinvara thought Dad was fucking her."

"Raff!" said Fizzy, sounding outraged.

"There's no need," said Torquil, "for that kind of language."

Everybody was carefully avoiding catching Robin's eye. She knew she had turned red.

"Seems odd, doesn't it?" Strike asked. "Your father asking you to come all the way down to Oxfordshire, when there were people far closer he could have asked to keep an eye on his wife? Didn't I hear that there was someone here overnight?"

Izzy piped up before Raphael could answer.

"Tegan *was* here that night—the stable girl—because Kinvara won't leave the horses without a sitter," she said, and then, correctly anticipating Strike's next question, "I'm afraid nobody's got any contact details for her, because Kinvara had a row with her right after Papa died, and Tegan walked out. I don't actually know where she's working now. Don't forget, though," said Izzy, leaning forwards and addressing Strike earnestly, "Tegan was probably fast asleep when Kinvara claims she came back here. This is a big house. Kinvara could have claimed to have come back any time and Tegan might not have known."

"If Kinvara was there with him in Ebury Street, why would he tell me to come and find her here?" Raphael asked, exasperated. "And how do you explain how she got here ahead of me?"

Izzy looked as though she would like to make a good retort to this, but appeared unable to think of one. Strike knew now why Izzy had

said that the content of Chiswell's phone call to his son "didn't matter": it further undermined the case for Kinvara as murderer.

"What's Tegan's surname?" he asked.

"Butcher," said Izzy.

"Any relation to the Butcher brothers Jimmy Knight used to hang
around with?" Strike asked.

Robin thought the three on the sofa seemed to be avoiding each
other's eyes. Fizzy then answered.

"Yes, as a matter of fact, but—"

"I suppose I could try and contact the family, see whether they'll
give me Tegan's number," said Izzy. "Yes, I'll do that, Cormoran,
and let you know how I get on."

Strike turned back to Raphael.

"So, did you set off immediately after your father asked you to go
to Kinvara?"

"No, I ate something, first, and showered," said Raphael. "I wasn't
exactly looking forward to dealing with her. She and I aren't each
other's favorite people. I got here around nine."

"How long did you stay?"

"Well, in the end, I was here for hours," said Raphael quietly. "A
couple of police arrived to break the news that Dad was dead. I could
hardly walk out after that, could I? Kinvara nearly coll—"

The door reopened and Kinvara walked back in, returned to her
hard-backed chair, her face set, tissues clutched in her hand.

"I've only got five minutes," she said. "The vet's just called, he's
in the area, so he'll pop in to see Romano. I can't stay."

"Could I ask something?" Robin asked Strike. "I know it might
be nothing at all," she said, to the room at large, "but there was a small
blue tube of homeopathic pills on the floor beside the minister when
I found him. Homeopathy didn't seem to be the kind of thing he'd—"

"What kind of pills?" asked Kinvara sharply, to Robin's surprise.

"Lachesis," said Robin.

"In a small blue tube?"

"Yes. Were they yours?"

"Yes, they were!"

"You left them in Ebury Street?" asked Strike.

"No, I lost them weeks ago . . . but I never had them *there*," she said, frowning, more to herself than to the room. "I bought them in London, because the pharmacy in Woolstone didn't have any."

She frowned, clearly reconstructing events in her mind.

"I remember, I tasted a couple outside the chemists, because I wanted to know whether he'd notice them in his feed—"

"Sorry, what?" asked Robin, unsure she had heard correctly.

"Mystic's feed," said Kinvara. "I was going to give them to Mystic."

"You were going to give homeopathic tablets to a *horse?*" said Torquil, inviting everyone else to agree that this was funny.

"Jasper thought it was a ludicrous idea, too," said Kinvara vaguely, still lost in recollection. "Yes, I opened them up right after I'd paid for them, took a couple, and," she mimed the action, "put the tube in my jacket pocket, but when I got home, they weren't there any more. I thought I must have dropped them somehow . . ."

Then she gave a little gasp and turned red. She seemed to be boggling at some inner, private realization. Then, realizing that everybody was still watching her, she said:

"I traveled home from London with Jasper that day. We met at the station, got the train together . . . he took them out of my pocket! He stole them, so I couldn't give them to Mystic!"

"Kinvara, don't be so utterly ridiculous!" said Fizzy, with a short laugh.

Raphael suddenly ground out his cigarette in the china ashtray at Robin's elbow. He seemed to be refraining from comment with difficulty.

"Did you buy more?" Robin asked Kinvara.

"Yes," said Kinvara, who seemed almost disoriented with shock, though Robin thought her conclusion as to what had happened to her pills very strange. "They were in a different bottle, though. That blue tube, that's the one I bought first."

"Isn't homeopathy just placebo effect?" Torquil inquired of the room at large. "How could a *horse*—?"

"Torks," muttered Fizzy, through gritted teeth. "Shut up."

"Why would your husband have stolen a tube of homeopathic pills from you?" asked Strike curiously. "It seems—"

"Pointlessly spiteful?" asked Raphael, arms folded beneath the picture of the dead foal. "Because you're so convinced you're right, and the other person's wrong, that it's OK to stop them doing something harmless?"

"Raff," said Izzy at once, "I know you're upset—"

"I'm not upset, Izz," said Raphael. "Very liberating, really, going back through all the shitty things Dad did while he was alive—"

"That's enough, boy!" said Torquil.

"Don't call me 'boy,'" said Raphael, shaking another cigarette out of his packet. "All right? Don't fucking call me 'boy.'"

"You'll have to excuse Raff," Torquil told Strike loudly, "he's upset with m'late father-in-law because of the will."

"I already knew I'd been written out of the will!" snapped Raphael, pointing at Kinvara. "*She* saw to that!"

"Your father didn't need any persuasion from me, I promise you!" said Kinvara, scarlet in the face now. "Anyway, you've got plenty of money, your mother spoils you rotten." She turned to Robin. "His mother left Jasper for a diamond merchant, after taking Jasper for everything she could lay her hands on—"

"Could I ask another couple of questions?" said Strike loudly, before a plainly fuming Raphael could speak.

"The vet will be here for Romano in a minute," said Kinvara. "I need to get back to the stable."

"Just a couple, and I'm done," Strike assured her. "Did you ever miss any amitriptyline pills? I think you were prescribed them, weren't you?"

"The police asked me this. I might have lost some," said Kinvara, with irritating vagueness, "but I can't be sure. There was a box I thought I'd lost and then I found it again and it didn't have as many pills in as I remembered, and I know I meant to leave a pack at Ebury Street in case I ever forgot when I was coming up from London, but when the police asked me I couldn't remember whether I'd actually done it or not."

"So you couldn't swear to it that you had pills missing?"

"No," said Kinvara. "Jasper might have stolen some, but I can't swear to it."

"Have you had any more intruders in your garden since your husband died?" asked Strike.

"No," said Kinvara. "Nothing."

"I heard that a friend of your husband's tried to call him early the morning that he died, but couldn't get through. D'you happen to know who the friend was?"

"Oh...yes. It was Henry Drummond," said Kinvara.

"And who's—?"

"He's an art dealer, very old friend of Papa's," interrupted Izzy. "Raphael worked for him for a little while—didn't you, Raff?—until he came to help Papa at the House of Commons."

"I can't see what Henry's got to do with anything," said Torquil, with an angry little laugh.

"Well, I think that's everything," said Strike, ignoring this comment as he closed his notebook, "except that I'd be glad to know whether you think your husband's death was suicide, Mrs. Chiswell."

The hand grasping the tissue contracted tightly.

"Nobody's interested in what I think," she said.

"I assure you, I am," said Strike.

Kinvara's eyes flickered from Raphael, who was scowling at the lawn outside, to Torquil.

"Well, if you want my opinion, Jasper did a very stupid thing, right before he—"

"Kinvara," said Torquil sharply, "you'd be best advised—"

"I'm not interested in your advice!" said Kinvara, turning on him suddenly, eyes narrowed. "After all, it's your advice that brought this family to financial ruin!"

Fizzy shot her husband a look across Izzy, warning him against retorting. Kinvara turned back to Strike.

"My husband provoked somebody, somebody I warned him he shouldn't upset, shortly before he died—"

"You mean Geraint Winn?" asked Strike.

"No," said Kinvara, "but you're close. Torquil doesn't want me to say anything about it, because it involves his good friend Christopher—"

"Bloody hell!" exploded Torquil. He got to his feet, again hitching up his mustard corduroys, and looking incensed. "My God, are we dragging total outsiders into this fantasy, now? What the bloody hell has Christopher got to do with anything? M'father-in-law killed himself!" he told Strike loudly, before rounding on his wife and sister-in-law. "I've tolerated this nonsense because you gels want peace of mind, but frankly, if this is where it's going to lead—"

Izzy and Fizzy set up an outcry, both trying to placate him and justify themselves, and in the midst of this mêlée, Kinvara got to her feet, tossed back her long red hair and walked towards the door, leaving Robin with the strong impression that she had lobbed this grenade into the conversation deliberately. At the door she paused, and the others' heads turned, as though she had called to them. In her high, clear, childish voice, Kinvara said:

"You all come back here and treat this house as though you're the real owners and I'm a guest, but Jasper said I could live here as long as I'm alive. Now I need to see the vet and when I get back, I'd like you all to have gone home. You aren't welcome here any more."

43

. . . I am afraid it will not be long before we hear something of the family ghost.

Henrik Ibsen, *Rosmersholm*

Robin asked whether she might use the bathroom before they departed from Chiswell House and was shown across the hall by Fizzy, who was still fuming at Kinvara.

"How dare she," said Fizzy, as they crossed the hall. "*How dare she? This is Pringle's house, not hers.*" And, in the next breath, "*Please* don't pay any attention to what she said about Christopher, she's simply trying to get a rise out of Torks, it was a disgusting thing to do, he's simply *livid.*"

"Who *is* Christopher?" Robin asked.

"Well—I don't know whether I should say," replied Fizzy. "But I suppose, if you—of course, he can't have anything to do with it. It's just Kinvara's spite. She's talking about Sir Christopher Barrowclough-Burns. Old friend of Torks' family. Christopher's a senior civil servant and he was that boy Mallik's mentor at the Foreign Office."

The lavatory was chilly and antiquated. As she bolted the door, Robin heard Fizzy striding back to the drawing room, doubtless to placate the angry Torquil. She looked around: the chipped, painted stone walls were bare except for many small dark holes in which the occasional nail still stuck out. Robin presumed Kinvara was responsible for the removal of a large number of Perspex frames from the wall, which now stood stacked on the floor facing the toilet. They contained a jumble of family photographs in messy collages.

After drying her hands on a damp towel that smelled of dog, Robin crouched down to flick through these frames. Izzy and Fizzy had been almost indistinguishable as children, making it impossible to tell which of them was cartwheeling on the croquet lawn, or jumping a pony at a local gymkhana, dancing in front of a Christmas tree in the hall or embracing the young Jasper Chiswell at a shooting picnic, the men all in tweeds and Barbours.

Freddie, however, was immediately recognizable, because unlike his sisters he had inherited his father's protuberant lower lip. As white-blond in youth as his niece and nephews, he featured frequently, beaming for the camera as a toddler, stony-faced as a child in a new prep school uniform, muddy and triumphant in rugby kit.

Robin paused to examine a group shot of teenagers, all dressed head to toe in white fencing jackets, Union Jacks ran down the sides of everyone's breeches. She recognized Freddie, who was standing in the middle of the group, holding a large silver cup. At the far end of the group was a miserable-looking girl whom Robin recognized immediately as Rhiannon Winn, older and thinner than she had been in the photograph her father had shown Robin, her slightly cringing air at odds with the proud smiles on every other face.

Continuing to search the boards, Robin stopped at the last one to examine the faded photograph of a large party.

It had been taken in a marquee, from what seemed to be a stage. Many bright blue helium balloons in the shape of the number eighteen danced over the crowd's heads. A hundred or so teenagers had clearly been bidden to face the camera. Robin scanned the scene carefully and found Freddie easily enough, surrounded by a large group of both boys and girls whose arms were slung around each other's shoulders, beaming and, in some cases, braying with laughter. After nearly a minute, Robin spotted the face she had instinctively sought: Rhiannon Winn, thin, pale and unsmiling beside the drinks table. Close behind her, half-hidden in shadow, were a couple of boys who were not in black tie, but jeans and T-shirts. One in particular was darkly handsome and long-haired, his T-shirt bearing a picture of The Clash.

Robin got out her mobile and took a picture of both the fencing team and the eighteenth birthday party photographs, then carefully replaced the stack of Perspex boards as she had found them, and left the bathroom.

She thought for a second that the silent hall was deserted. Then she saw that Raphael was leaning up against a hall table, his arms folded.

"Well, goodbye," said Robin, starting to walk towards the front door.

"Hang on a minute."

As she paused, he pushed himself off the table and approached her.

"I've been quite angry with you, you know."

"I can understand why," said Robin quietly, "but I was doing what your father hired me to do."

He moved closer, coming to a halt beneath an old glass lantern hanging from the ceiling. Half the lightbulbs were missing.

"I'd say you're bloody good at it, are you? Getting people to trust you?"

"That's the job," said Robin.

"You're married," he said, eyes on her left hand.

"Yes," she said.

"To Tim?"

"No . . . there isn't any Tim."

"You're not married to *him?*" said Raphael quickly, pointing outside.

"No. We just work together."

"And that's your real accent," said Raphael. "Yorkshire."

"Yes," she said. "This is it."

She thought he was going to say something insulting. The olive dark eyes moved over her face, then he shook his head slightly.

"I quite like the voice, but I preferred 'Venetia.' Made me think of masked orgies."

He turned and walked away, leaving Robin to hurry back out into the sunshine to rejoin Strike, who she presumed would be waiting impatiently in the Land Rover.

She was wrong. He was still standing beside the car's bonnet, while Izzy, who was standing very close to him, talked rapidly in an undertone. When she heard Robin's feet on the gravel behind her, Izzy took a step backwards with what, to Robin, seemed a slightly guilty, embarrassed air.

"Lovely to see you again," Izzy said, kissing Robin on both cheeks, as though this had been a simple social call. "And you'll ring me, won't you?" she said to Strike.

"Yep, I'll keep you updated," he said, moving around to the passenger seat.

Neither Strike nor Robin spoke as she turned the car around. Izzy waved them off, a slightly pathetic figure in her loose shirt dress. Strike raised a hand to her as they took the bend in the drive that hid her from their sight.

Trying not to upset the skittish stallions, Robin drove at a snail's pace. Glancing left, Strike saw that the injured horse had been removed from the field, but in spite of Robin's best intentions, as the noisy old car lurched past its field, the black stallion took off again.

"Who d'you reckon," said Strike, watching the horse plunge and buck, "first took a look at something like that and thought, 'I should get on its back'?"

"There's an old saying," said Robin, trying to steer around the worst of the potholes, "'the horse is your mirror.' People say dogs resemble their owners, but I think it's truer of horses."

"Making Kinvara highly strung and prone to lash out on slight provocation? Sounds about right. Turn right here. I want to get a look at Steda Cottage."

A bare two minutes later, he said:

"Here. Go up here."

The track to Steda Cottage was so overgrown that Robin had missed it entirely the first time they had passed it. It led deep into the woodland that lay hard up against the gardens of Chiswell House, but unfortunately, the Land Rover was only able to proceed for ten yards before the track became impassable by car. Robin cut the engine, privately worried about how Strike was going to manage a barely discernible path of earth and fallen leaves, overgrown with brambles and nettles, but as he was already getting out, she followed suit, slamming the driver's door behind her.

The ground was slippery, the tree canopy so dense that the track was in deep shade, dank and moist. A pungent, green, bitter smell filled their nostrils, and the air was alive with the rustle of birds and small creatures whose habitat was being rudely invaded.

"So," said Strike, as they struggled through the bushes and weeds. "Christopher Barrowclough-Burns. That's a new name."

"No, it isn't," said Robin.

Strike looked sideways at her, grinning, and immediately tripped on a root, remaining upright at some cost to his sore knee.

"*Shit*...I wondered whether you remembered."

"'Christopher didn't promise anything about the pictures,'" quoted Robin promptly. "He's a civil servant who mentored Aamir Mallik at the Foreign Office. Fizzy just told me."

"We're back to 'a man of your habits,' aren't we?"

Neither spoke for a short spell as they concentrated on a particularly treacherous stretch of path where whip-like branches clung willingly to fabric and skin. Robin's skin was a pale, dappled green in the sun filtered by the ceiling of leaves above them.

"See any more of Raphael, after I went outside?"

"Er—yes, actually," said Robin, feeling slightly self-conscious. "He came out of the sitting room as I was coming out of the loo."

"Didn't think he'd pass up another chance of talking to you," said Strike.

"It wasn't like that," Robin said untruthfully, remembering the remark about masked orgies. "Izzy whispering anything interesting, back there?" she asked.

Amused by the reciprocal jab, Strike took his eyes off the path, thereby failing to spot a muddy stump. He tripped for a second time, this time saving himself from a painful fall by grabbing a tree covered in a prickly climbing plant.

"*Fuck*—"

"Are you—?"

"I'm fine," he said, angry with himself, examining the palm that was now full of thorns and starting to pull them out with his teeth. He heard a loud snap of wood behind him and turned to see Robin holding out a fallen branch, which she had broken to make a rough walking stick.

"Use this."

"I don't—" he began, but catching sight of her stern expression, he gave in. "Thanks."

They set off again, Strike finding the stick more useful than he wanted to admit.

"Izzy was just trying to convince me that Kinvara could have sneaked back to Oxfordshire, after bumping off Chiswell between six and seven in the morning. I don't know whether she realizes there are multiple witnesses to every stage of Kinvara's journey from Ebury Street. The police probably haven't gone into detail with the family yet, but I think, once the penny drops that Kinvara can't have done it in person, Izzy'll start suggesting she hired a hitman. What did you make of Raphael's various outbursts?"

"Well," said Robin, navigating around a patch of nettles, "I can't blame him, getting annoyed with Torquil."

"No," agreed Strike, "I think old Torks would grate on me, too."

"Raphael seems really angry with his father, doesn't he? He didn't *have* to tell us about Chiswell putting that mare down. I thought he was almost going out of his way to paint his father as...well..."

"A bit of a shit," agreed Strike. "He thought Chiswell had stolen those pills of Kinvara's out of malice, too. That whole episode was bloody strange, actually. What made you so interested in those pills?"

"They seemed so out of place for Chiswell."

"Well, it was a good call. Nobody else seems to have asked questions about them. So what does the psychologist make of Raphael denigrating his dead father?"

Robin shook her head, smiling, as she usually did when Strike referred to her in this way. She had dropped out of her psychology course at university, as he well knew.

"I'm serious," said Strike, grimacing as his false foot skidded on fallen leaves and he saved himself, this time with the aid of Robin's stick. "*Bollocks*...go on. What d'you make of him putting the boot into Chiswell?"

"Well, I think he's hurt and furious," said Robin, weighing her words. "He and his father were getting on better than they ever had, from what he told me when I was at the House of Commons, but now Chiswell's dead, Raphael's never going to be able to get properly back on good terms with him, is he? He's left with the fact he was written out of the will and no idea of how Chiswell really felt about him. Chiswell was quite inconsistent with Raphael. When he was drunk and depressed, he seemed to lean on him, but otherwise he was pretty rude to him. Although I can't honestly say I saw Chiswell ever being nice to anybody, except maybe—"

She stopped short.

"Go on," said Strike.

"Well, actually," said Robin, "I was going to say he was quite nice to me, the day I found out all about the Level Playing Field."

"This was when he offered you a job?"

"Yes, and he said he might have a bit more work for me, once I'd got rid of Winn and Knight."

"Did he?" said Strike, curiously. "You never told me that."

"Didn't I? No, I don't suppose I did."

And like Strike, she remembered the week that he had been laid up at Lorelei's, followed by the hours at the hospital with Jack.

"I went over to his office, as I told you, and he was on the phone to some hotel about a money clip he'd lost. It was Freddie's. After Chiswell got off the phone, I told him about the Level Playing Field and he was happier than I ever saw him. 'One by one, they trip themselves up,'" he said.

"Interesting," panted Strike, whose leg was now killing him. "So you think Raphael's smarting about the will, do you?"

Robin, who thought she caught a sardonic note in Strike's voice, said:

"It isn't just money—"

"People always say that," he grunted. "It *is* the money, and it isn't. Because what *is* money? Freedom, security, pleasure, a fresh chance... I think there's more to be got out of Raphael," said Strike, "and I think you're going to have to be the one to do it."

"What else can he tell us?"

"I'd like a bit more clarity on that phone call Chiswell made to him, right before that bag went over his head," panted Strike, who was now in considerable pain. "It doesn't make much sense to me, because even if Chiswell knew he was about to kill himself, there were people far better placed to keep Kinvara company than a stepson she didn't like who was miles away in London.

"Trouble is, the call makes even less sense if it was murder. There's something," said Strike, "we aren't being t—ah. Thank Christ."

Steda Cottage had just come into view in a clearing ahead of them. The garden, which was surrounded by a broken-down fence, was now almost as overgrown as its surroundings. The building was squat, made of dark stone and clearly derelict, with a yawning hole in the roof and cracks in most of the windows.

"Sit down," Robin advised Strike, pointing him towards a large tree stump just outside the cottage fence. In too much pain to argue, he did as she instructed, while Robin picked her way towards the front door and gave it a little push, but found it locked. Wading through knee-length grass, she peered one by one through the grimy windows. The rooms were thick with dust and empty. The only sign of any previous occupant was in the kitchen, where a filthy mug bearing a picture of Johnny Cash sat alone on a stained surface.

"Doesn't look as though anyone's lived here for years, and no sign of anyone sleeping rough," she informed Strike, emerging from the other side of the cottage.

Strike, who had just lit a cigarette, made no answer. He was staring down into a large hollow in the woodland floor, around twenty feet square, bordered with trees and full of nettles, tangled thorn and towering weeds.

"Would you call that a dell?" he asked her.

Robin peered down into the basin-like indentation.

"I'd say it's more like a dell than anything else we've passed," she said.

"'He strangled the kid and they buried it, down in the dell by our dad's house,'" quoted Strike.

"I'll have a look," said Robin. "You stay here."

"No," said Strike, raising a hand to stop her, "you're not going to find anything—"

But Robin was already sliding her way down the steep edges of the "dell," the thorns snagging at her jeans as she descended.

It was extremely difficult to move around once she reached the bottom. Nettles came up almost to her waist and she held up her hands to avoid scratches and stings. Milk parsley and wood avens speckled the dark green with white and yellow. The long thorny branches of wild roses curled like barbed wire everywhere she trod.

"Watch yourself," said Strike, feeling impotent as he watched her struggle along, scratching or stinging herself at every other step.

"I'm fine," said Robin, peering at the ground beneath the wild vegetation. If anything had been buried here, it had long since been covered by plants, and digging would be a very difficult business. She said as much to Strike, as she bent low to see what lay underneath a dense patch of bramble.

"Doubt Kinvara would be happy with us digging, anyway," said Strike, and as he said it, he remembered Billy's words: *She wouldn't let me dig, but she'd let you.*

"Wait," said Robin, sounding tense.

In spite of the fact that he knew perfectly well she could not have found anything, Strike tensed.

"What?"

"There's something in there," said Robin, moving her head from side to side, the better to see into a thick patch of nettles, right in the center of the dell.

"Oh God."

"What?" Strike repeated. Although far higher up than her, he could make out nothing whatsoever in the nettle patch. "What can you see?"

"I don't know... I might be imagining it." She hesitated. "You haven't got gloves, I suppose?"

"No. Robin, don't—"

But she had already walked into the patch of nettles, her hands raised, stamping them down at the base wherever she could, flattening them as much as possible. Strike saw her bend over and pull something out of the ground. Straightening up, she stood quite still, her red-gold head bowed over whatever she had found, until Strike said impatiently:

"What is it?"

Her hair fell away from a face that looked pale against the morass of dark green in which she stood, as she held up a small, wooden cross.

"No, stay there," she ordered him, as he moved automatically towards the edge of the dell to help her climb out. "I'm fine."

She was, in fact, covered in scratches and nettle stings, but deciding that a few more would hardly count, Robin pushed her way more forcefully out of the dell, using her hands to pull herself up the steep sides until she came close enough for Strike to reach out a hand and help her the last few feet.

"Thanks," she said breathlessly.

"Looks like it's been there years," she said, rubbing earth from the bottom, which was pointed, the better to stick into the ground. The wood was damp and stained.

"Something was written on it," said Strike, taking it from her and squinting at the slimy surface.

"Where?" said Robin. Her hair grazed his cheek as they stood close beside each other, staring at the very faint residue of what looked like felt tip, long since washed away by rain and dew.

"That looks like a kid's writing," said Robin quietly.

"That's an 'S,'" said Strike, "and at the end... is that a 'g' or a 'y'?"

"I don't know," whispered Robin.

They stood in silence, contemplating the cross, until the faint, echoing barks of Rattenbury the Norfolk terrier pierced their reverie.

"We're still on Kinvara's property," said Robin nervously.

"Yeah," said Strike, keeping hold of the cross as he began to lumber back the way they had come, teeth gritted against the pain in his leg. "Let's find a pub. I'm starving."

44

But there are so many sorts of white horses in this world, Mrs. Helseth...

Henrik Ibsen, *Rosmersholm*

"Of course," said Robin, as they drove towards the village, "a cross sticking out of the ground doesn't mean there's anything buried beneath it."

"True," said Strike, who had needed most of his breath on the return walk for the frequent obscenities he uttered as he stumbled and skidded on the forest floor, "but it makes you think, doesn't it?"

Robin said nothing. Her hands on the steering wheel were covered in nettle stings that prickled and burned.

The country inn they reached five minutes later was the very image of picture-postcard England, a white, timbered building with leaded bay windows, moss-covered slates on the roof and climbing red roses around the door. A beer garden with parasols completed the picture. Robin turned the Land Rover into the small car park opposite.

"This is getting stupid," muttered Strike, who had left the cross on the dashboard and was now climbing out of the car, staring at the pub.

"What is?" asked Robin, coming around the back of the car to join him.

"It's called the White Horse."

"After the one up the hill," said Robin, as they set off across the road together. "Look at the sign."

Painted on the board atop a wooden pole was the strange chalk figure they had seen earlier.

"The pub where I met Jimmy Knight the first time was called the White Horse, too," said Strike.

"The White Horse," said Robin, as they walked up the steps into the beer garden, Strike's limp now more pronounced than ever, "is one of the ten most popular pub names in Britain. I read it in some article. Quick, those people are leaving—grab their table, I'll get the drinks."

The low-ceilinged pub was busy inside. Robin headed first for the Ladies where she stripped off her jacket, tied it around her waist and washed her smarting hands. She wished that she had managed to find dock leaves on the journey back from Steda Cottage, but most of her attention on the return walk had been given to Strike who had nearly fallen twice more and hobbled on looking furious with himself, repelling offers of assistance with bad grace and leaning heavily on the walking stick she had fashioned from a branch.

The mirror showed Robin that she was disheveled and grubby compared to the prosperous middle-aged people she had just seen in the bar, but being in a hurry to return to Strike and review the morning's activities, she merely dragged a brush through her hair, wiped a green stain off her neck and returned to queue for drinks.

"Cheers, Robin," said Strike gratefully, when she returned to him with a pint of Arkell's Wiltshire Gold, shoving the menu across the table to her. "Ah, that's good," he sighed, taking a swig. "So what's the most popular one?"

"Sorry?"

"The most popular pub name. You said the White Horse is in the top ten."

"Oh, right...it's either the Red Lion or the Crown, I can't remember which."

"The Victory's my real local," said Strike reminiscently.

He had not been back to Cornwall in two years. He saw the pub now in his mind's eye, a squat building of whitewashed Cornish stone, the steps beside it winding down to the bay. It was the pub in which he had first managed to get served without ID, sixteen years old and dumped back at his uncle and aunt's for a few weeks, while his mother's life went through one of its regular bouts of upheaval.

"Ours is the Bay Horse," said Robin, and she, too, had a sudden vision of a pub from what she would always think of as home, also white, standing on a street that led off the market square in Masham. It was there that she had celebrated her A-level results with her friends, the same night that Matthew and she had got into a stupid row, and he had left, and she had refused to follow, but remained with her friends.

"Why 'bay'?" asked Strike, now halfway down his pint and luxuriating in the sunshine, his sore leg stretched out in front of him. "Why not just 'brown'?"

"Well, there *are* brown horses," said Robin, "but bay means something different. Black points: legs, mane and tail."

"What color was your pony—Angus, wasn't it?"

"How did you remember that?" asked Robin, surprised.

"Dunno," said Strike. "Same as you remembering pub names. Some things stick, don't they?"

"He was gray."

"Meaning white. It's all just jargon to confuse non-riding plebs, isn't it?"

"No," said Robin, laughing. "Gray horses have black skin under the white hair. True whites—"

"—die young," said Strike, as a barmaid arrived to take their order. Having ordered a burger, Strike lit another cigarette and as the nicotine hit his brain, felt a wave of something close to euphoria. A pint, a hot day in August, a well-paid job, food on the way and Robin, sitting across from him, their friendship restored, if not entirely to what it had been before her honeymoon, then perhaps as close as was possible, now that she was married. Right now, in this sunny beer garden, and in spite of the pain in his leg, his tiredness and the unresolved mess that was his relationship with Lorelei, life felt simple and hopeful.

"Group interviews are never a good idea," he said, exhaling away from Robin's face, "but there were some interesting crosscurrents among the Chiswells, weren't there? I'm going to keep working on Izzy. I think she might be a bit more forthcoming without the family around."

Izzy will like being worked on, Robin thought, as she took out her mobile.

"I've got something to show you. Look."

She brought up her photograph of Freddie Chiswell's birthday party.

"That," she said, pointing at the girl's pale, unhappy face, "is Rhiannon Winn. She was at Freddie Chiswell's eighteenth birthday party. Turns out—" she scrolled back a picture, to show the group in white tunics, "they were on the British fencing team together."

"Christ, of course," said Strike, taking the phone from Robin. "The sword—the sword in Ebury Street. I bet it was Freddie's!"

"Of course!" echoed Robin, wondering why she hadn't realized that before.

"That can't be long before she killed herself," said Strike, scrutinizing more closely the miserable figure of Rhiannon Winn at the birthday party. "And—bloody hell, that's Jimmy Knight behind her. What's he doing at a public schoolboy's eighteenth?"

"Free drink?" suggested Robin.

Strike gave a small snort of amusement as he handed back Robin's phone.

"Sometimes the obvious answer is the right one. Was I imagining Izzy looking self-conscious when the story of Jimmy's teenage sex appeal came up?"

"No," said Robin, "I noticed that, too."

"Nobody wants us to talk to Jimmy's old mates the Butcher brothers, either."

"Because they know more than where their sister works?"

Strike sipped his beer, thinking back to what Chiswell had told him the first time they'd met.

"Chiswell said other people were involved in whatever he did to get blackmailed, but they had a lot to lose if it got out."

He took out his notebook and contemplated his own spiky, hard-to-read handwriting, while Robin sat peacefully enjoying the quiet chatter of the beer garden. A lazy bee buzzed nearby, reminding her of the lavender walk at Le Manoir aux Quat'Saisons, where she and Matthew had spent their anniversary. It was best not to compare how she felt now to the way she had felt then.

"Maybe," said Strike, tapping the open notebook with his pen, "the Butcher brothers agreed to take on horse-slashing duties for Jimmy while he was in London? I always thought he might have mates back down here who could've taken care of that side of things. But we'll let Izzy get Tegan's whereabouts out of them before we approach them. Don't want to upset the client unless it's absolutely necessary."

"No," agreed Robin. "I wonder...d'you think Jimmy met them when he came down here looking for Billy?"

"Could well have done," said Strike, nodding over his notes. "Very interesting, that. From what they said to each other on that march, Jimmy and Flick knew where Billy was at the time. They were off to see him when my hamstring went. Now they've lost him again...you know, I'd give a hell of a lot to find Billy. That's where all of this started and we're still—"

He broke off as their food arrived: a burger with blue cheese on it for Strike, and a bowl of chili for Robin.

"We're still?" prompted Robin, as the barmaid moved away.

"...none the wiser," said Strike, "about the kid he claims he saw die. I didn't want to ask the Chiswells about Suki Lewis, or not yet. Best not to suggest I'm interested in anyone but Chiswell's death right now."

He picked up his burger and took an enormous bite, his eyes unfocused, staring out over the road. After demolishing half of his burger, Strike turned back to his notes.

"Things to be done," he announced, picking up his pen again. "I want to find this cleaning woman Jasper Chiswell laid off. She had a key for a bit and she might be able to tell us how and when the helium got into the house.

"Hopefully Izzy will trace Tegan Butcher for us, and Tegan'll be able to shed some light on Raphael's trip down there on the morning his father died, because I'm still not buying that story.

"We'll leave Tegan's brothers for now, because the Chiswells clearly don't want us talking to them, but I might try and have a word with Henry Drummond, the art dealer."

"Why?" asked Robin.

"He was an old friend, did Chiswell a favor hiring Raphael. They must've been reasonably close. You never know, Chiswell might've told him what the blackmail was about. And he tried to reach Chiswell early on the morning Chiswell died. I'd like to know why.

"So, going forwards: you're going to have a bash at Flick at her jewelry shop, Barclay can stay on Jimmy and Flick, and I'll tackle Geraint Winn and Aamir Mallik."

"They'll never talk to you," said Robin at once. "Never."

"Want to bet?"

"Tenner says they won't."

"I don't pay you enough for you to throw tenners around," said Strike. "You can buy me a pint."

Strike took care of the bill and they headed back across the road to the car, Robin secretly wishing that there was somewhere else they needed to go, because the prospect of returning to Albury Street was depressing.

"We might be better off going back on the M40," said Strike, reading a map on his phone. "There's been an accident on the M4."

"OK," said Robin.

This would take them past Le Manoir aux Quat'Saisons. As she reversed out of the car park, Robin suddenly remembered Matthew's texts from earlier. He had claimed to have been messaging work, but she couldn't remember him ever contacting his office at a weekend before. One of his regular complaints about her job was that its hours and responsibilities bled into Saturday and Sunday, unlike his.

"What?" she said, becoming aware that Strike had just spoken to her.

"I said, they're supposed to be bad luck, aren't they?" repeated Strike, as they drove away from the pub.

"What are?"

"White horses," he said. "Isn't there a play where white horses appear as a death omen?"

"I don't know," said Robin, changing gear. "Death rides a white horse in Revelations, though."

"A pale horse," Strike corrected her, winding down the window so that he could smoke again.

"Pedant."

"Says the woman who won't call a brown horse 'brown,'" said Strike.

He reached for the grubby wooden cross, which was sliding about on the dashboard. Robin kept her eyes on the road ahead, determinedly focused on anything but the vivid image that had occurred to her when she had first spotted it, almost hidden in the thick, whiskered stems of the nettles: that of a child, rotting in the earth at the bottom of that dark basin in the woods, dead and forgotten by everyone except a man they said was mad.

45

It is a necessity for me to abandon a false and equivocal position.
Henrik Ibsen, *Rosmersholm*

Strike paid in pain for the walk through the woods at Chiswell House the next morning. So little did he fancy getting up out of bed and heading downstairs to work on a Sunday that he was forced to remind himself that, like the character of Hyman Roth in one of his favorite films, he had chosen this business freely. If, like the Mafia, private detection made demands beyond the ordinary, certain concomitants had to be accepted along with the rewards.

He had had a choice, after all. The army had been keen to keep him, even with half his leg missing. Friends of friends had offered everything from management roles in the close protection industry to business partnerships, but the itch to detect, solve and reimpose order upon the moral universe could not be extinguished in him, and he doubted it ever would be. The paperwork, the frequently obstreperous clients, the hiring and firing of subordinates gave him no intrinsic satisfaction — but the long hours, the physical privations and the occasional risks of his job were accepted stoically and with occasional relish. And so he showered, put on his prosthesis and, yawning, made his painful way downstairs, remembering his brother-in-law's suggestion that his ultimate goal ought to be sitting in an office while others literally did the legwork.

Strike's thoughts drifted to Robin as he sat down at her computer. He had never asked her what her ultimate ambition for the agency was, assuming, perhaps arrogantly, that it was the same as his: build up a sufficient bank balance to ensure them both a decent income while they took the work that was most interesting, without fear of losing everything the moment they lost a client. But perhaps Robin was waiting for him to initiate a talk along the lines that Greg had suggested? He tried to imagine her reaction, if he invited her to sit down on the farting sofa while he subjected her to a PowerPoint display setting out long-term objectives and suggestions for branding.

As he set to work, thoughts of Robin metamorphosed into memories of Charlotte. He remembered how it had been on days like this while they had been together, when he had required uninterrupted hours alone at a computer. Sometimes Charlotte had taken herself out, often making an unnecessary mystery about where she was going, or invented reasons to interrupt him, or pick a fight that kept him pinned down while the precious hours trickled away. And he knew that he was reminding himself how difficult and exhausting that behavior had been, because ever since he had seen her at Lancaster House, Charlotte had slid in and out of his disengaged mind like a stray cat.

A little under eight hours, seven cups of tea, three bathroom breaks, four cheese sandwiches, three bags of crisps, an apple and twenty-two cigarettes later, Strike had repaid all his subcontractors' expenses, ensured that the accountant had the firm's latest receipts, read Hutchins' updated report on Dodgy Doc and tracked several Aamir Malliks across cyberspace in search of the one he wanted to interview. By five o'clock he thought he had him, but the photograph was so far from "handsome," which was how Mallik had been described in the blind item online, that he thought it best to email Robin a copy of the pictures he had found on Google Images, to confirm that this was the Mallik he sought.

Strike stretched, yawning, listening to a drum solo that a prospective purchaser was banging out in a shop below in Denmark Street. Looking forward to getting back upstairs and watching the day's Olympic highlights, which would include Usain Bolt running the hundred meters, he was on the point of shutting off his computer when a small "ping" alerted him to the arrival of an email from

Lorelei@VintageVamps.com, the subject line reading simply: "You and me."

Strike rubbed his eyes with the heels of his palms, as though the sight of the new email had been some temporary aberration of sight. However, there it sat at the top of his inbox when he raised his head and opened his eyes again.

"Oh, shit," he muttered. Deciding that he might as well know the worst, he clicked on it.

The email ran to nearly a thousand words and gave the impression of having been carefully crafted. It was a methodical dissection of Strike's character, which read like the case notes for a psychiatric case that, while not hopeless, required urgent intervention. By Lorelei's analysis, Cormoran Strike was a fundamentally damaged and dysfunctional creature standing in the way of his own happiness. He caused pain to others due to the essential dishonesty of his emotional dealings. Never having experienced a healthy relationship, he ran from it when it was given to him. He took those who cared about him for granted and would probably only realize this when he hit rock bottom, alone, unloved and tortured by regrets.

This prediction was followed by a description of the soul-searching and doubts that had preceded Lorelei's decision to send the email, rather than simply tell Strike that their no-strings arrangement was at an end. She concluded that she thought it fairest to him to explain in writing why she, and by implication every other woman in the world, would find him unacceptable unless he changed his behavior. She asked him to read and think about what she had said "understanding that this doesn't come from a place of anger, but of sadness," and requested a further meeting so that they could "decide whether you want this relationship enough to try a different way."

After reaching the bottom of the email, Strike remained where he was, staring at the screen, not because he was contemplating a response, but because he was gathering himself for the physical pain he was anticipating upon standing up. At last he pushed himself up into a vertical position, flinching as he lowered his weight onto the prosthesis, then closed down his computer and locked up the office.

Why can't we can't end it by phone? he thought, heaving himself up the stairs by using the handrail. *It's obvious it's fucking dead, isn't it? Why do we have to have a post-mortem?*

Back in the flat, he lit another cigarette, dropped down onto a kitchen chair and called Robin, who answered almost immediately.

"Hi," she said quietly. "Just a moment."

He heard a door close, footsteps, and another door closing.

"Did you get my email? Just sent you a couple of pictures."

"No," said Robin, keeping her voice low. "Pictures of what?"

"I think I've found Mallik living in Battersea. Pudgy bloke with a monobrow."

"That's not him. He's tall and thin with glasses."

"So I've just wasted an hour," said Strike, frustrated. "Didn't he ever let slip where he was living? What he liked to do at the weekends? National Insurance number?"

"No," said Robin, "we barely spoke. I've already told you this."

"How's the disguise coming along?"

Robin had already told Strike by text that she had an interview on Thursday with the "mad Wiccan" who ran the jewelry shop in Camden.

"Not bad," said Robin. "I've been experimenting with—"

There was a muffled shout in the background.

"Sorry, I'm going to have to go," Robin said hastily.

"Everything OK?"

"It's fine, speak tomorrow."

She hung up. Strike remained with the mobile at his ear. He deduced that he had called during a difficult moment for Robin, possibly even a row, and lowered the mobile with faint disappointment at not having had a longer chat. For a moment or two, he contemplated the mobile in his hand. Lorelei would be expecting him to call as soon as he had read her email. Deciding that he could credibly claim not to have seen it yet, Strike put down his phone and reached instead for the TV remote control.

46

. . . I should have handled the affair more judiciously.
Henrik Ibsen, *Rosmersholm*

Four days later, at lunchtime, Strike was to be found leaning up against a counter in a tiny takeaway pizza restaurant, which was most conveniently situated for watching a house directly across the street. One of a pair of brown brick semi-detached houses, the name "Ivy Cottages" was engraved in stone over the twin doors, which seemed to Strike more fitting for humbler dwellings than these houses, which had graceful arched windows and corniced keystones.

Chewing on a slice of pizza, Strike felt his phone vibrate in his pocket. He checked to see who was calling before answering, because he had already had one fraught conversation with Lorelei today. Seeing that it was Robin, he answered.

"I'm in," said Robin. She sounded excited. "Just had my interview. The owner's dreadful, I'm not surprised nobody wants to work for her. It's a zero-hours contract. Basically, she wants a couple of people to fill in whenever she fancies not working."

"Flick still there?"

"Yes, she was manning the counter while I was talking to the shop owner. The woman wants to give me a trial tomorrow."

"You weren't followed?"

"No, I think that journalist has given up. He wasn't here yesterday either. Mind you, he probably wouldn't have recognized me even if he'd seen me. You should see my hair."

"Why, what have you done with it?"

"Chalk."

"What?"

"Hair chalk," said Robin. "Temporary color. It's black and blue. And I'm wearing a lot of eye makeup and some temporary tattoos."

"Send us a selfie, I could do with some light relief."

"Make your own. What's going on your end?"

"Bugger all. Mallik came out of Della's house with her this morning—"

"God, are they *living* together?"

"No idea. They went out somewhere in a taxi with the guide dog. They came back an hour ago and I'm waiting to see what happens next. One interesting thing, though: I've seen Mallik before. Recognized him the moment I saw him this morning."

"Really?"

"Yeah, he was at Jimmy's CORE meeting. The one I went to, to try and find Billy."

"How weird...D'you think he was acting as a go-between for Geraint?"

"Maybe," said Strike, "but I can't see why the phone wouldn't have done if they wanted to keep in touch. You know, there's something funny about Mallik generally."

"He's all right," said Robin quickly. "He didn't like me, but that was because he was suspicious. That just means he's sharper than most of the rest of them."

"You don't fancy him as a killer?"

"Is this because of what Kinvara said?"

"'My husband provoked somebody, somebody I warned him he shouldn't upset,'" Strike quoted.

"And why should anyone be particularly worried about upsetting Aamir? Because he's brown? I felt sorry for him, actually, having to work with—"

"Hang on," said Strike, letting his last piece of pizza fall back onto the plate.

The front door of Della's house had opened again.

"We're off," said Strike, as Mallik came out of the house alone, closed the door behind him, walked briskly down the garden path, and set off down the road. Strike headed out of the pizzeria in pursuit.

"Got a spring in his step now. He looks happy to be away from her..."

"How's your leg?"

"It's been worse. Hang on, he's turning left...Robin, I'm going to go, need to speed up a bit."

"Good luck."

"Cheers."

Strike crossed Southwark Park Road as quickly as his leg permitted, then turned into Alma Grove, a long residential street with plane trees planted at regular intervals, and Victorian terraced houses on both sides. To Strike's surprise, Mallik stopped at a house on the right, with a turquoise door, and let himself inside. The distance between his place of residence and that of the Winns' was five minutes' walk at most.

The houses in Alma Grove were narrow and Strike could well imagine loud noises traveling easily through the walls. Giving Mallik what he judged to be sufficient time to remove his jacket and shoes, Strike approached the turquoise door and knocked.

After a few seconds' wait, Aamir opened up. His expression changed from pleasant inquiry to shock. Aamir evidently knew exactly who Strike was.

"Aamir Mallik?"

The younger man did not speak at first, but stood frozen with one hand on the door, the other on the hall wall, looking at Strike with dark eyes shrunken by the thickness of the lenses in his glasses.

"What do you want?"

"A chat," said Strike.

"Why? What for?"

"Jasper Chiswell's family have hired me. They aren't sure he committed suicide."

Appearing temporarily paralyzed, Aamir neither moved nor spoke. Finally, he stood back from the door.

"All right, come in."

In Aamir's position, Strike too would have wanted to know what the detective knew or suspected, rather than wondering through fretful nights why he had called. Strike entered and wiped his feet on the doormat.

The house was larger inside than it had appeared outside. Aamir led Strike through a door on the left into a sitting room. The décor was, very obviously, the taste of a person far older than Aamir. A thick, patterned carpet of swirling pinks and greens, a number of chintz-covered chairs, a wooden coffee table with a lace cloth laid over it and an ornamental edged mirror over the mantelpiece all spoke of geriatric occupants, while an ugly electric heater had been installed in the wrought iron fireplace. Shelves were bare, surfaces denuded of ornaments or other objects. A Stieg Larsson paperback lay on the arm of a chair.

Aamir turned to face Strike, hands in the pockets of his jeans.

"You're Cormoran Strike," he said.

"That's right."

"It was your partner who was pretending to be Venetia, at the Commons."

"Right again."

"What d'you want?" Aamir asked, for the second time.

"To ask you a few questions."

"About what?"

"OK if I sit down?" asked Strike, doing so without waiting for permission. He noticed Aamir's eyes drop to his leg, and stretched out the prosthesis ostentatiously, so that a glint of the metal ankle could be seen above his sock. To a man so considerate of Della's disability, this might be sufficient reason not to ask Strike to get up again. "As I said, the family doesn't think Jasper Chiswell killed himself."

"You think I had something to do with his death?" asked Aamir, trying for incredulity and succeeding only in sounding scared.

"No," said Strike, "but if you want to blurt out a confession, feel free. It'll save me a lot of work."

Aamir didn't smile.

"The only thing I know about you, Aamir," said Strike, "is that you were helping Geraint Winn blackmail Chiswell."

"I wasn't," said Aamir at once.

It was the automatic, ill-considered denial of a panicked man.

"You weren't trying to get hold of incriminating photographs to use against him?"

"I don't know what you're talking about."

"The press are trying to break your bosses' super-injunction. Once the blackmail's out in the public domain, your part in it won't remain hidden for long. You and your friend Christopher—"

"*He's not my friend!*"

Aamir's vehemence interested Strike.

"D'you own this house, Aamir?"

"What?"

"Just seems a big place for a twenty-four-year-old on what can't be a big salary—"

"It's none of your business who owns this—"

"I don't care, personally," said Strike, leaning forwards, "but the papers will. You'll look beholden to the owners if you aren't paying a fair rent. It could seem like you owed them something, like you're in their pocket. The tax office will also consider it a benefit in kind if it's owned by your employers, which could cause problems for both—"

"How did you know where to find me?" Aamir demanded.

"Well, it wasn't easy," Strike admitted. "You don't have much of an online life, do you? But in the end," he said, reaching for a sheaf of folded paper in the inside pocket of his jacket, and unfolding them, "I found your sister's Facebook page. That *is* your sister, right?"

He laid the piece of paper, on which he had printed the Facebook post, on the coffee table. A plumply pretty woman in a hijab beamed up out of the poor reproduction of her photograph, surrounded by four young children. Taking Aamir's silence for assent, Strike said:

"I went back through a few years' worth of posts. That's you," he said, laying a second printed page on top of the first. A younger Aamir stood smiling in academic robes, flanked by his parents. "You took a first in politics and economics at LSE. Very impressive...

"And you got onto a graduate training program at the Foreign Office," Strike continued, placing a third sheet down on top of the first two. This showed an official, posed photograph of a small group of smartly dressed young men and women, all black or from other ethnic minorities, standing around a balding, florid-faced man. "There you are," said Strike, "with senior civil servant Sir Christopher Barrowclough-Burns, who at that time was running a diversity recruitment drive."

Aamir's eye twitched.

"And here you are again," said Strike, laying down the last of his four printed Facebook pages, "just a month ago, with your sister in that pizza place right opposite Della's house. Once I identified where it was and realized how close it was to the Winns' place, I thought it might be worth coming to Bermondsey to see whether I could spot you in the vicinity."

Aamir stared down at the picture of himself and his sister. She had taken the selfie. Southwark Park Road was clearly visible behind them, through the window.

"Where were you at 6 a.m. on the thirteenth of July?" Strike asked Aamir.

"Here."

"Could anyone corroborate that?"

"Yes. Geraint Winn."

"Had he stayed the night?"

Aamir advanced a few steps, fists raised. It could not have been plainer that he had never boxed, but nevertheless, Strike tensed. Aamir looked close to breaking point.

"All I'm saying," said Strike, holding up his hands pacifically, "is that 6 a.m. is an odd time for Geraint Winn to be at your house."

Aamir slowly lowered his fists, then, as though he did not know what else to do with himself, he backed away to sit down on the edge of the seat of the nearest armchair.

"Geraint came round to tell me Della had had a fall."

"Couldn't he have phoned?"

"I suppose so, but he didn't," said Aamir. "He wanted me to help him persuade Della to go to casualty. She'd slipped down the last few stairs and her wrist was swelling up. I went round there—they only live round the corner—but I couldn't persuade her. She's stubborn. Anyway, it turned out to be only a sprain, not a break. She was fine."

"So you're Geraint's alibi for the time Jasper Chiswell died?"

"I suppose so."

"And he's yours."

"Why would I want Jasper Chiswell dead?" asked Aamir.

"That's a good question," said Strike.

"I barely knew the man," said Aamir.

"Really?"

"Yes, really."

"So what made him quote Catullus at you, and mention Fate, and intimate in front of a room full of people that he knew things about your private life?"

There was a long pause. Again, Aamir's eye twitched.

"That didn't happen," he said.

"Really? My partner—"

"She's lying. Chiswell didn't know anything about my private life. Nothing."

Strike heard the numb drone of a hoover next door. He had been right. The walls were not thick.

"I've seen you once before," Strike told Mallik, who looked more frightened than ever. "Jimmy Knight's meeting in East Ham, couple of months ago."

"I don't know what you're talking about," said Mallik. "You've mistaken me for someone else." Then, unconvincingly, "Who's Jimmy Knight?"

"OK, Aamir," said Strike, "if that's how you want to play it, there's no point going on. Could I use your bathroom?"

"What?"

"Need a pee. Then I'll clear out, leave you in peace."

Mallik clearly wanted to refuse, but seemed unable to find a reason to do so.

"All right," said Aamir. "But—"

A thought seemed to have occurred to him.

"—wait. I need to move—I was soaking some socks in the sink. Stay here."

"Right you are," said Strike.

Aamir left the room. Strike wanted an excuse to poke around upstairs for clues to the entity or activity that might have caused animal noises loud enough to disturb the neighbors, but the sound of Aamir's footsteps told him that the bathroom lay beyond the kitchen on the ground floor.

A couple of minutes later, Aamir returned.

"It's through here."

He led Strike down the hall, through a nondescript, bare kitchen, and pointed him into the bathroom.

Strike entered, closed and locked the door, then placed his hand at the bottom of the sink. It was dry. The walls of the bathroom were pink and matched the pink bathroom suite. Grab rails beside the toilet and a floor-to-ceiling rail at the end of the bath suggested that this had been, some time in the recent past, the home of a frail or disabled person.

What was it that Aamir had wanted to remove or conceal before the detective entered? Strike opened the bathroom cabinet. It contained very little other than a young man's basic necessities: shaving kit, deodorant and aftershave.

Closing the cabinet, Strike saw his own reflection swing into view and, over his shoulder, the back of the door, where a thick navy toweling robe had been hung up carelessly, suspended from the arm hole rather than the loop designed for that purpose.

Flushing the toilet to maintain the fiction that he was too busy to nose around, Strike approached the dressing gown and felt the empty pockets. As he did so, the precariously placed robe slid off the hook.

Strike took a step backwards, the better to appreciate what had just been revealed. Somebody had gouged a crude, four-legged figure into the bathroom door, splintering the wood and paint. Strike turned on the cold tap, in case Aamir was listening, took a picture of the carving with his mobile, turned off the tap and replaced the toweling robe as he had found it.

Aamir was waiting at the end of the kitchen.

"All right if I take those papers with me?" Strike asked, and without waiting for an answer he returned to the sitting room and picked up the Facebook pages.

"What made you leave the Foreign Office, anyway?" he asked casually.

"I . . . didn't enjoy it."

"How did it come about, you working for the Winns?"

"We'd met," said Aamir. "Della offered me a job. I took it."

It happened, very occasionally, that Strike felt scruples about what he was driven to ask during an interview.

"I couldn't help noticing," he said, holding up the wad of printed material, "that you seemed to drop out of sight of your family for quite a long time after you left the Foreign Office. No more appearances in group shots, not even on your mother's seventieth birthday. Your sister stopped mentioning you, for a long time."

Aamir said nothing.

"It was as if you'd been disowned," said Strike.

"You can get out, now," said Aamir, but Strike didn't move.

"When your sister posted this picture of the pair of you in the pizza place," Strike continued, unfolding the last sheet again, "the responses were—"

"I want you to leave," repeated Aamir, more loudly.

" 'What you doing with that scumbag?' 'Your dad know you still seeing him?' " Strike read aloud from the messages beneath the picture of Aamir and his sister. " 'If my brother permitted *liwat*—' "

Aamir charged at him, sending a wild right-handed punch to the side of Strike's head that the detective parried. But the studious-looking Aamir was full of the kind of blind rage that could make a dangerous opponent of almost any man. Tearing a nearby lamp from its socket he swung it so violently that had Strike not ducked in time, the lamp base could have shattered, not on the wall that half-divided the sitting room, but on his face.

"Enough!" bellowed Strike, as Aamir dropped the remnants of the lamp and came at him again. Strike fended off the windmilling fists, hooked his prosthetic leg around the back of Aamir's leg, and threw him to the floor. Swearing under his breath, because this action had done his aching stump no good at all, Strike straightened up, panting, and said:

"Any more and I'll fucking deck you."

Aamir rolled out of Strike's reach and got to his feet. His glasses were hanging from one ear. Hands shaking, he took them off and examined the broken hinge. His eyes were suddenly huge.

"Aamir, I'm not interested in your private life," panted Strike, "I'm interested in who you're covering up for—"

"Get out," whispered Aamir.

"—because if the police decide it's murder, everything you're trying to hide will come out. Murder inquiries respect no one's privacy."

"*Get out!*"

"All right. Don't say I didn't warn you."

At the front door, Strike turned one last time to face Aamir, who had followed him into the hall, and braced himself as Strike came to a halt.

"Who carved that mark on the inside of your bathroom door, Aamir?"

"*Out!*"

Strike knew there was no point persisting. As soon as he had crossed the threshold, the front door slammed behind him.

Several houses away, the wincing Strike leaned up against a tree to take the weight off his prosthesis, and texted Robin the picture he had just taken, along with the message:

Remind you of anything?

He lit a cigarette and waited for Robin's response, glad of an excuse to remain stationary, because quite apart from the pain in his stump, the side of his head was throbbing. In dodging the lamp he had hit it against the wall, and his back was aching because of the effort it had taken to throw the younger man to the floor.

Strike glanced back at the turquoise door. If he was honest, something else was hurting: his conscience. He had entered Mallik's house with the intention of shocking or intimidating him into the truth about his relationship with Chiswell and the Winns. While a private detective could not afford the doctor's dictum "first, do no harm," Strike generally attempted to extract truth without causing unnecessary damage to the host. Reading out the comments at the bottom of that Facebook post had been a low blow. Brilliant, unhappy, undoubtedly tied to the Winns by something other than choice, Aamir Mallik's eruption into violence had been the reaction of a desperate man. Strike didn't need to consult the papers in his pocket to recall the picture of Mallik standing proudly in the Foreign Office, about to embark on a stellar career with his first-class degree with his mentor, Sir Christopher Barrowclough-Burns, by his side.

His mobile rang.

"Where on earth did you find that carving?" said Robin.

"The back of Aamir's bathroom door, hidden under a dressing gown."

"You're joking."

"No. What does it look like to you?"

"The white horse on the hill over Woolstone," said Robin.

"Well, that's a relief," said Strike, elbowing himself off the supporting tree and limping off along the street again. "I was worried I'd started hallucinating the bloody things."

47

*...I want to try and play my humble part in the struggles of
life.*

Henrik Ibsen, *Rosmersholm*

Robin emerged from Camden Town station at half past eight on
Friday morning and set off for the jewelry shop where she was to
have her day's trial, furtively checking her appearance in every window that she passed.

In the months following the trial of the Shacklewell Ripper, she
had become adept at makeup techniques such as altering the shape
of her eyebrows or over-painting her lips in vermillion, which made
a significant difference to her appearance when coupled with wigs
and colored contact lenses, but she had never before worn as much
makeup as today. Her eyes, in which she was wearing dark brown
contact lenses, were heavily rimmed with black kohl, her lips painted
pale pink, her nails a metallic gray. Having only one conventional
hole in each earlobe, she had bought a couple of cheap ear cuffs to
simulate a more adventurous approach to piercing. The short black
second-hand dress she had bought at the local Oxfam shop in Deptford still smelled slightly fusty, even though she had run it through
the washing machine the previous day, and she wore it with thick
black tights and a pair of flat black lace-up boots in spite of the
warmth of the morning. Thus attired, she hoped that she resembled
the other goth and emo girls who frequented Camden, an area of
London that Robin had rarely visited and which she associated
mainly with Lorelei and her vintage clothes store.

She had named her new alter ego Bobbi Cunliffe. When under-cover, it was best to assume names with a personal association, to which you responded instinctively. Bobbi sounded like Robin, and indeed people had sometimes tried to abbreviate her name that way, most notably her long-ago flirt in a temporary office, and her brother, Martin, when he wished to annoy her. Cunliffe was Matthew's surname.

To her relief, he had left for work early that day, because he was auditing an office out in Barnet, leaving Robin free to complete her physical transformation without undermining remarks and displea-sure that she was, again, going undercover. Indeed, she thought she might derive a certain pleasure from using her married name — the first time she had ever offered it as her own — while embodying a girl whom Matthew would instinctively dislike. The older he got, the more Matthew was aggravated by and contemptuous of people who did not dress, think or live as he did.

The Wiccan's jewelry shop, Triquetra, was tucked away in Cam-den Market. Arriving outside at a quarter to nine, Robin found the stallholders of Camden Lock Place already busy, but the store locked up and empty. After a five-minute wait, her employer arrived, puffing slightly. A large woman whom Robin guessed to be in her late fifties, she had straggly dyed black hair that showed half an inch of silver root, had the same savage approach to eyeliner as Bobbi Cunliffe and wore a long green velvet dress.

During the cursory interview that had led to today's trial, the shop owner had asked very few questions, instead speaking at length about the husband of thirty years who had just left her to live in Thailand, the neighbor who was suing her over a boundary dispute and the stream of unsatisfactory and ungrateful employees who had walked out on Triquetra to take other jobs. Her undisguised desire to extract the maximum amount of work for the minimum amount of pay, coupled with her outpourings of self-pity, made Robin wonder why anybody had ever wanted to work for her in the first place.

"You're punctual," she observed, when within earshot. "Good. Where's the other one?"

"I don't know," said Robin.

"I *don't need this*," said the owner, with a slight note of hysteria. "Not on the day I've got to meet Brian's lawyer!"

She unlocked the door and showed Robin into the shop, which was the size of a large kiosk, and as she raised her arms to start pulling up blinds, the smell of body odor and patchouli mingled with the dusty, incense-scented air. Daylight fell into the shop like a solid thing, rendering everything there more insubstantial and shabby by comparison. Dull silver necklaces and earrings hung in racks on the dark purple walls, many of them featuring pentagrams, peace symbols and marijuana leaves, while glass hookahs mingled with tarot cards, black candles, essential oils and ceremonial daggers on black shelves behind the counter.

"We've got *millions* of extra tourists coming through Camden right now," said the owner, bustling around the back of the counter, "and if she doesn't turn—*there you are*," she said, as Flick, who looked sulky, sloped inside. Flick was wearing a yellow and green Hezbollah T-shirt and ripped jeans, and carrying a large leather messenger bag.

"Tube was late," she said.

"Well, *I* managed to get here all right, and so did Bibi!"

"Bobbi," Robin corrected her, deliberately broadening her York-shire accent.

She didn't want to pretend to be a Londoner this time. It was best not to have to talk about schools and locales that Flick might know.

"—well, I need you two to be on top of things *all—the—time*," said the owner, beating out the last three words with one hand against the other. "All right, Bibi—"

"—Bobbi—"

"—yes, come here and see how the till works."

Robin had no difficulty grasping how the till worked, because she had had a Saturday job in her teens at a clothes shop in Harrogate. It was just as well that she did not need longer instruction, because a steady stream of shoppers began to arrive about ten minutes after they opened. To Robin's slight surprise, because there was nothing in the shop that she would have cared to buy, many visitors to Camden seemed to feel that their trip would be incomplete without a pair of pewter earrings, or a pentagram-embossed candle, or one of the small

hessian bags that lay in a basket beside the till, each of which pur-
ported to contain a magic charm.

"All right, I need to be off," the owner announced at eleven, while
Flick was serving a tall German woman who was dithering between
two packs of tarot cards. "Don't forget: one of you needs to be
focused on stock all the time, in case of pilfering. My friend Eddie
will be keeping an eye out," she said, pointing at the stall selling old
LPs just outside. "Twenty minutes each for lunch, taken separately.
Don't forget," she repeated ominously, "Eddie's watching."

She left in a whirl of velvet and body odor. The German customer
departed with her tarot cards and Flick slammed the till drawer shut,
the noise echoing in the temporarily empty shop.

"Old Steady Eddie," she said venomously. "He doesn't give a shit.
He could rob her blind and he wouldn't care. Cow," added Flick for
good measure.

Robin laughed and Flick seemed gratified.

"What's tha name?" asked Robin, in broad Yorkshire. "She
never said."

"Flick," said Flick. "You're Bobbi, yeah?"

"Yeah," said Robin.

Flick took out her mobile from her messenger bag, which she had
stowed beneath the counter, checked it, appeared not to see what she
had hoped to see, then stuffed it out of sight again.

"You must've been hard up for work, were you?" she asked Robin.

"Had to take what I could," Robin said. "I were sacked."

"Yeah?"

"Fookin' Amazon," said Robin.

"Those tax-dodging bastards," said Flick, slightly more interested.
"What happened?"

"Didn't make my daily rate."

Robin had lifted her story directly from a recent news report about
working conditions in one of the retail company's warehouses: the
relentless pressure to make targets, packing and scanning thousands
of products a day under unforgiving pressure from supervisors. Flick's
expression wavered between sympathy and anger as Robin talked.

"That's outrageous!" she said, when Robin had finished.

"Yeah," said Robin, "and no union or nothing, obviously. Me dad were a big trade union man back in Yorkshire."

"Bet he was furious."

"He's dead," said Robin, unblushingly. "Lungs. Ex-miner."

"Oh, shit," said Flick. "Sorry."

She was looking upon Robin with respect and interest now.

"See, you'll have been a worker, not an employee. That's how the bastards get away with it."

"What's the difference?"

"Fewer statutory rights," said Flick. "You might have a case against them if they deducted from your wages, though."

"Dunno if I could prove that," said Robin. "How come you know all this?"

"I'm pretty active in the labor movement," said Flick, with a shrug. She hesitated, "And my mother's an employment lawyer."

"Yeah?" said Robin, allowing herself to sound politely surprised.

"Yeah," said Flick, picking her nails, "but we don't get on. I don't see any of my family, actually. They don't like my partner. Or my politics."

She smoothed out the Hezbollah T-shirt and showed Robin.

"What, are they Tories?" asked Robin.

"Might as well be," said Flick. "They loved bloody Blair."

Robin felt her phone vibrate in the pocket of her second-hand dress.

"Is there a bog anywhere here?"

"Through here," said Flick, pointing to a well-hidden purple painted door with more racks of jewelry nailed to it.

Beyond the purple door Robin found a small cubbyhole with a cracked, dirty window. A safe sat beside a dilapidated kitchen unit with a kettle, a couple of cleaning products and a stiff J-cloth on top. There was no room to sit down and barely room to stand, because a grubby toilet had been plumbed into the corner.

Robin shut herself inside the chipboard cubicle, put down the toilet lid and sat down to read the lengthy text that Barclay had just sent to both her and Strike.

Billy's been found. He was picked up off street 2 weeks ago. Psychotic episode, sectioned, hospital in north London, don't know which yet. Wouldn't tell docs his next of kin till yesterday. Social worker contacted Jimmy this morning. Jimmy wants me to go with him to persuade Billy to discharge himself. Scared what Billy's going to tell the doctors, says he talks too much. Also, Jimmy's lost bit of paper with Billy's name on & he's shitting himself about it. Asked me if I'd seen it. He says it's handwritten, no other details, I don't know why so important. Jimmy thinks Flick's nicked it. Things bad between them again.

As Robin was reading this for a second time, a response came in from Strike.

Barclay: find out visiting arrangements at the hospital, I want to see Billy. Robin: try and search Flick's bag.

Thanks, Robin texted back, exasperated. **I'd never have thought of that on my own.**

She got up, flushed the toilet and returned to the shop, where a gang of black-clad goths were picking over the stock like drooping crows. As she sidled past Flick, Robin saw that her messenger bag was sitting on a shelf beneath the counter. When the group had finally left in possession of essential oils and black candles, Flick took out her phone to check it again, before sinking once more into a morose silence.

Robin's experience in many temporary offices had taught her that little bonded women more than discovering that they were not alone in their particular man-related miseries. Taking out her own phone, she saw a further text from Strike:

That's why I get paid the big money. Brains.

Amused against her will, Robin suppressed a grin and said:

"He must think I'm fooking stupid."

"Wassup?"

"Boyfriend. So-called," said Robin, ramming her phone back into her pocket. "S'posed to be separated from his wife. Guess where he was last night? Mate of mine saw him leaving hers this morning." She exhaled loudly and slumped down on the counter.

"Yeah, my boyfriend likes old women and all," said Flick, picking at her nails. Robin, who had not forgotten that Jimmy had been married to a woman thirteen years his senior, hoped for more confidences, but before she could ask more, another group of young women entered, chattering in a language that Robin did not recognize, though she thought it sounded Eastern European. They clustered around the basket of supposed charms.

"*Dziękuję ci,*" Flick said, as one of them handed over her money, and the girls laughed and complimented her on her accent.

"What did you just say?" asked Robin, as the party left. "Was that Russian?"

"Polish. Learned a bit from my parents' cleaner." Flick hurried on, as though she had given something away, "Yeah, I always got on better with the cleaners than I did with my parents, actually, you can't call yourself a socialist and have a cleaner, can you? Nobody should be allowed to live in a house too big for them, we should have forcible repossessions, redistribution of land and housing to the people who need it."

"Too right," said Robin enthusiastically, and Flick seemed reassured to be forgiven her professional parents by Bobbi Cunliffe, daughter of a dead ex-miner and Yorkshire trade unionist.

"Want a tea?" she offered.

"Aye, that'd be great," said Robin.

"Have you heard of the Real Socialist Party?" asked Flick, once she had come back into the shop with two mugs.

"No," said Robin.

"It's not your normal political party," Flick assured her. "We're more like a proper community-based campaign, like, back to the Jarrow marchers, that kind of thing, the real spirit of Labor movement, not an imperialist Tory-lite shower of shite like fucking 'New Labor.' We don't want to play the same old politics game, we want to change the rules of the game in favor of ordinary working—"

Billy Bragg's version of the "Internationale" rang out. As Flick reached into her bag, Robin realized that this was Flick's ringtone. Reading the caller's name, Flick became tense.

"You be all right on your own for a bit?"

"Course," said Robin.

Flick slid into the back room. As the door swung shut Robin heard her say:

"What's going on? Have you seen him?"

As soon as the door was securely shut, Robin hurried to where Flick had been standing, crouched down and slid her hand under the leather flap of the messenger bag. The interior resembled the depths of a bin. Her fingers groped through sundry bits of crumpled paper, sweet wrappers, a sticky lump of something Robin thought might be chewed gum, various lid-less pens and tubes of makeup, a tin with a picture of Che Guevara on it, a pack of rolling tobacco that had leaked over the rest of the contents, some Rizlas, some spare tampons and a small, twisted ball of fabric that Robin was afraid might be a pair of worn pants. Trying to flatten out, read and then re-crumple each piece of paper was time-consuming. Most seemed to be abandoned drafts of articles. Then, through the door behind her, she heard Flick say loudly:

"*Strike?* What the hell..."

Robin froze, listening.

"...paranoid...it alone now...tell them he's..."

"Excuse me," said a woman peering over the counter. Robin jumped up. The portly, gray-haired customer in a tie-dyed T-shirt pointed up at the shelf on the wall, "could I see that rather special *athame?*"

"Which?" asked Robin, confused.

"The *athame*. The ceremonial dagger," said the elderly woman, pointing.

Flick's voice rose and fell in the room behind Robin.

"...it, didn't you?...member you...pay me back...Chiswell's money..."

"Mmm," said the customer, weighing the knife carefully in her hand, "have you anything larger?"

"*You had it, not me!*" said Flick loudly, from behind the door.

"Um," said Robin, squinting up at the shelf, "I think this is all we've got. That one might be a bit bigger..."

She stood on tiptoe to reach the longer knife, as Flick said:

"*Fuck off, Jimmy!*"

"There you are," said Robin, handing over the seven-inch dagger.

With a clatter of falling necklaces, the door behind Robin flew open, hitting her in the back.

"Sorry," said Flick, seizing her bag and shoving the phone back inside it, breathing hard, her eyes bright.

"Yes, you see, I like the triple moon marking on the smaller one," said the elderly witch, pointing at the decoration on the hilt of the first dagger, unfazed by Flick's dramatic reappearance, "but I prefer the longer blade."

Flick was in that febrile state between fury and tears that Robin knew was one of the most amenable to indiscretion and confession. Desperate to get rid of her tiresome customer, she said bluntly in Bobbi's thick Yorkshire:

"Well, that's all we've got."

The customer chuntered a little more, weighing the two knives in her hands, and at last took herself off without buying either.

"Y'all right?" Robin asked Flick at once.

"No," said Flick. "I need a smoke."

She checked her watch.

"Tell her I'm taking lunch if she comes back, all right?"

Damn, thought Robin, as Flick disappeared, taking her bag and her promising mood with her.

For over an hour, Robin minded the shop alone, becoming increasingly hungry. Once or twice, Eddie at the record stall peered vaguely into the shop at Robin, but showed no other interest in her activities. In a brief lull between more customers, Robin nipped into the back room to make sure that there wasn't any food there that she had overlooked. There wasn't.

At ten to one, Flick strolled back into the shop with a dark, thuggishly handsome man in a tight blue T-shirt. He subjected Robin to the hard, arrogant stare of a certain brand of womanizer, melding appreciation and disdain to signal that she might be good-looking, but she would have to try a little harder than that to arouse his interest. It was a strategy that Robin had seen work on other young women in offices. It had never worked on her.

"Sorry I was so long," Flick told Robin. Her bad mood did not seem entirely dissipated. "Ran into Jimmy. Jimmy, this is Bobbi."

"All right?" said Jimmy, holding out a hand.

Robin shook it.

"You go," said Flick to Robin. "Go and get something to eat."

"Oh, right," said Robin. "Thanks."

Jimmy and Flick waited while, under cover of checking her bag for money, Robin crouched down and, hidden by the counter, set her mobile to record before placing it carefully at the back of the dark shelf.

"See tha in a bit, then," she said brightly, and strolled away into the market.

48

But what do you say to it all, Rebecca?

Henrik Ibsen, *Rosmersholm*

A whining wasp zigzagged from inner to outer rooms of Strike's office, passing between the two windows that were flung open to admit the fume-laden evening air. Barclay waved the insect away with the takeaway menu that had just arrived with a large delivery of Chinese food. Robin peeled lids off the cartons and laid them out on her desk. Over by the kettle, Strike was trying to find a third fork.

Matthew had been surprisingly accommodating when Robin had called him from Charing Cross Road three-quarters of an hour previously, to say that she needed to meet Strike and Barclay, and was likely to be back late.

"Fine," he had said, "Tom wants to go for a curry, anyway. I'll see you at home."

"How was today?" Robin asked, before he could hang up. "The office out in..."

Her mind went blank.

"Barnet," he said. "Games developer. Yeah, it was all right. How was yours?"

"Not bad," said Robin.

Matthew was so determinedly uninterested in the details of the Chiswell job after their many arguments about it that there seemed no point in telling him where she had been, who she was impersonating, or what had happened that day. After they had said goodbye,

Robin walked on through meandering tourists and Friday night drinkers, knowing that a casual listener would have taken the conversation to be that of two people connected merely by proximity or circumstance, with no particular liking for each other.

"Want a beer?" Strike asked her, holding up a four pack of Tennent's.

"Yes, please," said Robin.

She was still wearing her short black dress and lace-up boots, but had tied back her chalked hair, cleaned her face of its thick makeup and removed her dark lenses. Seeing Strike's face in a patch of evening sunlight, she thought he looked unwell. There were deeper lines than usual around his mouth and across his forehead, lines etched there, she suspected, by grinding, daily pain. He was also moving awkwardly, using his upper body to turn and trying to disguise his limp as he returned to her desk with the beer.

"What've you been up to today?" she asked Strike, as Barclay heaped his plate with food.

"Following Geraint Winn. He's holed up in a miserable B&B five minutes away from the marital home. He led me all the way into central London and back to Bermondsey again."

"Risky, following him," commented Robin. "He knows what you look like."

"All three of us could've been behind him and he wouldn't have noticed. He's lost about a stone since I last saw him."

"What did he do?"

"Went to eat in a place right by the Commons, called the Cellarium. No windows, like a crypt."

"Sounds cheerful," said Barclay, settling down on the fake leather sofa and starting on his sweet and sour pork balls.

"He's like a sad homing pigeon," said Strike, tipping the whole tub of Singapore noodles onto his own plate, "returning to the place of his former glories with the tourists. Then we went to King's Cross."

Robin paused in the act of helping herself to beansprouts.

"Blow job in a dark stairwell," said Strike matter-of-factly.

"Eurgh," muttered Robin, continuing to help herself to food.

"Did ye see it, aye?" asked Barclay with interest.

"Back view. Elbowed my way through the front door, then backed out with apologies. He was in no state to recognize me. After that, he bought himself some new socks from Asda and went back to his B&B."

"There are worse days out," said Barclay, who had already eaten half the food on his plate. Catching Robin's eye, he said through a mouthful, "Wife wants me home by half eight."

"All right, Robin," said Strike, lowering himself gingerly onto his own desk chair, which he had brought through to the outer office, "let's hear what Jimmy and Flick had to say to each other when they thought no one was listening."

He opened a notebook and took a pen from the pot on her desk, leaving his left hand free to fork Singapore noodles into his mouth. Still chewing vigorously, Barclay leaned forwards on the sofa, interested. Robin placed her mobile face up on the desk and pressed "play."

For a moment there was no sound except faint footsteps, which were Robin's, leaving the Wiccan's shop earlier in search of lunch.

"I thought you were here on your own?" said Jimmy's voice, faint but clear.

"She's having a day's trial," said Flick. "Where's Sam?"

"I told him I'll meet him at yours later. Right, where's your bag?"

"Jimmy, I haven't—"

"Maybe you picked it up by mistake."

More footsteps, a scraping of wood and leather, clattering, thunks and furtive rustlings.

"This is a fucking tip."

"I haven't got it, how many more times? And you've got no right to search that without my—"

"This is serious. I had it in my wallet. Where's it gone?"

"You've dropped it somewhere, haven't you?"

"Or someone's taken it."

"Why would *I* take it?"

"Insurance policy."

"That's a hell of an—"

"But if that's what you're thinking, you wanna remember, you fucking nicked it, so it incriminates you as much as me. More."

"I was only there in the first place because of you, Jimmy!"

"Oh, *that's* going to be the story, is it? Nobody bloody made you. You're the one who started all this, remember."

"Yeah and I wish I hadn't, now!"

"Too late for that. I want that paper back and so should you. It proves we had access to his place."

"You mean it proves a connection between him and Bill—ouch!"

"Oh, fuck off, that didn't hurt! You demean women who really are knocked around, playing the victim. I'm not kidding, now. If you've taken it—"

"Don't threaten me—"

"What're you going to do, run off to Mummy and Daddy? How're they going to feel when they find out what their little girl's been up to?"

Flick's rapid breathing now became sobs.

"You nicked money from him, and all," said Jimmy.

"You thought it was a laugh at the time, you said he deserved it—"

"Try that defense in court, see how far it gets you. If you try and save yourself by throwing me under the bus, I won't have any fucking problem telling the pigs you were in this thing *all the way*. So if that bit of paper turns up somewhere I don't want it to go—"

"I haven't got it, I don't know where it is!"

"—you've been fucking warned. Give me your front door key."

"What? Why?"

"Because I'm going over to that shithole you call a flat right now and I'm searching it with Sam."

"You're not going over there without me—"

"Why not? Got another Indian waiter sleeping off his hangover there, have you?"

"I never—"

"I don't give a shit," said Jimmy. "Screw whoever you like. Give me your key. *Give it me.*"

More footsteps; a tinkling of keys. The sound of Jimmy walking away and then a cascade of sobs that continued until Robin pressed pause.

"She cried until the shop owner came back," said Robin, "which was just before I did, and she hardly spoke this afternoon. I tried to walk back to the Tube with her, but she shook me off. Hopefully she'll be in a more talkative mood tomorrow."

"So, did you and Jimmy search her flat?" Strike asked Barclay.

"Aye. Books, drawers, under her mattress. Nothing."

"What exactly did he say you were looking for?"

"'Bit o' paper wi' handwriting an' Billy's name on,' he says. 'I had it in me wallet and it's gone.' Claims it's somethin' tae do with a drugs deal. He thinks I'm some ned who'll believe anythin'."

Strike put down his pen, swallowed a large mouthful of noodles and said:

"Well, I don't know about you two, but what jumps out at me is 'it proves we had access.'"

"I think I might know a bit more about that," said Robin, who had so far successfully concealed her excitement about what she was about to reveal. "I found out today that Flick can speak a bit of Polish, and we know she stole cash from her previous place of work. What if—?"

"'I do that cleaning,'" said Strike, suddenly. "That's what she said to Jimmy, on the march, when I was following them! 'I do that cleaning, and it's disgusting'...Bloody hell—you think she was—?"

"Chiswell's Polish cleaner," said Robin, determined not to be robbed of her moment of triumph. "Yes. I do."

Barclay was continuing to shovel pork balls into his mouth, though his eyes were suitably surprised.

"If that's true, it changes bloody everything," said Strike. "She'd have had access, been able to snoop around, take stuff into the house—"

"How'd she find out he wanted a cleaner?" asked Barclay.

"Must've seen the card he put in a newsagent's window."

"They live miles apart. She's in Hackney."

"Maybe Jimmy spotted it, snooping around Ebury Street, trying to collect his blackmail money," suggested Robin, but Strike was now frowning.

"But that's back to front. If she found out about the blackmailable offense when she was a cleaner, her employment must've pre-dated Jimmy trying to collect money."

"All right, maybe Jimmy didn't tip her off. Maybe they found out he wanted a cleaner while they were trying to dig dirt on him in general."

"So they could run an exposé on the Real Socialist Party website?" suggested Barclay. "That'd reach a good four or five people."

Strike snorted in amusement.

"Main point is," he said, "this piece of paper's got Jimmy very worried."

Barclay speared his last pork ball and stuck it in his mouth. "Flick's taken it," he said thickly. "I guarantee it."

"Why are you so sure?" asked Robin.

"She wants somethin' over him," said Barclay, getting up to take his empty plate over to the sink. "Only reason he's keepin' her around is because she knows too much. He told me the other day he'd be happy tae get shot of her if he could. I asked why he couldnae just dump her. He didnae answer."

"Maybe she's destroyed it, if it's so incriminating?" suggested Robin.

"I don't think so," said Strike. "She's a lawyer's daughter, she's not going to destroy evidence. Something like that paper could be valuable, if the shit hits the fan and she decides she's going to cooperate with the police."

Barclay returned to the sofa and picked up his beer.

"How's Billy?" Robin asked him, getting started at last on her own cooling meal.

"Poor wee bastard," said Barclay. "Skin and bone. The traffic cops caught him when he jumped a Tube barrier. He tried tae batter them, ended up bein' sectioned. The doctors say he's got delusions o' persecution. At first he thought he was bein' chased by the government and the medical staff were all part o' some giant conspiracy, but now he's back on his medication he's a wee bit more rational.

"Jimmy wanted tae take him home there and then, but the docs werenae gonna let that happen. What's really pissin' Jimmy off," said Barclay, pausing to finish his can of Tennent's, "is Billy's still obsessed wi' Strike. Keeps askin' for him. The doctors think it's part o' his delusion, that he's latched ontae the famous detective as part of his fantasy, like: the only person he can really trust. Couldnae tell them he and Strike have met. Not wi' Jimmy standin' there telling them it's all a load o' pish.

"The medics don't want anyone near him except family, and they're no keen on Jimmy any more, neither, not after he tried tae persuade Billy he's well enough to go home."

Barclay crushed his beer can in his hand and checked his watch. "Gotta go, Strike."

"Yeah, all right," said Strike. "Thanks for staying. Thought it would be good to have a joint debrief."

"Nae bother."

With a wave to Robin, Barclay departed. Strike bent to pick up his own beer off the floor and winced.

"You all right?" asked Robin, who was helping herself to more prawn crackers.

"Fine," he said, straightening up again. "I did a lot of walking again today, and I could have done without the fight yesterday."

"Fight? What fight?" asked Robin.

"Aamir Mallik."

"What!"

"Don't worry. I didn't hurt him. Much."

"You didn't tell me the argument got physical!"

"I wanted to do it in person, so I could enjoy you looking at me like I'm a complete bastard," said Strike. "How about a bit of sympathy for your one-legged partner?"

"You're an ex-boxer!" said Robin. "And he probably weighs about nine stone soaking wet!"

"He came at me with a lamp."

"*Aamir* did?"

She couldn't imagine the reserved, meticulous man she had known in the House of Commons using physical violence against anyone.

"Yeah. I was pushing him about Chiswell's 'man of your habits' comment and he snapped. If it makes you feel any better, I don't feel good about it," said Strike. "Hang on a minute. Need a pee."

He pulled himself awkwardly out of the chair and departed for the bathroom on the landing. As she heard the door close, Strike's mobile, which was charging on top of the filing cabinet beside Robin's desk,

rang. She got up to check it and saw, through the cracked and sellotaped screen, the name "Lorelei." Wondering whether to answer it,
Robin hesitated too long and the call went to voicemail. Just as she
was about to sit down again, a small *ping* declared that a text arrived.

**If you want a hot meal and a shag with no human emotions
involved, there are restaurants and brothels.**

Robin heard the bang of the bathroom door outside and stumbled
hastily back to her chair. Strike limped back inside the room, lowered
himself into his chair and picked up his noodles.

"Your phone just rang," said Robin. "I didn't pick up—"

"Chuck it over," said Strike.

She did so. He read the text with no change of expression, muted
the phone and put it in his pocket.

"What were we saying?"

"That you didn't feel good about the fight—"

"I feel fine about the fight," Strike corrected her. "If I hadn't
defended myself I'd have a face full of stitches."

He pronged a forkful of noodles.

"The bit I don't feel great about is when I told him I know he's
been ostracized by his family, barring one sister who's still talking to
him. It's all on Facebook. It was when I mentioned his family dropping him that I nearly got my head taken off with a table lamp."

"Maybe they're upset because they think he's with Della?" suggested Robin as Strike chewed his noodles.

He shrugged and made an expression indicative of "maybe," swallowed, and said, "Has it occurred to you that Aamir is literally the
only person connected with this case who's got a motive? Chiswell
threatened him, presumably with exposure. 'A man of your habits.'
'Lachesis knew when everyone's time was up.'"

"What happened to 'forget about motive, concentrate on means'?"

"Yeah, yeah," said Strike wearily. He set aside his plate, from
which he had eaten nearly all the noodles, took out his cigarettes and
lighter, and sat up a little straighter. "OK, let's focus on means.

"Who had access to the house, to anti-depressants and helium?

Who knew Jasper Chiswell's habits well enough to be sure he'd drink his orange juice that morning? Who had a key, or, who would he have trusted enough to let in in the early hours of the morning?"

"Members of his family."

"Right," said Strike, as his lighter flared, "but we know Kinvara, Fizzy, Izzy and Torquil can't have done it, which leaves us with Raphael and his story of being ordered down to Woolstone that morning."

"You really think he could have killed his father then driven coolly down to Woolstone to wait with Kinvara until the police arrived?"

"Forget psychology or probability: we're considering opportunity," said Strike, blowing out a long jet of smoke. "Nothing I've heard so far precludes Raphael being at Ebury Street at six in the morning. I know what you're going to say," he forestalled her, "but it wouldn't be the first time a phone call had been faked by a killer. He could have called his own mobile with Chiswell's to make it seem as though his father had ordered him down to Woolstone."

"Which means that either Chiswell didn't have a passcode on his mobile, or that Raphael knew it."

"Good point. That needs checking."

Clicking out the nib of his pen, Strike made a note on his pad. As he did it, he wondered whether Robin's husband, who had previously deleted her call history without her knowledge, knew her current passcode. These small matters of trust were often powerful indicators of the strength of a relationship.

"There's another logistical problem if Raphael was the killer," Robin said. "He didn't have a key, and if his father let him in, it would mean Chiswell was awake and conscious while Raphael pounded up anti-depressants in the kitchen."

"Another good point," said Strike, "but the pounding up of the pills has to be explained away with all of our suspects.

"Take Flick. If she was posing as the cleaner, she probably knew the house in Ebury Street better than most of the family. Loads of opportunities to poke around, and she had a restricted key for a while. They're hard to get copied, but let's say she managed it, so she could still let herself in and out of the house whenever she fancied.

"She creeps in in the early hours to doctor the orange juice, but crushing pills in a pestle and mortar is a noisy job—"

"—unless," said Robin, "she brought the pills already crushed up, in a bag or something, and dusted them around the pestle and mortar to make it look as though Chiswell had done it."

"OK, but we still need to explain why there were no traces of amitriptyline in the empty orange juice carton in the bin. Raphael could plausibly have handed his father a glass of juice—"

"—except that Chiswell's prints were the only ones on there—"

"—but would Chiswell not find it odd to come downstairs in the morning to a pre-poured glass of juice? Would *you* drink a glass of something you hadn't poured, and which appeared mysteriously in what you thought was an empty house?"

Down in Denmark Street, a group of young women's voices rose over the constant swish and rumble of traffic, singing Rihanna's "Where Have You Been?"

"*Where have you been? All my life, all my life…*"

"Maybe it *was* suicide," said Robin.

"That attitude won't get the bills paid," said Strike, tapping his cigarette ash onto his plate. "Come on, people who had the means to get into Ebury Street that day: Raphael, Flick—"

"—and Jimmy," said Robin. "Everything that applies to Flick applies to him, because she would've been able to give him all the information she had about Chiswell's habits and his house, and given him her copied key."

"Correct. So those are three people we know could have got in that morning," said Strike, "but this took much more than simply being able to get in through the door. The killer also had to know which anti-depressants Kinvara was taking, and arrange for the helium canister and rubber tubing to be there, which suggests close contact with the Chiswells, access to the house to get the stuff inside, or insider knowledge of the fact that the helium and tubing were already in there."

"As far as we know, Raphael hadn't been in Ebury Street lately and wasn't on terms with Kinvara to know what pills she was taking, though I suppose his father might have mentioned it to him," said

Robin. "Judged on opportunity alone, the Winns and Aamir seem to be ruled out...so, assuming she *was* the cleaner, Jimmy and Flick go to the top of our suspect list."

Strike heaved a sigh and closed his eyes.

"Bollocks to it," he muttered, as he passed a hand across his face, "I keep circling back to motive."

Opening his eyes again, he stubbed out his cigarette on his dinner plate and immediately lit another one.

"I'm not surprised MI5 are interested, because there's no obvious gain here. Oliver was right—blackmailers don't generally kill their victims, it's the other way around. Hatred's a picturesque idea, but a hot-blooded hate killing is a hammer or a lamp to the head, not a meticulously planned fake suicide. If it was murder, it was more like a clinical execution, planned in every detail. Why? What did the killer get out of it? Which also makes me wonder, why *then?* Why did Chiswell die *then?*"

"It was surely in Jimmy and Flick's best interests for Chiswell to stay alive until they could produce evidence that forced him to come across with the money they wanted. Same with Raphael: he'd been written out of the will, but his relationship with his father was showing some signs of improvement. It was in his interest for his father to stay alive.

"But Chiswell had covertly threatened Aamir with exposure of something unspecified, but probably sexual, given the Catullus quotation, and he'd recently come into possession of information about the Winns' dodgy charity. We shouldn't forget that Geraint Winn wasn't really a blackmailer: he didn't want money, he wanted Chiswell's resignation and disgrace. Is it beyond the realms of possibility that Winn or Mallik took a different kind of revenge when they realized the first plan had failed?"

Strike dragged heavily on his cigarette and said:

"We're missing something, Robin. The thing that ties all this together."

"Maybe it doesn't tie together," said Robin. "That's life, isn't it? We've got a group of people who all had their own personal tribulations and secrets. Some of them had reason not to like Chiswell, to resent him, but that doesn't mean it all joins up neatly. Some of it must be irrelevant."

"There's still something we don't know."

"There's a lot we don't—"

"No, something big, something...fundamental. I can smell it. It keeps almost showing itself. Why did Chiswell say he might have more work for us after he'd scuppered Winn and Knight?"

"I don't know," said Robin.

"'One by one, they trip themselves up,'" Strike quoted. "Who'd tripped themselves up?"

"Geraint Winn. I'd just told him about the missing money from the charity."

"Chiswell had been on the phone, trying to find a money clip, you said. A money clip that belonged to Freddie."

"That's right," said Robin.

"Freddie," repeated Strike, scratching his chin.

And for a moment he was back in the communal TV room of a German military hospital, with the television muted in the corner and copies of the *Army Times* lying on a low table. The young lieutenant who had witnessed Freddie Chiswell's death had been sitting there alone when Strike found him, wheelchair-bound, a Taliban bullet still lodged in his spine.

"...the convoy stopped, Major Chiswell told me to get out, see what was going on. I told him I could see movement up on the ridge. He told me to fucking well do as I was told.

"I hadn't gone more than a couple of feet when I got the bullet in the back. The last thing I remember was him yelling out of the lorry at me. Then the sniper took the top of his head off."

The lieutenant had asked Strike for a cigarette. He wasn't supposed to be smoking, but Strike had given him the half pack he had on him.

"Chiswell was a cunt," said the young man in the wheelchair.

In Strike's imagination he saw tall, blond Freddie swaggering up a country lane, slumming it with Jimmy Knight and his mates. He saw Freddie in fencing garb, out on the piste, watched by the indistinct figure of Rhiannon Winn, who was perhaps already entertaining suicidal thoughts.

Disliked by his soldiers, revered by his father: could Freddie be the thing that Strike sought, the element that tied everything together, that connected two blackmailers and the story of a strangled child? But the notion seemed to dissolve as he examined it, and the diverse strands of the investigation fell apart once more, stubbornly unconnected.

"I want to know what the photographs from the Foreign Office show," said Strike aloud, his eyes on the purpling sky beyond the office window. "I want to know who hacked the Uffington white horse onto the back of Aamir Mallik's bathroom door, and I want to know why there was a cross in the ground on the exact spot Billy said a kid was buried."

"Well," said Robin, standing up and beginning to clear away the debris of their Chinese takeaway, "nobody ever said you weren't ambitious."

"Leave that. I'll do it. You need to get home."

I don't want to go home.

"It won't take long. What are you up to tomorrow?"

"Got an afternoon appointment with Chiswell's art dealer friend, Drummond."

Having rinsed off the plates and cutlery, Robin took her handbag down from the peg where she'd hung it, then turned back. Strike tended to rebuff expressions of concern, but she had to say it.

"No offense, but you look terrible. Maybe rest your leg before you have to go out again? See you soon."

She left before Strike could answer. He sat lost in thought until, finally, he knew he must begin the painful journey back upstairs to his attic flat. Having heaved himself upright again, he closed the windows, turned off the lights and locked up the office.

As he placed his false foot on the bottom stair to the floor above, his phone rang again. He knew, without checking, that it was Lorelei. She wasn't about to let him go without at least attempting to hurt him as badly as he had hurt her. Slowly, carefully, keeping his weight off his prosthesis as much as was practical, Strike climbed the stairs to bed.

49

Rosmers of Rosmersholm—clergymen, soldiers, men who have filled high places in the state—men of scrupulous honor, every one of them...

Henrik Ibsen, *Rosmersholm*

Lorelei didn't give up. She wanted to see Strike face to face, wanted to know why she had given nearly a year of her life, as she saw it, to an emotional vampire.

"You owe me a meeting," she said, when he finally picked up the phone at lunchtime next day. "I want to see you. You owe me that."

"And what will that achieve?" he asked her. "I read your email, you've made your feelings clear. I told you from the start what I wanted and what I didn't want—"

"Don't give me that 'I never pretended I wanted anything serious' line. Who did you call when you couldn't walk? You were happy enough for me to act like your wife when you were—"

"So let's both agree I'm a bastard," he said, sitting in his combined kitchen-sitting room with his amputated leg stretched out on a chair in front of him. He was wearing only boxer shorts, but would soon need to get his prosthesis on and dress smartly enough to blend in at Henry Drummond's art gallery. "Let's wish each other well and—"

"No," she said, "you don't get out of it that easily. I was happy, I was doing fine—"

"I never wanted to make you miserable. I like you—"

"You *like* me," she repeated shrilly. "A year together and you *like* me—"

"What do you want?" he said, losing his temper at last. "Me to limp up the fucking aisle, not feeling what I should feel, not wanting it, wishing I was out of it? You're making me say what I don't want to say. I didn't want to hurt anyone—"

"But you did! You *did* hurt me! And now you want to walk away as though nothing happened!"

"Whereas you want a public scene in a restaurant?"

"I want," she said, crying now, "not to feel as though I could have been anyone. I want a memory of the end that doesn't make me feel disposable and cheap—"

"I never saw you that way. I don't see you like that now," he said, eyes closed, wishing he had never crossed the room at Wardle's party. "Truth is, you're too—"

"Don't tell me I'm too good for you," she said. "Leave us both with some dignity."

She hung up. Strike's dominant emotion was relief.

No investigation had ever brought Strike so reliably back to the same small patch of London. The taxi disgorged him onto the gently sloping pavement of St. James's Street a few hours later, with the red brick St. James's Palace ahead and Pratt's on Park Place to his right. After paying off the driver, he headed for Drummond's Gallery, which lay between a wine dealer's and a hat shop on the left-hand side of the street. Although he had managed to put his prosthesis on, Strike was walking with the aid of a collapsible walking stick that Robin had bought him during another period when his leg had become almost too painful to bear his weight.

Even if it had marked the end of a relationship he wanted to escape, the call with Lorelei had left its mark. He knew in his heart that he was, in the spirit if not in the letter, guilty of some of the charges she had laid against him. While he had told Lorelei at the outset that he sought neither commitment nor permanence, he had known perfectly well that she had understood him to mean "right now" rather than "never" and he had not corrected that impression, because he wanted a distraction and a defense against the feelings that had dogged him after Robin's wedding.

However, the ability to section off his emotions, of which Charlotte had always complained, and to which Lorelei had dedicated a lengthy paragraph of the email dissecting his personality, had never failed him yet. Arriving two minutes early for his appointment with Henry Drummond, he transferred his attention with ease to the questions he intended to put to the late Jasper Chiswell's old friend.

Pausing beside the black marble exterior of the gallery, he saw himself reflected in the window and straightened his tie. He was wearing his best Italian suit. Behind his reflection, tastefully illuminated, a single painting in an ornate golden frame stood on an easel behind the spotless glass. It featured a pair of what, to Strike, looked like unrealistic horses with giraffe-like necks and staring eyes, ridden by eighteenth-century jockeys.

The gallery beyond the heavy door was cool and silent, with a floor of highly polished white marble. Strike walked carefully with his stick among the sporting and wildlife paintings, which were illuminated discreetly around the white walls, all of them in heavy gilded frames, until a well-groomed young blonde in a tight black dress emerged from a side door.

"Oh, good afternoon," she said, without asking his name, and walked away towards the back of the gallery, her stilettos making a metallic click on the tiles. "Henry! Mr. Strike's here!"

A concealed door opened, and Drummond emerged: a curious-looking man, whose ascetic features of pinched nose and black brows were enclosed by rolls of fat around chin and neck, as though a puritan had been engulfed by the body of a jolly squire. With his mutton-chop whiskers and dark gray suit and waistcoat he had a timeless, irrefutably upper-class, appearance.

"How do you do?" he said, offering a warm, dry hand. "Come into the office."

"Henry, Mrs. Ross just called," said the blonde, as Strike walked into the small room beyond the discreet door, which was book-lined, mahogany-shelved and very tidy. "She'd like to see the Munnings before we close. I've told her it's reserved, but she'd still like—"

"Let me know when she arrives," said Drummond. "And could we have some tea, Lucinda? Or coffee?" he inquired of Strike.

"Tea would be great, thank you."

"Do sit down," said Drummond, and Strike did so, grateful for a large and sturdy leather chair. The antique desk between them was bare but for a tray of engraved writing paper, a fountain pen and an ivory and silver letter opener. "So," said Henry Drummond heavily, "you're looking into this appalling business for the family?"

"That's right. D'you mind if I take notes?"

"Carry on."

Strike took out his notebook and pen. Drummond swiveled gently from side to side in his rotating chair.

"Terrible shock," he said softly. "Of course, one thought immediately of foreign interference. Government minister, eyes of the world on London with the Olympics and so forth . . ."

"You didn't think he could have committed suicide?" asked Strike.

Drummond sighed heavily.

"I knew him for forty-five years. His life had not been devoid of vicissitudes. To have come through everything—the divorce from Patricia, Freddie's death, resignation from the government, Raphael's ghastly car accident—to end it *now*, when he was Minister for Culture, when everything seemed back on track . . .

"Because the Conservative Party was his life's blood, you know," said Drummond. "Oh, yes. He'd bleed blue. Hated being out, delighted to get back in again, rise to minister . . . we joked of him becoming PM in our younger days, of course, but that dream was gone. Jasper always said, 'Tory faithful likes bastards or buffoons,' and that he was neither one nor the other."

"So you'd say he was in generally good spirits around the time he died?"

"Ah . . . well, no, I couldn't say that. There were stresses, worries— but suicidal? Definitely not."

"When was the last time you saw him?"

"The last time we met face to face was here, at the gallery," said Drummond. "I can tell you exactly what date it was: Friday the twenty-second of June."

This, Strike knew, was the day that he had met Chiswell for the first time. He remembered the minister walking away towards Drummond's gallery after their lunch at Pratt's.

"And how did he seem to you that day?"

"Extremely angry," said Drummond, "but that was inevitable, given what he walked in on, here."

Drummond picked up the letter opener and turned it delicately in his thick fingers.

"His son—Raphael—had just been caught, for the second time—ah—"

Drummond balked for a second.

"—*in flagrante*," he said, "with the other young person I employed at that time, in the bathroom behind me."

He indicated a discreet black door.

"I had already caught them in there, a month prior to that. I hadn't told Jasper the first time, because I felt he had quite enough on his plate."

"In what way?"

Drummond fingered the ornate ivory, cleared his throat and said:

"Jasper's marriage isn't—wasn't…I mean to say, Kinvara is a handful. Difficult woman. She was badgering Jasper to put one of her mares in foal to Totilas at the time."

When Strike looked blank, Drummond elucidated:

"Top dressage stallion. Nigh on ten thousand for semen."

"Christ," said Strike.

"Well, quite," said Drummond. "And when Kinvara doesn't get what she wants…one doesn't know whether it's temperament or something deeper—actual mental instability—anyway, Jasper had a very difficult time with her.

"Then he'd been through the ghastly business of Raphael's, ah, accident—that poor young mother killed—the press, and so on and so forth, his son in jail…as a friend, I didn't want to add to his troubles.

"I'd told Raphael the first time it happened that I wouldn't inform Jasper, but I also said he was on a final warning and if he stepped out of line again, he would be out on his ear, old friend of his father's or not. I had Francesca to consider, too. She's my goddaughter, eighteen years old and completely smitten with him. I didn't want to have to tell her parents.

"So when I walked in and heard them, I really had no choice. I'd thought I was safe to leave Raphael in charge for an hour because Francesca wasn't at work that day, but of course, she'd sneaked in specially to see him, on her day off.

"Jasper arrived to find me pounding on the door. There was no way to hide what was going on. Raphael was trying to block my entrance to the bathroom here while Francesca climbed out of the window. She couldn't face me. I rang her parents, told them everything. She never came back.

"Raphael Chiswell," said Drummond heavily, "is a Bad Lot. Freddie, the son who died—my godchild too, incidentally—was worth a million of... well, well," he said, turning the penknife over and over in his fingers, "one shouldn't say it, I know."

The office door opened and the young blonde in the black dress entered with a tea tray. Strike compared it mentally to the tea he had in the office as she set down two silver pots, one containing hot water, bone china cups and saucers and a sugar bowl complete with tongs.

"Mrs. Ross has just arrived, Henry."

"Tell her I'm tied up for the next twenty minutes or so. Ask her to wait, if she's got time."

"So I take it," said Strike, when Lucinda had left, "that there wasn't much time for conversation that day?"

"Well, no," said Drummond, unhappily. "Jasper had come to see Raphael at work, believing that all was going splendidly, and to arrive in the middle of that scene... Totally on my side, obviously, once he grasped what was going on. He was the one who actually shoved the boy out of the way to get the bathroom door open. Then he turned a nasty color. He had a heart problem, you know, it had been grumbling on for years. Sat down on the toilet rather suddenly. I was very worried, but he wouldn't let me call Kinvara...

"Raphael had the decency to be ashamed of himself, then. Tried to help his father. Jasper told him to get out of it, made me close the door, leave him in there..."

Now sounding gruff, Drummond broke off and poured himself

and Strike tea. He was evidently in some distress. As he added three lumps to his own cup, the teaspoon rattled against the cup.

"'Pologise. Last time I ever saw Jasper, you see. He came out of the bathroom, ghastly color, still, shook my hand, apologized, said he'd let his oldest friend…let me down."

Drummond coughed again, swallowed and continued with what seemed an effort:

"None of it was Jasper's fault. Raphael learned such morals as he's got from the mother, and she's best described as a high-class…well, well. Meeting Ornella was really the start of all Jasper's problems. If he'd only stayed with Patricia…

"Anyway, I never saw Jasper again. I had some difficulty bringing myself to shake Raphael's hand at the funeral, if you want the truth."

Drummond took a sip of tea and Strike tried his own. It was far too weak.

"All sounds very unpleasant," the detective said.

"You may well say so," sighed Drummond.

"You'll appreciate that I have to ask about some sensitive matters."

"Of course," said Drummond.

"You've spoken to Izzy. Did she tell you that Jasper Chiswell was being blackmailed?"

"She mentioned it," said Drummond, with a glance to check that the door was shut. "He hadn't breathed a word to me. Izzy said it was one of the Knights…one remembers a family in the grounds. The father was an odd-job man, yes? As for the Winns, well, no, I don't think there was much liking between them and Jasper. Strange couple."

"The Winns' daughter Rhiannon was a fencer," said Strike. "She was on the junior British fencing team with Freddie Chiswell—"

"Oh yes, Freddie was awfully good," said Drummond.

"Rhiannon was a guest at Freddie's eighteenth birthday party, but she was a couple of years younger. She was only sixteen when she killed herself."

"How ghastly," said Drummond.

"You don't know anything about that?"

"How should I?" said Drummond, a fine crease between his dark eyes.

"You weren't at the eighteenth?"

"I was, as a matter of fact. Godfather, you know."

"You can't remember Rhiannon?"

"Goodness, you can't expect me to remember all the names! There were upwards of a hundred young people there. Jasper had a marquee in the garden and Patricia ran a treasure hunt."

"Really?" said Strike.

His own eighteenth birthday party, in a rundown pub in Shoreditch, had not included a treasure hunt.

"Just in the grounds, you know. Freddie always liked a competition. A glass of champagne at every clue, it was rather jolly, got things off with a swing. I was manning clue three, down by what the children always used to call the dell."

"The hollow in the ground by the Knights' cottage?" asked Strike casually. "It was full of nettles when I saw it."

"We didn't put the clue *in* the dell, we put it under Jack o'Kent's doormat. He couldn't be trusted to take care of the champagne, because he had a drink problem. I sat on the edge of the dell in a deck chair and watched them hunt and everyone who found the clue got a glass of champagne and off they went."

"Soft drinks for the under-eighteens?" asked Strike.

Faintly exasperated by this killjoy attitude, Drummond said:

"Nobody *had* to drink champagne. It was an eighteenth, a celebration."

"So Jasper Chiswell never mentioned anything to you that he wouldn't want to get into the press?" asked Strike, returning to the main point.

"Nothing whatsoever."

"When he asked me to find a way of countering his blackmailers, he told me that whatever he'd done happened six years ago. He implied to me that it wasn't illegal when he did it, but is now."

"I've no idea what that could have been. Jasper was a very law-abiding type, you know. Whole family, pillars of the community, churchgoers, they've done masses for the local area..."

A litany of Chiswellian beneficence followed, which rolled on for a couple of minutes and did not fool Strike in the slightest. Drummond was obfuscating, he was sure, because Drummond knew exactly what Chiswell had done. He became almost lyrical as he extolled the innate goodness of Jasper, and of the entire family, excepting, always, the scapegrace Raphael.

"... and hand always in his pocket," Drummond concluded, "minibus for the local Brownies, repairs to the church roof, even after the family finances ... well, well," he said again, in a little embarrassment.

"The blackmailable offense," Strike began again, but Drummond interrupted.

"There was no offense." He caught himself. "You just said it yourself. Jasper told you he had done nothing illegal. No law was broken."

Deciding that it would do no good to push Drummond harder about the blackmail, Strike turned a page in his notebook, and thought he saw the other relax.

"You called Chiswell on the morning he died," said Strike.

"I did."

"Would that have been the first time you'd spoken since sacking Raphael?"

"Actually, no. There had been a conversation a couple of weeks prior to that. M'wife wanted to invite Jasper and Kinvara over for dinner. I called him at DCMS, breaking the ice, you know, after the Raphael business. It wasn't a long conversation, but amicable enough. He said they couldn't make the night suggested. He also told me ... well, to be frank, he told me he wasn't sure how much longer he and Kinvara would be together, that the marriage was in trouble. He sounded tired, exhausted ... unhappy."

"You had no more contact until the thirteenth?"

"We had no contact even then," Drummond reminded him. "I phoned Jasper, yes, but there was no answer. Izzy tells me—" He faltered. "She tells me that he was probably already dead."

"It was early for a call," said Strike.

"I ... had information I thought he should have."

"Of what kind?"

"It was personal."

Strike waited. Drummond sipped his tea.

"It related to the family finances, which as I imagine you know, were very poor at the time Jasper died."

"Yes."

"He'd sold off land and remortgaged the London property, offloaded all the good paintings through me. He was right down to the dregs, at the end, trying to sell me some of old Tinky's leavings. It was...a little embarrassing, actually."

"How so?"

"I deal in Old Masters," said Drummond. "I do not buy paintings of spotted horses by unknown Australian folk artists. As a courtesy to Jasper, being an old friend, I had some of it valued with my usual man at Christie's. The only thing that had any monetary worth at all was a painting of a piebald mare and foal—"

"I think I've seen that," said Strike.

"—but it was worth peanuts," said Drummond. "Peanuts."

"How much, at a guess?"

"Five to eight thousand at a push," said Drummond dismissively.

"Quite a lot of peanuts to some people," said Strike.

"My dear fellow," said Henry Drummond, "that wouldn't have repaired a tenth of the roof at Chiswell House."

"But he was considering selling it?" asked Strike.

"Along with half a dozen others," said Drummond.

"I had the impression that Mrs. Chiswell was particularly attached to that painting."

"I don't think his wife's wishes were of much importance to him by the end...Oh dear," sighed Drummond, "this is all very difficult. I really don't wish to be responsible for telling the family something that I know will only cause hurt and anger. They're already suffering."

He tapped his teeth with a nail.

"I assure you," he said, "that the reason for my call cannot have any bearing on Jasper's death."

Yet he seemed in two minds.

"You must speak to Raphael," he said, clearly choosing his words with care, "because I think...possibly...I don't like Raphael," he said, as though he had not already made that perfectly clear, "but I think, actually, he did an honorable thing on the morning his father died. At least, I can't see what he personally had to gain by it, and I think he's keeping silent about it for the same reason as myself. Being in the family, he is better placed to decide what to do than I can be. Speak to Raphael."

Strike had the impression that Henry Drummond would rather Raphael made himself unpopular with the family.

There was a knock on the office door. Blonde Lucinda put her head inside.

"Mrs. Ross isn't feeling terribly well, Henry; she's going to go, but she'd like to say goodbye."

"Yes, all right," said Drummond, getting to his feet. "I don't think I can be of more use, I'm afraid, Mr. Strike."

"I'm very grateful for you seeing me," said Strike, also rising, though with difficulty, and picking up his walking stick again. "Could I ask one last thing?"

"Certainly," said Drummond, pausing.

"Do you understand anything by the phrase 'he put the horse on them'?"

Drummond appeared genuinely puzzled.

"Who put *what* horse ... where?"

"You don't know what that might mean?"

"I've really no idea. Terribly sorry, but as you've heard, I've got a client waiting."

Strike had no alternative but to follow Drummond back into the gallery.

In the middle of the otherwise deserted gallery stood Lucinda, who was fussing over a dark, heavily pregnant woman sitting on a high chair, sipping water.

As he recognized Charlotte, Strike knew that this second encounter could not be a coincidence.

50

. . . you have branded me, once for all — branded me for life.
Henrik Ibsen, *Rosmersholm*

"Corm," she said weakly, gaping at him over the rim of her glass. She was pale, but Strike, who would have put nothing past her to stage a situation that she could use to her advantage, including skipping food or applying white foundation, merely nodded.

"Oh, you know each other?" said Drummond, surprised.

"I must go," mumbled Charlotte, getting to her feet while the concerned Lucinda hovered. "I'm late, I'm meeting my sister."

"Are you sure you're well enough?" said Lucinda.

Charlotte gave Strike a tremulous smile.

"Would you mind walking me up the road? It's only a block."

Drummond and Lucinda turned to Strike, clearly delighted to offload responsibility for this wealthy, well-connected woman onto his shoulders.

"Not sure I'm the best person for the job," said Strike, indicating his stick.

He felt Drummond and Lucinda's surprise.

"I'll give you plenty of warning if I think I'm actually going into labor," said Charlotte. "Please?"

He could have said "No." He might have said, "Why don't you get your sister to meet you here?" A refusal, as she knew well, would make him appear churlish in front of people he might need to talk to again.

"Fine," he said, keeping his voice just the right side of brusque.

"Thanks so much, Lucinda," said Charlotte, sliding down from the chair.

She was wearing a beige silk trench coat over a black T-shirt, maternity jeans and sneakers. Everything she wore, even these casual things, was of fine quality. She had always favored monochrome colors, stark or classic designs, against which her remarkable beauty was thrown into relief.

Strike held open the door for her, reminded by her pallor of the occasion when Robin had turned white and clammy at journey's end, after deftly steering a hire car out of what could have been a disastrous crash on black ice.

"Thank you," he said to Henry Drummond.

"My pleasure," said the art dealer formally.

"The restaurant's not far," Charlotte said, pointing up the slope as the gallery door swung shut.

They walked side by side, passersby perhaps assuming that he was responsible for her bulging stomach. He could smell what he knew was Shalimar on her skin. She had worn it ever since she was nineteen and he had sometimes bought it for her. Once again, he remembered walking this way towards the argument with her father in an Italian restaurant so many years ago.

"You think I arranged this."

Strike said nothing. He had no desire to become enmeshed in disagreement or reminiscence. They had walked for two blocks before he spoke.

"Where is this place?"

"Jermyn Street. Franco's."

The moment she said the name, he recognized it as the very same one in which they had met Charlotte's father all those years previously. The ensuing row had been short but exceedingly vicious, for a vein of incontinent spite ran right through every member of Charlotte's aristocratic family, but then she and Strike had gone back to her flat and made love with an intensity and urgency that he now wished he could expunge from his brain, the memory of her crying even as she climaxed, hot tears falling onto his face as she shouted with pleasure.

"Ouch. Stop," she said sharply.

He turned. Cradling her belly with both hands, she backed into a doorway, frowning.

"Sit down," he said, resenting even having to make suggestions to help her. "On the step there."

"No," she said, taking deep breaths. "Just get me to Franco's and you can go."

They walked on.

The maître d'hôtel was all concern: it was clear that Charlotte was not well.

"Is my sister here?" Charlotte asked.

"Not yet," said the maître d' anxiously, and like Henry Drummond and Lucinda, he looked to Strike to share responsibility for this alarming and unsought problem.

Barely a minute later, Strike was sitting in Amelia's seat at the table for two beside the window, and the waiter was bringing a bottle of water, and Charlotte was still taking deep breaths, and the maître d' was putting bread down between them, saying uncertainly that Charlotte might feel better if she ate something, but also suggesting quietly to Strike that he could call an ambulance at any moment, if that seemed desirable.

At last they were left alone. Still, Strike did not speak. He intended to leave the moment her color improved, or her sister arrived. All around them sat well-heeled diners, enjoying wine and pasta amid tasteful wood, leather and glass, with black and white prints on the geometric white and red wallpaper.

"You think I arranged this," mumbled Charlotte again.

Strike said nothing. He was keeping lookout for Charlotte's sister, whom he had not seen for years and who doubtless would be appalled to find them sitting together. Perhaps there would be another tight-lipped row, hidden from their fellow diners, in which fresh aspersions would be cast upon his personality, his background and his motives in escorting his wealthy, pregnant, married ex-girlfriend to her dinner date.

Charlotte took a breadstick and began to eat it, watching him.

"I really didn't know you were going to be there today, Corm."

He didn't believe it for a second. The meeting at Lancaster House had been chance: he had seen her shock when their eyes met, but this was far too much of a coincidence. If he hadn't known it to be impossible, he would even have supposed that she knew he had split up with his girlfriend that morning.

"You don't believe me."

"It doesn't matter," he said, still scanning the street for Amelia.

"I got a real shock when Lucinda said you were there."

Bollocks. She wouldn't have told you who was in the office. You already knew.

"This happens a lot lately," she persisted. "They call them Braxton Hicks contractions. I hate being pregnant."

He knew he had not disguised his immediate thought when she leaned towards him and said quietly:

"I know what you're thinking. I didn't get rid of ours. I didn't."

"Don't start, Charlotte," he said, with the sensation that the firm ground beneath his feet was starting to crack and shift.

"I lost—"

"I'm not doing this again," he said, a warning note in his voice. "We're not going back over dates from two years ago. I don't care."

"I took a test at my mother's—"

"I said I don't care."

He wanted to leave, but she was if anything paler now, her lips trembling as she gazed at him with those horribly familiar, russet-flecked green eyes, now brimming with tears. The swollen belly still didn't seem part of her. He would not have been entirely surprised had she lifted her T-shirt to show a cushion.

"I wish they were yours."

"Fuck's sake, Charlotte—"

"If they were yours, I'd be happy about it."

"Don't give me that. You didn't want kids any more than I did."

Tears now tipped over onto her cheeks. She wiped them away, her fingers shaking more violently than ever. A man at the next table was trying to pretend that he wasn't watching. Always hyperaware of the effect that she was having on those around her, Charlotte threw the eavesdropper a look that made him return hurriedly to his tortellini, then tore off a piece of bread and put it in her mouth, chewing while crying. Finally she gulped water to help her swallow, then pointed at her belly and whispered:

"I feel sorry for them. That's all I've got: pity. I feel sorry for them, because I'm their mother and Jago's their father. What a start in life. In the beginning I tried to think up ways of dying without killing them."

"Don't be so fucking self-indulgent," Strike said roughly. "They're going to need you, aren't they?"

"I don't want to be needed, I never did. I want to be free."

"To kill yourself?"

"Yes. Or to try and make you love me again."

He leaned in towards her.

"You're married. You're having his children. We're finished, it's over."

She leaned in, too, her tear-stained face the most beautiful he had ever seen. He could smell Shalimar on her skin.

"I'll always love you better than anyone in this world," she said, stark white and stunning. "You know that's the truth. I loved you better than anyone in my family, I'll love you better than my children, I'll love you on my deathbed. I think about you when Jago and I—"

"Keep this up and I'm leaving."

She leaned back in her seat again and stared at him as though he were an approaching train and she was tied to the tracks.

"You know it's true," she said hoarsely. "You know it is."

"Charlotte—"

"I know what you're going to say," she said, "that I'm a liar. I *am*. I *am* a liar, but not on the big things, never on the big ones, Bluey."

"Don't call me that."

"You didn't love me enough—"

"Don't you dare fucking blame me," he said, in spite of himself. Nobody else did this to him: nobody even came close. "The end— that was all you."

"You wouldn't compromise—"

"Oh, I compromised. I came to live with you, like you wanted—"

"You wouldn't take the job Daddy—"

"I had a job. I had the agency."

"I was wrong about the agency, I know that now. You've done such incredible things...I read everything about you, all the time. Jago found it all on my search history—"

"Should have covered your tracks, shouldn't you? You were a damn sight more careful with me, when you were screwing him on the side."

"I wasn't sleeping with Jago while I was with you—"

"You got engaged to him two weeks after we finished."

"It happened fast because I made it happen fast," she said fiercely. "You said I was lying about the baby and I was hurt, furious—you and I would be married now if you hadn't—"

"Menus," said a waiter suddenly materializing beside their table, handing one to each of them. Strike waved his away.

"I'm not staying."

"Take it for Amelia," Charlotte instructed him, and he pulled the menu out of the waiter's hand and slapped it down on the table in front of him.

"We have a couple of specials today," said the waiter.

"Do we look like we want to hear specials?" Strike growled. The waiter stood for a second, frozen in astonishment, then wound his way back through the crowded tables, his back view affronted.

"All this romantic bullshit," Strike said, leaning in to Charlotte. "You wanted things I couldn't give you. Every single fucking time, you hated the poverty."

"I acted like a spoiled bitch," she said, "I know I did, then I married Jago and I got all those things I thought I deserved and I want to fucking die."

"It goes beyond holidays and jewelry, Charlotte. You wanted to break me."

Her expression became rigid, as it so often had before the worst outbursts, the truly horrifying scenes.

"You wanted to stop me wanting anything that wasn't you. That'd be the proof I loved you, if I gave up the army, the agency, Dave Polworth, every-bloody-thing that made me who I am."

"I never, ever wanted to break you, that's a terrible thing to—"

"You wanted to smash me up because that's what you do. You have to break it, because if you don't, it might fade away. You've got to be in control. If you kill it, you don't have to watch it die."

"Look me in the eye and tell me you've loved anyone, since, like you loved me."

"No, I haven't," he said, "and thank fuck for that."

"We had incredible times together—"

"You'll have to remind me what they were."

"That night on Benjy's boat in Little France—"

"—your thirtieth? Christmas in Cornwall? They were a whole lot of fucking fun."

Her hand fell to her belly. Strike thought he saw movement through the thin black T-shirt, and it seemed to him again that there was something alien and inhuman beneath her skin.

"Sixteen years, on and off, I gave you the best I had to give, and it was never enough," he said. "There comes a point where you stop trying to save the person who's determined to drag you down with them."

"Oh, *please*," she said, and suddenly, the vulnerable and desperate Charlotte vanished, to be replaced by somebody altogether tougher, cool-eyed and clever. "You didn't want to save me, Bluey. You wanted to *solve* me. Big difference."

He welcomed the reappearance of this second Charlotte, who was in every way as familiar as the fragile version, but whom he had far less compunction about hurting.

"I'm looking good to you now because I got famous and you married an arsehole."

She absorbed the hit without blinking, though her face became a little pinker. Charlotte had always enjoyed a fight.

"You're so predictable. I knew you'd say I came back because you're famous."

"Well, you do tend to resurface whenever there's drama, Charlotte," Strike said. "I seem to remember that the last time, I'd just got my leg blown off."

"You bastard," she said, with a cool smile. "That's how you explain me taking care of you, all those months afterwards?"

His mobile rang: Robin.

"Hi," he said, turning away from Charlotte to look out of the window. "How's it going?"

"Hi, just telling tha I can't meet tha tonight," said Robin, in a much thicker Yorkshire accent than usual. "I'm going out with a friend. Party."

"I take it Flick's listening?" said Strike.

"Yeah, well, why don't you try calling your wife if you're lonely?" said Robin.

"I'll do that," said Strike, amused in spite of Charlotte's cool stare from across the table. "D'you want me to yell at you? Give this some credibility?"

"No, *you* fook off," said Robin loudly, and she hung up.

"Who was that?" asked Charlotte, eyes narrowed.

"I've got to go," said Strike, pocketing the mobile and reaching for his walking stick, which had slipped and fallen under the table while he and Charlotte argued. Realizing what he was after, she leaned sideways and succeeded in picking it up before he could reach it.

"Where's the cane I gave you?" she said. "The Malacca one?"

"You kept it," he reminded her.

"Who bought you this one? Robin?"

Amidst all of Charlotte's paranoid and frequently wild accusations, she had occasionally made uncannily accurate guesses.

"She did, as a matter of fact," said Strike, but instantly regretted saying it. He was playing Charlotte's game and at once, she turned into a third and rare Charlotte, neither cold nor fragile, but honest to the point of recklessness.

"All that's kept me going through this pregnancy is the thought that once I've had them, I can leave."

"You're going to walk out on your kids, the moment they exit the womb?"

"For another three months, I'm trapped. They all want the boy so much, they hardly let me out of their sight. Once I've given birth, it'll be different. I can go. We both know I'll be a lousy mother. They're better off with the Rosses. Jago's mother's already lining herself up as a surrogate."

Strike held out his hand for the walking stick. She hesitated, then passed it over. He got up.

"Give my regards to Amelia."

"She's not coming. I lied. I knew you'd be at Henry's. I was at a private viewing with him yesterday. He told me you were going to interview him."

"Goodbye, Charlotte."

"Wouldn't you rather have had advance warning that I want you back?"

"But I don't want you," he said, looking down at her.

"Don't kid a kidder, Bluey."

Strike limped out of the restaurant past the staring waiters, all of whom seemed to know how rude he had been to one of their colleagues. As he slammed his way out into the street, he felt as though he was pursued, as though Charlotte had projected after him a succubus that would tail him until they met again.

51

Can you spare me an ideal or two?

Henrik Ibsen, *Rosmersholm*

"You've been brainwashed to think it's got to be this way," said the anarchist. "See, you need to get your head around a world without leaders. No individual invested with more power than any other individual."

"Right," said Robin. "So tha've *never* voted?"

The Duke of Wellington in Hackney was overflowing this Saturday evening, but the deepening darkness was still warm and a dozen or so of Flick's friends and comrades in CORE were happy to mill around on the pavement on Balls Pond Road, drinking before heading back to Flick's for a party. Many of the group were holding carrier bags containing cheap wine and beer.

The anarchist laughed and shook his head. He was stringy, blond and dreadlocked, with many piercings, and Robin thought she recognized him from the mêlée in the crowd on the night of the Paralympic reception. He had already shown her the squidgy lump of cannabis he had brought to contribute to the general amusement of the party. Robin, whose experience of drugs was restricted to a couple of long-ago tokes on a bong back in her interrupted university career, had feigned an intelligent interest.

"You're so naive!" he told her now. "Voting's part of the great democratic con! Pointless ritual designed to make the masses think they've got a say and influence! It's a power-sharing deal between the Red and Blue Tories!"

"What's th'answer, then, if it's not voting?" asked Robin, cradling her barely touched half of lager.

"Community organization, resistance and mass protest," said the anarchist.

"'Oo organizes it?"

"The communities themselves. You've been bloody brainwashed," repeated the anarchist, mitigating the harshness of the statement with a small grin, because he liked Yorkshire socialist Bobbi Cunliffe's plain-spokenness, "to think you need leaders, but people can do it for themselves once they've woken up."

"An' who's gonna wake 'em up?"

"Activists," he said, slapping his own thin chest, "who aren't in it for money or power, who want *empowerment* of the people, not *control*. See, even unions—no offense," he said, because he knew that Bobbi Cunliffe's father had been a trade union man, "same power structures, the leaders start aping management—"

"Y'all right, Bobbi?" asked Flick, pushing to her side through the crowd. "We'll head off in a minute, that was last orders. What're you telling her, Alf?" she added, with a trace of anxiety.

After a long Saturday in the jewelry shop, and the exchange of many (in Robin's case, wholly imaginary) confidences about their love lives, Flick had become enamored of Bobbi Cunliffe to the point that her own speech had become slightly tinged with a Yorkshire accent. Towards the end of the afternoon she had extended a two-fold invitation, firstly to that night's party, and secondly, pending her friend Hayley's approval, a rented half-share in the bedroom recently vacated by their ex-flatmate, Laura. Robin had accepted both offers, placed her phone call to Strike, and agreed to Flick's suggestion that, in the absence of the Wiccan, they lock up the shop early.

"'E's just telling me 'ow me dad was no better'n a capitalist," said Robin.

"Fuck's sake, Alf," said Flick, as the anarchist laughingly protested.

Their group straggled out along the pavement as they headed off through the night towards Flick's flat. In spite of his obvious desire to continue instructing Robin in the rudiments of a leaderless world, the anarchist was ousted from Robin's side by Flick herself, who wanted to talk about Jimmy. Ten yards ahead of them, a plump, bearded and pigeon-toed Marxist, who had been introduced to Robin as Digby, walked alone, leading the way to the party.

"Doubt Jimmy'll come," she told Robin, and the latter thought she was arming herself against disappointment. "He's in a bad mood. Worried about his brother."

"What's wrong wi' him?"

"It's schizophrenic affection something," said Flick. Robin was sure that Flick knew the correct term, but that she thought it appropriate, faced with a genuine member of the working classes, to feign a lack of education. She had let slip the fact that she had started a university course during the afternoon, seemed to regret it, and ever since had dropped her "h"s a little more consistently. "I dunno. 'E 'as delusions."

"Like what?"

"Thinks there's government conspiracies against him and that," said Flick, with a little laugh.

"Bloody 'ell," said Bobbi.

"Yeah, he's in 'ospital. He's caused Jimmy a lot of trouble," said Flick. She stuck a thin roll-up in her mouth and lit it. "You ever heard of Cormoran Strike?"

She said the name as though it were another medical condition.

"Who?"

"Private detective," said Flick. "He's been in the papers a lot. Remember that model who fell out of a window, Lula Landry?"

"Vaguely," said Robin.

Flick glanced over her shoulder to check that Alf the anarchist was out of earshot.

"Well, Billy went to see 'im."

"The fook for?"

"Because Billy's mental, keep up," said Flick, with another little laugh. "He thinks he saw something years ago—"

"What?" said Robin, quicker than she meant to.

"A murder," said Flick.

"Christ."

"He didn't, obviously," said Flick. "It's all bollocks. I mean, he *saw* something, but nobody bloody died. Jimmy was there, he knows. Anyway, Billy goes to this detective prick and now we can't get rid of him."

"What d'you mean?"

"'E beat Jimmy up."

"The detective did?"

"Yeah. Followed Jimmy on a protest we were doing, beat him up, got Jimmy fooking arrested."

"Bloody 'ell," said Bobbi Cunliffe again.

"Deep state, innit?" said Flick. "Ex-army. Queen and the flag and all that fucking shit. See, Jimmy and me had something on a Conservative minister—"

"Did you?"

"Yeah," said Flick. "I can't tell you what, but it was big, and then Billy fucked everything up. Sent Strike sniffing around, and we reckon he got in touch with the gov—"

She broke off suddenly, her eyes following a small car that had just passed them.

"Thought that was Jimmy's for a moment. It isn't. I forgot, it's off the road."

Her mood sagged again. During the slack periods in the shop that day, Flick had told Robin the history of her and Jimmy's relationship, which in its endless fights and truces and renegotiations might have been the story of some disputed territory. They seemed never to have reached an agreement on the relationship's status and every treaty had fallen apart in rows and betrayals.

"You're well shot of him, if you ask me," said Robin, who all day had pursued a cautious policy of trying to prize Flick free of the loyalty she clearly felt she owed the faithless Jimmy, in the hope of extracting confidences.

"Wish it were that easy," said Flick, lapsing into the cod-Yorkshire she had adopted towards the end of the day. "It's not like I wanna be *married* or anything—" she laughed at the very idea, "—he can sleep with who he likes and so can I. That's the deal and I'm fine with it."

She had already explained to Robin at the shop that she identified as both genderqueer and pansexual, while monogamy, properly looked at, was a tool of patriarchal oppression, a line that Robin suspected had been originally Jimmy's. They walked in silence for a while. In the denser darkness they entered an underpass, when Flick said with a flicker of spirit:

"I mean, I've had my own fun."

"Glad to hear it," said Robin.

"Jimmy wouldn't like it if he knew all of them, either."

The pigeon-toed Marxist walking ahead of them turned his head at that and Robin saw, by the light of a streetlamp, his little smirk as he glanced back at Flick, whose words he had clearly caught. The latter, being engaged in trying to dig her door keys out of the bottom of her cluttered messenger bag, seemed not to notice.

"We're up there," Flick said, pointing at three lit windows above a small sports shop. "Hayley's back already. Shit, I hope she remembered to hide my laptop."

The flat was reached from a back entrance, up a cold, narrow stairwell. Even from the bottom of the stairs, they could hear the persistent bass of "Niggas in Paris," and on reaching the landing, they found the flimsy door standing open and a number of people leaning up against the walls outside, sharing an enormous joint.

"*What's fifty grand to a muh-fucka like me,*" rapped Kanye West, from the dimly lit interior.

The dozen or so newcomers met a substantial number of people already inside. It was astonishing how many people could fit into such a small flat, which evidently comprised only two bedrooms, a minuscule shower room and a cupboard-sized kitchenette.

"We're using Hayley's room to dance in, it's the biggest, the one you'll share," Flick shouted in Robin's ear as they forced their way towards the dark room.

Lit only by two strings of fairy lights, and the small rectangles of lights emanating from the phones of those checking their texts and social media, the room was already thick with the smell of cannabis and lined with people. Four young women and a man were managing to dance in the middle of the floor. Her eyes growing gradually accustomed to the darkness, Robin saw the skeletal frame of a bunk bed, already supporting a few people sharing a joint on the top mattress. She could just make out an LGBT rainbow flag and a poster of *True Blood*'s Tara Thornton on the wall behind them.

Jimmy and Barclay had already combed this flat for the piece of paper Flick had stolen from Chiswell and not found it, Robin reminded herself, peering through the darkness for likely hiding places. Robin wondered whether Flick kept it permanently on her person, but Jimmy would surely have thought of that, and in spite of Flick's avowed pansexuality, Robin thought Jimmy better placed than herself to persuade Flick to strip. Meanwhile, the darkness might be Robin's friend as she slid her hand beneath mattresses and rugs, but the party was so densely packed that she doubted it would be possible to do without alerting somebody to her odd behavior.

"...find Hayley," Flick bellowed in Robin's ear, pressing a can of lager into her hand, and they edged out of the room again into Flick's own bedroom, which seemed even smaller than it really was because every inch of the walls and ceiling had been covered in political flyers and posters, the orange of CORE and the black and red of the Real Socialist Party predominating. A gigantic Palestinian flag was pinned over the mattress on the floor.

Five people were already inside this room, which was lit by a solitary lamp. A pair of young women, one black, one white, lay entwined on the mattress on the floor, while podgy, bearded Digby had taken up a position on the floor, talking to them. Two teenage boys stood awkwardly against the wall, furtively watching the girls on the bed, their heads close together as they rolled a joint.

"Hayley, this is Bobbi," said Flick. "She's interested in Laura's half of the room."

Both girls on the bed looked around: the tall, shaven-headed, sleepy-eyed peroxide blonde answered.

"I've already said Shanice can move in," said the blonde, sounding stoned, and the petite black girl in her arms kissed her on the neck.

"Oh," said Flick, turning in consternation to Robin. "Shit. Sorry."

"You're all right," said Robin, feigning bravery in the face of disappointment.

"Flick," someone called from the hall, "it's Jimmy downstairs."

"Oh, fuck," said Flick, flustered, but Robin saw the pleasure flare in her face. "Wait there," she said to Robin, and left for the press of bodies in the hall.

"*Bougie girl, grab her hand,*" rapped Jay-Z from the other room.

Pretending to be interested in the conversation between the girls on the bed and Digby, Robin slid down the wall to sit on the laminate floor, sipping her lager while she covertly surveyed Flick's bedroom. It had evidently been tidied for the party. There was no wardrobe, but a clothes rail holding coats and the occasional dress, while T-shirts and sweaters were halfheartedly folded in a dark corner. A small number of Beanie Babies sat on top of the chest of drawers, along with a clutter of makeup, while various placards stood jumbled in a corner. Jimmy and Barclay must surely have been thoroughly through this room. Robin wondered whether they had thought of searching behind all these flyers. Unfortunately, even if they hadn't, she could hardly start unpinning them now.

"Look, this is basic stuff," said Digby, addressing the girls on the bed. "You'll agree that capitalism depends in part on the poorly paid labor of women, right? So feminism, if it's to be effective, *must* also be Marxist, the one implies the other."

"Patriarchy is about more than capitalism," said Shanice.

Out of the corner of her eye, Robin saw Jimmy fighting his way through the narrow hall, his arm around Flick's neck. The latter appeared happier than she had all evening.

"Women's oppression is inextricably linked to their inability to enter the labor force," announced Digby.

The drowsy-eyed Hayley disentangled herself from Shanice to extend her hand towards the black-clad teenagers in a silent request. Their joint passed over Robin's head.

"Sorry 'bout the room," Hayley said vaguely to Robin, after taking a long toke. "Bastard getting a place in London, innit?"

"Total bastard," said Robin.

"—because you want to subsume feminism within the larger ideology of Marxism."

"There's no *subsuming*, the aims are identical!" said Digby, with an incredulous little laugh.

Hayley tried to give Shanice the joint, but the impassioned Shanice waved it away.

"Where are you Marxists when we're challenging the ideal of the heteronormative family?" she demanded of Digby.

"Hear, hear," said Hayley vaguely, snuggling closer to Shanice and shoving the teenagers' joint at Robin, who passed it straight back to the boys. Interested though they had been in the lesbians, they promptly left the bedroom before anybody else could offer their meager supply of drugs around.

"I used to have some of them," Robin said aloud, getting to her feet, but nobody was listening. Digby took the opportunity to peek up Robin's short black skirt as she passed close to him on her way to the chest of drawers. Under cover of the increasingly heated conversation about feminism and Marxism, and with the appearance of vaguely nostalgic interest, Robin picked up and put down each of Flick's Beanie Babies in turn, feeling through the thin plush to the plastic beads and stuffing within. None of them felt as though they had been opened up and re-sewn to conceal a piece of paper.

With a sense of slight hopelessness, she returned to the dark hall, where people stood pressed together, spilling out onto the landing.

A girl was hammering on the door of the bathroom.

"Stop shagging in there, I need a piss!" she said, to the amusement of various people standing around.

This is hopeless.

Robin slid into the kitchenette, which was hardly larger than two telephone boxes, where a couple was sitting on the side, the girl with her legs over the man's, who had his hand up her skirt, while the teenagers in black were now foraging with difficulty for something to eat. Under pretense of finding another drink, Robin sifted through empty cans and bottles, watching the progress of the teenagers through the cupboards and reflecting how insecure a hiding place a cereal box would make.

Alf the anarchist appeared in the kitchen doorway as Robin made to leave the room, now far more stoned than he had been in the pub.

"There she is," he said loudly, trying to focus on Robin. "Th' union leader's daughter."

"That's me," said Robin, as D'banj sang "*Oliver, Oliver, Oliver Twist*" from the second bedroom. She tried to duck under Alf's arm, but he lowered it, blocking her exit from the kitchen. The cheap laminate floor was vibrating with the stamping of the determined dancers in Hayley's room.

"You're hot," said Alf. "'M'I allowed to say that? I mean it in a fucking feminist way."

He laughed.

"Thanks," said Robin, succeeding on her second pass in dodging around him and getting back into the tiny hall, where the desperate girl was still pounding on the bathroom door. Alf caught Robin's arm, bent down and said something incomprehensible in her ear. When he straightened up again, some of her hair chalk had left a black stain on the end of his sweaty nose.

"What?" said Robin.

"I said," he shouted, "'wanna find somewhere quieter so we can talk more?'"

But then Alf noticed somebody standing behind her.

"All right, Jimmy?"

Knight had arrived in the hall. He smiled at Robin, then leaned up against the wall, smoking and holding a can of lager. He was ten years older than most of the people there, and some of the girls cast him sideways looks, in his tight black T-shirt and jeans.

"Waiting for the bog as well?" he asked Robin.

"Yeah," said Robin, because that seemed the simplest way to extricate herself from both Jimmy and Alf the anarchist, should she need to. Through the open door of Hayley's room, she saw Flick dancing, now clearly delighted with life, laughing at whatever was said to her.

"Flick says your dad was a trade union man," Jimmy said to Robin. "Miner, yeah?"

"Yeah," said Robin.

"Fuck's SAKE," said the girl who had been hammering on the

bathroom door. She danced on the spot in desperation for a few more seconds, then pushed her way out of the flat.

"There are bins to the left!" called one of the other girls after her.

Jimmy leaned closer to Robin, so that she could hear him over the thumping bass. His expression was, as far as she could see, sympathetic, even gentle.

"Died, though, didn't he?" he asked Robin. "Your dad. Lungs, Flick said?"

"Yeah," said Robin.

"I'm sorry," said Jimmy, quietly. "Been through something similar myself."

"Really?" said Robin.

"Yeah, my mum. Lungs, as well."

"Workplace related?"

"Asbestos," said Jimmy, nodding as he dragged on his cigarette. "Wouldn't happen now, they've brought in legislation. I was twelve. My brother was two, he can't even remember her. My old man drank himself to death without her."

"That's really rough," said Robin sincerely. "I'm sorry."

Jimmy blew smoke away from her face and pulled a grimace.

"Two of a kind," said Jimmy, clinking his can of lager against Robin's. "Class war veterans."

Alf the anarchist lurched away, swaying slightly, and disappeared into the dark room pierced with fairy lights.

"Family ever get compensation?" asked Jimmy.

"Tried," said Robin. "Mum's still pursuing it."

"Good luck to her," said Jimmy, raising his can and drinking. "Good bloody luck to her."

He banged on the bathroom door.

"Fucking hurry up, people are waiting," he shouted.

"Maybe someone's ill?" Robin suggested.

"Nah, it'll be someone having a quickie," said Jimmy.

Digby emerged from Flick's bedroom, looking disgruntled.

"I'm a tool of patriarchal oppression, apparently," he announced loudly.

Nobody laughed. Digby scratched his belly under his T-shirt, which Robin now saw featured a picture of Groucho Marx, and ambled into the room where Flick was dancing.

"He's a tool, all right," Jimmy muttered to Robin. "Rudolf Steiner kid. Can't get over the fact that nobody gives him stars for effort anymore."

Robin laughed, but Jimmy didn't. His eyes held hers just a fraction too long, until the bathroom door opened a crack and a plump, red-faced young girl peeked out. Behind her, Robin saw a man with a wispy gray beard replacing his Mao cap.

"Larry, you filthy old bastard," said Jimmy, grinning as the red-faced girl scuttled past Robin and disappeared into the dark room after Digby.

"Evening, Jimmy," said the elderly Trotskyist, with a prim smile, and he, too, left the bathroom to a couple of cheers from the young men outside.

"Go on," Jimmy told Robin, holding open the door and blocking anyone else's attempts to push past her.

"Thanks," she said, as she slid into the bathroom.

The glare of the strip light was dazzling after the dinginess of the rest of the flat. The bathroom barely had standing room between the smallest shower Robin had ever seen, with a grimy transparent curtain hanging off half its hooks, a small toilet in which a large amount of sodden tissue and a cigarette end was floating. A used condom glistened in the wicker bin.

Above the sink were three rickety shelves crammed with half-used toiletries and general clutter, crammed together so that one touch seemed likely to dislodge everything.

Struck by a sudden idea, Robin moved closer to these shelves. She was remembering how she had relied on the squeamish ignorance and avoidance of most men towards matters pertaining to menstruation when she had hidden the listening devices in a box of Tampax. Her eyes ran swiftly over half-used bottles of supermarket-brand shampoo, an old tub of Vim, a dirty sponge, a pair of cheap deodorants and a few well-used toothbrushes in a chipped mug. Very carefully, because everything was so tightly packed together, Robin eased out a small box of Lil-Lets that proved to have only one sealed tampon inside it. As she reached up to replace the box, she spotted the corner of a small, squashy bundle, encased in a plastic wrapper and hidden behind the Vim and a bottle of fruity shower gel.

With a sudden stab of excitement, she reached up and wriggled the white polythene parcel carefully out of the place it had been wedged, trying not to knock everything over.

Somebody hammered on the door.

"I'm fucking bursting!" shouted a new girl.

"Won't be long!" Robin shouted back.

Two bulky sanitary towels had been rolled up in their own unromantic wrapping ("for Very Heavy Flow"): the sort of thing a young woman was unlikely to steal, especially if wearing skimpy clothing. Robin extracted them. There was nothing odd about the first. The second, however, emitted a small, crisp cracking noise as Robin bent it. Her excitement mounting, Robin turned it sideways and saw that it had been slit with what had probably been a razor blade. Wriggling her fingers into the tissue-like foam within, she felt a thick, folded piece of paper, which she eased out and unfolded.

The writing paper was exactly the same as that on which Kinvara had written her farewell note, with the name "Chiswell" embossed across the top and a Tudor rose, like a drop of blood, beneath it. A few disjointed words and phrases were scrawled in the distinctive, cramped handwriting Robin had seen so often in Chiswell's office, and in the middle of the page one word had been circled many times.

251 Ebury Street
London
SW1W

Blanc de blanc

Suzuki ✔

~~Mother?~~

Bill

Odi et amo, quare id faciam, fortasse requiris? Nescio, sed fieri sentio et excrucior.

Hardly breathing in her excitement, Robin took out her mobile, took several pictures of the note, then refolded it, replaced it in the sanitary towel and returned the package to the place it had been on the shelf. She attempted to flush the toilet, but it was clogged and all she achieved was that the water rose ominously in the bowl, refusing to subside, the cigarette butt bobbing there in swirling tissue.

"Sorry," Robin said, opening the door. "Loo's blocked."

"Whatever," said the impatient, drunk girl outside, "I'll do it in the sink."

She pushed past Robin and slammed the door.

Jimmy was still standing outside.

"Think I'm going to take off," Robin told him. "I only really came t'see if that room was vacant, but soombody's got in ahead of me."

"Shame," said Jimmy lightly. "Come to a meeting some time. We could use a bit of Northern soul."

"Yeah, I might," said Robin.

"Might what?"

Flick had arrived, holding a bottle of Budweiser.

"Come to a meeting," said Jimmy, taking a fresh cigarette out of his pack. "You were right, Flick, she's the real deal."

Jimmy reached out and pulled Flick to him, pressing her to his side, and kissed her on the top of the head.

"Yeah, sh'iz," said Flick, smiling with real warmth as she wound her arm around Jimmy's waist. "Come to the next one, Bobbi."

"Yeah, I might," said Bobbi Cunliffe, the trade unionist's daughter, and she bade them goodbye, pushed her way out of the hall and out into the cold stairwell.

Not even the sight and smell of one of the black-clad teenagers vomiting copiously on the pavement just outside the main door could dampen Robin's jubilation. Unable to wait, she texted Strike the picture of Jasper Chiswell's note while hurrying towards the bus stop.

52

I can assure you, you have been on the wrong scent entirely,
Miss West.

Henrik Ibsen, *Rosmersholm*

Strike had fallen asleep, fully clothed, his prosthesis still attached, on top of the bedcovers in his attic bedroom. The cardboard folder containing everything pertaining to the Chiswell file was lying on his chest, vibrating gently as he snored, and he dreamed that he was walking hand in hand with Charlotte through an otherwise deserted Chiswell House, which they had bought together. Tall, slim and beautiful, she was no longer pregnant. She trailed Shalimar and black chiffon behind her, but their mutual happiness was evaporating in the damp chill of the shabby rooms through which they were wandering. What could have prompted the reckless, quixotic decision to purchase this drafty house, with the peeling walls and the wires dangling from the ceiling?

The loud buzz of a text arriving jerked Strike from sleep. For a fraction of a second he registered the fact that he was back in his attic room, alone, neither the owner of Chiswell House nor the lover of Charlotte Ross, before groping for the phone on which he was half lying in the full expectation that he was about to see a message from Charlotte.

He was wrong: it was Robin's name he saw when he peered groggily at the screen, and it was, moreover, one in the morning. Momentarily forgetting that she had been out at a party with Flick, Strike sat up hurriedly and the cardboard file that had been lying on his chest slid smoothly off him, scattering its various pages across the floorboards, while Strike squinted, blurry-eyed, at the photograph Robin had just sent him.

"Fuck me backwards."

Ignoring the mess of notes at his feet, he called her back.

"Hi," said Robin jubilantly, over the unmistakable sounds of a London night bus: the clatter and roar of the engine, the grinding of brakes, the tinny ding of the bell and the obligatory drunken laughter of what sounded like a gaggle of young women.

"How the *fuck* did you manage that?"

"I'm a woman," said Robin. He could hear her smile. "I know where we hide things when we really don't want them found. I thought you'd be asleep."

"Where are you—a bus? Get off and grab a cab. We can charge it to the Chiswell account if you get a receipt."

"There's no need—"

"Do as you're bloody told!" Strike repeated, a little more aggressively than he had intended, because while she had just pulled off quite a coup, she had also been knifed, out alone on the street after dark, a year previously.

"All right, all right, I'll get a cab," said Robin. "Have you read Chiswell's note?"

"Looking at it now," said Strike, switching to speakerphone so that he could read Chiswell's note while talking to her. "I hope you left it where you found it?"

"Yeah. I thought that was best?"

"Definitely. Where exactly—?"

"Inside a sanitary towel."

"Christ," said Strike, taken aback. "I'd never've thought to—"

"No, nor did Jimmy and Barclay," said Robin smugly. "Can you read what it says at the bottom? The Latin?"

Squinting at the screen, Strike translated:

"'*I hate and I love. Why do I do it, you might ask? I don't know. I just feel it, and it crucifies me . . .*' that's Catullus again. A famous one."

"Did you do Latin at university?"

"No."

"Then how—?"

"Long story," said Strike.

In fact, the story of his ability to read Latin wasn't long, merely (to most people) inexplicable. He didn't feel like telling it in the middle of the night, nor did he want to explain that Charlotte had studied Catullus at Oxford.

"'I hate and I love,'" Robin repeated. "Why would Chiswell have written that down?"

"Because he was feeling it?" Strike suggested.

His mouth was dry: he had smoked too much before falling asleep. He got up, feeling achy and stiff, and picked his way carefully around the fallen notes, heading for the sink in the other room, phone in hand.

"Feeling it for Kinvara?" asked Robin dubiously.

"Ever see another woman around while you were in close contact with him?"

"No. Of course, he might not have been talking about a woman."

"True," admitted Strike. "Plenty of man love in Catullus. Maybe that's why Chiswell liked him so much."

He filled a mug with cold tap water, drank it down in one, then threw in a tea bag and switched on the kettle, all the while peering down at the lit screen of his phone in the darkness.

"'Mother,' crossed out," he muttered.

"Chiswell's mother died twenty-two years ago," said Robin. "I've just looked her up."

"Hmm," said Strike. "'Bill,' circled."

"Not Billy," Robin pointed out, "but if Jimmy and Flick thought it meant his brother, people must sometimes call Billy 'Bill.'"

"Unless it's the thing you pay," said Strike. "Or a duck's beak, come to that...'Suzuki'...'Blanc de'...Hang on. Jimmy Knight's got an old Suzuki Alto."

"It's off the road, according to Flick."

"Yeah. Barclay says it failed its MOT."

"There was a Grand Vitara parked outside Chiswell House when we visited, too. One of the Chiswells must own it."

"Good spot," said Strike.

He switched on the overhead light and crossed to the table by the window, where he had left his pen and notebook.

"You know," said Robin thoughtfully, "I think I've seen 'Blanc de blanc' somewhere recently."

"Yeah? Been drinking champagne?" asked Strike, who had sat down to make more notes.

"No, but...yeah, I suppose I must've seen it on a wine label, mustn't I? Blanc de blancs...what does it mean? 'White from whites?'"

"Yeah," said Strike.

For nearly a minute, neither of them spoke, both examining the note. "You know, I hate to say this, Robin," said Strike at last, "but I think the most interesting thing about this is that Flick had it. Looks like a to-do list. Can't see anything here that proves wrongdoing or suggests grounds for blackmail or murder."

"'Mother, crossed out,'" Robin repeated, as though determined to wring meaning out of the cryptic phrases. "Jimmy Knight's mother died of asbestosis. He just told me so, at Flick's party."

Strike tapped his notepad lightly with the end of his pen, thinking, until Robin voiced the question that he was grappling with.

"We're going to have to tell the police about this, aren't we?"

"Yeah, we are," sighed Strike, rubbing his eyes. "This proves she had access to Ebury Street. Unfortunately, that means we're going to have to pull you out of the jewelry shop. Once the police search her bathroom, it won't take her long to work out who must've tipped them off."

"Bugger," said Robin. "I really felt like I was getting somewhere with her."

"Yeah," Strike agreed. "This is the problem with having no official standing in an inquiry. I'd give a lot to have Flick in an interrogation room...This bloody case," he said, yawning. "I've been going through the file all evening. This note's like everything else: it raises more questions than it answers."

"Hang on," said Robin, and he heard sounds of movement, "sorry—Cormoran, I'm going to get off here, I can see a taxi rank—"

"OK. Great work tonight. I'll call you tomorrow—later today, I mean."

When she had hung up, Strike set his cigarette down in the ashtray, returned to his bedroom to pick up the scattered case notes off the floor, and took them back to the kitchen. Ignoring the freshly boiled kettle, he took a beer from the fridge, sat back down at the table with the file and, as an afterthought, opened the sash window beside him a few inches, to let some clean air into the room while he kept smoking.

The Military Police had trained him to organize interrogations and findings into three broad categories: people, places and things, and Strike had been applying this sound old principle to the Chiswell file before falling asleep on the bed. Now he spread the contents of the file out over the kitchen table and set to work again, while a cold night breeze laden with petrol fumes blew across the photographs and papers, so that their corners trembled.

"People," Strike muttered.

He had written a list before he slept of the people who most interested him in connection with Chiswell's death. Now he saw that he had unconsciously ranked the names according to their degree of involvement in the dead man's blackmail. Jimmy Knight's name topped the list, followed by Geraint Winn's, and then by what Strike thought of as each man's respective deputy, Flick Purdue and Aamir Mallik. Next came Kinvara, who knew that Chiswell was being blackmailed, and why; Della Winn, whose super-injunction had kept the blackmail out of the press, but whose precise degree of involvement in the affair was otherwise unknown to Strike, and then Raphael, who had by all accounts been ignorant both of what his father had done, and of the blackmail itself. At the bottom of the list was Billy Knight, whose only known connection with the blackmail was the bond of blood between himself and the primary blackmailer.

Why, Strike asked himself, had he ranked the names in this particular order? There was no proven link between Chiswell's death and the blackmail, unless, of course, the threat of exposure of his unknown crime had indeed pushed Chiswell into killing himself.

It then occurred to Strike that a different hierarchy was revealed if he turned the list on its head. In this case Billy sat on top, a disinterested seeker, not of money or another man's disgrace, but of truth and justice. In the reversed order, Raphael came in second, with his strange and, to Strike, implausible story of being sent to his stepmother on the morning of his father's death, which Henry Drummond claimed grudgingly to have hidden some honorable motive as yet unknown. Della rose to third place, a widely admired woman of impeccable morality, whose true thoughts and feelings towards her blackmailing husband and to his victim remained inscrutable.

Read backwards, it seemed to Strike that each suspect's relation to the dead man became cruder, more transactional, until the list terminated with Jimmy Knight and his angry demand for forty thousand pounds.

Strike continued to pore over the list of names as though he might suddenly see something emerging out of his dense, spiky handwriting, the way unfocused eyes may spot the 3D image hidden in a series of brightly colored dots. All that occurred to him, however, was the fact that there was an unusual number of pairs connected to Chiswell's death: couples—Geraint and Della, Jimmy and Flick; pairs of full siblings—Izzy and Fizzy, Jimmy and Billy; the duo of blackmailing collaborators—Jimmy and Geraint; and the subsets of each blackmailer and his deputy—Flick and Aamir. There was even the quasi-parental pairing of Della and Aamir. This left two people who formed a pair in being isolated within the otherwise close-knit family: the widowed Kinvara and Raphael, the unsatisfactory, outsider son.

Strike tapped his pen unconsciously against the notebook, thinking. *Pairs.* The whole business had begun with a pair of crimes: Chiswell's blackmail and Billy's allegation of infanticide. He had been trying to find the connection between them from the start, unable to believe that they could be entirely separate cases, even if on the face of it their only link was in the blood tie between the Knight brothers.

Turning the page, he examined the notes he had headed "Places." After a few minutes spent examining his own jottings concerning access to the house in Ebury Street, and the locations, in several cases unknown, of the suspects at the time of Chiswell's death, he made a note to remind himself that he still hadn't received from Izzy contact details for Tegan Butcher, the stable girl who could confirm that Kinvara had been at home in Woolstone while Chiswell was suffocating in a plastic bag in London.

He turned to the next page, headed "Things," and now he set down his pen and spread Robin's photographs out so that they formed a collage of the death scene. He scrutinized the flash of gold in the pocket of the dead man, and then the bent sword, half hidden in shadow in the corner of the room.

It seemed to Strike that the case he was investigating was littered with objects that had been found in surprising places: the sword in the corner, the lachesis pills on the floor, the wooden cross found in a tangle of nettles at the bottom of the dell, the canister of helium and the rubber tubing in a house where no child's party had ever been held, but his tired mind could find neither answers nor patterns here.

Finally, Strike downed the rest of his beer, lobbed the empty can across the room into the kitchen bin, turned to a blank page in his notebook and began to write a to-do list for the Sunday of which two hours had already elapsed.

1. <u>Call Wardle</u>
Text note found in Flick's flat,
Update on police case if possible.
2. <u>Call Izzy</u>
Show her stolen note.
Ask: was Freddie's money clip ever found?
Tegan's details?
Need phone number for Raphael.
Also phone number, if poss, for Della Winn
3. <u>Call Barclay</u>
Give update.
Cover Jimmy + Flick again
When does Jimmy visit Billy?
4. <u>Call hospital</u>
Try and arrange interview with Billy when Jimmy not there.
5. <u>Call Robin</u>
Arrange interview with Raphael

6. _Call Della_
Try and arrange interview

After a little further thought, he finished the list with

7. Buy teabags/beer/bread

After tidying up the Chiswell file, tipping the overflowing ashtray into the bin, opening the window wider to admit more cold, fresh air, Strike went for a last pee, cleaned his teeth, switched off the lights and returned to his bedroom, where a single reading lamp still burned.

Now, with his defenses weakened by beer and tiredness, the memories he had sought to bury in work forced their way to the forefront of his mind. As he undressed and removed his prosthetic leg, he found himself going back over every word Charlotte had said to him across the table for two in Franco's, remembering the expression of her green eyes, the scent of Shalimar reaching him through the garlic fumes of the restaurant, her thin white fingers playing with the bread.

He got into bed between the chilly sheets and lay, hands behind his head, staring up into the darkness. He wished he could feel indifferent, but in fact his ego had stretched luxuriously at the idea that she had read all about the cases that had made his name and that she thought about him while in bed with her husband. Now, though, reason and experience rolled up their sleeves, ready to conduct a professional post-mortem on the remembered conversation, methodically disinterring the unmistakable signs of Charlotte's perennial will to shock and her apparently insatiable need for conflict.

The abandonment of her titled husband and newborn children for a famous, one-legged detective would certainly constitute the crowning achievement of a career of disruption. Having an almost pathological hatred of routine, responsibility or obligation, she had sabotaged every possibility of permanence before she had to deal with the threats of boredom or compromise. Strike knew all this, because he knew her better than any other human being, and he knew that their final parting had happened at the exact moment where real sacrifice and hard choices had to be made.

But he also knew — and the knowledge was like ineradicable bacteria in a wound that stopped it ever healing — that she loved him as she had never loved anyone else. Of course, the skeptical girlfriends and wives of his friends, none of whom had liked Charlotte, had told him over and over again, "That's not love, what she does to you," or, "Not being funny, Corm, but how do you know she hasn't said exactly the same to all the others she's had?" Such women saw his confidence that Charlotte loved him as delusion or egotism. They had not been present for those times of total bliss and mutual understanding that remained some of the best of Strike's life. They had not shared jokes inexplicable to any other human being but himself and Charlotte, or felt the mutual need that had drawn them back together for sixteen years.

She had walked from him straight into the arms of the man she thought would hurt Strike worst, and indeed, it *had* hurt, because Ross was the absolute antithesis of him and had dated Charlotte before Strike had even met him. Yet Strike remained certain her flight to Ross had been self-immolation, done purely for spectacular effect, a Charlottian form of *sati*.

> *Difficile est longum subito deponere amorem,*
> *Difficile est, verum hoc qua lubet efficias.*

> *It is hard to abruptly shrug off a long-established love*
> *Hard, but this, somehow, you must do.*

Strike turned off the light, closed his eyes and sank, once more, into uneasy dreams of the empty house where squares of unfaded wallpaper bore witness to the removal of everything of value, but this time he walked alone, with the strange sensation that hidden eyes were watching.

53

And then, in the end, the poignant misery of her victory...
Henrik Ibsen, *Rosmersholm*

Robin arrived home just before 2 a.m. As she crept around the kitchen, making herself a sandwich, she noticed on the kitchen calendar that Matthew was planning to play five-a-side football later that morning. Accordingly, when she slipped into bed with him twenty minutes later, she set the alarm on her phone for eight o'clock before plugging it in to charge. As part of her effort to try and keep the atmosphere amicable, she wanted to get up to see him before he left.

He seemed happy that she'd made the effort to join him for breakfast, but when she asked whether he wanted her to come and cheer from the sidelines, or meet him for lunch afterwards, he declined both offers.

"I've got paperwork to do this afternoon. I don't want to drink at lunchtime. I'll come straight back," he said, so Robin, secretly delighted, because she was so tired, told him to have a good time and kissed him goodbye.

Trying not to focus on how much lighter of heart she felt once Matthew had left the house, Robin occupied herself with laundry and other essentials until, shortly after midday, while she was changing the sheets on their bed, Strike called.

"Hi," said Robin, gladly abandoning her task, "any news?"

"Plenty. Ready to write some stuff down?"

"Yes," said Robin, hurriedly grabbing notebook and pen off the top of her dressing table and sitting down on the stripped mattress.

"I've been making some calls. First off, Wardle. Very impressed with your work in getting hold of that note—"

Robin smiled at her reflection in the mirror.

"—though he's warned me the police won't take kindly to us, as he put it, 'clodhopping all over an open case.' I've asked him not to say where he got the tip-off about the note, but I expect they'll put two and two together, given that Wardle and I are mates. Still, that's unavoidable. The interesting bit is that the police are still worried about the same features of the death scene as we are and they've been going deeper into Chiswell's finances."

"Looking for evidence of blackmail?"

"Yeah, but they haven't got anything, because Chiswell never paid out. Here's the interesting bit. Chiswell got an unexplained payment in cash of forty thousand pounds last year. He opened a separate bank account for it, then seems to have spent it all on house repairs and other sundries."

"He *received* forty thousand pounds?"

"Yep. And Kinvara and the rest of the family are claiming total ignorance. They say they don't know where the money came from or why Chiswell would've opened a separate account to take receipt of it."

"The same amount Jimmy asked for before he scaled down his request," said Robin. "That's odd."

"Certainly is. So then I called Izzy."

"You've been busy," said Robin.

"You haven't heard the half of it. Izzy denies knowledge of where the forty grand came from, but I'm not sure I believe her. Then I asked her about the note Flick stole. She's appalled that Flick might've been posing as her father's cleaner. Very shaken up. I think for the first time she's considering the possibility that Kinvara isn't guilty."

"I take it she never met this so-called Polish woman?"

"Correct."

"What did she make of the note?"

"She thinks it looks like a to-do list, as well. She assumes 'Suzuki' meant the Grand Vitara, which was Chiswell's. No thoughts on 'mother.' The one thing of interest I got from her was in relation to 'blanc de blanc.' Chiswell was allergic to champagne. Apparently it made him go bright red and hyperventilate. What's odd about that is, there was a big empty box labeled Moët & Chandon in the kitchen when I checked it, the morning Chiswell died."

"You never told me that."

"We'd just found the body of a government minister. An empty box seemed relatively uninteresting at the time, and it never occurred to me it might be relevant to anything until I spoke to Izzy today."

"Were there bottles inside?"

"Nothing, so far as I could see, and according to the family, Chiswell never entertained there. If he wasn't drinking champagne himself, why was the box there?"

"You don't think—"

"That's exactly what I think," said Strike. "I reckon that box was how the helium and the rubber tubing got into the house, disguised."

"Wow," said Robin, lying back on the unmade bed and looking up at the ceiling.

"Quite clever. The killer could've sent it to him as a gift, couldn't they, knowing he was highly unlikely to open and drink it?"

"Bit slapdash," said Robin. "What was to stop him opening it up anyway? Or re-gifting it?"

"We need to find out when it was sent," Strike was saying. "Meanwhile, one minor mystery's been cleared up. Freddie's money clip was found."

"Where?"

"Chiswell's pocket. That was the flash of gold in the photograph you took."

"Oh," said Robin, blankly. "So he must have found it, before he died?"

"Well, it'd be hard for him to find it *after* he died."

"Ha ha," said Robin sarcastically. "There *is* another possibility."

"That the killer planted it on the corpse? Funny you should say that. Izzy says she was very surprised when it turned up on the body, because if he'd found it, she would have assumed he'd have told her. He made a massive fuss about losing it, apparently."

"He did," Robin agreed. "I heard him on the phone, ranting on about it. They fingerprinted it, presumably?"

"Yeah. Nothing suspicious. Only his—but at this point, that means nothing. If there was a killer, it's clear they wore gloves. I also asked Izzy about the bent sword, and we were right. It was Freddie's old saber. Nobody knows how it got bent, but Chiswell's fingerprints were the only ones on there. I suppose it's possible Chiswell got it off the wall while drunk and sentimental and accidentally trod on it, but again, there's nothing to say a gloved killer couldn't have handled it as well."

Robin sighed. Her elation at finding the note appeared to have been premature.

"So, still no real leads?"

"Hold your horses," said Strike bracingly, "I'm leading up to the good stuff.

"Izzy managed to get a new phone number for that stable girl who can confirm Kinvara's alibi, Tegan Butcher. I want you to give her a ring. I think you'll seem less intimidating to her than I will."

Robin jotted down the digits Strike read out.

"And after you've called Tegan, I want you to phone Raphael," said Strike, giving her the second number he had got from Izzy. "I'd like to clear up once and for all what he was really up to, the morning his father died."

"Will do," said Robin, glad of something concrete to do.

"Barclay's going to go back onto Jimmy and Flick," said Strike, "and I..."

He left a small pause, deliberately dramatic, and Robin laughed.

"And you're..."

"...am going to interview Billy Knight and Della Winn."

"What?" said Robin, amazed. "How're you going to get into the hosp—and *she'll* never agree—"

"Well, that's where you're wrong," said Strike. "Izzy dug Della's number out of Chiswell's records for me. I just rang her. I admit, I was expecting her to tell me to piss off—"

"—in slightly more elevated language, if I know Della," Robin suggested.

"—and she sounded initially as though she wanted to," admitted Strike, "but Aamir's disappeared."

"What?" said Robin, sharply.

"Calm down. 'Disappeared' is Della's word. In reality, he resigned the day before yesterday and vacated his house, which hardly makes him a missing person. He's not picking up the phone to her. She's blaming me, because—her words again—I did 'a fine job' on him when I went round to question him. She says he's very fragile and it'll be my fault if he ends up doing himself a mischief. So—"

"You've offered to find him in exchange for her answering questions?"

"Right in one," said Strike. "She jumped at the offer. Says I'll be able to reassure him that he's not in trouble and that nothing unsavory I might have heard about him will go any further."

"I hope he's all right," said Robin, concerned. "He *really* didn't like me, but that just proves he's smarter than any of the rest of them. When are you meeting Della?"

"Seven o'clock this evening, at her house in Bermondsey. And tomorrow afternoon, if all goes to plan, I'm going to be talking to Billy. I checked with Barclay, and Jimmy's got no plans to visit then, so I called the hospital. I'm waiting for Billy's psychiatrist to call me back now and confirm."

"You think they'll let you question him?"

"Supervised, yeah, I think they will. They're interested in seeing how lucid he is if he gets to talk to me. He's back on his meds and greatly improved, but he's still telling the story of the strangled kid. If the psychiatric team's in agreement, I'm going to be visiting the locked ward tomorrow."

"Well, great. It's good to have things to be getting on with. God knows, we could use a breakthrough—even if it is about the death we're not being paid to investigate," she sighed.

"There might not be a death at the bottom of Billy's story at all," said Strike, "but it's going to bug me forever unless we find out. I'll let you know how I get on with Della."

Robin wished him luck, bade him goodbye and ended the call, though she remained lying on her half-made bed. After a few seconds, she said aloud:

"Blanc de blancs."

Once again, she had the sense of a buried memory shifting, issuing a gust of low mood. Where on earth had she seen that phrase, while feeling miserable?

"Blanc de blancs," she repeated, getting off the bed. "Blanc d—*ow!*"

She had put her bare foot down on something small and very sharp. Bending down, she picked up a backless diamond stud earring.

At first, she merely stared at it, her pulse unaltered. The earring wasn't hers. She owned no diamond studs. She wondered why she hadn't trodden on it when she climbed into bed with a sleeping Matthew in the early hours of the morning. Perhaps her bare foot had missed it, or, more probably, the earring had been in the bed and displaced only when Robin pulled off the undersheet.

Of course, there were many diamond stud earrings in the world. The fact remained that the pair to which Robin's attention had most recently been drawn had been Sarah Shadlock's. Sarah had been wearing them the last time Robin and Matthew had gone to dinner, the night that Tom had attacked Matthew with sudden and apparently unwarranted ferocity.

For what felt like a very long time, but was in reality little over a minute, Robin sat contemplating the diamond in her hand. Then she laid the earring carefully on her bedside cabinet, picked up her mobile, entered "Settings," removed her caller ID, then phoned Tom's mobile.

He answered within a couple of rings, sounding grumpy. In the background, a presenter was wondering aloud what the forthcoming Olympic closing ceremony would be like.

"Yah, hello?"

Robin hung up. Tom wasn't playing five-a-side football. She continued to sit, motionless, her phone in her hand, on the heavy matrimonial bed that had been so difficult to move up the narrow stairs of this lovely rented house, while her mind moved back over the clear signs that she, the detective, had willfully ignored.

"I'm so stupid," Robin said quietly to the empty, sunlit room. "*So* bloody stupid."

54

Your gentle and upright disposition, your polished mind, your unimpeachable honor, are known to and appreciated by everyone...

Henrik Ibsen, *Rosmersholm*

Though the early evening was still bright, Della's front garden lay in shadow, which gave it a placid, melancholy air in contrast to the busy, dusty road that ran beyond the gates. As Strike rang the doorbell, he noted two large dog turds on the otherwise immaculate front lawn and he wondered who was helping Della with such mundane tasks now that her marriage was over.

The door opened, revealing the Minister for Sport in her impenetrable black glasses. She was wearing what Strike's elderly aunt back in Cornwall would have called a housecoat, a knee-length purple fleece robe that buttoned to the high neck, giving her a vaguely ecclesiastic air. The guide dog stood behind her, looking up at Strike with dark, mournful eyes.

"Hi, it's Cormoran Strike," said the detective, without moving. Given that she could neither recognize him by sight nor examine any of the identification he carried, the only way she could know whom she was admitting to her house was by the sound of his voice. "We spoke on the phone earlier and you asked me to come and see you."

"Yes," she said, unsmiling. "Come in, then."

She stepped back to let him pass, one hand on the Labrador's collar. Strike entered, wiping his feet on the doormat. A swell of music, loud strings and woodwind instruments, cut through by the pounding of a kettle drum, issued from what Strike assumed was the sitting room. Strike, who had been raised by a mother who listened mainly to metal bands, knew very little about classical music, but there was a looming, ominous quality about this music he didn't particularly care for. The hall was dark, because the lights hadn't been turned on, and otherwise nondescript, with a dark brown patterned carpet that, while practical, was rather ugly.

"I've made coffee," said Della. "I'll need you to carry the tray into the sitting room for me, if you wouldn't mind."

"No problem," said Strike.

He followed the Labrador, which padded along at Della's heels, its tail wagging vaguely. The symphony grew louder as they passed the sitting room, the doorframe of which Della touched lightly as she passed, feeling for familiar markers to orient herself.

"Is that Beethoven?" asked Strike, for something to say.

"Brahms. Symphony Number One, C Minor."

The edges of every surface in the kitchen were rounded. The knobs on the oven, Strike noticed, had raised numbers stuck to them. On a cork noticeboard was a list of phone numbers headed IN CASE OF EMERGENCY, that he imagined were for the use of a cleaner or home help. While Della crossed to the worktop opposite, Strike extracted his mobile from his coat pocket and took a picture of Geraint Winn's number. Della's outstretched hand reached the rim of the deep ceramic sink, and she moved sideways, where a tray sat already laden with a mug and a cafetière of freshly brewed coffee. Two bottles of wine stood beside it. Della felt for both of these, turned and held them out to Strike, still unsmiling.

"Which is which?" she asked.

"Châteauneuf-du-Pape, 2010, in your left hand," said Strike, "and Château Musar, 2006, in your right."

"I'll have a glass of the Châteauneuf-du-Pape if you wouldn't mind opening the bottle and pouring it for me. I assumed that you wouldn't want a drink, but if you do, help yourself."

"Thanks," said Strike, picking up the corkscrew she had laid beside the tray, "coffee will be fine."

She set off silently for the sitting room, leaving him to follow with the tray. As he entered the room he caught the heavy scent of roses and was fleetingly reminded of Robin. While Della grazed furniture with her fingertips, feeling her way towards an armchair with wide wooden arms, Strike saw four large bunches of flowers positioned in vases around the room and punctuating the overall drabness with their vivid colors, red, yellow and pink.

Aligning herself by pressing the backs of her legs against the chair, Della sat down neatly, then turned her face towards Strike as he set the tray on the table.

"Would you put my glass here, on my right chair arm?" she said, patting it, and he did so, while the pale Labrador, which had flopped down beside Della's chair, watched him out of kind, sleepy eyes.

The strings of the violins in the symphony swooped and fell as Strike sat down. From the fawn carpet to the furniture, all of which might have been designed in the seventies, everything seemed to be in different shades of brown. Half of one wall was covered in built-in shelves holding what he thought must be at least a thousand CDs. On a table to the rear of the room was a stack of Braille manuscripts. A large, framed photograph of a teenage girl sat on the mantelpiece. It occurred to Strike that her mother could not even enjoy the bitter-sweet solace of looking at Rhiannon Winn every day, and he found himself filled with inconvenient compassion.

"Nice flowers," he commented.

"Yes. It was my birthday a few days ago," said Della.

"Ah. Many happy returns."

"Are you from the West Country?"

"Partly. Cornwall."

"I can hear it in your vowels," said Della.

She waited while he dealt with the cafetière and poured himself coffee. When the sounds of clinking and pouring had ceased, she said:

"As I said on the phone, I'm very worried about Aamir. He'll still be in London, I'm sure, because it's all he's ever known. Not with his family," she added, and Strike thought he heard a trace of contempt. "I'm extremely concerned about him."

She felt carefully for the wine glass next to her and took a sip.

"When you've reassured him that he isn't in any kind of trouble, and that anything Chiswell told you about him will go no further, you must tell him to contact me—urgently."

The violins continued to screech and whine in what, to the untutored Strike, was a dissonant expression of foreboding. The guide dog scratched herself, her paw thudding off the carpet. Strike took out his notebook.

"Have you got the names or contact details of any friends Mallik might have gone to?"

"No," said Della. "I don't think he has many friends. Latterly he mentioned someone from university but I don't remember a name. I doubt it was anyone particularly close."

The thought of this distant friend seemed to make her uneasy.

"He studied at the LSE, so that's an area of London he knows well."

"He's on good terms with one of his sisters, isn't he?"

"Oh, no," said Della, at once. "No, no, they all disowned him. No, he's got nobody, really, other than me, which is what makes this situation so dangerous."

"The sister posted a picture on Facebook of the two of them fairly recently. It was in that pizza joint opposite your house."

Della's expression betrayed not merely surprise, but displeasure.

"Aamir told me you'd been snooping online. Which sister was it?"

"I'd have to ch—"

"But I doubt he'd be staying with her," said Della, talking over him. "Not with the way the family as a whole has treated him. He *might* have contacted her, I suppose. You might see what she knows."

"I will," said Strike. "Any other ideas about where he might go?"

"He really doesn't have anyone else," she said. "That's what worries me. He's vulnerable. It's essential I find him."

"Well, I'll certainly do my best," Strike promised her. "Now, you said on the phone that you'd answer a few questions."

Her expression became slightly more forbidding.

"I doubt I can tell you anything of interest, but go on."

"Can we start with Jasper Chiswell, and your and your husband's relationship with him?"

By her expression, she managed to convey that she found the question both impertinent and slightly ludicrous. With a cold smile and raised eyebrows, she responded:

"Well, Jasper and I had a professional relationship, obviously."

"And how was that?" asked Strike, adding sugar to his coffee, stirring it and taking a sip.

"Given," said Della, "that Jasper hired you to try and discover disreputable information about us, I think you already know the answer to that question."

"You maintain that your husband wasn't blackmailing Chiswell, then, do you?"

"Of course I do."

Strike knew that pushing on this particular point, when Della's super-injunction had already shown what lengths she would go to in her own defense, would only alienate her. A temporary retreat seemed indicated.

"What about the rest of the Chiswells? Did you ever run across any of them?"

"Some," she said, a little warily.

"And how did you find them?"

"I barely know them. Geraint says Izzy was hardworking."

"Chiswell's late son was on the junior British fencing team with your daughter, I think?"

The muscles of her face seemed to contract. He was reminded of an anemone shutting in on itself when it senses a predator.

"Yes," she said.

"Did you like Freddie?"

"I don't think I ever spoke to him. Geraint was the one who ferried Rhiannon around to her tournaments. He knew the team."

The shadow stems of the roses closest to the window stretched like bars across the carpet. The Brahms symphony crashed stormily on in the background. Della's opaque lenses contributed to a feeling of inscrutable menace and Strike, though wholly unintimidated, was put in mind of the blind oracles and seers that peopled ancient myths, and the particular supernatural aura attributed by the able-bodied to this one particular disability.

"What was it that made Jasper Chiswell so eager to find out things to your disadvantage, would you say?"

"He didn't like me," said Della simply. "We disagreed frequently. He came from a background that finds anything that deviates from its own conventions and norms to be suspect, unnatural, even dangerous. He was a rich white Conservative male, Mr. Strike, and he felt the corridors of power were best populated exclusively by rich white Conservative males. He sought, in everything, to restore a status quo he remembered in his youth. In pursuit of that objective, he was frequently unprincipled and certainly hypocritical."

"In what way?"

"Ask his wife."

"You know Kinvara, do you?"

"I wouldn't say I 'know' her. I had an encounter with her a while ago that was certainly interesting in the light of Chiswell's public proclamations about the sanctity of marriage."

Strike had the impression that beneath the lofty language, and in spite of her genuine anxiety about Aamir, Della was deriving pleasure from saying these things.

"What happened?" Strike asked.

"Kinvara turned up unexpectedly late one afternoon at the ministry, but Jasper had already left for Oxfordshire. I think it was her aim to surprise him."

"When was this?"

"I should say . . . a year ago, at least. Shortly before Parliament went into recess, I think. She was in a state of great distress. I heard a commotion outside and went to find out what was going on. I could tell by the silence of the outer office that they were all agog. She was very emotional, demanding to see her husband. Initially I thought she must have had dreadful news and perhaps needed Jasper as a source of comfort and support. I took her into my office.

"Once it was just the two of us, she broke down completely. She was barely coherent, but from the little I could understand," said Della, "she'd just found out there was another woman."

"Did she say who?"

"I don't think so. She may have done, but she was—well, it was quite disturbing," said Della austerely. "More as though she had suffered a bereavement than the end of a marriage. 'I was just part of his game,' 'He never loved me' and so forth."

"What game did you take her to mean?" asked Strike.

"The political game, I suppose. She spoke of being humiliated, of being told, in so many words, that she had served her purpose...

"Jasper Chiswell was a very ambitious man, you know. He'd lost his career once over infidelity. I imagine he cast around quite clinically for the kind of new wife who'd burnish his image. No more Italian fly-by-nights now he was trying to get back into the cabinet. He probably thought Kinvara would go down very well with the county Conservatives. Well-bred. Horsey.

"I heard, later, that Jasper had bundled her off into some kind of psychiatric clinic not long afterwards. That's how families like the Chiswells deal with excessive emotion, I suppose," said Della, taking another sip of wine. "Yet she stayed with him. Of course, people do stay, even when they're treated abominably. He talked about her within my hearing as though she was a deficient, needy child. I remember him saying Kinvara's mother would be 'babysitting' her for her birthday, because he had to be in Parliament for a vote. He could have paired his vote, of course — found a Labor MP and struck a deal. Simply couldn't be bothered.

"Women like Kinvara Chiswell, whose entire self-worth is predicated on the status and success of marriage, are naturally shattered when everything goes wrong. I think all those horses of hers were an outlet, a substitute and — oh yes," said Della, "I've just remembered — the *very* last thing she said to me that day was that in addition to everything else, she now had to go home to put down a beloved mare."

Della felt for the broad, soft head of Gwynn, who was lying beside her chair.

"I felt very sorry for her, there. Animals have been an enormous consolation to me in my life. One can hardly overstate the comfort they give, sometimes."

The hand that caressed the dog still sported a wedding ring, Strike noticed, along with a heavy amethyst ring that matched her housecoat. Somebody, he supposed Geraint, must have told her that it was the same color and again, he felt an unwelcome pang of pity.

"Did Kinvara tell you how or when she'd found out that her husband had been unfaithful?"

"No, no, she simply gave way to an almost incoherent outpouring of rage and grief, like a small child. Kept saying, 'I loved him and he never loved me, it was all a lie.' I've never heard such a raw explosion of grief, even at a funeral or a deathbed. I never spoke to her again except for hello. She acted as though she had no memory of what had passed between us."

Della took another sip of wine.

"Can we return to Mallik?" Strike asked.

"Yes, of course," she said at once.

"The morning that Jasper Chiswell died—the thirteenth—you were here, at home?"

There was a lengthy silence.

"Why are you asking me that?" Della said, in a changed tone.

"Because I'd like to corroborate a story I've heard," said Strike.

"You mean, that Aamir was here with me, that morning?"

"Exactly."

"Well, that's quite true. I'd slipped downstairs and sprained my wrist. I called Aamir and he came over. He wanted me to go to casualty, but there was no need. I could still move all my fingers. I simply needed some help managing breakfast and so on."

"*You* called Mallik?"

"What?" she said.

It was the age-old, transparent "what?" of the person who is afraid they've made a mistake. Strike guessed that some very rapid thinking was going on behind the dark glasses.

"*You* called Aamir?"

"Why? What does he say happened?"

"He says your husband went in person to fetch him from his house."

"Oh," said Della and then, "of course, yes, I forgot."

"Did you?" asked Strike gently. "Or are you backing up their story?"

"I forgot," Della repeated firmly. "When I said I 'called' him I wasn't talking about the telephone. I meant that I called 'on' him. Via Geraint."

"But if Geraint was here when you slipped, couldn't he have helped you with your breakfast?"

"I think Geraint wanted Aamir to help persuade me to go to casualty."

"Right. So it was Geraint's idea to go to Aamir, rather than yours?"

"I can't remember now," she said, but then, contradicting herself, "I'd fallen rather heavily. Geraint has a bad back, naturally he wanted help and I thought of Aamir, and then the pair of them nagged me to go to A&E, but there was no need. It was a simple sprain."

The light was now fading beyond the net curtains. Della's black lenses reflected the neon red of the dying sun above the rooftops.

"I'm extremely worried about Aamir," she said again, in a strained voice.

"A couple more questions and I'm done," Strike replied. "Jasper Chiswell hinted in front of a roomful of people that he knew something disreputable about Mallik. Can you tell me anything about that?"

"Yes, well, it was that conversation," said Della quietly, "that first made Aamir think about resigning. I could feel him pulling away from me after it happened. And then *you* finished the job, didn't you? You went to his house, to taunt him further."

"There was no taunting, Mrs. Winn—"

"*Liwat*, Mr. Strike, did you never learn what that meant all the time you were in the Middle East?"

"Yeah, I know what it means," said Strike matter-of-factly. "Sodomy. Chiswell seemed to be threatening Aamir with exposure—"

"Aamir wouldn't suffer from exposure of the truth, I assure you!" said Della fiercely. "Not that it matters a jot, but he doesn't happen to be gay!"

The Brahms symphony continued on what, to Strike, was its gloomy and intermittently sinister course, horns and violins competing to jar the nerves.

"You want the truth?" said Della loudly. "Aamir objected to being groped and harassed, *felt up* by a senior civil servant, whose inappropriate touching of young men passing through his office is an open secret, even a joke! And when a comprehensive-educated Muslim boy loses his cool and smacks a senior civil servant, which of the two do you imagine finds themselves smeared and stigmatized? Which of them, do you think, becomes the subject of derogatory rumors, and is forced out of a job?"

"I'm guessing," said Strike, "*not* Sir Christopher Barrowclough-Burns."

"How did you know whom I was talking about?" said Della sharply.

"Still in the post, is he?" asked Strike, ignoring the question.

"Of course he is! Everybody knows about his *harmless* little ways, but nobody wants to go on the record. I've been trying to get something done about Barrowclough-Burns for years. When I heard Aamir had left the diversity program in murky circumstances, I made it my business to find him. He was in a pitiable state when I first made contact with him, absolutely pitiable. Quite apart from the derailing of what should have been a stellar career, there was a malicious cousin who'd heard some gossip and spread the rumor that Aamir had been fired for homosexual activity at work.

"Well, Aamir's father isn't the sort of man to look kindly on a gay son. Aamir had been resisting his parents' pressure to marry a girl they thought suitable. There was a terrible row and a complete breach. This brilliant young man lost everything, family, home and job, in the space of a couple of weeks."

"So you stepped in?"

"Geraint and I had an empty property around the corner. Both our mothers used to live there. Neither Geraint nor I have siblings. It had become too difficult to manage our mothers' care from London, so we brought them up from Wales and housed them together, around the corner. Geraint's mother died two years ago, mine this, so the house was empty. We didn't need the rent. It seemed only sensible to let Aamir stay there."

"And this was nothing but disinterested kindness?" Strike said. "You weren't thinking of how useful he might be to you, when you gave him a job and a house?"

"What d'you mean, 'useful'? He's a very intelligent young man, any office would be—"

"Your husband was pressuring Aamir to get incriminating information on Jasper Chiswell from the Foreign Office, Mrs. Winn.

Photographs. He was pressuring Aamir to go to Sir Christopher for pictures."

Della reached out for her glass of wine, missed the stem by inches and hit the glass with her knuckles. Strike lunged forwards to try and catch it, but too late: a whip-like trail of red wine described a parabola in the air and spattered the beige carpet, the glass falling with a thud beside it. Gwynn got up and approached the spill with mild interest, sniffing the spreading stain.

"How bad is it?" asked Della urgently, her fingers grasping the arms of her chair, her face inclined to the floor.

"Not good," said Strike.

"Salt, please...put salt on it. In the cupboard to the right of the cooker!"

Turning on the light as he entered the kitchen, Strike's attention was caught for the first time by an odd something he had failed to spot on his previous entry into the room: an envelope stuck high up on a wall-mounted cabinet to the right, too high for Della to reach. Having grabbed the salt out of the cupboard he made a detour to read the single word written on it: *Geraint.*

"To the right of the cooker!" Della called a little desperately from the sitting room.

"Ah, the right!" Strike shouted back, as he tugged down the envelope and slit it open.

Inside was a receipt from "Kennedy Bros. Joiners," for the replacement of a bathroom door. Strike licked his finger, dampened down the envelope flap, resealed it as best he could and stuck it back where he had found it.

"Sorry," he told Della, re-entering the room. "It was right in front of me and I didn't notice."

He twisted the top of the cardboard tub and poured salt liberally over the purple stain. The Brahms symphony came to an end as he straightened up, dubious as to the likely success of the home remedy.

"Have you done it?" Della whispered into the silence.

"Yeah," said Strike, watching the wine rising into the white and turning it a dirty gray. "I think you're still going to need a carpet cleaner, though."

"Oh dear...the carpet was new this year."

She seemed deeply shaken, though whether this was entirely due to the spilled wine was, Strike thought, debatable. As he returned to the sofa and set down the salt beside the coffee, music started up again, this time a Hungarian air that was no more restful than the symphony, but weirdly manic.

"Would you like more wine?" he asked her.

"I—yes, I think I would," she said.

He poured her another and passed it directly into her hand. She drank a little, then said shakily:

"How could you know what you just told me, Mr. Strike?"

"I'd rather not answer that, but I assure you it's true."

Clutching her wine in both hands Della said:

"You *have* to find Aamir for me. If he thought *I* sanctioned Geraint telling him to go to Barrowclough-Burns for favors, it's no wonder he—"

Her self-control was visibly disintegrating. She tried to set the wine down on the arm of her chair and had to feel for it with the other hand before doing so successfully, all the while shaking her head in little jerks of disbelief.

"No wonder he what?" asked Strike quietly.

"Accused me of...of smothering...controlling...well, of course, this explains everything...we were so close—you wouldn't understand—it's hard to explain—but it was remarkable, how soon we became—well, like family. Sometimes, you know, there's an instant affinity—a connection that years couldn't forge, with other people—

"But these past few weeks, it all changed—I could feel it—starting when Chiswell made that jibe in front of everyone—Aamir became distant. It was as though he no longer trusted me...I should have known...oh Lord, I should have known...you have to find him, you have to..."

Perhaps, Strike thought, the depth of her burning sense of need was sexual in origin, and perhaps on some subconscious level it had indeed been tinged with appreciation of Aamir's youthful masculinity. However, as Rhiannon Winn watched over them from her cheap gilt frame, wearing a smile that didn't reach her wide, anxious eyes, her teeth glinting with heavy braces, Strike thought it far more likely that Della was a woman possessed of that which Charlotte so conspicuously lacked: a burning, frustrated maternal drive tinged, in Della's case, with unassuageable regret.

"This as well," she whispered. "*This as well*. What hasn't he ruined?"

"You're talking about—"

"My husband!" said Della numbly. "Who else? My charity—our charity—but you know that, of course? It was you who told Chiswell about the missing twenty-five thousand, wasn't it? And the lies, the stupid lies, Geraint's been telling people? David Beckham, Mo Farah—all those impossible promises?"

"My partner found out."

"Nobody will believe me," said Della distractedly, "but I didn't know, I had no idea. I've missed the last four board meetings—preparations for the Paralympics. Geraint only told me the truth after Chiswell threatened him with the press. Even then he claimed it was the accountant's fault, but he swore to me the other things weren't true. Swore it, on his mother's grave."

She twisted the wedding ring on her finger, apparently distracted.

"I suppose your wretched partner tracked down Elspeth Lacey-Curtis, as well?"

"Afraid so," lied Strike, judging that a gamble was indicated. "Did Geraint deny that, too?"

"If he'd said anything to make the girls uncomfortable he felt awful, but he swore there was nothing else to it, no touching, just a couple of risqué jokes. But in this climate," said Della furiously, "a man ought to damned well think about what jokes he makes to a bunch of fifteen-year-old girls!"

Strike leaned forwards and grabbed Della's wine, which was in danger of being upended again.

"What are you doing?"

"Moving your glass onto the table," said Strike.

"Oh," said Della, "thank you." Making a noticeable effort to control herself, she continued, "Geraint was representing *me* at that event, and it will go the way it always goes in the press when it all comes out: it will have been my fault, all of it! Because men's crimes are *always* ours in the final analysis, aren't they, Mr. Strike? Ultimate responsibility *always* lies with the woman, who should have stopped it, who should have acted, who *must have known*. Your failings are really *our* failings, aren't they? Because the proper role of the woman is carer, and there's nothing lower in this whole world than a bad mother."

Breathing hard, she pressed her trembling fingers to her temples. Beyond the net curtains night, deep blue, was inching like a veil over the glaring red of sunset and as the room grew darker, Rhiannon Winn's features faded gradually into the twilight. Soon all that would be visible was her smile, punctuated by the ugly braces.

"Give me back my wine, please."

Strike did so. Della drank most of it down at once and continued to clasp the glass as she said bitterly:

"There are plenty of people ready to think all kinds of odd things about a blind woman. Of course, when I was younger, it was worse. There was often a prurient interest in one's private life. It was the first place some men's minds went. Perhaps you've experienced it, too, have you, with your one leg?"

Strike found that he didn't resent the blunt mention of his disability from Della.

"Yeah, I've had a bit of that," he admitted. "Bloke I was at school with. Hadn't seen him in years. It was my first time back in Cornwall since I got blown up. Five pints in, he asked me at what point I warned women my leg was going to come off with my trousers. He thought he was being funny."

Della smiled thinly.

"Never occurs to some people that it is we who should be making the jokes, does it? But it will be different for you, as a man...most people seem to think it in the natural order of things that the able-bodied woman should look after the disabled man. Geraint had to deal with that for years...people assuming there was something peculiar about him, because he chose a disabled wife. I think I may have tried to compensate for that. I wanted him to have a role...status...but it would have been better for both of us, in retrospect, if he had done something unconnected to me."

Strike thought she was a little drunk. Perhaps she hadn't eaten. He felt an inappropriate desire to check her fridge. Sitting here with this impressive and vulnerable woman, it was easy to understand how Aamir had become so entangled with her both professionally and privately, without ever intending to become so.

"People assume I married Geraint because there was nobody else who wanted me, but they're quite wrong," said Della, sitting up straighter in her chair. "There was a boy I was at school with who was smitten with me, who proposed when I was nineteen. I had a choice and I chose Geraint. Not as a carer, or because, as journalists have sometimes implied, my limitless ambition made a husband necessary...but because I loved him."

Strike remembered the day he had followed Della's husband to the stairwell in King's Cross, and the tawdry things that Robin had told him about Geraint's behavior at work, yet nothing that Della had just said struck him as incredible. Life had taught him that a great and powerful love could be felt for the most apparently unworthy people, a circumstance that ought, after all, to give everybody consolation.

"Are you married, Mr. Strike?"

"No," he said.

"I think marriage is nearly always an unfathomable entity, even to the people inside it. It took this...all of this mess...to make me realize I can't go on. I don't really know when I stopped loving him, but at some point after Rhiannon died, it slipped—"

Her voice broke.

"—slipped away from us." She swallowed. "Please will you pour me another glass of wine?"

He did so. The room was very dark now. The music had changed again, to a melancholy violin concerto which at last, in Strike's opinion, was appropriate to the conversation. Della had not wanted to talk to him, but now seemed reluctant to let the conversation end.

"Why did your husband hate Jasper Chiswell so much?" Strike asked quietly. "Because of Chiswell's political clashes with you, or—?"

"No, no," said Della Winn wearily. "Because Geraint has to blame somebody other than himself for the misfortunes that befall him."

Strike waited, but she merely drank more wine, and said nothing.

"What exactly—?"

"Never mind," she said loudly. "Never mind, it doesn't matter."

But a moment later, after another large gulp of wine, she said:

"Rhiannon didn't really want to do fencing. Like most little girls, what she wanted was a pony, but we—Geraint and I—we didn't come from pony-owning backgrounds. We didn't have the first idea what one does with horses. As I think back, I suppose there were ways around that, but we were both terribly busy and felt it would be impractical, so she took up fencing instead, and very good she was at it, too…

"Have I answered enough of your questions, Mr. Strike?" she asked a little thickly. "Will you find Aamir?"

"I'll try," Strike promised her. "Could you give me his number? And yours, so I can keep you updated?"

She had both numbers off by heart, and he copied them down before closing his notebook and getting back to his feet.

"You've been very helpful, Mrs. Winn. Thank you."

"That sounds worrying," she said, with a faint crease between the eyebrows. "I'm not sure I meant to be."

"Will you be—?"

"Perfectly," said Della, enunciating over-clearly. "You'll call me when you find Aamir, won't you?"

"If you don't hear from me before then, I'll update you in a week's time," Strike promised. "Er—is anyone coming in tonight, or—?"

"I see you aren't quite as hardened as your reputation would suggest," said Della. "Don't worry about me. My neighbor will be in to walk Gwynn for me shortly. She checks the gas dials and so forth."

"In that case, don't get up. Good night."

The near-white dog raised her head as he walked towards the door, sniffing the air. He left Della sitting in the darkness, a little drunk, with nothing else for company but the picture of the dead daughter she had never seen.

Closing the front door, Strike couldn't remember the last time he had felt such a strange mixture of admiration, sympathy and suspicion.

55

...let us at least fight with honorable weapons, since it seems we must fight.

Henrik Ibsen, *Rosmersholm*

Matthew, who had supposedly been out just for the morning, still hadn't come home. He had sent two texts since, one at three in the afternoon:

Tom got work troubles, wants to talk. Gone to pub with him (I'm on Cokes.) Back as soon as I can.

And then, at seven o'clock:

Really sorry, he's pissed, I can't leave him. Going to find him a taxi then come back. Hope you've eaten. Love you x

Still with her caller ID switched off, Robin had again phoned Tom's mobile. He had answered immediately. There was no background babble of a pub.

"Yes?" said Tom testily and apparently sober, "who is this?"

Robin hung up.

Two bags were packed and waiting in the hall. She had already phoned Vanessa and asked whether she could stay on her sofa for a couple of nights, before she got a new place to live. She found it strange that Vanessa didn't sound more surprised, but at the same time, was glad not to have to fend off pity.

Waiting in the sitting room, watching night fall outside the window, Robin wondered whether she would even have been suspicious had she not found the earring. Lately she had become simply grateful for time without Matthew, when she could relax, not having to hide anything, whether the work she was doing on the Chiswell case or the panic attacks that must be conducted quietly, without fuss, on the bathroom floor.

Sitting in the stylish armchair belonging to their absent landlord, Robin felt as though she were inhabiting a memory. How often were you aware, while it happened, that you were living an hour that would change the course of your life forever? She would remember this room for a long time, and she gazed around it now, with the aim of fixing it in her mind, thereby trying to ignore the sadness, the shame and the pain that burned and twisted inside her.

At just past nine o'clock, she heard, with a wave of nausea, Matthew's key in the lock and the sound of the door opening.

"Sorry," he shouted, before he'd even closed the door, "he's a silly sod, I had a job persuading the taxi driver to take—"

Robin heard his small exclamation of surprise as he spotted the suitcases. Safe, now, to dial, she pressed the number she had ready on her phone. He walked into the sitting room, puzzled, in time to hear her booking a minicab. She hung up. They looked at each other.

"What's with the cases?"

"I'm leaving."

There was a long silence. Matthew seemed not to understand.

"What d'you mean?"

"I don't know how to say it any more clearly, Matt."

"Leaving *me*?"

"That's right."

"Why?"

"Because," said Robin, "you're sleeping with Sarah."

She watched Matthew struggling to find words that might save him, but the seconds slid by, and it was too late for real incredulity, for astonished innocence, for genuine incomprehension.

"What?" he said at last, with a forced laugh.

"Please don't," she said. "There's no point. It's over."

He continued to stand in the doorway of the sitting room and she thought he looked tired, even haggard.

"I was going to go and leave a note," said Robin, "but that felt too melodramatic. Anyway, there are practical things we need to talk about."

She thought she could see him thinking, *How did I give it away? Who have you told?*

"Listen," he said urgently, dropping his sports bag beside him (full, no doubt, of clean, pressed kit), "I know things haven't been good between us, you and me, but it's you I want, Robin. Don't throw us away. Please."

He walked forwards, dropped into a crouch beside her chair and tried to take her hand. She pulled it away, genuinely astonished.

"You're sleeping with Sarah," she repeated.

He got up, crossed to the sofa and sat down, dropped his face into his hands and said weakly:

"I'm sorry. I'm sorry. It's been so shit between you and me—"

"—that you had to sleep with your friend's fiancée?"

He looked up at that, in sudden panic.

"Have you spoken to Tom? Does he know?"

Suddenly unable to bear his proximity, she walked away towards the window, full of a contempt she had never felt before.

"Even now, worried about your promotion prospects, Matt?"

"No—fuck—you don't understand," he said. "It's over between me and Sarah."

"Oh, really?"

"Yes," he said. "Yes! Fuck—this is so fucking ironic—we talked all day. We agreed it couldn't go on, not after—you and Tom—we've just ended it. An hour ago."

"Wow," said Robin, with a little laugh, feeling disembodied, "*isn't that ironic?*"

Her mobile rang. Dreamlike, she answered it.

"Robin?" said Strike. "Update. I've just seen Della Winn."

"How did it go?" she asked, trying to sound steady and bright, determined not to cut the call short. Her working life was now her entire life and Matthew would no longer impinge upon it. Turning her back on her fuming husband, she looked out onto the dark cobbled street.

"Very interesting on two counts," said Strike. "Firstly, she slipped up. I don't think Geraint was with Aamir the morning Chiswell died."

"That *is* interesting," said Robin, forcing herself to concentrate, aware of Matthew watching her.

"I've got a number for him and I tried it, but he's not picking up. I thought I'd see if he's still at the B&B down the road as I'm in the vicinity, but the owner says he's moved on."

"Shame. What was the other interesting thing?" asked Robin.

"Is that Strike?" asked Matthew loudly, from behind her. She ignored him.

"What was that?" asked Strike.

"Nothing," said Robin. "Go on."

"Well, the second interesting thing is that Della met Kinvara last year, who was hysterical because she thought Chiswell—"

Robin's mobile was pulled roughly out of her hand. She wheeled around. Matthew ended the call with a stab of his finger.

"How *dare* you?" shouted Robin, holding out her hand. "Give that back!"

"We're trying to save our fucking marriage and you're taking calls from him?"

"I'm not trying to save this marriage! *Give me back my phone!*"

He hesitated, then thrust it back at her, only to look outraged when she coolly phoned Strike back again.

"Sorry about that, Cormoran, we got cut off," she said, with Matthew's wild eyes on her.

"Everything all right there, Robin?"

"It's fine. What were you saying about Chiswell?"

"That he was having an affair."

"An affair!" said Robin, her eyes on Matthew's. "Who with?"

"Christ knows. Have you had any luck getting hold of Raphael? We know he's not that bothered about protecting his father's memory. He might tell us."

"I left a message for him, and for Tegan. Neither of them have called back."

"OK, well, keep me posted. This all sheds an interesting light on the hammer round the head, though, doesn't it?"

"Certainly does," said Robin.

"That's me at the Tube. Sure you're all right?"

"Yes, of course," said Robin, with what she hoped sounded like workaday impatience. "Speak soon."

She hung up.

"'Speak soon,'" Matthew imitated her, in the high-pitched, wispy voice he always used when impersonating women. "'Speak later, Cormoran. I'm running out on my marriage so I can be at your beck and call forever, Cormoran. I don't mind working for minimum wage, Cormoran, not if I can be your skivvy.'"

"Fuck off, Matt," said Robin calmly. "Fuck off back to Sarah. The earring she left in our bed is upstairs on my bedside table, by the way."

"Robin," he said, suddenly earnest, "we can get through this. If we love each other, we can."

"Well, the problem with that, Matt," said Robin, "is that I don't love you anymore."

She had always thought the idea of eyes darkening was literary license, but she saw his light eyes turn black as his pupils dilated in shock.

"You bitch," he said quietly.

She felt a cowardly impulse to lie, to back away from the absolute statement, to protect herself, but something stronger in her held on: the need to tell the unvarnished truth, when she had been lying to him and herself for so long.

"No," she said. "I don't. We should have split up on the honeymoon. I stayed because you were ill. I felt sorry for you. No," she corrected herself, determined to do the thing properly, "actually, we should never have gone on the honeymoon. I ought to have walked out of the wedding once I knew you'd deleted those calls from Strike."

She wanted to check her watch to see when her cab would arrive, but she was scared to take her eyes off her husband. There was something in his expression that recalled a snake peering out from under a rock.

"How do you think your life looks to other people?" he asked quietly.

"What d'you mean?"

"You bailed out on uni. Now you're bailing out on us. You even bailed out on your therapist. You're a fucking flake. The only thing you haven't run out on is this stupid job that's half-killed you, and you got sacked from *that*. He only took you back because he wants to get into your pants. And he probably can't get anyone else so cheap."

She felt as though he had punched her. Winded, her voice sounded weak.

"Thanks, Matt," she said, moving towards the door. "Thanks for making this so easy."

But he moved quickly to block her exit.

"It was a temping job. He paid you attention, so you kidded yourself that was the career for you, even though it's the last fucking thing you should've been doing, with *your* history—"

She was fighting tears now, but determined not to succumb.

"I wanted to do police work for years and years—"

"No, you fucking didn't!" jeered Matthew, "when did you ever—?"

"I had a life before you!" Robin shouted. "I had a home life where I said things you never heard! I never told you, Matthew, because I knew you'd laugh, like my dickhead brothers! I did psychology hoping it would take me to some kind of forensic—"

"You never said this, you're trying to justify—"

"I didn't tell you because I knew you'd sneer—"

"Bullshit—"

"It isn't bullshit!" she shouted. "I'm telling you the truth, this is the whole truth, and you're proving my point, you don't believe me! You liked it when I dropped out of uni—"

"The hell d'you mean?"

"'There's no hurry to go back,' 'you don't *have* to have a degree...'"

"Oh, so now I'm being fucking blamed for being sensitive!"

"You liked it, you liked me being stuck at home, why can't you admit it? Sarah Shadlock at uni and me underachieving back in Masham—it made up for me getting better A-levels than you, getting into my first choice of—"

"Oh!" he laughed humorlessly, "oh, you got better fucking *A-levels* than me? Yeah, that keeps me up at night—"

"If I hadn't been raped, we'd have split up years ago!"

"Is this what you learned in therapy? To tell lies about the past, to justify all your bullshit?"

"I learned to tell the truth!" shouted Robin, driven to the point of brutality. "And here's some more: I was falling out of love with you before the rape! You weren't interested in anything I was doing—my course, my new friends. All you wanted to know was whether any other blokes were making moves on me. But afterwards, you were so sweet, so kind...you seemed like the safest man in the world, the only one I could trust. That's why I stayed. We wouldn't be here, now, but for that rape."

They both heard the car pull up outside. Robin tried to slide past him into the hall, but he moved to block her again.

"No, you don't. You're not getting out of it that bloody easily. You stayed because I was *safe*? Fuck off. You loved me."

"I thought I did," said Robin, "but not anymore. Get out of the way. I'm leaving."

She tried to sidestep him, but he moved to block her again.

"No," he said again, and now he moved forwards, jostling her back into the sitting room. "You're staying here. We're having this out."

The minicab driver rang the doorbell.

"Coming!" Robin shouted, but Matthew snarled:

"You're not running away this time, you're going to stay and sort out your mess—"

"No!" shouted Robin, as though to a dog. She came to a halt, refusing to be backed further into the room, even though he was so close she could feel his breath on her face, and she was suddenly reminded of Geraint Winn, and was overwhelmed with revulsion. "Get away from me. *Now!*"

And like a dog Matthew took a step backwards, responding not to the order, but to something in her voice. He was angry, but scared, too.

"Right," said Robin. She knew she was on the edge of a panic attack, but she held on, and every second she did not dissolve was giving her strength, and she stood her ground. "I'm leaving. You try and stop me, I'll retaliate. I've fought off far bigger, meaner men than you, Matthew. You haven't even got a bloody knife."

She saw his eyes turn blacker than ever, and suddenly she remembered how her brother, Martin, had punched Matthew in the face, at the wedding. No matter what was coming, she vowed, in a kind of dark exhilaration, she'd do better than Martin. She'd break his damn nose if she had to.

"Please," he said, his shoulders suddenly sagging, "Robin—"

"You're going to have to hurt me if you want to stop me leaving, but I warn you, I'll prosecute you for assault if you do. *That* won't go down too well at the office, will it?"

She held his gaze for a few more seconds then walked back towards him, her fists already curling, waiting for him to block or grab her, but he moved aside.

"Robin," he said hoarsely. "Wait. Seriously, wait, you said there were things we had to discuss—"

"The lawyers can do it," she said, reaching the front door and pulling it open.

The cool night air touched her like a blessing.

A stocky woman was sitting at the wheel of a Vauxhall Corsa. Seeing Robin's cases, she got out to help her hoist them into the boot. Matthew had followed and was now standing in the doorway. As Robin made to get into the car, he called to her and her tears began to fall at last, but without looking at him, she slammed the door.

"Please, let's go," she said thickly, to the driver, as Matthew came down the steps and bent to speak to her through the glass.

"I still fucking love you!"

The car moved away over the cobbles of Albury Street, past the molded frontages of the pretty sea merchants' houses where she had never felt she belonged. At the top of the street she knew that if she looked back, she would see Matthew standing watching the vanishing car. Her eyes met those of the driver in the rearview mirror.

"Sorry," said Robin nonsensically, and then, bewildered by her own apology, she said, "I've—I've just left my husband."

"Yeah?" said the driver, switching on her indicator. "I've left two. It gets easier with practice."

Robin tried to laugh, but the noise turned into a loud wet hiccup, and as the car approached the lonely stone swan high on the corner pub, she began to cry in earnest.

"Here," said the driver gently, and she passed back a plastic-wrapped pack of tissues.

"Thanks," sobbed Robin, extracting one and pressing it to her tired, stinging eyes until the white tissue was sodden and streaked with the last traces of thick black eye makeup that she had worn to impersonate Bobbi Cunliffe. Avoiding the sympathetic gaze of the driver in the rearview mirror, she looked down into her lap. The wrapper on the tissues was that of an unfamiliar American brand: "Dr. Blanc."

At once, Robin's elusive memory dropped into view, as though it had been waiting for this tiny prod. Now she remembered exactly where she had seen the phrase "Blanc de Blanc," but it had nothing to do with the case, and everything to do with her imploding marriage, with a lavender walk and a Japanese water garden, and the last time she had ever said "I love you," and the first time she'd known she didn't mean it.

56

I cannot — I will not — go through life with a dead body on my back.

Henrik Ibsen, *Rosmersholm*

As Strike approached Henlys Corner on the North Circular Road the following afternoon, he saw, with a muttered oath, that traffic ahead had come to a halt. The junction, which was a notorious hotspot for congestion, had supposedly been improved earlier that year. As he joined the stationary queue, Strike wound down his window, lit a cigarette and glanced at his dashboard clock, with the familiar sensation of angry impotence that driving in London so often engendered. He had wondered whether it might be wiser to take the Tube north, but the psychiatric hospital lay a good mile from the nearest station, and the BMW was marginally easier on his still sore leg. Now he feared that he was going to be late for an interview that he was determined not to miss, firstly because he had no wish to disoblige the psychiatric team who were letting him see Billy Knight, and secondly because Strike didn't know when there would next be an opportunity to speak to the younger brother without fear of running into the older. Barclay had assured him that morning that Jimmy's plans for the day comprised writing a polemic on Rothschild's global influence for the Real Socialist website and sampling some of Barclay's new stash.

Scowling and tapping his fingers on the steering wheel, Strike fell back to ruminating on a question that had been nagging at him since the previous evening: whether or not the cut connection halfway through his call to Robin had really been due to Matthew snatching the phone out of her hand. He had not found Robin's subsequent assurances that all was well particularly convincing.

While heating himself baked beans on his one-ringed hob, because he was still attempting to lose weight, Strike had debated calling Robin back. Eating his meatless dinner unenthusiastically in front of the television, supposedly watching highlights of the Olympics closing ceremony, his attention was barely held by the sight of the Spice Girls zooming around on top of London cabs. *I think marriage is nearly always an unfathomable entity, even to the people inside it,* Della Winn had said. Perhaps Robin and Matthew were even now in bed together. Was pulling a phone out of her hand any worse than deleting her call history? She had stayed with Matthew after that. Where was her red line?

And Matthew was surely too careful of his own reputation and prospects to abandon all civilized norms. One of Strike's last thoughts before falling asleep the night before had been that Robin had successfully fought off the Shacklewell Ripper, a grisly reflection, perhaps, but one that brought a certain reassurance.

The detective was perfectly aware that the state of his junior partner's marriage ought to be the least of his worries, given that he so far had no concrete information for the client who was currently paying three full-time investigators to find out the facts about her father's death. Nevertheless, as the traffic finally moved on, Strike's thoughts continued to eddy around Robin and Matthew until at last he saw a signpost to the psychiatric clinic and, with an effort, focused his mind on the forthcoming interview.

Unlike the gigantic rectangular prism of concrete and black glass where Jack had been admitted a few weeks earlier, the hospital outside which Strike parked twenty minutes later boasted crocketed spires and byzantine windows covered with iron bars. In Strike's opinion it looked like the bastard offspring of a gingerbread palace and a gothic prison. A Victorian stonemason had carved the word "Sanatorium" into the dirty redbrick arch over the double doorway.

Already five minutes late, Strike flung open the driver's door and, not bothering to change his trainers for smarter footwear, locked the BMW and hurried, limping, up the grubby front steps.

Inside he found a chilly hallway with high, off-white ceilings, churchlike windows and a general suspicion of decay barely kept at bay by the fug of disinfectant. Spotting the ward number he had been given by phone, he set off along a corridor to the left.

Sunlight falling through the barred windows cast striped patches onto the off-white walls, which were hung crookedly with art, some of which had been done by former patients. As Strike passed a series of collages depicting detailed farmyard scenes in felt, tinsel and yarn, a skeletal teenage girl emerged from a bathroom alongside a nurse. Neither of them seemed to notice Strike. Indeed, the girl's dull eyes were focused, it seemed to him, inward upon a battle she was waging far from the real world.

Strike was faintly surprised to discover the double doors to the locked ward at the end of the ground floor corridor. Some vague association with belfries and Rochester's first wife had led him to picture it on an upper floor, hidden perhaps in one of those pointed spires. The reality was entirely prosaic: a large green buzzer on the wall, which Strike pressed, and a male nurse with bright red hair peering through a small glass window, who turned to speak to somebody behind him. The door opened and Strike was admitted.

The ward had four beds and a seating area, where two patients in day clothes were sitting, playing drafts: an older, apparently toothless man and a pale youth with a thickly bandaged neck. A cluster of people were standing around a workstation just inside the door: an orderly, two more nurses, and what Strike assumed to be two doctors, one male, one female. All turned to stare at him as he entered. One of the nurses nudged the other.

"Mr. Strike," said the male doctor, who was short, rather foxy in appearance and had a strong Mancunian accent. "How do you do? Colin Hepworth, we spoke on the phone. This is my colleague, Kamila Muhammad."

Strike shook hands with the woman, whose navy trouser suit reminded him of a policewoman's.

"We're both going to be sitting in on your interview with Billy," she said. "He's just gone to the bathroom. He's quite excited about seeing you again. We thought we'd use one of our interview rooms. It's right here."

She led him around the workstation, the nurses still watching avidly, into a small room containing four chairs and a desk that had been bolted to the floor. The walls were pale pink but otherwise bare.

"Ideal," said Strike. It was like a hundred interview rooms he had used in the military police. There, too, third parties had often been present, usually lawyers.

"A quick word before we start," said Kamila Muhammad, pulling the door to on Strike and her colleague, so that the nurses couldn't hear their conversation. "I don't know how much you know about Billy's condition?"

"His brother told me it's schizoid affective disorder."

"That's right," she said. "He went off his medication and ended up in a full-blown psychotic episode, which by the sounds of it is when he came to see you."

"Yeah, he seemed pretty disturbed at the time. He looked as though he'd been sleeping rough, as well."

"He probably had been. His brother told us he'd been missing around a week at that point. We don't believe Billy's psychotic anymore," she said, "but he's still quite closed down, so it's hard to gauge to what degree he's engaged with reality. It can be difficult to get an accurate picture of someone's mental state where there are paranoid and delusional symptoms."

"We're hoping that you can help us disentangle some of the facts from the fiction," said the Mancunian. "You've been a recurring motif in his conversation ever since he was sectioned. He's been very keen to talk to you, but not so much to any of us. He's also expressed fear of—of repercussions if he confides in anyone and, again, it's difficult to know whether that fear is part of his illness or, ah, whether there's someone who he genuinely has reason to fear. Because, ah—"

He hesitated, as though trying to choose his words carefully. Strike said:

"I'd imagine his brother could be scary if he chose to be," and the psychiatrist seemed relieved to have been understood without breaking confidentiality.

"You know his brother, do you?"

"I've met him. Does he visit often?"

"He's been in a couple of times, but Billy's often been more distressed and agitated after seeing him. If he seems to be similarly affected during your interview—" said the Mancunian.

"Understood," said Strike.

"Funny, really, seeing you here," said Colin, with a faint grin. "We assumed that his fixation with you was all part of his psychosis. An obsession with a celebrity is quite common with these kinds of disorders... As a matter of fact," he said candidly, "just a couple of days ago, Kamila and I were agreeing that his fixation with you would preclude an early discharge. Lucky you called, really."

"Yeah," said Strike drily, "that is lucky."

The redheaded male nurse knocked on the door and put his head in.

"That's Billy ready to talk to Mr. Strike."

"Great," said the female psychiatrist. "Eddie, could we get some tea in here? Tea?" she asked Strike over her shoulder. He nodded. She opened the door. "Come in, Billy."

And there he was: Billy Knight, wearing a gray sweatshirt and jogging pants, his feet in hospital slippers. The sunken eyes were still deeply shadowed, and at some point since he and Strike had last seen each other, he had shaven his head. The finger and thumb of his left hand were bandaged. Even through the tracksuit that somebody, presumably Jimmy, had brought him to wear, Strike could tell that he was underweight, but while his fingernails were bitten to bloody stubs and there was an angry sore at the corner of his mouth, there was no longer an animal stench about him. He shuffled inside the interview room, staring at Strike, then held out a bony hand, which Strike shook. Billy addressed the doctors.

"Are you two going to stay?"

"Yes," said Colin, "but don't worry. We're going to keep quiet. You can say whatever you like to Mr. Strike."

Kamila positioned two chairs against the wall and Strike and Billy sat down opposite each other, the desk between them. Strike could have wished for a less formal configuration of furniture, but his experience in Special Investigation Branch had taught him that a solid barrier between questioner and interviewee was often useful, and doubtless this was just as true on a locked psychiatric ward.

"I've been trying to find you, since you first came to see me," Strike said. "I've been quite worried about you."

"Yeah," said Billy. "Sorry."

"Can you remember what you said to me at the office?"

Absently, it seemed, Billy touched his nose and his sternum, but it was a ghost of the tic he had exhibited in Denmark Street, and almost as though he sought to remind himself how he had felt then.

"Yeah," he said, with a small, humorless smile. "I told you about the kid, up by the horse. The one I saw strangled."

"D'you still think you witnessed a child being strangled?" asked Strike.

Billy raised a forefinger to his mouth, gnawed at the nail and nodded.

"Yeah," he said, removing the finger. "I saw it. Jimmy says I imagined it because I'm—you know. Ill. You know Jimmy, don't you? Went to the White Horse after him, didn't you?" Strike nodded. "He was fucking livid. White Horse," said Billy, with a sudden laugh. "That's funny. Shit, that's funny. I never even thought of that before."

"You told me you saw a child killed 'up by the horse.' Which horse did you mean?"

"White Horse of Uffington," said Billy. "Big chalk figure, up on the hill, near where I grew up. Doesn't look like a horse. More like a dragon and it's on Dragon Hill, as well. I've never understood why they all say it's a horse."

"Can you tell me exactly what you saw up there?"

Like the skeletal girl Strike had just passed, he had the impression that Billy was staring inside himself, and that outer reality had temporarily ceased to exist for him. Finally, he said quietly:

"I was a little kid, proper little. I think they'd given me something. I felt sick and ill, like I was dreaming, slow and groggy, and they kept trying to make me repeat words and stuff and I couldn't speak properly and they all thought it was funny. I fell over in the grass on the way up. One of them carried me for a bit. I wanted to sleep."

"You think you'd been given drugs?"

"Yeah," said Billy dully. "Hash, probably, Jimmy usually had some. I think Jimmy took me up the hill with them to keep my father from knowing what they'd done."

"Who do you mean by 'they'?"

"I don't know," said Billy simply. "Grown-ups. Jimmy's ten years older'n me. Dad used to make him look after me all the time, if he was out with his drinking mates. This lot came to the house in the night and I woke up. One of them gave me a yogurt to eat. There was another little kid there. A girl. And then we all went out in a car...I didn't want to go. I felt sick. I was crying but Jimmy belted me.

"And we went to the horse in the dark. Me and the little girl were the only kids. She was howling," said Billy and the skin of his gaunt face seemed to shrink more tightly to his bones as he said it. "Screaming for her mum and *he* said, 'Your mum can't hear you now, she's gone.'"

"Who said that?" asked Strike.

"Him," whispered Billy. "The one that strangled her."

The door opened and a new nurse brought in tea.

"Here we go," she said brightly, her eager eyes on Strike. The male psychiatrist frowned at her slightly and she withdrew, closing the door again.

"Nobody's ever believed me," said Billy, and Strike heard the underlying plea. "I've tried to remember more, I wish I could, if I've got to think about it all the time I wish I could remember more of it.

"He strangled her to stop her making a noise. I don't think he meant it to go that far. They all panicked. I can remember someone shouting 'You've killed her!'...or him," Billy said quietly. "Jimmy said afterwards it was a boy, but he won't admit that now. Says I'm making it all up. 'Why would I say it was a boy when none of it ever fucking happened, you're mental.' It was a girl," said Billy stubbornly. "I don't know why he tried to say it wasn't. They called her a girl's name. I can't remember what it was, but it was a girl.

"I saw her fall. Dead. Limp on the ground. It was dark. And then they panicked.

"I can't remember anything about going back down the hill, can't remember anything after that except the burial, down in the dell by my dad's place."

"The same night?" asked Strike.

"I think so, I think it was," said Billy nervously. "Because I remember looking out of my bedroom window and it was still dark and they were carrying it to the dell, my dad and *him*."

"Who's 'him'?"

"The one who killed her. I think it was him. Big guy. White hair. And they put a bundle in the ground, all wrapped up in a pink blanket, and they closed it in."

"Did you ask your father about what you'd seen?"

"No," said Billy. "You didn't ask my dad questions about what he did for the family."

"For which family?"

Billy frowned in what seemed to be genuine puzzlement.

"You mean, for your family?"

"No. The family he worked for. The Chiswells."

Strike had the impression that this was the first time the dead minister's family name had been mentioned in front of the two psychiatrists. He saw two pens falter.

"How was the burial connected with them?"

Billy seemed confused. He opened his mouth to say something, appeared to change his mind, frowned around the pale pink walls and fell to gnawing his forefinger again. Finally, he said:

"I don't know why I said that."

It didn't feel like a lie or a denial. Billy seemed genuinely surprised by the words that had fallen out of his mouth.

"You can't remember hearing anything, or seeing anything, that would make you think he was burying the child for the Chiswells?"

"No," said Billy slowly, brow furrowed. "I just...I thought then, when I said it...he was doing a favor for...like I heard something, after..."

He shook his head.

"Ignore that, I don't know why I said it."

People, places and things, thought Strike, taking out his notebook and opening it.

"Other than Jimmy and the little girl who died," said Strike, "what can you remember about the group of people who went to the horse that night? How many of them would you say were there?"

Billy thought hard.

"I don't know. Maybe...maybe eight, ten people?"

"All men?"

"No. There were women, too."

Over Billy's shoulder, Strike saw the female psychiatrist raise her eyebrows.

"Can you remember anything else about the group? I know you were young," Strike said, anticipating Billy's objection, "and I know you might have been given something that disoriented you, but can you remember anything you haven't told me? Anything they did? Anything they were wearing? Can you remember anyone's hair or skin color? Anything at all?"

There was a long pause, then Billy closed his eyes briefly and shook his head once, as though disagreeing firmly with a suggestion only he could hear.

"She was dark. The little girl. Like..."

By a tiny turn of his head, he indicated the female doctor behind him.

"Asian?" said Strike.

"Maybe," said Billy, "yeah. Black hair."

"Who carried you up the hill?"

"Jimmy and one of the other men took turns."

"Nobody talked about why they were going up there in the dark?"

"I think they wanted to get to the eye," said Billy.

"The eye of the horse?"

"Yeah."

"Why?"

"I don't know," said Billy, and he ran his hands nervously over his shaven head. "There are stories about the eye, you know. He strangled her in the eye, I know that. I can remember that, all right. She pissed herself as she died. I saw it spattering on the white."

"And you can't remember anything about the man who did it?"

But Billy's face had crumpled. Hunched over, he heaved with dry sobs, shaking his head. The male doctor half rose from his seat. Billy seemed to sense the movement, because he steadied himself and shook his head.

"I'm all right," he said, "I want to tell him. I've got to know if it's real. All my life, I can't stand it anymore, I've got to know. Let him ask me, I know he's got to. Let him ask me," said Billy, "I can take it."

The psychiatrist sat slowly back down.

"Don't forget your tea, Billy."

"Yeah," said Billy, blinking away the tears in his eyes and wiping his nose on the back of his sleeve. "All right."

He took the mug between his bandaged hand and his good one, and took a sip.

"OK to continue?" Strike asked him.

"Yeah," said Billy quietly. "Go on."

"Can you remember anyone ever mentioning a girl called Suki Lewis, Billy?"

Strike had expected a "no." He had already turned the page to the list of questions written under the heading "Places" when Billy said:

"Yeah."

"What?" said Strike.

"The Butcher brothers knew her," said Billy. "Mates of Jimmy's from home. They did a bit of work round the Chiswells' place sometimes, with Dad. Bit of gardening and help with the horses."

"They knew Suki Lewis?"

"Yeah. She ran away, didn't she?" said Billy. "She was on the local news. The Butchers were excited because they seen her picture on the telly and they knew her family. Her mum was a headcase. Yeah, she was in care and she ran away to Aberdeen."

"Aberdeen?"

"Yeah. That's what the Butchers said."

"She was twelve."

"She had family up there. They let her stay."

"Is that right?" said Strike.

He wondered whether Aberdeen had seemed unfathomably

remote to the teenage Butchers of Oxfordshire, and whether they had been more inclined to believe this story because it was, to them, uncheckable and so, strangely, more believable.

"We're talking about Tegan's brothers, right?" asked Strike.

"You can see he's good," Billy said naively over his shoulder, to the male psychiatrist, "can't you? See how much he knows? Yeah," he said, turning back to Strike. "She's their little sister. They were like us, working for the Chiswells. There used to be a lot to do in the old days, but they sold off a lot of the land. They don't need so many people anymore."

He drank some more tea, the mug in both hands.

"Billy," said Strike, "d'you know where you've been since you came to my office?"

At once, the tic reappeared. Billy's right hand released the warm mug and touched his nose and chest in quick, nervous succession.

"I was...Jimmy doesn't want me to talk about that," he said, setting the mug clumsily back on the desk. "He told me not to."

"I think it's more important you answer Mr. Strike's questions than worry about what your brother thinks," said the male doctor, from behind Strike. "You know, you don't have to see Jimmy if you don't want to, Billy. We can ask him to give you some time here, to get better in peace."

"Did Jimmy visit you where you've been staying?" Strike asked.

Billy chewed his lip.

"Yeah," he said at last, "and he said I had to stay there or I'd cock everything up for him again. I thought the door had explosives round it," he said, with a nervy laugh. "Thought if I tried to go out the door I'd explode. Probably not right, is it?" he said, appearing to search Strike's expression for a clue. "I get ideas about stuff sometimes, when I'm bad."

"Can you remember how you got away from the place you were being kept?"

"I thought they switched off the explosives," said Billy. "The guy told me to run for it and I did."

"What guy was this?"

"The one who was in charge of keeping me there."

"Can you remember anything you did while you were being kept captive?" Strike asked. "How you spent your time?"

The other shook his head.

"Can you remember," said Strike, "carving anything, into wood?"

Billy's gaze was full of fear and wonder. Then he laughed.

"You know it all," he said, and held up his bandaged left hand. "Knife slipped. Went right in me."

The male psychiatrist added helpfully:

"Billy had tetanus when he came in. There was a very nasty infected gash on that hand."

"What did you carve into the door, Billy?"

"I really did that, then, did I? Carved the white horse on the door? Because afterwards I didn't know if I really did that or not."

"Yeah, you did it," said Strike. "I've seen the door. It was a good carving."

"Yeah," said Billy, "well, I used to—do some of that. Carving. For my dad."

"What did you carve the horse onto?"

"Pendants," said Billy, surprisingly. "On little circles of wood with leather through 'em. For tourists. Sold them in a shop over in Wantage."

"Billy," said Strike, "can you remember how you ended up in that bathroom? Did you go there to see someone, or did somebody take you there?"

Billy's eyes roamed around the pink walls again, a deep furrow between his eyes as he thought.

"I was looking for a man called Winner...no..."

"Winn? Geraint Winn?"

"Yeah," said Billy, again surveying Strike with astonishment. "You know *everything*. How do you know all this?"

"I've been looking for you," said Strike. "What made you want to find Winn?"

"Heard Jimmy talking about him," said Billy, gnawing at his nail again. "Jimmy said Winn was going to help find out all about the kid who was killed."

"Winn was going to help find out about the child who was strangled?"

"Yeah," said Billy, nervously. "See, I thought you were one of the people trying to catch me and lock me up, after I saw you. Thought you were trying to trap me and—I get like that, when I'm bad," he said hopelessly. "So I went to Winner—Winn—instead. Jimmy had a phone number and address for him written down, so I went to find Winn and then I got caught."

"Caught?"

"By the—brown-skinned bloke," mumbled Billy, with a half-glance back at the female psychiatrist. "I was scared of him, I thought he was a terrorist and he was going to kill me, but then he told me he was working for the government, so I thought the government wanted me kept there in his house and the doors and windows were wired with explosives... but I don't think they were, really. That was just me. He probably didn't want me in his bathroom. Probably wanted to get rid of me all along," said Billy, with a sad smile. "And I wouldn't go, because I thought I'd get blown up."

His right hand crept absently back to his nose and chest.

"I think I tried to call you again, but you didn't answer."

"You did call. You left a message on my answering machine."

"Did I? Yeah... I thought you'd help me get out of there... sorry," said Billy, rubbing his eyes. "When I'm like that, I don't know what I'm doing."

"But you're sure you saw a child strangled, Billy?" asked Strike quietly.

"Oh yeah," said Billy bleakly, raising his face. "Yeah, that never goes away. I know I saw it."

"Did you ever try and dig where you thought—?"

"Christ, no," said Billy. "Go digging right by my dad's house? No. I was scared," he said weakly. "I didn't want to see it again. After they buried her, they let it grow over, nettles and weeds. I used to have dreams like you wouldn't believe. That she climbed up out of the dell in the dark, all rotting, and tried to climb in my bedroom window."

The psychiatrists' pens moved scratchily across their papers.

Strike moved down to the category of "Things" that he had written on his notebook. There were only two questions left.

"Did you ever put a cross in the ground where you saw the body buried, Billy?"

"No," said Billy, scared at the very idea. "I never went near the dell if I could avoid it, I never wanted to."

"Last question," Strike said. "Billy, did your father do anything unusual for the Chiswells? I know he was a handyman, but can you think of anything else he—?"

"What d'you mean?" said Billy.

He seemed suddenly more frightened than he had seemed all interview.

"I don't know," said Strike carefully, watching his reaction. "I just wondered—"

"Jimmy warned me about this! He told me you were snooping around Dad. You can't blame us for that, we had nothing to do with it, we were kids!"

"I'm not blaming you for anything," said Strike, but there was a clatter of chairs: Billy and the two psychiatrists had got to their feet, the female's hand hovering over a discreet button beside the door that Strike knew must be an alarm.

"Has this all been to get me to talk? You trying to get me and Jimmy in trouble?"

"No," said Strike, hoisting himself to his feet, too. "I'm here because I believe you saw a child strangled, Billy."

Agitated, mistrustful, Billy's unbandaged hand touched his nose and chest twice in quick succession.

"So why're you asking what Dad did?" he whispered. "That's not how she died, it was nothing to do with that! Jimmy'll fucking tan me," he said in a broken voice. "He told me you were after him for what Dad did."

"Nobody's going to tan anyone," said the male psychiatrist firmly. "Time's up, I think," he said briskly to Strike, pushing open the door. "Go on, Billy, out you go."

But Billy didn't move. The skin and bone might have aged, but his face betrayed the fear and hopelessness of a small, motherless child whose sanity had been broken by the men who were supposed to protect him. Strike, who had met countless rootless and neglected children during his rackety, unstable childhood, recognized in Billy's imploring expression a last plea to the adult world, to do what grown-ups were meant to do, and impose order on chaos, substitute sanity for brutality. Face to face, he felt a strange kinship with the emaciated, shaven-headed psychiatric patient, because he recognized the same craving for order in himself. In his case, it had led him to the official side of the desk, but perhaps the only difference between the two of them was that Strike's mother had lived long enough, and loved him well enough, to stop him breaking when life threw terrible things at him.

"I'm going to find out what happened to the kid you saw strangled, Billy. That's a promise."

The psychiatrists looked surprised, even disapproving. It was not part of their profession, Strike knew, to make definitive statements or guarantee resolutions. He put his notebook back into his pocket, moved from behind the desk and held out his hand. After a few long moments' consideration, the animosity seemed to seep out of Billy. He shuffled back to Strike, took his proffered hand and held it over-long, his eyes filling with tears.

In a whisper, so that neither of the doctors could hear, he said:

"I hated putting the horse on them, Mr. Strike. I hated it."

57

Have you the courage and the strength of will for that, Rebecca?
Henrik Ibsen, *Rosmersholm*

Vanessa's one-bedroomed flat occupied the ground floor of a detached house a short distance from Wembley Stadium. Before leaving for work that morning, she had given Robin a spare key to her flat, along with a kindly assurance that she knew that it would take Robin longer than a couple of days to find a new place to live, and that she didn't mind her staying until she managed to do so.

They had sat up late drinking the night before. Vanessa had told Robin the full story of finding out that her ex-fiancé had cheated on her, a story full of twists and counter-twists that Vanessa had never told before, which included the setting up of two fake Facebook pages as bait for both her ex and his lover, which had resulted, after three months of patient coaxing, in Vanessa receiving nude pictures from both of them. As impressed as she was shocked, Robin had laughed as Vanessa reenacted the scene in which she passed her ex the pictures, hidden inside the Valentine card she had handed across a table for two in their favorite restaurant.

"You're too nice, girl," said Vanessa, steely-eyed over her Pinot Grigio. "At a bare minimum I'd have kept her bleeding earring and turned it into a pendant."

Vanessa was now at work. A spare duvet sat neatly folded at the end of the sofa on which Robin was sitting, with her laptop open in front of her. She had spent the entire afternoon scanning available rooms in shared properties, which were all she could possibly afford on the salary that Strike was paying her. The memory of the bunk bed in Flick's flat kept recurring as she scanned the adverts in her price range, some of which featured stark, barrack-like rooms with multiple beds inside them, others with photographs that looked as though they ought to feature attached to news stories about reclusive hoarders discovered dead by neighbors. Last night's laughter seemed remote now. Robin was ignoring the painful, hard lump in her throat that refused to dissolve, no matter how many cups of tea she consumed.

Matthew had tried to contact her twice that day. Neither time had she picked up and he hadn't left a message. She would need to contact a lawyer about divorce soon, and that would cost money she didn't have, but her first priority had to be finding herself a place to live and continuing to put in the usual number of hours on the Chiswell case, because if Strike had cause to feel she wasn't pulling her weight she would be endangering the only part of her life that currently had worth.

You bailed out on uni. Now you're bailing out on us. You even bailed on your therapist. You're a fucking flake.

The photographs of grim rooms in unknown flats kept dissolving before her eyes as she pictured Matthew and Sarah in the heavy mahogany bed that her father-in-law had bought, and when this happened Robin's insides seemed to turn to liquid lead and her self-control threatened to melt away and she wanted to phone Matthew back and scream at him, but she didn't, because she refused to be what he wanted to make her, the irrational, incontinent, uncontrolled woman, the *fucking flake*.

And anyway, she had news for Strike, news she was keen to impart once he had finished his interview with Billy. Raphael Chiswell had answered his mobile at eleven o'clock that morning and, after some initial coldness, had agreed to talk to her, but only at a place of his choosing. An hour later, she had received a call from Tegan Butcher, who had not required much persuasion to agree to an interview. Indeed, she seemed disappointed to be talking to the famous Strike's partner rather than the man himself.

Robin copied down the details of a room in Putney (*live-in land-lady, vegetarian household, must like cats*), checked the time and decided to change into the only dress she had brought with her from Albury Street, which was hanging, ironed and ready, from the top of Vanessa's kitchen door. It would take her over an hour to get from Wembley to the restaurant in Old Brompton Road, where she and Raphael had agreed to meet, and she feared that she needed more time than usual to make herself presentable.

The face staring out of Vanessa's bathroom mirror was white, with eyes still puffy with lack of sleep. Robin was still trying to paint out the shadows with concealer when her mobile rang.

"Cormoran, hi," said Robin, switching to speakerphone. "Did you see Billy?"

His account of the interview with Billy took ten minutes, during which time Robin finished her makeup, brushed her hair and pulled on the dress.

"You know," Strike finished, "I'm starting to wonder whether we shouldn't do what Billy wanted us to do in the first place: dig."

"Mm," said Robin, and then, "Wait—what? You mean...literally?"

"It might come to that," said Strike.

For the first time all day, Robin's own troubles were entirely eclipsed by something else, something monstrous. Jasper Chiswell's had been the first body she had seen outside the comforting, sanitized context of the hospital and the funeral parlor. Even the memory of the shrink-wrapped turnip head with its dark, gasping cavity for a mouth paled beside the prospect of earth and worms, a decaying blanket and a child's rotting bones.

"Cormoran, if you think there's genuinely a child buried in the dell, we should be telling the police."

"I might, if I thought Billy's psychiatrists would vouch for him, but they won't. I had a long talk with them after the interview. They can't say one hundred percent that the child strangling *didn't* happen—the old impossible-to-prove-a-negative problem—but they don't believe it."

"They think he's making it up?"

"Not in the normal sense. They think it's a delusion or, at best, that he misinterpreted something he saw when he was very young. Maybe even something on TV. It would be consistent with his overall symptoms. I think myself there's unlikely to be anything down there, but it would be good to know for sure.

"Anyway, how's your day been? Any news?"

"What?" Robin repeated numbly. "Oh—yes. I'm meeting Raphael for a drink at seven o'clock."

"Excellent work," said Strike. "Where?"

"Place called Nam something...Nam Long Le Shaker?"

"The place in Chelsea?" said Strike. "I was there, a long time ago. Not the best evening I've ever had."

"And Tegan Butcher rang back. She's a bit of a fan of yours, by the sound of it."

"Just what this case needs, another mentally disturbed witness."

"Tasteless," said Robin, trying to sound amused. "Anyway, she's living with her mum in Woolstone and working at a bar at Newbury Racecourse. She says she doesn't want to meet us in the village because her mum won't like her getting mixed up with us, so she wonders whether we could come and see her at Newbury."

"How far's that from Woolstone?"

"Twenty miles or so?"

"All right," said Strike, "how about we take the Land Rover out to Newbury to interview Tegan and then maybe swing by the dell, just for another look?"

"Um...yes, OK," said Robin, her mind racing over the logistics of having to return to Albury Street for the Land Rover. She had left it behind because parking places required a permit on Vanessa's street. "When?"

"Whenever Tegan can see us, but ideally this week. Sooner the better."

"OK," said Robin, thinking of the tentative plans she had made to view rooms over the next couple of days.

"Everything all right, Robin?"

"Yes, of course."

"Ring me when you've spoken to Raphael then, OK?"

"Will do," said Robin, glad to end the call. "Speak later."

58

. . . I believe two different kinds of will can exist at the same time in one person.

Henrik Ibsen, *Rosmersholm*

Nam Long Le Shaker had the feeling of a decadent, colonial–era bar. Dimly lit, with leafy plants and assorted paintings and prints of beautiful women, the décor mixed Vietnamese and European styles. When Robin entered the restaurant at five past seven, she found Raphael leaning up against the bar, wearing a dark suit and tieless white shirt, already halfway down a drink and talking to the long-haired beauty who stood in front of a glittering wall of bottles.

"Hi," said Robin.

"Hello," he responded with a trace of coolness, and then, "Your eyes are different. Were they that color at Chiswell House?"

"Blue?" asked Robin, shrugging off the coat she had worn because she felt shivery, even though the evening was warm. "Yes."

"S'pose I didn't notice because half the bloody lightbulbs are missing. What are you drinking?"

Robin hesitated. She ought not to drink while conducting an interview, but at the same time, she suddenly craved alcohol. Before she could decide, Raphael said with a slight edge in his voice:

"Been undercover again today, have we?"

"Why d'you ask?"

"Your wedding ring's gone again."

"Were your eyes this sharp in the office?" asked Robin, and he grinned, reminding her why she had liked him, even against her will.

"I noticed your glasses were fake, remember?" he said. "I thought at the time you were trying to be taken seriously, because you were too pretty for politics. So these," he indicated his deep brown eyes, "may be sharp, but this," he tapped his head, "not so much."

"I'll have a glass of red," said Robin, smiling, "and I'll pay, obviously."

"If this is all on Mr. Strike, let's have dinner," said Raphael at once. "I'm starving and skint."

"Really?"

After a day of trawling through the available rooms for rent on her agency salary, she was not in the mood to hear the Chiswell definition of poverty again.

"Yeah, really, little though you might believe it," said Raphael, with a slightly acid smile, and Robin suspected he knew what she had been thinking. "Seriously, are we eating, or what?"

"Fine," said Robin, who had barely touched food all day, "let's eat."

Raphael took his bottle of beer off the bar and led her through to the restaurant where they took a table for two beside the wall. It was so early that they were the only diners.

"My mother used to come here in the eighties," said Raphael. "It was well known because the owner liked telling the rich and famous to sod off if they weren't dressed properly to come in, and they all loved it."

"Really?" said Robin, her thoughts miles away. It had just struck her that she would never again have dinner with Matthew like this, just the two of them. She remembered the very last time, at Le Manoir aux Quat'Saisons. What had he been thinking while he ate in silence? Certainly he had been furious at her for continuing to work with Strike, but perhaps he had also been weighing in his mind the competing attractions of Sarah, with her well-paid job at Christie's, her endless fund of stories about other people's wealth, and her no doubt self-confident performance in bed, where the diamond earrings her fiancé had bought her snagged on Robin's pillow.

"Listen, if eating with me's going to make you look like that, I'm fine with going back to the bar," said Raphael.

"What?" said Robin, surprised out of her thoughts. "Oh—no, it isn't you."

A waiter brought over Robin's wine. She took a large slug.

"Sorry," she said. "I was just thinking about my husband. I left him last night."

As she watched Raphael freeze in surprise with the bottle at his lips, Robin knew herself to have crossed an invisible boundary. In her whole time at the agency, she had never used truths about her private life to gain another's confidence, never blended the private and the professional to win another person over. In turning Matthew's infidelity into a device to manipulate Raphael, she knew that she was doing something that would appall and disgust her husband. Their marriage, he would have thought, ought to be sacrosanct, a world apart from what he saw as her seedy, ramshackle job.

"Seriously?" said Raphael.

"Yes," said Robin, "but I don't expect you to believe me, not after all the crap I told you when I was Venetia. Anyway," she took her notebook out of her handbag, "you said you were OK with me asking some questions?"

"Er—yeah," he said, apparently unable to decide whether he was more amused or disconcerted. "Is this real? Your marriage broke up last night?"

"Yes," said Robin. "Why are you looking so shocked?"

"I don't know," said Raphael. "You just seem so...Girl Guidey." His eyes moved over her face. "It's part of the appeal."

"Could I just ask my questions?" said Robin, determinedly unfazed.

Raphael drank some beer and said:

"Always busy with the job. Turns a man's thoughts to what it would take to distract you."

"Seriously—"

"Fine, fine, questions—but let's order first. Fancy some dim sum?"

"Whatever's good," said Robin, opening her notebook.

Ordering food seemed to cheer Raphael up.

"Drink up," he said.

"I shouldn't be drinking at all," she replied, and indeed, she hadn't touched the wine since her first gulp. "OK, I wanted to talk about Ebury Street."

"Go on," said Raphael.

"You heard what Kinvara said about the keys. I wondered whether—"

"—I ever had one?" asked Raphael with equanimity. "Guess how many times I was ever in that house."

Robin waited.

"Once," said Raphael. "Never went there as a kid. When I got out of—you know—Dad, who hadn't visited me once while I was inside, invited me down to Chiswell House to see him, so I did. Brushed my hair, put on a suit, got all the way down to that hellhole and he didn't bother turning up. Detained by a late vote at the House or some crap. Picture how happy Kinvara was to have me on her hands for the night, in that bloody depressing house that I've had bad dreams about ever since I was a kid. Welcome home, Raff."

"I took the early train back to London. Following week, no contact from Dad until I get another summons, this time to go to Ebury Street. I considered just not bloody turning up. Why did I go?"

"I don't know," said Robin. "Why did you?"

He looked directly into her eyes.

"You can bloody hate someone and still wish they gave a shit about you and hate yourself for wishing it."

"Yes," said Robin quietly, "of course you can."

"So round I trot to Ebury Street, thinking I might get—not a heart to heart, I mean, you met my father—but maybe, you know, some human emotion. He opened the door, said 'There you are,' shunted me into the sitting room and there was Henry Drummond and I realized I was there for a job interview. Drummond said he'd take me on, Dad barked at me not to fuck it up and shoved me back out onto the street. First and last time I was ever inside the place," said Raphael, "so I can't say I've got fond associations with it."

He paused to consider what he'd just said, then let out a short laugh.

"And my father killed himself there, of course. I was forgetting that."

"No key," said Robin, making a note.

"No, among the many things I didn't get that day were a spare key and an invitation to let myself in whenever I fancied it."

"I need to ask you something that might seem as though it's slightly out of left field," said Robin cautiously.

"This sounds interesting," said Raphael, leaning forwards.

"Did you ever suspect that your father was having an affair?"

"What?" he said, almost comically taken aback. "No—but—*what?*"

"Over the last year or so?" said Robin. "While he was married to Kinvara?"

He seemed incredulous.

"OK," said Robin, "if you don't—"

"What on *earth* makes you think he was having an affair?"

"Kinvara was always very possessive, very concerned about your father's whereabouts, wasn't she?"

"Yeah," said Raphael, now smirking, "but you know why that was. That was *you.*"

"I heard that she broke down months before I went to work in the office. She told somebody that your father had cheated on her. She was distraught, by all accounts. It was around the time her mare was put down and she—"

"—hit Dad with the hammer?" He frowned. "Oh. I thought that was because of her not wanting the horse put down. Well, I suppose Dad was a ladies' man when he was younger. Hey—maybe that's what he was up to, the night I went down to Chiswell House and he stayed up in London? Kinvara was definitely expecting him back and she was furious when he cried off at the last minute."

"Yes, maybe," said Robin, making a note. "Can you remember what date that was?"

"Er—yeah, as a matter of fact, I can. You don't tend to forget the day you're released from jail. I got out on Wednesday the sixteenth of February last year, and Dad asked me to go down to Chiswell House on the following Saturday, so...the nineteenth."

Robin made a note.

"You never saw or heard signs there was another woman?"

"Come on," said Raphael, "you were there, at the Commons. You saw how little I had to do with him. Was he going to tell me he was playing around?"

"He told you about seeing the ghost of Jack o'Kent roaming the grounds at night."

"That was different. He was drunk then, and—morbid. Weird.

Banging on about divine retribution...I don't know, I suppose he could've been talking about an affair. Maybe he'd grown a conscience at last, three wives down the line."

"I didn't think he married your mother?"

Raphael's eyes narrowed.

"Sorry. Momentarily forgot I'm the bastard."

"Oh, come on," said Robin gently, "you know I didn't mean—"

"All right, sorry," he muttered. "Being touchy. Being left out of a parent's will does that to a person."

Robin remembered Strike's dictum about inheritance: *It is the money, and it isn't*, and in an uncanny echo of her thoughts, Raphael said:

"It isn't the money, although God knows I could use the money. I'm jobless, and I don't think old Henry Drummond's going to give me a reference, do you? And now my mother looks like she's going to settle permanently in Italy, so she's talking about selling the London flat, which means I'll be homeless. It'll come to this, you know," he said bitterly. "I'll end up as Kinvara's bloody stable boy. No one else will work for her and no one else'll employ me...

"But it's not just the money. When you're left out of the will...well, *left out*, that says it all. The last statement of a dead man to his family and I didn't rate a single mention and now I've got fucking Torquil advising me to piss off to Siena with my mother and 'start again.' Tosser," said Raphael, with a dangerous expression.

"Is that where your mother lives? Siena?"

"Yeah. She's shacked up with an Italian count these days, and believe me, the last thing he wants is her twenty-nine-year-old son moving in. He's showing no sign of wanting to marry her and she's starting to worry about her old age, hence the idea of flogging the flat here. She's getting a bit long in the tooth to pull the trick she did on my father."

"What d'you—?"

"She got pregnant on purpose. Don't look so shocked. My mother doesn't believe in shielding me from the realities of life. She told me the story years ago. I'm a gamble that didn't come off. She thought he'd marry her if she got pregnant, but as you've just pointed out—"

"I said I'm sorry," said Robin. "I am. It was really insensitive and—and stupid."

She thought perhaps Raphael was about to tell her to go to hell, but instead he said quietly:

"See, you *are* sweet. You weren't entirely acting, were you? In the office?"

"I don't know," said Robin. "I suppose not."

Feeling his legs shift under the table, she moved very slightly backwards again.

"What's your husband like?" Raphael asked.

"I don't know how to describe him."

"Does he work for Christie's?"

"No," said Robin. "He's an accountant."

"Christ," said Raphael, appalled. "Is that what you like?"

"He wasn't an accountant when I met him. Can we go back over your father calling you on the morning he died?"

"If you like," said Raphael, "but I'd much rather talk about you."

"Well, why don't you tell me what happened that morning and then you can ask me whatever you like," said Robin.

A fleeting smile passed over Raphael's face. He took a swig of beer and said:

"Dad called me. Told me he thought Kinvara was about to do something stupid and told me to go straight down to Woolstone and stop it. I *did* ask why it had to be me, you know."

"You didn't tell us that at Chiswell House," said Robin, looking up from her notes.

"Of course I didn't, because the others were there. Dad said he didn't want to ask Izzy. He was quite rude about her on the phone...he was an ungrateful shit, really he was," said Raphael. "She worked her fingers to the bloody bone and you saw how he treated her."

"What do you mean, rude?"

"He said she'd shout at Kinvara, upset her and make it worse or something. Pot and bloody kettle, but there you are. But the truth is," said Raphael, "that he saw me as a kind of upper servant and Izzy as proper family. He didn't mind me getting my hands dirty and it didn't matter if I pissed off his wife by barging into her house and stopping her—"

"Stopping her what?"

"Ah," said Raphael, "food."

The dim sum placed on the table before them, the waitress retreated.

"What did you stop Kinvara doing?" Robin repeated. "Leaving your father? Hurting herself?"

"I love this stuff," said Raphael, examining a prawn dumpling.

"She left a note," persisted Robin, "saying she was leaving. Did your father send you down there to persuade her not to go? Was he afraid Izzy would egg her on to leave him?"

"D'you seriously think I could persuade Kinvara to stay in the marriage? Never having to lay eyes on me again would've been one more incentive to go."

"Then why did he send you to her?"

"I've told you," said Raphael. "He thought she was going to do something stupid."

"Raff," said Robin, "you can keep playing silly buggers—"

He corpsed.

"Christ, you sound Yorkshire when you say that. Say it again."

"The police think there's something fishy about your story of what you were up to that morning," said Robin. "And so do we."

That seemed to sober him up.

"How do you know what the police are thinking?"

"We've got contacts on the force," said Robin. "Raff, you've given everyone the impression that your father was trying to stop Kinvara hurting herself, but nobody really buys that. The stable girl was there. Tegan. She could have prevented Kinvara from hurting herself."

Raphael chewed for a while, apparently thinking.

"All right," he sighed. "All right, here it is. You know how Dad had sold off everything that would raise a few hundred quid, or given it to Peregrine?"

"Who?"

"All right, *Pringle*," said Raphael, exasperated. "I prefer not to use their stupid bloody nicknames.

"He didn't sell off everything of value," said Robin.

"What d'you mean?"

"That picture of the mare and foal is worth five to eight—"

Robin's mobile rang. She knew from the ringtone that it was Matthew.

"Aren't you going to get that?"

"No," said Robin.

She waited until the phone had stopped ringing, then took it out of her bag.

"'Matt,'" said Raphael, reading the name upside down. "That's the accountant, is it?"

"Yes," said Robin, silencing the phone, but it immediately began to vibrate in her hand instead. Matthew had called back.

"Block him," suggested Raphael.

"Yes," said Robin, "good idea."

All that was important to her right now was keeping Raphael cooperative. He seemed to enjoy watching her block Matthew. She put the mobile back in her bag and said:

"Go on about the paintings."

"Well, you know how Dad had offloaded all the valuable ones through Drummond?"

"Some of us think five thousand pounds worth of picture is quite valuable," said Robin, unable to help herself.

"Fine, Ms. Lefty," said Raphael, suddenly nasty. "You can keep *sneering* about how people like me don't know the value of money—"

"Sorry," said Robin quickly, cursing herself. "I am, seriously. Look, I've—well, I've been trying to find a room to rent this morning. Five thousand pounds would change my life right now."

"Oh," said Raphael, frowning. "I—OK. Actually, if it comes to that *I'd* leap at the chance of five grand in my pocket right now, but I'm talking about *seriously* valuable stuff, worth tens and hundreds of thousands, things that my father wanted to keep in the family. He'd already handed them on to little *Pringle* to avoid death duties. There was a Chinese lacquer cabinet, an ivory workbox and a couple of other things, but there was also the necklace."

"Which—?"

"It's a big ugly diamond thing," said Raphael, and with the hand not spearing dumplings he mimed a thick collar. "Important *stones*. It's come down through five generations or something and the convention was that it went to the eldest daughter on her twenty-first, but my father's father, who as you might have heard was a bit of a playboy—"

"This is the one who married Tinky the nurse?"

"She was his third or fourth," said Raphael, nodding. "I can never remember. Anyway, he only had sons, so he let all his wives wear the thing in turn, then left it to my father, who kept the new tradition going. His wives got to wear it—even my mother got a shot—and he forgot about the handing on to the daughter on her twenty-first bit, Pringle didn't get it and he didn't mention it in his will."

"So—wait, d'you mean it's now—?"

"Dad called me up that morning and told me I had to get hold of the bloody thing. Simple job, kind of thing anyone would enjoy," he said, sarcastically. "Bust in on a stepmother who hates my guts, find out where she's keeping a valuable necklace, then steal it from under her nose."

"So you think your father believed that she was leaving him, and was worried that she was going to take it with her?"

"I suppose so," said Raphael.

"How did he sound on the phone?"

"I told you this. Groggy. I thought it was a hangover. After I heard he'd killed himself," Raphael faltered, ". . . well."

"Well?"

"To tell you the truth," said Raphael, "I couldn't get it out of my head that the last thing Dad wanted to say to me in this life was, 'run along and make sure your sister gets her diamonds.' Words to treasure forever, eh?"

At a loss for anything to say, Robin took another sip of wine, then asked quietly:

"Do Izzy and Fizzy realize the necklace is Kinvara's now?"

Raphael's lips twisted in an unpleasant smile.

"Well, they know it is legally, but here's the really funny thing: they think she's going to hand it over to them. After everything they've said about her, after calling her a gold-digger for years, slagging her off at every possible opportunity, they can't quite grasp that she won't hand the necklace over to Fizzy for Flopsy—damn it—*Florence*—because," he affected a shrill upper-class voice, "'Darling, even *TTS* wouldn't do that, it belongs in *the family*, she *must realize* she can't sell it.'

"Bullets would bounce off their self-regard. They think there's a kind of natural law in operation, where Chiswells get what they want and lesser beings just fall into line."

"How did Henry Drummond know you were trying to stop Kinvara keeping the necklace? He told Cormoran you went to Chiswell House for noble reasons."

Raphael snorted.

"Cat's really out of the bag, isn't it? Yeah, apparently Kinvara left a message for Henry the day before Dad died, asking where she could get a valuation on the necklace."

"Is that why he phoned your father that morning?"

"Exactly. To warn him what she was up to."

"Why didn't you tell the police all this?"

"Because once the others find out she's planning to sell it, the whole thing's going to turn nuclear. There'll be an almighty row and the family'll go to lawyers and expect me to join them in kicking the shit out of Kinvara, and meanwhile I'm still treated like a second-class citizen, like a fucking *courier*, driving all the old paintings up to Drummond in London and hearing how much Dad was getting for them, and not a penny of *that* did I ever see—I'm not getting caught up in the middle of the great necklace scandal, I'm not playing their bloody game. I should've told Dad to stuff it, the day he phoned," said Raphael, "but he didn't sound well, and I suppose I felt sorry for him, or something, which only goes to prove they're right, I'm *not* a proper bloody Chiswell."

He had run out of breath. Two couples had joined them in the restaurant now. Robin watched in the mirror as a well-groomed blonde did a double take at Raphael as she sat down with her florid, overweight companion.

"So, why did you leave Matthew?" Raphael asked.

"He cheated," said Robin. She didn't have the energy to lie.

"Who with?"

She had the impression he was seeking to redress some kind of power balance. However much anger and contempt he had displayed during the outburst about his family, she had heard the hurt, too.

"With a friend of his from university," said Robin.

"How did you find out?"

"A diamond earring, in our bed."

"Seriously?"

"Seriously," said Robin.

She felt a sudden wave of depression and fatigue at the idea of traveling all the way back to that hard sofa in Wembley. She had not yet called her parents to tell them what had happened.

"Under normal circumstances," said Raphael, "I'd be putting the moves on you. Well, not right now. Not tonight. But give it a couple of weeks..."

"Trouble is, I look at you," he raised a forefinger, and pointed first to her, and then to an imaginary figure behind her, "and I see your one-legged boss looming over your shoulder."

"Is there any particular reason you feel the need to mention him being one-legged?"

Raphael grinned.

"Protective, aren't you?"

"No, I—"

"It's all right. Izzy fancies him, too."

"I never—"

"Defensive, too."

"Oh, for God's sake," said Robin, half-laughing, and Raphael grinned.

"I'm having another beer. Drink that wine, why don't you?" he said, indicating her glass, which was still two-thirds full.

When he had procured another bottle, he said with a malevolent grin, "Izzy's always liked bits of rough. Did you notice the charged look from Fizzy to Izzy when Jimmy Knight's name was mentioned?"

"I did, actually," said Robin. "What was that about?"

"Freddie's eighteenth birthday party," said Raphael, smirking. "Jimmy crashed it with a couple of mates and Izzy—how do I put this delicately?—*lost* something in his company."

"Oh," said Robin, astonished.

"She was blind drunk. It's passed into family legend. I wasn't there. I was too young.

"Fizzy's so amazed at the idea that her sister could have slept with the estate carpenter's son that she thinks he must have some sort of supernatural, demonic sex appeal. *That's* why she thinks Kinvara was slightly on his side, when he turned up asking for money."

"What?" said Robin sharply, reaching for her notebook again, which had fallen closed.

"Don't get too excited," said Raphael, "I still don't know what he was blackmailing Dad about, I never did. Not a full member of the family, you see, so not to be fully trusted.

"Kinvara told you this at Chiswell House, don't you remember? She was alone at home, the first time Jimmy turned up. Dad was in London again. From what I've pieced together, when she and Dad first talked it over, she argued Jimmy's case. Fizzy thinks that's down to Jimmy's sex appeal. Would you say he's got any?"

"I suppose some people might think he has," said Robin indifferently, who was making notes. "Kinvara thought your father should pay Jimmy his money, did she?"

"From what I understand," said Raphael, "Jimmy didn't frame it as blackmail on the first approach. She thought Jimmy had a legitimate claim and argued for giving him something."

"When was this, d'you know?"

"Search me," said Raphael, shaking his head. "I think I was in jail at the time. Bigger things to worry about . . .

"Guess," he said, for the second time, "how often any of them have asked me what it was like in jail?"

"I don't know," said Robin cautiously.

"Fizzy, never. Dad, never—"

"You said Izzy visited."

"Yeah," he acknowledged, with a tip of the bottle to his sister. "Yeah, she did, bless her. Good old Torks has made a couple of jokes about not wanting to bend over in the shower. I suggested," said Raphael, with a hard smile, "that he'd know all about that kind of thing, what with his old pal Christopher sliding his hand between young men's legs at the office. Turns out it's serious stuff when some hairy old convict tries it, but harmless frolics for public schoolboys."

He glanced at Robin.

"I suppose you know now why Dad was taunting that poor bloke Aamir?"

She nodded.

"Which Kinvara thought was a motive for murder," said Raphael, rolling his eyes. "Projection, pure projection — they're all at it.

"Kinvara thinks Aamir killed Dad, because Dad had been cruel to him in front of a room full of people. Well, you should have heard some of the things Dad was saying to Kinvara by the end.

"Fizzy thinks Jimmy Knight might've done it because he was angry about money. *She's* bloody angry about all the family money that's vanished, but she can't say that in so many words, not when her husband's half the reason it's gone.

"Izzy thinks Kinvara must have killed Dad because Kinvara felt unloved and sidelined and disposable. Dad never thanked Izzy for a damn thing she did for him, and didn't give a toss when she said she was leaving. You get the picture?

"None of them have got the guts to say that they all felt like killing Dad at times, not now he's dead, so they project it all onto someone else. And *that*," said Raphael, "is why none of them are talking about Geraint Winn. He gets double protection, because Saint Freddie was involved in Winn's big grudge. It's staring them in the face that he had a real motive, but we're not supposed to mention that."

"Go on," said Robin, her pen at the ready. "Mention."

"No, forget it," said Raphael, "I shouldn't have —"

"I don't think you say much accidentally, Raff. Out with it."

He laughed.

"I'm trying to stop fucking over people who don't deserve it. It's all part of the great redemption project."

"Who doesn't deserve it?"

"Francesca, the little girl I — you know — at the gallery. She's the one who told me. She got it from her older sister, Verity."

"Verity," repeated Robin.

Sleep-deprived, she struggled to remember where she had heard that name. It was very like "Venetia," of course...and then she remembered.

"Wait," she said, frowning in her effort to concentrate. "There was a Verity on the fencing team with Freddie and Rhiannon Winn."

"Right in one," said Raphael.

"You all know each other," said Robin wearily, unknowingly echoing Strike's thought as she started writing again.

"Well, that's the joy of the public school system," said Raphael. "In London, if you've got the money, you meet the same three hundred people everywhere you go...Yeah, when I first arrived at Drummond's gallery, Francesca couldn't wait to tell me that her big sister had once dated Freddie. I think she thought that made the pair of us predestined, or something.

"When she realized I thought Freddie was a bit of a shit," said Raphael, "she changed tack and told me a nasty story.

"Apparently, at his eighteenth, Freddie, Verity and a couple of others decided to mete out some punishment to Rhiannon for having dared to replace Verity on the fencing team. In their view she was—I don't know—a bit common, a bit Welsh?—so they spiked her drink. All good fun. Sort of stuff that goes on the dorm, you know.

"But she didn't react too well to neat vodka—or maybe, from their point of view, she reacted really well. Anyway, they managed to take some nice pictures of her, to pass around among themselves...this was in the early days of the internet. These days I suppose half a million people would have viewed them in the first twenty-four hours, but Rhiannon only had to endure the whole fencing team and most of Freddie's mates having a good gloat.

"Anyway," said Raphael, "about a month later, Rhiannon killed herself."

"Oh my God," said Robin quietly.

"Yeah," said Raphael. "After little Franny told me the story, I asked Izzy about it. She got very upset, told me not to repeat it, ever—but she didn't deny it. I got lots of 'nobody kills themselves because of a silly joke at a party' bluster and she told me I mustn't talk about Freddie like that, it would break Dad's heart...

"Well, the dead don't have hearts to break, do they? And personally, I think it's about time somebody pissed on Freddie's eternal flame. If he hadn't been born a Chiswell, the bastard would've been in borstal. But I suppose you'll say I can talk, after what I did."

"No," said Robin gently. "That isn't what I was going to say."

The pugnacious expression faded from his face. He checked his watch.

"I'm going to have to go. I've got to be somewhere at nine."

Robin raised her hand to signal for the bill. When she turned back to Raphael, she saw his eyes moving in routine fashion over both the other women in the restaurant, and in the mirror she saw how the blonde tried to hold his gaze.

"You can go," she said, handing over her credit card to the waitress. "I don't want to make you late."

"No, I'll walk you out."

While she was still putting her credit card back into her handbag, he picked up her coat and held it up for her.

"Thank you."

"No problem."

Out on the pavement, he hailed a taxi.

"You take this one," he said. "I fancy a walk. Clear my head. I feel as though I've had a bad therapy session."

"No, it's all right," said Robin. She didn't want to charge a taxi all the way back to Wembley to Strike. "I'm going to get the Tube. Goodnight."

"'Night, Venetia," he said.

Raphael got into the taxi, which glided away, and Robin pulled her coat more tightly around herself as she walked off in the opposite direction. It had been a chaotic interview, but she had managed to get much more than she had expected out of Raphael. Taking out her mobile again, she phoned Strike.

59

We two go with each other...

Henrik Ibsen, Rosmersholm

When he saw Robin was calling him, Strike, who had taken his note-book out to the Tottenham for a drink, pocketed the former, downed the remainder of his pint in one and took the call out onto the street.

The mess that building works had made of the top of Tottenham Court Road—the rubble-strewn channel where a street had been, the portable railings and the plastic barricades, the walkways and planks that enabled tens of thousands of people to continue to pass through the busy junction—were so familiar to him now that he barely noticed them. He had not come outside for the view, but for a cigarette, and he smoked two while Robin relayed everything that Raphael had told her.

Once the call was over, Strike returned his mobile to his pocket and absentmindedly lit himself a third cigarette from the tip of the second and continued to stand there, thinking deeply about everything she had said and forcing passersby to navigate around him.

A couple of things that Robin had told him struck the detective as interesting. Having finished his third cigarette and flicked it into the open abyss in the road, Strike retreated inside the pub and ordered himself a second pint. A group of students had now taken his table, so he headed into the back, where high bar stools sat beneath a stained-glass cupola whose colors were dimmed by night. Here,

Strike took out his notebook again and re-examined the list of names over which he had pored in the early hours of Sunday, while he sought distraction from thoughts of Charlotte. After gazing at it again in the manner of a man who knows something is concealed there, he turned a few pages to reread the notes he had made of his interview with Della.

Large, hunch-backed and motionless but for the eyes flicking along the lines he had scribbled in the blind woman's house, Strike unknowingly repelled a couple of timid backpackers who had considered asking whether they might share his table and take the weight off their blistered feet. Fearing the consequences of breaking his almost tangible concentration, they retreated before he noticed them.

Strike turned back to the list of names. Married couples, lovers, business partners, siblings.

Pairs.

He flicked further backwards to the pages to find the notes he had made during the interview with Oliver, who had taken them through the forensic findings. A two-part killing, this: amitriptyline and helium, each potentially fatal on its own, yet used together.

Pairs.

Two victims, killed twenty years apart, a strangled child and a suffocated government minister, the former buried on the latter's land.

Pairs.

Strike turned thoughtfully to a blank page and made a new note for himself.

Francesca—confirm story

60

. . . you really must give me some explanation of your taking this matter—this possibility—so much to heart.

Henrik Ibsen, *Rosmersholm*

The following morning, a carefully worded official statement about Jasper Chiswell appeared in all the papers. Along with the rest of the British public, Strike learned over his breakfast that the authorities had concluded that no foreign power or terrorist organization had been involved in the untimely death of the Minister for Culture, but that no other conclusion had yet been reached.

The news that there was no news had been greeted online with barely a ripple of interest. The local postboxes of Olympic winners were still being painted gold, and the public was basking in the satisfied afterglow arising from a triumphant games, its unspent enthusiasm for all things athletic now concentrated on the imminent prospect of the Paralympics. Chiswell's death had been filed away in the popular mind as the vaguely inexplicable suicide of a wealthy Tory.

Keen to know whether this official statement indicated that the Met investigation was close to concluding, Strike called Wardle to find out what he knew.

Unfortunately, the policeman was no wiser than Strike himself. Wardle added, not without a certain irritability, that he had not had a single day off in three weeks, that the policing of the capital while the city heaved under the weight of millions of extra visitors was complex and onerous past Strike's probable understanding, and that he didn't have time to go ferreting for information on unrelated matters on Strike's behalf.

"Fair enough," said Strike, unfazed. "Only asking. Say hello to April for me."

"Oh yeah," said Wardle, before Strike could hang up. "She wanted me to ask you what you're playing at with Lorelei."

"Better let you go, Wardle, the country needs you," said Strike, and he hung up on the policeman's grudging laugh.

In the absence of information from his police contacts, and with no official standing to secure him the interviews he desired, Strike was temporarily stymied at a crucial point in the case, a frustration no more pleasant for being familiar.

A few phone calls after breakfast informed him that Francesca Pulham, Raphael's sometime colleague and lover from Drummond's gallery, was still studying in Florence, where she had been sent to remove her from his pernicious influence. Francesca's parents were currently on holiday in Sri Lanka. The Pulhams' housekeeper, who was the only person connected with the family that Strike was able to reach, refused point blank to give him telephone numbers for any of them. From her reaction, he guessed the Pulhams might be the kind of people who'd run for lawyers at the very idea of a private detective calling their house.

Having exhausted all possible avenues to the holidaying Pulhams, Strike left a polite request for an interview on Geraint Winn's voicemail, the fourth he had made that week, but the day wore on and Winn didn't call back. Strike couldn't blame him. He doubted that he would have chosen to be helpful, had he been in Winn's shoes.

Strike had not yet told Robin that he had a new theory about the case. She was busy in Harley Street, watching Dodgy Doc, but on Wednesday she called the office with the welcome news that she had arranged an interview with Tegan Butcher on Saturday at Newbury Racecourse.

"Excellent!" said Strike, cheered by the prospect of action, and striding through to the outer office to bring up Google Maps on Robin's computer. "OK, I think we're going to be looking at an overnighter. Interview Tegan, then head over to Steda Cottage once it gets dark."

"Cormoran, are you serious about this?" said Robin. "You genuinely want to go digging in the dell?"

"That sounds like a nursery rhyme," said Strike vaguely, examining B roads on the monitor. "Look, I don't think there's anything there. In fact, as of yesterday, I'm sure of it."

"What happened yesterday?"

"I had an idea. I'll tell you when I see you. Look, I promised Billy I'd find out the truth about his strangled child. There's no other way to be totally sure, is there, other than digging? But if you're feeling squeamish, you can stay in the car."

"And what about Kinvara? We'll be on her property."

"We'll hardly be digging up anything important. That whole area's waste ground. I'm going to get Barclay to meet us there, after dark. I'm not much good for digging. Will Matthew be OK if you're away overnight Saturday?"

"Fine," said Robin, with an odd inflection that made Strike suspect that he wouldn't be fine about it at all.

"And you're OK to drive the Land Rover?"

"Er—is there any chance we could take your BMW instead?"

"I'd rather not take the BMW up that overgrown track. Is there something wrong with the—?"

"No," said Robin, cutting across him. "That's fine, OK, we'll take the Land Rover."

"Great. How's Dodgy?"

"In his consulting rooms. Any news on Aamir?"

"I've got Andy trying to find the sister he's still on good terms with."

"And what are you up to?"

"I've just been reading the Real Socialist Party website."

"Why?"

"Jimmy gives quite a lot away in his blog posts. Places he's been and things he's seen. You OK to stay on Dodgy until Friday?"

"Actually," said Robin, "I was going to ask whether I could take a couple of days off to deal with some personal business."

"Oh," said Strike, brought up short.

"I've got a couple of appointments I need—I'd rather not miss," said Robin.

It wasn't convenient to Strike to have to cover Dodgy Doc himself, partly because of the continuing pain in his leg, but mainly because he was eager to continue chasing down confirmation of his theory on the Chiswell case. This was also very short notice to ask for two days' leave. On the other hand, Robin had just indicated a willingness to sacrifice her weekend to a probable wildgoose chase into the dell.

"Yeah, OK. Everything all right?"

"Fine, thanks. I'll let you know if anything interesting happens with Dodgy. Otherwise, we should probably leave London at eleven-ish on Saturday."

"Barons Court again?"

"Would it be all right if you meet me at Wembley Stadium station? It would just be easier, because of where I'm going to be on Friday night."

This, too, was inconvenient: a journey for Strike of twice the length and involving a change of Tube.

"Yeah, OK," he said again.

After Robin had hung up, he remained in her chair for a while, pondering their conversation.

She had been noticeably tight-lipped about the nature of the appointments that were so important that she didn't want to miss them. He remembered how particularly angry Matthew had sounded in the background of his calls to Robin, to discuss their pressured, unstable and occasionally dangerous job. She had twice sounded distinctly underwhelmed about the prospect of digging in the hard ground at the bottom of the dell, and now asked to drive the BMW rather than the tank-like Land Rover.

He had almost forgotten his suspicion of a couple of months ago, that Robin might be trying to get pregnant. Into his mind swam the vision of Charlotte's swollen belly at the dinner table. Robin wasn't the kind of woman who'd be able to walk away from her child as soon as it left the womb. If Robin was pregnant...

Logical and methodical as he usually was, and aware in one part of himself that he was theorizing on scant data, Strike's imagination nevertheless showed him Matthew, the father-to-be, listening in on Robin's tense request for time off for scans and medical checks, gesticulating angrily at her that the time had come to stop, to go easy on herself, to take better care.

Strike turned back to Jimmy Knight's blog, but it took him a little longer than usual to discipline his troubled mind back into obedience.

61

Oh, you can tell me. You and I are such friends, you know.

Henrik Ibsen, *Rosmersholm*

Fellow Tube travelers gave Strike a slightly wider berth than was necessary on Saturday morning, even allowing for his kit bag. He generally managed to cut a path easily through crowds, given his bulk and his boxer's profile, but the way he was muttering and cursing as he struggled up the stairs at Wembley Stadium station—the lifts weren't working—made passersby extra careful to neither jostle nor impede him.

The primary reason for Strike's bad mood was Mitch Patterson, whom he had spotted that morning from the office window, skulking in a doorway, dressed in jeans and a hoodie entirely unsuited to his age and bearing. Puzzled and angered by the private detective's reappearance, but having no route out of the building except by the front door, Strike had called a cab to wait for him at the end of the street, and left the building only once it was in position. Patterson's expression when Strike had said "Morning, Mitch" might have amused Strike, if he hadn't been so insulted that Patterson had thought he could get away with watching the agency in person.

All the way to Warren Street station, where he asked the cab to drop him, Strike had been hyper-alert, worried that Patterson had been there as a distraction or decoy, enabling a second, less obtrusive tail to follow him. Even now, as he clambered, panting, off the top of the stairs at Wembley, he turned to scrutinize the travelers for the one who ducked down, turned back or hastily concealed their face. None of them did so. On balance, Strike concluded that Patterson had been working alone; victim, perhaps, of one of the manpower problems so familiar to Strike. The fact that Patterson had chosen to cover the job rather than forgo it suggested that somebody was paying him well.

Strike hoisted his kit bag more securely onto his shoulder and set off towards the exit.

Having pondered the question during his inconvenient journey to Wembley, Strike could think of three reasons why Patterson had reappeared. The first was that the press had got wind of some interesting new development in the Met investigation into Chiswell's death, and that this had led a newspaper to rehire Patterson, his remit to find out what Strike was up to and how much he knew.

The second possibility was that someone had paid Patterson to stalk Strike, in the hopes of impeding his movements or hampering his business. That suggested that Patterson's employer was somebody that Strike was currently investigating, in which case, Patterson doing the job himself made sense: the whole point would be to destabilize Strike by letting him know that he was being watched.

The third possible reason for Patterson's renewed interest in him was the one that bothered Strike most, because he had a feeling it was most likely to be the true one. He now knew that he had been spotted in Franco's with Charlotte. His informant was Izzy, whom he had called in the hope of fleshing out details of the theory he hadn't yet confided to anyone.

"So, I hear you had dinner with Charlotte!" she had blurted, before he had managed to pose a question.

"There was no dinner. I sat with her for twenty minutes because she was feeling ill, then left."

"Oh—sorry," said Izzy, cowed by his tone. "I—I wasn't prying—Roddy Fforbes was in Franco's and he spotted the pair of you..."

If Roddy Fforbes, whoever he was, was spreading it around London that Strike was taking his heavily pregnant, married ex-fiancée out for dinner while her husband was in New York, the tabloids would definitely be interested, because wild, beautiful and aristocratic Charlotte was news. Her name had peppered gossip columns since she was sixteen years old, her various tribulations—running away from school, the stints in rehab and in psychiatric clinics—were well documented. It was even possible that Patterson had been hired by Jago Ross, who could certainly afford it. If the side effect of policing his wife's movements was ruining Strike's business, Ross would undoubtedly consider that a bonus.

Robin, who was sitting a short distance away from the station in the Land Rover, saw Strike emerge onto the pavement, kit bag over his shoulder, and registered that he looked as bad-tempered as she had ever seen him. He lit a cigarette, scanning the street until his eye found the Land Rover at the end of a series of parked vehicles and he began to limp, unsmiling, towards her. Robin, whose own mood was perilously low, could only assume that he was angry at having to make the long trip to Wembley with what appeared to be a heavy bag and a sore leg.

She had been awake since four o'clock that morning, unable to get back to sleep, cramped and unhappy on Vanessa's hard sofa, thinking about her future, and about the row she had had with her mother by phone. Matthew had called the house in Masham, trying to reach her, and Linda was not only desperately worried, but furious that Robin hadn't told her what was going on first.

"Where are you staying? With Strike?"

"Of course I'm not staying with Strike, why on earth would I be—?"

"Where, then?"

"With a different friend."

"Who? Why didn't you tell us? What are you going to do? I want to come down to London to see you!"

"Please don't," said Robin through gritted teeth.

Her guilt about the expense of the wedding she and Matthew had put her parents to, and about the embarrassment her mother and father were about to endure in explaining to their friends that her marriage was over barely a year after it had begun, weighed heavily on her, but she couldn't bear the prospect of Linda badgering and cajoling, treating her as though she were fragile and damaged. The last thing she needed right now was her mother suggesting that she go back to Yorkshire, to be cocooned in the bedroom that had witnessed some of the worst times of her life.

After two days viewing a multitude of densely packed houses, Robin had put down a deposit on a box room in a house in Kilburn, where she would have five other housemates, and into which she would be able to move the following week. Every time she thought of the place, her stomach turned over in trepidation and misery. At the age of almost twenty-eight, she would be the oldest housemate.

Trying to propitiate Strike, she got out of the car and offered to help him with the kit bag, but he grunted at her that he could manage. As the canvas hit the metal floor of the Land Rover she heard a loud clattering of heavy metal tools and experienced a nervous spasm in her stomach.

Strike, who had taken fleeting stock of Robin's appearance, had his worst suspicions strengthened. Pale, with shadows beneath her eyes, she managed to look both puffy and drawn and also seemed to have lost weight in the few days since he'd last seen her. The wife of his old army friend Graham Hardacre had been hospitalized in the early stages of pregnancy because of persistent vomiting. Perhaps one of Robin's important appointments had been to address that problem.

"You all right?" Strike asked Robin roughly, buckling up his seatbelt.

"Fine," she said, for what felt like the umpteenth time, taking his shortness as annoyance at his long Tube journey.

They drove out of London without talking. Finally, when they had reached the M40, Strike said:

"Patterson's back. He was watching the office this morning."

"You're kidding!"

"Has there been anyone round your place?"

"Not that I know of," said Robin, after an almost imperceptible hesitation. Perhaps this was what Matthew had been calling her about, when he had tried to reach her in Masham.

"You didn't have any trouble getting away this morning?"

"No," said Robin, honestly enough.

In the days that had elapsed since she'd walked out, she had imagined telling Strike that her marriage was over, but had not yet been able to find a form of words that she knew she would be able to deliver with the requisite calm. This frustrated her: it ought, she told herself, to be easy. He was the friend and colleague who had been there when she'd called off the wedding and who knew about Matthew's previous infidelity with Sarah. She ought to be able to tell him casually mid-conversation, as she had with Raphael.

The problem was that on the rare occasions when she and Strike had shared revelations about their love lives, it had been when one of them had been drunk. Otherwise, a profound reserve on such matters had always lain between them, in spite of Matthew's paranoid conviction that they spent most of their working lives in flirtation.

But there was more to it than that. Strike was the man she had hugged on the stairs at her wedding reception, the man with whom she had imagined walking out on her husband before the marriage could be consummated, the man for whom she had spent nights of her honeymoon wearing a groove in the white sand as she paced alone, wondering whether she was in love with him. She was afraid of giving herself away, afraid of betraying what she had thought and felt, because she was sure that if he ever had the merest suspicion of what a disruptive factor he had been, in both the beginning and the end of her marriage, it would surely taint their working relationship, as certainly as it would surely prejudice her job if he ever knew about the panic attacks.

No, she must appear to be what he was—self-contained and stoic, able to absorb trauma and limp on, ready to face whatever life flung at her, even what lay at the bottom of the dell, without flinching or turning away.

"So what d'you think Patterson's up to?" she asked.

"Time will tell. Did your appointments go all right?"

"Yes," said Robin, and to distract herself from the thought of her tiny new rented room, and the student couple who had shown her around, casting sideways glances at the strangely grown-up woman who was coming to live with them, she said, "There are biscuits in the bag back there. No tea, sorry, but we can stop if you like."

The thermos was back in Albury Street, one of the things she had forgotten to sneak out of the house when she had returned while Matthew was at work.

"Thanks," said Strike, though without much enthusiasm. He was wondering whether the reappearance of snacks, given his self-proclaimed diet, might not be further proof of his partner's pregnancy.

Robin's phone rang in her pocket. She ignored it. Twice that morning, she had received calls from the same unknown number and she was afraid that it might be Matthew who, finding himself blocked, had borrowed another phone.

"D'you want to get that?" asked Strike, watching her pale, set profile.

"Er—not while I'm driving."

"I can answer it, if you want."

"No," she said, a little too quickly.

The mobile stopped ringing but, almost at once, began again. More than ever convinced that it was Matthew, Robin took the phone out of her jacket, saying:

"I think I know who it is, and I don't want to talk to them just now. Once they hang up, could you mute it?"

Strike took the mobile.

"It's been put through from the office number. I'll turn it to speakerphone," said Strike helpfully, given that the ancient Land Rover didn't have a functioning heater, let alone Bluetooth, and he did so, holding the mobile close to her mouth, so that she could make herself heard over the rattle and growl of the drafty vehicle.

"Hello, Robin here. Who's this?"

"Robin? Don't you mean *Venetia*?" said a Welsh voice.

"Is that Mr. Winn?" said Robin, eyes on the road, while Strike held the mobile steady for her.

"Yes, you nasty little bitch, it is."

Robin and Strike glanced at each other, startled. Gone was the unctuous, lascivious Winn, keen to charm and impress.

"Got what you were after, haven't you, eh? Wriggling up and down that corridor, sticking your tits in where they weren't wanted, 'oh, Mr. Winn—'" he imitated her the same way Matthew did, high-pitched and imbecilic, "'—oh, help me, Mr. Winn, should I do charity or should I do politics, let me bend a bit lower over the desk, Mr. Winn.' How many men have you trapped that way, how far do you go—?"

"Have you got something to tell me, Mr. Winn?" asked Robin loudly, talking over him. "Because if you've just called to insult me—"

"Oh, I've got plenty to bloody tell you, *plenty to bloody tell you*," shouted Winn. "You are going to *pay*, Miss Ellacott, for what you've done to me, *pay* for the damage you've done to me and my wife, you don't get off that easily, you broke the law in this office and I'm going to see you in court, do you understand me?" He was becoming almost hysterical. "We'll see how well your wiles work on a judge, shall we? Low-cut top and 'oh, I think I'm overheating—'"

A white light seemed to be encroaching on the edges of Robin's vision, so that the road ahead turned tunnel-like.

"NO!" she shouted, taking both hands off the wheel before slamming them back down again, her arms shaking. It was the "no" she had given Matthew, a "no" of such vehemence and force that it brought Geraint Winn up short in exactly the same way.

"Nobody made you stroke my hair and pat my back and ogle my chest, Mr. Winn, that wasn't what *I* wanted, though I'm sure it gives you a bit of a kick to think it was—"

"Robin!" said Strike, but he might as well have been one more creak of the car's ancient chassis, and she ignored, too, Geraint's sudden interjection, "Who else is there? Was that Strike?"

"—you're a creep, Mr. Winn, a *thieving* creep who stole from a charity and I'm not only happy I got the goods on you, I'll be delighted to tell the world you're flicking out pictures of your dead daughter while you're trying to peer down young women's shirts—"

"How dare you!" gasped Winn, "are there no depths—you *dare* mention Rhiannon—it's all going to come out, Samuel Murape's family—"

"Screw you and screw your bloody grudges!" shouted Robin. "You're a pervy, thieving—"

"If you've got anything else to say, I suggest you put it in writing, Mr. Winn," Strike shouted into the mobile, while Robin, hardly knowing what she was doing, continued to yell insults at Winn from a distance. Ending the call with a jab of the finger, Strike grabbed the wheel as Robin again removed both hands from it to gesticulate.

"Fuck's sake!" said Strike, "pull over—pull over, now!"

She did as he told her automatically, the adrenaline disorientating her like alcohol, and when the Land Rover lurched to a halt she threw off her seatbelt and got out on the hard shoulder, cars whizzing past her. Hardly knowing what she was doing she began to stumble away from the Land Rover, tears of rage sliding down her face, trying to outpace the panic now lapping at her, because she had just irrevocably alienated a man they might need to talk to again, a man who had already been talking about revenge, who might even be the one paying Patterson...

"Robin!"

Now, she thought, Strike, too, would think her a flake, a damaged fool who should never have taken on this line of work, the one who ran when things got tough. It was that which made her wheel around to face him as he hobbled along the hard shoulder after her, and she wiped her face roughly on her sleeve and said, before he could tell her off, "I know I shouldn't have lost it, I know I've fucked up, I'm sorry." But his answer was lost in the pounding in her ears and, as though it had been waiting for her to stop running, the panic now engulfed her. Dizzy, unable to order her thoughts, she collapsed on the verge, dry bristles of grass prickling through her jeans as, eyes shut and head in hands, she tried to breathe herself back to normality as the traffic zoomed past.

She wasn't quite sure whether one minute or ten had elapsed, but finally her pulse slowed, her thoughts became ordered and the panic ebbed away, to be replaced by mortification. After all her careful pretense that she was coping, she had blown it.

A whiff of cigarette smoke reached her. Opening her eyes, she saw Strike's legs sticking out on the ground to her right. He, too, had sat down on the verge.

"How long have you been having panic attacks?" he asked conversationally.

There seemed no point dissembling any more.

"About a year," she muttered.

"Been getting help with them?"

"Yes. I was in therapy for a bit. Now I do CBT exercises."

"Do you, though?" Strike asked mildly. "Because I bought vegetarian bacon a week ago, but it's not making me any healthier, just sitting there in the fridge."

Robin began to laugh and found that she couldn't stop. More tears leaked from her eyes. Strike watched her, not unkindly, smoking his cigarette.

"I could have been doing them a bit more regularly," Robin admitted at last, mopping her face again.

"Anything else you fancy telling me, now we're getting into things?" asked Strike.

He felt he ought to know the worst now, before he gave her any advice on her mental condition, but Robin seemed confused.

"Any other health matters that might affect your ability to work?" he prompted her.

"Like what?"

Strike wondered whether a direct inquiry constituted some kind of infringement of her employment rights.

"I wondered," he said, "whether you might be, ah, pregnant."

Robin began to laugh again.

"Oh God, that's funny."

"Is it?"

"No," she said, shaking her head, "I'm not pregnant."

Strike now noticed that her wedding and engagement rings were missing. He had become so used to seeing her without them as she impersonated Venetia Hall and Bobbi Cunliffe that it had not occurred to him that their absence today might be significant, yet he didn't want to pose a direct question, for reasons that had nothing at all to do with employment rights.

"Matthew and I have split up," Robin said, frowning at the passing traffic in an effort not to cry again. "A week ago."

"Oh," said Strike. "Shit. I'm sorry."

But his concerned expression was at total odds with his actual feelings. His dark mood had lightened so abruptly that it was akin to having moved from sober to three pints down. The smell of rubber and dust and burned grass recalled the car park where he had accidentally kissed her, and he drew on his cigarette again and tried hard not to let his feelings show in his face.

"I know I shouldn't have spoken to Geraint Winn like that," said Robin, tears now falling again. "I shouldn't have mentioned Rhiannon, I lost control and—it's just, *men*, bloody *men*, judging everyone by their bloody selves!"

"What happened with Matt—?"

"He's been sleeping with Sarah Shadlock," said Robin savagely. "His best friend's fiancée. She left an earring in our bed and I—oh *bugger*."

It was no use: she buried her face in her hands and, with a sense of having nothing to lose now, cried in earnest, because she had thoroughly disgraced herself in Strike's eyes, and the one remaining piece of her life that she had been seeking to preserve had been tainted. How delighted Matthew would be to see her falling apart on a motorway verge, proving his point, that she was unfit to do the job she loved, forever limited by her past, by having, twice, been in the wrong place, at the wrong time, with the wrong men.

A heavy weight landed across her shoulders. Strike had put his arm around her. This was simultaneously comforting and ominous, because he had never done that before, and she was sure that this was the precursor to him telling her that she was unfit to work, that they would cancel the next interview and return to London.

"Where have you been staying?"

"Vanessa's sofa," said Robin, trying frantically to mop her streaming eyes and nose: snot and tears had made the knees of her jeans soggy. "But I've got a new place now."

"Where?"

"Kilburn, a room in a shared house."

"Bloody hell, Robin," said Strike. "Why didn't you tell me? Nick and Ilsa have got a proper spare room, they'd be delighted—"

"I can't sponge off your friends," said Robin thickly.

"It wouldn't be sponging," said Strike. He jammed his cigarette in his mouth and started searching his pockets with his free hand. "They like you and you could stay there for a couple of weeks until— aha. I thought I had one. It's only creased, I haven't used it—don't think so, anyway—"

Robin took the tissue and, with one hearty blow of her nose, demolished it.

"Listen," Strike began, but Robin interrupted at once:

"Don't tell me to take time off. Please don't. I'm fine, I'm fit to work, I hadn't had a panic attack in ages before that one, I'm—"

"—not listening."

"All right, sorry," she muttered, the sodden tissue clutched in her fist. "Go on."

"After I got blown up, I couldn't get in a car without doing what you've just done, panicking and breaking out in a cold sweat and half suffocating. For a while I'd do anything to avoid being driven by someone else. I've still got problems with it, to tell the truth."

"I didn't realize," said Robin. "You don't show it."

"Yeah, well, you're the best driver I know. You should see me with my bloody sister. Thing is, Robin—oh, bollocks."

The traffic police had arrived, pulling up behind the abandoned Land Rover, apparently puzzled as to why the occupants were sitting fifty yards away on the verge, to all appearances unconcerned with the fate of their poorly parked vehicle.

"Not in too much of a hurry to get help, then?" said the portlier of the two sarcastically. He had the swagger of a man who thinks himself a joker.

Strike removed his arm from around Robin's shoulders and both stood up, in Strike's case, clumsily.

"Car sickness," Strike told the officer blandly. "Careful, or she might puke on you."

They returned to the car. The first officer's colleague was peering at the tax disk on the ancient Land Rover.

"You don't see many of this age still on the roads," he commented.

"It's never let me down yet," said Robin.

"Sure you're all right to drive?" Strike muttered, as she turned the ignition key. "We could pretend you're still feeling ill."

"I'm fine."

And this time, it was true. He had called her the best driver he knew, and it might not be much, but he had given her back some of her self-respect, and she steered seamlessly back onto the motorway.

There was a long silence. Strike decided that further discussion of Robin's mental health ought to wait until she wasn't driving.

"Winn said a name at the end of the call there," he mused, taking out his notebook. "Did you hear?"

"No," muttered Robin, shamefaced.

"It was Samuel something," Strike said, making a note. "Murdoch? Matlock?"

"I didn't hear."

"Cheer up," said Strike bracingly, "he probably wouldn't have blurted it out if you hadn't been yelling at him. Not that I recommend calling interviewees thieving perverts in future..."

He stretched around in his seat, reaching for the carrier bag in the back. "Fancy a biscuit?"

62

. . . I do not want to see your defeat, Rebecca.

Henrik Ibsen, *Rosmersholm*

The car park at Newbury Racecourse was already jam-packed when they arrived. Many of the people heading for the ticket marquee were dressed for comfort, like Strike and Robin, in jeans and jackets, but others had donned fluttering silk dresses, suits, padded waistcoats, tweed hats and corduroy trousers in shades of mustard and puce that reminded Robin of Torquil.

They queued for tickets, each lost in their thoughts. Robin was afraid of what was coming once they reached the Crafty Filly, where Tegan Butcher worked. Certain that Strike had not yet had his full say on her mental health, she was afraid that he had merely postponed the announcement that he wanted her to return to a desk job in the office.

In fact, Strike's mind was temporarily elsewhere. The white railings glimpsed beyond the small marquee where the crowd queued for tickets, and the abundance of tweed and corduroy, were reminding him of the last time he had been at a racecourse. He had no particular interest in the sport. The one constant paternal figure in his life, his uncle Ted, had been a footballing and sailing man, and while a couple of Strike's friends in the army had enjoyed a bet on the horses, he had never seen the attraction.

Three years previously, though, he had attended the Epsom Derby with Charlotte and two of her favorite siblings. Like Strike,

Charlotte came from a disjointed and dysfunctional family. In one of her unpredictable effusions of enthusiasm, Charlotte had insisted on accepting Valentine and Sacha's invitation, notwithstanding Strike's lack of interest in the sport and his barely cordial feelings towards both men, who considered him an inexplicable oddity in their sister's life.

He had been broke at the time, setting up the agency on a shoestring, already being chased by lawyers for repayment of the small loan he had taken from his biological father, when every bank had turned him down as a bad risk. Nevertheless, Charlotte had been incensed when, after losing a fiver on the nose on the favorite, Fame and Glory, who had come in second, he had refused to place another bet. She had refrained from calling him puritanical or sanctimonious, plebeian or penny-pinching, as she had done previously when he had refused to emulate the reckless and ostentatious spending of her family and friends. Egged on by her brothers, she had chosen to lay larger and larger bets herself, finally winning £2500 and insisting that they visit the champagne tent, where her beauty and high spirits had turned many heads.

As he walked with Robin up a wide tarmacked thoroughfare that ran parallel from the racetrack itself behind the towering stands, past coffee bars, cider stalls and ice cream vans, the jockeys' changing rooms and owners' and trainers' bar, Strike thought about Charlotte, and gambles that came off, and gambles that didn't, until Robin's voice pulled him back to the present.

"I think that's the place."

A painted sign showed the head of a dark, winking filly in a snaffle bit hung on the side of a one-story brick bar. The outdoor seating area was crowded. Champagne flutes clinked amid a buzz of talk and laughter. The Crafty Filly overlooked the paddock where horses would shortly be paraded, around which a further crowd had begun to congregate.

"Grab that high table," Strike told Robin, "and I'll get drinks and tell Tegan we're here."

He disappeared into the building without asking her what she wanted.

Robin sat down at one of the tall tables with its metal bar-chairs, which she knew Strike preferred because getting on and off them would be easier on his amputated leg than the low wickerwork sofas. The whole outside area sat beneath a canopy of polyurethane to protect drinkers from non-existent rain. The sky was cloudless today, the day warm with a light breeze that barely moved the leaves of the topiary plants at the entrance to the bar. It would be a clear night for digging in the dell outside Steda Cottage, Robin thought, always assuming that Strike wasn't about to cancel the expedition, because he thought her too unstable and emotional to take along.

That thought turned her insides even colder and she fell to reading the printed lists of runners they had been given, along with their cardboard entry tags, until a half-bottle of Moët & Chandon landed unexpectedly in front of her and Strike sat down, holding a pint of bitter.

"Doom Bar on draft," he said cheerfully, tipping his glass to her before taking a sip. Robin looked blankly at the little bottle of champagne, which she thought resembled bubble bath.

"What's this for?"

"Celebration," said Strike, having taken a sizable gulp of his beer. "I know you're not supposed to say it," he went on, rummaging through his pockets for cigarettes, "but you're well shot of him. Sleeping with his mate's fiancée in the marital bed? He deserves everything that's coming to him."

"I can't drink. I'm driving."

"That's just cost me twenty-five quid, so you can take a token swig."

"Twenty-five quid, for this?" said Robin, and taking advantage of Strike lighting his cigarette, she surreptitiously wiped her leaking eyes again.

"Tell me something," said Strike, as he waved his match, extinguishing it. "D'you ever think about where you see the agency going?"

"What d'you mean?" said Robin, looking alarmed.

"My brother-in-law was giving me the third degree about it, night the Olympics started," said Strike. "Banging on about reaching a point where I didn't have to go out on the street any more."

"But you wouldn't want that, would y—wait," said Robin,

panicking. "Are you trying to tell me I've got to go back to the desk and answering the phones?"

"No," said Strike, blowing smoke away from her, "I just wondered whether you give the future any thought."

"You want me to leave?" asked Robin, still more alarmed. "Go and do something el—?"

"Bloody hell, Ellacott, no! I'm asking you whether you think about the future, that's all."

He watched as Robin uncorked the little bottle.

"Yes, of course I do," she said uncertainly. "I've been hoping we can get the bank balance a bit healthier, so we aren't living hand to mouth all the time, but I love the—" her voice wobbled, "—the job, you know I do. That's all I want. Do it, get better at it and...I suppose make the agency the best in London."

Grinning, Strike clinked his beer glass against her champagne.

"Well, bear in mind we want exactly the same thing while I'm saying the next bit, all right? And you might as well drink. Tegan can't take a break for forty minutes, and we've got a lot of time to kill before we head over to the dell this evening."

Strike watched her take a sip of champagne before going on.

"Pretending you're OK when you aren't isn't strength."

"Well, that's where you're wrong," Robin contradicted him. The champagne had fizzed on her tongue and seemed to give her courage even before it hit her brain. "Sometimes, acting as though you're all right, makes you all right. Sometimes you've got to slap on a brave face and walk out into the world, and after a while it isn't an act any-more, it's who you are. If I'd waited to feel ready to leave my room after—you know," she said, "I'd still be in there. I had to leave before I was ready. And," she said, looking him directly in the eyes, her own bloodshot and swollen, "I've been working with you for two years, watching you plow on no matter what, when we both know any doctor would have told you to put your leg up and rest."

"And where did that get me, eh?" asked Strike reasonably. "Inva-lided out for a week, with my hamstring screaming for mercy every time I walk more than fifty yards. You want to draw parallels, fine. I'm dieting, I've been doing my stretches—"

"And the vegetarian bacon, rotting away in the fridge?"

"Rotting? That stuff's like industrial rubber, it'll outlive me. Listen," he said, refusing to be deflected, "it'd be a bloody miracle if you hadn't suffered any after-effects from what happened last year." His eyes sought the tip of the purple scar on her forearm, visible beneath the cuff of her shirt. "Nothing in your past precludes you from doing this job, but you need to take care of yourself if you want to keep doing it. If you need time off—"

"—that's the last thing I want—"

"This isn't about what you want. It's about what you need."

"Shall I tell you something funny?" said Robin. Whether because of the mouthful of champagne, or for some other reason, she had experienced a startling lift in mood that made her loose-tongued. "You'd have thought I'd have had panic attacks galore over the last week, wouldn't you? I've been trying to find a place to live, looking round flats, traveling all over London, I've had loads of people coming up unexpectedly behind me—that's a major trigger," she explained. "People behind me, when I don't know they're there."

"Don't think we need Freud to explain that one."

"But I've been fine," said Robin. "I think it's because I haven't had to—"

She stopped short, but Strike thought he knew what the end of the sentence would have been. Taking a chance, he said:

"This job becomes well-nigh impossible if your home life's screwed up. I've been there. I know."

Relieved to have been understood, Robin drank more champagne then said in a rush:

"I think it's made me worse, having to hide what's going on, having to do the exercises in secret, because any sign I wasn't a hundred percent and Matthew would be yelling at me again for doing this job. I thought it was him trying to reach me on the phone this morning, that's why I didn't want to take the call. And when Winn started calling me those names, it—well, it felt as though I *had* taken the call. I don't need Winn to tell me I'm basically a pair of walking tits, a stupid, deluded girl who doesn't realize that's my only useful attribute."

Matthew's been telling you that, has he? thought Strike, imagining a few corrective measures from which he thought Matthew might benefit. Slowly and carefully he said:

"The fact that you're a woman...I *do* worry about you more when you're out alone on a job than I would if you were a bloke. Hear me out," he said firmly, as she opened her mouth in panic. "We've got to be honest with each other, or we're screwed. Just listen, will you?

"You've escaped two killers using your wits and remembering your training. I'd lay odds bloody Matthew couldn't've managed that. But I don't want a third time, Robin, because you might not be so lucky."

"You *are* telling me to go back to a desk job—"

"Can I finish?" he said sternly. "I don't want to lose you, because you're the best I've got. Every case we've worked since you arrived, you've found evidence I couldn't have found and got round people I couldn't have persuaded to talk to me. We're where we are today largely because of you. But the odds are always going to be against you if you come up against a violent man and I've got responsibilities here. I'm the senior partner, I'm the one you could sue—"

"You're worried I'd *sue*—?"

"No, Robin," he said harshly, "I'm worried you'll end up fucking dead and I'll have to carry that on my conscience for the rest of my life."

He took another swig of Doom Bar, then said:

"I need to know you're mentally healthy if I'm putting you out on the street. I want a cast-iron guarantee from you that you're going to address these panic attacks, because it isn't only you who has to live with the consequences if you're not up to it."

"Fine," muttered Robin, and when Strike raised his eyebrows, she said, "I mean it. I'll do what it takes. I will."

The crowd around the paddock was becoming ever denser. Evidently the runners in the next race were about to be paraded.

"How are things with Lorelei?" Robin asked. "I like her."

"Then I'm afraid I've got even more bad news for you, because you and Matthew aren't the only people who split up last weekend."

"Oh, shit. Sorry," said Robin, and she covered her embarrassment by drinking more champagne.

"For someone who didn't want that, you're getting through it quite fast," said Strike, amused.

"I didn't tell you, did I?" said Robin, remembering suddenly, as she held up the little green bottle. "I know where I saw Blanc de Blancs before, and it wasn't on a bottle—but it doesn't help us with the case."

"Go on."

"There's a suite at Le Manoir aux Quat'Saisons called that," said Robin. "Raymond Blanc, you know, the chef who started the hotel? Play on words. Blanc de Blanc—no 's.'"

"Is that where you had your anniversary weekend?"

"Yeah. We weren't in 'Blanc de Blanc,' though. We couldn't afford a suite," said Robin. "I just remember walking past the sign. But yes...that's where we celebrated our paper anniversary. Paper," she repeated, with a sigh, "and some people make it to platinum."

Seven dark thoroughbreds were appearing one by one in the paddock now, jockeys in their silks perched atop them like monkeys, stable girls and lads leading the nervy creatures, with their silken flanks and their prancing strides. Strike and Robin were some of the few not craning their necks for a better view. Before she had time to second-guess herself, Robin introduced the subject she most wanted to discuss.

"Was that Charlotte I saw you talking to at the Paralympic reception?"

"Yeah," said Strike.

He glanced at her. Robin had had occasion before now to deplore how easily he seemed to read her thoughts.

"Charlotte had nothing to do with me and Lorelei splitting. She's married now."

"So were Matthew and I," Robin pointed out, taking another sip of champagne. "Didn't stop Sarah Shadlock."

"I'm not Sarah Shadlock."

"Obviously not. If you were that bloody annoying I wouldn't be working for you."

"Maybe you could put that on the next employee satisfaction review. 'Not as bloody annoying as the woman who shagged my husband.' I'll have it framed."

Robin laughed.

"You know, I had an idea about Blanc de Blancs myself," said Strike. "I was going back over Chiswell's to-do list, trying to eliminate possibilities and substantiate a theory."

"What theory?" said Robin sharply, and Strike noted that even halfway down the bottle of champagne, with her marriage in splinters and a box room in Kilburn to look forward to, Robin's interest in the case remained as acute as ever.

"Remember when I told you I thought there was something big, something fundamental, behind the Chiswell business? Something we hadn't spotted yet?"

"Yes," said Robin, "you said it kept 'almost showing itself.'"

"Well remembered. So, a couple of things Raphael said—"

"That's me on my break, now," said a nervous female voice behind them.

63

It is a purely personal matter, and there is not the slightest necessity to go proclaiming it all over the countryside.

Henrik Ibsen, *Rosmersholm*

Short, square and heavily freckled, Tegan Butcher wore her dark hair scraped back in a bun. Even in her smart bar uniform, which comprised a gray tie and a black shirt on which a white horse and jockey were embroidered, she had the air of a girl more at home in muddy Wellington boots. She had brought a milky coffee out of the bar to drink while they questioned her.

"Oh—thanks very much," she said, when Strike went to fetch an extra chair, clearly gratified that the famous detective would do as much for her.

"No problem," said Strike. "This is my partner, Robin Ellacott."

"Yeah, it was you that contacted me, wasn't it?" said Tegan as she got up onto the bar chair, making slightly heavy weather of the climb, being so short. She seemed simultaneously excited and fearful.

"You haven't got long, I know," said Strike, "so we'll get straight to it, if you don't mind, Tegan?"

"No. I mean, yeah. That's fine. Go on."

"How long did you work for Jasper and Kinvara Chiswell?"

"I was doing it part time for them while I was still at school, so counting that...two and a half years, yeah."

"How did you like working for them?"

"It was all right," said Tegan cautiously.

"How did you find the minister?"

"He was all right," said Tegan. She appeared to realize that this wasn't particularly descriptive, and added, "My family've known him for ages. My brothers done a bit of work up at Chiswell House for years, on and off."

"Yeah?" said Strike, who was making notes. "What did your brothers do?"

"Repairing fences, bit of gardening, but they've sold off most of the land now," said Tegan. "The garden's gone wild."

She picked up her coffee and took a sip, then said anxiously:

"My mum would do her nut if she knew I was meeting you. She told me to keep well out of it."

"Why's that?"

"'Least said, soonest mended,' she always says. That and 'least seen, most admired.' That's what I got if I ever wanted to go to the young farmers' disco."

Robin laughed. Tegan grinned, proud to have amused her.

"How did you find Mrs. Chiswell as an employer?" asked Strike.

"All right," said Tegan, yet again.

"Mrs. Chiswell liked to have someone sleeping at the house if she was away for the night, is that right? To be near the horses?"

"Yeah," said Tegan, and then, volunteering information for the first time, "she's paranoid."

"Wasn't one of her horses slashed?"

"You can call it slashed if you want," said Tegan, "but I'd call it more of a scratch. Romano managed to get his blanket off in the night. He was a sod for doing that."

"You don't know anything about intruders in the garden, then?" asked Strike, his pen poised over his notebook.

"Weelll," said Tegan slowly, "she *said* something about it, but..."

Her eyes had strayed to Strike's Benson & Hedges, which were lying beside his beer glass.

"Can I have a smoke?" she asked, greatly daring.

"Help yourself," said Strike, taking out a lighter and pushing it towards her.

Tegan lit up, took a deep drag on the cigarette, and said:

"I don't think there was ever anyone in the gardens. That's just

Mrs. Chiswell. She's—" Tegan struggled to find the right word. "Well, if she was a horse you'd call her spooky. *I* never heard anyone when I was there overnight."

"You slept over at the house the night before Jasper Chiswell was found dead in London, didn't you?"

"Yeah."

"Can you remember what time Mrs. Chiswell got back?"

"'Bout eleven. I got a right shock," said Tegan. Now that her nerves were wearing off, a slight tendency to garrulity was revealed. "Because she was s'posed to be staying up in London. She went off on one when she walked in, because I'd had a fag in front of the telly—she doesn't like smoking—and I'd had a couple of glasses of wine out the bottle in the fridge, as well. Mind, she'd told me to help myself to anything I wanted before she left, but she's like that, always shifting the goalposts. What was right one minute was wrong the next. You had to walk on eggshells, you really did.

"But she was already in a bad mood when she arrived. I could tell from the way she came stomping down the hall. The fag and the wine, that just gave her an excuse to have a go at me. That's what she's like."

"But you stayed the night, anyway?"

"Yeah. She said I was too drunk to drive, which was rubbish, I weren't drunk, and then she told me to go and check on the horses, because she had a phone call to make."

"Did you hear her make the call?"

Tegan rearranged herself in the too-high chair, so that the elbow of her smoking arm was cupped in her free hand, her eyes slightly narrowed against the smoke, a pose she evidently thought appropriate while dealing with a tricky private detective.

"I dunno if I should say."

"How about I suggest a name and you can nod if it's the right one?"

"Go on, then," said Tegan, with the mingled mistrust and curiosity of one who has been promised a magic trick.

"Henry Drummond," said Strike. "She was leaving a message to say that she wanted a valuation on a necklace?"

Impressed against her will, Tegan nodded.

"Yeah," she said. "That's right."

"So you went out to check on the horses...?"

"Yeah, and when I got back Mrs. Chiswell said I should stay over anyway, because she needed me early, so I did."

"And where did *she* sleep?" asked Robin.

"Well—upstairs," said Tegan, with a surprised laugh. "Obviously. In her bedroom."

"You're sure she was there all night?" asked Robin.

"Yeah," said Tegan, with another little laugh. "Her bedroom was next to mine. They're the only two with windows that face the stables. I could hear her going to bed."

"You're sure she didn't leave the house during the night? Didn't drive anywhere, as far as you know?" asked Strike.

"No. I'd've heard the car. There are potholes everywhere round that house, you can't leave quietly. Anyway, I met her next morning on the landing, heading for the bathroom in her nightie."

"What time would that have been?"

"'Bout half-seven. We had breakfast together in the kitchen."

"Was she still angry with you?"

"Bit ratty," admitted Tegan.

"You didn't happen to hear her take another call, round about breakfast time?"

Frankly admiring, Tegan said:

"You mean, from Mr. Chiswell? Yeah. She went out of the kitchen to take it. All I heard was 'No, I mean it this time, Jasper.' Sounded like a row. I've told the police this. I thought they must've argued in London and that's why she'd come home early instead of staying up there.

"Then I went outside to muck out, and she came out and she was schooling Brandy, that's one of her mares, and then," said Tegan, with a slight hesitation, "*he* arrived. Raphael, you know. The son."

"And what happened then?" asked Strike.

Tegan hesitated.

"They had a row, didn't they?" said Strike, mindful of how much of Tegan's break was slipping away.

"Yeah," said Tegan, smiling in frank wonderment. "You know *everything*!"

"D'you know what it was about?"

"Same thing she was phoning that bloke about, night before."

"The necklace? Mrs. Chiswell wanting to sell it?"

"Yeah."

"Where were you when they were having the row?"

"Still mucking out. He got out of his car and went marching up to her in the outdoor school—"

Robin, seeing Strike's perplexity, muttered, "Like a paddock where you train horses."

"Ah," he said.

"—yeah," said Tegan, "that's where she was schooling Brandy. First they were talking and I couldn't hear what they were saying and then it turned into a proper shouting match and she dismounted and yelled at me to come and untack Brandy—take off the saddle and bridle," she added kindly, in case Strike hadn't understood, "and they marched off into the house and I could hear them still having a go at each other as they disappeared.

"She never liked him," said Tegan. "Raphael. Thought he was spoiled. Always slagging him off. *I* thought he was all right, personally," she said, with a would-be dispassionate air at odds with her heightened color.

"Can you remember what they were saying to each other?"

"A bit," said Tegan. "He was telling her she couldn't sell it, that it belonged to his dad or something, and she told him to mind his own business."

"Then what happened?"

"They went inside, I kept mucking out, and after a bit," said Tegan, faltering slightly, "I saw a police car coming up the drive and... yeah, it was awful. Policewoman come and asked me to go inside and help. I went in the kitchen and Mrs. Chiswell was white as a sheet and all over the place. They wanted me to show them where the teabags were. I made her a hot drink and he—Raphael—made her sit down. He was really nice to her," said Tegan, "considering she'd just been calling him every name under the sun."

Strike checked his watch.

"I know you haven't got long. Just a couple more things."

"All right," she said.

"There was an incident over a year ago," said Strike, "where Mrs. Chiswell attacked Mr. Chiswell with a hammer."

"Oh, God, yeah," said Tegan. "Yeah...she really lost it. That was right after Lady was put down, start of the summer. She was Mrs. Chiswell's favorite mare and Mrs. Chiswell come home and the vet had already done it. She'd wanted to be there when it happened and she went crazy when she come back and seen the knacker's van."

"How long had she known that the mare would have to be put down?" asked Robin.

"Those last two, three days, I think we all knew, really," said Tegan sadly. "But she was such a lovely horse, we kept hoping she'd pull through. The vet had waited for hours for Mrs. Chiswell to come home, but Lady was suffering and he couldn't wait around all day, so..."

Tegan made a gesture of hopelessness.

"Any idea what made her go up to London that day, if she knew Lady was dying?" asked Strike.

Tegan shook her head.

"Can you talk us through exactly what happened, when she attacked her husband? Did she say anything first?"

"No," said Tegan. "She come into the yard, seen what had happened, ran towards Mr. Chiswell, grabbed the hammer and just swung for him. Blood everywhere. It was horrible," said Tegan, with patent sincerity. "Awful."

"What did she do after she'd hit him?" asked Robin.

"Just stood there. The expression on her face...it was like a *demon* or something," said Tegan unexpectedly. "I thought he was dead, thought she'd killed him.

"They put her away for a couple of weeks, you know. She went off to some hospital. I had to do the horses alone...

"We were all gutted about Lady. I loved that mare and I thought she was going to make it, but she'd given up, she lay down and wouldn't eat. I couldn't blame Mrs. Chiswell for being upset, but...she could've killed him. Blood everywhere," she repeated. "I wanted to leave. Told my mum. Mrs. Chiswell scared me, that night."

"So what made you stay?" asked Strike.

"I dunno, really . . . Mr. Chiswell wanted me to, and I was fond of the horses. Then she came out of hospital and she was really depressed and I suppose I felt sorry for her. I kept finding her crying in Lady's empty stall."

"Was Lady the mare that Mrs. Chiswell wanted to — er — what's the right term?" Strike asked Robin.

"Put in foal?" Robin suggested.

"Yeah . . . put in foal to the famous stallion?"

"Totilas?" said Tegan, with the ghost of an eye roll. "No, it was Brandy she wanted to breed from, but Mr. Chiswell was having none of it. Totilas! He costs a fortune."

"So I heard. She didn't by any chance mention using a different stallion? There's one called 'Blanc de Blancs,' I don't know whether—"

"Never heard of him," said Tegan. "No, it *had* to be Totilas, he was the best, she was fixated on using him. That's what she's like, Mrs. Chiswell. When she gets an idea in her head you can't shift it. She was going to breed this beautiful Grand Prix horse and . . . you know she lost a baby, don't you?"

Strike and Robin nodded.

"Mum felt sorry for her, she thought the thing about getting a foal was, you know, a sort of substitute. Mum thinks it was all to do with the baby, how Mrs. Chiswell's mood went up and down all the time.

"Like, one day, a few weeks after she came out of hospital, I remember, she was *manic*. I think it was the drugs they had her on. High as a kite. Singing in the yard. And I said to her, 'You're cheerful, Mrs. C,' and she laughed and said, 'Oh, I've been working on Jasper and I think I'm nearly there, I think he's going to let me use Totilas after all.' It was all rubbish. I asked him and he was really grumpy about it, said it was wishful thinking and he could hardly afford as many horses as she'd already got."

"You don't think he might've surprised her," said Strike, "by offering her a different stallion to breed from? A cheaper one?"

"That would just've annoyed her," said Tegan. "It was Totilas or nothing." She stubbed out the cigarette Strike had given her, checked her watch and said regretfully, "I've only got a couple more minutes."

"Two more things, and we're done," said Strike. "I've heard that your family knew a girl called Suki Lewis, years ago? She was a runaway from care—"

"You know *everything!*" said Tegan again, delightedly. "How did you know that?"

"Billy Knight told me. D'you happen to know what happened to Suki?"

"Yeah, she went to Aberdeen. She was in our Dan's class at school. Her mum was a nightmare: drink and drugs and all sorts. Then the mum goes on a real bender and that's how Suki got put into care. She ran away to find her dad. He worked on the North Sea rigs."

"And you think she found her father, do you?" asked Strike.

With a triumphant air, Tegan reached into her back pocket for her mobile. After a few clicks, she presented Strike with the Facebook page she had brought up for a beaming brunette, who stood posing with a posse of girlfriends in front of a swimming pool in Ibiza. Through the tan, the bleached smile and the false eyelashes, Strike discerned the palimpsest of the thin, buck-toothed girl from the old photograph. The page was captioned "Susanna McNeil."

"See?" said Tegan happily. "Her dad took her in with his new family. 'Susanna' was her proper name but her mum called her 'Suki.' My mum's friends with Susanna's auntie. Says she's doing great."

"You're quite sure this is her?" asked Strike.

"Yeah, of course," said Tegan. "We were all pleased for her. She was a nice girl."

She checked her watch again.

"'M'sorry, but that's my break over, I've got to go."

"One more question," said Strike. "How well did your brothers know the Knight family?"

"Quite well," said Tegan. "The boys were in different years at school but yeah, they knew them through working at Chiswell House."

"What do your brothers do now, Tegan?"

"Paul's managing a farm over near Aylesbury now and Dan's up in London doing landscape—why are you writing this down?" she said, alarmed for the first time at the sight of Strike's pen moving across his notebook. "You mustn't tell my brothers I've spoken to you! They'll go mad if they think I've talked about what went on up at the house!"

"Really? What *did* go on up there?" Strike asked.

Tegan looked uncertainly from him to Robin and back again.

"You already know, don't you?"

And when neither Strike nor Robin responded she said:

"Listen, Dan and Paul just helped out with transporting them. Loading them up and that. And it was legal back then!"

"What was legal?" asked Strike.

"I *know* you know," said Tegan, half-worried, half-amused. "Someone's been talking, haven't they? Is it Jimmy Knight? He was back not long ago, sniffing around, wanting to talk to Dan. Anyway, everyone knew, locally. It was supposed to be hush-hush, but we all knew about Jack."

"Knew *what* about him?" asked Strike.

"Well... that he was the gallows maker."

Strike absorbed the information without so much as a quiver of the eyelid. Robin wasn't sure her own expression had remained as impassive.

"But you already knew," said Tegan. "Didn't you?"

"Yeah," said Strike, to reassure her. "We knew."

"Thought so," said Tegan, relieved and sliding down, inelegantly, from her chair. "But if you see Dan, don't tell him I said. He's like Mum. 'Least said, soonest mended.' Mind, none of us think there was anything wrong with it. This country'd be better with the death penalty, if you ask me."

"Thanks for meeting us, Tegan," said Strike. She blushed slightly as she shook first his hand, then Robin's.

"No problem," she said, now seeming reluctant to leave them. "Are you going to stay for the races? Brown Panther's running in the two-thirty."

"We might," said Strike, "we've got a bit of time to kill before our next appointment."

"I've got a tenner on Brown Panther," Tegan confided. "Well... bye, then."

She had gone a few steps when she wheeled around and returned to Strike, now even pinker in the face.

"Can I have a selfie with you?"

"Er," said Strike, carefully not catching Robin's eye, "I'd rather not, if it's all the same to you."

"Can I have your autograph, then?"

Deciding that this was the lesser of two evils, Strike wrote his signature on a napkin.

"Thanks."

Clutching her napkin, Tegan departed at last. Strike waited until she had disappeared into the bar before turning to Robin, who was already busy on her phone.

"Six years ago," she said, reading from the mobile screen, "an EU directive came in banning member states from exporting torture equipment. Until then, it was perfectly legal to export British-made gallows abroad."

64

Speak so that I can understand you.

Henrik Ibsen, *Rosmersholm*

"'I acted within the law and in accordance with my conscience,'" Strike quoted Chiswell's gnomic pronouncement back in Pratt's. "So he did. Never hid the fact that he was pro-hanging, did he? I suppose he provided the wood from his grounds."

"And the space for Jack o'Kent to build them—which is why Jack o'Kent warned Raff not to go into the barn, when he was a child."

"And they probably split the profits."

"Wait," said Robin, remembering what Flick had shrieked after the minister's car, the night of the Paralympic reception. "'He put the horse on them'...Cormoran, d'you think—?"

"Yeah, I do," said Strike, his thoughts keeping pace with hers. "The last thing Billy said to me at the hospital was 'I hated putting the horse on them.' Even in the middle of a psychotic episode, Billy could carve a perfect White Horse of Uffington into wood...Jack o'Kent had his boys carving it onto trinkets for tourists and onto gallows for export...nice little father-son business he had going, eh?"

Strike clinked his beer glass against her little champagne bottle and downed the last dregs of his Doom Bar.

"To our first proper breakthrough. If Jack o'Kent was putting a little bit of local branding on the gallows, they were traceable back to him, weren't they? And not only to him: to the Vale of the White Horse, and to Chiswell. It all fits, Robin. Remember Jimmy's placard, with the pile of dead black children on it? Chiswell and Jack o'Kent were flogging them abroad—Middle East or Africa, probably. But Chiswell can't have known they had the horse carved into them—Christ, no, he *definitely* didn't," said Strike, remembering Chiswell's words in Pratt's, "because when he told me there were photographs, he said 'there are no distinguishing marks, so far as I'm aware.'"

"You know how Jimmy said he was owed?" said Robin, following her own train of thought. "And how Raff said Kinvara thought he had a legitimate claim for money, at first? What d'you think are the chances that Jack o'Kent left some gallows ready for sale when he died—"

"—and Chiswell sold them without bothering to track down and pay off Jack's sons? Very smart," said Strike, nodding. "So for Jimmy, this all started as a demand for his rightful share of his father's estate. Then, when Chiswell denied he owed them anything, it turned into blackmail."

"Not a very strong case for blackmail, though, when you think about it, is it?" said Robin. "D'you really think Chiswell would have lost a lot of voters over this? It *was* legal at the time he sold them, and he was publicly pro-death penalty, so nobody could say he was a hypocrite. Half the country thinks we should bring back hanging. I'm not sure the kind of people who vote for Chiswell would have thought he did much wrong."

"Another good point," conceded Strike, "and Chiswell could probably have brazened it out. He'd survived worse: impregnating his mistress, divorce, an illegitimate kid, Raphael's drugged-up car crash and imprisonment...

"But there were 'unintended consequences,' remember?" Strike asked thoughtfully. "What did those pictures at the Foreign Office show, that Winn was so keen to get hold of? And who's that 'Samuel' Winn just mentioned on the phone?"

Strike pulled out his notebook and jotted down a few sentences in his dense, hard-to-read handwriting.

"At least," said Robin, "we've got confirmation of Raff's story. The necklace."

Strike grunted, still writing. When he'd finished, he said, "Yeah, that was useful, as far as it went."

"What d'you mean, 'as far as it went'?"

"Him heading down to Oxfordshire to stop Kinvara running off with a valuable necklace is a better story than the trying-to-stop-her-topping-herself one," said Strike, "but I still don't think we're being told everything."

"Why not?"

"Same objection as before. Why would Chiswell send Raphael down there as his emissary, when his wife hated him? Can't see why Raphael would be any more persuasive than Izzy."

"Have you taken against Raphael, or something?"

Strike raised his eyebrows.

"I haven't got personal feelings for him one way or the other. You?"

"Of course not," said Robin, a little too quickly. "So, what was that theory you mentioned, before Tegan arrived?"

"Oh, yeah," said Strike. "Well, it might be nothing, but a couple of things Raphael said to you jumped out at me. Got me thinking."

"What things?"

Strike told her.

"I can't see what's significant about any of that."

"Maybe not in isolation, but try putting it together with what Della told me."

"Which bit?"

But even when Strike reminded her what Della had said, Robin remained confused.

"I don't see the connection."

Strike got up, grinning.

"Mull it over for a while. I'm going to ring Izzy and tell her Tegan's let the cat out of the bag about the gallows."

He walked away and disappeared into the crowds in search of a quiet spot from which to make his call, leaving Robin to swill the now-tepid champagne around in the miniature bottle and ponder what Strike had just said. Nothing coherent emerged from her exhausted attempts to connect the disparate pieces of information, and after a few minutes she gave up and simply sat there, enjoying the warm breeze that lifted the hair from her shoulders.

In spite of her tiredness, the shattered state of her marriage and her very real apprehension about going digging in the dell later that night, it was pleasant to sit here, breathing in the smells of the racecourse, of soft air redolent of turf, leather and horse, catching trails of perfume from the women now moving away from the bar towards the stands, and the smoky whiff of venison burgers cooking in a van nearby. For the first time in a week, Robin realized that she was actually hungry.

She picked up the cork of the champagne bottle and turned it over in her fingers, remembering another cork, the one she had saved from her twenty-first birthday party, for which Matthew had come home from university with a bunch of new friends, Sarah among them. Looking back, she knew that her parents had wanted to throw a big party for her twenty-first in compensation for her not having the graduation party they had all been expecting.

Strike was taking a long time. Perhaps Izzy was spilling all the details, now that they knew what the substance of the blackmail had been about, or perhaps, Robin thought, she simply wanted to keep him on the phone.

Izzy isn't his type, though.

The thought startled her a little. She felt slightly guilty for giving it headspace and even more uncomfortable when it was jostled out of the way by another.

All his girlfriends have been beautiful. Izzy isn't.

Strike attracted remarkably good-looking women, when you considered his generally bearlike appearance and what he himself had referred to in her hearing as "pube-like" hair.

I bet I look gross, was Robin's next, inconsequential thought. Puffy-faced and pale when she had got in the Land Rover that morning, she had cried a lot since. She was half-deliberating whether she had time to find a bathroom and at least brush her hair, when she spotted Strike walking back towards her holding a venison burger in each hand and a betting slip in his mouth.

"Izzy isn't picking up," he informed her through clenched teeth. "Left a message. Grab one of these and come on. I've just put a tenner each way on Brown Panther."

"I didn't realize you're a betting man," said Robin.

"I'm not," said Strike, removing the betting slip from his teeth and pocketing it, "but I'm feeling lucky today. Come on, we'll watch the race."

As Strike turned away, Robin slid the champagne cork discreetly into her pocket.

"*Brown* Panther," Strike said through a mouthful of burger, as they approached the track. "Except he isn't, is he? Black mane, so he's—"

"—a bay, yes," said Robin. "Are you upset he isn't a panther, either?"

"Just trying to follow the logic. That stallion I found online—Blanc de Blancs—was chestnut, not white."

"Not gray, you mean."

"Fuck's sake," muttered Strike, half-amused, half-exasperated.

65

I wonder how many there are who would do as much—who dare do it?

Henrik Ibsen, *Rosmersholm*

Brown Panther came in second. They spent Strike's winnings among the food and coffee tents, killing the hours of daylight until it was time to head for Woolstone and the dell. While panic fluttered in Robin's chest every time she thought of the tools in the back of the Land Rover and the dark basin full of nettles, Strike distracted her, whether intentionally or not, by a persistent refusal to explain how the testimony of Della Winn and Raphael Chiswell fitted together, or what conclusions he had drawn from it.

"Think," he kept saying, "just think."

But Robin was exhausted, and it was easier to simply push him to explain over successive coffees and sandwiches, all the while savoring this unusual interlude in their working lives, for she and Strike had never before spent hours together unless at some time of crisis.

But as the sun sank ever closer to the horizon, Robin's thoughts darted more insistently towards the dell, and each time they did so her stomach did a small backflip. Noticing her increasingly preoccupied silences, Strike suggested for the second time that she stay in the Land Rover while he and Barclay dug.

"No," said Robin tersely. "I didn't come to sit in the car."

It took them three-quarters of an hour to reach Woolstone. Color was bleeding rapidly out of the sky to the west as they descended for the second time into the Vale of the White Horse, and by the time they had reached their destination a few feeble stars were spotting the dust-colored heavens. Robin turned the Land Rover onto the overgrown track leading to Steda Cottage and the car rocked and pitched its way over the deep furrows and tangled thorns and branches, into the deeper darkness bestowed by the dense canopy above.

"Get as far in as you can," Strike instructed her, checking the time on his mobile. "Barclay's got to park behind us. He should've been here already, I told him nine o'clock."

Robin parked and cut the engine, eyeing the thick woodland that lay between the track and Chiswell House. Unseen they might be, but they were still trespassing. Her anxiety about possible detection was as nothing, however, to her very real fear of what lay beneath the tangled nettles at the bottom of that dark basin outside Steda Cottage, and so she returned to the subject she had been using as a distraction all afternoon.

"I've told you — *think*," said Strike, for the umpteenth time. "Think about the lachesis pills. You're the one who thought they were significant. Think about all those odd things Chiswell kept doing: taunting Aamir in front of everyone, saying Lachesis 'knew when everyone's number would be up,' telling you 'one by one, they trip themselves up,' looking for Freddie's money clip, which turned up in his pocket."

"I have thought about those things, but I still don't see how—"

"The helium and tubing entering the house disguised as a crate of champagne. Somebody knew he wouldn't want to drink it, because he was allergic. Ask yourself how Flick knew Jimmy had a claim on Chiswell. Think about Flick's row with her flatmate Laura—"

"How can *that* have anything to do with this?"

"Think!" said Strike, infuriatingly. "No amitriptyline was found in the empty orange juice carton in Chiswell's bin. Remember Kinvara, obsessing over Chiswell's whereabouts. Have a guess what little Francesca at Drummond's art gallery is going to tell me if I ever get her on the phone. Think about that call to Chiswell's constituency office about people 'pissing themselves as they die'—which isn't conclusive in itself, I grant you, but it's bloody suggestive when you stop to think about it—"

"You're winding me up," said the incredulous Robin. "Your idea connects all of that? And makes sense of it?"

"Yep," said Strike smugly, "and it also explains how Winn and Aamir knew there were photographs at the Foreign Office, presumably of Jack o'Kent's gallows in use, when Aamir hadn't worked there in months and Winn, so far as we know, had never set foot—"

Strike's mobile rang. He checked the screen.

"Izzy calling back. I'll take it outside. I want to smoke."

He got out of the car. Robin heard him say, "Hi," before he slammed the door. She sat waiting for him, her mind buzzing. Either Strike had genuinely had a brainwave, or he was taking the mickey, and she slightly inclined to the latter, so utterly disconnected did the separate bits of information he had just listed seem.

Five minutes later, Strike returned to the passenger seat.

"Our client's unhappy," he reported, slamming the door again. "Tegan was supposed to be telling us that Kinvara crept back out that night to kill Chiswell, not confirming her alibi and blabbing about Chiswell flogging gallows."

"Izzy admitted it?"

"Didn't have much choice, did she? But she didn't like it. Very insistent on telling me that exporting gallows was legal at the time. I put it to her that her father had defrauded Jimmy and Billy out of their money, and you were right. There were two sets of gallows built and ready to sell when Jack o'Kent died and nobody bothered to tell his sons. She liked admitting that even less."

"D'you think she's worried they'll mount a claim on Chiswell's estate?"

"I can't see that it'd do Jimmy's reputation much good in the circles he moves in, accepting money made from hanging people in the Third World," said Strike, "but you never know."

A car sped past on the road behind them and Strike craned around hopefully.

"Thought that might be Barclay..." He checked his watch. "Maybe he's missed the turning."

"Cormoran," said Robin, who was far less interested in either Izzy's mood or Barclay's whereabouts than in the theory Strike was withholding from her, "have you *seriously* got an idea that explains everything you just told me?"

"Yeah," said Strike, scratching his chin, "I have. Trouble is, it brings us closer to *who*, but I'm still damned if I can see *why* they did it, unless it was done out of blind hatred—but this doesn't feel like a red-blooded crime of passion, does it? This wasn't a hammer round the head. This was a well-planned execution."

"What happened to 'means before motive'?"

"I've been concentrating on means. That's how I got here."

"You won't even tell me 'he' or 'she'?"

"No good mentor would deprive you of the satisfaction of working it out for yourself. Any biscuits left?"

"No."

"Lucky I've still got this, then," Strike said, producing a Twix from his pocket, unwrapping it and handing her half, which she took with a bad grace that amused him.

Neither spoke until they had finished eating. Then Strike said, far more soberly than hitherto:

"Tonight's important. If there's nothing buried in a pink blanket at the bottom of the dell, the whole Billy business is finished: he imagined the strangling, we've set his mind at rest and I get to try and prove my theory about Chiswell's death, unencumbered by distractions, without worrying where a dead kid fits in and who killed her."

"Or him," Robin reminded Strike. "You said Billy wasn't sure which it was."

As she said it, her unruly imagination showed her a small skeleton wrapped in the rotten remains of a blanket. Would it be possible to tell whether the body had been male or female from what was left? Would there be a hair grip or a shoelace, buttons, a hank of long hair?

Let there be nothing, she thought. *God, let there be nothing there.*

But aloud, she asked:

"And if there *is*—something—someone—buried in the dell?"

"Then my theory's wrong, because I can't see how a child strangling in Oxfordshire fits with anything I've just mentioned."

"It doesn't have to," said Robin reasonably. "You could be right about who killed Chiswell, and this could be an entirely separate—"

"No," Strike said, shaking his head. "It's too much of a coincidence. If there's something buried in the dell, it connects to everything else. One brother witnessing a murder as a child, the other blackmailing a murdered man twenty years later, the kid being buried on Chiswell's land . . . if there's a child buried in the dell, it fits in somewhere. But I'll lay odds there's nothing there. If I seriously thought there was a body in the dell, I'd've tried to persuade the police to do the job. Tonight's for Billy. I promised him."

They sat watching the track fade gradually from sight in the darkness, Strike occasionally checking his mobile.

"Where's bloody Barclay got—? Ah!"

Headlights had just swung onto the track behind them. Barclay advanced an old Golf up the track and braked, turning off his lights. In her wing mirror, Robin watched his silhouette leave the car, turning into the flesh and blood Barclay as he reached Strike's window, carrying a kit bag just like the detective's.

"Evenin'," he said laconically. "Nice night for a grave robbin'."

"You're late," said Strike.

"Aye, I know. Just got a call from Flick. Thought you'd want tae hear what she's got tae say."

"Get in the back," Strike suggested. "You can tell us while we're waiting. We'll give it ten minutes, make sure it's properly dark."

Barclay clambered into the back of the Land Rover and closed the doors. Strike and Robin twisted around in their seats to talk to him.

"So, she calls me, greetin'—"

"English translation, please."

"Cryin', then—not to mention shittin' herself. The police came calling today."

"'Bout bloody time," said Strike. "And?"

"They searched the bathroom and found Chiswell's note. She's been interviewed."

"What was her explanation for having it?"

"Didnae confide in me. All she wanted was to know where Jimmy is. She's in a right fuckin' state. It was all 'just tell Jimmy they've got it, he'll know whut I mean.'"

"Where is Jimmy, d'you know?"

"Havenae a scooby. Saw him yesterday and he didnae mention any plans, but he told me he'd pissed off Flick by askin' if she had Bobbi Cunliffe's number. He took a liking to young Bobbi," said Barclay, grinning at Robin. "Flick told him she didnae know and wanted to know why he was so interested. Jimmy said he was jus' tryin' to get Bobbi along to a Real Socialist meetin', but, y'know, Flick's not that fuckin' dumb."

"D'you think she realizes it was me who tipped off the police?" asked Robin.

"Not yet," said Barclay. "She's panickin'."

"All right," said Strike, squinting up at the little of the sky they could see through the foliage overhead, "I think we should get started. Grab that bag beside you, Barclay, I've got tools and gloves in there."

"How're ye gonnae dig wi' your leg like that?" asked Barclay skeptically.

"You can't do it on your own," said Strike, "we'll still be here tomorrow night."

"I'm digging, too," said Robin firmly. She felt braver after Strike's assurances that they were highly unlikely to find anything in the dell. "Pass me those wellies, Sam."

Strike was already extracting torch and walking stick from his kit bag.

"I'll carry it," offered Barclay, and there was a sound of heavy metal tools shifting as he hoisted Strike's bag onto his shoulder along with his own.

The three of them set off along the track, Robin and Barclay matching their pace to Strike's, who progressed carefully, focusing the beam of his torch on the ground and making regular use of the stick, both to lean on and push obstacles out of his way. Their footsteps were deadened by the soft ground, but the quiet night amplified the chink and clatter of the tools carried by Barclay, the rustling of tiny, unseen creatures fleeing the giants who had invaded their wilderness and, from the direction of Chiswell House, the barking of a dog. Robin remembered the Norfolk terrier, and hoped he wasn't loose.

When they reached the clearing, Robin saw that night had turned the derelict cottage into a witch's lair. It was easy to imagine figures lurking behind the cracked windows and, telling herself firmly that the situation was quite creepy enough without imagining fresh horrors, she turned away from it. With a soft "ooft," Barclay let the kit bags fall onto the ground at the lip of the dell and unzipped both. By the light of the torch, Robin saw a wide array of tools: a pick, a mattock, two pinchbars, a fork, a small ax and three spades, one of them with a pointed head. There were also several pairs of thick gardening gloves.

"Aye, that should do us," said Barclay, squinting into the dark basin below them. "We'll want to clear that before we've got any chance o' breakin' the ground."

"Right," said Robin, reaching for a pair of gloves.

"Ye sure about this, big man?" Barclay asked Strike, who had done the same.

"I can pull up nettles, for Christ's sake," said Strike irritably.

"Bring the ax, Robin," said Barclay, grabbing the mattock and a pinchbar. "Some o' those bushes'll need hacked down."

The three of them slid and stumbled down the steep side of the dell and set to work. For nearly an hour they hacked at sinewy branches and tugged up nettles, occasionally swapping tools or returning to the upper ground to fetch different ones.

In spite of the gathering cool of the night, Robin was soon sweating, peeling off layers as she worked. Strike, on the other hand, was devoting a considerable amount of energy to pretending that the constant bending and twisting on slippery, uneven ground wasn't hurting the end of his stump. The darkness concealed his winces, and he was careful to rearrange his features whenever Barclay or Robin turned on the torch to check on their progress.

Physical activity was helping dispel Robin's fear of what could be hidden beneath their feet. Perhaps, she thought, this was what it was like in the army: hard manual work and the camaraderie of your colleagues helping you focus on something other than the grisly reality of what might lie ahead. The two ex-soldiers had bent to their task methodically and without complaint except for occasional curses as stubborn roots and branches tore at fabric and flesh.

"Time tae dig," said Barclay at last, when the bottom of the basin was as clear as they could reasonably make it. "Ye'll need to get out of it, Strike."

"I'll start, Robin can take over," said Strike. "Go on," he said to her, "take a break, hold the torch steady for us and pass me down the fork."

Growing up with three brothers had taught Robin valuable lessons about the male ego, and about picking her fights. Convinced that Strike's order was dictated more by pride than by sense, she never-theless complied, clambering up the steep side of the dell, there to sit and hold the beam of the torch steady while they worked, occasion-ally passing down different tools to help them remove rocks and tackle particularly hard stretches of ground.

It was a slow job. Barclay dug three times as fast as Strike, who Robin could see was immediately struggling, especially with pressing the pointed head spade down into the earth with a foot, his prosthesis being unreliable if asked to support his entire weight on the uneven ground, and excruciating when pressed down against resistant metal. Minute by minute she held off intervening, until a muttered "*fuck*" escaped Strike, and he bent over, grimacing in pain.

"Shall I take over?" she suggested.

"Think you're going to have to," he muttered ungraciously.

He dragged himself back out of the dell, trying not to put any more weight on his stump, taking the torch from a descending Robin and holding it steady for the other two as they worked, the end of his stump throbbing and, he suspected, rubbed raw.

Barclay had created a short channel a couple of feet deep before he took his first break, clambering out of the hole to fetch a bottle of water from his kit bag. While he drank and Robin took a rest, lean-ing on the handle of her spade, the sound of barking reached them again. Barclay squinted towards the unseen Chiswell House.

"What kind of dogs has she got in there?" he asked.

"Old Lab and a yappy bastard of a terrier," said Strike.

"Don't like our chances if she lets them oot," said Barclay, wiping his mouth on his arm. "Terrier'll get straight through those bushes. They've got fuckin' good hearin', terriers."

"Better hope she doesn't let them out, then," said Strike, but he added, "Give it five, Robin," and turned off the torch.

Robin, too, climbed out of the basin and accepted a fresh bottle of water from Barclay. Now that she was no longer digging, the chill made her exposed flesh creep. The fluttering and scurrying of small creatures in the grass and trees seemed extraordinarily loud in the darkness. Still the dog barked, and, distantly, Robin thought she heard a woman shout.

"Did you hear that?"

"Aye. Sounded like she was telling it to shut up," said Barclay.

They waited. At last, the terrier stopped barking.

"Give it a few more minutes," said Strike. "Let it fall asleep."

They waited, the whispering of every leaf magnified in the darkness, until Robin and Barclay lowered themselves back into the dell and began to dig again.

Robin's muscles were now begging for mercy, her palms beginning to blister beneath the gloves. The deeper they dug, the harder the job became, the soil compacted and full of rocks. Barclay's end of the trench was considerably deeper than Robin's.

"Let me do a bit," Strike suggested.

"No," she snapped, too tired to be anything but blunt. "You'll bugger your leg completely."

"She's nae wrong, pal," panted Barclay. "Gie's another drink of water, I'm gaspin'."

An hour later, Barclay was standing waist deep in soil and Robin's palms were bleeding beneath the overlarge gloves, which were rubbing away layers of skin as she used the blunt end of the mattock to try and prize a heavy rock out of the ground.

"Come—*on*—you—bloody—thing—"

"Want a hand?" offered Strike, readying himself to descend.

"Stay there," she told him angrily. "I'm not going to be able to help carry you back to the car, not after this—"

A final, involuntary yelp escaped her as she succeeded in overturning the small boulder. A couple of tiny, wriggling insects attached to the underside slid away from the torchlight. Strike directed the beam back on Barclay.

"Cormoran," said Robin sharply.

"What?"

"I need light."

Something in her voice made Barclay stop digging. Rather than direct the beam back at her, and disregarding her warning of a moment ago, Strike slid back down into the pit, landing on the loose earth. The torchlight swung around, blinding Robin for a second.

"What've you seen?"

"Shine it here," she said. "On the rock."

Barclay clambered towards them, his jeans covered from hem to pockets in soil.

Strike did as Robin asked. The three of them peered down at the encrusted surface of the rock. There, stuck to the mud, was a strand of what was plainly not vegetable matter, but wool fibers, faintly but distinctly pink.

They turned in unison to examine the indentation left in the ground where the rock had sat, Strike directing the torchlight into the hole.

"Oh, shit," gasped Robin, and without thinking she clapped two muddy garden gloves to her face. A couple of inches of filthy material had been revealed, and in the strong beam of the torch, it, too, was pink.

"Give me that," said Strike, tugging the mattock out of her hand.

"No—!"

But he almost pushed her aside. By the deflected torchlight she could see his expression, forbidding, furious, as though the pink blanket had grievously wronged him, as though he had suffered a personal affront.

"Barclay, you take this."

He thrust the mattock at his subcontractor.

"Break this up, as much as you can. Try not to puncture the blanket. Robin, go to the other end. Use the fork. And mind my hands," Strike told Barclay. Sticking the torch in his mouth so that he could see by its light, he fell to his knees in the dirt and began to move earth aside with his fingers.

"Listen," whispered Robin, freezing.

The sound of the terrier's frenzied barking reached them once again through the night air.

"I yelled, didn't I, when I overturned the rock?" whispered Robin. "I think I woke it up again."

"Never mind that now," said Strike, his fingers prizing dirt away from the blanket. "Dig."

"But what if——?"

"We'll deal with that if it happens. *Dig.*"

Robin plied the fork. After a couple of minutes, Barclay swapped the mattock for a shovel. Slowly, the length of the pink blanket, its contents still buried too deep to remove, was revealed.

"That's no adult," said Barclay, surveying the stretch of filthy blanket.

And still, the terrier continued to yap, distantly, from the direction of Chiswell House.

"We should call the polis, Strike," said Barclay, pausing to wipe sweat and mud out of his eyes. "Are we no disturbing a crime scene, here?"

Strike didn't answer. Feeling slightly sick, Robin watched his fingers feeling the shape of the thing that was hidden beneath the filthy blanket.

"Go up to my kit bag," he told her. "There's a knife in there. Stanley knife. Quickly."

The terrier was still yapping distractedly. Robin thought it sounded louder. She clambered up the steep side of the dell, groped around in the dark depths of the bag, found the knife and slid back down to Strike.

"Cormoran, I think Sam's right," she whispered. "We should leave this to the——"

"Give me the knife," he said, holding out his hand. "Come on, quick, I can feel it. This is the skull. *Quickly!*"

Against her better instincts, she handed over the blade. There was a sound of puncturing fabric and then a ripping.

"What are you doing?" she gasped, watching Strike tugging at something in the ground.

"Jesus fuck, Strike," said Barclay angrily, "are ye tryin' to rip off its——?"

With a dreadful crunching noise, the earth gave up something large and white. Robin gave a small yelp, stepped backwards and fell, half-sitting, into the wall of the dell.

"Fuck," repeated Barclay.

Strike shifted the torch to his free hand so as to shine it onto the thing he had just dragged out of the earth. Stunned, Robin and Barclay saw the discolored and partially shattered skull of a horse.

66

Do not sit here musing and brooding over insoluble conundrums.
                              Henrik Ibsen, *Rosmersholm*

Protected through the years by the blanket, the skull shone pale in the torchlight, weirdly reptilian in the length of its nose and the sharpness of its mandibles. A few blunt teeth remained. There were cavities in the skull in addition to the eyeholes, one in the jaw, one to the side of the head, and around each, the bone was cracked and splintered.

"Shot," said Strike, turning the skull slowly in his hands. A third indentation showed the course of another bullet, which had fractured but not penetrated the horse's head.

Robin knew she would have been feeling far worse had the skull been human, but she was nonetheless shaken by the noise it had made when released from the earth, and by the unexpected sight of this fragile shell of what had once lived and breathed, stripped bare by bacteria and insects.

"Vets euthanize horses with a single shot to the forehead," she said. "They don't spray them with bullets."

"Rifle," said Barclay authoritatively, clambering nearer to examine the skull. "Someone's took pot shots at it."

"Not that big, is it? Was it a foal?" Strike asked Robin.

"Maybe, but I think it looks more like a pony, or a miniature horse."

He turned it slowly in his hands and all three of them watched the skull moving in the torchlight. They had expended so much pain and effort digging it out of the ground that it seemed to hold secrets beyond those of its mere existence.

"So Billy *did* witness a burial," said Strike.

"But it wasn't a child. You won't have to rethink your theory," said Robin.

"Theory?" repeated Barclay, and was ignored.

"I don't know, Robin," said Strike, his face ghostly beyond the torchlight. "If he didn't invent the burial, I don't think he invented—"

"Shit," said Barclay. "She's done it, she's let those fucking dogs out."

The yapping of the terrier and the deeper, booming barks of the Labrador, no longer muffled by containing walls, came ringing through the night. Without ceremony, Strike dropped the skull.

"Barclay, grab all the tools and get out of here. We'll hold the dogs off."

"What about—?"

"Leave it, there's no time to fill it in," said Strike, already clambering out of the dell, ignoring the excruciating pain in the end of his stump. "Robin, come on, you're with me—"

"What if she's called the police?" Robin said, reaching the top of the dell first and turning to help heave Strike up.

"We'll wing it," he panted, "come on, I want to stop the dogs before they get to Sam."

The woods were dense and tangled. Strike had left his walking stick behind. Robin held his arm as he limped as fast as he could, grunting with pain every time he asked his stump to bear his weight. Robin glimpsed a pinprick of light through the trees. Somebody had come out of the house with a torch.

Suddenly, the Norfolk terrier burst through the undergrowth, barking ferociously.

"Good boy, yes, you found us!" Robin panted.

Ignoring her friendly overture it launched itself at her, trying to bite. She kicked out at it with her Wellingtoned foot, holding it at bay while sounds reached them of the heavier Labrador crashing towards them.

"Little fucker," said Strike, trying to repel the Norfolk terrier as it darted around them, snarling, but seconds later the terrier had caught wind of Barclay: it turned its head towards the dell and, before either of them could stop it, took off again, yapping frenziedly.

"Shit," said Robin.

"Never mind, keep going," said Strike, though the end of his stump was burning and he wondered how much longer it would support him.

They had managed only a few more paces when the fat Labrador reached them.

"Good boy, yes, good boy," Robin crooned, and the Labrador, less enthusiastic about the chase, allowed her to secure a tight grip on its collar. "Come on, come with us," said Robin, and she half dragged it, with Strike still leaning on her, towards the overgrown croquet lawn where they now saw a torch bobbing ever nearer through the darkness. A shrill voice called:

"Badger! Rattenbury! Who's that? Who's there?"

The silhouette behind the torchlight was female and bulky.

"It's all right, Mrs. Chiswell!" called Robin. "It's only us!"

"Who's 'us'? Who are you?"

"Follow my lead," Strike muttered to Robin, and he called, "Mrs. Chiswell, it's Cormoran Strike and Robin Ellacott."

"What are you doing here?" she shouted, across the diminishing space between them.

"We were interviewing Tegan Butcher in the village, Mrs. Chiswell," called Strike, as he, Robin and the reluctant Badger made their laborious way through the long grass. "We were driving back this way and we saw two people entering your property."

"What two people? Where?"

"They entered the woods back there," said Strike. From the depths of the trees, the Norfolk terrier was still frenziedly barking. "We didn't have your number, or we'd have called to warn you."

Within a few feet of her now, they saw that Kinvara was wearing a thick, padded coat over a short nightdress of black silk, her legs bare above Wellington boots. Her suspicion, shock and incredulity met Strike's total assurance.

"Thought we ought to do something, seeing as we were the only people who witnessed it," he gasped, wincing a little as he hobbled up to her with Robin's assistance, self-deprecatingly heroic. "Apologies," he added, coming to a halt, "for the state of us. Those woods are muddy and I fell over a couple of times."

A cold breeze swept the dark lawn. Kinvara stared at him, flummoxed, suspicious, then turned her face in the direction of the terrier's continued barking.

"RATTENBURY!" she shouted. "*RATTENBURY!*"

She turned back to Strike.

"What did they look like?

"Men," invented Strike, "young and fit from the way they were moving. We knew you'd had trouble with trespassers before—"

"Yes. Yes, I have," said Kinvara, sounding frightened. She seemed to take in Strike's condition for the first time, as he leaned heavily on Robin, face contorted with pain.

"I suppose you'd better come in."

"Thanks very much," said Strike gratefully, "very kind of you."

Kinvara jerked the Labrador's collar out of Robin's grip and bellowed, "RATTENBURY!" again, but the distantly barking terrier did not respond, so she dragged the Labrador, which was showing signs of rebellion, back towards the house, Robin and Strike following.

"What if she calls the police?" Robin muttered to Strike.

"Cross that bridge when we come to it," he responded.

A floor-to-ceiling drawing room window stood open. Kinvara had evidently followed her frantic dogs through it, as the quickest route to the woods.

"We're pretty muddy," Robin warned her, as they crunched their way across the gravel path that encircled the house.

"Just leave your boots outside," said Kinvara, stepping into the drawing room without bothering to remove her own. "I'm planning to change this carpet, anyway."

Robin tugged off her wellies, followed Strike inside and closed the window.

The cold, dingy room was illuminated by a single lamp.

"Two men?" Kinvara repeated, turning again to Strike. "Where exactly did you see them coming in?"

"Over the wall at the road," said Strike.

"D'you think they knew you'd seen them?"

"Oh yeah," said Strike. "We pulled up, but they ran into the woods. Think they might've bottled it once we followed them, though, don't you?" he asked Robin.

"Yes," said Robin, "we think we heard them running back towards the road when you let the dogs out."

"Rattenbury's still chasing someone—of course, that could be a fox—he goes crazy about the foxes in the woods," said Kinvara.

Strike's attention had just been caught by a change to the room since the last time he had seen it. There was a fresh square of dark crimson wallpaper over the mantelpiece, where the painting of the mare and foal had hung.

"What happened to your picture?" he asked.

Kinvara turned to see what Strike was talking about. She answered, perhaps a few seconds too late:

"I sold it."

"Oh," said Strike. "I thought you were particularly fond of that one?"

"Not since what Torquil said that day. I didn't like having it hanging there, after that."

"Ah," said Strike.

Rattenbury's persistent barking continued to echo from the woods where, Strike was certain, it had found Barclay, struggling back to his car with two kit bags full of tools. Now that Kinvara had released her hold on its collar, the fat Labrador let out a single booming bark and trotted to the window, where it began whining and pawing at the glass.

"The police won't get here in time even if I call them," said Kinvara, half worried, half angry. "I'm never top priority. They think I make it all up, these intruders."

"I'm going to check on the horses," she said, coming to a decision, but instead of going out through the window, she stomped out of the drawing room into the hall and from there, as far as they could hear, into a different room.

"I hope the dog hasn't got Barclay," Robin whispered.

"Better hope he hasn't brained it with a spade," muttered Strike.

The door reopened. Kinvara had returned, and to Robin's consternation, she was carrying a revolver.

"I'll take that," said Strike, hobbling forwards and taking the revolver out of her startled grip. He examined it. "Harrington & Richardson 7-shot? This is illegal, Mrs. Chiswell."

"It was Jasper's," she replied, as though this constituted a special permit, "and I'd rather take—"

"I'll come with you to check on the horses," said Strike firmly, "and Robin can stay here and keep an eye on the house."

Kinvara might have liked to protest, but Strike was already opening the drawing room window. Seizing its opportunity, the Labrador lumbered back out into the dark garden, its deep barks echoing around the grounds.

"Oh, for God's sake—you shouldn't have let him out—Badger!" shouted Kinvara. She whipped back around to Robin, said, "mind you stay in this room!" then followed the Labrador back into the garden, Strike limping after her with the rifle. Both disappeared into the darkness. Robin stood where they had left her, struck by the vehemence of Kinvara's order.

The open window had admitted plenty of night air into what was already a chilly interior. Robin approached the log basket beside the fire, which was temptingly full of newspaper, sticks, logs and firelighters, but she could hardly build a fire in Kinvara's absence. The room was as shabby in every respect as she remembered it, the walls now denuded of everything but four prints of Oxfordshire landscapes. Outside in the grounds the two dogs continued to bark, but inside the room the only sound, which Robin hadn't noticed on her last visit, due to the family's talking and bickering, was the loud ticking of an old grandfather clock in the corner.

Every muscle in Robin's body was starting to ache after the long hours of digging, and her blistered hands were smarting. She had just sat down on the sagging sofa, hugging herself for warmth, when she heard a creak overhead that sounded very like a footstep.

Robin stared up at the ceiling. She had probably imagined it. Old houses made strange noises that sounded human until they were familiar to you. Her parents' radiators made chugging noises in the night and their old doors groaned in the central heating. It was probably nothing.

A second creak sounded, several feet from where the first had occurred.

As she got to her feet, Robin scanned the room for anything she could use as a weapon. A small, ugly bronze frog ornament sat on a table beside the sofa. As her fingers closed over the cold pock-marked surface, she heard a third creak from overhead. Unless she was imagining it, the footsteps had now moved all the way across a room directly above the one in which she was.

Robin stood quite still for almost a minute, straining her ears. She knew what Strike would say: stay put. Then she heard another tiny movement overhead. Somebody, she was sure, was creeping around upstairs.

Moving as quietly as possible in her socked feet, Robin edged around the drawing room door without touching it, in case it creaked, and walked quietly into the middle of the stone-flagged hall, where the hanging lantern cast a patchy light. She came to a halt beneath it, straining her ears, heart bumping erratically, imagining an unknown person standing above her, also standing, frozen, listening, waiting. Bronze frog still clutched in her right hand, she moved to the foot of the stairs. The landing above her was in darkness. The sound of the dogs' barking echoed from deep in the woods.

She was halfway towards the upper landing when she thought she heard another small noise above her: the scuff of a foot on carpet followed by the swish of a closing door.

She knew that there was no point calling out "Who's there?" If the person hiding from her had been prepared to show their face, they would hardly have let Kinvara leave the house alone to face whatever had set off the dogs.

Reaching the top of the stairs, Robin saw that a vertical strip of light lay like a spectral finger across the dark floor, emanating from the only lit room. Her neck and scalp prickled as she crept towards it, afraid that the unknown lurker was watching from one of the three dark rooms with open doors she was passing. Constantly checking over her shoulder, she pushed the door of the lit bedroom with the tips of her fingers, raised the bronze frog high and entered.

This was clearly Kinvara's room: messy, cluttered and deserted. A single lamp burned on the bedside table nearest the door. The bed was unmade, with an air of having been left in a hurry, the cream quilted eiderdown lying crumpled on the floor. The walls were covered with many pictures of horses, all of them of significantly lesser quality, even to Robin's untutored eye, than the missing picture in the drawing room. The wardrobe doors stood open, but only a Lilliputian could have been hidden among the densely packed clothes within.

Robin returned to the dark landing. Taking a tighter grip on the bronze frog, she oriented herself. The sounds she had heard had come from a room directly overhead, which meant that it was probably the one with the closed door, facing her.

As she reached out her hand towards the doorknob, the terrifying sensation that unseen eyes were watching intensified. Pushing the door open, she felt around on the interior wall without entering, until she found a light switch.

The stark light revealed a cold, bare bedroom with a brass bedstead and a single chest of drawers. The heavy curtains on their old fashioned brass rings had been drawn, hiding the grounds. On the double bed lay the painting, "Mare Mourning," the brown and white mare forever nosing the pure white foal curled up in the straw.

Groping in the pocket of her jacket with the hand not holding the bronze paperweight, Robin found her mobile and took several photographs of the painting lying on the bedspread. It had the appearance of having been hastily placed there.

She had a sudden feeling that something had moved behind her. She whipped around, trying to blink away the shining impression of the gilded frame burned into her retina by the flash on her camera. Then she heard Strike's and Kinvara's voices growing louder in the garden and knew that they were returning to the drawing room.

Slapping off the light in the spare room, Robin ran as quietly as possible back across the landing and down the stairs. Fearing that she wouldn't be able to reach the drawing room in time to greet them, she darted to the downstairs bathroom, flushed the toilet, and then ran back across the hall, reaching the drawing room just as her hostess re-entered it from the garden.

67

. . . I had good reason enough for so jealously drawing a veil of concealment over our compact.

Henrik Ibsen, *Rosmersholm*

The Norfolk terrier was struggling in Kinvara's arms, its paws muddy. At the sight of Robin, Rattenbury set up a volley of barking again and struggled to get free.

"Sorry, I was dying for the loo," panted Robin, the bronze frog hidden behind her back. The old cistern backed up her story, making loud gushing and clanking noises that echoed through the stone-flagged hallway. "Any luck?" Robin called to Strike, who was climbing back into the room behind Kinvara.

"Nothing," said Strike, now haggard with pain. After waiting for the panting Labrador to hop back into the room, he closed the window, the revolver in his other hand. "There were definitely people out there, though. The dogs knew it, but I think they've taken off. What were the odds of us passing just as they were climbing over the wall?"

"Oh, do *shut up*, Rattenbury!" shouted Kinvara.

She set the terrier down and, when it refused to stop yapping at Robin, she threatened it with a raised hand, at which it whimpered and retreated into a corner to join the Labrador.

"Horses OK?" Robin asked, moving to the end table from which she had taken the bronze paperweight.

"One of the stable doors wasn't fastened properly," said Strike, wincing as he bent to feel his knee. "But Mrs. Chiswell thinks it might have been left like that. Would you mind if I sat down, Mrs. Chiswell?"

"I—no, I suppose not," Kinvara said gracelessly.

She headed to a table of bottles sitting in the corner of the room, uncorked some Famous Grouse and poured herself a stiff measure of whisky. While her back was turned, Robin slid the paperweight back onto the table. She tried to catch Strike's eyes, but he had sunk down onto the sofa with a faint groan, and now turned to Kinvara.

"I wouldn't say no, if you're offering," he said shamelessly, wincing again as he massaged his right knee. "Actually, I think this is going to have to come off, do you mind?"

"Well—no, I suppose not. What do you want?"

"I'll have a Scotch as well, please," said Strike, setting the revolver down on the table beside the bronze frog, rolling up his trouser leg and signaling with his eyes that Robin, too, should sit down.

While Kinvara sloshed another measure into a glass, Strike started to remove the prosthesis. Turning to give him his drink, Kinvara watched in queasy fascination as Strike worked on the false leg, averting her eyes at the point it left the inflamed stump. Panting as he propped the prosthesis against the ottoman, Strike allowed his trouser leg to fall back over his amputated leg.

"Thanks very much," he said, accepting the whisky from her and taking a swig.

Trapped with a man who couldn't walk, to whom she ought in theory to be grateful, and to whom she had just given a drink, Kinvara sat down, too, her expression stony.

"Actually, Mrs. Chiswell, I was going to phone you to confirm a couple of things we heard from Tegan earlier," said Strike. "We could go through them now if you like. Get them out of the way."

With a slight shiver, Kinvara glanced at the empty fireplace, and Robin said helpfully, "Would you like me to—?"

"No," snapped Kinvara. "I can do it."

She went to the deep basket standing beside the fireplace, from which she grabbed an old newspaper. While Kinvara built a structure of small bits of wood over a mound of newspaper and a firelighter, Robin succeeded in catching Strike's eye.

"There's somebody upstairs," she mouthed, but she wasn't sure he had understood. He merely raised his eyebrows quizzically, and turned back to Kinvara.

A match flared. Flames erupted around the little pile of paper and sticks in the fireplace. Kinvara picked up her glass and returned to the drinks table, where she topped it up with more neat Scotch, then, coat wrapped more tightly around herself, she returned to the log basket, selected a large piece of wood, dropped it on top of the burgeoning fire, then fell back onto the sofa.

"Go on, then," she said sullenly to Strike. "What do you want to know?"

"As I say, we spoke to Tegan Butcher today."

"And?"

"And we now know what Jimmy Knight and Geraint Winn were blackmailing your husband about."

Kinvara evinced no surprise.

"I told those stupid girls you'd find out," she said with a shrug. "Izzy and Fizzy. Everyone round here knew what Jack o'Kent was doing in the barn. Of course somebody was going to talk."

She took a gulp of whisky.

"I suppose you know all of it, do you? The gallows? The boy in Zimbabwe?"

"You mean Samuel?" asked Strike, taking a punt.

"Exactly, Samuel Mu—Mudrap or something."

The fire caught suddenly, flames leaping up past the log, which shifted in a shower of sparks.

"Jasper was worried they were his gallows the moment we heard the boy had been hanged. You know all of it, do you? That there were two sets? But only one made it to the government. The other lot went astray, the lorry was hijacked or something. That's how they ended up in the middle of nowhere.

"The photographs are pretty grisly, apparently. The Foreign Office thinks it was probably a case of mistaken identity. Jasper didn't see how they could be traced to him, but Jimmy said he could prove they were.

"I *knew* you'd find out," said Kinvara, with an air of bitter satisfaction. "Tegan's a horrible gossip."

"So, to be clear," said Strike, "when Jimmy Knight first came here to see you, he was asking for his and Billy's share for two sets of gallows his father had left completed when he died?"

"Exactly," said Kinvara, sipping her whisky. "They were worth eighty thousand for the pair. He wanted forty."

"But presumably," said Strike, who remembered that Chiswell had talked of Jimmy returning a week after his first attempt to get money, and asking for a reduced amount, "your husband told him he'd only ever received payment for one of them, as one set got stolen en route?"

"Yes," said Kinvara, with a shrug. "So then Jimmy asked for twenty, but we'd spent it."

"How did you feel about Jimmy's request, when he first came asking for money?" Strike asked.

Robin wasn't sure whether Kinvara had turned a little pinker in the face, or whether it was the effects of the whisky.

"Well, I saw his point, if you want the truth. I could see why he felt he had a claim. Half the proceeds of the gallows belonged to the Knight boys. That had been the arrangement while Jack o'Kent was alive, but Jasper took the view that Jimmy couldn't expect money for the stolen set, and given that he'd been storing them in his barn, and bearing all the costs of transportation and so on...and he said that Jimmy couldn't sue him even if he wanted to. He didn't like Jimmy."

"No, well, I suppose their politics were very different," said Strike.

Kinvara almost smirked.

"It was a bit more personal than that. Haven't you heard about Jimmy and Izzy? No...I suppose Tegan's too young to have heard that story. Oh, it was only once," she said, apparently under the impression that Strike was shocked, "but that was quite enough for Jasper. A man like Jimmy Knight, deflowering his darling daughter, you know...

"But Jasper couldn't have given Jimmy the money even if he'd wanted to," she went on. "He'd already spent it. It took care of our overdraft for a while and repaired the stable roof. I never knew," she added, as though sensing unspoken criticism, "until Jimmy explained it to me that night, what the arrangement between Jasper and Jack o'Kent had been. Jasper had told me the gallows were his to sell and I believed him. *Naturally* I believed him. He was my husband."

She got up again and headed back to the drinks table as the fat Labrador, seeking warmth, left its distant corner, waddled around the ottoman and slumped down in front of the now roaring fire. The Norfolk terrier trotted after it, growling at Strike and Robin until Kinvara said angrily:

"*Shut up*, Rattenbury."

"There's are a couple more things I wanted to ask you about," said Strike. "Firstly, did your husband have a passcode on his phone?"

"Of course he did," said Kinvara. "He was very security-conscious."

"So he didn't give it out to a lot of people?"

"He didn't even tell *me* what it was," said Kinvara. "Why are you asking?"

Ignoring the question, Strike said:

"Your stepson's now told us a different story to account for his trip down here, on the morning of your husband's death."

"Oh, really? What's he saying this time?"

"That he was trying to stop you selling a necklace that's been in the family for—"

"Come clean, has he?" she interrupted, turning back towards them with a fresh whisky in her hands. With her long red hair tangled from the night air, and her flushed cheeks, she had a slight air of abandon now, forgetting to hold her coat closed as she headed back to the sofa, the black nightdress revealing a canyon of cleavage. She flopped back down on the sofa. "Yes, he wanted to stop me doing a flit with the necklace, which, by the way, I'm *perfectly* entitled to do. It's mine under the terms of the will. Jasper should have been a bit more bloody careful writing it if he didn't want me to have it, shouldn't he?"

Robin remembered Kinvara's tears, the last time they had been in this room, and how she had felt sorry for her, unlikable though she had shown herself to be in other ways. Her attitude now had little of the grief-stricken widow about it, but perhaps, Robin thought, that was the drink, and the recent shock of their intrusion into her grounds.

"So you're backing up Raphael's story that he drove down here to stop you taking off with the necklace?"

"Don't you believe him?"

"Not really," said Strike. "No."

"Why not?"

"It rings false," said Strike. "I'm not convinced your husband was in a fit state that morning to remember what he had and hadn't put in his will."

"He was well enough to call me and demand to know whether I was really walking out on him," said Kinvara.

"Did you tell him you were going to sell the necklace?"

"Not in so many words, no. I said I was going to leave as soon as I could find somewhere else for me and the horses. I suppose he might have wondered how I'd manage that, with no real money of my own, which made him remember the necklace."

"So Raphael came here out of simple loyalty to the father who'd cut him off without a penny?"

Kinvara subjected Strike to a long and penetrating look over her whisky glass, then said to Robin:

"Would you throw another log on the fire?"

Noting the lack of a "please," Robin nevertheless did as she was asked. The Norfolk terrier, which had now joined the sleeping Labrador on the hearthrug, growled at her until she had sat down again.

"All right," said Kinvara, with an air of coming to a decision. "All right, here it is. I don't suppose it matters any more, anyway. Those bloody girls will find out in the end and serve Raphael right.

"He *did* come down to try and stop me taking the necklace, but it wasn't for Jasper, Fizzy or Flopsy's sake—I suppose," she said aggressively to Robin, "you know all the family nicknames, don't you? You probably had a good giggle at them, while you were working with Izzy?"

"Erm—"

"Oh, don't pretend," said Kinvara, rather nastily, "I know you'll have heard them. They call me 'Tinky Two' or something, don't they? And behind his back, Izzy, Fizzy and Torquil call Raphael 'Rancid.' Did you know that?"

"No," said Robin, at whom Kinvara was still glaring.

"Sweet, isn't it? And Raphael's mother is known to all of them as the Orca, because she dresses in black and white.

"Anyway... when the Orca realized Jasper wasn't going to marry her," said Kinvara, now very red in the face, "d'you know what she did?"

Robin shook her head.

"She took the famous family necklace to the man who became her *next* lover, who was a diamond merchant, and she had him prize out the really valuable stones and replace them with cubic zirconias. Man-made diamond substitutes," Kinvara elucidated, in case Strike and Robin hadn't understood. "Jasper never realized what she'd done and I certainly didn't. I expect Ornella's been having a jolly good laugh every time I've been photographed in the necklace, thinking I'm wearing a hundred thousand pounds' worth of stones.

"Anyway, when my darling stepson got wind of the fact that I was leaving his father, and heard that I'd talked about having enough money to buy land for the horses, he twigged that I might be about to get the necklace valued. So he came hotfooting it down here, because the last thing he wanted was for the family to find out what his mother had done. What would be the odds of him wheedling his way back into his father's good books after that?"

"Why haven't you told anyone this?" asked Strike.

"Because Raphael promised me that morning that if I didn't tell his father what the Orca had done, he'd maybe manage to persuade his mother to give the stones back. Or at least, give me their value."

"And are you still trying to recover the missing stones?"

Kinvara squinted malevolently at Strike over the rim of her glass.

"I haven't done anything about it since Jasper died, but that doesn't mean I won't. Why should I let the bloody Orca waltz off with what's rightfully mine? It's down in Jasper's will, the contents of the house that haven't been spefi—specif—spe-cif-ically excluded," she enunciated carefully, thick-tongued now, "belong to me. So," she said, fixing Strike with a gimlet stare, "does *that* sound more like Raphael to you? Coming down here to try and cover up for his darling mama?"

"Yes," said Strike, "I'd have to say it does. Thank you for your honesty."

Kinvara looked pointedly at the grandfather clock, which was now showing three in the morning, but Strike refused to take the hint.

"Mrs. Chiswell, there's one last thing I want to ask and I'm afraid it's quite personal."

"What?" she said crossly.

"I spoke to Mrs. Winn recently. Della Winn, you know, the—"

"Della-Winn-the-Minister-for-Sport," said Kinvara, just as her husband had done, the first time Strike met him. "Yes, I know who she is. Very odd woman."

"In what way?"

Kinvara wriggled her shoulders impatiently, as though it should be obvious.

"Never mind. What did she say?"

"That she met you in a state of considerable distress a year ago and that from what she could gather, you were upset because your husband had admitted to an affair."

Kinvara opened her mouth then closed it again. She sat thus for a few seconds, then shook her head as though to clear it and said:

"I...thought he was being unfaithful, but I was wrong. I got it all wrong."

"According to Mrs. Winn, he'd said some fairly cruel things to you."

"I don't remember what I said to her. I wasn't very well at the time. I was overemotional and I got everything wrong."

"Forgive me," said Strike, "but, as an outsider, your marriage seemed—"

"What a dreadful job you've got," said Kinvara shrilly. "What a really nasty, *seedy* job you do. Yes, our marriage was going wrong, what of it? Do you think, now he's dead, now he's *killed himself*, I want to relive it all with the pair of *you*, perfect strangers whom my stupid stepdaughters have dragged in, to stir everything up and make it ten times worse?"

"So you've changed your mind, have you? You think your husband committed suicide? Because when we were last here, you suggested Aamir Mallik—"

"I don't know what I said then!" she said hysterically. "Can you not understand what it's been like since Jasper killed himself, with the police and the family and *you*? I didn't think this would happen,

I had no idea, it didn't seem real—Jasper was under enormous pressure those last few months, drinking too much, in an awful temper—the blackmail, the fear of it all coming out—yes, I think he killed himself and I've got to live with the fact that I walked out on him that morning, which was probably the final straw!"

The Norfolk terrier began to yap furiously again. The Labrador woke with a start and started barking, too.

"Please leave!" shouted Kinvara, getting to her feet. "Get out! I never wanted you mixed up in this in the first place! Just go, will you?"

"Certainly," said Strike politely, setting down his empty glass. "Would you mind waiting while I get my leg back on?"

Robin had already stood up. Strike strapped the false leg back on while Kinvara watched, chest heaving, glass in hand. At last, Strike was ready to stand, but his first attempt had him falling back onto the sofa. With Robin's assistance, he finally achieved a standing position.

"Well, goodbye, Mrs. Chiswell."

Kinvara's only answer was to stalk to the window and fling it open again, shouting at the dogs, which had got up excitedly, to stay put.

No sooner had her unwelcome guests stepped out onto the gravel path than Kinvara slammed the window behind them. While Robin put her Wellington boots back on, they heard the shriek of the brass curtain rings as Kinvara dragged the drapes shut, then called the dogs out of the room.

"Not sure I'm going to be able to make it back to the car, Robin," said Strike, who wasn't putting weight on his prosthesis. "In retrospect, the digging might've...might've been a mistake."

Wordlessly, Robin took his arm and placed it over her shoulders. He didn't resist. Together they moved slowly off across the grass.

"Did you understand what I mouthed at you back there?" asked Robin.

"That there was someone upstairs? Yeah," he said, wincing horribly every time he put down his false foot. "I did."

"You don't seem—"

"I'm not surpr—wait," he said abruptly, still leaning on her as he came to a halt. "You didn't go up there?"

"Yes," said Robin.

"*For fuck's sake—*"

"I heard footsteps."

"And what would've happened if you'd been jumped?"

"I took a weapon and I wasn't—and if I hadn't gone up there, I wouldn't have seen this."

Taking out her mobile, Robin brought up the photo of the painting on the bed, and handed it to him.

"You didn't see Kinvara's expression, when she saw the blank wall. Cormoran, she didn't realize that painting had been moved until you asked about it. Whoever was upstairs tried to hide it while she was outside."

Strike stared at the phone screen for what felt like a long time, his arm heavy on Robin's shoulders. Finally, he said:

"Is that a piebald?"

"Seriously?" said Robin, in total disbelief. "Horse colors? Now?"

"Answer me."

"No, piebalds are black and white, not brown and—"

"We need to go to the police," said Strike. "The odds on another murder just went up exponentially."

"You aren't serious?"

"I'm completely serious. Get me back to the car and I'll tell you everything...but don't ask me to talk till then, because my leg's fucking killing me."

68

I have tasted blood now...

Henrik Ibsen, *Rosmersholm*

Three days later, Strike and Robin received an unprecedented invitation. As a courtesy for having chosen to aid rather than upstage the police in passing on information about Flick's stolen note and "Mare Mourning," the Met welcomed the detective partners into the heart of the investigation at New Scotland Yard. Used to being treated by the police as either inconveniences or showboaters, Strike and Robin were surprised but grateful for this unforeseen thawing of relations.

On arrival, the tall blonde Scot who was heading the team ducked out of an interrogation room for a minute to shake hands. Strike and Robin knew that the police had brought two suspects in for questioning, although nobody had yet been charged.

"We spent the morning on hysterics and flat denial," DCI Judy McMurran told them, "but I think we'll have cracked her by the end of the day."

"Any chance we could give them a little look, Judy?" asked her subordinate, DI George Layborn, who had met Strike and Robin at the door and brought them upstairs. He was a pudgy man who reminded Robin of the traffic policeman who had thought he was such a card, back on the hard shoulder where she'd had her panic attack.

"Go on, then," said DCI McMurran, with a smile.

Layborn led Strike and Robin around a corner and through the first door on their right into a dark and cramped area, of which half one wall was a two-way mirror into an interrogation room.

Robin, who had only ever seen such spaces in films and on TV, was mesmerized. Kinvara Chiswell was sitting on one side of a desk, beside a thin-lipped solicitor in a pinstriped suit. White-faced, devoid of makeup, wearing a pale gray silk blouse so creased she might have slept in it, Kinvara was weeping into a tissue. Opposite her sat another detective inspector in a far cheaper suit than the solicitor's. His expression was impassive.

As they watched, DCI McMurran re-entered the room and took the vacant chair beside her colleague. After what felt like a very long time, but was probably only a minute, DCI McMurran spoke.

"Still nothing to say about your night at the hotel, Mrs. Chiswell?"

"This is like a nightmare," whispered Kinvara. "I can't believe this is happening. I can't believe I'm here."

Her eyes were pink, swollen and apparently lashless now that she had wept her mascara away.

"Jasper killed himself," she said tremulously. "He was depressed! Everyone will tell you so! The blackmail was eating away at him...have you talked to the Foreign Office yet? Even the idea that there might be photographs of that boy who was hanged—can't you see how scared Jasper was? If that had come out—"

Her voice cracked.

"Where's your evidence against me?" she demanded. "Where is it? *Where?*"

Her solicitor gave a dry little cough.

"To return," said DCI McMurran, "to the subject of the hotel. Why do you think your husband called them, trying to ascertain—"

"It isn't a crime to go to a hotel!" said Kinvara hysterically, and she turned to her solicitor, "This is ridiculous, Charles, how can they make a case against me because I went to a—"

"Mrs. Chiswell will answer any questions you've got about her birthday," the solicitor told DCI McMurran, with what Robin thought was remarkable optimism, "but equally—"

The door of the observation room opened and hit Strike.

"No problem, we'll shift," Layborn told his colleague. "Come on, gang, we'll go to the incident room. Got plenty more to show you."

As they turned a second corner, they saw Eric Wardle walking towards them.

"Never thought I'd see the day," he said, grinning as he shook Strike's hand. "Actually invited in by the Met."

"You staying, Wardle?" asked Layborn, who seemed faintly resentful at the prospect of another policeman sharing the guests he was keen to impress.

"Might as well," said Wardle. "Find out what I've been assisting in, all these weeks."

"Must've taken its toll," said Strike, as they followed Layborn into the incident room, "passing on all that evidence we found."

Wardle sniggered.

Used as she was to the cramped and slightly dilapidated offices in Denmark Street, Robin was fascinated to see the space that Scotland Yard devoted to the investigation into a high profile and suspicious death. A whiteboard on the wall carried a timeline for the killing. The adjacent wall bore a collage of photographs of the death scene and the corpse, the latter showing Chiswell freed from his plastic wrapping, so that his congested face appeared in awful close-up, with a livid scratch down one cheek, the cloudy eyes half open, the skin a dark, mottled purple.

Spotting her interest, Layborn showed her the toxicology reports and phone records that the police had used to build their case, then unlocked the large cupboard where physical evidence was bagged and tagged, including the cracked tube of lachesis pills, a grubby orange juice carton and Kinvara's farewell letter to her husband. Seeing the note that Flick had stolen, and a printout of the photograph of "Mare Mourning" lying on a spare bed, both of which Robin knew had now become central to the police case, she experienced a rush of pride.

"Right then," said DI Layborn, closing the cupboard and walking over to a computer monitor. "Time to see the little lady in action."

He inserted a video disk in the nearest machine, beckoning Strike, Robin and Wardle closer.

The crowded forecourt of Paddington station was revealed, jerky black and white figures moving everywhere. The time and date showed in the upper left corner.

"There she is," said Layborn, hitting "pause" and pointing a stubby figure at a woman. "See her?"

Even though blurred, the figure was recognizable as Kinvara. A bearded man had been caught in the frame, staring, probably because her coat hung open, revealing the clinging black dress she had worn to the Paralympian reception. Layborn pressed "play" again.

"Watch her, watch her — gives to the homeless —"

Kinvara had donated to a swaddled man holding a cup in a doorway.

"— watch her," Layborn said unnecessarily, "straight up to the railway worker — pointless question — shows him her ticket . . . watch her, now . . . off to the platform, stops and asks another bloke a question, making sure she's remembered every bloody step of the way, even if she's not caught on camera . . . *aaaand* . . . onto the train."

The picture twitched and changed. A train was pulling into the station at Swindon. Kinvara got off, talking to another woman.

"See?" said Layborn. "Still making damn sure people remember her, just in case. And —"

The picture changed again, to that of the car park at Swindon station.

"— there she is," said Layborn, "car's parked right near the camera, conveniently. In she gets and off she goes. Gets home, insists the stable girl stays overnight, sleeps in the next room, goes outside next morning to ride within sight of the girl . . . cast-iron alibi.

"Course, like you, we'd already come to the conclusion that if it was murder, it must have been a two-person job."

"Because of the orange juice?" asked Robin.

"Mostly," said Layborn. "If Chiswell" (he said the name as it was spelled) "had taken amitriptyline unknowingly, the most likely explanation was that he'd poured himself doctored juice out of a carton in the fridge, but the carton in the bin was undoctored and only had his prints on."

"Easy to get his prints on small objects once he was dead, though," said Strike. "Just press his hand onto them."

"Exactly," said Layborn, striding over to the wall of photographs and pointing at a close-up of the pestle and mortar. "So we went back to this. The way Chiswell's prints are positioned and the way the powdered residue was sitting there pointed to it being faked, which meant the doctored juice could have been fixed up hours in advance, by somebody who had a key, who knew which anti-depressants the wife was on, that Chiswell's sense of taste and smell were impaired and that he always drank juice in the mornings. Then all they'd need to do is have the accomplice plant an undoctored juice carton in the bin with his dead handprint on, and take away the one with the amitriptyline residue in it.

"Well, who's better positioned to know and do all of that, than the missus?" asked Layborn rhetorically. "But here she was, with her cast-iron alibi for time of death, seventy-odd miles away when he was gulping down anti-depressants. Not to mention she's left that letter, trying to give us a nice clean story: husband already facing bankruptcy and blackmail realizes his wife's leaving him, which tips him over the edge, so he tops himself.

"But," said Layborn, pointing at the enlarged picture of the dead Chiswell's face, stripped of its plastic bag, revealing a deep red scrape on the cheek, "we didn't like the look of *that*. We thought from the first that was suspicious. Amitriptyline in overdose can cause agitation as well as sleepiness. That mark looked as though somebody else forced the bag over his head.

"Then there was the open door. The last person in or out didn't know there was a trick to closing it properly, so it didn't look like Chiswell was the last person to touch it. Plus, the packaging on the pills being absent—that smelled wrong from the start. Why would Jasper Chiswell get rid of it?" asked Layborn. "Just a few little careless mistakes."

"It nearly came off," said Strike. "If only Chiswell had been put to sleep by the amitriptyline as intended, and if they'd thought the thing through right to the finest details—close the door properly, leave the pill packaging *in situ*—"

"But they didn't," said Layborn, "and *she's* not smart enough on her own to talk herself out of this."

"'I can't believe this is happening,'" Strike quoted. "She's consistent. On Saturday night she told us 'I didn't think this would happen,' 'it didn't seem real—'"

"Try that in court," said Wardle quietly.

"Yeah, what were you expecting, love, when you crushed up a load of pills and put them in his orange juice?" said Layborn. "Guilty is as guilty does."

"Amazing, the lies people can tell themselves when they're drifting along in the wake of a stronger personality," said Strike. "I'll bet you a tenner that when McMurran finally breaks her, Kinvara'll say they started off hoping Chiswell would kill himself, then trying to pressure him into doing it, and finally reached a point when there didn't seem much difference between trying to push him into suicide, and putting the pills in his orange juice herself. I notice she's still trying to push the gallows business as the reason he'd top himself."

"That was very good work of yours, connecting the dots on the gallows," admitted Layborn. "We were a bit behind you on that, but it explained a hell of a lot. This is highly confidential," he added, taking a brown envelope off a nearby desk and tipping out a large photograph, "but we had this from the Foreign Office this morning. As you can see—"

Robin, who had gone to look, half-wished she hadn't. What was there to be gained, really, from seeing the corpse of what seemed to be a teenage boy, whose eyes had been picked out by carrion birds, and hanging from a gallows in a rubble-strewn street? The boy's dangling feet were bare. Somebody, Robin guessed, had stolen his trainers.

"The lorry containing the second pair of gallows was hijacked. Government never took delivery and Chiswell never got payment for them. This picture suggests they ended up being used by rebels for extrajudicial killings. This poor lad, Samuel Murape, was in the wrong place at the wrong time. British student, gap year, out there to visit family. It's not particularly clear," Layborn said, "but see there, just behind his foot—"

"Yeah, that could be the mark of the white horse," said Strike.

Robin's mobile, which was switched to silent, vibrated in her pocket. She was waiting for an important call, but it was only a text from an unknown number.

I know you've blocked my phone, but I need to meet you. An urgent situation's come up and it's to your advantage as much as mine to sort it out. Matt

"It's nothing," Robin told Strike, returning the mobile to her pocket.

This was the third message Matthew had left that day.

Urgent situation, my arse.

Tom had probably found out that his fiancée and his good friend had been sleeping together. Maybe Tom was threatening to call Robin, or drop in on the office in Denmark Street, to find out how much she knew. If Matthew thought that constituted an "urgent situation" to Robin, who was currently standing beside multiple pictures of a drugged and suffocated government minister, he was wrong. With an effort, she refocused on the conversation in the incident room.

"...the necklace business," Layborn was saying to Strike. "Far more convincing story than the one he told us. All that guff about wanting to stop her hurting herself."

"It was Robin who got him to change his story, not me," said Strike.

"Ah—well, good work," Layborn said to Robin, with a hint of patronage. "I thought he was an oily little bastard when I took his initial statement. Cocky. Just out of jail, and all. No bloody remorse for running over that poor woman."

"How are you getting on with Francesca?" Strike asked. "The girl from the gallery?"

"We managed to get hold of the father in Sri Lanka and he's not happy. Being quite obstructive, actually," said Layborn. "He's trying to buy time to get her lawyered up. Bloody inconvenient, the whole family being abroad. I had to get tough with him over the phone. I can understand why he doesn't want it all coming out in court, but too bad. Gives you a real insight into the mindset of the upper classes, eh, case like this? One rule for them..."

"On that subject," said Strike, "I assume you've spoken to Aamir Mallik?"

"Yeah, we found him exactly where your boy—Hutchins, is it?—said he was. At his sister's. He's got a new job—"

"Oh, I'm glad," said Robin inadvertently.

"—and he wasn't overjoyed to have us turning up at first, but he ended up being very frank and helpful. Said he found that disturbed lad—Billy, is it?—on the street, wanting to see his boss, shouting about a dead child, strangled and buried on Chiswell's land. Took him home with the idea of getting him to hospital, but he asked Geraint Winn's advice first. Winn was furious. Told him on no account to call an ambulance."

"Did he, now?" said Strike, frowning.

"From what Mallik's told us, Winn was worried association with Billy's story would taint his own credibility. He didn't want the waters muddied by a psychotic tramp. Blew up at Mallik for taking him into a house belonging to the Winns, told him to turf him out on the street again. Trouble was—"

"Billy wouldn't go," said Strike.

"Exactly. Mallik says he was clearly out of his mind, thought he was being held against his will. Curled up in the bathroom most of the time. Anyway," Layborn took a deep breath, "Mallik's had enough of covering up for the Winns. He's confirmed that Winn wasn't with him on the morning of Chiswell's death. Winn told Mallik afterwards, when he put pressure on Mallik to lie, he'd had an urgent phone call at 6 a.m. that day, which is why he left the marital home early."

"And you've traced that call?" said Strike.

Layborn picked up the printout of phone records, rifled through them, then handed a couple of marked pages to Strike.

"Here you go. Burner phones," he said. "We've got three different numbers so far. There were probably more. Used once, never used again, untraceable except for the single instance we got on record. Months in the planning.

"A single-use phone was used to contact Winn that morning, and two more were used to call Kinvara Chiswell on separate occasions during the previous weeks. She 'can't remember' who called her, but both times—see there?—she talked to whoever it was for over an hour."

"What's Winn got to say for himself?" asked Strike.

"Closed up like an oyster," said Layborn. "We're working on him, don't worry. There are porn stars who've been fucked fewer different ways than Geraint W—sorry, love," he said, grinning, to Robin, who found the apology more offensive than anything Layborn had said. "But you take my point. He might as well tell us everything now. He's screwed every which w—well," he said, floundering once more. "What interests me," he started up again, "is how much the wife knew. Strange woman."

"In what way?" asked Robin.

"Oh, you know. I think she plays on this a bit," said Layborn, with a vague gesture towards his eyes. "Very hard to believe she didn't know what he was up to."

"Speaking of people not knowing what their other halves are up to," interposed Strike, who thought he detected a martial glint in Robin's eye, "how's it going with our friend Flick?"

"Ah, we're making very good progress there," said Layborn. "The parents have been helpful in *her* case. They're both lawyers and they've been urging her to cooperate. She's admitted she was Chiswell's cleaner, that she stole the note and took receipt of the crate of champagne right before Chiswell told her he couldn't afford her anymore. Says she put it in a cupboard in the kitchen."

"Who delivered it?"

"She can't remember. We'll find out. Courier service, I shouldn't wonder, booked on another burner phone."

"And the credit card?"

"That was another good spot of yours," admitted Layborn. "We didn't know a credit card had gone missing. We got details through from the bank this morning. The same day Flick's flatmate realized the card was gone, somebody charged a crate of champagne and bought a hundred quid's worth of stuff on Amazon, all to be sent to an address in Maida Vale. Nobody took delivery, so it was returned to the depot where it was picked up that afternoon by someone who had the failed delivery notice. We're trying to locate the staff who can identify the person who collected it and we're getting a breakdown on what was bought on Amazon, but my money's on helium, tubing and latex gloves.

"This was all planned months in advance. *Months*."

"And that?" Strike asked, pointing to the photocopy of the note in Chiswell's handwriting, which was lying on the side in its polythene bag. "Has she told you why she nicked it yet?"

"She says she saw 'Bill' and thought it meant her boyfriend's brother. Ironic, really," said Layborn. "If she hadn't stolen it, we wouldn't have cottoned on nearly so fast, would we?"

The "we," thought Robin, was daring, because it had been Strike who had "cottoned on," Strike who had finally cracked the significance of Chiswell's note, as they drove back to London from Chiswell House.

"Robin deserves the bulk of the credit there, too," said Strike. "She found the thing, she noticed 'Blanc de Blanc' and the Grand Vitara. I just pieced it together once it was staring me in the face."

"Well, we were just behind you," said Layborn, absentmindedly scratching his belly. "I'm sure we'd have got there."

Robin's mobile vibrated in her pocket again: somebody was calling, this time.

"I need to take this. Is there anywhere I can—?"

"Through here," said Layborn helpfully, opening a side door.

It was a photocopier room, with a small window covered in a Venetian blind. Robin closed the door on the others' conversation and answered.

"Hi, Sarah."

"Hi," said Sarah Shadlock.

She sounded totally unlike the Sarah whom Robin had known for nearly nine years, the confident and bombastic blonde whom Robin had sensed, even in their teens, was hoping that some mischance might befall Matthew's long-distance relationship with his girlfriend. Always there through the years, giggling at Matthew's jokes, touching his arm, asking loaded questions about Robin's relationship with Strike, Sarah had dated other men, settling at last for poor tedious

Tom, with his well-paid job and his bald patch, who had put diamonds on Sarah's finger and in her ears, but never quelled her yen for Matthew Cunliffe.

All her swagger had gone today.

"Well, I've asked two experts, but," she said, sounding fragile and fearful, "and they can't say for sure, not from a photograph taken on a phone—"

"Well, obviously not," said Robin coolly. "I said in my text, didn't I, that I wasn't expecting a definitive answer? We're not asking for a firm identification or valuation. All we want to know is whether somebody might have credibly believed—"

"Well, then, yes," said Sarah. "One of our experts is quite excited about it, actually. One of the old notebooks lists a painting done of a mare with a dead foal, but it's never been found."

"What notebooks?"

"Oh, sorry," said Sarah. She had never sounded so meek, so frightened, in Robin's vicinity. "Stubbs."

"And if it *is* a Stubbs?" asked Robin, turning to look out of the window at the Feathers, a pub where she and Strike had sometimes drunk.

"Well, this is entirely speculative, obviously... but *if* it's genuine, *if* it's the one he listed in 1760, it could be a lot."

"Give me a rough estimate."

"Well, his 'Gimcrack' went for—"

"—twenty-two million," said Robin, feeling suddenly lightheaded. "Yes. You said so at our house-warming party."

Sarah made no answer. Perhaps the mention of the party, where she had brought lilies to her lover's wife's house, had scared her.

"So if 'Mare Mourning' is a genuine Stubbs—"

"It'd probably make more than 'Gimcrack' at auction. It's a unique subject. Stubbs was an anatomist, as much scientist as artist. If this is a depiction of a lethal white foal, it might be the first recorded instance. It could set records."

Robin's mobile buzzed in her hand. Another text had arrived.

"This has been very helpful, Sarah, thanks. You'll keep this confidential?"

"Yes, of course," said Sarah. And then, in a rush:

"Robin, listen—"

"No," said Robin, trying to stay calm. "I'm working a case."

"—it's over, it's finished, Matt's in pieces—"

"Goodbye, Sarah."

Robin hung up, then read the text that had just arrived.

Meet me after work or I'm giving a statement to the press.

Eager as she was to return to the group next door and relay the sensational information she had just received, Robin remained where she stood, temporarily flummoxed by the threat, and texted back:

Statement to the press about what?

His response came within seconds, littered with angry typos.

The mail called the office this morning g and left a message asking how I feel about my dive shacking up with Cornish Strike. The sun's been one this afternoon. You probably know he's two timing you but maybe you don't give a shit. I'm not having the papers calling me at work. Either meet me or I'm go give a statement to get them off my back.

Robin was rereading the message when yet another text arrived, this time with an attachment.

In case you haven't seen it

Robin enlarged the attachment, which was a screenshot of a diary item in the *Evening Standard*.

THE CURIOUS CASE OF CHARLOTTE CAMPBELL AND CORMORAN STRIKE

A staple of the gossip columns ever since she ran away from her first private school, Charlotte Campbell has lived out her life in a glare of publicity. Most people would choose a discreet spot for their consultation with a private detective, but the pregnant Ms. Campbell—now Mrs. Jago Ross—chose the window table of one of the West End's busiest restaurants.

Were detective services under discussion during the intense heart-to-heart, or something more personal? The colorful Mr. Strike, illegitimate son of rock star Jonny Rokeby, war hero and modern-day Sherlock Holmes, also happens to be Campbell's ex-lover.

Campbell's businessman husband will doubtless be keen to solve the mystery—business or pleasure?—upon his return from New York.

A mass of uncomfortable feelings jostled inside Robin, of which the dominant ones were panic, anger and mortification at the thought of Matthew speaking to the press in such a way as to leave open, spitefully, the possibility that she and Strike were indeed sleeping together.

She tried to call the number, but it went straight to voicemail. Two seconds later, another angry text appeared.

I'M WITH A CLIENT I DON'T WANT TO TALK ABOUT THIS IN FRONT OF HIM JUST MEET ME

Angry now, Robin texted:

And I'm at New Scotland Yard. Find a quiet corner.

She could imagine Matthew's polite smile as the client watched, his smooth "just the office, excuse me," while he hammered out his furious replies.

We've got stuff to sort out and you're acting like a child refusing to meet me. Either you come talk to me or I'm ringing the papers at eight. I notice you're not denying your sleeping with him, by the way

Furious, but feeling cornered, Robin typed back:

Fine, let's discuss it face to face, where?

He texted her directions to a bar in Little Venice. Still shaken, Robin pushed open the door to the incident room. The group was now huddled around a monitor showing a page of Jimmy Knight's blog, from which Strike was reading aloud:

"...'in other words, a single bottle of wine at Le Manoir aux Quat'Saisons can cost more than a single, out-of-work mother receives per week to feed, clothe and house her entire family.' Now that," said Strike, "struck me as a weirdly specific choice of restaurant, if he wanted to rant about Tories and their spending. *That's* what made me think he'd been there recently. Then Robin tells me 'Blanc de Blanc' is the name of one of their suites, but I didn't put that together as quickly as I should've done. It hit me a few hours later."

"He's a hell of a bloody hypocrite on top of everything else, isn't he?" said Wardle, who was standing, arms folded, behind Strike.

"You've looked in Woolstone?" Strike asked.

"The shithole in Charlemont Road, Woolstone, everywhere," said Layborn, "but don't worry. We've got a line on one of his girlfriends down in Dulwich. Checking there right now. With luck, we'll have him in custody tonight."

Layborn now noticed Robin, standing with her phone in her hand.

"I know you've already got people looking at it," she told Layborn, "but I've got a contact at Christie's. I sent her the picture of 'Mare Mourning' and she's just called me back. According to one of their experts, it *might* be a Stubbs."

"Even I've heard of Stubbs," Layborn said.

"What would it be worth, if it is?" Wardle asked.

"My contact thinks upwards of twenty-two million."

Wardle whistled. Layborn said, "Fuck me."

"Doesn't matter to us what it's worth," Strike reminded them all. "What matters is whether somebody might've spotted its potential value."

"Twenty-two fucking million," said Wardle, "is a hell of a motive."

"Cormoran," said Robin, picking her jacket off the back of the chair where she'd left it, "could I have a quick word outside? I'm going to have to leave, sorry," she said to the others.

"Everything OK?" Strike asked, as they re-entered the corridor together and Robin had closed the door on the group of police.

"Yes," said Robin, and then, "Well—not really. Maybe," she said, handing him her phone, "you'd better just read this."

Frowning, Strike scrolled slowly through the interchange between Robin and Matthew, including the *Evening Standard* clip.

"You're going to meet him?"

"I've got to. This must be why Mitch Patterson's sniffing around. If Matthew fans the flames with the press, which he's more than capable of doing…They're already excited about you and—"

"Forget me and Charlotte," he said roughly, "that was twenty minutes that she coerced me into. He's trying to coerce *you*—"

"I know he is," said Robin, "but I *have* got to talk to him sooner or later. Most of my stuff's still in Albury Street. We've still got a joint bank account."

"D'you want me to come?"

Touched, Robin said:

"Thanks, but I don't think that would help."

"Then ring me later, will you? Let me know what happened."

"I will," she promised.

She headed off alone towards the lifts. She didn't even notice who had just walked past her in the opposite direction until somebody said, "Bobbi?"

Robin turned. There stood Flick Purdue, returning from the bathroom with a policewoman, who seemed to have escorted her there. Like Kinvara, Flick had cried away her makeup. She appeared small and shrunken in a white shirt that Robin suspected her parents had insisted she wear, rather than her Hezbollah T-shirt.

"It's Robin. How are you, Flick?"

Flick seemed to be struggling with ideas too monstrous to utter.

"I hope you're cooperating," said Robin. "Tell them everything, won't you?"

She thought she saw a tiny shake of the head, an instinctive defiance, the last embers of loyalty not yet extinguished, even in the trouble Flick found herself.

"You must," said Robin quietly. "He'd have killed *you* next, Flick. You knew too much."

69

I have foreseen all contingencies — long ago.

Henrik Ibsen, *Rosmersholm*

A twenty-minute Tube ride later, Robin emerged at Warwick Avenue underground station in a part of London she barely knew. She had always felt a vague curiosity about Little Venice, as her extravagant middle name, "Venetia," had been given to her because she had been conceived in the real Venice. Doubtless she would henceforth associate this area with Matthew and the bitter, tense meeting she was sure awaited her, down by the canal.

She walked down a street named Clifton Villas, where plane trees spread leaves of translucent jade against square cream-colored houses, the walls of which glowed gold in the evening sun. The quiet beauty of this soft summer evening made Robin feel suddenly, overwhelmingly melancholy, because it recalled just such a night in Yorkshire, a decade previously, when she had hurried up the road from her parents' house, barely seventeen years old and wobbling on her high heels, desperately excited about her first date with Matthew Cunliffe, who had just passed his driving test and would be taking her into Harrogate for the evening.

And here she was walking towards him again, to arrange the permanent disentanglement of their lives. Robin despised herself for feeling sad, for remembering, when it was preferable to concentrate on his unfaithfulness and unkindness, the joyful shared experiences that had led to love.

She turned left, crossed the street and walked on, now in the chilly shadow of the brick that bordered the right-hand side of Blomfield Road, parallel to the canal, and saw a police car speeding across the top of the street. The sight of it gave her strength. It felt like a friendly wave from what she knew now was her real life, sent to remind her what she was meant to be, and how incompatible that was with being the wife of Matthew Cunliffe.

A pair of high black wooden gates was set into the wall, gates that Matthew's text had told her led to the canal-side bar, but when Robin pushed at them, they were locked. She glanced up and down the road, but there was no sign of Matthew, so she reached into her bag for her mobile, which, though muted was already vibrating with a call. As she took it out, the electric gates opened and she walked through them, raising the mobile to her ear as she did so.

"Hi, I'm just—"

Strike yelled in her ear.

"*Get out of there, it isn't Matthew—*"

Several things happened at once.

The phone was torn out of her hand. In one frozen second, Robin registered that there was no bar in sight, only an untidy patch of canal bank beneath a bridge, hemmed by overgrown shrubs, and a dark barge, *Odile*, sitting squat and shabby in the water below her. Then a fist hit her hard in the solar plexus, and she jack-knifed, winded. Doubled over, she heard a splash as her phone was lobbed into the canal, then somebody grabbed a fistful of her hair and the waistband of her trousers and dragged her, while she still had no air in her lungs to scream, towards the barge. Thrown through the open doorway of the boat, she hit a narrow wooden table and fell to the floor.

The door slammed shut. She heard the scrape of a lock.

"Sit down," said a male voice.

Still winded, Robin pulled herself up onto a wooden bench at the table, which was covered in a thin cushioned pad, then turned, to find herself looking into the barrel of a revolver.

Raphael lowered himself into the chair opposite her.

"Who just rang you?" he demanded and she deduced that in the physical effort to get her on the boat, and his terror that she might make a noise that the caller could hear, he had not had time or opportunity to check the screen on her mobile.

"My husband," lied Robin in a whisper.

Her scalp was burning where he had pulled her hair. The pain in her midriff was such that she wondered whether he had cracked one of her ribs. Still fighting to draw air into her lungs, Robin seemed for a few disoriented seconds to see her predicament in miniature, from far away, encased in a trembling bead of time. She foresaw Raphael tipping her weighted corpse into the dark water by night, and Matthew, who had apparently lured her to the canal, being questioned and maybe accused. She saw the distraught faces of her parents and her brothers at her funeral in Masham, and she saw Strike standing at the back of the church, as he had at her wedding, furious because the thing he had feared had come to pass, and she was dead due to her own failings.

But as each gasp re-inflated Robin's lungs, the illusion that she was watching from afar dissolved. She was here, now, on this dingy boat, breathing in its fusty smell, trapped within its wooden walls, with the dilated pupil of the revolver staring at her, and Raphael's eyes above it.

Her fear was a real, solid presence in the galley, but it must stand apart from her, because it couldn't help, and would only hinder. She must stay calm, and concentrate. She chose not to speak. It would give her back some of the power he had just taken from her if she refused to fill the silence. This was the trick of the therapist: let the pause unspool; let the more vulnerable person fill it.

"You're very cool," Raphael said finally. "I thought you might get hysterical and scream. That's why I had to punch you. I wouldn't have done that otherwise. For what it's worth, I like you, Venetia."

She knew that he was trying to re-impersonate the man who had charmed her against her will at the Commons. Clearly, he thought the old mixture of ruefulness and remorse would make her forgive, and soften, even with her burning scalp, and her bruised ribs, and the gun in her face. She said nothing. His faint, imploring smile disappeared and he said bluntly:

"I need to know how much the police know. If I can still blag my way out of what they've got, then I'm afraid you," he raised the gun a fraction to point directly at Robin's forehead (and she thought of vets and the one clean shot that the horse in the dell had been denied) "are done for. I'll muffle the shot in a cushion and put you overboard once it's dark. But if they already know everything, then I'll end it, here, tonight, because I'm never going back to prison. So you can see how it's in your best interests to be honest, can't you? Only one of us is getting off this boat."

And when she didn't speak, he said fiercely:

"Answer me!"

"Yes," she said. "I understand."

"So," he said quietly, "were you really just at Scotland Yard?"

"Yes."

"Is Kinvara there?"

"Yes."

"Under arrest?"

"I think so. She's in an interrogation room with her solicitor."

"Why have they arrested her?"

"They think the two of you are having an affair. That you were behind everything."

"What's 'everything'?"

"The blackmail," said Robin, "and the murder."

He advanced the gun so that it was pressing against her forehead. Robin felt the small, cold ring of metal pressing into her skin.

"Sounds like a crock of shit to me. How're we supposed to have had an affair? She hated me. We were never alone together for two minutes."

"Yes, you were," said Robin. "Your father invited you down to Chiswell House, right after you got out of jail. The night he was detained in London. You and she were alone together, then. That's when we think it started."

"Proof?"

"None," said Robin, "but I think you could seduce anyone if you really put your—"

"Don't try flattery, it won't work. Seriously, 'that's when we think it started'? Is that all you've got?"

"No. There were other signs of something going on."

"Tell me the signs. All of them."

"I'd be able to remember better," said Robin steadily, "without you pressing a gun into my forehead."

He withdrew it, but still pointing the revolver at her face, he said: "Go on. Quickly."

Part of Robin wanted to succumb to her body's desire to dissolve, to carry her off into blissful unconsciousness. Her hands were numb, her muscles felt like soft wax. The place where Raphael had pressed the gun into her skin felt cold, a ring of white fire for a third eye. He hadn't turned on the lights in the boat. They were facing each other in the deepening darkness and perhaps, by the time he shot her, she would no longer be able to see him clearly...

Focus, said a small, clear voice through the panic. *Focus. The longer you keep him talking, the more time they'll have to find you. Strike knows you were tricked.*

She suddenly remembered the police car speeding across the top of Blomfield Road and wondered whether it had been circling, looking for her, whether the police, knowing that Raphael had lured her to the area, had already dispatched officers to search for them. The fake address had been some distance away along the canal bank, reached, so Raphael's texts had said, through the black gates. Would Strike guess that Raphael was armed?

She took a deep breath.

"Kinvara broke down in Della Winn's office last summer and said that someone had told her she'd never been loved, that she was used as part of a game."

She must speak slowly. Don't rush it. Every second might count, every second that she could keep Raphael hanging on her words, was another second in which somebody might come to her aid.

"Della assumed she was talking about your father, but we checked and Della can't remember Kinvara actually saying his name. We think you seduced Kinvara as an act of revenge towards your father, kept the affair going for a couple of months, but when she got clingy and possessive, you ditched her."

"All supposition," said Raphael harshly, "and therefore bullshit. What else?"

"Why did Kinvara go up to town on the day her beloved mare was likely to be put down?"

"Maybe she couldn't face seeing the horse shot. Maybe she was in denial about how sick it was."

"Or," said Robin, "maybe she was suspicious about what you and Francesca were up to in Drummond's gallery."

"No proof. Next."

"She had a kind of breakdown when she got back to Oxfordshire. She attacked your father and was hospitalized."

"Still grieving her stillborn, excessively attached to her horses, generally depressed," Raphael rattled off. "Izzy and Fizzy will fight to take the stand and explain how unstable she is. What else?"

"Tegan told us that one day Kinvara was manically happy again, and she lied when asked why. She said your father had agreed to put her other mare in foal to Totilas. We think the real reason was that you'd resumed the affair with her, and we don't think the timing was coincidental. You'd just driven the latest batch of paintings up to Drummond's gallery for valuation."

Raphael's face became suddenly slack, as though his essential self had temporarily vacated it. The gun twitched in his hand and the fine hairs on Robin's arms lifted gently as though a breeze had rippled over them. She waited for Raphael to speak, but he didn't. After a minute, she continued:

"We think that when you loaded up the paintings for valuation, you saw 'Mare Mourning' close up for the first time and realized that it might be a Stubbs. You decided to substitute a different painting of a mare and foal for valuation."

"Evidence?"

"Henry Drummond's now seen the photograph I took of 'Mare Mourning' on the spare bed at Chiswell House. He's ready to testify that it wasn't among the pictures he valued for your father. The painting he valued at five to eight thousand pounds was by John Frederick Herring, and it showed a black and white mare and foal. Drummond's also ready to testify that you're sufficiently knowledgable about art to have spotted that 'Mare Mourning' might be a Stubbs."

Raphael's face had lost its mask-like cast. Now his near-black irises swiveled fractionally from side to side, as though he were reading something only he could see.

"I must've accidentally taken the Frederick Herring inste—"

A police siren sounded a few streets away. Raphael's head turned: the siren wailed for a few seconds, then, as abruptly as it had started, was shut off.

He turned back to face Robin. He didn't seem overly worried by the siren now it had stopped. Of course, he thought that it had been Matthew on the phone when he grabbed her.

"Yeah," he said, regaining the thread of his thought. "That's what I'll say. I took the painting of the piebald to be valued by mistake, never saw 'Mare Mourning,' had no idea it might be a Stubbs."

"You can't have taken the piebald picture by mistake," said Robin quietly. "It didn't come from Chiswell House and the family's prepared to say so."

"The family," said Raphael, "don't notice what's under their fucking noses. A Stubbs has been hanging in a damp spare bedroom for nigh on twenty years and nobody noticed, and you know why? Because they're such fucking arrogant snobs... 'Mare Mourning' was old Tinky's. She inherited it from the broken-down, alcoholic, gaga old Irish baronet she married before my grandfather. She had no idea what it was worth. She kept it because it was horsey and she loved horses.

"When her first husband died, she hopped over to England and pulled the same trick, became my grandfather's expensive private nurse and then his even more expensive wife. She died intestate and all her crap—it *was* mostly crap—got absorbed into the Chiswell estate. The Frederick Herring could easily have been one of hers and nobody noticed it, stuck away in some filthy corner of that bloody house."

"What if the police trace the piebald picture?"

"They won't. It's my mother's. I'll destroy it. When the police ask me, I'll say my father told me he was going to flog it now he knew it was worth eight grand. 'He must've sold it privately, officer.'"

"Kinvara doesn't know the new story. She won't be able to back you up."

"This is where her well-known instability and unhappiness with my father works in my favor. Izzy and Fizzy will line up to tell the world that she never paid much attention to what he was up to, because she didn't love him and was only in it for the money. Reasonable doubt is all I need."

"What's going to happen when the police put it to Kinvara that you only restarted the affair because you realized she might be about to become fantastically wealthy?"

Raphael let out a long, slow hiss.

"Well," he said quietly, "if they can make Kinvara believe that, I'm fucked, aren't I? But right now, Kinvara believes her Raffy loves her more than anything in the world, and she's going to take a *lot* of convincing that's not true, because her whole life's going to fall apart otherwise. I drilled it into her: if they don't know about the affair, they can't touch us. I virtually had her reciting it while I fucked her. And I warned her they'd try and turn us against each other if either one of us was suspected. I've got her very well-schooled and I said, when in doubt, cry your eyes out, tell them nobody ever tells you anything and act bloody confused."

"She's already told one silly lie to try and protect you, and the police know about it," said Robin.

"What lie?"

"About the necklace, in the early hours of Sunday morning. Didn't she tell you? Maybe she realized you'd be angry."

"*What did she say?*"

"Strike told her he didn't buy the new explanation for you going down to Chiswell House the morning your father died—"

"What d'you mean, he didn't buy it?" said Raphael, and Robin saw outraged vanity mingled with his panic.

"*I* thought it was convincing," she assured him. "Clever, to tell a story that you'd appear to give up only unwillingly. Everyone's always more disposed to believe something they believe they've uncovered for themsel—"

Raphael raised the gun so that it was close to her forehead again and even though the cold ring of metal had not yet touched her skin again, she felt it there.

"What lie did Kinvara tell?"

"She claimed you came to tell her that your mother removed diamonds from the necklace and replaced them with fakes."

Raphael appeared horrified.

"What the fuck did she say that for?"

"Because she'd had a shock, I suppose, finding Strike and me in the grounds when you were hiding upstairs. Strike said he didn't believe the necklace story, so she panicked and made up a new version. The trouble is, this one's checkable."

"The stupid cunt," said Raphael quietly, but with a venom that made the back of Robin's neck prickle. "That stupid, stupid cunt...why didn't she just stick to our story? And...no, wait..." he said, with the air of a man suddenly making a welcome connection, and to Robin's mingled consternation and relief, he withdrew the gun from where it had been almost touching her, and laughed softly. "*That's* why she hid the necklace on Sunday afternoon. She gave me some fucking guff about not wanting Izzy or Fizzy to sneak in and take it...well, she's stupid, but she's not hopeless. Unless someone checks the stones, we're still in the clear...And they'll have to take apart the stable block to find it. OK," he said, as though talking to himself, "OK, I think all of that's recoverable."

"Is that it, Venetia? Is that all you've got?"

"No," said Robin. "There's Flick Purdue."

"I don't know who that is."

"Yes, you do. You picked her up months ago, and fed her the truth about the gallows, knowing she'd pass the information to Jimmy."

"What a busy boy I've been," said Raphael lightly. "So what? Flick won't admit to shagging a Tory minister's son, especially if Jimmy might find out. She's as besotted with him as Kinvara is with me."

"That's true, she didn't want to admit it, but somebody must have spotted you creeping out of her flat next morning. She tried to pretend you were an Indian waiter."

Robin thought she saw a minute wince of surprise and displeasure. Raphael's *amour propre* was wounded at the thought that he could have been so described.

"OK," he said, after a moment or two, "OK, let's see...what if it *was* a waiter Flick shagged, but she's maliciously claiming it was me because of her class warrior bullshit and the grudge her boyfriend's got against my family?"

"You stole her flatmate's credit card out of her bag in the kitchen."

She could tell by the tightening of his mouth that he had not expected this. Doubtless he had thought that given Flick's lifestyle, suspicion would fall on anyone passing through her tiny, over-crowded flat, and perhaps especially Jimmy.

"Proof?" he said again.

"Flick can provide the date you were at her flat and if Laura testifies her credit card went missing that night—"

"But with no firm evidence I was ever there—"

"How did Flick find out about the gallows? We know she told Jimmy about them, not the other way around."

"Well, it can't have been me, can it? I'm the only member of the family who never knew."

"You knew everything. Kinvara had the full story from your father, and she passed it all to you."

"No," said Raphael, "I think you'll find Flick heard about the gallows from the Butcher brothers. I'm reliably informed that one of them lives in London now. Yeah, I think I've heard a rumor one of them shagged their mate Jimmy's girlfriend. And believe me, the Butcher brothers aren't going to come over well in court, pair of shifty oiks driving gallows around under cover of darkness. I'm going to look a lot more plausible and presentable than Flick and the Butchers if this comes to court, I really am."

"The police have got phone records," Robin persisted. "They know about an anonymous call to Geraint Winn, which was made around the time Flick found out about the gallows. We think you tipped off Winn anonymously about Samuel Murape. You knew Winn had a grudge against the Chiswells. Kinvara told you everything."

"I don't know anything about that phone call, Your Honor," said Raphael, "and I'm very sorry that my late brother was a prize cunt to Rhiannon Winn, but that's nothing to do with me."

"We think *you* made that threatening call to Izzy's office, the first day you were there, talking about people pissing themselves as they die," said Robin, "and we think it was *your* idea for Kinvara to pretend she kept hearing intruders in the grounds. Everything was designed to create as many witnesses as possible to the fact that your father had reason to be anxious and paranoid, that he might crack under extreme pressure—"

"He *was* under extreme pressure. He *was* being blackmailed by Jimmy Knight. Geraint Winn *was* trying to force him out of his job. Those aren't lies, they're facts and they're going to be pretty sensational in a courtroom, especially once the Samuel Murape story gets out."

"Except that you made stupid, avoidable mistakes."

He sat up straighter and leaned forwards, his elbow sliding a few inches, so that the nozzle of the gun grew larger. His eyes, which had been smudges in the shadow, became clearly defined again, onyx black and white. Robin wondered how she had ever thought him handsome.

"What mistakes?"

As he said it, Robin saw, out of the corner of her eye, a flashing blue light glide over the bridge just visible through the window to her right, which was blocked from Raphael's view by the side of the boat. The light vanished and the bridge was reabsorbed by the deepening darkness.

"For one thing," said Robin carefully, "it was a mistake to keep meeting Kinvara in the lead-up to the murder. She kept pretending she'd forgotten where she was meeting your father, didn't she? Just to get a couple of minutes with you, just to see you and check up on you—"

"That's not proof."

"Kinvara was followed to Le Manoir aux Quat'Saisons on her birthday."

His eyes narrowed.

"Who by?"

"Jimmy Knight. Flick's confirmed it. Jimmy thought your father was with Kinvara and wanted to confront him publicly about not giving him his money. Obviously, your father wasn't there, so Jimmy went home and wrote an angry blog about how High Tories spend their money, mentioning Le Manoir aux Quat'Saisons by name."

"Well, unless he saw me sneaking into Kinvara's hotel suite," said Raphael, "which he didn't, because I took fucking good care to make sure nobody did, that's all supposition, too."

"All right," said Robin, "what about the *second* time you were overheard having sex in the gallery bathroom? That wasn't Francesca. You were with Kinvara."

"Prove it."

"Kinvara was in town that day, buying lachesis pills and pretending she was angry that your father was still seeing you, which was all part of the cover story that she hated you. She rang your father to check that he was having lunch elsewhere. Strike overheard that call. What you and Kinvara didn't realize was that your father was having lunch only a hundred yards away from where you were having sex.

"When your father forced his way into the bathroom, he found a tube of lachesis pills on the floor. That's why he nearly had a heart attack. He knew that's what she'd come to town for. He knew who'd just been having sex with you in the bathroom."

Raphael's smile was more of a grimace.

"Yeah, that was a fuck-up. The day he came into our office, talking about Lachesis—'knows when everyone's number's up'—I realized later, he was trying to put the frighteners on me, wasn't he? I didn't know what the hell he was on about at the time. But when you and your crippled boss mentioned the pills at Chiswell House, Kinvara twigged: they fell out of her pocket while we were screwing. We hadn't known what first tipped him off...it was only after I heard he was ringing Le Manoir about Freddie's money clip that I knew he must have realized something was going on. Then he invited me over to Ebury Street and I knew he was about to confront me about it, and we needed to get a move on, killing him."

The entirely matter-of-fact way he discussed patricide chilled Robin. He might have been talking about wallpapering a room.

"He must've been planning to produce those pills during his big 'I know you're fucking my wife' speech...why didn't I spot them on the floor? I tried to put the room straight afterwards, but they must've rolled out of his pocket or something...it's harder than you'd think," said Raphael, "tidying up around a corpse you've just dispatched. I was surprised, actually, how much it affected me."

She had never heard his narcissism so clearly. His interest and sympathy was entirely for himself. His dead father was nothing.

"The police have taken statements from Francesca and her parents, now," Robin said. "She absolutely denies being in the bathroom with you that second time. Her parents never believed her, but—"

"They didn't believe her because she's even fucking dumber than Kinvara."

"The police are combing through security camera footage from the shops she says she was in, while you and Kinvara were in the bathroom."

"OK," said Raphael, "well, worst comes to the worst, and they can prove she wasn't with me, I might have to come clean about the fact that it was *another* young lady I was with in the bathroom that day, whose reputation I've been chivalrously trying to defend."

"Will you really be able to find a woman to lie for you, in court, on a murder charge?" asked Robin, in disbelief.

"The woman who owns this houseboat is mad for me," said Raphael softly. "We had a thing going before I went inside. She visited me in jail and everything. She's in rehab right now. Crazy bitch, loves drama. Thinks she's an artist. She drinks too much, she's a real pain in the arse, actually, but she fucks like a rabbit. She never bothered taking the spare key to this place off me, and she keeps a key to her mummy's house in that drawer over there—"

"It wouldn't happen to be her mother's house where you had the helium, tubing and gloves delivered, would it?" asked Robin.

Raphael blinked. He hadn't expected that.

"You needed an address that didn't seem connected to you. You made sure it was delivered while the owners were away, or at work, then you could let yourself in, collect the failed delivery card…"

"Pick it up, disguised and get it couriered it off to dear old Dad's house, yeah."

"And Flick took delivery and Kinvara made sure she hid it from your father until it was time to kill him?"

"That's right," said Raphael. "You pick up a lot of tips in jail. Fake

IDs, vacant buildings, empty addresses, you can do a hell of a lot with them. Once you're dead—" Robin's scalp prickled—"nobody's going to connect me with any of the addresses."

"The owner of this barge—"

"Is going to be telling everyone she was having sex with me in Drummond's bathroom, remember? She's on my team, Venetia," he said quietly, "so it's not looking good for you, is it?"

"There were other mistakes," said Robin, her mouth dry.

"Like?"

"You told Flick your father needed a cleaner."

"Yeah, because it makes her and Jimmy look fishy as hell, that she wheedled her way into my father's house. The jury'll be focused on that, not how she found out he wanted a cleaner. I've already told you, she's going to look like a grubby little tart with a grudge in the dock. That's just one more lie."

"But she stole a note from your father, a note he wrote while he was trying to check Kinvara's story with Le Manoir aux Quat'Saisons. I found it in her bathroom. She'd lied, told him her mother was going to the hotel with her. They'd never normally give out information about guests, but he was a government minister and he'd previously been there, so we think he managed to trick them into agreeing that they could remember the family vehicle there and that it was a shame her mother hadn't made it. He made a note of the suite Kinvara was in, probably pretending he'd forgotten it, and he was trying to get hold of the bill, to see whether there was any sign of two lots of breakfast or dinner, I suppose. When the prosecution produce the note and the bill in court—"

"*You* found that note, did you?" said Raphael.

Robin's stomach turned over. She had not meant to give Raphael another reason to shoot her.

"I knew I'd underestimated you after that dinner we had, at Nam Long Le Shaker," said Raphael. It wasn't a compliment. His eyes were narrowed, his nostrils flared in dislike. "You were a mess, but you were still asking fucking inconvenient questions. You and your boss were cozier with the police than I expected, too. And even after I tipped off the *Mail*—"

"That was *you*," said Robin, wondering how she had never realized. "*You* put the press and Mitch Patterson back on us..."

"I told them you'd left your husband for Strike, but that he was still shagging his ex. Izzy had given me that bit of gossip. I thought you needed slowing down, you two, because you kept poking away at my alibi...but after I've shot you,"—an icy chill ran the length of Robin's body—"your boss'll be busy answering the press's questions about how your body ended up in a canal, won't he? I think that's called killing two birds with one stone."

"Even if I'm dead," said Robin, her voice as steady as she could make it, "there'll still be your father's note and the hotel's testimony—"

"OK, so he was worried about what Kinvara was doing at Le Manoir," said Raphael roughly. "I've just told you, nobody saw me on the premises. The stupid cow did ask for two glasses with the champagne, but she could've been with someone else."

"You aren't going to have any opportunity to cook up a new story with her," said Robin, her mouth drier than ever, her tongue sticking to the roof of her mouth as she tried to sound calm and confident. "She's in custody now, she isn't as clever as you—and you made other mistakes," Robin rushed on, "stupid ones, because you had to enact the plan in a hurry once you realized your father was onto you."

"Like?"

"Like Kinvara taking away the packaging on the amitriptyline, after she'd doctored the orange juice. Kinvara forgetting to tell you the trick to closing the front door properly. And," said Robin, aware that she was playing her very last card, "her throwing the front door key to you, at Paddington."

In the wordless space that now stretched between them, Robin thought she heard footsteps close at hand. She didn't dare look out of the window in case she alerted Raphael, who appeared too appalled by what she had just said to take in anything else.

"'Throwing the front door key to me?'" repeated Raphael, with fragile bravado. "What the hell are you talking about?"

"The keys to Ebury Street are restricted, almost impossible to copy. The pair of you only had access to one: hers, because your father was suspicious of you both by the time he died, and he'd made sure the spare was out of your reach.

"She needed the key to get into the house and doctor the orange juice and you needed it to go in early next morning and suffocate him. So you cobbled together a plan at the last minute: she'd pass you the key at a prearranged spot at Paddington, where you'd be disguised as a homeless person.

"You were caught on camera. The police have got people enlarging and clarifying the image right now. They think you must have bought things from a charity shop in haste, which might produce another useful witness. The police are now combing CCTV footage for your movements from Paddington onwards."

Raphael said nothing at all for nearly a minute. His eyes were moving fractionally from left to right, as he tried to find a loophole, an escape.

"That's...inconvenient," he said finally. "I didn't think I was on camera, sitting there."

Robin thought she could see hope slipping away from him now. Quietly, she continued, "As per your plan, Kinvara arrived home in Oxfordshire, called Drummond and left a message that she wanted the necklace valued, to set up that whole back-up story.

"Early next morning, another burner phone was used to call both Geraint Winn and Jimmy Knight. Both were lured out of their houses, presumably with a promise of information on Chiswell. That was you, making sure they were in the frame if murder was suspected."

"No proof," muttered Raphael automatically, but still his eyes darted this way and that, searching for invisible lifelines.

"You let yourself into the house very early in the morning, expecting to find your father almost comatose after his early morning orange juice, but—"

"He *was* out of it, at first," said Raphael. His eyes had become glazed, and Robin knew that he was remembering what had happened, watching it, inside his head. "He was slumped on the sofa, very groggy. I walked straight past him into the kitchen, opened my box of toys—"

For a sliver of a second, Robin saw again the shrink-wrapped head, the gray hair pressed around the face so that only the gaping black hole of the mouth was visible. Raphael had done that; Raphael, who currently had a gun pointing at her face.

"—but while I'm arranging everything, the old bastard wakes up, sees me fixing the tubing onto the helium canister and comes back to fucking life. He staggers up, grabs Freddie's sword off the wall and tries to fight, but I got it off him. Bent the blade doing it. Forced him down into the chair—he was still struggling—and—"

Raphael mimed putting the bag over his father's head.

"*Caput.*"

"And then," said Robin, her mouth still dry, "you made those phone calls from his phone that were supposed to establish your alibi. Kinvara had told you his passcode, of course. And you left, without closing the door properly."

Robin didn't know whether she was imagining movement out of the porthole to her left. She kept her eyes fixed on Raphael, and the slightly wavering gun.

"Loads of this is circumstantial," he muttered, eyes still glazed. "Flick and Francesca have both got motives for lying about me . . . I didn't end it well with Francesca . . . I might still have a chance . . . I might . . ."

"There's no chance, Raff," said Robin. "Kinvara isn't going to lie for you much longer. When they tell her the truth about 'Mare Mourning,' she's going to put everything together for the first time. I think *you* insisted she move it into to the drawing room, to protect it from the damp in the spare room. How did you manage that? Did you make up some rubbish about it reminding *you* of her dead mare? Then she's going to realize you started up the affair again once you knew its true value, and that all the dreadful things you said to her when you ended it were true. And worst of all," said Robin, "she's going to realize that when the two of you heard intruders in the grounds—real ones, this time—you let the woman you were supposedly madly in love with walk out into the grounds in the dark, in her nightdress, while you stayed behind to protect—"

"*All right!*" he shouted suddenly and he advanced the gun nozzle until it pressed into her forehead again. "Stop fucking *talking*, will you?"

Robin sat quite still. She imagined how it would feel when he pressed the trigger. He had said he would shoot her through a cushion to muffle the sound, but perhaps he had forgotten, perhaps he was about to lose control.

"D'you know what it's like in jail?" he asked.

She tried to say "no," but the sound wouldn't come.

"The noise," he whispered. "The smell. The ugly, dumb people— like animals, some of them. Worse than animals. I never knew there were people like it. The places they make you eat and shit. Watching your back all the time, waiting for violence. The clanging, the yelling and the fucking squalor. I'd rather be buried alive. I won't do it again...

"I was going to have a dream life. I was going to be free, totally free. I'd never have to kowtow to the likes of fucking Drummond again. There's a villa on Capri I've had my eye on for a long time. View out over the Gulf of Naples. Then I'd have a nice pad in London...new car, once my fucking ban's lifted...imagine walking along and knowing you could buy anything, do anything. A dream life...

"Couple of little problems to get out of the way before I was completely sorted...Flick, easy: late night, dark road, knife in the ribs, victim of street crime.

"And Kinvara...once she'd made a will in my favor, after a few years, she'd have broken her neck riding an unsuitable horse or drowned out in Italy...she's a terrible swimmer...

"And then all of them could fuck themselves, couldn't they? The Chiswells, my whore of a mother. I'd need nothing from anyone. I'd have everything...

"But that's all gone," he said. Dark-skinned though he was, she saw that he had turned ashen, the dark shadows beneath his eyes hollow in the half-light. "It's all gone. You know what, Venetia? I'm going to blow your fucking brains out, because I've decided I don't like you. I think I'd like to see your fucking head explode before mine comes off—"

"Raff—"

"*Raff... Raff...*" he bleated, imitating her, "why do women all think they're different? You're not different, none of you."

He was reaching for the limp cushion beside him.

"We'll go together. I'd like to arrive in hell with a sexy girl on my ar—"

With a great splintering of wood, the door crashed open. Raphael spun around, pointing the gun at the large figure that had just fallen inside. Robin launched herself over the table to grab his arm, but Raphael knocked her backwards with his elbow and she felt blood spurt as her lip split.

"Raff, no, don't—*don't!*"

He had stood up, stooped in the cramped space, the barrel of the gun in his mouth. Strike, who had shouldered in the door, stood panting feet away from him, and behind Strike was Wardle.

"Go on and do it, then, you cowardly little fuck," said Strike.

Robin wanted to protest, but couldn't make a noise.

There was a small, metallic click.

"Took out the bullets at Chiswell House, you stupid bastard," said Strike, hobbling forwards and smacking the revolver out of Raphael's mouth. "Not half as clever as you thought you were, eh?"

There was a great ringing in Robin's ears. Raphael was spitting oaths in English and Italian, screaming threats, thrashing and twisting as Strike helped bend him over the table for Wardle to cuff him, but she stumbled away from the group as though in a dream, backwards towards the kitchen area of the galley, where pots and pans were hanging and white kitchen roll sat, ludicrously ordinary, beside a tiny sink. She could feel her lip swelling where Raphael had hit her. She tore off some kitchen roll, ran it under the cold tap and pressed it to her bleeding mouth, while through the porthole she watched uniformed officers hurrying through the black gates, taking possession of the gun and of the struggling Raphael, whom Wardle had just dragged onto the bank.

She had just been held at gunpoint. Nothing seemed real. Now the police were stomping in and out of the barge, but it was all noise and echo, and now she realized that Strike was standing beside her, and he seemed the only person with any reality.

"How did you know?" she asked thickly, through the cold wedge of tissue.

"Twigged five minutes after you left. The last three digits on that number you showed me on those supposed texts from Matthew were the same as one of the burner phone numbers. Went after you but you were already gone. Layborn sent panda cars out and I've been calling you nonstop ever since. Why didn't you pick up?"

"My phone was on silent in my bag. Now it's in the canal."

She craved a stiff drink. Maybe, she thought vaguely, there really was a bar somewhere nearby...but of course, she wouldn't be allowed to go to a bar. She was facing hours back at New Scotland Yard. They would need a long statement. She would have to relive the last hour in detail. She felt exhausted.

"How did you know I was here?"

"Called Izzy and asked if Raphael knew anyone in the vicinity of that fake address he was trying to get you to. She told me he'd had some posh druggie girlfriend who owned a barge. He was running out of places to go. The police have been watching his flat for the last two days."

"And you knew the gun was empty?"

"I *hoped* it was empty," he corrected her. "For all I knew, he'd checked it and reloaded."

He groped in his pocket. His fingers shook slightly as he lit a cigarette. He inhaled, then said:

"You did bloody well to keep him talking that long, Robin, but next time you get a call from an unknown number, you bloody well call it back and check who's on the other end. And don't you ever—*ever*—tell a suspect anything about your personal life again."

"Would it be OK if I have *two minutes*," she asked, pressing the cold kitchen roll against her swollen and bleeding lip, "to enjoy not being dead, before you start?"

Strike blew out a jet of smoke.

"Yeah, fair enough," he said, and pulled her clumsily into a one-armed hug.

ONE MONTH LATER

EPILOGUE

Your past is dead, Rebecca. It has no longer any hold on you—has nothing to do with you—as you are now.

Henrik Ibsen, *Rosmersholm*

The Paralympics had been and gone, and September was doing its best to wash away the memory of the long, Union-Jacked summer days, when London had basked for weeks in the world's attention. Rain was pattering against the Cheyne Walk Brasserie's high windows, competing with Serge Gainsbourg as he crooned "Black Trombone" from hidden speakers.

Strike and Robin, who had arrived together, had only just sat down when Izzy, who had chosen the restaurant for its proximity to her flat, arrived in a slightly disheveled flapping of Burberry trench coat and sodden umbrella, the latter taking some time to collapse at the door.

Strike had only spoken to their client once since the case had been solved, and then briefly, because Izzy had been too shocked and distressed to say much. They were meeting today at Strike's request, because there was one last piece of unfinished business in the Chiswell case. Izzy had told Strike by phone, when they arranged lunch, that she had not been out much since Raphael's arrest. "I can't face people. It's all so dreadful."

"How are you?" she said anxiously, as Strike maneuvered himself out from behind the white-clothed table to accept a damp embrace. "And oh, poor Robin, I'm so sorry," she added, hurrying around the other side of the table to hug Robin, before saying distractedly, "Oh yes, please, thank you," to the unsmiling waitress, who took her wet raincoat and umbrella.

Sitting down, Izzy said, "I promised myself I wouldn't cry," then grabbed a napkin from the table and pressed it firmly to her tear ducts. "Sorry...keep doing this. *Trying* not to be embarrassing..."

She cleared her throat and straightened her back.

"It's just been such a shock," she whispered.

"Of course it has," said Robin, and Izzy gave her a watery smile.

"*C'est l'automne de ma vie*," sang Gainsbourg. "*Plus personne ne m'étonne...*"

"You found this place OK, then?" Izzy said, scrabbling to find conventional conversational ground. "Quite pretty, isn't it?" she said, inviting them to admire the Provençal restaurant which Strike had thought, as he entered, had a feeling of Izzy's flat about it, translated into French. Here was the same conservative mix of traditional and modern: black and white photographs hung on stark white walls, chairs and benches covered in scarlet and turquoise leather, and old-fashioned bronze and glass chandeliers with rose-colored lampshades.

The waitress returned with menus and offered to take their drink order.

"Should we wait?" Izzy asked, gesturing at the empty seat.

"He's running late," said Strike, who was craving beer. "Might as well order drinks."

After all, there was nothing more to find out. Today was about explanations. An awkward silence fell again as the waitress walked away.

"Oh, gosh, I don't know whether you've heard," Izzy said suddenly to Strike, with an air of being relieved to have found what to her was standard gossip. "Charlie's been admitted to hospital."

"Really?" he said, with no sign of particular interest.

"Yah, bed rest. She had something—leak of amniotic fluid, I think—anyway, they want her under observation."

Strike nodded, expressionless. Ashamed of herself for wishing to know more, Robin kept quiet. The drinks arrived. Izzy, who seemed too keyed up to have noticed Strike's unenthusiastic response to what was, for her, a safe subject of mutual interest, said:

"I heard Jago hit the roof when he saw that story about the two of you in the press. Probably delighted to have her where he can keep an eye—"

But Izzy caught something in Strike's expression that made her desist. She took a slug of wine, checked to see whether anyone at the few occupied tables was listening, and said:

"I suppose the police are keeping you informed? You know Kinvara's admitted everything?"

"Yeah," said Strike, "we heard."

Izzy shook her head, her eyes filling with tears again.

"It's been so awful. One's friends don't know what to say...I still can't *believe* it. It's just so incredible. *Raff*...I wanted to go and see him, you know. I really *needed* to see him...but he refused. He won't see anyone."

She gulped more wine.

"He must have gone mad or something. He must be ill, mustn't he? To have done it? Must be mentally ill."

Robin remembered the dark barge, where Raphael had spoken in holy accents of the life he wanted, of the villa in Capri, the bachelor pad in London, and the new car, once the ban imposed for running over a young mother had been lifted. She thought how meticulously he had planned his father's death, the errors made only because of the haste with which the murder was to be enacted. She pictured his expression over the gun, as he had asked her why women thought there was any difference between them: the mother whom he called a whore, the stepmother he had seduced, Robin, whom he was about to kill so that he didn't have to enter hell alone. Was he ill in any sense that would put him in a psychiatric institution rather than the prison that so terrified him? Or had his dream of patricide been spawned in the shadowy wasteland between sickness and irreducible malevolence?

"...he had an awful childhood," Izzy was saying, and then, though neither Strike nor Robin had responded, "he *did*, you know, he really did. I don't want to speak ill of Papa, but Freddie was *everything*. Papa wasn't kind to Raff and the Orca—I mean, Ornella, his mother—well, Torks always says she's more like a high-class hooker than anything else. When Raff wasn't at boarding school she dragged him around with her, always chasing some new man."

"There are worse childhoods," said Strike.

Robin, who had just been thinking that Raphael's life with his mother sounded not unlike the little she knew about Strike's early years, was nevertheless surprised to hear him express this view so bluntly.

"Plenty of people go through worse than having a party girl for a mother," he said, "and they don't end up committing murder. Look at Billy Knight. No mother at all for most of his life. Violent, alcoholic father, beaten and neglected, ends up with serious mental illness and he's never hurt anyone. He came to my office in the throes of psychosis, trying to get justice for someone else."

"Yes," said Izzy hastily, "yes, that's true, of course."

But Robin had the impression that even now, Izzy could not equate the pain of Raphael and Billy. The former's suffering would always evoke more pity in her than the latter's, because a Chiswell was innately different to the kind of motherless boy whose beatings were hidden in the woods, where estate workers lived according to the laws of their kind.

"And here he is," said Strike.

Billy Knight had just entered the restaurant, raindrops glittering on his shorn hair. Though still underweight, his face was fuller, his person and clothes cleaner. He had been released from hospital only a week previously, and was currently living in Jimmy's flat on Charlemont Road.

"Hello," he said to Strike. "Sorry I'm late. Tube took longer'n I thought."

"No problem," said the two women, at the same time.

"You're Izzy," said Billy, sitting down beside her. "Haven't seen you 'n a long time."

"No," said Izzy, a little over-heartily. "It's been quite a while, hasn't it?"

Robin held out a hand across the table.

"Hi, Billy, I'm Robin."

"Hello," he said again, shaking it.

"Would you like some wine, Billy?" offered Izzy. "Or beer?"

"Can't drink on my meds," he told her.

"Ah, no, of course not," said Izzy, flustered. "Um...well, have some water, and there's your menu...we haven't ordered yet..."

Once the waitress had been and gone, Strike addressed Billy.

"I made you a promise when I visited you in hospital," he said. "I told you I'd find out what happened to the child you saw strangled."

"Yeah," said Billy apprehensively. It was in the hopes of hearing the answer to the twenty-year-old mystery that he had traveled from East Ham to Chelsea in the rain. "You said on the phone that you'd worked it out."

"Yes," said Strike, "but I want you to hear it from someone who knew, who was there at the time, so you get the full story."

"You?" Billy said, turning to Izzy. "You were *there*? Up at the horse?"

"No, no," said Izzy hastily. "It happened during the school holidays."

She took a fortifying gulp of wine, set down her glass, drew a deep breath and said:

"Fizz and I were both staying with school friends. I—I heard what happened, afterwards...

"What happened was...Freddie was home from university and he'd brought a few friends back with him. Papa left them in the house because he had some old regimental dinner to attend in London...

"Freddie could be...the truth is, he was awfully naughty sometimes. He brought up a lot of good wine from the cellar and they all got sloshed and then one of the girls said she'd wanted to try the truth of that story about the white horse...you know the one," she said to Billy, the Uffington local. "If you turn three times in the eye and make a wish..."

"Yeah," said Billy, with a nod. His haunted eyes were huge.

"So they all left the house in the dark, but being Freddie...he *was* naughty...they made a detour through the woods to *your* house. Steda Cottage. Because Freddie wanted to buy some, ah, marijuana, was it, your brother grew?"

"Yeah," said Billy, again.

"Freddie wanted to get some, so they could smoke it, up at the horse while the girls were making wishes. Of course, they shouldn't have been driving. They were already drunk.

"Well, when they got to your house, your father wasn't there—"

"He was in the barn," said Billy suddenly. "Finishing a set of... you know."

The memory seemed to have forced its way to the front of his mind, triggered by her recital. Strike saw Billy's left hand holding tightly to his right, to prevent the recurrence of the tic that seemed for Billy to have something of the significance of warding off evil. Rain continued to lash the restaurant windows and Serge Gainsbourg sang, "*Oh, je voudrais tant que tu te souviennes...*"

"So," said Izzy, taking another deep breath, "the way I heard it, from one of the girls who was there...I don't want to say who," she added a little defensively to Strike and Robin, "it's a long time ago and she was traumatized by the whole thing...well, Freddie and his friends clattering into the cottage woke you up, Billy. There was quite a crowd of them in there, and Jimmy rolled them a joint before they set off...Anyway," Izzy swallowed, "you were hungry, and Jimmy...or maybe," she winced, "maybe it was Freddie, I don't know...they thought it would be funny to crumble up some of what they were smoking and put it in your yogurt."

Robin imagined Freddie's friends, some of them perhaps enjoying the exotic thrill of sitting in that dark workman's cottage with a local lad who sold drugs, but others, like the girl who had told Izzy the story, uneasy about what was going on, but too young, too scared of their laughing peers to intervene. They had seemed like adults to the five-year-old Billy, but now Robin knew that they had all been nineteen to twenty-one at most.

"Yeah," said Billy quietly. "I knew they'd gave me something."

"So, then, Jimmy wanted to join them, going up the hill. I heard he'd taken a bit of a fancy to one of the girls," said Izzy primly. "But you weren't very well, after being fed that yogurt. He couldn't leave you alone in that state, so he took you with him.

"You all piled into a couple of Land Rovers and off you went, to Dragon Hill."

"But...no, this is wrong," said Billy. The haunted expression had returned to his face. "Where's the little girl? She was already there. She was with us in the car. I remember them taking her out when we got to the hill. She was crying for her mum."

"It—it wasn't a girl," said Izzy. "That was just Freddie's—well, it was his idea of humor—"

"It *was* a girl. They called her by a girl's name," said Billy. "I remember."

"Yes," said Izzy miserably. "Raphaela."

"That's it!" said Billy loudly, and heads turned across the restaurant. "That's it!" Billy repeated in a whisper, his eyes wide. "Raphaela, that's what they called her—"

"It wasn't a girl, Billy . . . it was my little—it was my little—"

Izzy pressed the napkin to her eyes again.

"*So* sorry . . . it was my little brother, Raphael. Freddie and his friends were supposed to be babysitting him, with my father away from home. Raff was awfully cute when he was little. He'd been woken up by them, too, I think, and the girls said they couldn't leave him in the house, they should take him with them. Freddie didn't want to. He wanted to leave Raff there on his own, but the girls promised they'd take care of him.

"But once they were up there, Freddie was awfully drunk and he'd had a lot of weed and Raff wouldn't stop crying and Freddie got angry. He said he was ruining everything and then . . ."

"He throttled him," said Billy, with a panicked expression. "It was real, he killed—"

"No, no, he didn't!" said Izzy, distressed. "Billy, you know he didn't—you *must* remember Raff, he came to us every summer, he's alive!"

"Freddie put his hands round Raphael's neck," said Strike, "and squeezed until he was unconscious. Raphael urinated. He collapsed. But he didn't die."

Billy's left hand was still gripping his right tightly.

"I *did* see it."

"Yeah, you did," said Strike, "and, all things considered, you were a bloody good witness."

The waitress returned with their meals. Once everyone was

served, Strike with his rib-eye steak and chips, the two women with their quinoa salads and Billy with the soup, which was all he seemed to have felt confident ordering, Izzy continued her story.

"Raff told me what had happened when I got back from the holidays. He was so little, so upset, I tried to bring it up with Papa, but he wouldn't listen. He just sort of brushed me off. Said Raphael was whiny and always...always complaining...

"And I look back," she said to Strike and Robin, her eyes filling with tears again, "and I think about it all...how much hate Raff must've felt, after things like that..."

"Yeah, Raphael's defense team will probably try and use that kind of thing," said Strike briskly, as he attacked his steak, "but the fact remains, Izzy, that he didn't act on his desire to see your father dead until he found out there was a Stubbs hanging upstairs."

"A disputed Stubbs," Izzy corrected Strike, pulling a handkerchief out of her cuff and blowing her nose. "Henry Drummond thinks it's a copy. The man from Christie's is hopeful, but there's a Stubbs aficionado in the States who's flying over to examine it, and he says it doesn't match the notes Stubbs made of the lost painting...but honestly," she shook her head, "I don't give a damn. What that thing's led to, what it's done to our family...it can go in a skip for all I care. There are more important things," said Izzy croakily, "than money."

Strike had an excuse for making no reply, his mouth being full of steak, but he wondered whether it had occurred to Izzy that the fragile man beside her was living in a tiny two-roomed flat in East Ham with his brother, and that Billy was, properly speaking, owed money from the sale of the last set of gallows. Perhaps, once the Stubbs was sold, the Chiswell family might consider fulfilling that obligation.

Billy was eating his soup in an almost trancelike state, his eyes unfocused. Robin thought his deeply contemplative state seemed peaceful, even happy.

"So, I must've got confused, mustn't I?" Billy asked at last. He spoke now with the confidence of a man who feels firm footing in reality. "I saw the horse being buried and thought it was the kid. I got mixed up, that's all."

"Well," said Strike, "I think there might be a bit more to it than that. You knew that the man who'd throttled the child was the same one burying the horse in the dell with your father. I suppose Freddie wasn't around much, being so much older than you, so you weren't completely clear who he was...but I think you've blocked out a lot about the horse and how it died. You conflated two acts of cruelty, perpetrated by the same person."

"What happened," asked Billy, now slightly apprehensive, "to the horse?"

"Don't you remember Spotty?" asked Izzy.

Amazed, Billy set down his soup spoon and held his hand horizontally perhaps three feet off the ground.

"That little—yeah...didn't it graze the croquet lawn?"

"She was an *ancient*, miniature spotted horse," Izzy explained to Strike and Robin. "She was the last of Tinky's lot. Tinky had awful, kitschy taste, even in horses..."

(...*nobody noticed, and you know why? Because they're such fucking arrogant snobs...*)

"...but Spotty was awfully sweet," Izzy admitted. "She'd follow you around like a dog if you were in the garden...

"I don't think Freddie *meant* to do it...but," she said hopelessly, "oh, I don't know anymore. I don't know what he was thinking...he always had a terrible temper. Something had annoyed him. Papa was out, he took Papa's rifle out of the gun cabinet, went up on the roof and started shooting at birds and then...well, he told me afterwards he hadn't meant to hit Spotty, but he must have been aiming near her, mustn't he, to kill her?"

He was aiming at her, thought Strike. *You don't put two bullets in an animal's head from that distance without meaning to.*

"Then he panicked," said Izzy. "He got Jack o'—I mean, your father," she told Billy, "to help him bury the body. When Papa came home Freddie pretended Spotty had collapsed, that he'd called the vet who'd taken her away, but of course, that story didn't stand up for two minutes. Papa was *furious* when he found out the truth. He couldn't abide cruelty to animals.

"I was heartbroken when I heard," said Izzy sadly. "I loved Spotty."

"You didn't by any chance put a cross in the ground where she'd been buried, did you, Izzy?" asked Robin, her fork suspended in mid-air.

"How on *earth* did you know that?" asked Izzy, astonished, as tears trickled out of her eyes again, and she reached again for her handkerchief.

The downpour continued as Strike and Robin walked away from the brasserie together, along Chelsea Embankment towards Albert Bridge. The slate-gray Thames rolled eternally onwards, its surface barely troubled by the thickening rain that threatened to extinguish Strike's cigarette, and soaked the few tendrils of hair that had escaped the hood of Robin's raincoat.

"Well, that's the upper classes for you," said Strike. "By all means throttle their kids, but don't touch their horses."

"Not entirely fair," Robin reproved him. "Izzy thinks Raphael was treated appallingly."

"Nothing to what he's got coming to him in Dartmoor," said Strike indifferently. "My pity's limited."

"Yes," said Robin, "you made that abundantly clear."

Their shoes smacked wetly on the shining pavement.

"CBT still going all right?" Strike asked, who was limiting the question to once weekly. "Keeping up your exercises?"

"Diligently," said Robin.

"Don't be flippant, I'm serious—"

"So am I," said Robin, without heat. "I'm doing what I've got to do. I haven't had a single panic attack for weeks. How's your leg?"

"Getting better. Doing my stretches. Watching my diet."

"You just ate half a potato field and most of a cow."

"That was the last meal I can charge to the Chiswells," said Strike. "Wanted to make the most of it. What are your plans this afternoon?"

"I need to get that file from Andy, then I'll ring the guy in Finsbury Park and see whether he'll talk to us. Oh, and Nick and Ilsa said to ask if you want to come for a takeaway curry tonight."

Robin had caved in to the combined insistence of Nick, Ilsa and Strike himself that going to live in a box room in a house full of strangers was undesirable in the immediate aftermath of being taken hostage at gunpoint. In three days' time, she would be moving into a room in a flat in Earl's Court, which she would share with a gay actor friend of Ilsa's whose previous partner had moved out. Her new flatmate's stated requirements were cleanliness, sanity and tolerance of irregular hours.

"Yeah, great," said Strike. "I'll have to head back to the office first. Barclay reckons he's got Dodgy bang to rights this time. Another teenager, going in and out of a hotel together."

"Great," said Robin. "No, I don't mean great, I mean—"

"It *is* great," said Strike firmly, as the rain splashed over and around them. "Another satisfied client. The bank balance is looking uncharacteristically healthy. Might be able to hike your salary up a bit. Anyway, I'm going up here. See you at Nick and Ilsa's later, then."

They parted with a wave, concealing from each other the slight smile that each wore once safely walking away, pleased to know that they would meet again in a few short hours, over curry and beer at Nick and Ilsa's. But soon Robin had given over her thoughts to the questions needing answers from a man in Finsbury Park.

Head bowed against the rain, she had no attention left to spare for the magnificent mansion past which she was walking, its rain-specked windows facing the great river, its front doors engraved with twin swans.

ACKNOWLEDGMENTS

For reasons not entirely related to the complexity of the plot, *Lethal White* has been one of the most challenging books I've written, but it's also one of my favorites. I truly couldn't have done it without the help of the following people.

David Shelley, my wonderful editor, allowed me all the time I needed to make the novel exactly what I wanted it to be. Without his understanding, patience and skill, there might not be a *Lethal White* at all.

My husband Neil read the manuscript while I was writing it. His feedback was invaluable and he also supported me in a thousand practical ways, but I think I'm most grateful for the fact that he never once asked why I decided to write a large, complex novel while also working on a play and two screenplays. I know he knows why, but there aren't many people who would have resisted the temptation.

Mr. Galbraith still can't quite believe his luck at having a fantastic agent who is also a dear friend. Thank you, The Other Neil (Blair).

Many people helped me research the various locations Strike and Robin visit during the course of this story and gave me the benefit of their experience and knowledge. My deepest thanks to:

Simon Berry and Stephen Fry, who took me for a fabulous, memorable lunch at Pratt's and enabled me to look at the betting book; Jess Phillips MP, who was incredibly helpful, gave me an insider's tour of the Commons and Portcullis House and, with Sophie Francis-Cansfield, David Doig and Ian Stevens, answered innumerable questions about life at Westminster; Baroness Joanna Shields, who was so kind and generous with her time, showed me inside DCMS, answered all my questions and enabled me to visit Lancaster House; Raquel Black, who couldn't have been more helpful, especially in taking pictures when I ran out of battery; Ian Chapman and James Yorke, who gave me a fascinating tour of Lancaster House; and Brian Spanner, for the daytrip to Horse Isle.

I'd be totally lost without my office and home support team. Huge thanks, therefore, to Di Brooks, Danni Cameron, Angela Milne, Ross Milne and Kaisa Tiensuu for their hard work and good humor, both of which are deeply appreciated.

After sixteen years together, I hope Fiona Shapcott knows exactly how much she means to me. Thank you, Fi, for everything you do.

My friend David Goodwin has been an unfailing source of inspiration and this book would not be what it is without him.

The QSC, on the other hand, have just got in the way.

To Mark Hutchinson, Rebecca Salt and Nicky Stonehill, thank you for holding everything together this year, especially those bits when you were holding *me* together.

Last but never, ever, least: thanks to my children, Jessica, David and Kenzie, for putting up with me. Having a writer for a mother isn't always an easy shift, but the real world wouldn't be worth living in without you and Dad.

CREDITS